The Seven Stones

The Seven Stones

Written by Mark J. P. Wolf

**Story by Mark J. P. Wolf
and Glenn R. Engelbart**

Maps drawn by the author.

Aurochs Press
South Milwaukee, Wisconsin

Set in Times New Roman.

ISBN: 979-8-35093-496-0

The Seven Stones

Book IV: Swamp and Sorrow 257

Book V: Sieges and Sorcery 367

KINGDOM OF
ITHARIA
AND SURROUNDING LANDS

N

THE SILVER SEA

NAVROGENAYA

TO TOLGARD AND PHAMIAR

VOL GURVETH
TESKA
GREAT GATES
ARINZEI VALLEY
FARRENHALE
TO ORDSKELL
LOOKOUT PATH & TOWERS
MOUNT HARBASH

VESKWOOD FOREST

RIVER SARYL

RIVER GURVETH
KAIHL
HALLOWAY
NORTH ROAD

KRAZ
KARZELL

KING NEHNCAZZAR'S TOMB

EDGENOOK
RAVENIA
KRONIVAR
BEGGAR'S BAY

GREENSWARD

CASTLE FROSTHELM
RUINED EAST ROAD

TO AORINTHEL'S ISLAND

SABLE SARRET
OKIARY
RIVER EMRIL
CROWCAW
GOMIRRÉ
SOUTH ROAD

FROSTHELM MOUNTAINS

GEVHRA DESERT

UPPER YANDL

FOREST

LAKE RUNDLEMERE

MUSSET

LOWER YANDL

RIVER YANDL

BOTTOMCLIFFE

ONEWAY

SOUTH ROAD

RUNDLEWOOD

FOREST ROAD

GRAY YANDL

"THE ROCKS"
HIGHWATER
OAKITSBURROW
HILLBROOK

LAKE GRAYLOCH

RIVER RHIL

LAKE EIHALO

TO ARTHEL HALL

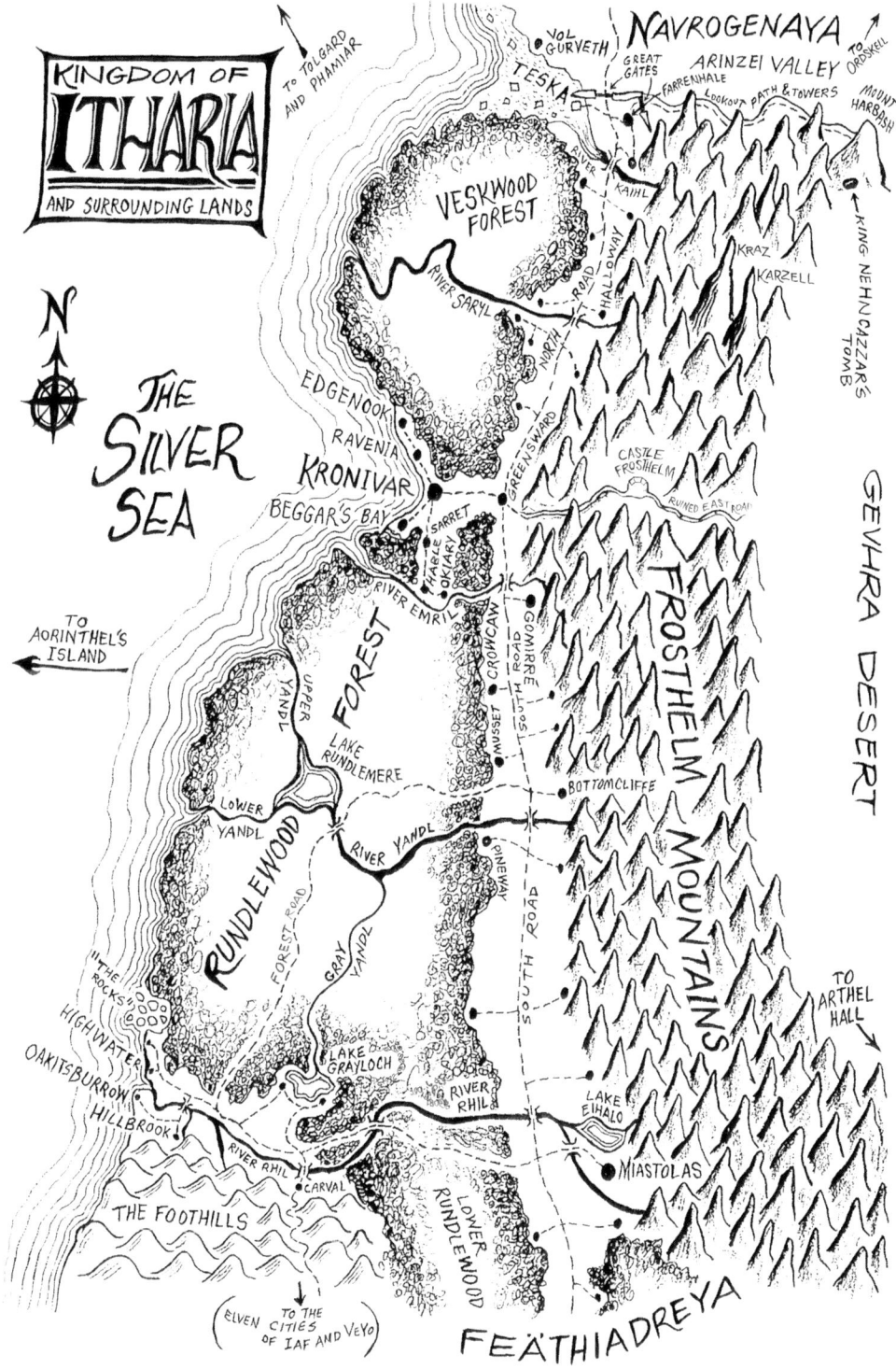

RIVER RHIL

CARVAL

THE FOOTHILLS

LOWER RUNDLEWOOD

MIASTOLAS

(ELVEN CITIES OF IAF AND VEYO)
TO THE

FEÄTHIADREYA

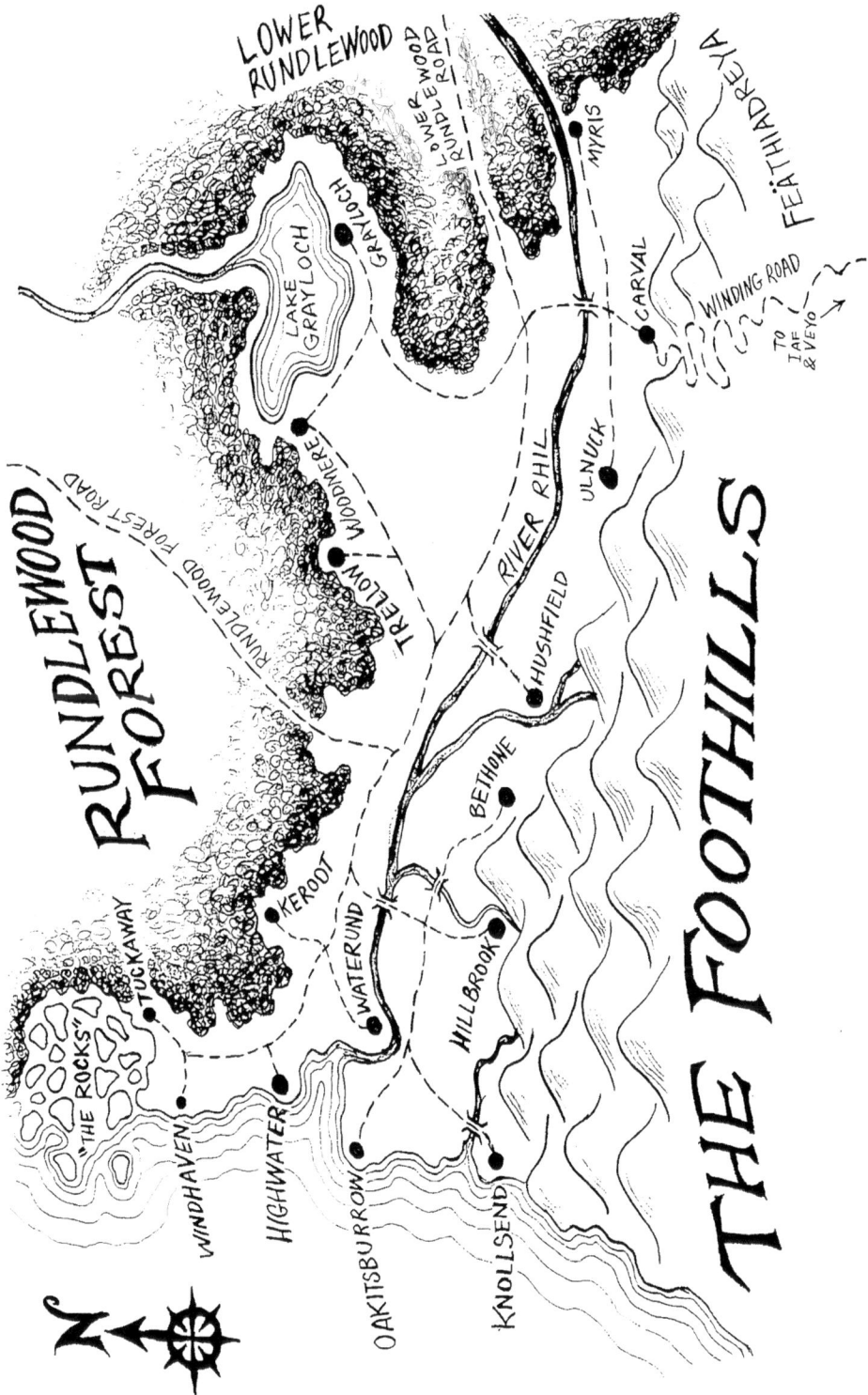

Prologue

The comet fell through the black depths of space. A distant star beckoned, writhing fiery filaments erupting in violent coronas. Harsh white starlight grazed the comet's gray bulk, solar winds sanding it away into a shimmering tail of silvery dust. As the star's hold increased, the comet accelerated, its tail long and bright.

Lured near an immense outer planet of murky, swirling storms, the comet skimmed its clouds, eluding its grasp. In the realm of the star's inner planets it plunged into the orbit of a small, blue-green world, veering sharply in a tightening arc, bound by the planet's gravity. It tore through the dense atmosphere, glowing brighter and hotter, the whisper of its passage becoming a deafening roar. Its silver-gray exterior flared to a brilliant orange, blazing away in a trail of fire and smoke.

Burning its hottest, the comet smashed into the edge of a continental landmass, impacting molten earth under enormous pressure and heat. A shock front rolled out through the planet's crust, splintering rock and scattering debris. Billowing clouds of dust and smoke blossomed as a thunderous boom echoed around the planet's surface.

Great rushing torrents of ocean filled the comet's gigantic crater, churning up the silvery dust that had settled there. Some time later when the basin had finally filled, only the uplift at the crater's center remained above water, forming a small island. Life soon returned, and flourished. Like a slumbering giant's deep, labored breathing, the tide's endless ebb and flow slowly eroded the crater's rim. Rivers ran down from the mountains, finding their way into the sea. Calm returned to the planet's surface for many thousands of years while the great Stone lay buried.

Book I: Swords and Stories

Chapter 1.
Long Night in Teska

In the orange glow of the firebowl's dying embers, Cedric Redthorn sat on a bench by the wall, tired yet anxious. The long day had left him exhausted, his spirit bowed with the burden of all he had learned. Almost everyone he had known was dead and gone; he felt abandoned and alone. Lulled by the loom's rhythmic clacking and shifting, he tried to rest. His gaze wandered across dozens of tapestries hung on the far wall, trying to make out their images in the haze of candlelight. Some depicted scenes of Teska, some the lands of the Goblins or the Elves; others might have been of Tolgard or Phamiar, and a few he recognized as Itharia. The images seemed unrelated and random: a shipwreck on a deserted shore; an empty throne gleaming in an elegant hall of soft shadow and fading sunlight; a long-tailed comet falling from a starry sky; a beardless old man in a strange, high-ceilinged prison room. Cedric had seen most of the weavings up close already. Those woven of fine thread contained the most intricate detail, while others of coarser weave remained vague and impressionistic. He wondered what they meant and what they forebode.

At last the sound of the loom ceased. Her trance broken, the withered old Teskan slumped back in her chair weak and weary, her spidery fingers stiff from the prolonged effort. Letha attended to his grandmother, and then began removing the new weaving from the loom. In the sudden quiet, Cedric could again hear the water lapping against the poles beneath the room, an uneasy reminder of their suspension over the swamp.

He got up and decided to wait for Letha in the back room, where Wendolin was still poring over the weaving from the day before. The old wizard was the only familiar face Cedric had seen in Teska, and probably the only one still alive after all that had happened. And now Wendolin would soon be leaving.

Cedric pushed aside the doorway curtain and passed through. Wendolin sat at the long, wooden table where the weaving lay illuminated by six wide candles all burned low. It depicted a forest scene at night, perhaps on the edge of a clearing. Dark trees rose into a blackened sky. Lying on the ground was an ornate sword, with three gaping holes aligned in its hilt. Beyond, in the dark, six eerie green figures bore a litter upon which lay a young, blond-bearded dwarf. They carried him into the woods like pallbearers in a funeral procession.

"Gnomes," said Wendolin. "It seems one of the swords will be lost, or is already lost."

"But who could have found them?" said Cedric. "I hid them well enough. If I can find them again—"

"It may have already happened, or it may be something yet to happen. Most of these weavings are of events to come. We must try to keep the swords safe for now, provided they are still there. You must take them south and lay low and wait for me."

Cedric stared at the weaving. "Maybe it can be avoided, then," he said.

"Perhaps," said Wendolin.

But neither spoke with any conviction.

The curtain moved aside as Letha entered with the new weaving. He unrolled it on top of the other one. "Looks like your friend here, Master Wendolin," he said.

"*Prenthii*, Teska Letha." Wendolin nodded to Letha as he departed.

The new weaving was of a small cottage on a green field under a bright blue sky. To one side was a tree, and on the other a large lilac bush grew in front of the cottage, spreading under the eaves. Smoking his pipe in a rocking chair on the porch was an old dwarf with a white beard who looked like Cedric.

"Is it me?" said Cedric. "What do you think it means?"

"It appears to be," said Wendolin. He looked long at the weaving, trying to divine its meaning. "It could very well be in the Foothills. At any rate that is where I am sending you. Find the swords and wait for me there."

"We'll eventually take them to the King, won't we?"

"We must bide our time. It would be unsafe to reveal them until we know more regarding Maëlveronde. He will be searching for them."

Wendolin stared at the image awhile longer, searching in vain for some significant detail that might have eluded him. At last he leaned back in resignation.

"I had hoped we would get something more useful than this," said Wendolin, "But it will have to do; we cannot afford to wait any longer. Zhindarren is keeping watch. He may have seen us together. I will leave tonight and go north, and draw him away. Wait until morning and then be off at once, but do not seem hurried. Leave with other dwarves, if you can. Retrieve the swords and go south, to in the Foothills. No one must suspect."

"And you?" said Cedric, "You say Maëlveronde's powers are well beyond your own by now. And what of Zhindarren's? Is it not dangerous to let him follow you?"

"It is," said Wendolin, "Yet through Zhindarren I may learn of Maëlveronde's whereabouts and find him."

"That's what I'm afraid of."

In the quiet that followed, Wendolin gave no sign of reassurance and Cedric's heart grew cold.

"Lie low in the south. I will come for you. It may be awhile, but I will come for you."

Since his arrival in Teska, Cedric longed to return to solid ground, but he was reluctant to part with Wendolin now. Though he saw the wisdom of Wendolin's plan and had never doubted the old wizard's great powers, he knew in his heart that once he left Teska he would never see his old friend again.

Chapter 2.
Last Days of the Ambersheath Farm

As the sun set, Iaven Ambersheath wandered the barren fields of his family's farm. Memories of harvests and summers long gone returned to bid farewell: wagonloads of mushrooms, cabbages, and corn; hot, lazy afternoons spent fishing in the River Rhil; barefoot races through soft grasses; the dusky incense of cattails burning to ward off bugs; full moons serenaded by fields of crickets. Those were the bright days of childhood before his father was lost at sea. Now he walked alone across the broken furrows, and in the deepening gloam the empty, rolling plains of black soil resembled a dark ocean frozen in time. Beyond them stood trees he had known all his life, their leaves already edged with fiery autumn colors. Iaven looked around and knew this was the Ambersheath family's last harvest. His mother Sara was remarrying and selling the farm.

Farm life on the outskirts of Hillbrook was the only one Iaven knew. Although they still carried on many traditions of their ancestors, the Dwarves of southern Itharia had long since given up the way of the warrior, trading sword and shield for hammer and tongs, rake and hoe, loom and chisel. They had settled in small villages and towns across the far southwestern end of Itharia, around the Rhil and all the way south to the Toes of the Foothills. Their arts and crafts had become domestic, their talk turning inward from news of distant warring kingdoms to the local harvest and latest town gossip. Hillbrook life was quiet, leisurely paced and uncomplicated. Iaven liked his life there and did not want to leave it. Nor did he have anywhere else to go.

In a way, Iaven thought, his father's success was to blame. The farm had grown so much that Iaven could not take it on by himself, now that his mother and brother wanted to sell it. Hagen Ambersheath had been a good husband, father, and provider; he and Sara had raised their identical twin sons Iaven and Orven on returns from the farm. After many years, the farm had grown in size and reputation, along with demand for its sumptuous mushrooms and savory red cabbage. Hagen sold his crops all over the Foothills area, even out to Oakitsburrow and up to Highwater. His warmth and charisma brought him new customers, and he came to love traveling. Sometimes he even took a trip north to the great port city of Kronivar, where both Dwarves and Men had settled, or east to Miastolas, summer capital of the Elven kingdom of Feäthiadreya. Iaven remembered how long it seemed, waiting for his father's return, and how excited he was to see the beautiful Elven artifacts his father brought back with him. He smiled, recalling the handfuls of trinkets he and Orven always fought over, and how they longed to one day go traveling with their father.

As the twins grew up, they took on more and more of the farm work. Hagen had brought on a hired hand, an old dwarf named Cedric Redthorn, who still resided in the little cottage they had built for him. Cedric had once worked at Castle Frosthelm up in the mountains, where he had been an apprentice to the King's great Master-Forger. His metalworking skills came in handy around the farm, and Hagen loved hearing his tales of the old days (Cedric claimed to be nearing his one hundred and seventy-first birthday, but they thought he must be joking). Cedric was like a grandfather to the twins, a dear friend to Sara and Hagen, and an honorary member of the Ambersheath family.

Around the time the farm reached the height of its prosperity Hagen was offered passage on the *Yoner*, a ship setting sail across the Silver Sea to kingdoms on the far shores. To the surprise of family and friends, he accepted. The Dwarves of Itharia distrusted boats, using them only when necessary, preferring solid ground beneath their feet, and few of them could swim. Yet Hagen was curious about Tolgard, Phamiar, Elluria, Ghoomhar, and other lands around the sea. Merchants had sold his mushrooms in other lands, but he had traveled little. It seemed the opportunity might never come again. Sara reluctantly agreed to it. With Cedric's help, she and the twins took care of the farm once or twice a year during his trips to Kronivar. The sea voyage would be longer, but they would manage.

As the weeks passed, they expected to see him returning, coming down the road in from town. The twins would run to greet him, Sara hurrying behind them. But he never came. Three months passed without any sign of him. Iaven and Orven's hearts grew heavy, their mother became withdrawn, and Cedric tried to keep them from giving up hope. Later, word reached them that the ship never arrived at its destination. Nor had it turned back; at best it could only be considered lost. Iaven remembered crying in his pillow on those long, quiet summer nights, struggling in vain to believe that his father had survived.

Summer went by, harvest season came, and the Ambersheaths' farm endured. The townsfolk spoke less of Hagen's fate; there was no question that the ship had sunk. Winter passed and spring appeared. Sara accepted Hagen's death and slowly recovered, while Cedric and the twins kept the farm running. Hagen's friends paid their respects and continued their patronage, but neither Iaven nor Orven could match their father's charisma or success. In the months following, Orven came to accept the fact of their father's death. Iaven still refused to give up hope though he no longer spoke of it.

Eleven years went by and the farm declined. The circle of Hagen's customers shrunk back to the immediate localities. When times were hard, fields were sold; and many of those that remained suffered from neglect. With Hagen gone, Cedric worked even harder than before, tiring more quickly as his years caught up with him. Sara lost enthusiasm for the farm and responsibilities fell to Iaven and Orven, who had come of age. Iaven recalled how his mother had suffered over those years, sometimes sitting alone in sorrow when she thought no one was watching.

Time passed and daily routines wore on. Sara emerged from her gloom, finding solace in her work. After nine years of being alone, she began accepting visits from Rory Applegate, the town's blacksmith. Two more years passed, and Rory asked Sara to marry him. Orven was happy for her but Iaven was wary of it, seeing it as an end of the life he knew. It had taken him a long time to accept his father's death, and he had found consolation in the chores that now fell to him. Tomorrow his mother would marry Rory and move to his house in the village, leaving the farm up for sale. Whatever she hadn't sold was all packed away, ready for the move. The house was left for Iaven and Orven until someone bought it, or in case they decided to keep the farm and try to make a go of it.

Iaven stood watching the sun descend into the haze of the western horizon. A chill wind blew as the sun's glowing rim disappeared behind distant treetops. He turned and started walking back to the house. With a lot of work the farm could prosper again, he thought. If they worked together. He and Orven were often at odds with each other, but they were still brothers. They would have to alternate traveling to sell their crops, and new help could be trained by Cedric. It could be done, if only Orven wanted to stay.

Orven had tired of the farm but remained to help his mother and Cedric, and because he had nowhere else to go. Like Iaven, he'd always listened with rapt attention to tales of distant corners of the kingdom and the lands of Elves, Men, and Goblins that lay beyond them. There were tales of the Dwarves' ancestors, who had come across the desert and settled in the mountains; wars with Goblins in the north and dealings with Elves in the south; ships sailing westward over the Silver Sea; castles, kings, and battles; cities rising and crumbling into dust; endless dark forests and distant mountain peaks. They filled Iaven's daydreams while he worked, but he had no desire to leave the security of the farm; if anything, he appreciated it more. But the same tales had kindled Orven's longing to see the world, leaving him restless for adventure. No riding a horse cart full of produce, like his father; he wanted to venture off to find his fortune, living by his wits and going where he would. His sense of duty kept him at the farm though he had long since ceased to enjoy it. Now that the farm had declined he was eager to sell it.

Iaven walked home. The Ambersheath homestead was a small but sturdy house, set between the fields and the road to town. An unremarkable place, weathered and worn, the only one Iaven had ever called home. The house was dark in the paling twilight, a soft light flickering inside the window. Iaven stepped indoors, feeling the warmth from the fireplace. Orven was kneeling and stoking the logs, gazing into the flames. He eased a log into place, listening to the fire's soft roar and crackle. A warm, orange glow bathed his face, his eyes half-lidded in the dry heat. As identical twins, Iaven and Orven were both of average build, with sandy blond hair, short beards, and deep blue eyes. But of late Orven's demeanor had taken on a quieter, more serious tone as he pondered his future in which the farm would play no part. Iaven stood watching Orven a moment, until Orven turned and looked at him.

"Cedric gone in already?" Orven asked.

"A while ago. I was out for a walk."

"Rory said they'll look after him, maybe move him over to the smithy. There's a lot they could learn from him there."

Iaven sighed and went to the window overlooking the lawn. Chairs and tables lined the grass, strings of lanterns hung tree to tree, and a canopied tent was pitched in back, all for the next day's wedding festivities. "We could take care of him here," Iaven said.

Orven grunted, knowing where this was leading. He went and sat down in one of the oak chairs across the room from Iaven. "He's worked enough. Let him spend his last few years in peace. Or months, seeing as how he's been lately. Mother and Rory have a room for him—"

"What if he wants to stay?" Iaven turned from the window.

"Then we'll let him, until the place sells. If it sells..."

"If we sell it," said Iaven. "We could hire new help, I could go into town to sell—"

"Then you'll have to do it alone. I've had it with farming." Contempt crept into Orven's voice. "Maybe you could get Zammond to help you. Or Wilbur— he's the stay-at-home type. Wilbur and you could run the place —if you could get him to leave Oakitsburrow!"

"Leave them out of it!" Iaven sank into a wooden armchair along the wall. "What would Dad say, what would he think..."

"Iaven..." Orven's tone softened, "don't hang on to it like this. He would have wanted you to move on."

They sat awhile in silence listening to the snapping flames. Firelight danced across the bare walls, hauntingly empty now that their mother's bric-a-brac was packed away into crates.

"You were the same way when mother wanted to remarry," Orven reminded him. "I'm sure Dad would have wanted her to."

"I know, I know. But this is different; my life's here. So is yours—"

"It was. And it was a good one. But times have changed... the Kingdom's changed. Some say we'll probably have to go to war. Old Henshaw claims there's Goblin spies camped as far south as the forests outside of Kronivar..."

"I doubt even he believes half the things he says," said Iaven. "And even if Goblins could come that far south, there couldn't be very many. They wouldn't get past Kronivar, and certainly not way down here. Why would they want to come to Hillbrook anyway?"

"Who knows?" Orven turned toward the fireplace. "Maybe they wouldn't. It doesn't matter." He paused, watching the fire. "But I'm not staying here."

Iaven looked at his brother. "So where will you go?"

"I don't know... yet. But there's no point in staying here. The farm's done for. Mother's gone, and Cedric... well, it's a wonder he's still alive, old as he is."

Iaven nodded. Over the last few years Cedric's health was waning. He had taken ill during the last harvest, and now spent most of his time resting. Iaven looked out the window towards his cottage, and saw Cedric's curtain was drawn.

"He could watch over the new help," Iaven said.

"If he's still around next spring," Orven pointed out.

"Of course he'll be!" Iaven wanted to argue with Orven, but knew it would only erupt into a shouting match that would wake their mother. It was her last night in the house, and neither of them wanted to spoil it.

"Well, I won't be," said Orven, getting up. Iaven stood looking out the window after Orven had gone in to bed. He looked at Cedric's cottage in the distance, dim now under the darkening sky, and knew Orven was right.

The following day began with the final preparations for the wedding, which was to be held in the garden by the line of great oaks at the end of the yard. Tables and chairs were readied, and food was arriving. Cooks built fires for roasting chickens and hung kettles for the fish boil. Huge baskets of vegetables and fruit lay on tables under shade trees. Heaping platters of the best mushrooms from the Ambersheaths' last harvest were brought out for everyone to sample. Rory's nieces and nephews came early to decorate, and gardeners did last minute trimming as guests began arriving. Rory had an enormous table for wedding gifts set up near the house, much larger than what was necessary.

Rory had spared no expense for his wedding and made sure everyone knew it. Besides the fact that he had no room for such a gathering, he and Sara decided to have the wedding at the Ambersheath farmstead hoping someone would realize what a fine place it was and decide to buy it (in addition to friends and family, Rory had invited wealthier townsfolk and other prospective buyers). Iaven walked amidst the bustling activity, thinking he had never seen the yard done up so well or so full of life.

As morning went on, guests trickled in, all in high spirits. Shortly before noon, the groom's party arrived, and Rory was all smiles and handshakes. He was a big, jovial, bear of a fellow, beefy forearms pumping up and down, shaking hands and clapping the backs of old friends. His florid face was flushed with joy and pride, his eyebrows bushier than ever. Sara readied herself in the house, chatting and laughing with the bridesmaids, happier than Iaven had seen her in a long time.

At last the guests all gathered in the garden and the ceremony was held, the sun shining on the crowd surrounding bride and groom. Glad but solemn songs were followed by a hushed silence while the vows were taken. The symbolic yoke was placed on the couple's shoulders, the water sprinkled, and the greens distributed. Afterward, there were more songs, moving and spirited. Iaven feigned his joy as uneasiness gnawed at him, and everything went by in a blur as he contemplated his uncertain future. He was ashamed that he could be so selfish and tried to put it out of his mind. The crowd's infectious spirit brightened his mood a little, but he still experienced everything at a distance.

It was late afternoon by the time dinner was served, and a while before all the guests were seated and fed. Long lines formed near the food and everyone filed through, filling their plates. Over the next hour or so, people relaxed and talked, eating and going for seconds, thirds, and more. Iaven and Orven sat at the main table with the wedding party for the meal and toasts, but later, for the desserts and after-dinner drinks, each of the twins went and sat at a table among his friends, away from the scrutiny of the guests. Iaven had a cold mug of beer with his good friends Zammond, Hobley, and Tillmore and began to feel more at ease.

When the meal wound down and most people were pleasantly sedated (some unable to move without great difficulty), after-dinner speeches began. A tinkling of glasses got people's attention, until Rory rose, waving his hands to quiet everyone who had taken up spoons to add to the tinkling.

"On behalf of myself and my wife," he boomed, "I would like to thank you all for coming to celebrate with us," —some clapped at this— "and we hope you'll stay into the evening, as we have plenty of good drink, thanks to our friends the Spurros at *The Riverbank Inn*. And there'll be music and dancing as well. As I'm not one for long speeches, I'll leave it at that, though I believe Mayor Ebbleaf has something to add." Surprised that Rory hadn't spoken at length about selling the farm, the audience broke into more applause.

At this, Norbin Ebbleaf, a short, stout dwarf, stood and nodded thanks to Rory who sat down. "My dear citizens," he began in a loud, official voice, as though a long speech was to follow, "Friends, I wish the best to our dear Rory and Sara. Times have been good to Hillbrook, and continue to be. It's true, there have been more reports from Kronivar of Goblin spies in the Kingdom, and rumors of activity in the north. But the Gates and Wall near Teska still hold strong, and I've just received word today that troops have been sent up to Farrenhale from Kronivar, doubling the watch there. As for Hillbrook, we've just added another new deputy, Tad Greenwold," —he motioned and Tad stood reluctantly— "and we are prepared to start a watch around our own Seven Bridges should the necessity arise. So there's no reason to worry. Our Kingdom is safe and strong, thanks to our good King. And thank you very—"

"Here's to King Jordgen!" came a loud shout. Iaven saw to his horror that Orven, a bit drunk judging from the bottles at his table, was standing and holding his mug aloft. "And to his army at the Castle!" Orven continued.

"Hear, hear!" murmured some in the crowd, taken aback by the suddenness of the toast.

Orven looked around at them. "And I am proud to announce that I am going to join them, for the sake of the Kingdom!" He raised his mug higher in salute, and then drank. After a moment the crowd erupted into applause, when it became clear a noble intention lay behind what had first appeared to be merely a drunken stunt.

Zammond, Hobley, and Tillmore began clapping, but Iaven sat with his arms folded, glaring in Orven's direction.

Always has to be the center of attention, Iaven thought. He wondered if Orven would really go through with it. He had a feeling Orven would do it, just to spite him, and it made him angry.

"Come on, Iaven, aren't you glad to have so valiant a brother?" Zammond teased, elbowing Iaven. The twins' friends knew how much Iaven would put up with in order to keep the farm going, though most agreed with Orven that it was a lost cause.

"I think it's a good idea," said Hobley, clapping with the crowd. He was considering going as well, but had not mentioned it to Iaven. Tillmore and Zammond joined in with him. Iaven clapped his hands a few times, and then slouched back in his chair with folded arms.

The mayor was motioning Orven over to his table, encouraging him to make a speech. Orven, realizing he had said enough, declined and made his way to the beer kegs instead. Seeing the speechmaking was at an end, the diners began milling about again, snatching up the last of the desserts, clearing tables out of the way, and lighting strings of lanterns as the musicians warmed up.

On his way to the kegs and back to his seat, Orven gladly accepted slaps on the back and handshakes of congratulations, acting more like a war hero returning rather than someone about to enlist. Iaven groaned. There wouldn't be a war anyway. Orven just wanted to leave Hillbrook, and his plans sealed Iaven's fate as well.

Iaven quickly tired of people telling him what a fine decision his brother had made. Worse still were those who mistook Iaven for Orven, congratulating him and slapping him on the back. Very soon he had had enough and managed to slip away back to the house.

While the evening continued with boisterous laughter and song beneath colored paper lanterns strung from the trees, Iaven sat alone in the darkened farmhouse. Eventually Zammond found him there. Iaven had no desire to be cheered up, but let Zammond join him. Gregarious and energetic, Zammond Brockleberry had wild, coppery hair and keen, sharp eyes that seemed to debate letting you in on the joke. A mischievous smile crept across his face.

"There he is! The twin brother of Hillbrook's own Orven Ambersheath!" Zammond exclaimed. "Why aren't you out there paying your honors?" He set down his mug and pulled up a chair by Iaven. "Come on, Iaven, don't sour the evening. I know you're still mourning the farm…"

"It isn't just that," Iaven grumbled. He had already tried to entice Zammond into helping him run the farm.

"Oh, I know," Zammond said, "but really, Iaven, it wouldn't have worked out anyway. Even if Orven stayed, I mean, knowing how the two of you get along."

The door banged open and Hobley ambled in. "Hey, Iaven! Here you go." He handed Iaven an extra mug. Hobley Elderthorn was burly and broad-shouldered, his wide hands belying his great ease with knife and bow, skills all four of the Elderthorn brothers possessed, as they were avid bowhunters. Despite his size, his three younger brothers were even larger than him, though his skills were greater than theirs, and his laugh the heartiest. Relaxed but not lazy, Hobley rarely let things trouble him and always raised his friends' spirits when he could.

Behind him came his best friend, Tillmore Hooth, who was tall, thin, and angular, with keen eyes and the cool attitude of a bemused aristocrat. Tillmore came from a long line of woodcarvers, though he professed to have little interest in the family trade, preferring instead to live by his wits, if he could; but he had yet to find another occupation.

Zammond eyed the mug. "None for me?" he cried, looking to Hobley in mock surprise.

"Better none than not enough," said Tillmore, "and with you, it's never enough!"

"Thanks, Hob," said Iaven.

"Sure thing, Iaven. Cheers!" Hobley raised his mug to Iaven. "You'll find something soon. I'm sure Rory has work at the smithy."

Iaven took a sip and set the mug down again. "I suppose. But I don't know much about it, and it isn't what I want to do."

Hobley pulled up a chair near Iaven, and Tillmore sat across from them. "You know, it's not such a bad idea, going off to the Castle," said Hobley, "We're going to have to fight anyway, if there's a war."

"Let's organize a guard right here," Zammond interrupted. "They say Goblin spies are prowling around the kingdom. What if they come down here?"

"With Teska in the north and the Castle in the mountains, the Kingdom's secure enough. And even if they got in, what would they want with us?" asked Tillmore.

"Not much to spy on in Hillbrook," said Hobley.

"How would they know without looking?" Zammond sat back and took a drink. "Alright, so it's not such a great idea..."

Tillmore raised a toast. "Zammond, your greatness cannot be underestimated!" As Tillmore drank, Zammond raised his mug in agreement, puzzled at the compliment, suddenly stopping as he realized what it actually meant.

"Either way, I don't think I'd make much of a warrior," said Iaven.

They sat awhile in silence, no one knowing what to say. Hobley finished his beer, and Iaven just sipped at his. Zammond fidgeted impatiently.

"Let's go back to the rest of the party. I'm tired of sitting around in the dark." Zammond stood, waiting for Iaven, and the others got up as well.

"In a bit… I don't feel like it just yet." Iaven walked them to the door. "I think I'll go see Cedric awhile. Maybe I'll join you later." A lit window glowed in the dim silhouette of the little cottage out by the fields.

"Alright, then, good night!" Hobley said. They left the house, and as Iaven went off to Cedric's cottage, they all knew they wouldn't see him any more that evening.

Iaven found Cedric sitting by the fireside, dozing in his chair. He was wrapped in his favorite blanket, with just his boots, head, and white beard exposed. Though worn now from years of use, the blanket's fine weave of colorful threads still formed a finely detailed picture. One day when Iaven had come to visit, Cedric was out smoking his pipe on his porch, and Iaven realized he was looking at the very scene the blanket depicted. When Iaven told him about it, Cedric had not been surprised; he just looked bemused and said, "She was right."

Cedric stirred and woke. He had been at the party earlier and knew how Iaven was feeling. "Ah, the brother of our noble Orven," he teased.

"So I've been told— too often, lately." Iaven sighed. "I still don't know what to do."

Cedric shifted around, his arms appearing from under the blanket as he sat up in the chair. "Well, it won't be the farm any more, you know that."

Iaven looked away into the blaze in the fireplace. "I know," he said.

Cedric smiled as though he understood things about Iaven that even Iaven did not know. Crow's-feet wrinkles appeared around his alert blue eyes. "I'm sure you'll amount to something. Something your father would have been proud of."

Iaven looked at him, wondering what he was thinking. "You think I should work for Rory? If a war does come the smithy will be busier than ever." He leaned back in his chair. "I don't think I'd like it. Then again, I've never tried it. I don't know. I suppose I could look for work on another farm, but it wouldn't be the same."

"Things could be worse." Cedric leaned forward to get his pipe from the mantle, and Iaven jumped up and reached it for him. "You and Orven, and even your parents, for that matter, didn't have to grow up or live during a war. Hasn't been one in ninety-odd years now, or so; people have forgotten what it was like." He lit his pipe and puffed at it. "I worked in the Castle, up in the mountains, as an apprentice to Angkelwen the Master-Forger. Orglen Frosthelm, Jordgen's grandfather, was King back then. When war was near, we in the forge worked day and night preparing. What beautiful and terrible things were wrought there. I tremble to think of it. Gold, silver, iron, bronze— the metals sang in Angkelwen's hammer and tongs. Would that I could look upon works like those again!"

"Do they still make such things at the Castle today?" Iaven asked.

"I doubt it. Angkelwen was old even then, and would have died long ago; he was probably killed in the attack on the Castle. And all the other apprentices would be dead by now, too, if any of them survived."

"Then how is it that you still are—"

The door swung open and Orven strode into the room. Expecting him to be drunk and wild, Iaven tensed, ready for confrontation, but Orven was strangely sober. "Cedric," he said, and then saw Iaven and turned toward him. "You're not begging him to save the farm, are you?" Contempt filled his voice. "Take it if you want, you can have it. I'm taking my fair share and going off to the Castle. Do what you want with yours."

"Leave me alone!" Iaven got up. He was the same size as Orven but didn't like to fight, and had never been as good a fighter as Orven. Even as children, Orven usually won; he was always willing to be more ruthless than Iaven was, and Iaven knew it.

"I mean, I don't expect *you* to become a soldier!" Orven taunted him, "You may as well take your—"

"Stop, stop, don't fight now!" Cedric waved at them, amused. "I asked Orven to come here tonight, I wanted you both to be here. But not to fight! I have something I've been waiting to give you."

"Well, alright, I'm sorry, but Iaven's been moping about the farm instead of thinking what he could be doing." Orven pulled up a chair and sat near the fireplace, across from Iaven and Cedric. He and Iaven glared at each other a moment, as the firewood crackled in the silence.

With an effort, Cedric leaned forward and got out of his chair. Grasping a knotted wooden cane, he made his way over to a wooden chest and motioned the twins over. Orven cleared away the pile of Cedric's things on top of the chest, and Iaven helped him open it. Very reverently, Cedric reached in and handed an oblong bundle wrapped in fine linen to Iaven, and an identical one to Orven, and then bid everyone back to the chairs by the fireside.

Once they were seated again, the twins unwrapped their bundles. Iaven unrolled the linen and was surprised to find an ornate sword and scabbard. He looked over and saw that Orven's bundle was the same. Cedric, beaming, was unable to contain himself. "Twin swords, Halix and Gorflange. Iaven's is Halix, and Orven has Gorflange."

Except for the crackle from the fireplace, the room was silent as Iaven and Orven examined their gifts. At first glance, they seemed like ordinary swords; but in the glow of firelight the gleaming metal revealed craftsmanship far superior to anything they had ever thought possible. Each sword had been forged of silvery metal, an alloy they had never seen, which on closer inspection almost appeared to have fine veins of gold running through it. The scabbard was of the same metal, wood-lined inside, its exterior wrapped in rose-colored leather laced with intricate designs in golden thread. Orven drew his sword out and held it aloft, the bright, broad blade gleaming and flashing in the room. The hilt of the sword had an elegant, gently curving cross with rounded ends inset with brilliant Tigersmilk pearls. It had an ample grip, and a pommel with a small, blue-green gem set in the very tip of its round end. Along the hilt ran elaborate patterns and designs worked into the metal that appeared delicate but were as solid as the blade itself. On the grip these designs formed interlacing vines with detailed miniature leaves spread flat against its surface. These leafy vines surrounded three holes along the axis of the grip, which looked as though they were made to house large gems inside the handle. Orven noticed that Iaven's sword was also missing these gems.

Iaven raised Halix, turning it over and feeling the weight of it in his hand. He wondered what history it had seen, and how it had come to Cedric. Orven gripped Gorflange and tried wielding it, awed by its beauty. Cedric smiled as he watched the twins playing with the swords, and wondered if they realized the irony of such a gift.

"Cedric, thank you!" Orven said, still gazing at the sword. "Where did you get these? How long have you had them? What happened to the gems for the swords? Have you got them?"

"These swords were made by Angkelwen, weren't they?" asked Iaven.

"Yes," said Cedric, "Angkelwen made them to unite the Elven and Dwarven Kingdoms against the Goblins during the war."

Orven was shocked. "You mean these are *the* Lost Swords of the Alliance? But I thought they were only a legend!" Orven exclaimed. "They say the swords were never completed, and then lost."

"Lost? Yes, but they were completed; all except for the gems, that is. And the gems are still lost," said Cedric. "The swords were for some time, too, but how I got them, and why I'm giving them to you is a long story, so I might as well begin..."

Chapter 3.
Tales by Fireside

Iaven and Orven settled into their chairs by fireside. Cedric sat back, drawing on his pipe. "First, you should know about the gems, since the swords were made for them. You've heard of Arthel Hall? Out east beyond the Elves, in the southern mountains, where the wizards are —the *Oswai*, as they were called. Though I've never been there, and it's been some time since I last saw Wendolin."

"You knew one? When you lived at the Castle?" Orven wondered why Cedric had never mentioned it before.

"Yes... but Arthel Hall is where their Council meets, and where they have their archives and libraries. They were there long before the Dwarves came across the desert. Wizards have a hand in the affairs of Elves, Dwarves, Men, and even the Goblins. Their number is small and they do little out in the open. Their work is subtle, their advice good. At least that's the way Wendolin was. But our tale begins some time even before him.

"A long time ago a wizard named Aorinthel lived in Arthel Hall. He was the greatest and wisest among them, and tired of their debates. Some on the Council wanted a stronger hand in world events, thinking themselves the most capable in such matters, while others argued for greater seclusion, centered on their own affairs and studies. As time went on, the divide deepened and they all took sides. They were eager to see whom Aorinthel would side with, but he favored a balance and would side with neither group. He was very outspoken, made some enemies, and soon could not continue his work undisturbed.

"He longed for a quiet, remote place to work, and had seen such a place once in his travels, an island out at the center of the Silver Sea. No one lived there, and no Kingdom had claimed it, since most trade routes in those days went port to port and rarely so far from shore. So Aorinthel moved to the island, and had the Dwarves build him a tower there. This was during the reign of King Varlen II, before I was born, and the Dwarves knew how to build and craft stone then. Aorinthel had aided King Varlen II on several occasions, and the tower was to be a token of the King's gratitude. Cartloads of the best stone were quarried, taken down to Kronivar, and brought over to the island, along with the finest craftsmen from the Castle. They cut the stone, laid the courses, and the tower rose above the island. From the top you could see out to sea on all sides —and be forewarned of any visitors approaching. They built a garden at the top, and another on one of the large balconies, convenient for growing spices and vegetables enough for Aorinthel and his apprentices. Aorinthel thanked Varlen, promising to come to the Dwarves' aid whenever they needed him.

"But the building of the tower was not without difficulties. While setting the foundations, the Dwarves tunneled deep into the ground as they did in the mountains, digging several levels of cellars beneath the tower. There they found a strange kind of stone they'd never seen before. Curious, they mined deeper down, and loaded some in their boats to take back with them. Then they found what seemed to be an enormous ball of gemstone lodged deep within the rock itself. They tried to pry it loose, but it was brittle and shattered into seven large pieces. Aorinthel took the shards in to study them. No one had ever seen their like before. The dwarves dug deeper, eager to find more. But in doing so, they struck water. The sea poured in and filled their tunnels, and some drowned. They sealed off one or two of the cellars just below ground, but the rest was flooded.

"The dwarves returned home saddened. They cursed the stone they'd mined, dumping it overboard, and told the Men whose boats they rode in that they'd never leave the mainland again."

"What became of the gem shards?" asked Orven.

"They couldn't tell the gemstone's color when it was buried," Cedric continued, "Each shard had shifting iridescent colors that changed. Eventually, after studying them a long time, Aorinthel fashioned the shards into gems, fixing a single color in each one. There was a red one, a blue one, a violet one, an orange one, a yellow one, a green one, and an indigo one. Aorinthel found them such an interesting object of study that his other projects fell by the wayside over the years. He became reclusive, returning to Arthel Hall less and less, until the boat he kept at the island fell into neglect. Even the messages he sent out by bird were shorter. Among the Council, many thought his obsession with the gems had grown unhealthy. And, of course, they were also quite curious about them."

"How often did he write back?" Iaven asked.

"Only rarely," said Cedric, "There was a room at the top of the tower where messenger-pigeons, doves, and other birds were kept, and these carried messages back and forth to Arthel Hall, Castle Frosthelm, or wherever they had been trained to fly. Since he had the birds, he must have felt it less necessary to return to the mainland. As Aorinthel grew older he traveled very little and in his last years he had become rather frail. But his skills and power grew in strength, which he attributed to his solitary life on the island. He had put a great deal of his time and himself into the gems, enhancing and shaping their powers, and they in turn increased his abilities.

"Magically, the gems were very powerful, but they were still somewhat fragile, making them difficult to work with. Aorinthel tried to strengthen them, but the attempt ended in disaster, and the indigo gem, the most beautiful of the seven, crumbled into dust. After that, he was extremely careful with the others. His failing health and backlog of work began to weary him, so he sent for apprentices from Arthel Hall. This, of course, pleased Arthel Hall, as they were very curious and wanted to keep an eye on him. The two factions could not agree on any one individual, so two apprentices were sent, one from each side; Wendolin and Maëlveronde, who both eventually became powerful wizards in their own right."

"What were the gems like?" asked Orven. "What kinds of powers did they have?"

Cedric furrowed his brow. "Wendolin didn't say much, but I could tell he was intrigued by them, maybe even revered them. They were unlike anything he had ever known. I think there was much about them that he suspected but would not say. Aorinthel was very protective of them, and usually gave his apprentices other tasks instead. He let them work with the gems on occasion, but never alone. And so the gems came to be."

Cedric paused. Flames crackled in the silence. A breeze blew softly under the eaves and in through a window left ajar, laden with the aroma of a far-off hickory fire. Orven wondered about the gems, half-expecting Cedric to reach into his pocket and produce them for the swords. But now it appeared they had met some tragic end.

"So then he made the swords for the gems?" asked Orven.

"You said they were for the war—" Iaven added.

"I'm coming to that." Cedric waved off their impatience, deliberately pausing and drawing on his pipe. "Now you already know Dwarven history concerning the Great War with the Goblins." The twins nodded. They had always listened with rapt attention to the lore Cedric passed onto them; tales of their ancestors journeying across the desert and settling in the mountains, the beginnings of Itharia, how the kingdom had spread westward down to the seashore where Kronivar was established, and finally to the north and south to the Foothills. The Elves of Feäthiadreya had aided the Dwarves' kingdom, ceding many lands to them, but not without a price. The Dwarves became allies of the Elves, who were often at war with Navrogenaya, the Goblin kingdom to the north. Itharia became the territory between the Elven and Goblin kingdoms, and the Goblin front was now the Dwarves' responsibility. The Dwarves hated the Goblins and had fought them in the mountains, so they had been quick to agree to the alliance. Itharia expanded northward to the swamps where the eleven tribes of the Teskans lived in pole-villages built over the water. The Teskans had been persecuted and almost wiped out by the Goblins, so the Dwarven occupation had been the lesser of two evils. To watch the border, the Dwarves had established an outpost near the border town of Farrenhale, alongside Teska, the Teskans' largest pole-village.

"In those days, we didn't have the North and East Gates and the wall running from the mountains to the swamps," Cedric said. "There were only the Teskan and Dwarven guards to keep Goblins from getting into the Kingdom. Not that the Goblins could do so easily, considering how the swamps are; and Goblins are less fond of boats than we are. Nowadays the guard is stronger there, and with the wall and the gates, people find it hard to believe rumors of Goblins spies wandering in the Kingdom."

"Are there any?" said Orven. "Some claim they're in the forest. Could they have found a way in?"

"It's possible," Cedric admitted. "But as far as Rundlewood is concerned, some people are just afraid of the forest and think they see things in there, like the Gnomes."

"But you were saying, about the war..." Iaven encouraged him.

"Well, the Goblins were kept at bay, and Itharia flourished. We kept a strong border guard with the Teskans and all was well. Without the concerns of war, the Kingdom grew. Kronivar was soon a great port city, as Men came from across the Sea; we traded with them and let them build there. Dwarves may not care for boating, but we love building and trade as much as anyone, and Kronivar grew. Other dwarves left the mountains and settled to the south, bringing their smithing and stonecraft with them, and they also took up farming, woodworking, and other trades. Sword and shield were put on the mantle or hung over the fireplace, and the Dwarves became accustomed to peaceful living. King Orglen still kept an army at the Castle, but a smaller one, and there was no threat of war for some time.

"Itharia enjoyed abundance; it was the first the Dwarves had known for many generations. They were not used to it, and were lulled into complacency —so some of the older dwarves in the Castle complained. The Goblins sensed this as well and planned their attack. For generations they had been crafting the *Auglweiz* —the Augglins— whole clans of unfortunate Goblins taken from the margins of their society and collectively inbred for size, strength, and mindlessness, until they were a race unto themselves, a slave labor work force for the Goblins.

"As the Goblins' forces grew, gangs of Trolls from the northeast and even some Men from Tolgard joined them. The Elves began to worry, and tensions rose between them and the Dwarves, who had come to dislike Elven interference in their affairs. The alliance became an uneasy one, and Arthel Hall sensed the danger of the whole situation.

"King Orglen, remembering the vow made to his father, asked Aorinthel for his aid, and Arthel Hall sent word to the island that efforts were required to repair the alliance, as war with the Goblins seemed imminent. They decided that twin swords would be forged, one for the Dwarves and one for the Elves, to represent the alliance and unify their forces. Elven craftsmen came to Castle Frosthelm, where the swords were to be forged by the great Master-Forger Angkelwen, and I was one of his apprentices at the time."

Cedric smiled and puffed his pipe as the twins regarded him anew. He was like a grandfather to them, and to think he had been present at such momentous events took some stretch of the imagination.

Cedric remained lost in thought awhile and his face grew grave again. "Those were truly dark times. Goblin forces were massing quickly. The Elves did little, expecting the Dwarves to hold the Goblins back. But the forces at Teska were not large enough to stave off an entire army and Kronivar was slow to mobilize. Dwarves from every town in the Kingdom came to the Castle's defense, though most were largely untrained.

"The mood at the Castle was a grim one, and nothing could be done fast enough. The great furnaces burned full blast as new weapons were forged. Hammers rang out day and night. Angkelwen set to work on the swords. Aorinthel sent Wendolin to the Castle to assist him, while he and Maëlveronde prepared the gems on his island. The swords took time, and time was short. I became Angkelwen's right-hand man, overseeing everything that went on that he could not attend to. Had he died before they were done, I would have had to finish the swords; but even at their peak, my skills were still less than a shadow of the great Master-Forger's."

"So the swords were made with the gems in mind?" Orven asked.

"They were. Aorinthel had grown quite attached to the gems, but he agreed to sacrifice them to fulfill his vow to King Orglen. He also realized how obsessed he was with them.

"Each sword was to contain three of the remaining gems. The swords were made sensitive to their powers, controlling and directing them. Aorinthel spent great efforts on the gems, so their powers are likely well beyond what Wendolin told me, maybe even beyond what he knew. But I'm afraid we may never know."

"The swords weren't used in the war?" said Orven.

Cedric drew slowly on his pipe. "No."

The twins stared at him. "Why not?" Iaven asked.

Cedric lowered his pipe and continued. "When the time came to forge the swords, the gems were not yet ready. Wendolin came to the Castle with Aorinthel's instructions for the swords' making, so they'd be finished along with the gems. That's how I met him.

"But you should know a little about him first. Wendolin and Maëlveronde were as different as night and day. Each represented one side of the schism in Arthel Hall, and each had different interests and abilities; but this was useful to Aorinthel. Wendolin was a tall, lanky fellow with a bushy beard and stately manner, even then. He was very bright, very sharp, sometimes a bit slow to act, but wise and perceptive. We became good friends. I showed him around the Castle and told him what was going on, while he told me about Arthel Hall and tales of distant lands. There wasn't much time, but we got to be fast friends. He also told me about Maëlveronde, the other apprentice.

"Maëlveronde was tall and striking of countenance, with a commanding presence and great charisma that drew people to him. I could tell Wendolin admired Maëlveronde, from the way he spoke of Maëlveronde's intensity and dedication, and his drive to master whatever had caught his interest. But Wendolin felt he was too brash at times, and undiplomatic; although when he wished he could be eerily convincing and persuasive. Maëlveronde loved training hawks and his prized gyrfalcon, Aegelred. Wendolin thought Maëlveronde was rather like a bird of prey himself. He was very clever, and I think Wendolin sometimes found him intimidating.

"Anyway, the swords were complicated enough that Wendolin had to go off to the Castle, while Maëlveronde stayed behind to help Aorinthel with the gems. But Maëlveronde had developed a great interest in the gems and was determined to learn all he could about them. Before he came to the island, Maëlveronde had been deep into his study of the Angkhadra, an ancient race, but soon the gems became the center of his attention and his sole desire. When the request for the swords came and Aorinthel agreed, Maëlveronde must have been bitterly upset, and realized he might never see them again. Even if the Goblins were defeated, the swords would remain in their respective Kingdoms afterward, out of his reach.

"Wendolin suspected that Maëlveronde slowed down Aorinthel's progress on the gems, gaining time. For Maëlveronde, each passing day became more maddening as the gems were slipping away. But once Wendolin was gone, he could act.

"Aorinthel must have suspected as well, though his trust may have blinded him. At any rate, Aorinthel was occupied with readying the gems as time grew ever shorter. Goblin troops were massing near the northern border, just out of sight of Teska, so it was difficult to judge their number. Unbeknownst to us at the time, more troops were gathering in an outpost on the far side of the mountains, on the desert's edge, waiting.

"Then one night the onslaught began. Teska was attacked and their bridge to the mainland was cut. Goblin regiments held Teska back, creating an opening for the rest to march south. Others came south through the desert. Both armies entered the mountains and closed in from east and west, besieging the Castle. King Orglen's army held them off, but the link to Kronivar was severed. And we hadn't counted on the sheer numbers they had marshaled; they must have been building up for years."

"But how could they attack over such a distance?" asked Orven, "And climb the Mountain Road? They would've had to have kept up their pace for days."

"That," said Cedric, "was due in part to the Augglins. We had never seen their like before. They were frightening in their size and mindless obedience to their masters. At one point the Goblins themselves killed dozens of them just to use their bodies to block a mountain road. The Augglins were beasts of burden, and when needed, fierce and unstoppable monsters with no sense of self-preservation. And they kept coming and coming. When word finally got through to Kronivar from Teska that the Goblins were on their way, Teska had underestimated their speed, and Kronivar was caught by surprise. The Goblins had started up into the mountains and held the road against the oncoming Kronivar troops.

"Soon Goblin troops arrived at the Castle and the battle began. When we saw them arriving from both sides, and sooner than expected, we feared Kronivar had failed. Our morale fell. The Goblins used the Augglins with no concern for them whatsoever, and their attacks were relentless. Defeat seemed certain. But messenger-birds had been sent out to the Elves. If we could hold out until they arrived, the Kingdom might not be lost. Our alliance had become an uneasy one, but we had faith they would come. It was our only hope, at any rate."

"What about the swords?" asked Orven.

"The swords were finished, but the gems never arrived," Cedric continued. "The swords were too valuable to let fall into enemy hands, so Wendolin summoned me and sent me to hide them in the mountains, in the event that the Castle would be taken before the Elves arrived. The Castle was still holding, but our losses were growing.

"So Wendolin wrapped up the swords and lowered me by rope down the sheer drop of the northern wall and cliff, into the valley. I was to hide the swords far enough away from the Castle, and then return; I could later retrieve them when the time was right.

"After working my way north, I found a suitable hiding-place, in a little rock cove near a tall, snow-covered pine. I looked around to remember the place as best I could. When I returned to the cliffside, the rope was gone. Not only did the war block any chance I had of getting back inside, but the terrain was against me as well. There was no safe way to get back up to the Castle unseen. I had heard tales about the Stone Giants who lived in the mountains near Kraz and Karzell, and took comfort in the fact that they did not seem to live anywhere near the Castle. I had to try to get back up, and there was no assurance that victory would be ours.

"I worked my way east but the ground was unyielding. I had to turn back and find another way several times. Night fell and was bitter cold. The battle echoed in the mountains; fainter now than before, and I judged that I had gone a good distance.

"The next day I went on, but slopes were steep and I was veering away from the Mountain Road. I had to get up to the road, to move toward the Castle and see what was happening. If the Goblins were still there, I would wait, though I had no idea what I would do if they'd won.

"But the Elves were on their way. Kronivar had gained ground and the Goblins suffered heavy losses and were retreating into the mountains. There the Goblins had some advantage, but Kronivar continued their slow advance. The Elves soon joined them, and were fresher. The Goblins retreated into the mountains and joined the encampment around the Castle for one last stand. They fought bitterly, and many Elves fell or were captured. At last the tide turned. Soon the Castle was regained. The Elves routed the Goblins, who took prisoners and began a retreat down the Eastern Mountain Road towards the desert."

"Of course, I found all that out much later," said Cedric, "I didn't know it at the time. I had finally worked my way up to the road, and was on my way to the Castle. Great shouts and cries erupted ahead of me, and they were Goblin cries. They were moving fast, and I had nowhere to run. I hid behind an outcropping of rock off the road, hoping they wouldn't see me in their haste.

"Most of them passed without looking back, shouting and raging. Some rode on Augglins or on carts pulled by them, the poor beasts straining under Goblin whips. I shuddered behind the rock, certain they would find me. They were so close I could smell them.

"And then it happened. An enormous Goblin captain went past on foot, barking orders to those behind him. He turned and caught sight of me crouching behind the rock. I thought I was done for. "What's a dwarf doing out here?" he growled, and threw me on a passing cart. A Goblin held me down, a knife against my neck. The Goblin captain laughed, barking something at others on the cart, and they grunted at the joke. They must have thought I was a prisoner who had escaped during the retreat."

"Old Henshaw says Goblins enslave their captives before they torture and kill them," said Orven.

"Yes, that occupied my thoughts at the time," Cedric said. "My hope was that the Elves would continue their rout to save us. But with the Augglins our speed was faster, so it seemed we would be well into Goblin territory before they caught up.

"We traveled night and day, stopping briefly to rest only when the Augglins had slowed and tired. I was bound and kept under constant watch. Eventually we descended from the mountains into the desert. We drove north alongside the mountains for several days, and came upon the ruins of a city built up into the mountain's edge, by Mount Harbash, near the border. The Goblins were excavating the ruins for treasure, and had an outpost there, where they were stationed just before the attack. And there was no hope for escape at night because of the *enkrida*, the large, black crablike creatures that roam the desert.

"They took me and the other captives into the back of the outpost, up a short way into the mountains. They had a prison there and kept us alive to torture us, to find out what we knew. And when no one could account for me as a prisoner, they were curious as to what I was doing so far down the road. They sensed I had been up to something."

Cedric paused, troubled by bad memories. Iaven was about to say something, when Cedric suddenly resumed.

"I won't describe what went on there. They had other prisoners there, dwarves, men, even some goblins. They'd stare at you, with glazed eyes and skin pale and sagging, just waiting to die. At night it was the worst— the ceaseless muttering and whispering, the scratching and scraping at the walls. New captives were left in their cells a few days, amidst it all, to weaken them before questioning began.

"But the greatest shock came when I learned that they knew about the swords. I overheard them questioning other dwarves. They must have had spies, or tortured it out of someone; I don't know. I feared they would suspect me and try to wring it out of me. And they had many, many ways to do it."

"The first session was a short one. They were getting some idea who knew what and who they had there. They demanded to know why I was out so far from the Castle. I began to think they already knew, and were just toying with me. I wondered if not telling them would make any difference. The next session was longer and far, far worse. I couldn't even crawl after they threw me back in the cell."

Cedric stopped again in recollection. The fire snapped in the silence, and the twins were still. Crickets shrilled softly outside.

"I began to lose hope," Cedric continued, "With each passing day, there seemed less chance the Elves would come. Then one afternoon the Goblin captain and his guard came and took me from the cell. As we left, others came running, shouting furiously. The captain grabbed me and hurried us off in a different direction, further into the mountains. The Elves had reached the outpost and were beginning their rout. The Goblin captain realized I knew something, and took me along into hiding. Perhaps I would be the trade by which he would get away; or maybe they would elude the Elves and take me north into Navrogenaya.

"The Goblin captain led us into the mountains. Soon the Elves found our trail and came after us. The captain saw we were trapped. The only path leading further into the mountains was a narrow rock ledge over a steep drop into a mist-covered valley. He forced us onto the ledge, trying to move us around the bend before the Elves came. We crept around the curving rock until we could not be seen from the path. The ledge narrowed and crumbled, but he forced us onward. Finally the rocks gave way and we all fell down into the valley."

Cedric sat and puffed on his pipe, the twins waiting for him to continue.

"I don't remember hitting bottom, though I must have. Just a few sharp moments of raw panic, and then blackness. A long, long blackness, a strange uneasy sleep riddled with curious dreams. Or at least I thought they were dreams. In one I was lying on a cold hard floor, in great pain. I did not open my eyes, the pain rose and fell, and I drifted away again.

"In another, I was laid out on a stone slab, in a huge chamber. Patterns of sunlight fell on enormous stone walls that rose up high around me. My pain was dulled, and my mind seemed numb as well. I was weary and dazed, fading in and out of the blackness. These dreams came in between what seemed like long periods of darkness. Sometimes, lying on the stone bed, I would sense a wide, open space around where I lay, and other times a faint, sweet aroma. At times I felt I was not alone; a presence was watching over me. But my memories were so hazy I couldn't even say what I was imagining.

"Then one day, I awoke in a meadow. I tried to get up, but I was very, very stiff. I sat there, wondering what had happened to me and where I was. I remember feeling very hungry. I rubbed my neck, stretched, and walked around a little. Soon I came to a path, which overlooked a wide valley. I saw Goblin huts in the distance, and realized it was the Arinzei Valley, the far southern edge of Navrogenaya! I was on the mountainside path which runs west, all the way to Teska; the very northern boundary of Itharia."

"How did you get there?" Orven asked.

"I don't know," said Cedric, "But when I saw Goblin huts below in the valley, it all came back to me; the war, the outpost, our chase into the mountains. Yet the place where we had fallen was mountains away from where I was. There was no time to think about it, though; I didn't know what became of the Goblins, or if I was safe there. For all I knew, they could have brought me there on their way back to Navrogenaya, and this would be my only chance to escape. So I went down the path toward Farrenhale and Teska.

"Along the way, I thought about it more. The Goblins who had fallen with me— surely they were dead. On the other hand, I wasn't, so I couldn't be sure. As I walked along, the valley seemed quiet; perhaps the Goblin troops had all been killed. I continued on alone, and after a few days, reached Teska.

"Upon arriving, I noticed that a high wall with a large iron gate had been erected at the end of the mountainside path, where it descended toward Farrenhale. It looked like it had been there awhile, but I had never heard of it.

The guards at the gate saw that I was a dwarf, and let me in. They seemed to regard me with suspicion, so I thought it best to say nothing. Perhaps they thought I was a deserter during the battle at the Castle. After all, Wendolin was the only one who knew about the hiding of the swords. And the swords! I had to get back to the Castle and retrieve them.

"I approached the bridge to Teska and stopped. The bridge had been rebuilt, stronger and twice as wide as before. Beyond it Teska was almost double the size it had been. I had been there once, a year or so right before the war, and wondered how they could have built onto it so much in so little time. Nor was there any sign of the battle that had taken place here during the Goblin invasion.

"I began to wonder if my sleep of blackness had been longer than a few days. I crossed the bridge and walked through the city, marveling at how large it had become. I found the inn there, and upon entering, realized I had no money.

"I almost left the place, when someone called my name. It was Wendolin! I almost didn't recognize him. He looked so much older, more weathered, his hair had gone from silver to white, and the lines near his eyes ran deeper. Had he been in captivity? He greeted me with greater joy than I had thought possible of him, almost with abandon. He took me in, ordered food for us, and took me to his room.

"Wendolin demanded to know what had happened to me, and I told him. Afterward he explained that I had not been dreaming; I had been in the care of the Stone Giants after my fall. There was no other explanation. Very little is known about the Stone Giants and what they do, though some in Arthel Hall may have an idea. But it was clear that they had healed me. The time of my stay however, had been *eighty-three years*... apparently, the Stone Giants experience time much differently than we do. They healed me and I had aged very little while in their care."

"You don't remember anything more of what it was like?" Orven asked.

"Just what I told you— it was dreamlike, you know. Anyway, Wendolin was happy to see me; he thought for sure I was dead. He told me all that happened, how Orglen had been killed in the war during the last battle, the arrival of the Elves and the winning of the war, and how they routed the Goblins through the mountains and cleared out the outpost. Wendolin did not know of my capture, he thought I'd died somewhere, lost in the mountains or fallen to my death."

Cedric sat back and smiled. The twins sat listening, enthralled. At twenty-five, they could not imagine the passage of eighty-three years, or what it would be like to return to the world after so long.

"Wendolin was still alive after all that time?" asked Orven.

"Wizards live longer than anybody —except Stone Giants, of course; we don't even know how long they live, or if they can die. But wizards can live a couple hundred years. Wendolin would be pretty old, now, if he's still alive... but I'm coming to that."

"So he sent you to get the swords?" asked Orven.

"And what became of the gems?" added Iaven.

"Yes, yes, the gems..." Cedric resumed, "Wendolin said that after the war, he returned to Aorinthel's island, after having received no word from Aorinthel concerning the gems, and no answer to his messages. Suspecting something had gone wrong, he sent word to Arthel Hall, asking if they had heard from Aorinthel, and told them he would go check on him.

"In Kronivar, Wendolin found a friend of his, a younger wizard named Nerander, who accompanied him. Together they found a ship willing to take them to the island, and set sail.

"As Aorinthel's tower rose over the horizon, Wendolin suspected the worst and knew they could not avoid being seen; but there was nothing they could do about it. Arriving at the island, he had Nerander stay near the ship until he found out what was going on.

"He found the tower open and empty, Maëlveronde and Aorinthel both gone. Wendolin decided to see whether birds had been sent out, and if his messages had reached them. But on his way up to the top of the tower, he noticed something strange in Aorinthel's workroom.

"Aorinthel's books lay scattered and open, pages blowing in the breeze. Papers, quills, and inkpots were lying about; an unusual sight, quite unlike Aorinthel. There were many freshly written pages at the desk, all in Maëlveronde's hand. And strangest of all, the gems were lying out in the open on the desktop, but there was no sign of Aorinthel anywhere. Wendolin climbed to the top of the tower to look for him out over the island, but spied something else instead. Out at the far end of the island beyond the forest, Maëlveronde was finishing repairs on Aorinthel's boat, but Aorinthel was nowhere in sight.

"Wendolin stood at the top of the tower watching Maëlveronde, his tiny black-garbed figure working at the side of the boat, and could faintly hear his hammer echoing. Only one explanation seemed likely; Maëlveronde had somehow taken the gems away from Aorinthel. But he would've had to have killed Aorinthel first. Although the older wizard was more powerful, he trusted Maëlveronde, blind to the faults that Wendolin saw. Perhaps Maëlveronde had killed Aorinthel while he slept; in any event, he would never have seen it coming.

"Suddenly, Maëlveronde turned and looked to the top of the tower where Wendolin stood. He dropped the hammer and started for the tower. Realizing he had been seen, Wendolin went down to the workroom, but there was no time to get back to the ship. Bolting the workroom door, he took the gems to the top of the tower, just as Maëlveronde was entering below. Wendolin looked out toward the ship, signaling Nerander to hurry to the tower.

"Maëlveronde was on his way up, and the locked door would not stop him for long. Wendolin had to do something with the gems; hiding them or dropping them from the tower was too risky, but keeping them was not safe, since Maëlveronde could overpower him. There was only one thing to do.

"Maëlveronde had just opened the locked door, when he heard ravens calling. He ran out on the balcony, only to see six large ravens, black against the sky, flying off to the mainland. Cursing, he brought out Aegelred, his gyrfalcon, and five hawks onto the balcony, releasing them in pursuit of the ravens. Each raven carried a gem, and they were on their way to Castle Frosthelm.

"Once the hawks were sent off on the chase, Maëlveronde went up to the top of the tower to battle Wendolin. Wendolin was able to hold out for some time, until Nerander arrived. Maëlveronde had not been expecting him and was taken by surprise. Together, after quite a struggle, Wendolin and Nerander were able to subdue Maëlveronde.

"Meanwhile, Arthel Hall had received Wendolin's message and had sent out several wizards, who arrived at the island later that day. Despite Nerander's testimony, both Maëlveronde and Wendolin were taken into custody and held for trial. Aorinthel's tower was emptied out, its contents sealed into crates and taken back to Arthel Hall for safekeeping. And a search of the island turned up what appeared to be Aorinthel's remains, which Maëlveronde had disposed of in a shallow grave.

"The trial was held at Arthel Hall, and in the end, Wendolin and Nerander were released. Maëlveronde was found guilty and sentenced to a ninety-nine-year imprisonment, after which time a new trial would be held to determine whether he was fit to return. They decided that the tower, now empty, would be the ideal place for his confinement. They took away everything Maëlveronde owned, leaving him nothing to work with, greatly reducing his power. He was locked in the tower, which was sealed magically by several wizards. All he had were the balcony gardens for his food, and one small messenger-pigeon, trained to fly only to Arthel Hall. He was to report to them once a week; if he failed to do so, they would come out to the island and check on him. Lest any ship attempt to come to the island, even inadvertently, a series of maelstroms were made to encircle the island, rendering the waters unsafe for any attempted landing. Thus was Maëlveronde jailed."

"So he's imprisoned out there?" Orven said.

"Hold on—" said Iaven, "If you were in the Stone Giant's care eighty-three years, and we've known you for another fourteen, or so, at least, that would mean the ninety-nine years are almost over."

"They would be, yes, but it doesn't matter anymore," Cedric replied.

"He escaped?" said Orven, "With his powers so limited?"

"And no one could get to him?" Iaven added.

Cedric eyed the twins shrewdly. "Remember, I was gone eighty-three years— quite a bit can happen in that time! So Maëlveronde was imprisoned on the island, and promptly sent the messenger-pigeon out with his weekly messages, which were often bitter and sardonic in tone. And Arthel Hall would send the same pigeon back with *their* message, which usually amounted to news of events at Arthel Hall and questions concerning Maëlveronde's solitary life. After while, the messages kept coming, but he ignored their questions altogether, choosing instead to send curses and strange poems. They didn't like it, but it fulfilled his obligation just the same.

"Then one day the pigeon, which had done its duty for a long time, died after delivering one of Maëlveronde's poems to Arthel Hall. When they sent a new one in its place a strange thing happened; the pigeon was gone awhile, and when it returned, Arthel Hall's message was still attached. They thought the bird had made a mistake, but the same thing happened when they sent it out again. Finally, Arthel Hall sent Wendolin and several other wizards out to the island to have a look.

"When they got there, the tower seal had been broken, and Maëlveronde was nowhere to be found. At the top of the tower, they found piles of feed, left for the pigeon, and neat rows of little paper scrolls, each tied up with black thread. Nearby was a cage with a pile of unopened scrolls from Arthel Hall inside. Maëlveronde had trained the pigeon to deposit the scroll from Arthel Hall and pick up a new scroll on every visit it made. When the bird was replaced, the new one didn't do anything but eat and fly back. The wizards read the scrolls that were left; the last one told of his escape, and was even so bold as to hint at how he'd done it.

"They didn't need the message though, since they were on the island already. Wendolin found a small tin of bones there —bird's bones— and was able to guess what had happened."

Orven blurted out, "But the pigeon—"

"The bones," continued Cedric, "were too large to be those of a pigeon. They were those of a much larger bird; Aegelred, Maëlveronde's prized gyrfalcon, who eventually had returned to him. Aegelred was far better trained than the five hawks he had sent out; they might have caught up to and stopped their prey, but they never made it back. But Aegelred was as tenacious as Maëlveronde, and returned with the dead raven as well as the gem it carried.

"Once he had a gem, Maëlveronde began to renew and rebuild his powers, until he was able to escape from the tower. Getting off the island, though, would be a different matter. He may have been able to divert one of the maelstroms enough to escape, but he still would have needed some means of travel across the sea. Perhaps he lured some passing ship, enchanting its crew with empty promises, or even built a vessel of his own.

"The wizards returned from the island and reported back to Arthel Hall. Soon after, Wendolin went out to search for Maëlveronde, and for a long time there was no sign of him. Wendolin had to move on to other things, but he never gave up and was always on the alert for news of Maëlveronde. The gems were lost and had likely fallen somewhere within the kingdom, except for the one Maëlveronde had. Wendolin knew that Maëlveronde would attempt to find the others, though it would be almost impossible without the swords. Since only I knew the swords' whereabouts, it seemed the swords, too, were lost. But seeing me in Teska, Wendolin felt there was a chance again."

"So that was what Wendolin told me in Teska; it was a lot to take in," Cedric said. "I learned other news of the kingdom, and together we went to see the Silkspinner, an old friend of his whom he often consulted in grave matters. She was a gaunt, old spidery woman who lived in a back room in Teska, and her loom could foretell things. She goes into a trance while weaving and doesn't know what will come out. She would weave ornate tapestries, with pictures in them —and that's how I got my blanket here."

"So that's why you came to Hillbrook?" asked Orven.

"No," said Cedric, "We didn't even know for certain if the dwarf pictured in it was me; the weave was too coarse. Wendolin was disappointed with it, and told me to take the swords into hiding. At that time Aardgen, Orglen's son, was still King, and Wendolin did not want him to get the swords just yet. He knew Aardgen would make an all-out search for the gems, attracting Maëlveronde's attention. Nor was Wendolin as fond of Aardgen as he had been of Aardgen's father. So I was to find the swords and go south, where I could lie low, until he could come for me when all was well. And that's how I came to Hillbrook."

"Didn't you have trouble finding the swords after all that time had passed?" asked Orven. He turned Gorflange over in the firelight, thinking of all the years it had lain hidden in the mountains.

"It didn't seem that long to me," said Cedric, "But the place had changed in eighty-three years. And I didn't want the dwarves in the Castle to see what I was doing. They would have taken the swords from me, had they known. I worked my way down, trying to remember. I searched for some time, and at last I found the small rock cove, and the swords, just where I had hidden them."

"And what became of Wendolin? I take it he never returned for the swords," said Orven.

"Alas, no, I waited for him all these years, and he never came. He may even be dead, for all I know. Perhaps he found Maëlveronde, or maybe Maëlveronde found him. My years are finally catching up with me, and I'm afraid I will never know."

"So you're giving us the swords. Do you want us to wait for Wendolin? Or if he isn't coming, what should we do with them?" Iaven asked, "Without the gems they're just ordinary swords, aren't they?"

"Wait a minute—" Orven sat up, "You said the King would have made an all-out search for the gems *if he had the swords...*"

"That's right." Cedric beamed. "Aorinthel designed the swords so that they could help find the gems if they were ever lost. Do you see that small blue-green gemstone set into the end of the pommel?" Iaven and Orven picked up their swords, turning them over, until they found the stone set into the tip of the hilt. "Each sword can sense the gems, when the blade is pointing toward them."

Orven held his sword horizontally, moving it slowly. As he pointed it to the north a very faint blue-green light began to flicker in the depths of the stone.

"I see it!" Orven said. "There's a gem to the north of us somewhere." Iaven had found the same direction and was looking at the light in the stone.

"There's another one to the east, probably near Miastolas," said Cedric, and the twins swung their swords around to find it. "We must be some distance away from either of them, since the light is so faint. Once you are closer, the light in the stone will grow brighter, even when the sword is not pointing right at a gem, if it is close enough."

"What happens after you put a stone into the sword?" asked Orven, "Does the light keep glowing then?"

"Oh, no," said Cedric, "If it did, you wouldn't be able to find the others. The sword shields the gems. Once one is set in place, it will no longer cause the glow, allowing the other gems to be found."

The twins looked in wonderment at the swords as they thought of the lost gems. Both were silent awhile, and then Orven spoke in a quiet, curious voice. "Why are you giving them to us?"

"Who else?" Cedric laughed. "I'm too old to take them to the Castle myself, though I consider King Jordgen a good king. Wendolin might be dead, and I won't be living much longer. Besides, you're like grandsons to me, and now you're leaving. No better time to hand them over. And no better dwarves to hand them over to."

"Do you want us to take them to the King?" asked Iaven.

"I'd rather go looking for the gems myself!" said Orven.

"If you join his army, you'll probably have to hand the sword over anyway," said Iaven.

Orven smiled. "With this sword, and three gems in it, they'll *have* to give me high rank, or else I won't join."

Iaven looked at his sword, bowed by the responsibility it brought. He briefly thought of selling it and using the money to keep the farm going, but knew how foolish that would be with the shadow of war hanging over them. He even considered giving it to Orven, but something told him that was a bad idea.

"Why don't you want to help the Kingdom?" Orven chided. "Come along with me and find the gems, and when we have them, we'll be heroes in the war!"

"I'm no warrior, and I'd gladly turn my sword over to the King," said Iaven. "Maybe he'd even reward me."

"You're a coward!" Orven snapped. "You'd sit on this farm until Goblins overran the fields. You're thinking only of yourself!"

"I am not!" Iaven retorted, "All you want is power and glory! I'm willing to give my sword over to the Kingdom—"

"Orven, Iaven, come on now!" said Cedric. "I didn't give you the swords so you could duel. Do what you think is best with them, even if you don't agree on the same thing. But whatever you do, remember the war we may be facing."

Orven was quieter now. "They won the last war without the swords."

"Just barely," Cedric pointed out. "Maëlveronde was young then, and on the island. He's been gone a long time, and has one of the gems with him. At least one. Who knows what he's been doing? And the Kingdom has grown since then, and the Goblin Kingdom has too."

"If Maëlveronde was so powerful back then, what would he be like today?" Iaven asked.

Cedric shrugged. "I wouldn't want to run into him."

The three of them were silent. In the fireplace, glowing embers crumbled into ash. After a moment Cedric leaned forward, got to his feet, and made his way across the room. "Well, I'm off to bed! Good night!"

The twins sheathed the swords and got up. They wished Cedric good night, thanking him again. They started out the door, when suddenly Orven looked troubled and turned back.

"One last thing," he asked Cedric, "If we follow the sword and go after a gem, how will we know that it isn't the one that Maëlveronde has?"

Cedric smiled. "Ah, well, be careful! It could be. There is no way to know."

Chapter 4.
A Parting of Ways

The following afternoon found Iaven and Orven busy cleaning up after the wedding party, which had gone on long into the night. By noon the last remaining guests had woken up and left, embarrassed and dazed. Flies buzzed scraps of food on the lawn and spilled beer on the tabletops. Flaps of the pavilion tent waved lazily in the midday breeze.

Tables and chairs on loan from the Spurros' Riverbank Inn had to be returned, and Iaven cleared and wiped them clean while Orven took down the lanterns. As Iaven worked, visions of Cedric's tales still burned in his mind's eye. His thoughts broke off when a frightened squirrel leapt from under a toppled chair. Iaven watched the squirrel bounding away across the lawn.

"Thinking of the swords?" said Orven. "And Cedric. So much we never knew about him."

"I wonder how much he told Dad. Do you think he told him about the swords?" Iaven said.

"Dad wouldn't have said anything if Cedric had asked him not to."

"I know. To think he had them here all the while..." That morning, Iaven had examined Halix. In the bright sunlight, the sword seemed more real and concrete, not just some object of lore. He had hefted it around in his hands wondering how it would feel to use it in a fight. He couldn't imagine himself amidst the frenzy of battle.

"I would have never let them lay hidden for so long," Orven said. "Wendolin may be long dead, and Maëlveronde might already have all the gems." Orven stepped down from the chair, a string of lanterns in his hand. He, too, had raised his sword that morning, feeling its power and running his fingers along the shining blade. The dark, gaping holes in Gorflange's hilt called to him like open mouths crying out for the gems, and he longed to see them filled.

"So you're still joining the army, then?" said Iaven.

"As soon as I can," said Orven. "With a sword like that, I'm sure to rise in the ranks. Of course, I'll have to find three gems before I go." Orven rolled a big iron fish-boil kettle and stacked it on another. "What are you doing with yours, anyway?"

"My sword? I don't know..."

"You weren't thinking of selling it, or something, were you?"

"No!" Iaven snapped back, too ashamed to admit the thought had crossed his mind.

"So what're you going to do with it? Max is coming with me, I'm sure he could use—"

"I'm not just giving it away. It's too important. And what if we did have to go to war?"

"I thought you didn't believe in that," Orven said. "You can't just hang it over the mantle and forget about it. It was made for the defense of the Kingdom."

"I know," said Iaven. "But you act like you're more interested in your own glory than anything else."

"You want me to find the gems and then hand the sword over to them? Why should I? It's mine now. Sure, I'll use it to fight for the Kingdom, but it'll be mine. And if you won't do anything with yours or take it to the King, then give it to someone who will!"

Iaven glared at Orven. "Thinking only of yourself! Like always. Even when we were young—"

"You're the one who can't see past the farm fields," Orven retorted. "Afraid of anything that might force you to change!" Both twins were yelling now, locked in a shouting match that almost always ended in a fight. Sara and Hagen had seen it happen too many times, and little had improved as the twins grew older. As adults they were more civil despite their differences, but their fights, though fewer, were more bitter and stubborn as tempers flared and neither would back down.

As they fought, neither one noticed Zammond approaching, watching and smiling. He usually found their disputes mildly amusing. In childhood he had been more a friend of Orven's and sometimes even picked on Iaven together with him. As they grew older, Zammond had drifted more toward thoughtful and even-tempered Iaven, gradually finding he had less in common with Orven. He and Iaven were best friends now, but he knew both twins well and was not beyond accusing Iaven of being a stick-in-the-mud when the occasion called for it. Finally, the twins turned to see what he wanted, annoyed at the interruption.

"Swords!" said Zammond. "Your fights *are* getting serious! What's all this talk of swords?"

Iaven and Orven looked at each other, knowing Zammond would eventually get it out of them. "Famous swords," Iaven grunted. "The Lost Swords of the Alliance, actually."

"You're joking!" Zammond looked to Orven, who nodded.

"It's true," said Orven. For once, Zammond was speechless.

Iaven began telling Zammond about the swords and gems, with Orven interrupting whenever he felt Iaven had left out important details. Zammond listened, noticing how both twins were really presenting their ideas of what should be done with the swords. Zammond much preferred the idea of an adventure but said nothing. The twins, however, kept pressing him for an opinion.

"Unbelievable... Maybe worth a trip to the Castle, eh?" Zammond looked to Iaven. "Can I see them, the swords?"

They all went in the house and Iaven brought Halix out to show Zammond.

"*Halix* and *Gorflange*... Pretty fancy swords, to be given names." Zammond held Halix in his hands, marveling at the craftsmanship, and knew Orven was right about what should be done with the swords. He immediately considered how he might persuade Iaven to take Halix to the Castle, or at least let him do so. He was still enthralled as Iaven took it back, when a loud knock at the door broke him from his reverie.

It was Maxmire Huffe, a burly farmhand whom Orven often went hunting with. "Hey Orven… Iaven, Zammond..." Max said, stepping inside. "What's going on here?" Neither Iaven nor Zammond seemed a likely candidate for bearing a sword.

"I'll tell you all about it," said Orven, shutting the door. "But first, I've got something to show you." Orven went into his room and Max followed, glancing at Halix as he went.

"Last night Max was talking about joining the army with Orven," Zammond told Iaven, *"Beer encourages bold deeds*, as they say, or at least promises of them. But I bet he will now, seeing the swords."

"Well he's not getting mine, whatever Orven thinks," said Iaven. He took Halix back into his room, sheathed it, and after a moment's thought, put it in a drawer where it might be less of a temptation.

"You're going to do *something* with it, aren't you?" asked Zammond.

"I suppose," said Iaven, as he left the room and the conversation.

Zammond let it rest, for the moment. He could bide his time. In the front room Iaven stood looking out the window. Across the lawn, three people were approaching from town. Iaven stepped outdoors to greet them and Zammond followed.

It was Sara and Rory, and talking with them, old Horace Henshaw. Iaven had never liked old Henshaw, whose shifty eyes made him seem perpetually suspicious. He had always liked the layout of the Ambersheath farm, so Iaven feared the worst and his heart sank as he watched them approach.

"Iaven, good news! Call Orven!" said Sara, as Rory began booming "Orven! Orven!" in his gruff baritone. Henshaw grinned at Iaven, and Iaven cringed.

Orven and Max came out of the house. "Iaven, Orven... We've sold the farm!" shouted Sara. "Horace just agreed on the price. And you'll both be getting a share."

"What about Cedric?" asked Iaven.

"He can stay, if he wants," said Rory. "Or move in by the smithy with us; it's up to him." He turned to Henshaw, "Let's go tell him the news." Rory led Henshaw away, discussing other farm matters that needed resolving.

"Horace said you could stay and work on their farm, if you want," Sara told Iaven when they had gone. "Though I know you were never fond of him."

"I couldn't work for someone else on our farm," said Iaven. "And certainly not the Henshaws. I suppose I could work for Rory. I don't know..."

"And there is the inheritance," Sara reminded him.

"It couldn't come at a better time," said Orven. "I'll need it for traveling."

"We certainly will." Max smiled. Orven threw him a sidelong glance.

"Well, Iaven, it'll give you time to think of what to do." Sara smiled. Iaven knew she was proud of Orven even though it pained her to see him go, and sensed she expected the same of him.

That week Sara and Rory removed the last of their belongings and the Henshaws began bringing things over. Iaven took what little he had over to the smithy and found himself visiting Cedric quite often. Cedric had decided to stay on in his cottage, giving advice as needed and enjoying walks around the countryside while he still could. He said he was too old to be moving again, and joked that he probably wouldn't be there very long anyway. His health had been failing of late, and Iaven knew he would miss Cedric terribly when his time came. Zammond often accompanied Iaven to Cedric's, brightening the visits and trying to convince Iaven to go off to the Castle and take the sword to King Jordgen. Zammond's persistence was wearing Iaven down and he had run out of excuses. At last they sat talking on the porch of Cedric's cottage.

"Maybe I'll go," said Iaven, "if Wilbur will come with us."

"Wilbur?" said Zammond, annoyed. Wilbur Millow was less likely to go than Iaven was. He lived in the tiny village of Oakitsburrow, by the Sea, and hadn't even come for the wedding, having given some excuse as usual. Since the Millows had moved away to Oakitsburrow they had seen much less of him.

"So you really don't intend to go," Zammond said. "You might as well say that, if it depends on Wilbur."

"I've been thinking of going to Oakitsburrow, to get away from everything and think things over," said Iaven, "Might as well ask him, don't you think?"

Zammond remained skeptical, looking at Iaven as if he were using one of Wilbur's excuses.

"Alright," Iaven said, "just let me go to Oakitsburrow and think it over. I don't really want to work at the smithy, and something's got to be done with the sword."

Iaven got up to leave and Zammond smiled, pleased he was making progress.

One morning later that week, a cold breeze blew as Orven, Max, and their friend Aaron Spurro arrived at Cedric's cottage. They spread out some of Hagen Ambersheath's old traveling maps in the sunlight on the table and began poring over them. Cedric sat smoking his pipe as he told them about various places and answered questions.

"The sword points north, into Rundlewood. Or is it pointing *through* the forest, to Kronivar?" Orven looked to Cedric. Max held the sword steady to the north, looking at the faint glow in the small blue-green stone set into the tip of the pommel.

"Might be," said Cedric, "but seeing how far away Kronivar is, I'd guess it's probably in the forest, from the look of it. Never saw the gems and swords together, you know."

"So we'll have to go through the forest," said Orven. Between Kronivar and the Foothills lay great expanses of the Rundlewood Forest. In the deep woods lived the Rundlewood Gnomes, a fierce tribal people the Dwarves considered primitive but feared all the same. The Gnomes rarely left the forest and were only seen by unlucky travelers passing through Rundlewood and in the nightmares of frightened children whose parents told them stories to keep them from wandering off into the woods.

On the map, a solitary road led northward through the forest from the Foothills area. Just before it reached the center of the forest it veered east, towards the mountains, reemerging onto the South Road near Bottomcliffe. Everyone knew the story of the Forest Road. Over two hundred forty-some years ago when the Foothills were still being settled, the Dwarves had wanted a more direct route to Kronivar than the South Road that ran alongside the mountains. They began building a road into the forest, but less than halfway in they fell under constant attacks by the Gnomes. Forced to give up the northerly route, they cut the road eastward, the attacks lessening as the road went east. The Gnomes appeared to live mainly around Lake Rundlemere and the river deltas, and in the lands south of Kronivar and westward to the cliffs overlooking the Silver Sea. They kept to themselves, deep in the forest. As long as you stayed on the road, you'd be alright, or so travelers were always told.

Orven looked at the vast spread of forest on the map. Except for the lake, the region lacked interior detail except where the tiny thread of the Forest Road and the rivers wove their way through it. The forest was another reason the Dwarves of the Foothills were not worried about Goblin spies. It seemed unlikely anyone would take the trouble to pass through the forest to come so far south.

"Too dangerous, with the Gnomes," said Cedric, "Why don't you look for the gem in Miastolas?"

"The Elves must have it already," said Orven, "I want one for the sword. It's probably just lost in the forest somewhere. The gnomes wouldn't even know what it was."

"Have any of you actually seen the Gnomes?" said Aaron. "I haven't, but then I've only been through Lower Rundlewood, by the Rhil, and they say the Gnomes don't go down that far south." Aaron Spurro was a year younger than Orven and Max, of smaller build, with steel-gray eyes and a quick, keen mind. Orven had invited him along for his clear thinking and culinary skills learned at his parents' inn. Aaron was usually quiet and withdrawn, and Orven hoped the trip would let them get to know him better.

"From what I've heard they're mostly north of the Yandl," said Max. "But who knows. You hear all kind of stories. Like about the *orrems* that walk the forest. Though I don't know anyone who's actually seen one."

"Oh, the Gnomes are there alright," said Cedric. Everyone had heard stories of Gnomes watching travelers from the trees, their beady eyes gleaming with green fire. Others fell victim to tiny, poisoned arrows that left them paralyzed and open to plunder. Rumors circulated of babies carried off into the woods, or dwarves who had succumbed to the Gnomes' wiles and been lured away to their deaths. Some claimed to see them canoeing under the Yandl Bridge, or climbing about high above in tree branches, always watching. Others said the road was safe, if you never strayed from it. Still other tales told of ghosts and wraiths wandering Rundlewood, or the *orrems*, the tall wooden creatures with long, jointed legs that the Gnomes brought to life and rode through the depths of the forest.

"My grandmother's neighbor, Erlen, something happened to him," said Aaron, "He and his father were returning from Bottomcliffe by the Forest Road. They wanted to get through Rundlewood as quickly as they could and took turns driving the cart. The old man was driving while Erlen lay in the hay in back, trying to nap. He woke after his father had stopped the cart. When he gets up, the old man's gone. He calls out, but there's no reply. A shriek and a moan make him jump. The horse is restless, wanting to get out of there. And weeds by the woods are moving. Erlen walks over slowly, his pitchfork trembling in his hands. His father's dagger is lying on the grass. Noises are coming from the woods; horrible soft whimperings. Something terrible is going on in there.

"He takes another step forward and the noises stop. He's all nerves, his heart's pounding. Then suddenly he thinks he sees gnomes watching him. The forest was dark, but he was sure of it. He drops the pitchfork and runs. Unhitching the horse, he rides off on it, at a gallop, getting as far away as he can without stopping."

"And no one ever saw the old man again?" Orven asked.

"Sometime later, two miners were driving on the Forest Road," Aaron continued, "About midday they came across someone staggering around in the road. Moving all funny like; not normal, you know. His skin was pale, he looked shriveled, all his hair gone white. His eyes were blank, like his mind was gone. They approached him slowly, but the old man screamed and ran off into the forest, like a wild animal. No one ever saw him after that."

"Maybe the old man was already crazy" said Orven.

"Your dad's friend Bill, saw something, too," said Cedric. "When he was young, he and two friends were traveling the Forest Road on foot, with their hunting dog, Grum. They walked all day, camping at night by the road. They'd stayed on the road and hadn't seen anyone, so they were feeling fairly safe, even though they were quite far north. That afternoon they were talking and joking and everything was fine, when Grum starts barking and looking off the roadside. At first they think he's spotted a rabbit or something, so they tell him to go after it. But he doesn't go; he's afraid of it. So they go over to see what it is.

"Bill looks in, sees it, and shouts. It looks like a dead body, but then he realizes it isn't. It's a stone statue lying there, so detailed he thought it was a real dwarf. The dwarf's head was at an angle, looking away, and his clothes, boots, his hands folded on his chest, they all looked so real; whoever carved it was a master, he thought.

"Well, he's looking at it, and the other two come over by it, but the dog won't. It stands and barks like it wants them to get away from it. They decide it's quite a find and decide to drag it onto the road, into the sun, to get a better look at it. So one takes hold of the feet, and Bill kneels near the arms to help pull it out. But as he kneels down, he looks the statue in the eye and suddenly pulls back. The others ask him what's wrong. 'He looked at me' he says, 'He could see me.' Well, they think he's crazy, but they go over by the statue, and get the same feeling. Now they don't want to touch it or go by it at all. 'It may be stone, but it's not carved,' one of them says.

"They left it there and swore they'd never take the Forest Road again. Bill says he'll never forget those sad and pleading eyes, begging him to help. He said maybe they ought to have broken it up, but they didn't even do that, so maybe he's still alive, lying out there somewhere to this day."

"We'll let you know if we see him," said Orven.

"Orven, I'm quite serious," said Cedric. The woven image from Teska flashed in his mind; the dwarf in it had looked like Orven. "Promise me you won't go after the gem in the forest. If you must take the forest path, never leave it. Set double watches at night. But I'd rather you didn't go in there at all."

"We'll be careful," said Orven.

"Will you promise me?"

"Alright," Orven relented. "But you needn't worry about us. We'll all be armed, too."

"And there'll be five of us," said Max, "Roy and Ripley are going, too. I talked them into it just yesterday."

"They still haven't decided to join the King's army with us," said Orven.

"They will," said Max, "once they see the Castle and the mountains. Besides, they'd have to come back without us." He leaned back, looking at Cedric. "That must have really been something, to be there for the Great War. Orven was telling me about it all."

"People have forgotten," Cedric said. "Those were dark times; nothing was a sure thing. The Goblins almost took the Castle. Many lives were lost."

"We'll be ready for them this time," said Max. "They say the border guard in Teska is better than it was in the old days. The Gates are sure to hold."

"Mmmhhh," Cedric shrugged, drawing on his pipe. "Let's hope so."

Orven was still contemplating the wide expanse of unknown that was Rundlewood, weighing tales he'd heard about the forest and the Gnomes, wondering how much of it was true. He was about to ask Cedric something when a knock came at the door and Iaven entered, a pack slung over his shoulder. He seemed in high spirits for the first time in days.

"I'm off to Wilbur's," said Iaven. "Been a while since I've seen him. I wonder what he'll make of all this."

"Running away, eh?" Orven chided. "I suppose compared to Wilbur, you do seem adventurous. What would Wilbur do with the sword? Perhaps you could ask his advice!"

"I was going to, actually," Iaven said. "He's quite sensible about things."

"And likely to agree with you, too!" Max added. He and Orven laughed.

"I haven't reached a decision," Iaven snapped back. "I'm going to Oakitsburrow, and I'm in no hurry." He turned to Cedric. "About the smithy work— I'd like to ask you more about it when I get back."

"I'll be here," said Cedric. "Take your time, think it over." He smiled and puffed on his pipe, rocking slowly in his chair.

"But don't deliberate too long," added Orven. "War is coming and the swords are dearly needed. I don't expect you to join the troops, but don't forget the Kingdom, either. If serving in the smithy is your way, then so be it. But let the sword serve its purpose in battle, even if you don't."

Orven's contempt made Iaven burn. Yet he saw the truth in what Orven said. Max looked at Iaven as if he had a right to Halix. Unconsciously, Iaven touched his hand to the hilt, as if to reassure himself it was still there. For a moment he seemed ready to draw it to defend himself. He stood glaring at Orven. "Wherever I serve, it'll be the Kingdom I serve, not my own hunger for glory."

Orven rose from the table, leering at Iaven. Cedric shifted in his chair and stood. "And we'll all fight together, won't we," he said, leaning on his cane and crossing between the twins. He started laughing, his amusement breaking the tension. "Always sparring, the two of you. If only the whole Kingdom were as ready to fight!" The moment passed and they were calm again, at least for Cedric's sake.

Iaven turned to Cedric, who was poking a log in the fireplace with the tip of his cane. "I'll stop by when I get back," he said. He hoisted the pack higher up on his shoulder and left.

"Still the same. Worse since your dad died. Takes a brother to raise one's ire like that. If anyone can get him to fight, it's you," said Cedric.

"Maybe," said Orven, sitting back down. "Though I doubt he'd be much good in a fight. He's better off in the smithy, I suppose."

"And I was so hoping to get that sword." Max smiled.

Cedric returned and sat down again. "You and your brother are still a lot alike," Cedric said. "Oh, you have your differences, but you Ambersheaths have a lot in common. Your dad could be stubborn, too. Give Iaven time, he'll decide."

Orven grunted, returning to the map. "That'll be a day long in coming. There aren't enough gems for both swords anyway, if Maëlveronde has one of them. Now let's have a look at the South Road."

Cedric tapped out his pipe and set it aside. "Long way to the Castle, by any road."

"Father was gone a few weeks when he went to Kronivar," Orven said. "And that was with the cart." He followed the roads leading out of the Foothills and the long South Road that ran along the mountains on its way north to the crossroads. Orven's eyes wandered back to the Rundlewood Forest again, the thin, wavering line of a road there offering a shortcut. The great expanse of unknown fascinated him. And in the heart of those dark woods a gem lay beckoning him.

Chapter 5.
By the Shore of the Silver Sea

Iaven had traveled to Oakitsburrow with his father and by himself when he was older. He and Orven usually alternated trips out of Hillbrook (his father had taken them both once, but tired of their bickering). Iaven always chose the Oakitsburrow trips, so he could visit Wilbur and look out over the Silver Sea. After their father's passing, Orven did most of the traveling, but Iaven still took the Oakitsburrow trips. Even after the farm's decline he had gone a few times. On foot the journey took all day, and Iaven enjoyed the solitude of the bright sunlit meadows.

The road bounded over hills, wound through overgrown fields, and past swards of flowering trees dropping their last blossoms. Sometimes it veered north, the River Rhil glittering in the distance, or south, through long stretches of fallow land and thickets surrounding farmland. In good pasturelands, hedgerows of trees and bushes lined the borders of neighboring fields. Cows and goats grazed on farms whose small houses sat atop distant hills, or straddled rivers with waterwheels turning at their sides. Birds chirped from high branches and flew in lazy swoops over the rolling ground. Broad, tilting arms of horizontal windmills creaked and turned in the breeze. From higher swells of land Iaven saw distant sun-dappled ponds where cows drank. Occasionally he passed horse-drawn carts loaded with the season's last produce. His shadow lengthened behind him as the sun sank into the west.

The day waned into twilight, and Iaven reached the outlying areas of Oakitsburrow where farms grew smaller and more frequent. Farmers herded animals into enclosures and bundled firewood for the evening's light and warmth. Iaven quickened his pace, shivering a little as cooling evening air from the west blew around him.

Night fell. Thin plumes of smoke rose from stone chimneys throughout the land. The aroma of hickory fires lingered like incense, lulling Iaven to dream of fireside warmth. Fire-lit windows of farmhouses glowed where families rested together at the day's end. Many were the days Iaven had trudged home through darkening fields after a long day's labor, toward the lighted windows of the Ambersheath homestead. They'd gather inside, his mother ladling soup from kettles hanging over the fire. After plates of steaming food, he'd rest by fireside, half-dozing and pleasantly sated. He envied those returning home whose worries did not extend beyond the borders of their farms. His steps heavier, Iaven gazed down the road into gray dimness. A cool, moist breeze blew stronger now as he neared the Silver Sea.

A small lane took him south and then westward again. Soon he rounded a hill and looked up at the long, rambling wooden building on it, its windows bright and full of voices and laughter that carried even to where he was passing. Old Fothergill's Inn was where his father had always stayed in Oakitsburrow. The Inn brewed its own beer and its fish fries brought folks in from all over the Foothills. Old Fothergill himself was fond of the Ambersheaths' mushrooms, and Hagen often returned with a keg of beer in trade. Though Iaven usually stayed overnight at Wilbur's, his father had taken him inside the Inn to meet his friends there. Iaven remembered Old Fothergill, a rotund, stubbly-cheeked dwarf with a bright eye and a ready laugh, who liked people and conversed just as easily with a child as with dwarves his own age or older. Iaven wondered if Old Fothergill was still there and whether things would be as he remembered them. He was tempted to go in and see, but the sky was darkening, a chill was growing, and the Millow homestead still lay a short way ahead.

The road led downhill away from the Inn and turned down a dark tree-lined lane. Iaven passed houses set back into the woods, and soon came upon the modest thatched-roof house where the Millows resided. Wilbur and his little brother Theo sat on the porch, watching swirls of smoke rising from the glowing end of Theo's burning cattail. Wilbur caught sight of Iaven and got up.

"Iaven! Sorry to hear about the farm. I just got your letter earlier today."

"Well, I'm glad it got here in time. Hello, Theo!" Iaven bent to sniff the smoke as Theo smiled up at him.

"Had any supper?" asked Wilbur, opening the door for Iaven. Iaven entered the Millow household, the rich scent of lard and onions bringing past childhood visits to mind.

As they stepped inside, Wilbur's mother Emma bid Iaven to lay his pack aside and sit down. She fixed him a hot plate of food, all the while chiding Wilbur for his inattentiveness to his guest while she did everything for him. Wilbur grunted and acquiesced. Iaven finished eating and thanked Mrs. Millow, noticing Wilbur's eagerness to leave and talk elsewhere. Having always liked the Silver Sea, he suggested they go there, and Wilbur agreed.

Soon they walked down the darkened lane and hillside. Wilbur was withdrawn and Iaven could not fathom his expression in the dark. Wilbur had put on weight since he had last seen him, but Iaven decided not to mention it.

"I'm tired of it," Wilbur said at last, "Even though Lann and father fight constantly over the store, I'll never really have any part of it for myself."

Iaven nodded. Wilbur's ailing father owned a dry goods store, which he had begun turning over to Lann, his eldest son, who was six years older than Wilbur. Lann, however, had different ideas as to how to run the store and did not hesitate to put them into practice. This upset Mr. Millow who wanted things done his way; after all, there was still young Theo and little Gretta to consider. Yet he dearly needed Lann's help and couldn't do without him, so they were always at loggerheads. And when Wilbur had suggested that he might run the store while Lann began a business of his own, both Lann and his father had scoffed at the idea. Wilbur made a fine counterman, they said, but managing the store was quite a different matter; and besides, as the eldest, Lann was most entitled to it anyway. Wilbur was welcome (and expected) to work for him as second-in-command, but letting him run it was out of the question. Wilbur admitted he wasn't one for haggling and competition —Lann had always gotten everything first in their family— so he had finally agreed and that was the end of it.

"Maybe I wouldn't be all that good at it, but I'd like to try. Or at least I could run it along with Lann, instead of just working for him."

"So what are you going to do?" asked Iaven.

Wilbur shrugged. "Keep going like I am, I suppose. Maybe I'll get used to it." Wilbur sighed. "I guess I shouldn't complain."

They arrived at the bluffs. Stone steps, pale in the starlight, led down the steep hill curving toward the beach, where large rocks lined the water's edge. A breeze blew over the waves rolling into shore. Iaven and Wilbur crossed the sand, climbed onto the rocks, and sat gazing out over the dark, shimmering expanse of the Silver Sea.

As they relaxed, the sea rippled and sparkled with starlight, washing onto shore and drawing back out again with a soft hushing roar like the slow breath of a giant deep in slumber. Waves splashed the rocks, rising between them, and then pulled out to join the waters stretching away into darkness. Only pinpoints of stars and their soft, wavering reflections gave any hint as to where the water ended and the sky began.

Iaven sat awhile in contemplation until Wilbur spoke. "What about you— what are you going to do now that the farm's sold?"

Iaven leaned back on the rocks. "Zammond wants to go traveling," he said, and told Wilbur about Cedric, the swords, the gemstones, and Orven's plans. Wilbur lay watching the stars and saying little, yet prompting Iaven if he paused for too long. At the end of the tale Wilbur remained silent. Iaven thought he had dozed off, until he finally spoke again.

"Well I wouldn't go into Rundlewood either," said Wilbur, "And the Castle *is* far away..."

"So I told Zammond. In fact, I said I'd only go if—"

"Though it would be something to see, wouldn't it?" Wilbur sat up again. "My Uncle Leo used to work unloading ships in Kronivar, until he got too old and moved back here; we've heard his stories many times. Dad considering going, but never had the time —or the inclination, I think." He slumped back onto his elbows. "It is kind of far, though. Lann wanted to go up to Kronivar last year, but Dad said it would take too long, he needed him here." Wilbur shifted his weight as resentment crept into his voice. "I said I could take care of it, but no; it had to be Lann. He just wanted to keep him here, that's all. He's afraid Lann will like it up there, or something, and lose interest in the store. I could never move away from here, but do you think that means anything to him?"

"Well, if you don't want to go, I can understand," said Iaven.

"Oh, I didn't say that." Wilbur gazed across the sea. "Maybe a short trip would be nice. I wouldn't go all the way to the Castle, and even Kronivar is pretty far. We wouldn't be going after the gems, right? I'd hate to run into Maëlveronde. Hard to imagine, all that going on, way out there on the island." They looked westward into the blackness, even though the island was much too far away to be seen. Iaven thought about all that had happened there, until he could almost sense the island's presence, invisible in the darkness beyond the horizon. Aorinthel's tower had long lain empty now, perhaps overgrown by vines or inhabited by rodents and birds. Iaven wished Maëlveronde was still imprisoned there, and the need to deliver the sword to the Castle seemed all the more urgent.

Maëlveronde, of course, had escaped from the island long before Iaven was born. Yet the dark waters held Iaven's gaze, his mind drifting to the day, eleven years ago, when his father left for Highwater, where he boarded the *Yoner* and set sail. The evening before his departure from Hillbrook, Hagen had come in late, returning home after saying goodbye to friends at the Riverbank Inn. Sara was waiting up for him, getting his pack ready. Hagen's friend Dorand Ell was coming for him early the next morning, to take him to Highwater. Iaven and Orven were already in bed. The twins' room was at the end of the hall, and soft firelight from the kitchen spilled under the bedroom door. Iaven lay awake in the dark. He saw the light on the floor flicker as his father came in from outside, and heard the door close behind him.

"Careful, dear," he heard his mother say in hushed tones. "The twins are asleep."

"Yes, dear, of course," said his father. "Oh, look at all this, how sweet of you... so much, though!"

"You'll need fresh clothes," his mother said, "This will be longer than you've ever been away." Her voice wavered. "You have to go... oh, I know, it's just so long."

"There, there," said his father. Iaven imagined his father putting his arms around his mother, reassuring her. "No different than any of the other long trips. The twins and Cedric can take care of the farm alright, and before long I'll be back. I'm only going this once, and they'll be buying after that. The harvest will be bigger next year."

"It's not your fault," said his mother, "We've had bad weather, Cedric said so. You can't blame yourself."

"I know, I know," his father spoke softly. "Whatever it is, this will help us out. It's for the best."

"It's not your fault," his mother repeated, her voice breaking.

Iaven heard his mother sniffle, and tensed, feeling her sorrow. It was so unlike her to cry, he thought. She had always been so calm and comforting whenever he needed her, and made everything alright again.

"And you've never gone by ship before," his mother said, tears in her voice now, "and so far away…"

"They travel by ship all the time," said his father, "The Men do anyway, and a few dwarves have tried it. I wouldn't trust those smaller boats either, but the *Yoner* is a big merchant vessel, bigger than a house and stronger, too. We'll be fine." They were silent awhile, and Iaven heard nothing but the faint crackle of the fire. He imagined them standing together, arms around each other, his mother's head on his father's shoulder.

"I'll miss you," his mother said, her voice muffled.

"You'll be fine," his father said, and then kissed her. "So will the twins. Iaven will be fine."

Iaven's heart sank as his name was mentioned. Why did his father name him specifically? They didn't need to worry about him any more than Orven. He was just as tough and could bear the same hardships, couldn't he? There was no need to single him out. He was suddenly glad Orven was asleep, Orven who would gloat over it and tease him about it for weeks to come. He almost wished he had been asleep, too, and not overheard anything. But maybe it was better to know, Iaven thought. He would work harder and prove himself, and his father would take notice. But the chance never came.

The following morning everyone arose early to see Hagen off. Sara made breakfast without a hint of her sorrow from the night before. Iaven and Orven were both tense about their father's departure, and Iaven knew she didn't want to make it any harder for them. Cedric, too, helped keep everyone's spirits up.

Just as they were finishing breakfast, Dorand Ell's wagon arrived, loaded down with apples and plums he was taking to market in Highwater. Hagen kissed Sara and hugged everyone goodbye, and soon he and Dorand were on their way. Iaven and Orven stood in the road, waving as the wagon disappearing overhill. Sara went back into the house, and Cedric motioned the twins off to work in the fields.

Iaven lay back on the rocks. The soft, rushing waves lapped against the stones. Iaven wondered if his father's ill-fated sea journey had made him more cautious and reluctant to leave Hillbrook, and he resolved to go to the Castle regardless of what Wilbur decided.

Iaven looked over to where Wilbur lay. That Wilbur hadn't entirely rejected the idea of a journey surprised him, and he now hoped that Wilbur *would* want to come along. "You've been quiet," said Iaven, "What are you thinking about over there?"

"What? Oh, nothing really," Wilbur said, "The sea reminds me of Uncle Leo's old stories and sea-songs. I loved hearing them; they made me want to travel and see the world. But I've never left the Foothills. Maybe that's why they always interested me so much."

They sat awhile in silence. A bracing wind blew a spray of fine mist off the water. "How I miss Uncle Leo," Wilbur continued, "What a life he must have had, in that great port city; people coming and going, ships from far-off lands bearing strange goods, so many buildings, so close together. I wondered half the time if he was making some of it up."

"So now you'd like to see Kronivar?" asked Iaven.

"Oh, I don't know." Wilbur laughed. "Maybe. His stories did scare me, sometimes. But this talk of war is worse. Friends of mine have been talking about joining the King's troops. '*You'll get a better position if you go early*' they say, '*And why not if we're going to have to go, eventually?*', though I wonder if we're really all that close to war." He paused, considering the possibility. "Has there been much talk of it in Hillbrook?"

"Some," said Iaven, "Everything from rumors at the Castle to Goblins in the woods. I don't believe a lot of it —or at least the tale-tellers, anyway."

"It's always something, isn't it? Someone loses a cat or dog near the woods, and blames the Gnomes. Now with war looming, it's Goblins." Wilbur sighed. "Kronivar... well, that would be interesting…"

Wilbur drifted off into thought. Iaven sensed his struggle and was about to say something when Wilbur burst out, "All right, why not, I'll take a week off. Let's go!" Iaven was glad to hear it. It would take more than a few weeks, Iaven thought, but he said nothing.

Iaven stayed at Wilbur's for three days. On the fourth they rose early and set out for Hillbrook. Wilbur's father was surprised but did not object to the trip; he even seemed pleased Wilbur was going. "I'd see the Castle myself," he told them, "were not my leaving so bad for business here." Lann, who had just come in, heard the remark and fell to arguing with his father. After a few days at the Millows, Iaven understood how even Wilbur could become restless.

The morning was bright and brisk, good walking weather. Iaven and Wilbur followed the road past Oakitsburrow's farms and through the uncultivated lands beyond them. They spent the day talking and hiking, but spoke little of the swords or the impending war, both of which seemed far removed from the quiet meadows around them. Now and then thoughts of war dimmed Iaven's mood the way shadows of small clouds drift over a sunlit field, darkening it briefly as they pass.

By nightfall they reached the outlying farms around Hillbrook. Iaven became morose as they neared the old farmstead Iaven could no longer call home.

"Let's go see Cedric, as long as we're close by," said Iaven, leading the way to the cottage by the fields where a light burned in the window. They knocked and went in. Cedric sat by the fireplace, mending a cloak. He set it aside as they pulled up chairs and sat down with him.

"Wilbur Millow," said Cedric, "What brings you to Hillbrook? Been quite a while, hasn't it?"

"I suppose it has," said Wilbur, a bit flush at Cedric's quick recognition.

"Couple years now, if I remember rightly," Cedric said, reaching for his pipe on the mantle. "So what brings you by again? A last look at the place?"

"Well," said Wilbur, glancing at Iaven, "we're going to the Castle."

"Wonderful!" Cedric lit his pipe and puffed at it. He leaned back in his chair, smiling, his cheeks rising into crow's feet wrinkles around his eyes. "So did Iaven convince you to go, or was it the other way around?"

"We both decided on it," said Iaven, before Wilbur could answer.

"Orven left this morning," Cedric said, "Along with Max, Ripley, Roy, and Aaron. They went east, towards Miastolas."

"Cedric," Iaven said, "I've been meaning to ask you— did you ever tell Dad about the swords?"

Cedric smiled now as if forced to reveal a guilty secret. "Oh sure, he saw them. He laughed and said it was harder to imagine you two fighting alongside each other instead of against each other. I had to agree with him. I told him not to tell you, in case Wendolin should return for the swords, so he didn't. If only he could've lived to see you get them. I wonder what he would have said."

There was a knock at the door and Zammond peeked inside.

"Iaven! You're back!" Zammond stepped in at Cedric's bidding. "And Wilbur! Well I'll be. Talked him into it did you? They won't believe it."

"They? Who?" Iaven looked annoyed.

"Hob and Tillmore," said Zammond. "They're just about packed for the trip, and neither one thought Wilbur would go. I would've never guessed it either."

"Hob and Tillmore are coming? But I never said I was going!" said Iaven.

"Well you are now, aren't you? I told them ahead of time so we could leave sooner. It wasn't too hard to convince them to go. Anyway, I just came by to see if Cedric had any more of those magic berries, or whatever that stuff was, that he gave Orven before they left."

"Wilderberry *leaf*," said Cedric. "The berries are poisonous; it's the leaves you want, for the healing of wounds. You make a tea out of them, and drink it." He puffed on his pipe. "And yes, I was saving some for Iaven, just in case."

"In case I ended up going."

Cedric shrugged. "You and your brother aren't all that different. Proud, stubborn, won't take any counsel..."

"Alright, alright," said Iaven, "So now that we're going —the five of us, it seems— we may as well figure out what we're going to need."

Delighted, Zammond pulled up a chair, anxious to hear about the road that lay ahead. Cedric refilled his pipe, ready with advice for the young fire-lit faces waiting to hear tales of what lay beyond their own little corner of the world.

Morning crept into Hillbrook. Clouds brightened in the east. Mists lingered on roads and hovered over fields, like groggy sleepers slow to awaken. The air was still, pierced by birds' cries. Behind a woodshop, a stout, black-bearded dwarf loaded wooden chairs onto his horse cart. Elway Nollins, a friend of Rory's, was taking a load of furniture to Woodmere, up near Lake Grayloch, where his cousin's family was moving. He had agreed to take five dwarves along for part of the journey, as a favor to Rory. Seeing the gray morning, he hoped the added weight wouldn't slow him down too much; looked like rain, he thought. He threw a burlap tarp over the furniture, leaving room on the end of the cart for his passengers, and departed.

Having packed the night before, Iaven and his friends gathered outside Rory's smithy. Soon they were riding out of Hillbrook. Houses and storefronts were shuttered, still in repose. The dwarves passed the town hall with its new bell tower, the cobbler's, the butcher's, and the bakery, where scents of fresh bread baking hung thick and warm in the humid air. Buildings dimmed into the mists behind them, until the hollow clomp of hoof on wood told them they were leaving town over the Rhil Bridge. Iaven took a last look at Hillbrook across the river, with a sudden pang of nostalgia as if he would never see it again.

The morning cleared as the mists settled. The sun, a pale ball of gold, drifted behind veils of cloud, emerging to shine now and then in patches of blue sky. The wind gusted in great yawning breaths, shuddering tree limbs and releasing dried leaves.

The dwarves spoke little, watching the countryside roll past. Iaven was still apprehensive, yet relieved to have started the trip. Zammond sat bolt upright, alert and exhilarated, while Hobley and Tillmore relaxed, imagining what was to come. Even Wilbur was enthusiastic.

They rode into the morning, the rising sun brightening their mood. Fields lay dotted with pumpkins ripe on the vine and corn set out to dry and harden. Farmers sowed wheat seed that would lie dormant until the spring thaw. At last the cultivated land gave way to pastures, and fields of wildflowers past their time of blooming, leaving only asters, snapdragons, and the seedpods of milkweed and wisteria. Bushes and trees gathered into small runs of forest revealing only glimpses of the land beyond them. The dwarves rode listening to the twittering and warbling of birds, soothed by the easy clip-clop rhythm of the horse's hooves. Nollins appeared lost in thought as he drove, and no one felt the need to say anything and break the spell of the morning.

By early afternoon, the road curved and took them over and around hills and finally forked, one branch continuing eastwards, the other winding northwards to Lake Grayloch. Nollins brought the cart to a halt. The five young dwarves got off, shouldering their packs after removing a few apples and bread for lunch.

"Well, here's where I'm turning. Wish the King health and a long life for me, if you see him." Nollins smiled, knowing these rascals would never be granted an audience with the King. "Keep to the roads, and fare you well."

The dwarves went on foot, feeling their journey had really begun now that they were alone. Iaven thought his father would have been excited for them, telling them about places where they were headed. He also wondered if his father would have thought of his journey any differently than Orven's, resolving to complete it and dispel any lingering doubts, even if they were just his own.

It was a beautiful day, brisk but nice for early October, and Iaven soon relaxed again. The sky was strewn with puffs of white cloud. The dwarves had eaten a good lunch and were content. The lands around them were calm and tranquil, but felt strangely empty.

"So how long will it take to get to the South Road?" Wilbur asked.

"About a day or two to Lower Rundlewood, and couple more through the forest. At least that's how it looks on the map," Iaven replied.

"I hope they're right about the Gnomes not coming that far south," said Wilbur.

"We could take the Forest Road if you want to see some," said Zammond. "We'd have a better chance of getting a gem there, too. Even if the one in Miastolas hasn't been found, Orven will get there before us. Wouldn't you rather present the sword to the King with some gems already in it?"

"Apart from remaining alive to present the sword, it would be nice to present it *before* the war begins, or at least before it's over," said Tillmore, "That may prove enough of a challenge even without side-tracking."

"If we found the gems on our way there, that wouldn't be so bad would it? Or if they were a *little* out of the way?" said Zammond.

"Depends how far 'a little' is," Tillmore said.

"I'm eager to see the Castle," said Hobley. "I may even join the troops. Wouldn't mind a look at it all first, though."

"I'll do whatever I can to help the Kingdom," said Wilbur, "But I doubt I'd make a good soldier. And the thought of war scares me." Those days most dwarves carried some sort of weapon when traveling longer distances, especially through the woods. Iaven had Halix; Hobley carried his axe; Tillmore, a long-bladed dagger; and Zammond and Wilbur had short swords from Rory's smithy. Wilbur fingered the hilt of his as he walked and could not quite picture himself using it in battle.

"I don't like it either," Hobley admitted.

In the peaceful countryside, war seemed as remote as old legends. The Foothills, by virtue of their great distance from the northern border, seemed a safe enough place, the impending war little more than an interesting rumor to spice up the monotony of daily chores and routines. Yet the more people tried to reassure themselves, the more doubts grew. By the time news reached Hillbrook it was not always reliable, but it never failed to spark lively debate and wild speculation. Now Iaven and his friends silently weighed all they had heard.

Iaven imagined Hillbrook overrun by Goblins; houses and fields set afire, dwarves fleeing with their families, the less fortunate slaughtered and left behind. How easily they could be caught off guard, and how fast panic would spread, he thought. Hillbrook was as unprepared for war as any town could be.

As autumn settled in, the Dwarves hoped to safely endure the next few months, thinking the Goblins would not risk mounting a winter campaign. As they walked, their talk died down and their thoughts turned inward. The land seemed wide and empty again, making them feel alone and vulnerable. A chill wind blew, whispering through trees and grasses that summer was over. All was quiet, the serenity broken only by distant choruses of geese honking and calling. In long lines forming straggling V-formations they flew south for the winter, their straining cries echoing through the cooling sky.

The sun began its slow descent. Breezes from the west urged the dwarves onward. Their lengthening shadows stretched down the road before them as a fine golden light etched everything in sharp detail. Starred glints of sunlight on metal winked in the distance, where a small band of around two dozen Dwarven soldiers marched toward them. Banners fluttered bearing the King's insignia, a white dragon against a field of purple. Two soldiers carried halberds, blades wide and sharp; another two held glaives. Their captain strode in front, empty-handed, a long broadsword ready at his belt. "Hail, young fellows!" he called.

The Captain was an older dwarf, weathered but sharp-eyed, a chestnut beard curling down his chest. Like the others, his helm of steel was damascened with gold and bronze, an aventail of steel mesh spread across his broad shoulders. Beneath his hauberk he wore a doublet of crimson and purple, with trim worked in gold and silver thread. The designs of the Captain's doublet were more intricate than those of the others, and his bearing more stately. Iaven and his friends unconsciously straightened their posture as they came into his presence.

"I am Captain Edron Halgreve, of His Majesty King Jordgen's army, at your service. And what brings you out into this fair countryside on so fine an evening?" he called, his beard glowing reddish-orange in the dying light.

"We're off to the Castle, sir," Zammond replied, "Any news from there?" Iaven glanced at Zammond, annoyed at his over-eagerness.

The Captain smiled. "Ah, excellent! To serve his majesty, I hope? Well done, young sir." His tone grew grave. "We come to the Foothills bearing tidings from the King. The shadow of war darkens, and all must prepare. We bring news of movements in the north, and hope to raise troops, lads like yourselves, for the King, ere we have to march —or be marched upon."

"Such fears are not unfounded," said a dark-haired dwarf near the Captain. "We keep watch on the northern border, from watchtowers in Teska, the Gates, and the mountainside path. Though the Arinzei Valley is part of Navrogenaya, the Goblins tend to keep their distance, beyond where our lookouts can see. Lately, however, there's been activity in the valley. Not much, but enough to portend trouble. Our spies went to peer where our watchtowers could not. The few who returned reported massing and encampments in the west, just beyond our sight. Their number and purpose remain uncertain, but the threat is clear."

"They say there are Goblin spies in Itharia," Iaven said.

"Yes, despite their denials, the Goblins are still sending spies into our Kingdom," said the Captain. "No one knows how they are doing it. We've doubled the guard at the North Gate and Mountain Gate, which bar the way along with Teska and the mountains. And the Teskans are very vigilant in watching the swamps. The only other way into the Kingdom is the Ruined East Road through the mountains, which the Castle keeps watch over. The border is secure, yet somehow spies are slipping inside. The Goblins already know the lay of the Kingdom; so why they come remains a mystery. Be warned; and tell others. We hope to spread the word, enlisting troops throughout the Foothills as we may."

"We'll do whatever we can," Zammond said.

"Captain," Wilbur inquired, "on your way through Lower Rundlewood, did you happen to see any Gnomes?"

"No," said the Captain, "But other dangers abound. Not all strangers are friendly these days. Stay together and beware." He glanced at the sky. "We've a way to go before setting camp. So have you, it would seem; the South Road is still several days' walk from here." With a nod to his men he departed, the others following in step.

Iaven and his friends watched them go, bidding them farewell. The soldiers marched into the west, toward a deep red-orange sun just above the horizon. The Captain turned back and raised his hand to them. "Take care as you go. Keep a lookout about you. And Godspeed your journey to the Castle!"

The dwarves walked on toward the night rising in the eastern sky. All grew dim around them, and in another hour or so they would have to set up camp. Tired, they spoke less, and their pace slowed. Their mood had dampened considerably, and the sword on Iaven's belt had never seemed as heavy as it did now.

Book II: Stones and Searches

Chapter 6.
The Road to Miastolas

Iaven pulled his cloak around himself and shivered. The eastern sky was lightening but the sun had yet to climb into view. Zammond had wanted to get an early start into the forest and Iaven had agreed. The woods were still dark, the air cool, moist and still. The dwarves plodded along, warmed by the tea Zammond had boiled on a small fire while they were getting up.

"Well, the second night out was better than the first, wasn't it?" Zammond had more enthusiasm than the rest of them combined.

"True," said Tillmore, "no rain or hornet's nest this time."

"I'm still stiff," Wilbur complained. "Not like yesterday, but I can't take many more days of this pace. We're not really in any hurry, are we?"

"I suppose not. We wouldn't make it through Lower Rundlewood in one day," said Tillmore, "No matter how early we started."

The day after meeting Captain Halgreve, Iaven and his friends had hiked the meadowlands, setting camp at the forest's edge. In the morning light Lower Rundlewood was less daunting, but its shadowy interior, an endless hall of innumerable dark pillars with thick undergrowth, lost none of its mystery. Now branches crowded together high overhead, leaving the travelers in deep shade. The air was heavy and motionless, filled with bird cries and the soft chirping of insects. Trees stood tall and dark, rows of silent sentinels standing guard. Lacy veils of spider webs hung from branch and stem, bejeweled with dew.

They walked in silence, listening to leaves rustle and whisper, the trees overhead creaking in the wind. The road turned and ran through corridors of dense, scented pine, and later opened onto long lanes carpeted with fallen leaves. Above and below them the leaves were a dazzling array of bright yellow, crimson, pumpkin orange, saffron, fire ant red, russet, and deep mahogany. The day warmed, though only to the pleasant cool of early October. Now and then honking flocks of geese passed high overhead. By noon, daylight filled the forest with a soft glow. Bright sun-spattered patches of leaves flashed where light slipped down between the trees. The dwarves soon came to a small river, a tributary of the Rhil, and stopped for lunch by some large rocks near the bridge.

While they ate, Zammond couldn't help eyeing Halix on Iaven's belt. "You think Orven's found the gem yet?"

Iaven bit his apple and grunted. He relented and pulled Halix from its scabbard. Zammond took it and began scanning the forest to the east. "Still there! And the light seems a little brighter, too."

"We're not going after them, are we?" said Wilbur.

"Don't you want to see Miastolas?" asked Zammond.

"It's farther east than we're going," said Tillmore, "And if the gem's there, someone's probably already found it."

"I've always wanted to go there, anyway," said Zammond. "Isn't it just over the river?"

"It is out of the way," said Iaven, taking Halix back. "Maybe on the way home."

"The whole point is to see if we can find the gem," said Zammond. "Even if we can't have it, we could at least see it, couldn't we?"

Finishing his lunch, Hobley leaned forward on his axe and got up. "Iaven's right, we ought to get the sword to the King as soon as we can," he said, "We should head for the Castle."

They sat relaxing awhile, 'letting the food settle after a good feed', as Wilbur's father often put it. When the dwarves had rested and were ready to go, Tillmore went down to the riverbank. "Might as well refill our water while we can," he told them.

The others followed his lead, spreading out along the river and finding places in the reeds and cattails close to the running water. Iaven, lagging behind, had to go the farthest to find an opening. He stepped in and squatted down, reaching into the stream and trying to avoid getting water bugs in his flask. The river ran around the rushes and cattails, the riverbed visible a foot or two below the surface. Iaven leaned forward a little more, dipping his flask further in where the water ran faster. As it filled, he relaxed and his gaze wandered. Something caught his eye in the reeds downriver. As recognition hit, Iaven jerked back and fell onto the wet embankment, pulling away up into the tall grasses. Hobley jumped up. "Iaven! What happened? What is it?"

Iaven calmed down, slightly embarrassed. He returned to the water's edge as Hob approached. Hob followed Iaven's stare and his gaze darkened.

"Over there," Iaven said under his breath, his heart still pounding. Half-submerged in the river lay a dead dwarf, stretched out as if he had fallen while running. His neck bent back, his head was turned sideways, half-sunken into the water. Dressed simply, he was perhaps a traveling farmer or craftsman who had been passing through the forest. A dank, swampy stench hung in the air, and flies were buzzing and landing on the dead body. His hair was wet and matted, his beard swaying underwater like dark kelp, and his clothes were soaked and muddy. Ants crawled across his pale, waterlogged face, and over the open eye that remained an inch above water staring at them, glassy, cold, and blank.

The other dwarves arrived behind Hobley. They stopped there, frozen and silent. "Look, on his back," Hobley said. Small black arrows with pointed tailfeathers protruded from the dwarf's stained cloak. "Goblins," Tillmore said gravely.

They stood there, not knowing what to do. Finally, Hobley suggested they bury him. But the prospect of going near the body, much less touching and moving it, was difficult to bear. In the woods nearby they found a small, shallow depression of moist ground, and used sticks to turn up the soil as best they could. Hobley and Zammond dragged the dwarf out of the water by his ankles to avoid seeing his face. The body was stiff and waterlogged, much heavier than they expected. When they moved it the smell grew worse, like a roiled cesspool, turning their stomachs. Wilbur sickened and turned away. The underside of the body was bloated and softened, pierced with insect bites and small teeth marks. Quickly they pulled the body up the bank and laid it in its shallow grave. Solemnly they piled dirt and leaves over it, until it was completely covered. For a while they stood in silence, looking at the small mound.

A rustle of leaves startled them. To the north, between two trees, a stag stood watching them, his sleek, graceful head crowned with a magnificent rack of dark antlers. When they moved, the stag turned and leapt back into the woods, leaving them shaken. Suddenly feeling like trespassers in the forest, they left the grave and went back to the road.

Near the bridge they stopped at the rocks where they had sat lunching earlier. No one felt like talking or going onward. Thoughts of returning home even crossed their minds. After a while they went over the bridge and down the road, their pace more sluggish than before.

"So now what?" said Wilbur, "Are we camping in the forest tonight?"

"He was alone," Zammond said. "There are five of us. And who knows how he got there? Maybe he blundered into them; he was on way back to the bridge, not running from it."

"Maybe he wasn't alone. We really don't know what happened," said Tillmore. "Whatever the case, there's no question of Goblin spies coming this far south."

No one said anything more as they walked. Even Wilbur wanted to keep going, now that they had begun, though all were eager to leave the forest for open lands as soon as possible.

The day drew on. Steeped in their wariness of the forest, the dwarves tensed and drew to the roadside as they heard a wagon approach around the bend in the road behind them. They stood ready, hand on hilt, waiting to see who was coming. The wagon's sound was reassuring; Goblin spies would most likely be on foot, and off the road. Then again, spies could have stolen a wagon. The clip-clop of the horse's hooves was slow and leisurely, and the dwarves' tension grew as they waited.

At last the wagon rounded the corner and the dwarves relaxed a little. Two men were aboard, traders probably, and behind them a cartload of wooden crates covered with a dark burlap tarp. At the reins sat a slightly heavyset man dressed in a dark green shirt, open at the collar, who slowed the horses upon seeing the dwarves. He was nearly forty or so, with light, graying hair and a beard that rimmed his chin with a fringe of gray, though his upper lip was shaven. He smiled at the dwarves, a sparkle in his eye revealing a youthful quality that belied his otherwise sedate appearance. He exchanged a few words with the man beside him, and looked back again, bemused. The other man's clothes and looks were similar to the driver, though he was slimmer, a few years older, and had no beard. He did not smile and was more wary of the dwarves, making them a bit nervous under his gaze. As the wagon neared, the dwarves stepped aside to let it pass, and a moment later it came to a halt in front of them.

"The Splide Brothers, at your service," said the man at the reins. "I'm Lexter, and this is my brother Leland." Leland nodded and said nothing, continuing his scrutiny of the dwarves. "Which way are you fellows headed?" said Lexter.

Iaven and his friends looked at each other, trying to gain consensus as to whether the strangers could be trusted. They seemed to speak Tharic almost as well as Dwarves, but with a slight northern accent. "Eastward, to the South Road," Iaven replied. The awkward moment passed when Hobley stepped forward. "Hobley Elderthorn, pleased to meet you," he said.

The tension eased. The other dwarves introduced themselves, and the two men seemed more relaxed now as well. "Thought we might be getting ambushed," Lexter admitted, smiling at them, "Seeing you fellows standing off the road, weapons in hand."

"These days one never knows," added Leland.

"First time through the forest?" asked Lexter.

The dwarves were unsure if they should reveal their inexperience but their pause had already given them away. "Yes," Iaven replied.

"Always safer traveling together," said Lexter, "We're heading east as well, if you care to ride along with us."

Again the dwarves looked each other. The men appeared friendly enough, but could they be trusted? On the other hand, the prospect of a night or two spent camping in the forest was an unpleasant one; they could keep an eye on the Splides, and outnumbered them better than two to one. So they agreed to the ride, which had been offered in exchange for their assistance should the wagon meet Goblins or an ambush along the way.

Lexter and Leland slid crates over to the side of the wagon, restacked a few, making room for the dwarves. Iaven and the others climbed on, and soon they were off again down the forest road. As they rode, Leland turned to them. "So you're from the Foothills, aren't you?"

"Hillbrook and Oakitsburrow," said Iaven.

"Thought so, by your accents. We just drove in from Iaf and Veyo," Leland said, "up Winding Road, from northern Feäthiadreya," he added, when he saw they did not recognize the old Elven villages.

"Outran a few bandits in the Foothills Pass," added Lexter. "Roads just aren't safe anymore."

"Well at least we're still in Itharia," said Zammond.

"Ah, Itharia, Kingdom of the Dwarves!" said Lexter in lighthearted mock reverence.

"A pleasant notion, certainly, this idea of kingdoms," said Leland with a slight, amused smile. "But what does it mean? A few villages here and there, many miles apart, and it's a country. They perch a castle on a mountaintop —a mere ornament!— and call themselves a kingdom, even being so bold as to name the mountains after themselves. Then there's a war or a rockslide or something, and it crumbles, and their whole kingdom becomes little more than a legend or song, if anyone cares to remember it at all. Have you any idea how large the mountains are, how high, how far away? Or the forests; the Dwarves have barely set foot in Rundlewood —quite rightly, too, considering how long the Gnomes have been there. And what about the legendary Stone Giants in the eastern mountains? And then there are the Teskans and their swamps and marshes. Do you suppose any of them call Itharia home? Or perhaps I should say, *call their home 'Itharia'?* Ah, yes, 'Kingdoms'; the wonderful invention of map-makers and kings!"

"Just a few lines on a map that everyone agrees upon," said Lexter, "Of course, they don't always agree. Although I will admit your countrymen do a fair job of guarding the northern border, with the Gates and the Wall. Yet it seems a few Goblins are slipping in somewhere, so I've heard..."

"But we needn't worry, with these fellows along!" Leland smiled at the dwarves. He looked at them, and the weapons they carried, his eyes stopping on Iaven's belt where Halix was sheathed. "Nice sword you have there, Iaven. May I have a closer look at it?"

Iaven froze, his hand on the hilt of the sword. Could Leland have recognized it? He didn't think so. But hesitating too long might look suspicious, too, like he was hiding something. The others watched to see what he would do. Iaven decided to show that he trusted the Splides, for now at least, and drew the sword from its sheath and handed it to Leland.

"Beautiful craftsmanship." Leland turned the sword over in his hands, caressing and examining the fine detail. "Rarely have I seen anything like it. Looks like you're missing a few gemstones here," he said, fingering the holes in the hilt rimmed with fine metalwork leaves. Iaven grew anxious, watching Leland and trying to hide his uneasiness.

"It belonged to his grandfather," Zammond blurted out, "a family heirloom."

"Yes, they certainly don't make anything like that anymore." Leland handed the sword back to Iaven, his eyes still upon it.

"Do you know much about Dwarven swords?" asked Iaven, relieved to have it back but curious just how much Leland knew.

"Oh, we've bought and sold a few," Leland said, turning and smiling a little to Lexter who returned the grin. Leland looked back to the dwarves. "We're traders, buying and selling, importing and exporting. Getting the right items to the right people can win you a fair amount." He smiled at them and laughed a little. "Right now, we're on our way to the great Harvest Festival in Miastolas, always a good place for trade."

"Have you been there before? What's it like?" Wilbur asked.

"The festival, or the city?" said Leland.

"Both. We were thinking of stopping there ourselves," said Zammond.

"A beautiful city," said Lexter, "and one of the Elves' largest. It's the northern capital of their kingdom, you know. One of the few places that invites visitors, every now and then. And certainly one of the easier ones to find."

"Elven villages are unlike those of Dwarves or Men," Leland explained, "They aren't really 'cities' as we think of them. Instead of cutting up trees into logs and boards and nailing them together, they bend nature to their will, causing trees and branches to grow as they need them to, weaving them, adding a few things here and there, but mainly letting nature build their abodes, under their guiding hand. Branches growing out around the trunk of a tree may form a natural staircase leading up into it, or trees growing in a circle might widen into walls and stretch a leafy, living dome over its occupants. These are no mere forest tree-huts like the Gnomes are said to build; they are homes as secure and comfortable as any you'll find among Dwarves or Men. The old methods, slow as they can be, still continue, honed and refined over centuries. Dwellings have been passed on in families for generations, and are still growing."

"That's why they can be hard to find," said Lexter, "Sometimes they blend right into the rest of the forest. But Miastolas is one of the great cities, quite beautiful to see, with its waterways and orchards, and Zwiatij Keh, the Northern Palace and Gardens that serve as the summer home of Queen Perla. You really must come and see it."

"The festivals are twice a year, the Spring Festival in late April and the Harvest Festival in early October," Leland told them. "For nine days, the Elves host Dwarves and Men and all celebrate the autumn harvests, trading, sharing produce, with music and dancing, eating and drinking, day and night. People come from as far away as Tolgard and Phamiar for it."

As Leland talked, Zammond caught the glances of the other dwarves, until they, too, admitted their desire to go and see the city.

"And there's a nice place to stay?" said Wilbur, "With food and a bed..."

"There's an old inn, *The Waxing Crescent*, across the river from the festival grounds" said Lexter. "The Dwarves and Elves built it together, for housing foreigners who come to the Festival. It must be over a hundred years old by now; the Festival's a very old tradition. We've stayed there before, and it's comfortable enough, even if it is a strange blend of Dwarvish and Elvish craft."

"How long until we get there?" asked Iaven.

"Quite a while yet," said Leland, "On foot it would have taken you a few days. But we'll be driving all night. With the two of us alternating at the reins we make pretty good time. So just sit tight, and maybe we'll get there by morning."

Spending the night trying to sleep on a moving wagon did not appeal to the dwarves, but it was better than sleeping in the forest. At least they would continue moving, Iaven thought. Now a stop in Miastolas didn't seem so bad, and Iaven looked forward to it. He recalled his father's stories of the colors, the scents, and the landscaped groves and hillsides reaching up into the mist-shrouded, pine-laden mountains to the east.

They rode all afternoon and into the evening, stopping only to eat and drink and change driver every few hours, or to rest their horse. The forest, still foreboding, passed by around them, endless and immense. Leland drove the wagon into the early evening as the day dimmed into a gray haze. After dark he hung a lantern on a pole, angling it forward and off to the side of the wagon. The pale, flickering glow it cast was just enough to see a few yards down the road ahead and the dark branches and undergrowth off the road on either side. Lexter stretched out by the crates, behind the dwarves, and had no trouble dozing in the creaking, rocking wagon. Zammond and Hobley sat nearby, listening to the whoops and calls of night birds and the low, rough pulse of toads croaking in nearby bogs. Wilbur, who had been yawning contagiously an hour after dark, was sound asleep. Tillmore was lost in thought, resting his head on folded arms. Iaven leaned against one of the crates, floating in and out of consciousness, between dreaming and waking. The night sounds, rocking motion, and his own exhaustion lulled him into drowsiness. He wondered what he was getting himself into, but his mind was too tired to focus and too sluggish to grasp the passing thoughts as they drifted through his mind like smoke.

Iaven awoke when the wagon stopped to change driver again. The forest was completely dark outside the circle of lantern light, except for tiny blue-green streaks of fireflies glowing and fading. Leland got in the back of the wagon and Lexter climbed into the driver's seat. Iaven had no idea how late at night it was since branches overhead obscured the stars. Yet he felt strangely rested and more alert now. Stiff from lying in back, he decided to ride up front and climbed into the bench next to Lexter, and soon they were underway again.

"Doesn't your horse get tired?" Iaven asked after riding in silence awhile. The Splides' horse was a great powerful animal, sleek of coat and wide of shoulder, but they had given her little rest, especially after adding so much to the load.

"She can sleep when we get there," said Lexter. "We got a late start this morning too, leaving from Carval. She's used to it." Lexter thought a moment and then spoke again. "Better to keep moving and get through soon as we can. Some folks in Carval warned us about the roads. Some even said Goblins were about. Well, no matter what, you've got to be careful traveling. The festival can attract some unseemly characters about it, unscrupulous types laying in wait for unwary travelers." He smiled at Iaven, his expression difficult to see in the faint lantern light.

"Let's hope they're all asleep and won't hear us passing," said Iaven, looking ahead again and shivering in the brisk night air. "How much longer, do you think, till we get there?"

"Oh, maybe a little before morning, the load's a bit heavier than usual. But we'll get there, and stop at the inn. I hope there'll be rooms open."

"I look forward to it," said Iaven. He felt like talking, yet was leery of the all-encompassing dark of the endless forest around them.

The horse continued plodding along through the night. The road appeared out of the blackness and disappeared into the dark behind them. Pale lantern light edged their faces and clothes. Dulled highlights gleamed on the fine metalwork of Iaven's sword, as though it had just come out of the furnace newly-forged, still reflecting the fire within. Lexter's gaze was drawn now and then to the hilt's ornate designs. Iaven caught Lexter eyeing the sword twice but did not let on that he noticed, thinking it better to say nothing, given the circumstances.

The hour was still before dawn when Iaven began nodding off again. He was ready to climb in back and lay down when the road widened and a vast starred blackness opened above them as they emerged into a meadow. A thin sliver of moon cast a faint, ghostly radiance. The air was moving, cool and fresh, and Iaven was relieved to be free of the oppressive closeness of the forest. They rode on awhile, coming at last to the crossroads where their road met the South Road running down from the north. A few buildings of stone and wood dotted the landscape, their windows dark and shuttered in repose.

Gradually the land rose and took them onto a small hilltop where Lexter brought the wagon to a halt. From there the hills fell away to the river, where the road crossed a wide wooden bridge arching gracefully over slow-moving waters. Beyond the river and reflected in its shimmering surface were the lights of the festival, dozens of many-colored torches and lanterns. Flames leapt and danced in the night breezes, lighting crowds of musicians, dancers, and merrymakers who thronged and mingled on the grounds of the far shore. To the north, on Lake Eihalo, a flock of slender Elven vessels lay moored with lanterns strung from their masts and celebrations on their decks. Faint sounds of laughter, song, and high-spirited talk could be heard across the river even at that distance.

"The festival's already started," said Lexter, "We had to miss the first few days, but we're staying for the rest." He shook the reins and they started downhill toward the river. In the distance beyond the festival grounds Iaven could see wide groves of trees with interweaving branches. Many were lit from within by ethereal golden light; the homes of the Elves, he guessed, and the edge of Miastolas. The groves extended off to the right, away into the valley, and far back into the hills where the land rose steadily. Beyond them the mountains towered above all, their peaks silhouetted in the paling eastern sky. The vastness of gently rolling land glimmered softly as if the stars themselves had come down and nestled there, slumbering in beds of leafy branches that muted their sparkle to a sleepy glow. Iaven breathed deeply, longing to enter the land, when suddenly the wagon rode lower and turned into the woods near the river, blocking his view.

Now they were heading towards a long, dark building where firelight flickered in a few windows. As they neared, Iaven saw that several large oak trees were not just growing near the building, but were worked into the design. Tree trunks acted as pilasters and branches formed ceiling beams like ribs down the length of the building. Closer still, and he could make out Dwarven carvings and woodworking fitted in between the trees, designed to match the work of the Elves without losing their Dwarven character. Above the main entrance hung a wooden sickle-shaped moon painted white.

"*The Waxing Crescent*, there she is, same as ever. Funny old place, but it suits our needs. It's either that or camping," said Lexter. The dwarves were stirring and Leland also woke. The wagon came to a stop, and Iaven stepped to the ground. He looked all around him and through the dark trees surrounding the inn, straining to catch another glimpse of the ethereal vision he had seen across the river and knew to be Miastolas.

Chapter 7.
The Gnomes of Rundlewood

The Forest Road was nowhere near as straight or as short as it had looked on the map. Orven and his friends realized they had underestimated the size of Rundlewood and how long their trip through it would take. The road ran long and straight at first, and then turned and wound around hills, through shallow valleys, and along steep ridges where the land fell away into wooded gullies. Dark, deep and quiet, the woods teemed with hidden life and unexplored places that beckoned temptingly. The road widened and narrowed as it went, thickly overgrown in places. Sometimes the trees parted and sunlight fell warm and bright onto open ground flooded with fallen leaves. Elsewhere the woods closed in around them, heavy and ancient.

The silence and the loneliness of the forest made them uneasy. Unlike the country roads between villages and towns of the Foothills, the Forest Road was little traveled. They had been walking three days now, expecting to see an occasional cart or wagon coming from Bottomcliffe, or a hunting party returning home, but had encountered no one. Nor was there any sign of the Gnomes; after a day or two their fears subsided and a sense of isolation set in. They marched on, talking less, weary of endless corridors of trees, the slowly winding turns revealing more road, and the ever-present shuffling crunch of dried leaves underfoot.

Next to Orven walked Roy Goldbeard, who was blond with a fair complexion, his dark blue eyes clouded over with thought. He drew his cloak tighter as the wind gusted around him. If he was uncomfortable, he gave no indication. Roy's cloak was new and fur-lined, the best of any of theirs. His family had money; his father was a skilled metalworker whose work was in demand throughout the Foothills. The Goldbeard family had been miners in the mountains before Roy's grandparents had moved to Hillbrook, and it was rumored that they'd brought gold and silver with them. If they were wealthy, Roy never flaunted it. He took some interest in his father's craft, which he was expected to continue, but wasn't ready to settle down with it yet. Despite his love of comfort, he had become restless and was determined to see the Kingdom before surrendering to his apprenticeship.

Alongside Roy walked Ripley Ironshard. Long-limbed and rail-thin, his wild streak was evident in his dark, hungry eyes and unruly straight black hair. The first day out he had been tense and anxious, eager for a fight. Orven remembered thinking Ripley too abrasive and not liking him when they had first met as children. Ripley and Roy were old friends, so Orven had come to know him anyway. He got to like Ripley, at first only in smaller doses. Roy, it seemed, was the only one who could quiet him down or talk sense into him, even when Ripley was in his wilder moods. Orven worried about Ripley's impulsiveness but was glad to have him along just the same.

The afternoon paled as night drew near. Soon they would need a place to camp again. Orven slowed and drew Gorflange, pointing the sword north-northwest of them. He had done so twice since entering the forest, with little change in the direction the sword indicated. This time, however, the little blue-green stone set in the tip of the pommel glowed when the sword pointed west into the forest.

"We're closer, look how bright it is!" Orven said. "It can't be far from here. Let's go get it."

"You promised Cedric we wouldn't go after the gem," said Aaron.

"No, I agreed to promise him that I wouldn't, but then I never made the promise," said Orven.

"If you promise to make a promise about something, it's the same thing," said Aaron.

"So we *are* going after the gem?" Max said.

"As long as we're here, and isn't too far from the road, why not?" said Orven, "Especially if it's somewhere where there aren't any gnomes."

"How far off the road is it? You don't really know, do you?" Max asked.

Orven stood roadside, peering into the forest shadows. "Probably not too far in," he said, nonchalantly and unconvincingly. He glanced back at the others. "We'll follow the sword in a straight line in to where the gem is, and then turn around and walk the same straight line back out again. We'll follow our own trail back; we can't get lost."

The others drew closer, hesitating. They looked into the forest and then at Orven, who was already a few steps into the woods.

"It won't take long," Orven assured them. "It could have been worse; it could have been at the bottom of a lake, or further north in Gnome country." He walked a few strides into the forest and turned back when he didn't hear them following. "Well?"

"We haven't seen any gnomes or crossed the Yandl," said Roy. "But I'd still rather not leave the road."

After a pause, Ripley drew his sword and strode into the forest behind Orven. "Come on, what're you afraid of?" He stood with his sword parting the weeds, making their hesitance seem ridiculous. Orven marched further in, and the others followed.

"We'll be back on the road in time to set camp," Max told Roy and Aaron as he brought up the rear of the party. "After all, isn't this what we came for?" No one could argue with that, so they went single file behind Orven into the woods.

Inside, the forest had already grown dim and shadowy. The cool, damp air was heavy with the smell of ferns and wet moss, cobwebbed bark and moist earth. Strange birds hooted and whooped deeper in. Unseen animals rustled leaves on the forest floor. In the paling light the forest looked endless in depth, dark and alive. The trees, taller and older than those of the Foothills, crowded their branches together high above ground, choking out all most of the paling light. Only fireflies remained, dancing pinpoints of blue-green glow that flared and faded, vanishing just as they caught your eye.

The going was slow, and Orven and Ripley tried to clear the way. They ducked under branches and stepped over sharp bushes of thistle and underbrush.

The onset of dusk made it harder to see what lay ahead. Strands of spider webs clung to their faces as they passed between the trees. Soon they came upon a ravine and eased their way down into it and back up the other side, trying to move in as straight a line as possible. They trudged onward, until Orven stopped to look at Gorflange's pommel.

"Is it here?" asked Ripley.

Orven paused. "The light's faded," he said. He angled the sword slightly and the light shined bright again. "We must have gone a little off course when we crossed that ravine," Orven began walking again, "But I've got the right direction now."

They followed Orven awhile until he stopped, readjusting the sword again. He turned and walked on without saying anything.

"Well how far off were we?" asked Max.

"Not much," Orven said. "We must be close, it's the brightest I've ever seen it." Right after Orven spoke, the blue-green glow flickered and brightened again as Orven angled the sword even more.

"We're bending too much to the left," Aaron said. He stopped walking and the others halted.

Orven turned to them. "It can't be far from here."

"You've been saying that since we left the road," said Max.

"Just a little further," said Orven, pushing through the undergrowth. Ripley and Roy followed and Max and Aaron reluctantly joined them.

After more wandering they emerged into a clearing. Night had fallen, and in the dim starlight the clearing looked to be about thirty yards across, a field of short grasses strewn with large, round, pale rocks. Orven moved across it and was about to reenter the woods when he noticed the others were not coming.

"We'll never find the road again tonight," said Aaron. "We might as well set camp here; we're unlikely to come across a better place."

"I'd have to agree," said Max, "Seems like we've been going in circles."

"We can always get it tomorrow," said Roy, sitting on one of the rocks.

Orven stood poised at the edge of the clearing. Ripley waited to see what he would do.

"I'll be right back, then," said Orven, turning into the woods. He paused. The pommel's light had dimmed. He moved the sword and found it glowed brightest just off to the left again.

"You haven't even changed position," said Aaron, "It looks like the gem is circling us."

They all stood still. Crickets shrilled their *crrikcrrikcrrikcrrik*, and solitary cries of night birds echoed.

"Maybe someone's carrying it around," said Ripley.

"Or maybe some animal picked it up," said Orven, "Or maybe not. Either way, we should set a watch tonight. I'll take the first shift." Thoughts of Maëlveronde occurred to each of them but no one said anything.

Max and Ripley collected kindling, and Aaron lit a fire for warmth. Uneasy, they all turned in for the night. Orven leaned back against a rock as the others dropped off to sleep. He caught himself nodding, lulled by the crickets and his tiredness, so he drew Gorflange from its sheath. He lay back, gripping the cold metal hilt on his chest, the blade pointing toward his feet, on the ready should anything startle him. The feel of the sword and its weight were reassuring, so much so that his eyelids drooped and he began to doze again.

How long he sat like this he could not tell. Nor did he notice a soft rustling noise in the woods as a small dark figure emerged from the forest, its beady eyes bright and alert. Carrying a spear twice its own height of three feet or so, the figure slipped through the clearing, right up to Orven's feet, attracted by starlight glinting on Gorflange's blade.

Orven lay half-asleep, but the blue-green glow from the sword's pommel brightened until it filtered through his eyelids and woke him. His eyes snapped open, momentarily blinded from the glow, and he saw the shape of the gnome standing before him. His heart raced as he raised Gorflange, struggling to his feet and calling out to awaken the others.

The gnome tensed and leapt on a rock, wildly wielding his spear with fierce shrieks and curses. The dwarves drew their swords. Atop the rock, the gnome kept Orven at bay, but the others closed in, surrounding him. With a quick, shrewd glance the gnome scanned and assessed the dwarves. In a flash of movement his hand dropped to his belt, loosed something, and flung it with a snap of his wrist. Before he saw it coming, the dart bit into Roy's neck and his senses reeled. Blacking out, he weakened and collapsed, watching the gnome point the spear and leap at him. As Roy hit the ground, the spear struck the grass in front of his face, and the gnome vaulted over his body. On instinct Roy grabbed the spear, feeling it bend as the gnome released it. His hand loosened, the spear fell to the ground, and he heard the gnome running off into the woods as everything blurred into darkness.

Still on edge, the others watched the gnome vanish and then rushed to where Roy lay. Ripley tried reviving him with cold water, and laid him near the fire's smoldering embers. They watched and waited anxiously. Finally Roy came to, dazed and drowsy.

Orven sheathed Gorflange and set the camp in order, picking up the carving tools the gnome had stolen and dropped. He found the dart that had stung Roy, a crude little wooden stick with one end sharpened to a poison-tipped point. Nearby lay the gnome's spear, which was pointed and weighted with a knot of wood near the tip to make it fly true. Orven broke the spear in half under his knee and hurled the dart into the woods. He went over where Aaron was sitting with Roy while he recovered. The dwarves were calmer now, overcome with profound tiredness and weariness. Orven sat on a rock and pulled his cloak around him.

"We were so close," Orven said, "He must have had it; the glow was the brightest when he was standing right there in front of me. It woke me up."

"We'll find him again," said Max, "During the daytime, tomorrow."

"Can we?" Orven said morosely. "And he probably won't be alone, either."

"Which way did he go?" said Aaron, "Not that I have any idea which way is north or south anymore. But it might give us some idea."

Orven looked around, trying to remember where they had stood. He drew Gorflange and pointed it, watching for the glow in the pommel's stone. He swung it around and the glow was strong; too bright, as if the gnome still lurked somewhere near them. Orven panicked and stood ready, straining his eyes, but he could see nothing in the dark beyond the clearing. He moved the sword about and came across the broken spear. Picking it up, Orven tested it and found the knot of wood near the spearhead made the sword glow brightest.

"It's here!" he cried, startling the others. "It's worked into the spearhead." He brought it over as they gathered to see it. The knot of wood was thick and heavy, its sinews grown around the gem itself. Orven blunted the spear's point and tore at the knot, but it was tough and unyielding. For nearly ten minutes Orven scraped and sawed the knot with no luck. The others watched Orven, eager to get back to sleep; the night was cold and they were all weary. Orven was tired as well, and could not break open the knot. Finally in frustration, he snapped the knot off the end of the spear and thrust it deep into his pocket.

"I'll get it tomorrow," he said. "We'd better get some rest. Besides, I want to get a good look at the gem in the light before we put it into the sword."

"Well at least we have it now," said Max, at his patience's end. "Sleep well!" he called, and rolled over at once.

Ripley was still too on edge to sleep. "Go ahead," he told Orven, "I'll take the rest of the watch." Orven nodded in agreement, bundled up, and lay down. He felt the knot of wood in his pocket, eager for the gem, and before long he drifted into a deep and dreamless slumber.

Ripley sat up straight, relaxed but alert, looking at the pale rocks strewn about the clearing, the dark jagged line of trees rising around them, and the broad circle of night sky filled with constellations. He hurled a stone into the woods, angry at himself for not doing more. Like the rest, he had stood with his sword drawn, hesitant to advance since the spear's reach was greater than his sword. The gnome wailing and cursing at them in some strange tongue had frightened him. Before he realized what had happened, Roy had fallen to the ground and the gnome was gone. Ripley had always thought himself good in a fight, and was ashamed of how shaken he had been. Roy could have been killed because he'd held back. He wanted a second chance to prove himself, but all he could do now was stay awake and keep watch.

As night wore on, Ripley thought less about the gnome and more about the sword and gems, of deeds they would do and the glory that would be theirs after the war. He imagined the Castle, the cities, and the mountains, wondering where he would make his stand and prove his worth. While he dreamed a slight breeze blew, bearing a fragrant scent in the cool, moist night air; a soothing aroma like incense burning, faint but sharp. Ripley breathed it in, calm and relaxed. Soon he lay back against the rock, sound asleep, dreaming of adventures yet to come.

Six small pairs of green eyes watched Ripley from the shadowy forest interior, where tendrils of smoke rose from a tiny dish and were fanned into the clearing. When they saw Ripley was fast asleep, the gnomes came creeping through the camp, searching and taking whatever interested them. The gnome who had been to their camp earlier came upon Orven, who lay deep in slumber. He hissed sharply, motioning the rest over. They stood around Orven's inert form, three on a side. Another gnome took out a pouch and sprinkled Orven with a dark, pungent dust that fell onto his skin and into his mouth. They waited and watched. "*Sgrasi sha*," the gnome with the pouch muttered. The others whispered noises of eager assent. They bent over Orven and their small hands set to work. Two of them unsheathed Gorflange and set it aside on the ground, out of reach. Others lifted Orven's back and arms and slid wooden spears underneath him, and under his head and legs. When all was ready they gathered around, crouching. "*Kraa!*" growled the lead gnome, and together they hoisted the spears onto their shoulders, lifting Orven off the ground. As they carried him into the woods, moving silently into the dark, the other dwarves slept deeply and peacefully, completely at rest.

Orven awoke, startled at the motion and the dim shapes of trees moving overhead in the darkness. At the corners of his eyes he saw the gnomes' moving shapes surrounding him in the dark. Orven wanted to cry out but found his throat too dry and hoarse to make a sound. He tried to move but his arms and legs were stiff and cold, heavy as dead weight. Fear flooded through him, a raw panic he was unable to express or release. His heart raced as he lay paralyzed on the gnomes' spears, rocking and swaying as they moved through the forest. Orven wondered if his friends had been taken, or even killed. Powerless and terrified, he stared up at the trees passing indifferently in the darkness, certain he would never see them again.

Ripley, Max, Aaron, and Roy slept well the rest of the night, until the gray, clouded dawn broke slowly in the east. Snug and warm in his blanket, Aaron lay listening to the honking of geese passing overhead, full of the longing and yearning he understood so well. He wished he could fly south with them, far from the dark forest and the war looming over them like the oncoming winter. He rolled over and opened his eyes to the dim skies and morning light. Aaron froze as he noticed movement throughout the campsite. He turned and saw it was a flock of geese that had landed to rest. They browsed the clearing, all identical, brown feathers speckled with white. Some craned their black necks to pull at the grass, while others still slept, beaks tucked under wings in repose. A few walked around honking softly, stretching their wings and drinking dew from shallow depressions on the rocks. Aaron sat up slowly, watching them. Nearby geese walked out of his reach, calm and unconcerned. Aaron watched the flock, wishing he could commune with them somehow.

Max awoke and propped his head upon his elbow, watching Aaron and the geese. Moments later Ripley woke and stood up, with a determined look in his eye that made Aaron and Max uneasy. Ripley appeared to be waiting for the right moment to pounce and catch the dwarves a poultry dinner. He was about to lunge at the geese when the entire flock flapped its wings and took to the air, roused into flight by a loud clapping noise.

"What'd you do that for?" he snapped at Aaron. "We could've had a tasty dinner there, what's the matter with you?"

"There's enough rabbit in these woods to feed an army," Aaron said, lying back down with his hands behind his head. "Let 'em go, if they know enough to fly south."

Roy woke up, rubbing his eyes. He looked about the campsite. "Where's Orven?"

They looked around, worried, and called into the woods for him. Max almost suggested that Orven had just gone for a walk when he saw Gorflange lying unsheathed on the ground, an ill omen they all were staring at now.

"He wouldn't have forgotten it," said Max. "Who was the last to see him? Who was on the watch?"

"Ripley never woke me for my watch," said Aaron, turning to him.

Ripley stood dumbfounded. "I... I must have dozed off... I don't know how..."

"It must have been the gnomes, then," said Max, standing up. "We've got to stay calm and think. Is there any trace of where they might have taken him? Was there a struggle?" They checked the campsite, but apart from missing items, everything was in order.

"Nothing. They could have gone in any direction," said Aaron. "I'm not even sure which direction *we* came from."

"We should have never left the road! We should have waited until morning." Roy sat down on the rocks. "Do you think Orven's still alive?"

"Of course he's alive!" said Max, pacing about the clearing. *But so was the dwarf they found turned to stone*, he thought.

"He didn't even get a chance to put the gem into the sword," said Ripley.

"The sword!" Max walked over and picking up Gorflange. "Orven had the gem in his pocket last night." Max moved the sword in an arc, watching the stone in the pommel, until he saw a tiny blue-green light flicker and hold steady. "He's in that direction," said Max, pointing into the forest.

"If he still has the gem," said Aaron.

"Let's hope he does," said Max, packing his things and Orven's. "And that we're not already too late."

The dwarves followed Max's lead through the forest as he carried Gorflange. They found they could not simply make a beeline through the woods in the direction the sword indicated; the land forced them to detour around fallen logs, thickets, and undergrowth, or veer around drumlins and eskers. After walking an hour, they came to a hilltop and stopped to rest, using their vantage point to scan the woods about them. Max, who carried Orven's pack as well as his own, sat down on the grass.

"We're getting closer," he said, glancing at the sword, "It's much brighter than when we started."

Ripley and Aaron peered down the slopes into the endless mosaic of autumn colors.

"Look, over there," Aaron pointed off to the northwest.

In the distance, tiny figures hiked through the woods, three gnomes returning from somewhere. Two of them, carrying spears, went south while the third approached a tree trunk and scampered up it like a squirrel. A shaggy tree-hut lodged in the branches like a giant bird's nest, a large, round, grassy ball with weeds and vines hanging from it like fur. The gnome ducked into a hole in the side of the tree-hut and disappeared. From the tree-hut ropy bridges extended to other trees, where more tree-huts hung in the branches with rope bridges leading to still other trees. Here and there fallen logs provided bridges or inclines for the gnomes, and some had carven faces and figures on them. With deepening fear, the dwarves slowly realized just how extensive the gnomes' dwellings were.

"There could be hundreds of them," Aaron said, gazing into the trees.

"We'd better get going before they see us," Max said. "We won't have to cross through it all, at least right here. But we may have to go a long way around them."

Ripley drew his sword. "And if we can't? We'd better be ready for them." The others unsheathed their swords, glancing about them, and returned down the back of the hill.

As the morning light brightened and birds called, Orven gradually awoke. He could move his arms and legs, only they now were bound firmly with twine. Looking around the forest, he saw he was high up off the ground, tied tightly to the trunk of a tree. His arms were pinned to his sides, his legs and ankles likewise bound. Gorflange was gone from its scabbard. He stretched his fingers to touch his pocket, feeling the bulge where the knot of wood with the gem was. They hadn't been after the gem, he thought; perhaps they didn't even know it was there. He looked around again. No one seemed to be about. To his left was a lake, which came right up to the tree to which he was tied. Below him to the right was a small clearing where some cut logs lay amidst strange carven ceremonial talismans and small wooden vessels.

Straining his neck forward, Orven looked straight down. He was about ten feet off the ground. He struggled trying to loosen the rope and stopped when the tree rocked slightly. He looked down again and then up. There were no branches above him, and the trunk of the tree ended abruptly a few feet above his head. It wasn't a tree at all, he realized, but a large log standing on end, balancing next to the water's edge. If he struggled too hard, the log could topple into the lake, drowning him, or fall forward into the clearing, crushing him underneath it. Orven stopped struggling.

The ropes were too tight for him to pull his arms out, and there was still the drop to the ground. He concentrated on moving his arm. His wrist was bound to the log, and he could only bend his hand up and down. He watched as a large, stringy mosquito landed on the back of his hand. The itchy tingle of its sting grew as it bit him. He shook his hand, but the mosquito stayed there until it finished. Orven's hand itched terribly and he grunted in frustration and anger. He struggled until the log wobbled, and then, frightened, he froze again.

Orven remained still for some time, breathing hard, trying to think of what he could do. It was hopeless. He would have to wait until the gnomes came for him, and he resisted imagining what they would do with him, or why they had kept him alive. Orven wondered whether Max and the others had suffered similar fates, and how far he had been taken away from them. Perhaps they were already dead; it appeared he soon would be.

Orven closed his eyes, trying to calm himself as panic turned to despair. He felt like he woud faint, and even imagined he heard familiar voices below him. "Somewhere around here," said Max, "but there's only the trees, and the lake."

"Probably Lake Rundlemere, from the size of it," said Aaron. Morning sunlight sparkled on the lake, a lovely and inviting sight after so many days in the Forest.

"So where is he?" Roy asked.

"Maybe they buried him," said Ripley.

"Ripley! Stop that!" Max chided.

"Up here!" shouted Orven, stretching his neck to look down at them. "They carried me away last night. I don't remember much; but here I am. I guess they didn't want me just yet. Lucky thing they left Gorflange, I see."

"How are we going to get you down from there?" said Max.

Ripley, Roy, and Aaron paced the clearing, thinking. Ripley stood near the log, and Orven became nervous, craning his neck to see what Ripley was doing.

"Don't climb it. It's balancing and could tip over too easily," Orven warned.

"We could try to catch it," said Ripley, handling the log as if he were contemplating pushing it over.

"It's too heavy," said Roy, "Even the four of us couldn't stop it, or slow it down, without getting crushed underneath. It's too big."

"The other trees are too far away to reach over from," said Max.

"We could drop it into the water," Ripley suggested.

"I can't swim!" Orven cried, "I can't even move, as it is. If I wouldn't be crushed, I'd drown!"

"We can't catch the log ourselves, but we could build a brace to hold it," said Aaron, "Something to catch the log, and let us lower it slowly."

"It must be quite heavy," said Max. "But we could try."

"There, see, by that stump? We could make a hole and put a short log into it on the other side, and then lay two longer logs across them making a kind of X-shaped brace, to catch Orven's log in." Aaron indicated the end of the clearing where the shorter logs lay.

"The ground by the water is soft enough, it shouldn't take long to dig out a hole," said Roy.

"Alright, let's give it a try," Max said, and went over where Aaron was digging. Roy and Ripley started hauling logs over.

"What if it falls apart?" said Orven. "This log's thicker and taller. You're also going to have to turn it around so I'm not on the side falling to the ground."

"We'll take care of it, don't worry," said Max as they widened the hole and tried to fit the short log into it, only to find it was still too small. Ripley and Roy leaned one of the logs on the tree stump, and dragged the other one over to set in place. Max glanced up at Orven. "We'll get you down before the Gnomes even know we're here," he said.

"Too late," Aaron said, pointing out onto the lake. "Look!" A few hundred feet from shore four gnomes with short wide paddles rowed a dugout canoe carved from a log. They rowed with long, powerful alternating strokes, and the sides of the canoe, carved smooth for speed, helped them close the distance fast. Behind them, farther away on the lake, a second canoe with four more gnomes was coming to join them.

Max and Aaron tore at the ground, pushing their log into the hole as Roy and Ripley laid the last log in place. Roy stood by, waiting to secure the logs together as Max straightened the short one in the hole. Ripley ran behind Orven's log, ready to push it forward. "Hurry! They're coming!" he shouted, rocking the log back and forth.

"No, Ripley, wait!" Roy shouted, "We're not done yet!"

"Wait!" Orven cried, "Turn the log around, or I'll fall right into the ground! Turn it so I'm on the backside of—" The log began falling forward and Orven screamed. The ground angled in at him as he fell face down into it, like a wide wall he was about to slam into. The log's shadow darkened as the ground rushed at him. Orven squeezed his eyes shut and tried to turn away. The others jumped back in horror out of the log's way. With a great thud and cracking sound the end of the log fell onto the brace, stopping just a foot or two above the ground. Orven opened his eyes and saw dried leaves and dirt right in front of him. Heart pounding, he let out a sigh, which was cut short by a low scraping sound.

"It didn't hold, it's coming off!" Max shouted, as the log began moving again. The brace had collapsed on the side near the water, the log rolling down it, turning Orven up from the ground and around to the top of the log where he lay staring skyward. After a sloshing plop, the log angled off with a strange buoyant motion into the lake. With sickening panic, Orven felt the water pull the log and saw treetops passing over and the sky opening above them.

As it slipped away, Ripley and Roy ran to the log and jumped for it. They climbed onto the log trying to stop it, but the force of them landing on it succeeded only in pushing it further out into the water. They started shouting and Max and Aaron ran to catch up. Left with no other choice, they slung their packs over their shoulders and forced themselves to leap onto the log with the others just as it floated into the lake.

The dwarves gripped the log in horror as it moved away from shore, trying to balance on it and keep Orven from rolling underwater. At first they only made matters worse, until they got a hold of themselves and the log. Ripley edged forward to where Orven lay tied to the log, drawing his sword to cut him loose. But just before he reached Orven, the gnomes in the canoe pulled up next to the log, raising spears and bows with arrows. Ripley gave a shout, leaping from the log onto the canoe and brandishing his sword. The gnomes stopped his blade with their paddles and spears, hissing and cursing as they tried to spear him or knock him into the water. Max and Roy drew their swords and tumbled onto the canoe, knocking a gnome overboard and narrowly saving Ripley from a spear thrust. The canoe rocked wildly under their weight as they fought the gnomes while struggling to keep their balance. At last they wounded one gnome and sent two more overboard into the water.

Aaron clung to the end of Orven's log as it rocked side to side, threatening to roll over.

"No! Up more! Hold it steady!" Orven yelled as water rushed up on either side of him.

"I'm doing the best I can!" Aaron held on, breathing hard. He steadied it as he could, but the current was carrying them away from the canoe and further out into the lake. The second canoe was advancing on them, the gnomes rowing together with strong swift strokes.

"Get their paddles!" Max shouted as the fighting continued. He swung his sword in a wide arc, catching one of the gnome's spears. Ripley grabbed the remaining gnome's paddle and pushed him overboard. Roy fished another paddle out of the water, wrenching it away from gnomes who had surfaced near the canoe. When at last the canoe was theirs, Max, Roy, and Ripley sat down and nervously began paddling after Orven's log, which was now some distance away. Lacking the gnomes' smooth, experienced strokes, they paddled hard but moved slowly until they found the right rhythm and started working together. Finally they made some progress toward the log as it drifted across the lake.

"It's heading for the river's mouth. We've got to catch it before it gets away downriver!" said Max, rowing and trying to steer the canoe while Roy and Ripley paddled. But the other canoe was gaining on them and looked like it might beat them to the log.

"What happened?" cried Orven, "Where are we?"

"We're being carried into the river," said Aaron, "I can barely steer this thing, much less slow it down!" The lake around them started to narrow as they reached the river delta, the current picking up speed as the river swept them into the forest. Orven saw trees reaching overhead and their shadows passed over his face. Bracing cold spray misted Orven as the log rushed downstream.

"How far are they behind us? We'll never get back to the— *Hey! Careful!*" he shouted as turbulence shook the log, threatening to roll him into the cold waters coursing past. Aaron righted the log, struggling to maintain his hold. Atop the log once more, Orven breathed a sigh of relief, but tensed when a sudden *thwok-thwok-thwok-thwok* sounded as small wooden arrows bit into the log only inches from his right arm. In tree-huts high above them, gnomes were shrieking and firing arrows at them as they sped past. Gulping down short breaths and heart beating hard, Aaron slunk down into the water at the end of the log to avoid getting hit. Now only his arms and head were above water, and he grasped the log, trying to keep it from rolling as he hung on.

"To the side! Turn me away from them!" shouted Orven. Aaron rotated the log too far, plunging Orven into the icy torrents rushing past. Orven squeezed his eyes shut and thought they would freeze solid in his head. The water rumbled loudly in his ears and ran into his nose and mouth, until Aaron finally righted the log again.

Orven recovered, coughing, gasping, and swearing at Aaron. Wet twine tightened around him and ice-cold water soaked his clothes. Another rain of arrows hit with a shivering *thwok-thwok-thwok* nearby on his right while icy waters sped past only inches away on his left. Aaron struggled to keep his grip as he dragged along in the water, dodging arrows and trying to balance the log at the same time.

Max, Roy, and Ripley dug furiously at the water with their paddles, their speed increasing as they entered the river delta. Max sat in front watching the log far ahead of them, while Ripley held the rear, shouting as their pursuers closed the gap. Their surge of speed into the river kept them out of range of the gnomes' bows and spears, but only for a moment.

"Arrows ahead, on the left!" Max warned as they passed into the forest shadows. They readied themselves, crouching down while rowing, and slid their packs onto their left shoulders like shields as arrows rained down on them from the trees. The canoe tilted as they leaned in, their packs filling with arrows. An arrowhead grazed Max's leg and in moments it ached and grew numb. The dwarves struggled to keep the canoe upright, fearing the icy waters as much as the gnomes' attack.

The current swept them along at a good pace now. Roy held up his paddle to ward off arrows, and it vibrated in his hand as they bit into it. Max and Ripley continued pulling madly at the water, trying to narrow the twenty yards between their canoe and Orven's log.

They passed deeper into the forest and soon the fall of arrows ceased on Orven's log and on their canoe. They saw no tree-huts along the banks, so Roy returned to rowing. When they came within ten yards of Orven's log, Ripley gave a shout, as the gnomes in the second canoe closed in behind them.

"Faster! They're pulling their bows!" Ripley yelled over the roaring river, swinging his paddle and turning to face them. Two gnomes were shooting while the others paddled to bring them closer. The turbulent river made aiming difficult, but they kept closing the distance. Ripley managed to bat away most of the arrows, and in a burst of anger he flung his paddle right at them, throwing one of them off balance. The gnomes' canoe pulled closer and they readied their spears.

"Ripley! We need those!" Max shouted when he saw Ripley had thrown the paddle away.

Orven's log was right in front of them now, and Aaron had climbed back onto it, drenched and shivering as he clung to the bark. He brushed wet hair out of his eyes and peered into the shadows ahead to see what was downriver, glancing behind him to see how close Max was getting. Max reached his paddle forward and Aaron grabbed it, and they pulled the log and canoe together.

Max climbed onto the log, and Aaron gripped his shoulder, pointing downriver. "Up ahead!" he yelled, and Max looked downstream as far as he could. About a hundred yards away, rocks lined both banks of the river. Tall stones stood out into the water, one on each side, supports for a span of bridge long gone. "Get everyone on the log, we'll have to steer through those!" Aaron yelled above the rushing river. Max nodded and motioned to Roy who crawled forward, careful not to lose his balance or separate the log and canoe as he came across. Following Roy, Ripley backed up to the front of the canoe, still shouting at the gnomes.

The log shot straight down the river, the rocks approaching fast. Max kept them on course, ready with his paddle, glancing back to make sure Roy and Ripley were on the log. Both saw the pass between the rocks and helped steady the log. Just as they were about to shoot through the pass, Ripley grabbed Roy's paddle. Turning back, he lurched forward and struck the empty canoe hard on the side, sending it angling away in the water. The log shot between the rocks as the empty canoe turned sideways, hitting the rocks broadside with a loud thumping boom. An instant later the gnomes' canoe came crashing into it head on, throwing the gnomes into the water, while the dwarves' log sped away downriver.

Ripley gave a ferocious shout of victory and brandished the paddle high in the air, almost falling off the log and taking Roy with him.

"Are they gone? What happened?" Orven snapped, as Max sawed away at the wet twine with his sword. The twine fell away from Orven and he sat up rubbing his arms as Max freed his legs. Aaron and Roy used the paddles to keep the log upright and try to slow its speed. The paddles added some drag, but the log was still speeding downriver at a dangerous pace.

"We did it!" Ripley shouted with abandon.

"Yes," said Orven, "But now we've got to get off this log." Max handed Gorflange back to Orven, who examined it briefly and then slid it back into its sheath. "Any suggestions?"

Max stared down the river, ignoring Orven. Orven turned and looked. Fifty yards away on the right bank and approaching fast was a large tree overhanging the river. They would either have to duck it or try to catch its branches, and soon. "Jump for the tree!" Orven shouted.

The dwarves, however, were lined up one behind the other, so it was not as simple as Orven thought. As the tree passed over them, Orven and Max sprang up, grabbing the branches. Behind them, Aaron, Roy, and Ripley did the same, slamming into them and each other as the log disappeared downriver beneath them. Aaron and Roy hung onto Max and Orven, and Ripley hung onto Aaron and Roy, his legs dangling and splashing in the river. The branch bowed under their weight, creaking and ready to give way at any moment.

"Move over!" said Orven, "Ripley, swing over to shore, can you?"

Ripley stretched out a foot, but it was too far to reach. He started swinging back and forth to catch a foothold on the bank. The tree branch swayed and made a slow cracking sound.

"Not that much!" Max shouted. The wood splintered and the branch swung down as it tore from the tree, bringing them closer to the bank and lowering them all into the cold, rushing water. They hung onto the branch and each other, and began the laborious climb up the weed-choked bank.

At last they lay on the grass exhausted, shivering and trying to dry off. They sat around for some time, idling picking arrows out of their packs, discovering what had been lost or damaged in the chase, and eating what remained of their food.

"How are we going to get back to the road?" said Roy, "Or are we?"

"We could follow the river," Aaron suggested.

"But not back to the Gnomes," Orven added. "And it would take several days through the forest just to get back there, anyway. Let's follow the river west, to the Silver Sea. From there, we can follow the shoreline north, until we reach Beggar's Bay and the towns around Kronivar. That might be the easiest. And the safest."

"As long as it's the shortest," said Roy, "I've had enough of this forest!"

"What about the gem?" Ripley asked, "Did they take it?"

Orven smiled and took the knot of wood from his pocket, holding it up for all to see. He fished a knife out of his pack and peeled the rest of the wood away, breaking it open at last.

The gem slipped out of its wood casing and lay on the palm of his hand. It was about the size of a robin's egg, a deep rich green, clear as an emerald, verdant and lush. The forest light glinted and sparkled off the facets Aorinthel had cut on its surface long ago, and ancient fire seemed to glow deep within its heart. Orven gazed down in wonderment at it, entranced. The others gathered around him staring at it. Moments later, Gorflange rang as Orven unsheathed it. He held the gem near one of the holes in the hilt, the gem reflecting green in the metal. As Orven brought it closer, the tiny metalwork leaves rimming the holes rotated and withdrew slightly, allowing the gem to be set into the sword.

Once the gem dropped in, the leaves resumed their position. Orven hefted the sword again. It seemed lighter now, and moved with his hand as though it anticipated his movements. He looked at the sword anew, as if he were seeing it for the first time, or as if he sensed a power in himself he had never felt before. At last, with an effort, he sheathed it again.

"It's beautiful!" said Max. He looked up at Orven. "So where's the next one?"

Orven drew Gorflange again and began pointing it around them. The light in the stone set into the pommel's tip flickered briefly as the sword passed from north to east. Guiding it back, he pinpointed the direction as somewhere north-northeast of them, the dimness of the light indicating it was still a good distance away.

"Kronivar, maybe?" Orven said.

"Whatever the case, it'll be awhile before we're out of the forest, or even to the Silver Sea," said Aaron. No one wanted to get moving just yet, and so they sat resting in their wet clothes, tired and dreading the rest of their detour through the forest.

Chapter 8.
A Stay in Miastolas

By day Miastolas was no less beautiful than the vision Iaven had seen across the river at night. Around noontime, Lexter, Leland, and the dwarves crossed over the bridge and into the festival grounds. All along Lake Eihalo's southern shores throngs of merrymakers were meeting, dealing, eating, and drinking. Mingling there were Northern Elves and Elves from the southern archipelagos, sea-dwellers, and merchants; Dwarves and Men from the Foothills, Kronivar, and the Northern Provinces; and travelers from as far away as Tolgard, Phamiar, and Elluria. Musicians played and singers wandered amidst appreciative shouts and applause. Spaces opened in crowds where dancers, tumblers, or jugglers performed. Merchants and traders haggled and bargained, sampling each other's wares. Farmers proudly displayed livestock and produce. Scents of fresh food beckoned; spits of poultry roasting over open flames, fish sizzling in skillets, and soups steaming in cauldrons. Bakers drew trays of fragrant hot bread and pastries from brick ovens. The whole shoreline was a vast array of color and light, out to the great flower gardens on the lake's eastern end. Many wore their brightest, most festive garments for the occasion: colorful silks, furs, even feathers, dazzling designs old, new, and startlingly different. On Lake Eihalo graceful Elven vessels with high curved prows lay at anchor, sleek and elegant, their tall thin sails furled or fluttering in the breeze.

The dwarves sat breakfasting on rocks by the water's edge while Leland and Lexter told them about the festival and the city. Afterward they strolled about, enjoying all the festival had to offer. Songs enlivened the air, lifting Iaven's spirits and carrying them along:

> *Come one, come all,*
> *A-dancing and a-singing*
> *Strings a-humming, fingers strumming,*
> *Here the stranger lingers dreaming,*
> *Under moon and sun a-beaming,*
> *Wondering and wandering,*
> *Hear the clearest bells a-ringing,*
> *Near the mountain rivers streaming,*
> *Waters springing, prancing, gleaming*
> *Dancers answer with their wheeling*
> *Singers sing and voice the feeling*
> *Come one, come all, and take a chance!*
> *Give over all to happenstance,*
> *Oh, come and join our song and dance!*
>
> *Come one, come all,*
> *A-dining and a-drinking*
> *Now the harvest's taken in, now the festivals begin,*
> *Dough is rising, grapes are crushing,*

Fruit is ripening, water rushing,
Folks are toasting, feasting, roasting,
While the autumn sun is sinking
Near the mountain waters churning
Spits are turning, fires burning,
Fork and knife are all a-clatter,
Dancing in each dish and platter,
Come one, come all, your friends invite!
Give over all to appetite,
Oh, eat and drink with us tonight!

The light, loose rhythms reminded Iaven of songs his father had sung after trips to Miastolas. As they worked in the fields, Hagen would sing for the twins, humming the parts he'd forgotten. Iaven delighted in the songs, hoping to one day travel and see the city for himself. Now he wished his father could have been there with him.

The festival enchanted the dwarves, and they found Lexter and Leland to be good company. The Splides in turn liked guiding the dwarves and watching them experience everything for the first time. They even knew a few elves and introduced them to the dwarves.

Elven visits to the Foothills were infrequent and Iaven rarely had had a chance to see any Elves up close. Tall, light-skinned and fair-haired, the Elves had a keen alertness and youthful quality whatever their age. Their lithe, graceful bearing appeared effortless; swift but not hurried, relaxed yet guarded and watchful. As hosts they remained discreet and unassuming; yet they deftly saw to everyone's needs and let nothing get out of hand. Some served as guards, with long thin blades sheathed at their belts and bows and quivers slung over their shoulders. Their subtle presence deterred many a rogue or pickpocket, and generations of such care and vigilance had made the Miastolas Harvest Festival one of the most cherished celebrations around the Silver Sea.

During the festival and the weeks before it, Elven guards also patrolled the border shared with the Dwarves, the roads by which travelers came into Miastolas, and the southern end of Lower Rundlewood. Late that afternoon Iaven saw several of these guards returning over the bridge. They were dressed like the festival guards but with light shirts of ring-mail over green doublets. As they entered the grounds, crowds gasped and heads turned. People stepped back to let them pass. Musicians and singers grew silent. The company's Captain strode in front, a tall, stern veteran whose eyes, clear and sharp, bore a fierceness that belied his age. As the crowd pulled away, Iaven saw that the Captain carried, on outstretched arm, a severed Goblin head which he gripped by its wild, wiry black hair. Yellow, glazed eyes stared from its pallid, expressionless face. Its jaw hung open, points of sharp, curving teeth rising behind a thick lower lip.

"Behold!" the Captain shouted. "He who was wandering in Lower Rundlewood!" He held the head up for all to see. "And he is not the only one. Yet some claim the Goblin threat is still far off; that war is not imminent. Or that our allies, the Dwarves, will be able to hold them back." The Captain drew cold stares from dwarves in the crowd. "The northern border with Navrogenaya is secure, they tell us, the Gates will hold. And I do not doubt the Teskans are vigilant. Yet here are Goblins, in Lower Rundlewood!"

Leland leaned in toward Iaven and the others. "That's Captain Perialhe of the Forest Guard, and this is meant, I assume, as a kind of warning to Queen Perla," he explained, "and to all those who feel no need to mobilize. Many, like her, believe the Elves to be safe, with the Dwarves to the north. But not everyone has the same faith in your kingdom."

"We should not wait nor rely on others who are unable to contain them," the Captain continued, scanning the crowd. "Goblins are massing near the border. We must prepare now!" Some guards voiced their approval, along with others in the crowds. "We cannot wait!" shouted the Captain, "They are here!" He raised the head, drawing the audience's eyes to it. The crowd fell to murmuring among themselves. Concerned Elves of the festival guard who had been conversing together stepped forward by the Captain, and one turned to address the crowds.

"Captain Perialhe has set a high standard for all to follow; an exemplar for all who would fight the Goblins. May Dwarves and Elves alike take his example to heart! May we fight side by side when the time comes!" Applause drowned out the murmuring, as the festival guards escorted the forest troops off like heroes, the Captain leaving reluctantly.

"Well, well!" said Lexter when tension had subsided, "Quite a serious business! You fellows had better stay out of trouble. Looks like Dwarves have fallen out of favor here!" Lexter seemed almost amused as if the threat of war mattered little to him, or as if he even relished the idea. "You'd better keep your swords sheathed while you're here. A drawn blade may say more than you intend. Or better still, leave your swords at the inn." Lexter smiled.

"We'll keep them sheathed," said Iaven.

That afternoon the festival continued very much as it had before, but many a conversation led back to the Goblin threat. Prices rose, and folk from farther away planned to leave early. Though dwarves met with no hostility, many resented the chiding and felt put on the defensive. They supposed the Elves saw the Dwarves as having failed them, as irresponsible, or worse, weak and ineffectual. Iaven and his friends encountered no ill will from the Elves, but the festival's mood had subtly altered for them.

As the sun lowered in the west, the festival showed no signs of slowing down. After strolling the grounds, Iaven and Zammond made their way back to meet their friends and the Splide brothers for a light supper near where the Elven boats were moored. Iaven came to enjoy the Splides' company and found them to be useful guides in Miastolas. Still, he did not mention Halix around the Splides or talk about it openly in front of them, and neither did his friends.

Having collected their favorite foods, Lexter, Leland, and the dwarves enjoyed a light yet satisfying supper. Afterwards, Lexter suggested seeing more of Miastolas while it was still light out, so they all wandered along the shore of Lake Eihalo.

At the lake's far eastern end lay the great Eihalo Flower Gardens, spread around the curving shores and up the slopes to great rushing waterfalls where mountain streams fed into the lake. The Gardens' variety and meticulous landscaping had made them Hagen Ambersheath's favorite place to visit on trips to Miastolas. Once he had even managed to obtain seeds from the Gardens —a gift from an elf-friend— and had tried growing them around the oak trees in the Ambersheaths' yard. His love for the Gardens made Iaven anxious to see them.

But summer had passed and most flowers would be done blooming, thought Iaven. There'd only be the late-bloomers; asters, chrysanthemums, sweet alyssum, oberelias, and marigolds, until early-morning frosts came. Yet it might be his only chance to see the Gardens.

As they crossed a small bridge over a waterway the air grew sweet-scented, and before them the gardens lay like an immense tapestry rolling over the hills. It took Iaven's breath away. By some art or magic many flowers remained blooming beyond the swiftly passing days of summer. Azaleas flashed blood-red and lemon-yellow. Stalks of lavender hyacinths reached skyward. Bluebells, daisies, and violets scattered beneath magnolia branches bowed with blossoms. Basket-of-gold daffodils opened along with dahlias, dazzling white lilies, and billowing chrysanthemums, all in intricate patterns pleasing to the eye. Footpaths wove through dense banks of color and around fountains, out to the water's edge or far back to the white falls tumbling into the river. Paths led into hidden coves and natural gazebos woven from the branches of living trees. Large flagstones rose from the ground forming benches where one could breathe in sweet fragrances like waking dreams. Suddenly Iaven wanted to visit more of Feäthiadreya and was no longer in a hurry to get to the Castle.

In time the dwarves and the Splides found themselves resting in the shade of linden trees ringed with crimson roses, overlooking a pond spread with wide, white water lilies.

"I wish Itharia had something like this," said Hobley.

"You have other things to be proud of," said Leland, "There's nothing in Feäthiadreya like the Carven Halls of Gomirré, or the Great Gates near Teska, or Castle Frosthelm up in the mountains. The Elves are different that way; I heard a story once of an Elven merchant who traded a golden urn full of jewels for a little branch bearing the cocoon of a rare butterfly."

"Strange folk!" Lexter laughed. "But though they value such things more than gemstones and gold, they're aware of what Dwarves and Men value and can be shrewd traders."

"Which reminds me," said Leland, "there's a few people we have to see this evening, so we'd better get going while it's still light out."

They left the Gardens and crossed over a waterway, which they followed south through the orchards where it split into three tiny streams. Before the dwarves realized it, they had entered the city itself. Around them rose trees whose sculpted branches hid the dwellings of the Elves. Bright autumn leaves and flowering vines garnished their limbs, and fruit grew within reach of the Elves' windows. Branches overlapped and gracefully interlocked, making it difficult to tell where each abode began and ended. Some towered to several stories and extended over many trees. Often trees grew close together, rimming the edges of clearings like circular clearings where gardens bloomed, footpaths ran, and herbs, vegetables, and other crops grew. As Leland and Lexter led the dwarves down the trails, they passed through natural arches formed by trees. One circular area opened to them after another, some large, some small, always surrounded by trees and their curving branches. Tree roots dove out of the ground, forming short bridges over waterways that brought the Elves' water and irrigated their fields. Where each trail led back into the trees, braided branches arched over the passageway, framing the garden-circle beyond it.

The dwarves gazed around in wonderment, having lost their way after all the turnings, archways, and circles. At last they emerged where a wide road passed in front of an ornate gateway arch. The gate itself was made of crisscrossing boughs, with a huge mosaic of colored gemstones curving above it. Thin but wiry branches held the gems in place, letting light in behind them, and the entire mosaic glowed in glorious colors. Together, several thousand gems created an elaborate scene depicting a caravan of Elves marching across woodlands and out of mountain valleys into the forest, all under a blazing orange sun. The gate below the mosaic was closed, and beyond it the path led into a large circular meadow filled with wildflowers. In the meadow's center, rows of trees ran on each side of the path, forming a darkening corridor into the forest. Trees framing the corridor entrance were inscribed with Elven runes, which were not carved but formed directly by the ridges of the trees' bark.

"This leads out to Zwiatij Keh, the Northern Palace and summer home of Queen Perla, who departs for her Winter Palace in the south after a parade at the festival's end. Until then some of it's open to visitors. We really ought to come back here tomorrow and see it." Leland gazed through the gate and then turned to the dwarves. "Shall we meet here, around noon-time tomorrow, then?"

"Meet here? We'll be lucky if we can find our way back tonight!" said Iaven.

"Oh, we didn't take the shortest way in; far from it," said Lexter, "We just wanted you to see more of the place. This road we just crossed, here in front, leads back to the festival grounds."

"Rather inconvenient for a parade, if it were otherwise," said Leland. "Come on, it'll be getting dark soon, let's head back. We'll meet again here tomorrow."

The dwarves agreed and walked down the wide, curving road. Soon it opened out into the orchards and swung past the Gardens. At last it came to the festival, where they enjoyed themselves long into the night.

Less than an hour after the dwarves had finally turned in, Zammond became restless again. "Well, Iaven, how about it? You obviously can't fall asleep either, with Wilbur's snoring."

"True," Iaven admitted. The rooms at *The Waxing Crescent* were small but adequate and each had two beds. The Splides had taken the room next door, and Hobley and Tillmore had the room across the hall, so Wilbur had ended up on a cot in their room. He was dead tired after the long day and had no trouble falling into a boisterous slumber.

"It's a wonder he doesn't wake himself up," said Zammond, sitting up in bed. "So what do you say? We'll just narrow it down a bit. With all those jewels and gems everywhere, we might even get to see it up close."

"And that's all," said Iaven, "We aren't thieves!"

"Of course. I'd just like to see it. After all you've heard, don't you want to see one? As long as we're here... Maybe we could even get it in trade! I'll look for a cocoon..."

"I doubt it," said Iaven, swinging his legs out of bed. "But we'll try." Some attempt would have to be made before Zammond would be satisfied. But Iaven, too, was curious about the gem. "Alright, let's go," he said, "But we're not drawing the sword where anyone might see it. Nor are we prowling around like thieves. And settle down, before you wake everyone up!"

Moments later they were ready. Iaven had Halix at his belt and stepped out into the darkened hall. It was hours before sunrise and the inn was quiet. Zammond grabbed his cloak and slammed the door as he left.

"Zammond!" Iaven called in a hoarse whisper.

"Sorry! You're a little nervous about this, aren't you?"

"I just don't want you waking anyone up, that's all."

They stood in the hall in silence. After a moment Wilbur's snoring resumed, muffled behind the door and regular as ever.

"He'll never even know we're gone," said Zammond.

Iaven and Zammond crossed the river and walked along the edge of the festival grounds. The crowds had not thinned at all, and they paused to watch a few night-time entertainments; fire-eaters and jugglers with flaming batons, illusionists who performed only at night, and fireworks over the lake. Tall, thin torches on poles lined the lakeshore and lanterns hung from the trees. Further down along the beach bonfires burned merrily.

They walked on past the Gardens, away from the light and noise of the festival. Soft lights glowed and lovers lingered there.

Iaven and Zammond kept going, over a garden bridge and south through the orchards. Iaven stopped and looked around, making sure they were alone. "Alright," he said. He slipped Halix out of its sheath and aimed the blade into the woods, moving it in an arc. "Look," he said, "It's south of here. Somewhere in the Elves' trees. We'd get lost in that maze, so that's as far as we can go." He sheathed the sword.

"That's it?" said Zammond. "Let's go a little further and see if we can narrow it down!"

"Go where?" said Iaven, "Those trails were confusing enough in daylight, much less in the dark. And what would we say if someone saw us? We can't go in there."

Zammond paused. "Well, what about that mosaic, at least? It's right off the road."

"And then that's it? We'll go right back?"

"Yes!" Zammond lied.

They went down the road to the palace. A few trees shed a soft orange-yellow light from above, where the Elves' homes were. Except for night sounds of crickets and frogs, all was quiet. Iaven was afraid someone would appear around the bend and ask where they were going, but no one did. After a long curving walk they arrived at the gate. Iaven peered through into the meadow-circle. The entrance to Zwiatij Keh lay in darkness. Two slim torches framed the tree-lined corridor, their needles of flame shedding a faint light.

There was a faint *shing!* as Iaven drew Halix. He stepped back to face the palace gate and raised the sword toward the mosaic, and the stone set into the pommel glowed brighter than it ever had before.

It was difficult to make out the figures in the mosaic; the gems and jewels were all dark now, and only through careful discernment of their shapes and positions could one see the image they produced. Iaven aimed the sword around the mosaic. At one point the glow intensified. He directed the sword back to it and stopped.

"Right there," said Zammond. "Remember the orange sun in the picture, the one the Elves were marching under? I think that's it." Iaven peered up to where Zammond was pointing. It was several feet above them, out of their reach, even with the sword.

"Which one is it?" said Iaven. The mosaic was a wall of gemstones, closely packed, and he could hardly believe Zammond had narrowed it down to the gem they were looking for.

"Well, I remember the sun was made from a large gem surrounded by many smaller ones. It was the largest one in that part of the picture. And the only one, I think, big enough to fit the sword," said Zammond.

Iaven looked up at the stones in the mosaic. After a moment he lowered the sword again and sheathed it. "So there it is," he said disappointedly. "Well, we've found it, at least. I suppose we'd better head back now."

Zammond stared up at the dark mosaic, wondering how to get the gem down from it.

"Come on," said Iaven, "We'll leave it for the Elves. It's been there for who knows how long."

With an effort Zammond tore himself away and he and Iaven ambled down the curving road. "For the Elves?" he said, "You're not thinking of turning the sword over to them, too, are you?"

"Maybe," said Iaven, "It might help repair the alliance somewhat; that *was* the reason the swords were made, anyway. What if Goblin spies attacked us on our way to the Castle, and the sword fell into their hands? And the Castle really is a lot farther away than we'd thought."

"Iaven! You're saying this is it, you're going back to Hillbrook from here? How can you?"

Iaven was silent and kept on going. Zammond walked beside him, waiting.

"And besides, why should the Elves get the sword? It was never actually theirs, even if it was originally meant to be. Let King Jordgen present it to them, not you! And what makes you think you could get an audience with the Queen, anyway?"

"I don't know," said Iaven finally, "I suppose you're right. We probably couldn't get an audience, and we should give Halix to the King. He probably won't grant us an audience either, but at least we could see the Castle... What was that?"

Iaven turned at a small cracking sound from the woods on their right. "Is someone there?"

Zammond looked around. "I don't see anyone. You're just nervous."

"Well you're more used to sneaking around than I am," said Iaven. "Let's head back. I'm tired." They plodded off down the road and through the orchard. Iaven wished the gem was merely lost or buried where they could have simply taken it. He reminded himself that it wasn't the reason they had come to Miastolas, and realized how much he really wanted to get a gem for the sword.

The following morning the dwarves woke late and breakfasted on the festival grounds. The sun rose high in the clear sky, and near its zenith they remembered they were meeting Leland for a tour of the Palace grounds. They headed through the orchards, over waterways, and down the wide curving road to the Palace Gate. It was open now, and Leland stood inside the meadow-circle, admiring the wildflowers blanketing the ground around the path.

As they approached, the dwarves looked at the gateway mosaic in the sunlight, and then passed through the gate. Zammond lingered outside, gazing up at the mosaic and the jeweled image of the sun, now brilliantly lit from behind by the sun itself. The whole mosaic was alive with molten light, shimmering and sparkling. Zammond stared at the large orange gem, certain it was one of the seven Aorinthel had fashioned so long ago.

While Hobley and Tillmore greeted Leland, Iaven stepped out and nudged Zammond. "Come on! He's waiting." Zammond nodded and followed Iaven through the gate. Before they passed through, Iaven shot a glance up at the orange gem shining in all its glory, feeling a pang of desire for it again.

"Well, there they are. I trust you all slept well enough?" Leland smiled at them. "Lexter's still asleep, but he's seen it all anyway, so he won't be joining us. Shall we go up to the Palace?" Leland turned and led the way.

Inside the wide meadow-circle, the path led straight through to where rows of trees began, their branches arching over the path. Guards stood on each side; tall, blond, sharp-featured Elves with watchful eyes. They held ornamental glaives at attention and wore ring-mail over their green doublets. As Palace guards, they also bore the Queen's insignia, an orange seahorse on a field of blue. Leland and the dwarves felt their scrutiny as they passed.

At first the trees ran like pillars on either side of them, the sunlit spread of wildflowers shining between their trunks. As they walked the trees grew closer together, their branches interweaving more tightly overhead until it almost seemed as if they were indoors. The path rose up an incline to the top of a hill.

There the tunnel opened into an immense high dome of crisscrossing branches that let in airy shafts of golden sunlight. Vines wove around the branches, their broad leaves able to filter light or deflect rain as the Elves desired. Water trickled and tumbled in fountains along the walls of the dome, where curling branches of large, ornamental trees swung low to the ground, forming stairways leading to other areas.

At the back of the dome, tall archways overlooked the valley where the palace grounds ran to meet the wooded hills leading into the mountains. Hedges and waterways encircled fruit trees and sweet-scented herbs, delicate ferns, and intricately plotted floral displays which had only now reached their final week of blooming. The Palace Gardens were broader, lovelier, and more formal than the Eihalo Gardens, which the dwarves realized were only the Palace Gardens' nursery. Visitors wandered throughout the Palace grounds, the summer home of peacocks and colorful, long-legged birds. Elves were stationed talking with their guests, answering questions and giving directions.

"So this is the Palace of Zwiatij Keh!" said Iaven.

"Oh, no, not at all." Leland led them out of the arch into the sunlight and directed their gaze up over the trees to the right. "This dome is merely a greeting-room for visitors. Zwiatij Keh itself, where the Queen resides, is just beyond those trees."

The Palace of Zwiatij Keh rose up over the forest in the distance and was the size of a small city, climbing well over three hundred feet into the sky. Tree trunks and branches of many colors grew in interlocking spirals widening and winding gracefully into curving onion domes billowing out and tapering up into the air. Tall, broad trees like towers ended in branches shaped into ball-like enclosures, curtained with greenery. Waterfalls sparkled and fell from the sides of terraced towers hung with flowering vines. Wreaths of leafy foliage encircled tall redwoods and cedars growing far beyond their usual heights. Huge plumes of ferns sprouted at the tops of steeples and spires, and flowers ringed many tall arched windows. Elves could be seen passing along slender walkways or standing at balconies. Even at that distance one could see the towers and domes were decorated with elaborate natural woodwork designs. Iaven's gaze was drawn to the Palace like some ethereal dream hanging before him, unreal and remote yet visible and looming large in the distance, and he longed to draw nearer to it. The whole Palace seemed to float in the mid-day haze, a mirage towering up into the heavens.

They went out on the lawn of the Palace Gardens, but Iaven barely noticed. The vision of the Palace held sway over him, and he sat down with the others under a shade tree. With an effort he turned to them again.

"Can we go there?" Iaven asked Leland.

"Visitors usually aren't allowed in the Palace itself, which is a shame since the throne room is so magnificent. The festival ends in three days and the Queen is no doubt preparing to depart for the Winter Palace. Her court is probably quite busy with festival matters." Leland smiled. "But we know a few important folks, so after lunch we'll give it a try."

Iaven was elated, and even considered turning the sword over to the Elves as an excuse to get in. He saw Zammond knew what he was thinking, and decided against it.

"All I've heard about Miastolas and the Palace, and now here we are!" Hobley exclaimed. "I'm glad we came. I would have hated to miss it."

"Me, too!" said Wilbur. "What's for lunch?"

"Well, for starters," said Leland, drawing out a small flask and tiny silver cups from his shoulder-bag, "You should try some Oshberry Nectar while you're here." He gave each of the dwarves a little silver cup and poured the nectar into them one by one. "A toast to new adventures, and new friends," he said. He finished and tipped the flask, filling Tillmore's cup. "Ah, just enough for the five of you!" he said, disappointed.

Hobley offered his to Leland, but Leland declined. "No, that's all right, go ahead. Lexter and I have had plenty of it already, and we stock up on it every time we come. We buy it for trading, but always seem to drink it all ourselves!" Leland laughed. "Excellent stuff, and this was a particularly good year for it, too, so I'm told."

"To adventures and friends!" Zammond raised his cup. The others joined him, clinking the cups' rims together, and they all drank.

Iaven sipped his cautiously, as he always did with drinks he had never tasted before. The liquid was sweet and soothing in his mouth. It had a light, sweet taste that lingered on the tongue, and he savored the rest, thinking he could drink a whole flask of the nectar. Even after he had swallowed the last drop, the taste remained. Filled with contentment and warmth, he lay back on the sunlit grass, staring at the sky.

"It's delicious!" Iaven exclaimed in a quiet voice, letting the smooth, sweet feeling wash over him. He closed his eyes and stretched out his legs, and decided to buy a flask of the stuff himself, maybe two if he could afford it. The flavor continued to sweeten and he breathed deeply, feeling lighter and more peaceful than he had in a long time.

Iaven heard birds cawing and chirping, and opened his eyes. The sun had moved and he realized he had been lying there for some time. The others were all stretched out on the grass, too, and Leland was gone. Iaven sensed something amiss and woke the others. Groggy and annoyed at being disturbed, they sat rubbing sleep from their eyes.

Iaven got to his feet, his trepidation growing.

"Iaven, look!" said Zammond.

Iaven saw Halix's empty scabbard hanging from his belt. A wave of angry denial and frustration shot through him.

"No!—Oh, why did we—I can't believe it!" Iaven sat down hard on the grass.

Hobley stood and scanned the landscape. "Maybe he hasn't gone too far, we could try to find him."

The dwarves got up from the grass. "Hard to say how long we've been dozing," Zammond said. "Great stuff, though, whatever that nectar was!"

"At least it wasn't poisonous," said Tillmore.

"Could the Elves have taken the sword away from him? He was carrying it unsheathed. Maybe it looked suspicious," said Wilbur.

"We might as well try to look for him," said Iaven, feeling it was already too late.

They all went back into the visitors' dome and down the walkway through the rows of trees. Soon they emerged in the meadow-circle near the mosaic gate.

"How could we have trusted him?" said Zammond. "What fools we were!"

"We should have taken his advice and not trusted anyone!" said Wilbur.

They walked back to the orchards and the festival. Iaven said little, burning with anger at himself and crushed by a dread responsibility for whatever happened to the sword.

"Well, there's five of us, and only two of them, maybe we can find them," said Hobley.

"It's either that or return to Hillbrook," Tillmore agreed.

"The inn!" said Zammond. "He might have gone back to the inn. Maybe we can still catch them." And so they bypassed the festival and crossed the bridge to *The Waxing Crescent*.

The innkeeper was a burly, older dwarf with wild and unkempt graying hair, a round, reddened nose, and a wide chin. "The Splides?" he said, "In the room next to yours? Pulled out just a little while ago, they did. The one with the beard, he was loading up the wagon, and just as he's done the other comes by. Said they had to go quick. Gave a nice tip, too," he said, expecting the dwarves to do likewise for the news. This was lost on all of them except Tillmore, who reached into his pocket and handed the man a few coins.

"You wouldn't know where they were headed, would you?" Tillmore inquired.

"No," said the innkeeper. "Can't say I was sorry to see them go, either. They're the dangerous type, what with the wares they're lugging."

"What do you mean?" asked Iaven.

"All those chests," he explained, "They asked us to keep an eye on 'em, paid us extra, even. One was hurrying to leave, the other comes back with a sword. Opened one of the crates, and it was full of weaponry; swords, axes, broadswords, daggers, and all; and them both foreigners looking to sell. Festival gets all sorts, you know. Stolen goods, probably. Most smithies serve King or Queen, but weapons change hands, some for a fair price."

"Well thank you very much, sir," said Tillmore, flipping the innkeeper another coin as an afterthought.

"Many thanks! Staying a few more nights, are you?" said the innkeeper.

"Maybe," said Iaven, as they all trudged back out.

The dwarves spent what was left of the afternoon searching the festival grounds, just in case. Everything that had once seemed cheerful and relaxing now seemed noisy, heavy, and crowded. They stayed until evening, but there was no sign of Leland or Lexter anywhere to be found.

It was late at night in the forests of Miastolas, and as the sixth day of the Great Harvest Festival had ended, many Elves were deep in slumber. Far fewer lights glowed in the trees than the first few nights had seen, for even the Elves tired after nearly a week of merrymaking. The road curving through the forest to the mosaic gate was also darker as a result, but this did not ease the minds of the two men traveling along it.

"I don't like it, it's too risky," said Leland.

"It was above the gate," said Lexter, "They were standing there. And the end of the sword was glowing." Lexter opened his coat and brought Halix out. He lifted it towards the gate as Iaven had done, and the stone set into the pommel glowed bright blue-green. "Don't you think it's worth the risk?"

Leland laughed. "So you believe me now, eh? I thought it might be an Angkelwen sword, the first time I saw it. You don't see craftsmanship like that today. And in such excellent condition for its age. That alone would have been a find in itself."

"But if it really *is* one of the 'Lost Swords of the Alliance' as some call them..." said Lexter.

"Well, I suppose it's possible," said Leland, "but it's more than likely just the stuff of legends, after all. A claim made to strengthen the Alliance at the time. After the war, they couldn't find the swords; some said they were destroyed or left unfinished, or never even forged at all. And anyway, how could they lose swords like that? Just diplomats making promises. We don't even know for certain what those swords looked like."

"We know enough about Dwarven swords to have some idea, and the two or three Angkelwen swords we've owned briefly—"

"I agree it's one of his; I just doubt it's one of the two 'Lost' ones," Leland interrupted. "How would those dwarves have come across it anyway? They'd never even been out of the Foothills!"

"Here it is," said Lexter. They stood beneath the mosaic above the closed gate. Lexter extended his arm with the sword, the end of which cast a ghostly blue-green glow onto his upturned face. But the gems were too high, out of reach. "It's up there somewhere," he said.

"Something's making the sword glow like that, but what is it? And is it important? We don't have much time. I don't like having the wagon so far in."

"Harald will look after it," said Lexter, still gazing upward. He lowered his arm.

"I don't think we can trust him for long, and someone's bound to see it," said Leland.

"Harald's alright," said Lexter, getting out a length of rope and aiming at a thick tree branch several feet above the mosaic. "We owe him enough. You can always trust a man to want his money back. Besides, this will only take a few minutes."

"It better," Leland said. He watched as Lexter tossed the rope up into the tree, trying to get it over the branch. Finally it went over. Lexter lowered the end of the rope hanging down and held it taut, testing to see if it would support his weight. With Halix tucked under his arm, Lexter grasped the rope and began walking up the gate, until he was in front of the mosaic.

Seeing Lexter was holding steady, Leland left. "I'm going to check on Harald," he said.

"Go ahead, I'll be done in a moment." Lexter gripped the rope with one arm and used the other to pry gems out of the mosaic with the sword, letting them fall to the ground. The gem the dwarves had talked about was there, but he didn't know what it looked like, so he'd just take a few handfuls of gems and sort through them later.

Gems torn from the mosaic lay scattered on the ground like dark constellations. Lexter finished and lowered himself to the ground. They'd planned to split the gems half and half, but since Leland couldn't even wait for him, Lexter decided to pocket a few choice ones right away; he'd earned them. It had all been his idea anyway, and he was the one who had followed the dwarves at night and found out about the sword. He bent down and was about to touch the gems, when he heard a footfall and a gleaming steel point appeared near his face.

"Drop the sword!" Zammond shouted. Lexter straightened with Zammond's blade aimed at his throat, and the four other dwarves had him surrounded.

Lexter paused and dropped Halix onto the ground by his feet. Zammond started to come forward to pick it up when Lexter jumped back and drew his own sword, which Zammond had forgotten about. Lexter swung his sword and it rang against Zammond's, catching him by surprise and throwing him off balance. Zammond lost his footing and fell to the ground on top of Halix. Lexter was ready to strike Zammond again when Hobley blocked Lexter with his axe as Tillmore held him at bay with his long-bladed dagger. As they fought, Zammond crawled back and pulled Halix out of the pile of gems and picked up his own sword as well. Wilbur stood ready with his sword drawn, near Iaven, who was unarmed and wielding a stick. Lexter backed off from Hobley and Tillmore, and slashed at Wilbur, who jumped aside nervously. He aimed a blow that Iaven countered with his stick. Just as Zammond recovered and joined in again, Lexter swung wildly, opening a way between Wilbur and Iaven and slipping through. He turned on them now, no longer surrounded. At that moment Leland came running around the bend of the road, sword drawn.

"Iaven!" Zammond tossed Halix to Iaven, but Leland and Lexter were on to them. Iaven swung Halix and bit steel with Leland's sword, while Hobley and Tillmore held off Lexter's strokes and thrusts. Zammond and Wilbur backed up Iaven, holding Leland off, but the Splides were taller than the dwarves and much more experienced swordsmen. The dwarves realized they had lost their advantage. Iaven had Halix back now, and it occurred to each of them that fleeing was their best choice at the moment.

As soon as they could they made a break for it. "Let's go!" Iaven yelled, as they ran off down the road. The Splides came after them, but without the dwarves' youth they were soon out of breath. Now they were back where the Elves' homes began, and had to be quiet. "Let them go," said Leland, "We'll find them." Lexter headed back to pick up the pile of gems from the ground.

Leland looked down the road, breathing hard, and then caught up to Lexter to be sure he got his fair share of the gems.

The dwarves had slowed to walking by the time they got to the orchards, and half-expected Lexter and Leland to appear at any time and overtake them. When he saw the Splides weren't behind them anymore, Iaven wondered if they'd taken a different route to lay in wait for the dwarves somewhere. "We can't go back to the inn," he said, "Not yet."

Until dawn, the safest place seemed to be the festival grounds. They mingled in the crowds, pausing to see the entertainments but constantly watchful, glancing at anyone who looked even remotely like the Splides. The dwarves were tired, having spent long hours waiting for the Splides, but they could not sleep. Now that they had Halix back they planned to pack up and leave as soon as possible, despite their desire to stay and see more of Miastolas.

In the morning light, things seemed calmer and safer. The dwarves wondered if they'd overestimated the danger of the night before. Tired and heavy, they trudged back to the inn, passing over the bridge to the *Crescent*.

"There he is!" whispered Lexter. He and Leland had hidden for some time behind a hedge by the inn, waiting for just this moment. "Better to wait," said Leland, "They'll clear out of here this morning, I'm sure of it. We'll get them on the road. Too many people here." They watched as the dwarves went inside past Elven guards standing by the door.

"Fine," Lexter said. "I wouldn't mind getting out of here myself —that *was* the plan, anyway."

"Until you lost the sword!" Leland snapped back. Now that the dwarves were inside, the Splides stepped out into the open. "I think we should wait further down the road. The wagon's ready to go, and we really don't want to be seen much, after taking those gems."

"No one saw us but the dwarves," Lexter said.

"You don't know that. Elves might have seen us from the trees —what with all the noise you were making!"

"It doesn't matter now," said Lexter, "We were supposed to leave right away, right after!"

"Maybe we should have," said Leland, "We've got the gems, let's leave the sword—"

"I want both!" Lexter shot back, trying not to raise his voice.

Leland glared at Lexter, used to his younger brother's stubbornness but despising it all the same. Both had been up all night and were more than a little ornery.

"I'll move the wagon into the woods and wait for you there. Don't be too obvious when following them!" He turned and left before Lexter could respond.

The dwarves relaxed, flopping down on their beds awhile before packing up and leaving. Zammond walked over to the doorway of the room, looking out. As Iaven stood by his bed, waiting to see if Zammond saw anything, an idea struck him. He drew Halix and pointed it out the door. The blue-green light in the pommel glowed brightly. Iaven sheathed the sword again as Zammond turned to see what he was doing.

"He's out there, and close by, too!" Iaven said.

Zammond looked curious. "I didn't see anyone."

Iaven walked to the door. "Call in those guards that were out front."

Zammond went out and returned with guards, and Iaven and Zammond talked with them inside the room.

"We have a description of the thief from two witnesses who were passing through," said one of the guards, "But we do not know his whereabouts."

"He robbed us as well," Iaven told them. "We want him caught as much as you do."

"And you claim he's outside somewhere? Alright then." The guards waited for Iaven and Zammond, and together they went outdoors.

In the bright sunlight Iaven felt safer than he had at night. Knowing the Splides were nearby, he looked for hiding places where they could keep an eye on the inn. Iaven, Zammond, and the guards spread out, searching. Iaven sprang around a corner and caught Lexter slipping away.

In a flash Iaven drew Halix, and Lexter spun and met it with his blade. Lexter fought well; despite nearing middle age and being more than a bit on the heavy side, he was a fair swordsman. Iaven, lacking experience, nervously backed off, yet managed to hold his own much to his surprise. The sword was heavy in his hand but moved well, and he could tell it was no ordinary sword.

Lexter pressed forward harder, causing Iaven to panic, but Zammond and the guards caught up with them. After a moment they had Lexter subdued. Iaven's heart was beating hard, and he sheathed Halix and watched as the guards bound Lexter's hands.

"I've done nothing!" Lexter protested. One of the guards searched his pockets and came up with a handful of gems.

"It's him all right," said one guard to the other. "Fits the description, too."

Others came to help escort Lexter away. The remaining guard spoke to Iaven and Zammond.

"Your help is appreciated," he told them, "There'll be a short trial, and he'll be held until the festival's end. After that, he will be made to leave the city, as it is closed to foreigners after the festival." He nodded. "Once again, we thank you," he added as he left.

"Well, Iaven," Zammond smiled, "pretty good for someone who's never wielded a sword before!" He elbowed Iaven, and Iaven nudged him back, pleased by the compliment, even though he knew Lexter could have killed him had Zammond and the guards appeared a moment too late.

"I wish I could have seen it," said Hobley, "I knew Iaven had it in him!"

"Oh, sure you did! You're just as surprised as I am!" said Zammond.

"So they're letting Lexter go?" asked Wilbur.

"Only when the festival's over, so we'll have a few days' head start, if he decides to come after us," said Iaven.

"And Leland?" asked Tillmore.

"Still out there somewhere," said Zammond.

"We'd better get going," Iaven said, starting to pack. "We're all tired but we ought to get as far north as we can. Leland seemed the smarter of the two, and I'd like to get as far away from the Splides as possible."

They all were morose and slow to pack, catching moments of shut-eye in between, and an hour later they paid for their room and were off down the road.

The dwarves descended the shallow hills that lay between the inn and the crossroads where the South Road came down from the north. As they passed, none of them noticed a man standing in the forest off the road, watching them.

On their way to the Castle, Leland thought to himself. He had dealings that evening —with Lexter held for trial he could stay, and the Bottomcliffe deal sounded too good to pass up— but after that he was willing to leave the festival a day or two early to pursue the dwarves. He would need to leave a message for Lexter to rendezvous in one of the towns along the South Road. The dwarves were on foot and he could easily catch up to them with the wagon. He smiled to himself, relishing the challenge. The dwarves passed overhill and out of sight as he watched, but Leland knew that he had not seen the last of them yet.

Chapter 9.
Meetings in Bottomcliffe

During the next four days, both of the twins' parties traveled northward. Orven's party followed alongside the Upper Yandl towards the sea through the unending forests of Rundlewood, while Iaven's party journeyed up the South Road near the mountains. The weather cooled as the wind bore autumn southward, rustling trees and rattling dried leaves, sighing in resignation to the inevitable onset of winter.

That afternoon, after leaving Miastolas, the dwarves walked in silence, tired and irritable after a sleepless night. Almost losing Halix had shaken their confidence. It hung sheathed at Iaven's side, and for some time no one cared to talk about it or the gems; their search for the gem had resulted in the ruining of the mosaic, and almost the loss of the sword.

As the day wore on, only Zammond regained his high spirits, which the others found annoying. But they let him soften their somber mood, and gradually conversation picked up again. Iaven's spirits still sagged, so he was glad when Zammond fell to the back of the party with Wilbur, since he did not feel like being cheered up. Tillmore walked with Iaven now.

"This morning I heard you say you were thinking of joining the King's troops," said Iaven. "I was rather surprised."

"So was I," said Tillmore. "I wasn't going to tell anyone, but I'm worried about Hob. He's been fey of late. He hides well, drowning it in drink, even his family doesn't know. He's tired of Hillbrook life and sees how the long years of bricklaying and ditch-digging have worn out his father almost into the grave. He expects his life to be pretty much the same. His family's poorer than he lets on, and knows they're looked down upon. So he's leaving without any hope of coming back. Dying in the war will bring honor on his family and put him to rest; that's how he sees it. So I've come along to look after him."

"You're hoping to talk him out of it?" said Iaven.

"At first I was," said Tillmore, "But he really does want to help the kingdom. He's always been generous that way. It looks like I'll have to see it through with him, keeping him safe if I can. He's the kind who'll take foolish risks to prove his bravery."

"I know what you mean," said Iaven, recalling childhood dares.

A hush fell over them as Hobley approached.

"Leland knew we're going to the Castle," Hobley said. "Would he come after us without Lexter?"

"Maybe," said Iaven, "to keep from losing track of us."

"He could have the gem, since the Elves only caught Lexter," said Tillmore, "They both might have been out there that morning. He might come after the sword."

"I wish we hadn't gone after the gem," Iaven said, "It was Zammond's idea, and he—"

"Hey Iaven!" Zammond called, dashing up and slapping him hard on the back in a friendly but provoking manner. "What're we talking about?"

"You're in high spirits," Hobley complained.

"Terribly high," said Tillmore.

"How about it?" said Zammond, "We've waited long enough. C'mon, Iaven, let's see where the next gem is!"

They stopped and Wilbur caught up to them. Iaven reluctantly withdrew Halix, knowing he would have to sooner or later. He aimed it south towards Miastolas, expecting to see a faint glow. To his surprise, the stone in the pommel was very bright, even in the sunlight.

"Leland," said Hobley, readying his axe as Wilbur drew his sword.

Iaven looked down the road. No one was anywhere near them. He moved the sword side to side to pinpoint the gem's location, but the sword glowed equally bright in all directions. Puzzled, Iaven turned a full circle, with no change in results.

"Somewhere nearby, isn't it?" Zammond said, watching Iaven. After several frustrating minutes, Iaven suddenly handed Hobley the sword. "You try it," he said. Hobley took it and moved it around. Now it seemed to glow only when pointed at Iaven.

"Just as I thought," said Iaven, smiling reluctantly.

Hobley searched alongside Iaven, and then reached into Iaven's hood and removed the orange gem.

"Zammond! You had it all the while?" Iaven chided, his voice betraying his gladness.

"Remember when I picked Halix up off the ground? It was right there, so I couldn't resist." Zammond moved in closer, staring down at the gem with the others.

The gem was a rich, brilliant orange like a glowing ember. Light danced on its surface as it lay in Hobley's palm. It seemed ancient yet very alive, with secret powers resting in its depths, its glittering facets holding their gaze. Iaven took Halix back from Hobley and took the gem, thrilled as his fingertips touched it. As he brought the gem near, the tiny metalwork leaves rimming the holes rotated and withdrew, and he set the gem into the sword. The leaves resumed their positions, locking the gem firmly in place. Iaven raised the sword and it seemed less clumsy in his hand now, and lighter. He moved it about easily, confident he would be able to wield it. It flowed with his movements, and a strange excitement made him feel eager to use it. He became aware of how he was playing with the sword while the others watched him, and sheathed it again.

"Why didn't you let on sooner that you had it?" Iaven asked.

"And have you turn it over to the Elves? You would have, wouldn't you? So I had to wait until we were far enough away from Miastolas. And then I thought of this. Well, aren't you glad now that I took it?" Zammond said, grinning.

Iaven looked at Zammond. "We've come too far to take it back, I suppose."

"They won't miss it!" said Zammond, "Besides, it wasn't theirs anyway, they must have found it somewhere. It was meant to be with the swords."

"I'm amazed you were able to keep it secret for so long," said Tillmore. "No wonder you've been so annoyingly cheerful."

"It was grating on me, too!" said Wilbur.

"Let's find another one," Zammond motioned towards Halix. "I know, we're not going out of our way for them. I just want to see where they are."

Iaven drew Halix and was about to hand it to Zammond, when he decided to look for the gems himself. Iaven pointed the sword across the land like a sailor surveying the horizon. He stopped, moved Halix back a little, and stopped again. The light from the pommel stone was dim, but with his hand cupped around it, a faint blue-green flicker was visible.

"North and to the west," said Zammond, "must be near Kronivar."

"It's awfully faint," added Tillmore, "maybe it's further out, lost at sea, or something."

"We're still stopping there anyway, in Kronivar, aren't we?" asked Wilbur.

"It's out of our way," said Iaven, "Though I wouldn't mind seeing it myself. But we've still a long, long way to go."

The day after the Harvest Festival ended more carts and wagons were traveling north, and Iaven and his friends found a few rides. But many drivers turned them away or wouldn't stop, unsure who could be trusted. Most travelers were too busy hurrying home to the villages and hamlets along the South Road. There was little stopping and talking when strangers met, unlike in summers past before the shadow of war had spread over Itharia. Iaven and the others soon grew somber and no longer attempted conversation with their fellow travelers.

On their second day out from Miastolas, Iaven had seen a family with a weatherworn cart loaded down with all their belongings; they were moving south where they thought life would be safer. Soldiers from the Castle traveled in small companies of half a dozen or so, going town to town to raise troops, and dwarves Iaven's age or younger left with them. Many went off to the Castle in groups with their friends, naïvely eager for adventure and a chance to prove their loyalty to the crown, or to find relief from the monotony of their provincial lives.

Seeing others going off to join the troops, and knowing they probably thought he was doing likewise, Iaven began to feel he was shirking his duty. He still planned to return to Hillbrook after delivering the sword to the Castle and thought the rest of his duty could be fulfilled working in Rory's smithy. Why should everyone have to serve at the front, or even in the King's troops? But somehow he could not entirely convince himself it was as simple as that.

For many miles the road ran straight, wide, and long in front of them. To the left were meadowlands, and beyond them the dark forests of Rundlewood. On the right, the range of the Frosthelm Mountains rose in the distance, their broad shoulders catching the day's last light. Now and then side roads led away from the South Road to villages and farms, half-hidden behind hills and set far enough away from the road to be left alone. Many of the villages were too small to have an inn, and these days strangers were looked on with suspicion or sent away. Near well-traveled roads folks kept to themselves, and Iaven wondered whether they'd help travelers in need.

As the fourth day after they left Miastolas drew to a close, the road emptied and the dwarves had it all to themselves. The sun sank quickly into the forest and shadow crept out, spilling across the meadows, across the road, and gradually up the mountains until only their peaks were tinged with crimson. The wind was soft but swift and cold. The dwarves wrapped their cloaks tight and spoke little. Mournful wolf howls, long and lonely, echoed in the dusky gloom. Iaven's heart sank and a shiver ran down his spine. His hands were cold and he thrust them in his pockets. Night fell, and he hoped there was not much farther to go.

Earlier that day Iaven's party had stopped off the road in an orchard for lunch. While they ate, a horse-drawn wagon passed by heading north on the far side of the road. The dwarves had not seen the driver, nor did he see them. Leland was in a hurry to get to Bottomcliffe where an important deal awaited him.

In Miastolas, Leland had met with men and dwarves looking for weaponry, but instead of the usual piecemeal sale or trade, they had insinuated (after Leland feigned a lack of interest) that they might buy an entire wagon-load, paid for in gold. They set a date in Bottomcliffe and told him to be there. With war imminent, Leland expected demand to rise, but this surpassed his hopes. He sensed something big going on, something shady and underhanded perhaps, which meant there'd be more money involved. The following day he left Miastolas, leaving a message for Lexter with a mutual friend. Lexter would understand. After the Elves released him, he could ride with Harald on his way back up to Gomirré and catch up in Bottomcliffe.

During the ride, Leland's mind kept returning to the same questions. What was going on in Bottomcliffe? Why were so many weapons needed? They claimed it was for the upcoming war, but he remained unconvinced; other motives lurked beneath the surface. He and Lexter had done enough such dealings to recognize deceit in others. But the money was good, and answers would come soon enough, he thought. No time for chasing dwarves who Lexter imagined to have one of the Lost Swords of the Alliance. Lexter had always been a dreamer. Leland often wondered where Lexter would have ended up without his older brother's guidance and good business sense.

Late that afternoon Leland's wagon turned onto a side road leading in to Bottomcliffe. Bottomcliffe was a mining town at the foot of the mountains, almost as old as Kronivar, though it looked even older. Clapboard houses stood on stone foundations, crowding together near the roads and further apart beyond the edge of town. Most were built around a central fireplace which rose into a massive chimney; single-family dwellings, some with small shops attached. Leland rode down Bottomcliffe's main street and to the central town square, where roads crisscrossed a great rectangular lawn and encircled a well where a few women were drawing water for the night. Leland drove around the square, looking for the inn. In back of the town rose the large, rugged shapes of the millhouses and furnaces, and beyond them the mine entrances, cut into the high wall of steep gray cliffs.

At last Leland came to the inn, *The Copper Dragon*, and drove into the fenced-in dooryard behind it. A man sat on a stoop polishing urns and tinware, and Leland flipped him a coin to watch the horse and wagon. The man caught it deftly and nodded.

The Copper Dragon had been a fixture in the heart of Bottomcliffe since the early days of King Aardgen's reign, renowned for its ample portions if not its cleanliness. Inside and out, the *Dragon* proclaimed its success and its patrons' support. Iron grillwork framed its windows, and two ornate castings of long, thin dragons extending their claws stood poised by the doors in the flickering lamplight outside the front entrance. Inside, metal tankards lined high shelves, and shields bearing crests of Bottomcliffe's important families hung in the corners of the main common room.

Leland entered into the noisy, smoky room where mining dwarves talked, ate, and drank. Apart from a few hostile glances, the miners took little notice of him. At the back of the room he found an empty table along the wall surrounded by high-backed benches of dark wood. Leland slid around the table to have his back to the wall and keep watch for whomever he was supposed to meet. Right after dark, they'd said, so he ordered a beer and sat back and waited.

Leland relaxed and was enjoying his beer when he noticed a thin, suspiscious-looking dwarf glancing in his direction and making his way over to the table. His gaunt features and cheerless expression seemed out of place in the inn. He came to Leland's table, hesitating.

"Mr. Splide?"

"Correct," said Leland, setting down his beer. "And who might you be?"

The dwarf looked him over, as though judging Leland's appearance and finding it lacking. "Wait here. They will arrive in a moment." He turned and disappeared back into the crowd.

Leland sighed and sipped his beer. Again he wondered who these people were. And what they were willing to pay. The windows had grown dim now and a barmaid was lighting candles on the tables and in wall sconces. Leland drank and took in the other patrons from where he sat; practically all dwarves, big sturdy types from the mines or foundries. The few Men there were most likely traders from Kronivar or visitors from across the sea, though not many ventured beyond the port cities. Fond of eavesdropping, Leland listened to fragments of conversations and arguments above the din.

"Why sit and wait?" said a short, heavyset dwarf with a wide brow overhanging dark, wild eyes. "No reason to let them build up. Ought to go up there and put a stop to it right away."

"What, and try to take the valley?" a red-faced older dwarf with graying hair replied. "What a waste of lives that would be! And what of the Gates and Wall, then? All bluff, the Goblins are; trying to scare us."

"They're waiting for the right moment," said a third, "The Castle's been too slow to respond. Something's got to be done."

"More than what the King's done," said the first dwarf, "What's he waiting for, I'd like to know."

"They've held off the Goblins since before your father was born!" the gray-haired dwarf retorted.

"'*The young crave action, while the old favor diplomacy,*' as they say," said the wild-eyed dwarf, the youngest at the table, "true enough, maybe, but Jordgen's an old king and not prone to either anymore. Puts us all in danger. The Castle least so, perhaps, cut off as they are."

"Hrrrmmph!" the gray-haired dwarf grunted in contempt, chewing his food and tired of the conversation but wanting the last word anyway.

Leland was so distracted that he didn't notice the strangers drawing near. The thin dwarf was leading three others to the table; a dark-haired, tall, brawny fellow of noble bearing in a long brown cloak, a shorter, balding dwarf with a short yellow beard and bad teeth, and a tall, older man with a long gray beard who was dressed in a coat of dark crimson. The two dwarves sat on Leland's right, while the brawny fellow and the old man sat on Leland's left. They sat down before Leland had said anything, and now he was trapped behind the table. He wondered if that was their intent.

"We hear you have weaponry for sale," said the tall brawny fellow, in a low but careful voice. His long vowels revealed him to be from Kronivar, and now at close range Leland could better see his features. Part Man, part Dwarf, he thought; but many such half-breeds and quarter-breeds populated Kronivar these days, since the great influx of foreigners. "Thon Aranstone," he added. He met Leland's gaze and extended his hand.

"Leland Splide, pleased to do business with you." Leland smiled as Aranstone's large hand enclosed his in a firm grip. "Javin said you were interested in several crates' worth?"

Aranstone's gaze shifted to the old man, then back to Leland. "We are," he admitted.

"Javin speaks too rashly," the old man spoke suddenly, "too eager to deal and unworthy of trust; a fool. But yes, we are. What else did he tell you?" The old man stared at Leland. Gleaming points of reflected candle flame danced in his eyes, his manner exuding strength and immense virility. Under the weight of the old man's steady gaze, Leland knew his approval would be needed before the dealings began.

Aranstone smiled. "This is Greywood, my trusted advisor. And to your right is Olmic," —the balding dwarf nodded at Leland— "and next to him, Trelt." Trelt continued his scrutiny of Leland but made no sign of acknowledgement.

"Javin didn't tell me very much," said Leland, turning back to Aranstone. "Wouldn't say what you needed until after I'd turned him down twice." He looked to Greywood. "So I hope it was worth coming all the way up here."

Greywood merely smiled at Leland's attempt at arrogance. "Come now, Mr. Splide, you sensed there was something, didn't you? You're not as impulsive as your brother, are you, riding all the way up here? Too bad he couldn't join us tonight."

Leland wondered where this was leading. "You seem to know quite a bit about my brother and I," he said, "yet I know nothing about you. Or whether I can trust you."

Olmic laughed. "We could have slit your throats while you slept in Miastolas!"

"Enough of your joking, Olmic!" Aranstone said. "He's not serious, Mr. Splide. I am sorry we must seem so secretive. We wanted to be sure you were who you said you were. Who are we? We are citizens of Kronivar, concerned about the war that is brewing. If Teska fell, a march on Kronivar could happen. Unlikely? Perhaps; but war does seem inevitable, and we should not place all our trust in the Wall and Gates in the north."

"Yet you aren't quite a part of the King's army," Leland ventured.

"Not yet," said Olmic, "Of course, we would defend the Kingdom together. Certainly. But Kronivar is large enough to need its own guard, and Itharia needs us as well. Many dwarves feel King Jordgen has been slow to mobilize."

"The Castle's army has grown small over the years," said Greywood, "and now they are hurrying to rebuild it as they can. They may be too slow, and too small, to stand alone."

"Some think they ought to have kept up an army all these years," said Olmic, "But too many dwarves have come down from the mountains. Now it's a question of how quickly everything can be pulled together again. And so we add our efforts alongside those of the Castle."

"I see," said Leland, leaning back to think. Kronivar, Itharia's largest city, had grown tremendously since the last war, while the number of dwarves living in the mountains had declined, especially during King Aardgen's reign. Leland had heard rumors that a growing number of dwarves and men wanted Kronivar to become its own nation-state, following ideas that were once only the idle musings of extremists. Dwarven politics mattered little to him, but knowledge of them was useful for doing business.

"And you intend to pay in gold? The full amount?" Leland said.

"Yes," Aranstone said, "upon delivery of the entire shipment, of course."

"Of course. Fair enough." Leland sipped his beer. A barmaid arrived to take orders, and the tension loosened for a moment. Leland sat back, drinking and appearing calm, but his mind was racing. Could it be as good as it sounded? What would they need? What prices to ask? He thought they might be able to get a little more than usual this time. They seemed straightforward, yet he couldn't help feeling something more was going on. Did that matter? Not with enough gold, he thought. He wished Lexter was there; Lexter was always good in negotiations. Sometimes he'd ask for the most outrageous things and he'd be taken seriously and get them. Leland arranged meetings and made sure everything went smoothly, but it was Lexter who was good at haggling and dealing.

"For a deal of this magnitude, I would prefer to have my brother present," Leland said once the barmaid left. "Can you stay a day or two? He should be on his way."

"We aren't completing the transaction tonight," said Greywood. "Nor are we staying here. Our only intent this evening is to arrange for the delivery, at a later date."

"Here?" Leland inquired.

"In Kronivar," Aranstone replied. A pause brought all eyes to Leland. "Is that all right?" Aranstone added, watching him.

"Kronivar? Yes, certainly. That's fine." Leland relaxed again.

"Good," said Olmic. He smiled, glancing to Aranstone and Greywood and then back to Leland. "Then let's begin discussing the details."

"Ten days from tomorrow should give you and your brother enough time," said Greywood, sitting back again, as the barmaid returned with their tankards. "We'll arrange everything tonight but the final prices, which we can determine when we see the merchandise."

Leland drank the last of his beer and ordered another. The others sipped their drinks, and even Trelt no longer regarded Leland with apprehension. Leland took a deep breath and braced himself for the long night of dealings ahead.

"So how much farther is it?" asked Hobley. The walking always seemed colder and slower after the sun had gone down.

"Bottomcliffe should be up ahead, across from the Rundlewood road," said Iaven, "On the map, anyway. We haven't passed it yet. That might be it there." Half a mile away they could just make out clusters of dark shapes with lit windows in the gloom. Further back huge buildings towered like shadows against the walls of steep cliffs. All lay in darkness now, only the lights of the town beckoning them onward.

They came to the crossroads and turned east. Soon they were walking the streets of Bottomcliffe. Pale circles of lamplight led the way. Broad-shouldered dwarves, dust-blackened from the mines, cast suspicious glances at Iaven. Weatherworn buildings seethed with dull menace in the dim light. They kept going. Finally, they asked where they might find the inn, and were pointed in the general direction.

The warmth of the candlelit glow behind the ironwork windows drew them forward. The copper dragons around the doors seemed alive in the flickering light and shadow, ready to pounce. Iaven and his friends passed through the heavy doors, into the atmosphere of food, drink, smoke, warmth, and noise. After the quiet road, the crowd of strangers seemed close and threatening. Hobley found a table in the middle of the common room where miners were getting up to leave. A barmaid was already wiping the table. They set aside their packs, sat down, and placed their orders right away.

"Warmth," said Wilbur. "And food. I've had enough camping outdoors to last me a lifetime."

"I'm tired, too," Zammond admitted, "but it's a good tired, like after a long day's hard work."

"And how would you know about that?" said Tillmore.

"It's about time he's tired," Wilbur grumbled.

98

They sat chatting awhile, anticipating the meal. The warmth made Iaven drowsy and his eyelids heavy. He looked forward to a night indoors.

Soon the barmaid returned with mugs and steaming plates of food: slabs of beef, fresh vegetables, soup, and hot bread with butter. It was the best meal they had seen in days and the dwarves hungrily set to work.

"So you think we'll see Orven?" said Hobley. "I wonder if he came this way. I thought we might see him in Miastolas."

"I don't know," said Iaven, enjoying his food too much to bother about his brother. He idly scanned the room, looking for Orven and his friends. His eyes stopped on a booth along the back wall, his nerves tensing with a cold tingle. He strained to make sure of what he saw; Leland Splide, sitting and talking with men and dwarves. As Iaven watched, Leland glanced up and met his gaze. Their eyes locked. A moment later the others looked in Iaven's direction to see what Leland was staring at.

"Iaven, what is it?" said Zammond.

"They're here, and they've seen us!" Iaven turned back as Zammond looked to the booth.

"Who, Orven?" asked Wilbur.

"Leland. He's got his men with him. We've got to leave right away!"

"Right now?" Wilbur's words were muffled by a mouthful of food.

"I agree," said Zammond, "There's five of them, and they'll know the town, too. We'd better go now." He ate a big forkful of meat and took one of the dinner rolls.

"Now? But—" Rather than waste time protesting, Wilbur ate as much as he could as they pulled their packs together. Each threw a few coins on the table, enough to cover the meal and a bit extra. Most of the food was left on the plates, still steaming and untouched.

"What a shame, a real shame!" Wilbur said, stuffing his roll and Tillmore's roll into his pockets as they pulled him along. People began looking askance at them as they hurried out. "Another night under the stars," said Tillmore.

Seeing the dwarves, Leland's desire for the sword returned in a flash. A pity they'd seen him, he thought; he could have finished his meeting and followed them up to their room. They wouldn't have suspected anything and it would have been easy to get the sword. But it was too late.

When Iaven broke off eye contact, Leland realized everyone at his table was staring at Iaven's party. Greywood turned back to him. "Friends of yours?" he inquired like someone who believes he has stumbled onto a valuable secret.

Leland turned to meet Greywood's gaze. "Not particularly." He tried to sound casual and offhand. "Did business with them once." He shrugged, feeling a pang of loss as he watched the dwarves shoulder their packs and leave.

Greywood gave no sign of what he thought. He tried to get a better look at the dwarves, but the last one had just left. He turned back to Leland and Aranstone.

"Then let us continue with the business at hand," he said, noting Leland's reactions.

The streets of Bottomcliffe were dark and winding, and only the tall, ashen walls of the cliffs to the east kept them from losing their way. Iaven led the way as fast as he could without drawing too much attention. They followed the cliff wall, hoping to find good camping ground outside of town. They kept glancing back to see if anyone was following them, but no one was.

"Can we slow down a little?" Wilbur had fallen behind, out of breath. "I don't think they're coming."

At last they came to the edge of town. Houses were fewer and farther apart, and they had only the stars to light their way. The land rose and the cliffs loomed higher as they approached. To the south stood the mills and mine entrances. The cliff wall angled off to the northeast, the incline growing steeper as they went.

Finally, too tired to go any farther, they reached flatter ground where a shallow depression in the cliffside which seemed as good a place as any to set camp. Soon they sat close around a small fire burning bright and casting great, dancing shadows on the cliff wall behind them.

"More camping," Wilbur complained, eating one of his dinner rolls. "I had hoped for four walls tonight, but one will have to do!"

Despite disappointment and sparse accommodations, the dwarves had no trouble falling asleep. Near the end of the first watch, Wilbur leaned against the cliff wall, gazing at the fire, which had burned low. Blackened wood crackled and sparks leapt out, floating up on rising currents of air. He was still hungry, but cries of wolves echoing in the mountains spoke of hungers deeper than his own.

Wilbur sat back, trying to stay awake. Wind rustled dry leaves on the trees and whispered through the grasses. A nightjar's churring sounded some distance away. *We could have done worse, I suppose*, he thought. *Tomorrow night I'll insist*— His thought broke off as he heard a low, growling sound nearby. He straightened up, scanning the dark land. Nothing moved and all was quiet, except for intermittent crickets chirping.

A black shape crept between the bushes. Wilbur tried to see where it had gone, but the fire was low and the hillside full of the vague forms of trees, bushes, and rocks. The low growl came again, he turned, and saw the shape just as it stopped moving. Fifteen feet away from their camp a mountain lion stood watching to see what Wilbur would do, perhaps debating whether he was worth going after. Wilbur froze and waited. The lion moved its head, surveying the camp, never letting Wilbur out of its gaze.

Moving carefully keeping an eye on the mountain lion, Wilbur nudged Zammond with his foot. "Zammond! Wake up!" he whispered. The lion stepped closer to see what he was doing.

"What, already?" Zammond woke, annoyed and bleary-eyed.

"Look!" Wilbur gasped. The mountain lion had wandered another few feet closer to the camp. Zammond sat squinting at it. The lion moved again, letting out a low, purring growl. Zammond pulled himself out of his blanket and grabbed his sword. Wilbur shouted and woke the others.

Zammond motioned Wilbur back along the cliff wall and tried to keep the lion at bay. It was playing with them now, watching them and moving with cold, wild grace, alert and poised to pounce. Its fearless confidence made Zammond's sword arm shake. The lion growled and lurched forward, swinging a big paw that caught Zammond's forearm, tearing his shirt and gouging his arm.

Zammond yelled and jumped back. Suddenly Iaven was next to him with Halix drawn, and Hobley raised his axe. Wilbur moved along the cliff wall behind the fire, and Tillmore followed, making room for Iaven and Hobley to back up and join them. The mountain lion growled loudly now, stalking them as they edged away against the wall. Zammond pulled in by Tillmore, clutching his bleeding arm, and Iaven and Hobley held the rear along the cliff wall.

"It's forcing us away from the fire," said Tillmore. The mountain lion followed them, ready to leap at any moment. It growled and claws scratched iron as Hobley fended off a swipe of the lion's paw.

Iaven's heart was pounding yet his sword arm was not shaking. Halix seemed easier to wield with the gem in it, and Iaven's fear was muted by his awe of the sword. Without thinking what he was doing, he stepped forward and swung Halix in a short, precise arc, nicking the mountain lion's shoulder. Roaring, the lion recoiled, refocusing its attention on Iaven, but he was ready for another parry with it. "Iaven, be careful, don't get too close!" yelled Hobley, impressed by Iaven's quick move.

All of a sudden a dog was barking. A branch snapped, dropped into their fire, and rose out flaming brightly. A booming, angry shout came from behind the branch, distracting the lion. Iaven dashed in again and Hobley swung his axe the moment it turned away. The lion jumped sideways at the blows, snarling in pain and anger. The flaming branch waved at the lion from the other side, and it leapt away between them, up the rocks and through the bushes, and was gone. The barking dog, a big, sleek, black hunting dog, stood at the camp's edge watching it go, barking and snarling as if he alone had frightened it away.

The flaming branch was now held aloft like a torch, its light revealing a burly dwarven miner in a dark woolen shirt, a bushy black beard spreading onto his wide chest. Once the lion was gone he stood glaring at the dwarves.

"Thanks!" said Hobley, still tense from the encounter.

"What are you doing on my land?" thundered the miner, in a deep voice no friendlier than the mountain lion. Big and bearlike, he stood almost a head taller than any of them. His stern face glowered in the half-light of the burning branch and his eyes, dull and bloodshot, held the dwarves in their steady gaze. He was angry and appeared to be somewhat drunk. "What are you doing here?" he demanded again, and they all jumped. No one knew what to say. The hunting dog faced them, too, growling and waiting for his master's command to attack.

"We didn't know this was your land," Tillmore volunteered. The miner turned and stared at him. They wondered if it only made him angrier.

"You're not from Bottomcliffe, are you? Any of you?" he said, and they tried to guess whether he thought this a good thing or if it made matters worse.

"No, none of us," said Hobley, standing straight and returning the miner's gaze. He held his axe by the neck, resting its handle on the ground, waiting to see what would happen.

Iaven realized his sword was still drawn and sheathed Halix, hoping this would help calm the situation. "We're from Hillbrook," he added.

"Hillbrook?" The miner seemed amused. "Why aren't you staying in town?" he said, still not satisfied with the trespassers' excuses.

Zammond grunted and held his wounded arm, pulling his torn sleeve around it to stop the bleeding. Now that the fight was over he was beginning to feel his injury more. He was more concerned with his pain than their present situation.

The hunting dog barked once, turned to look at his master, and then back to the dwarves again. The miner lowered the branch, which was burning out, and tossed it into the fire. He stood there, weighing and deciding something, his face shadowed and unreadable.

"We'd better get your friend inside." His voice was calmer. "Barg!" he shouted, and the dog turned and ran off. The miner motioned the dwarves to come along and they followed him.

On the way to his cabin, the tension eased as they talked with the miner. His name was Broden, and he had lived in Bottomcliffe all his life and worked in the mines for many years, until a back injury forced him out to a foreman's job in the mill. That evening in his cabin, they also learned his wife had died of illness, and of two sons who had died in a mining accident. For the past nine years he had lived alone outside of town, with his dog Barg.

Broden's log cabin was small but comfortable, with wood plank flooring and a wide fireplace of stone quarried from the cliffs. Pelts of wolves and foxes hung on the walls, and the room smelled of fresh apples and heavy pipe smoke. In the years since his wife's death, Broden had returned to his bachelor lifestyle, though his sparse decor left little that could be in disarray.

After he bandaged Zammond's arm, which was only badly scratched, Broden asked them where they were headed. Iaven described their journey to the Castle, leaving out any mention of Halix, and referring to Leland as someone who had tried to rob them. Broden sat listening with interest. When he heard they hadn't eaten, he gave them apples and put out plates of meat, bread, and potatoes, and a jar of cider. The dwarves thanked him and ate heartily. Broden was more relaxed now, more sober, and Iaven realized that he seldom had any visitors and was glad to have some company. Iaven guessed that he and his friends were about the ages Broden's sons would have been.

While they ate by the fire, Broden told them about Bottomcliffe, and mining, even how the ore was ground and smelted. He talked of smithies around the town, where tankards, pots, pans, irons, pokers, silverware, plows, and other metalwork was made. And many of these he had along his walls or in cabinets, including the tankards he toasted with them. Seeing they were simple folk like himself and interested in what he told them, Broden grew more at ease, talking of goings-on in town, troubles with his health, and whatever else came to mind.

He explained why he had been worried about trespassers: there had been brawling in town over what people thought of the King and the Goblin threat. Rabble-rousers had led secret rallies in the woods, and so he had wondered what Iaven and his friends were doing on his land.

"Most of the wild ones have gone on to Kronivar, but there's still some around here. Not many, but enough for trouble." He took a gulp of cold beer.

"But what have they got against King Jordgen?" asked Iaven.

"Well, it's more the idea of the Castle, I suppose, so far away but controlling their fates," Broden replied. "That goes back to King Varlen's days. We have mining songs about it, ballads that have grown over the years." Clearing his throat with a sound like muted thunder, he began singing in low, rolling rhythms like hammers swinging to and fro, reshaping the mountains:

> In ancient days before us
>> The mountains hid their treasure,
> Their silver, gold, and jewels
>> And riches without measure,
> Inside great walls of granite
>> Without a crack or fissure,
> Asleep within the dark rock,
>> Such was their will and pleasure.
>
> One day the Dwarves went westward
>> And from the heights descended,
> They settled by the waters,
>> Their kingdom they extended.
> But those who mined were restless,
>> Their claims they all rescinded,
> They packed and ventured southward,
>> And there their roaming ended.
>
> They crossed through grassy meadows,
>> And took no notice of them,
> Until the mountains steeply
>> Rose towering above them.
> They cut deep shafts and tunnels,
>> Took what the mines would give them,
> The cliffs became their homesteads
>> And all the miners loved them.
>
> The mines begat the foundries
>> And Bottomcliffe was founded.
> Soon gravel paths and roadways
>> By houses were surrounded.
> The King learned of the mining
>> And tribute was demanded,

As fortunes grew enormous
The royal trumpets sounded.

But deep inside the mineshafts,
Down tunnels now forbidden,
The Dwarves disturbed a strange race
Of tiny people hidden.
As tunnels burrowed deeper,
They lost the stone they lived in,
And turned against the Dwarves who
Had come to them unbidden.

They lived within the granite
As fish live in the ocean,
They echoed miners' hammers
And set the rocks in motion.
They set the tunnel trembling
In terrible vibration,
It crumbled and collapsed in
A thundering explosion.

More than a few dwarves perished,
The tragedy was vaster;
And more might have been rescued
Had they received help faster.
Neglected by the Castle,
Left like a wound to fester!
More tribute was demanded
Despite the great disaster.

The hammers still are swinging,
The millstones keep on turning,
The mines have all grown deeper,
And deeper is our yearning.
We honor those entombed here
And we shall heed their warning,
They will not be forgotten,
Their fires are still burning.

"That's just the start of it," Broden told them, "The song moves in cycles, with new verses added like links on a chain. That was back in King Varlen's day, over two hundred years ago. Varlen was Orglen's great-grandfather, you know, and Orglen was Jordgen's grandfather. Things have changed since then, though there are always people who feel the Castle don't do enough for them. Me, I think we'll make do as we can. With enough fellows like you joining the troops,

I think we'll be alright. But now maybe you want to get some sleep; you're welcome to stay, if you like."

At this, the dwarves' expressions brightened, and Broden smiled. "Three of you can stay out here, the other two can take my boys' room."

Iaven and his friends thanked Broden and they all got up. Broden let out a broad yawn they all found contagious. "It's late, isn't it?" he said. "We'll have a place ready for you in no time." Hobley and Tillmore followed him into the back room. Zammond, Wilbur, and Iaven spread their blankets near the fireplace where the floor was warmer. Zammond and Wilbur dozed off, and Iaven turned in as well. Soon Broden came to check if the fire was low enough. He went to his room and shut the door, and then all was dark and quiet.

Iaven stretched out and was settled on his pillow when he heard the small clicking sound of Barg's toenails as the dog walked across the wood floor. Barg lay down on a blanket spread for him in the corner. He sat staring at Iaven across the darkened room, tiny points of firelight in his eyes. Even after Broden had warmed to them, the dog still was apprehensive and upset at the intrusion. *My master may trust you, but I don't* his attitude seemed to say, making Iaven uneasy now that Broden was gone.

As he lay on the floor, Iaven shut his eyes and tried to relax, but could not stop thinking. He recalled with wonderment how he had wielded Halix against the mountain lion, and thrilled to think what the sword might be like with two or even three gems in it. He imagined fighting in the war with it, though he had no intention or desire to do so. Iaven still found it strange that some Itharians were loath to support the King, since most people in Hillbrook felt as he did. He still did not know when he would return to Hillbrook, and what he would do when he got back. Eventually so many thoughts entangled his mind demanding attention that they all became hazy and he promptly fell asleep.

Chapter 10.
The Crossing

"We'd better look for a place to camp." No one had spoken for a long time and Orven's voice startled them out of their thoughts. They were worn out, dragging along, and the light filtering into the forest was growing dim.

"The forest's denser around the river, we'll have to look inland," said Max.

"I suppose so," Orven said without turning around.

The deep woods north of the Yandl were thicker and more ancient than the southern ones, making the dwarves' passage slow and laborious. The cool, damp October air worsened the colds they had caught during the night spent in their wet clothes after climbing out of the river. In the days that followed, they tried to stay as close to the Upper Yandl as they could while it wound its way westward. The land rose and fell, leading them away from the river, or right up to the bank only to block their way, forcing them to backtrack. At times the forest closed around them, daring them to advance, while at other times broad hillsides or deep valleys opened but led away from the river.

They made little progress and their colds persisted, tiring them after only a few hours of hiking. Often they moved in silence, awed by the vastness and mystery of the unexplored forest around them. Far off whoops and growls of unseen animals kept them tense, and in the leafy canopy high above them cries of strange birds echoed. Occasionally strange, brightly colored insects would land on them briefly, startling in their unfamiliarity. And everywhere around them, silent but ever-present, falling leaves sailed down to the ground.

Without the river they would have been hopelessly lost. They now thought less of maps and gave up on any idea of Rundlewood as a part of Itharia to which Dwarves could lay claim. The Castle and the war seemed remote and insignificant here. No one said anything, but they all wished they had stayed on the Forest Road or traveled up the South Road instead. Their encounter with the gnomes left them feeling ill-prepared for joining the King's troops, and their morale was low. Tensions among them might have erupted into fights if not for their waning energy. They pushed on, hoping the worst was behind them.

During the days they followed the river, Orven said little and his manner was brusque. He kept thinking of how easily the gnomes had captured him, and worse, how helpless he had been. A smoldering shame rose like bile within him, and a shapeless anger made him want to lash out at something. It was the forest's fault; it was the circumstances. Being tied up and needing to be rescued made him look foolish. Before that, he had led the others. He led them out of Hillbrook and into the forest. He had gotten them lost, too, but no matter. The important thing was that he led them. And then they had to come rescue him, and all he could do was shout directions from where he lay, bound to the tree like some trophy of the Gnomes. They all could have been killed, because of him. How could they take him seriously after that?

Orven longed to escape the forest. He wearied of the unending trees, gnarled roots underfoot, and thick veils of foliage pressing close around them. Branches and underbrush barred their way, scratching them as they pushed through, as narrow trails and shady passes tried to lure them astray, away from the river and deeper into the winding depths of the forest.

Orven wanted another chance to fight and prove himself, to regain what he had lost in his friends' eyes. He had given in to fear during the skirmish with the gnome. He admitted it to himself now; the shock of seeing the gnome close at hand, strange and unearthly, and the spear brandished in his face. He remembered pulling back from the gnome, a fierce, strange being half-visible in the dark, wild, feral and menacing. He should have charged, unhesitating, and killed it on the spot. But he hadn't. And the gnomes had come back for him.

It sickened Orven to think he was nothing like the warrior he thought he was. Never again would he let fear get the better of him. One moment of weakness was all the enemy needed for an advantage. It wouldn't happen again; he would see to that. If they came across danger, he would be the first to confront it. As Orven's anger and disgust ebbed and flowed, he pushed on through the woods, trying to stay several paces ahead of the others, where he could be alone with his doubts and shame, and still feel he was leading them.

Max walked a few strides behind Orven, keeping pace. He wanted to move up and talk with Orven, but knew Orven wanted time alone. Max was drowsy from his cold and glad to have Orven leading them again. Even now Orven seemed to forge ahead with determination and know where they were going. These woods were too different, too foreign, unlike any he had known. He and Orven had gone on hunting trips over the years, mostly in smaller woods around the Foothills. He'd always enjoyed the peace of the woods, the rustle of game in the underbrush, and when night fell, their venison roasting over the fire. But here he didn't feel safe at all. They weren't supposed to be here, Max thought.

He peered all around them for any sign of the Gnomes. Maybe they were out of Gnome territory, as Orven said, but there was no way to be certain. Tired as they were, they had gotten very little sleep their first few nights along the Yandl. Farther down the river, rest came more easily, as fatigue overpowered their fears. They agreed to shifts of two watchmen at a time, to keep each other awake, and what little sleep they had was troubled. The Gnomes haunted their dreams, their dreams blended with the forest, and weariness blurred what was real or imagined.

Max knew they were far from ready to join the King's troops. If it came to war with the Goblins, they'd at least be fighting a foe they could see, out in the open, and they'd be trained and prepared. He didn't blame Orven at all for what had happened with the Gnomes; none of them had been ready. Max knew they were lucky to get Orven back and realized more than ever what his friend meant to him.

It took longer than usual that evening to find an open area where they could camp for the night. At last they came to a small, grassy clearing, some twenty feet across, just enough to part the overreaching tree branches and let in a little night sky between them. Roy and Aaron yawned sighs of relief and set their packs down in the grass. Max still shouldered his, watching Orven as he was deciding something. On the edge of the clearing two downed trees had fallen together, one on top of the other. Big arching branches reached up from their sides and bent to the ground. Their trunks, splintered and cracked, widened into thick masses of tangled roots torn from the ground. The tree on top was heavier and appeared to have fallen and taken the other tree down with it.

"Maybe we'd be better off under here," Orven said, indicating the ground beneath the fallen trees. The branches were still full of leaves, dried and shriveled husks still clinging to the deadwood. The arching limbs formed a kind of cover, a leafy hollow into which the dwarves could crawl and sleep. Orven went inside, and the others reluctantly followed. There was no need to explain why the shelter was safer, but they were weary of the closeness of the forest and longed to sleep stretched out under the stars. Everyone was too tired to argue and in the end one place was as good as any other once they were fast asleep.

They slept because they were dead tired, but uneasily. Strange noises surrounded them; eerie prolonged cries of night birds, itinerant whirring and chickering of insects, and occasional low rustlings along the forest floor. The forest watched and tolerated them, ready to close in at any moment.

Orven and Roy had the first watch of the night. Orven continued brooding, lost in thought, while Roy was quiet and unreadable, reluctant to say what was on his mind. They sat, leaning against the fallen logs, looking into the depths of the woods or trying to catch glimpses of stars hidden beyond the treetops.

"So when do you think we'll reach Kronivar?" Roy asked, making the question sound as casual as possible, afraid Orven might take it as criticism.

"I don't know," Orven replied. He fought the urge to make excuses or encouraging promises. His last ones had sounded empty and hollow. He didn't know when they'd reach Kronivar; he no longer trusted his guesses about the forest. It took all his effort to dispel his own doubts which threatened the certainty he felt he should have as their leader. If only he could—

"Orven, did you hear that?" Roy whispered. He was looking over the logs in the direction of the clearing.

Orven sat up and turned the same way Roy was facing. "Hear what?"

Roy was silent, listening. A light wind blew around the logs, cooling their faces. Orven heard only the usual night sounds around them. Then he noticed a faint whispering sound, like a slow pulse. A low, barely audible sound, regular and repeated, *usssh, usshh, usshh, usshh*, like something striding through tall grasses, brushing them aside as it went. Something tall with a long stride, moving in their direction.

Orven hunched down behind the fallen logs, peering between them, trying to stay out of sight but morbidly curious to see what was approaching. The sounds slowly grew louder, and others were alternating with it now — *ushhushhhushhushushh*— whatever was coming was not alone. A rabbit that had been sitting still scampered away across the clearing. Bird calls around them ceased and one bird flew off from its perch.

"Orven? What is it? Do you hear that?" whispered Roy. "We'd better wake the others..." But Orven's hand came down on his shoulder, stopping him. One quick sidelong glance from Orven told him not to move or speak or do anything until whatever it was had passed.

Orven eased Roy back down until he was behind the logs. Roy did not resist and stopped just high enough to see between the tree trunks with Orven. The sounds grew louder until individual footfalls could be heard. Orven's heart was pounding in his ears, almost obscuring the sound. In the great blooming darkness of the forest opening in front of them, Orven began to discern movement, like that of poles waving or bending. Long wooden legs swung out of the thickets and into the clearing. In the faint light the orrems were tall, gangly things, with long, jointed wooden legs that carried a short log-like body high up off the ground. At both ends of the body rose shapes vaguely like horse heads, oddly stylized and crudely hewn from wood. They were too high up in the dark for Orven to make out clearly, but he did see that four gnomes rode on the back of each orrem, straddled across it one behind the other.

The first orrem passed through the clearing and was about to reenter the woods when the second one stopped, one of its riders giving a shrill, snapping whistle that called the first one to a halt.

A gnome from the second orrem said something and scurried down the orrem's leg, while the other three strung arrows and pulled their bows. The gnome on the ground drew a long bone knife and sniffed the air. He moved a step forward, a step back, turning to determine the source of what he smelled. Two more orrems carrying gnomes entered the clearing and stopped.

Panic gripped Orven. He struggled to fight the fear seeping through his limbs. Roy was shaking now, and Orven kept his hand on Roy's shoulder to still him. They could neither run nor fight; waiting was their only hope. Orven's heart beat heavy and quick, flush with tension. Waiting was difficult for him; he wanted a fight that he had a chance of winning.

Orven remained tense, caressing the hilt of his sword without thinking about it. He wanted more than anything to draw Gorflange and leap into action, but held back, waiting to see what would happen. The odds were clearly against them; in seconds they'd all be fired upon from above and killed. It occurred to him that Max, Ripley, or Aaron could wake at any time and give their position away. Even if they were quiet —not likely, with Ripley along— they might easily be seen. The gnomes' high vantage point from atop the orrems' backs made it difficult to hide. If it weren't for the fallen tree, they would have been seen already, Orven thought.

Max stirred and lifted his head, looking at Orven. He was about to speak when Orven raised his hand in a small, quick gesture. Max remained still and silent.

The gnome with the knife seemed indecisive now. "*Sha-ri, nes sha-ri,*" he called up to his fellows in a tremulous unearthly voice that made Orven shudder. They muttered something back, and he sheathed his knife and climbed back up the orrem. "*Lka!*" he shouted, and the orrems began moving again.

Orven breathed easier, but only in shallow, silent breaths. The orrems passed in single file into the murky depths of the forest, until the low shushing sound of their passage died away. When it was quiet again, Orven fell back from the logs and exhaled. Roy let go and lay down on his back, closing his eyes and uttering a soft moan of relief.

It was Max and Ripley's turn for the next watch, and after awhile they woke Ripley and told him what happened.

"Orrems?! Why didn't you wake me up?" Ripley said, stunned and mildly offended that he had missed the highlight of the evening.

The rest of the night passed uneventfully, much to their relief, and they were off again in the morning. Unsure how far they had gone or how much there was to go, their morale and pace dropped even lower. With renewed worries of the gnomes and orrems, little was said as they went along, apart from complaints when the forest grew unbearable.

Gradually they were forced away from the river until they could no longer hear it, and by late afternoon the forest changed around them. Atop a swell of land ahead, blue sky glowed between the tree trunks. A moist breeze drew them closer, the light brightened, and the muted, rolling sound of waves lapping the shore greeted them. Their spirits lifted, they hurried to the bluff's edge.

They were high up, more than a hundred feet, and the bluff fell steeply down to the sea. Trees and bushes growing out of steep slopes blocked their view of the water's edge below them, but farther off a broad plain of deep blue water rippled and sparkled in the sunlight, a welcome sight that made their hearts ache with the desire to go down to the shore. At that moment they might have even boarded a treacherous rowboat just to be rid of the forest. They all sat on the cliff's edge, relaxing and looking out over the sea.

"Is this the closest we can get to the water? We'll have to follow the shore, somehow, all the way up to Kronivar," said Aaron.

Orven saw what Aaron meant. They could not reach the shore, and the bluff continued north as far as they could tell. How far Kronivar was to the north he did not know, nor how long it would take to get there. Orven sighed and looked over the open sea, feeling like a prisoner gazing out at the bright shining world between the iron bars of his cell's window.

The following day they went north keeping as close to the bluff's edge as they could. In the early morning mist was rolling in from the sea, which cleared up after sunrise. The low sound of the sea to their left gave them some comfort and made them feel less surrounded by the forest. They guessed that the gnomes did not venture this close to the sea; at least they wanted to believe that was true. At any rate they felt one step further along their journey out of the forest.

They pressed onward. Orven and Max were again in the vanguard, with Roy, Aaron, and Ripley following. Roy was miserable with his cold, and anxious to leave the forest. He thought about the war, and Orven and Max enlisting. Ripley would join the troops too, and he realized how much he'd miss him. Aaron seemed unlikely to join, so he guessed the two of them would find a way back to Hillbrook. He was sure the war was not for him. His lack of experience and motivation would only hinder the efforts of others. If Hillbrook was to have a guard, that seemed the place for him to serve. Roy wouldn't mention it to Orven, though. He had seen Orven and Iaven argue about it and knew what Orven thought of staying in Hillbrook while others went off to fight. Orven would laugh at him and lump him together with Iaven, and he did not want that. Roy was glad to know someone like Orven and could even picture Orven as a captain leading a squadron. Roy could see himself leading the guard in Hillbrook, a position he half-expected because of his father's reputation, but that would only be sentinel duty, not likely to involve combat. Did that make him a coward? As he walked in silence, the debate raged in his head.

Aaron had misgivings from the moment they had left the road, but as their mishaps often fulfilled his expectations, he felt strangely vindicated and somehow could not blame them for proving him right. Now it seemed up to him to try and help Orven find the quickest way out of the forest. He had, it was true, bit back his comments after sensing Orven's humiliation. Some of them were justly deserved, though he was ashamed to feel this way. He had never doubted Orven's bravery; his ability to plan, however, was another matter. Orven could be too forceful or stubborn; useful attributes sometimes, but not always.

Deeper into the forest, Aaron had grown more aware of the seriousness of their situation, including the foolish risks they had taken. Even he had underestimated the Gnomes, cautious as he was. He no longer had the same self-assurance or faith in the group and saw the importance of Orven's leadership to their small party. Aaron prided himself on his quick thinking, but realized it took more than good ideas to lead others and gain their trust and respect. He thought about Orven's capture by the Gnomes; he knew he would not have done as well as Orven had. The past week's events had raised Aaron's opinion of Orven, but it never occurred to him to let Orven know about it.

They tried to keep near the shoreline as they traveled north, despite the sloping and curving land. It was now mid-October and the leaves had turned their deepest colors. The dwarves were still awed by the forest, the breadth and depth and endlessness of it. Ancient trees of enormous girth reached to lofty heights, and everywhere rolling hills and valleys tempting them to stray and wander. Only the soft, soothing pulse of the Silver Sea gave them any sense of bearings amidst it all.

The dwarves hiked north, weakened and tired, recovering from their colds. In the afternoon of the following day the sound of rushing water grew louder. They emerged from the trees by a cliff and below them a wide river tumbled down a shallow waterfall into a widening delta flowing out to the Silver Sea. The air was moist and cool and sunlight danced on the water.

"This must be the Emril River," said Roy, "It runs down from the mountains near Gomirré."

"Which means we aren't far from the villages south of Kronivar, are we?" said Orven.

"I remember Cedric pointing it out," said Max, "Hable and Okiary were the furthest south, just outside the forest. They're inland, away from the sea, but not far north of the Emril."

"Well, we can't cross right here anyway," said Orven, watching the rushing waters spreading before them.

They had no choice but to follow the river shoreline eastward, back into the forest, and hope they were far enough north to be a good distance away from the Gnomes. Orven felt frustrated and confined by the river, wanting badly to cross it, and wondered just how far they would have to travel before they could do so. He was weary of the forest, and wondered how much longer they could keep going, but led them onward.

Ripley strode at the rear of the group, the place he had occupied for some time. He was convinced there would eventually be an ambush from behind and wanted to be ready when the time came. He relished a good fight and had grown uneasy and restless over the past few days, waiting for someone or something to show themselves. Waves of anxiety and irritability alternated with stretches of tiredness and boredom. Their worst enemy was the endlessness of the forest itself, and nothing could be done to alleviate that.

He, too, had been frightened of the Gnomes, but at least he could see them and strike out at them. Quieter now, he understood how serious their situation was. He believed Orven would lead them safely to Kronivar, yet the forest was much vaster than they had expected. Ripley looked into the depths of the woods for any trace of the Gnomes. He wanted to encounter them again, in a good, fair fight, to release the restlessness and anxiety hanging over him like a dark cloud, even though he had to admit he was afraid of them.

The forest was unyielding, forcing the dwarves to backtrack, making the journey much longer than it would have been had they known where they were going. Evening fell, they camped again, and continued on the following day. By late afternoon they came to a low hilltop that looked out over a sweeping expanse of the river as it cut through the woods. The river spread wide and appeared to be shallow enough to cross. Greatly relieved, Orven announced that they would wade through and head north again. The sun was going down and it would be good to get across and on their way before nightfall.

Orven led them down the sloping north side of the hill, which was lined with pines and low bushes and shrubs. He made his way cautiously, tired as he was. Looking up to assess where the crossing might be best, he stopped. The others descended the hill behind him and saw Orven crouching down, motioning them to stay low.

Max moved near Orven, following his gaze. Across the river, just inside the forest, a small fire was burning at a campsite. Two packs lay nearby, the shade of the trees making it difficult to see much detail. No one seemed to be there.

"Other dwarves camping?" said Roy.

"Out here?" said Orven.

"If we're close to the southern towns," said Roy.

"What's that? Look!" Max whispered.

As they watched, something moved in the forest behind the fire. A large figure, taller than a dwarf and more than twice the height of a gnome, came forward and moved to the side. Another emerged from the forest and sat down near the packs.

"Goblins!" Roy gasped. They could just make them out in the gloom between the trees; large figures clad in brown and dark green, weapons hanging ready at their belts. The standing one stoked the fire, threw a few sticks on it, and sat down. The faint smell of meat roasting wafted across the river. Max's stomach growled with hunger.

"Right where we could have crossed!" said Roy.

"We're not going any farther east, we'll have to cross here," Orven said, "We've come far enough. Who knows how far we'd have to go to find another way across?"

The others agreed. They were tired, not yet over their colds, and in need of a rest.

"The river's too wide for us to take them by surprise," said Max. "We'll need some plan of attack. Goblin spies are armed and well trained. They won't hesitate to kill to keep their presence in the forest a secret." Max wondered what they were doing and what information they had collected. He shuddered to think what would happen if Orven lost Gorflange to them.

"We could wait them out. They might be gone by morning," Aaron said. "Max is right, and we're not in any condition to fight them tonight." No one liked hearing it put so bluntly, but neither did anyone disagree.

"Spies can't stay long in one place," said Roy, "They're sure to move on. Let's camp tonight and wait them out." Ripley glared at the Goblin campsite, consumed by a wave of anger dulled by fatigue. Here was the enemy he had waited for, and he would fight them if they weren't gone by morning.

"We'll set camp over the hill, out of sight, and keep a double watch again," Orven said. He tried to sound confident that this was the best thing to do, but a part of him chided himself for not leading an attack that evening, no matter how tired they were.

They set camp and their watches continued into the night. Orven took the first watch with Aaron and had no trouble staying awake as he pondered plan after plan of how they would confront the Goblin spies. Each time he imagined the Goblins' response and what could go wrong with the dwarves' attack. Whenever he thought he had a workable plan he told it to Aaron who listened and pointed out something Orven had overlooked. In the end Orven was upset at not having found a solution and was ready for a good long rest when Max relieved him of the watch.

In the light of morning their spirits lifted. They all discussed what to do, despite an unspoken agreement that the goblins were probably gone already anyway. Their morning was a leisurely one, as if they were giving the goblins plenty of time to move along. Finally, the dwarves cleaned up, assembled their packs, and proceeded over the hill, expecting to find the way clear.

The Goblin camp was still there. The dwarves crouched behind the bushes, hating to hide but having to in the bright noonday sun. The goblins had long since put out their fire and one was walking about the camp, turning around occasionally and talking to the other who was sitting off to the side, obscured from their view. They did not appear to be packing or preparing to leave.

"At least it looks like there's only the two of them," said Max.

"They must be far enough in from the towns to escape notice," said Roy.

The dwarves sat, watching and waiting. Despite all their plans of the night before, it was difficult to decide on a clear course of action.

"Why are they still here?" asked Aaron. "Are they waiting for something, or someone?"

"Maybe other spies," said Ripley, "We shouldn't wait. This might be our only chance before more of them show up!"

Orven wanted to act but they would be at a disadvantage crossing the river without cover. And the goblins would be ready for them.

"They can't stay there forever," said Aaron, "Something's got to happen. I say we wait a bit and see what they do." No one objected or had any better ideas, so the dwarves went back over the hill but continued their watch.

The day wore on. The goblins stayed around their camp, and brought out a map, which they unfolded and sat looking at awhile. Later, one drew a short black arrow into his bow and brought down a fleeing rabbit with a single shot. As the afternoon waned, the other went into the woods, returned with some kindling, and threw it on a pile.

"Looks like they're staying," Orven said. Max kept watch with Orven, while the others remained back behind the hill. "We've really got to do something."

"I agree," said Max. The waiting was getting to him and the others were anxious as well. "But if we're going to do something, we'd better do it before dark."

"I know," said Orven. "Let's see what everyone thinks. I've got a few ideas."

They climbed over the hill and met with the others, who were bored and eager to do something. "All right, here's what I'm thinking," Orven began. "They'll probably start a fire and have supper soon. When one of them is gone, we'll cross over. Taking them on one at a time, I think we can defeat them."

"Let 'em both try," Ripley snapped, "We can beat 'em!"

"You don't understand," Orven said, irritated. "These spies are trained in combat; we're not. We outnumber them, yes, but we need whatever advantages we can get. We won't know how long we have before the other one returns. And even if there's only one it won't be easy. In the time it takes us to cross the river, he could send a dozen arrows our way. As soon as he sees us we've got to act fast, and act together. No hesitation."

"Who's hesitating? Let's go!" Ripley said, getting up as he spoke.

"No, wait!" Orven tugged him back. "We've got to work together." On a wide, flat rock Orven and Max laid small stones and arranged their battle plan. Aaron and Roy gave their opinions and suggestions, and Ripley watched impatiently, eager to get on with it.

When the plan was finalized, they readied their weapons and crept back over the hill. Across the river the goblins were discussing something. The sun was sinking, but they were in no hurry to start their fire. The dwarves waited behind bushes, hearts pounding, watching for one of the goblins to leave and wondering how much more waiting they could endure. Orven worried that Ripley would grow restless and charge early. Slowly, the angle of the light grew shallower as the sun set.

At last one goblin stood and handed flint to the one seated by the kindling. He began striking the flint over dried grasses, while the other walked off into the forest.

Orven signaled and the dwarves descended the hill as quickly and quietly as they could. Orven watched the goblin lighting the fire. He sat in the shade with his back turned, and Orven had the uneasy feeling that he would turn around and see them at any moment. The dwarves made their way down to the water's edge and stopped. All was quiet except for the rushing of the Emril flowing past, a few birdcalls, and the muted clicking of the goblin's flint across the river.

Orven surveyed the water in front of them. It looked shallow enough halfway in, and he hoped it would stay like that all the way across. They had to take that chance. He motioned to them, and they began crossing, hoping the river's sound would muffle their own. Amazingly, the goblin still sat with his back turned. A moment later the striking of the flint stopped and he sat up straight again. Orven tensed, wondering if he had heard something, and then realized the goblin had lit the fire. Orven still expected the goblin to turn around, or the other one to return too soon.

At last they were halfway across the river. Orven let Max pass him, looking for shallow places to cross, and did not take his eyes off the seated goblin. A few steps more, and they were ten yards from the far shore. The goblin shifted his position and moved one of his legs out from under him. Orven was sure the goblin must have heard them, yet still he did not turn around. Orven saw the goblin's armor of leather and small, lacquered wooden plates, realizing a bow and arrow would not have helped as he had thought it might. The goblin watched the fire, and Orven sensed their luck would give out soon. His hand trembled on Gorflange's hilt as he waded through the water.

They were now five yards from shore. The goblin, his back still turned, leaned forward and stood up, still seeming to watch the fire. Orven's heart was pounding hard and he could feel it in his ears. To his horror, Orven saw from the corner of his eye that Ripley was moving in long strides across the water, passing Max on the way to shore. Ripley's sword was drawn, his arm bent as he grasped its hilt. He was not watching for Orven's signal to charge. Orven realized if he did not give the signal soon, Ripley would be off and running without them. Orven turned back and saw the goblin was looking into the forest. Then a sound to his left; Ripley running across the shore. The goblin whirled around and his sword was out in a flash.

"Now!" shouted Orven, and they were all in motion, out of the river and over the bank, converging on the goblin. He was ready for them, a sword in one hand and in the other a large iron mace he had snatched up from the ground nearby. "*Kasrac!*" he called into the forest in a frightening, urgent growl. The other goblin came running and the dwarves knew they would have to divide their attack. They thrust at the goblin from three sides, but he anticipated them and fended them off faster than they expected, sword clanging and mace swinging. The goblin even nicked Ripley's sword arm, spurring Ripley on and intensifying his attack. Ripley, Max, and Orven held the goblin at bay while Roy and Aaron angled around behind him. The goblin tried to move the dwarves closer together, but they spread out and stood their ground.

Just as they gained position, the other goblin arrived, thrusting his sword at Orven. Orven swung and met the blade in time, thrilled at how light and easy Gorflange was to wield, rising and falling and arcing through the air. It seemed to anticipate his actions and he was more at one with it than any weapon or tool he had ever used.

When the second goblin arrived, the dwarves could not help Orven without compromising their position. Aaron wavered between them, but found more openings on the first goblin. Orven was surprised to be holding his own against the second goblin and continued fending off blows and getting in thrusts of his own, even causing the goblin to step back. Energy surged through him as he concentrated on the fight. He marveled at the feel of the sword in his hand, and it seemed he could think and react faster with it.

Max, Roy, Ripley, and Aaron had the first goblin squarely between them and were landing blows on his armor. Ripley charged in whenever he could. While Roy and Max distracted the goblin, Ripley smashed a loose armor plate and stabbed the goblin in the side. The goblin kept fighting as if he felt little pain, but Max landed another blow, and through their concerted efforts the four of them brought him down. They knocked the mace from his hand and snatched away his sword as he lay on the ground, and Ripley kicked and beat him to make sure he stayed down. Finally the goblin lay still. Max stood over him with his sword drawn, its point only inches from the goblin's head.

Roy and Aaron went to help Orven, who was still holding his own. Orven swung and dodged a blow, Gorflange swinging in flashing arcs whirling around and clanging against the goblin's blade. Just as Ripley came to help, Orven swung Gorflange around in a wide quick slash, catching the goblin by surprise and knocking the sword from his hand. Orven was as surprised as everyone else at the sudden reaction he had not even planned. Without stopping or thinking he thrust forward and stabbed the shocked goblin in the right shoulder, knocking him to the ground.

Ripley leapt forward to aid Orven, but Orven was faster and was at the fallen goblin's side. With a quick swing, Ripley cut a gash in the goblin's hairy forearm. The goblin lay on his back, breathing hard and fast, his shoulder and arm bleeding onto his doublet and armor. He looked up at Orven and was about to say something, when Orven brought Gorflange down through his throat, killing him. Orven let another blow fall to make sure he was dead, and then stood, staring down at the goblin and trembling.

The others watched, shocked at what Orven had done. Even Ripley was stunned by Orven's ferocity. After a moment Ripley released a long howl of victory, waving his sword high in the air. The loud, joyous wail snapped the others out of their amazement, and they joined in the victory shout. Only Orven did not join in; he stood looking down on the goblin he had slain, still breathing hard, his face flushed. Beads of sweat ran down his face, chilling his skin in the cool October air. The goblin had been down, subdued, and he had struck him and slain him. He had killed the goblin and now stood unbelieving, as though expecting the goblin to stir again. Blood seeped from the goblin's wounds, his face contorted in pain, lifeless eyes rolled back in their baggy sockets. Orven had the strangest sensation, as though Gorflange were pulsing in his hand, and then realized it was his own heart beating hard. He looked at the sword, which glinted at him in the dull light. He had never been in a fight like that. He had never really fought with a sword at all, and certainly not in a battle of life and death. He moved Gorflange around slowly, amazed at what he had done with it. The others were staring at him in awe, and he did his best to hide his wonderment.

Orven saw the other goblin lying on the ground under the point of Max's sword. "He's still alive?" Orven asked.

"Yes, what shall we do with him?" Max looked down at his captive. The goblin was gasping and scowling at them, pained by his wounds and his shame of lying there before them. Orven looked down upon him and burned with anger towards the goblin, as if he had dared to remain alive after fighting them.

"We could bind him up and take him into Kronivar," said Max, "They'd be able to—"

"Too dangerous," said Orven distractedly. He moved closer to where the goblin lay. Again his fury rose up, along with hatred, the same hatred mixed with shame and naked fear he had felt while bound to the tree as a captive of the Gnomes. All his frustrated anger and bile came back, until he was hot with rage. Before he knew it, he raised Gorflange high and brought it down in a crushing chop, slaying the goblin at Max's feet.

Max jumped back, stunned by Orven's sudden behavior. The light was fading fast now around them and he looked at his friend in the dusky light. "Orven…" He was at a loss for words, almost afraid. "We could have just taken him in to town, he was already wounded…"

Orven looked up. "He would have died anyway, by the time we got him there. They wouldn't have gotten much out of him."

Max looked at Orven. It seemed a vicious and unnecessary act, but Orven had been worked up into a frenzy, fighting the other goblin almost by himself. Max knew it must have been terrifying. He looked down at the dead goblin, its heavy features spattered with blood, imagining how Orven must have felt, losing control after facing a terrible foe alone. Somehow the whole fight had been soured by the unnecessary killing, but Max said nothing since he had not been in Orven's situation.

Tired and starting to feel the pains and scrapes sustained in battle, the dwarves sheathed their weapons and staggered around the campsite, calming down. Aaron and Roy went back over the hill and brought their packs and piled them on the ground. They looked through the goblins' packs but found nothing of interest or value in them, apart from a map, a few knives, and pieces of flint. But they felt strange about taking anything.

As it grew dark the dwarves decided they did not want to leave the goblins corpses lying out, nor did they want to drag them anywhere or even touch them. They just heaped dirt and leaves over them until they were covered, and left them that way. Night had fallen and none of them wanted to camp anywhere near the goblin mounds, so they pushed northward through the forest to put some distance between themselves and the river.

All were quiet as they passed through the darkness of the woods. Orven went over the evening's events. He felt uneasy about what he had done. He tried not to think about it; it was what he had to do. *We're at war*, he thought, *he would have killed me just the same*. At the same time, it seemed as if a great weight had been lifted from him; all doubts had fled and his leadership was restored twice over. Gorflange, too, had surpassed his wildest expectations, and there were still two gems missing from it. Orven's desire for more gems burned even stronger than before.

But there was something more. He had fought and survived. Orven sensed he had lost something irretrievably now, and he knew he was ready to join the troops and go to war. In his mind's eye he saw the goblin lying on the ground, and felt the swing of the sword downward and the sound it had made. It was as if he had cut something loose or released something. He walked with the other dwarves through the dark. The forest no longer seemed threatening. He still had the oddest, uneasy feeling that something had changed, or that he had, and decided they were all very tired and in need of rest. If they could only press on further, they might even make it to an inn, and that seemed worth the extra effort and the walk in the dark, cool woods.

The dwarves kept going and soon the forest loosened its hold on them. At last it relented, and great relief swept through them when the night sky opened wide above them and they saw the lights of the town of Hable in the distance.

Chapter 11.
The Streets of Kronivar

It was a bright, sunny day, windy and heavy with the cool drowsiness of deepening autumn. From the Crossroads, the West Road to Kronivar led through a broad meadowland, with the Veskwood Forest visible far off in the north and the northern end of Upper Rundlewood away to the south. Iaven's party was nearing Kronivar and eager to see the city they'd heard so much about.

Several days earlier, after leaving Broden's cabin, Iaven's party had traveled up the South Road on foot and later by cart. Further north, rides had been easier to come by, giving them a chance to rest and keeping them from getting sidetracked. The dwarves had wearied of travel and every little roadside village or hamlet seemed a welcome stopping point. As they approached the Emril Bridge, Zammond grew anxious to go see the Great Carven Halls of Gomirré, but they were perched on the back of a merchant's cart and would not abandon their ride.

The farmer who had given them a ride that morning was heading north and let them off in Greensward. Greensward, or the Crossroads as it was sometimes called, was the oldest city in Itharia outside of the mountains. When the Dwarves of old had reached the western edge of the mountains, they descended into the meadows and established a town. It was from Greensward that the West, North, and South Roads extended into the lands they would soon claim for the kingdom. At one time, some three hundred years ago, Greensward had been the bustling center of business, trade, and travel. But as Kronivar grew on the western shore, Greensward had declined into a much smaller settlement. Some weathered buildings still stood where the roads met, and several shops were still busy and flourishing. The two inns there, an ancient one that had been expanded and a newer one, were the center of the town's prosperity, and with all the travel to the Castle both had been doing well in the last few months.

It was late morning when Iaven's party stopped in Greensward for a light lunch before continuing west to try to reach Kronivar before nightfall. The last few days of the journey had been uneventful and the dwarves were regaining their morale. At the same time, however, they had become more aware of the growing concern regarding the impending war. Villages were more watchful, and travelers more hurried. Attempts were made to secure farms and property, children were brought indoors early, and grazing livestock were not allowed out as far and free as they once had been. Rumors of Goblin activity in the north and spies roaming unchecked throughout the land served only to deepen the worries of people living between Kronivar and the mountains. Many saw themselves as vulnerable in the event of a march on the city. They also sensed undercurrents of growing tension between the Castle and Kronivar, though most felt certain the kingdom would pull together when the time came.

Iaven's party found a ride going west. The wind picked up, gusting through their hair, cold and fresh. By late afternoon, as the sun sank into the land ahead of them, they passed farms on the farthest reaches of town. Buildings grew more numerous and at last they entered the main square of Kronivar's Old Town area.

The Old Town neighborhood was the oldest part of Kronivar, and some of the original structures remained. Having no interest in boating or sailing, the dwarves who had first settled Kronivar had been content to build a good distance away from the water's edge, on higher ground commanding an excellent view of the bay. The town grew and flourished, expanding into the lands around the original settlement as well as down the western slopes toward the sea. Foreign merchant vessels found they could sell their wares to the growing community, and the Dwarves began building closer to the sea to accommodate the traders who anchored in the bay and brought their wares ashore. Some foreigners found the new land to their liking and stayed with the Dwarves' welcome, building near the water and extending the city out to the seashore. Eventually Kronivar became the kingdom's largest city.

Wilbur was aglow with anticipation, and the others were also eager to explore the city. Iaven's own curiosity had grown in the past few weeks. As they entered the town square, the heart of Old Town opened wide before them. At the center of the square stood a great old well, set in the middle of a broad green lawn with roads leading into it from all sides. The main thoroughfares lining the square led past an array of shops, smithies, and stables, all busy with customers and trade. On the avenues and by the green peddlers with pushcarts hawked their wares. Over the general murmur of buyers and sellers rose shouts of town criers and the snap of whips and clip-clop of horses pulling carts up and down the avenues, their wooden wheels clattering over the cobblestones. Seagulls, crying shrilly, circled high above it all. The streets thronged with people who darted in and out of shops and avoided colliding with horse carts passing within a few feet of each other. The day's end was nearing and activity had reached its fever peak as everyone hurried to finish up the day's business before sundown.

Walking through the streets, Iaven and his friends found themselves lost amidst the bustle of the town, overwhelmed by it all. Their sense of wonderment was broken by angry shouts of drivers and pushcarts telling them to get out of the way. They stepped onto the green and out of traffic.

"If only we had business like this back home!" said Wilbur. He gazed around at all the shops, the buildings set so close together that some shared an outer wall. They were all of an older style, half-timbered with narrow windows and built of heavy dark wood. Some had second and even third stories, and Wilbur gazed at them, wondering what the town square would look like from up so high.

"We still have time to see the docks," said Tillmore.

Iaven nodded. He suggested they get a room at an inn nearby and then, unencumbered, explore what they could of the city before it got too dark. Everyone agreed and soon they discovered *The Brown Badger*, located right off the town square. It was a solid old place, very much still in use, and to their liking. They secured a room, unshouldered their packs, and were off again down the avenues.

The lure of the sea drew them westward. They descended the slope and entered an even larger and newer town square, twice as wide as the one in Old Town. Iaven remembered seeing one of his father's maps of the city and hearing how the new town square had become the center of trade and was now the heart of Kronivar. Whereas Old Town was still mainly populated by Dwarves, the newer areas were settled by Dwarves and the Human Men who had come across the sea from other lands. Iaven had been uncomfortable among the crowds in Old Town, and here he was even more out of place. The endless rows of buildings, the people, the horse carts and wagons, everything in motion; it overwhelmed him, even as it fascinated him.

The New Town Square, as it was called, was actually long and rectangular. Large, wide grassy squares ran down the middle, separated by avenues joining the main roads that ran around them. The squares were also set with wells, footpaths, large shade trees ringed with flowers, and merchants' pushcarts here and there. The downtown crowded around the squares on all sides, and at the far north end was the broad façade of Kronivar City Hall, a tall bell tower rising up proudly in the center of it. A large clock face with ornate wrought-iron hands overlooked the square from the tower. The clock had been installed only a dozen or so years earlier, during the time of Hagen Ambersheath's last trip to the city. Iaven remembered his father's description of the strange wooden gear-works, which had come from some far-off land across the sea. He had seen them being hoisted up and installed behind the clock face. It was the only clock in Itharia, and still considered by many to be a curiosity and an oddity, though in the city few people's lives were left unaffected by its tolling bells.

Iaven and his friends sat on a stone bench near a tree in one of the park squares, watching all the activity around them. Iaven wondered if the city was busier because of the war preparations, or if the pace was always so fast. Dwarves and many Human Men mingled here, going about their business. Iaven watched people bearing armloads and cartloads of merchandise and produce. Try as he might, he was unable to see any pattern or make sense of it all. He found it intimidating and sat back taking it in.

"It's all bigger than I expected," said Zammond, "The buildings are right up against each other, and so many of them!"

"How can people live like this?" asked Wilbur.

"You'd think they'd want more peace and quiet," said Hobley.

"Can you imagine living like this this every day?" added Tillmore, "Yet I suppose some people actually *enjoy* it."

The dwarves started as a loud, long peal broke from the bell tower as the ringing of the hour began. Deep tones rang and reverberated, rolling over the din of buyers, sellers, and cart traffic. Accustomed as they were to the relative quiet of the countryside, it was almost too much for them.

Iaven got up, eager to move on. "There's the docks to see yet, if we can," he said.

"Yes, let's get going." Zammond sprang up.

The dwarves wove their way through traffic and went down a side street. As they neared the waterfront, they passed men and dwarves returning as the docks' workday ended. The sun was setting over the Silver Sea, silhouetting the many-masted ships anchored in the bay against a red-orange sky. Sea-bells clanged in the evening breeze and seagulls cried and wheeled in the air. A cooper rolled some barrels down a plank. Wilbur and Zammond led the way to a railed boardwalk by the sea where fishermen were reeling in their lines.

Men came ashore from vessels moored at the docks, and Iaven was surprised to see a few dwarves among them. Most dwarves working at the docks were longshoremen or shipbuilders, but a small number, mostly half-breeds and mixed bloods, dared life as a sailor. Their families had lived in Kronivar for many generations, watching ships arriving at port and setting off for the open sea. They were said to be a rough and rowdy bunch, scoffing at their countrymen who always stayed ashore. Their motives varied: for many, their love of gold was stronger than their fear of water; others had succumbed to their curiosity or wanderlust; while some merely did so for reasons known only to them.

Looking out across the Silver Sea with trepidation and wonderment, Iaven contemplated what it would be like to venture out to sea, sailing into the unknown. He recalled the bittersweet memory of his father anticipating his voyage on the *Yoner*. Iaven understood his father's desire, but shared none of it. Miastolas, Bottomcliffe, Kronivar, and the Castle would be more than enough travel for him. And yet, despite their troubles, he was enjoying their journey. Iaven ached with the loss of his father as he regarded ships moored in the harbors and anchored in the bay. Hagen had always encouraged the twins to try new things, but was never forceful when they were reluctant. Iaven imagined how delighted his father would have been with his trip and how eager he would have been for details.

Remembering the gem, Iaven drew the sword and pointed it around them, keeping an eye out for anyone who might find it suspicious. He pointed Halix out to sea and got no response. When he aimed the sword back into Kronivar, however, a bright blue-green glow appeared in the pommel's stone.

"It's in the city somewhere." Iaven sheathed the sword again.

"Told you it wasn't out to sea," said Zammond.

"It may as well be," said Tillmore, "unless you're hoping to steal this one, too."

They walked back into the city and Zammond tried to keep them in line with the direction the sword had indicated. Darkness was falling now, and fewer people were out in the streets. Inns and pubs were lit up and busy, voices and laughter floating out their doors. Lamplighters were lighting lanterns hung from poles at wide intervals along the streets. The dwarves went along, trying not to attract attention as they stepped around a corner or into an alleyway, drawing the sword again to stay on course.

At last they arrived back in the Old Town neighborhood. The street-lanterns here were older and hung farther apart. As the area was mostly dwarves, Iaven and the others were more at ease.

"Back to where we started!" Wilbur said. "And time to rest, too."

"Let's have a look around first," said Iaven.

They pointed the sword across the town square towards the inn, and the pommel stone glowed a bright blue-green. They walked across the square to the inn and pointed the sword at it again, but got only a very faint light in the stone.

They turned back and pointed it in a new direction across the square, and the glow brightened again.

"Could be in one of the shops," said Tillmore, "More than we can afford, no doubt."

They walked over to the shops, but there, too, the light weakened.

"Well, the glow is still there, it's not far from here," said Iaven.

"So is our room," Wilbur yawned, "and that's where I'm going. It's been a long day." He started towards the inn and the others followed, except Zammond.

"Wait! I think I've got it," Zammond exclaimed. Iaven, tired and beginning to agree with Wilbur, looked at Zammond and handed him the sword. Zammond pointed it in one direction, crossed the square, only to find the light had dimmed. He tried it again, crisscrossing the square twice. "Well that's strange," he said, frustrated and tired.

"We'll look more tomorrow," Iaven said, reaching for Halix as Zammond handed it back.

They entered *The Brown Badger* and ate a good supper of hunter's stew, vegetables, and beer, served with a basket of hot bread and butter. They left a good tip for the barmaid, who was amused by their enthusiasm. Afterward they all went upstairs to their room, where the cot they had requested was already set up as a fifth bed in the corner. They drew straws and Tillmore got the cot, and after the obligatory complaint he was soon fast asleep on it. Everyone else was drowsy after eating, and it wasn't long before they blew out the candles and dozed off.

In the middle of the night, Iaven lay awake, gazing at the unfamiliar ceiling. He was glad to have a bed under a roof, and thought about his journey's end. He didn't mind returning to Hillbrook, though working in Rory's smithy did not appeal to him. And there was still the question of where to live. Moving in with his mother and Rory seemed intrusive. Iaven wanted to marry and start his own homestead, though he knew of no likely matches in either Hillbrook or the surrounding towns. And without a livelihood, he was not much of a prospect anyway. He thought of Horace Henshaw's offer to work on the farm, and rejected the idea immediately. It would be too strange to be only a hired hand in what had always been his home. Cedric would be there at least, but little else would seem the same.

Iaven took comfort in knowing he could talk to Cedric about what to do. Cedric was sure to have good advice. Iaven decided to go see him as soon as he returned.

As Iaven lay in bed his mind raced and pondered, imagining various futures and possibilities. He wanted to sleep but could not still his restless mind. He lay there for some time, he wasn't even sure how long, his thoughts always returning to the same worries and unanswered questions.

Across the room, Zammond sat up in bed, wide-eyed. He appeared to have woken from a dream, but Iaven feared it was something else. Iaven shut his eyes and pretended to be asleep.

"Iaven," Zammond said.

"What?" Iaven moaned, sounding as irritated as he could.

"I think I know where it is."

Zammond sat on the edge of his bed, and Iaven rolled over and looked at him. "Where what is? ... Now?! You want to go looking for the gem right now? Why do we always have to do this in the middle of the night?"

Zammond started getting dressed. "If it is where I think it is, we won't be able to get it during the day. And we won't be stealing it from anyone either, if I'm right!"

Iaven lay in bed, unwilling to go out into the chilly night air. It occurred to him that maybe some activity would distract him and tire him out, allowing him to get some rest. He got up. "This better not take too long," he said.

They got dressed and went outside. Iaven drew Halix and handed it to Zammond. Zammond began pointing it around the square, raising and lowering the blade.

"We kept the blade level when we moved it around before," Zammond explained.

"You think it's up high in some building, or what?" asked Iaven.

"No, look!" Zammond said, showing him the light in the stone set into the pommel. As he pointed it into the square and lowered the blade, the glow intensified. "We kept going past it. It's right near the center of the square."

"Is it buried?" Iaven asked.

"That's what I want to find out," said Zammond. He walked onto the grass, watching the blue-green light in the pommel. They came to the well at the center of the square, and Zammond aimed the sword down the well. The light shined even brighter.

"Looks like it's down there alright," Zammond said. He turned and handed Halix to Iaven. "Let's get it, what do you say? Before anyone sees us?"

Iaven took the sword and gazed down into the well. It was four or five feet across inside, the thick, damp rings of stone masonry descending down into total darkness, like a bottomless pit. Iaven shivered just looking into its depths. He dropped a small pebble into it, to hear how deep it was. The pebble disappeared into the blackness, a moment passed, and a tiny echoing splash was heard.

"I wonder who threw the gem down there, and why," Iaven said. "Too bad..."

"What do you mean, 'too bad'? We've found it! We'll have *two* gems for the sword now," Zammond exclaimed.

"You want to go down there and try to get it?" Iaven noticed Zammond smiling at him. "You want *me* to go down there? Oh no..."

"Oh come on Iaven, it won't be that hard, look how big the water bucket is, and the rope is thick enough..."

"You want me to sit on the edge of the bucket, and be lowered into the well? It's pitch black down there, and we have no idea how deep the water is!" Iaven protested.

"It won't take that long, and it won't be dark; you've got the sword." He indicated the blue-green glow emanating from the pommel's stone. "That'll light the way. Besides, I'll be operating the winch, and you'll be down and up again in no time. Come on, Iaven! For King and Country!"

Iaven hated the idea, but it was his sword and his responsibility. As long as Halix pointed at the gem, the sword would light the way. And he really did want another gem.

"All right," Iaven said, "but if I decide I want to come back up, you're pulling me straight up, right away."

"Of course!" Zammond said. "Yes... yes, I will, I promise."

Iaven looked at Zammond, doubting his intent, and then climbed onto the edge of the well. "You sure this rope is strong enough?" But he knew it was; and the bucket was sturdy and wide enough for him to sit on the edge of it, to one side of the handle. Nervously, Iaven got onto it, gripping the rope and sitting on the bucket's rim, until he was swinging over the gaping hole of the well. The rope held fine, and everything was ready for the descent.

"Now if I call out or something happens, you bring me right back up, all right?"

"Just as you say," Zammond reassured him. He turned the winch slowly, holding it back with great effort as he lowered Iaven into the well.

Iaven felt a moment of panic as layers of stone rose up around him until the night sky was just a small circle above him. The well was cold and damp, and very old. Iaven gripped Halix, pointing the blade downward. The blue-green glow lit the heavy gray walls surrounding him, allowing him to see but making him feel even more closed in.

Lower and lower he went, one course of stone after another rising through the circle of blue-green light. At last when he was some twenty or more feet underground he saw the water sparkling dully several feet below him, looking black and opaque in the pale glow. After a few more minutes, his feet got wet, and then his legs. The bottom of the bucket touched the water, and he called up for Zammond to stop.

Iaven hung onto the rope as he lowered himself off the bucket and into the dark water. It was impossible to gauge how deep it was, and he hoped to touch bottom right away. The water was ice cold and soaked him right through his clothes, numbing his feet. Once he was in the water he held on, set Halix down into the bucket, blade first, to keep the light glowing, and grabbed the rope with both hands. As he lowered himself deeper in, the icy, heavy wetness gripped him. He was in up to his thighs now and trembled with the cold. Waist deep, he still had not touched bottom. He shuddered, biting back a surge of panic as cold water pressed in around his ribs. He wondered if he should call for Zammond to reel him up and consider the gem lost. He eased his way down more, until he was in up to his shoulders. At last, to his relief, his feet touched solid ground.

Having found his footing he stood still, heart pounding, his feet almost numb now and the rest of him shivering. He let go of the rope and reached for Halix. Pointing the blade into the water, he scanned the bottom of the well, and touched something with his foot. It felt like a small rock, and tapping his foot nearby, he found other stones around it, in a circle. He pulled at one and felt the others move, as if they were connected in a necklace of some kind.

Careful not to move from his position, he placed Halix back in the bucket, and tried picking up the necklace with his foot. He got his foot under part of it, but only succeeded in pushing it around. He tried using his other foot to maneuver it, and nearly lost his balance.

The water was very cold and he was afraid of losing the necklace. There seemed to be no other way to get it. He reached out his hand, inching down further into the water, shivering as he lowered himself in. Blindly, he reached down toward his feet, for the necklace. Balancing on bended knees, he was up to his chin in the water, but still his groping hand touched nothing. He moved his foot to make sure the necklace was there, all the while stretching to keep his face out of the water. Still he could not reach it. He pressed his lips shut and lowered them into the water, and it was not enough.

"Iaven! Is it down there? What are you doing?" Zammond's voice echoed.

Steeling himself, Iaven squeezed his eyes shut, gasped in a breath, and plunged himself under the cold water. He bounced down and up, remaining underwater as little as possible, the water rumbling in his ears. His hand touched bottom, but did not hit the necklace. Cringing and shivering, he tried again and caught one of the stones on the necklace, pulling it up as he stood.

When he held the necklace near the sword's blade, the blue-green glow brightened, and he could make it out a little better. It was an older style of metalwork, with ornate, tarnished clasps and links in which the stones were set. The largest stone was the right size and similar in shape to the orange gem. Iaven tried to make out what color it was, but in the blue-green glow it appeared dark and opaque.

Since the gem was set in the necklace, Iaven could not put it into the sword. Nor did he want to lose the only source of light he had in that dark, dank hole of water and wet stone. He gripped the necklace in his hand, the gem resting on his palm, and pulled himself back up onto the side of the water bucket, much heavier now that he was soaking wet. He left Halix where it was, its blade and hilt rising out of the bucket, and held the necklace down low near the end of the blade, making the sword's light brighter. When he was settled in place on the bucket's rim, his free arm gripping the rope firmly, he called up to Zammond to reel him in.

"You found it!" Zammond shouted, his voice echoing strangely in the well. He grunted and wound the winch. Iaven sat shivering, water dripping off him, lurching up bit by bit until the water below disappeared in the darkness.

Iaven watched the cold, damp stone inching downwards around him in the pale blue-green radiance, his feet starting to regain feeling. He imagined himself dry and warm by the fireplace at the inn, examining the necklace. They would pry the gem out and—

With a sudden yank the bucket came to a sharp halt. The rope loosened and Iaven and the bucket dropped two or three feet. The rope caught again and held, Iaven yelling in horror as Halix was jolted out of the bucket. It tipped over the edge, its light dimming as it fell out of sight and splashed into the dark water.

"Zammond! Wait! It—" Iaven stopped cold as Zammond cried out. He looked up and saw a figure leaning over and watching as someone else worked the winch until Iaven was a few feet from the top of the well. The stranger's outline, black against the starry night sky, was familiar.

"Well, well, well!" The stranger gazed down at Iaven.

"Orven!" Bitter frustration crushed Iaven.

"I misjudged you! Didn't think you were interested in the gems. And here you are," Orven laughed, "soaking wet and dangling by a rope! However did Wilbur talk you into it?" Laughter erupted behind Orven outside the well. Muted sounds of a struggle told Iaven they were holding Zammond back.

Iaven looked at his brother's face half hidden in the shadows and peering down into the well. It was hard to make out his expression, but Orven seemed genuinely surprised, maybe even pleased, to find Iaven out looking for the gems.

"It's in the necklace, isn't it?" Orven eyed the string of jewels hanging from Iaven's hand. Iaven lowered his hand, knowing it was too late.

"So you were watching us," Iaven said. "Waiting for us to get the gem out for you?"

Orven smiled guiltily. "Let's say we were just lucky to have come by at the right time. I would have never guessed it was you and Zammond! Anyone else come along with you two? Oh, besides *Wilbur*, I mean!"

Resentment boiled up in Iaven. He held the necklace out over the water. "I could drop it back in," he said.

"Then I'd have to send you back down for it. Say, where is Halix? Got any other gems for it?" Orven laughed at the empty scabbard hanging from Iaven's belt.

Iaven held the necklace out a moment longer and then pulled it back into his lap. Orven gazed down at him with what seemed like amusement, yet there was something else, something more serious. Iaven could feel how determined Orven was to get the gems. His heart beat hard and the quickness of his anger surprised him, but the feeling was not unfamiliar.

Once when they were young children, working in the fields on a bright, sunny afternoon, Iaven had found an ancient Elven arrowhead in the furrows, the first he'd ever come across. He examined it with awe, running his fingertips over the serrated edges and its once-sharp point. Orven came by to see what he had found and Iaven proudly held it up to show him. "Wait till Dad sees this!" Iaven exclaimed, as Orven took it for a closer look.

"It's just a pointed rock," Orven sneered, and before Iaven could say anything he threw it into the weeds on the meadow's edge. With a flash of panic, Iaven ran to get it, unsure where it had landed in the tall grass. After several fruitless hours searching, he fell behind on his chores, and his father had scolded him. Iaven said nothing about the arrowhead to his father but he had been mad at Orven for weeks afterward. As he hung on the rope in the cold dark hole of the well, anger burned through Iaven again, as searing as it had been that summer afternoon.

"Come on, Iaven, hand it over," Orven chided, "I'll put it to better use than you ever would. See, look, I've got one already!" He held Gorflange up and Iaven saw a gem twinkle in one of the hilt's holes. Then with a slow, deliberate motion, Orven turned the sword over until his hand was on the hilt and the blade pointed down into the well, threatening Iaven. The pale blue-green glow from Gorflange's pommel underlit Orven's face, and greed shone in his eyes.

"Give it to me," Orven said, all playfulness gone from his voice now. He leaned in and gave the rope a shove, sending Iaven swinging and bumping against the damp stone walls. Orven smiled as Iaven struggled to regain his balance. "Hand it up to me. Now." Orven extended his hand into the well.

For a moment Iaven considered grabbing Orven's hand and pulling him down into the well. Chances were they'd both fall in and start fighting, Orven pushing Iaven underwater and holding him there. They'd both get hurt, and maybe Orven would even find Halix at the bottom.

Iaven handed Orven the necklace. Anger and revulsion surged through him, leaving him trembling.

"Beautiful!" Orven held the necklace up out of the well, gazing at the gem and watching moonlight wink on its dark facets. When Orven raised it so the white light of the waxing moon shined through it, a dark, rich violet hue flashed in his hand.

"Good work, Iaven!" Orven smiled down at his brother. He stood up from the well, and just as Iaven was about to say something, the rope shuddered as Orven unlatched the winch. At once Iaven felt the drop and its uneasy lightness as the rope unwound and the winch clattered away. He plunged back down into darkness, his shouting drowning out Orven's fading laughter.

Orven had little remorse about taking the gem from Iaven. He had simply come upon it late, he thought, but fortunately not too late. He was quite surprised to find Iaven pursuing the gems and wondered if he'd found any others. "Too bad Iaven didn't have Halix with him," he told his friends as they returned to *The Gnarled Oak*, their inn on the southern end of the New Town Square. "But he had the gem. And now we have it. Seems our business here is at an end."

It was early morning and still dark out, so they turned in again. After nights of camping on the forest floor, the inn's beds were too comfortable to abandon at daybreak, so they slept until almost noon.

Once they were all awake, Orven brought out the necklace and held the gem up in the light. The necklace itself was old, corroded prongs grasping jewels set amidst its links. They were small and pretty in their own right, but none could compare to Aorinthel's gem, which occupied the place of prominence. It was a beautiful shade of violet, sparkling, dark and mysterious, drawing the eye into its alluring depths. Orven pried it out of the necklace and let the others see it. After impatiently awaiting its return, he put it into the sword. When the metalwork leaves resumed their position locking the gem in place, Orven lifted the sword as though to wield it. It seemed even lighter and easier in his hand, and his desire to find a third gem increased a hundredfold. He could feel its power, its readiness, its responsiveness to his will, and his need to use it again was strong.

"And where are we off to today?" Max was anxious to find the third gem, and wondered if Orven would continue looking for a fourth one.

Orven leveled the sword and swept it across the room, watching the pommel as he cupped his hand around it. "East of here," he said, finding a faint blue-green flicker. "Looks far away."

"Due East?" said Max, "Probably up at the Castle, then."

"I hope so," said Roy, "I'd hate to go climbing around the mountains looking for it."

"If it is at the Castle, they aren't going to just give it away," said Aaron. "It would be much better if it *were* lost in the mountains."

"Well there's only one way to find out," said Orven. He sheathed Gorflange and starting packing his things.

They had a late breakfast in the common room, and soon were traveling again. The road to Greensward would be easy going, but beyond that it climbed into the mountains, winding its way east toward the Castle. On foot it was several days' journey, though the road between Kronivar and Castle was well traveled by carts and wagons going their way.

"Still going to join the King's troops?" Max asked Orven as they walked.

"Maybe, once I have a third gem for Gorflange. Imagine what I'll be able to do with it then." Along with the violet gem, his confidence had returned and a high position in the Dwarven army seemed even more certain now. Orven knew he could not settle for anything less.

In another inn, overlooking the central square of Kronivar's Old Town neighborhood, Iaven, Zammond, Wilbur, Hobley, and Tillmore sat sullenly at breakfast.

"Well at least we have the orange gem," said Zammond. "Maybe the King has more to add to it, since the sword's pointing there."

"He'll soon have a sword, too," said Iaven.

"Aren't you going to miss it?" asked Hobley.

Iaven considered. "A bit," he admitted. They all sat in silence, thinking about the last leg of their journey and how quickly the rest of it had gone.

"We could stay on a few more nights and see the city," said Wilbur.

The others nodded. No one needed convincing.

They sat around the table, somber in the sunlit morning. Even the barmaid serving them noticed the change in their attitude from the night before.

"Morning, fellows... Why so glum today?" she inquired. "What can I get you?"

"Oh, just tired, I suppose," Iaven answered. She was so cheerful and kind that he had a strange urge to tell her all that had happened, but thought better of it. "Long night yesterday," he added.

"I see," she replied with a hint of a smile. She repeated the morning's menu, and they all placed their orders. Iaven sat back, thinking of the gem he had lost, the end of his journey to the Castle, the unanswered questions awaiting him in Hillbrook, and the dark cloud of war that hung over and threatened it all.

Chapter 12.
Visitors in the Night

In Hillbrook and the other villages of the Foothills, news and rumors of the impending war circulated rapidly. A dozen of Hillbrook's own dwarves had joined Captain Halgreve's company and more were leaving for the troops gathering in Kronivar and at the Castle. Mayor Ebbleaf doubled the Bridge Guard, and everyone waited for what now seemed inevitable, although most business continued as usual. There was talk of massing Goblin forces north of the border, spy activity around Kronivar, and even several reports of people having seen something, which they thought were Goblins, in the southern edges of Rundlewood. Whether or not the rumors were true, they made for good small talk when neighbors or strangers met, and many other worries were forgotten.

Although most talk on front porches and over back fences had to do with the impending war, once in a while the town's gossip would turn to some local happening, providing momentary relief. One such occurrence was Daren Muldern's wife throwing him out after an argument, right in front of his cronies. The story circulated for weeks, and Daren thought he would never live it down, when at last another local story took hold of Hillbrook's interest.

Everyone knew the hired hand who lived on the Ambersheath farm was quite old, but now that he had finally died, word got around as to just how old he really was. He was said to have almost reached his one hundred and seventieth birthday, though some found that too hard to believe; after all, he only looked around a hundred or so. But most people were proud that the oldest known dwarf in all of Itharia had lived in their town. "Right here in Hillbrook!" said the baker to an out-of-towner, "It's the food, of course!" Others accounted for his old age with a variety of ideas, with no end to speculation. Daren even found he could go back to his favorite tavern without getting harassed too badly. "Couldn't have come at a better time!" he said to those who commented on his good fortune.

Word of Cedric's death and his great old age spread across the countryside, and talk of it would have died down, had it not been for what happened a little over a week later. On the tenth of October, the same night Iaven saw Leland in *The Copper Dragon* and one of the many nights Orven spent in Rundlewood, a strange figure strode along the outskirts of Hillbrook after dark. "Too tall to be a gnome, too thin to be a goblin, and probably not a dwarf, either," said Emma Moffenbyer, who claimed to have seen it from her bedroom window. "She never saw a thing," said Aggie Hocker, who had a falling out with Emma every other week. "She'd only said she'd seen something *after* the break-in, so I doubt she really did." None of the bridge guards had seen anything, despite their vigilance. They concluded that the stranger must have been a very wily one indeed, if he wasn't entirely the product of unfounded rumor.

The stranger passed through the edges of town, lingering a moment in the shadows beyond the circle of lamplight outside the Riverbank Inn. He watched as a solitary dwarf emerged and began stumbling his way home. As soon as the dwarf had moved out into the semidarkness beyond the Inn's lantern, the stranger confronted him.

The dwarf, an old cobbler by the name of Cornus Highbog, trembled with fear at the sudden appearance of the stranger whose steady gaze impaled his soul. The stranger was an old man whose long white beard disappeared into the folds of his cloak. His bright, undimmed eyes stared out of his weathered old face, and the cobbler could neither tear his eyes away nor guard any secrets demanded of him.

"Where might I find the Ambersheath farm?" the stranger inquired in a low, quiet voice like a velvet growl.

Relieved that the stranger's request was such a simple one, Cornus muttered the directions as best he could, straining his mind to be as clear and coherent as possible. He repeated everything as if to verify what he had just said, hoping the stranger would leave him. The stranger thanked him and departed. Cornus stood watching him go, shaking so much he nearly lost his balance. At first his story was disregarded as drunken fabrication, but later it seemed to fit in with other reports and was more likely to be believed.

The stranger moved through Hillbrook and arrived at the farmstead. He came to the small cottage on the edge of the fields, finding its door locked. With a small gesture and whispered word from him, the bolt slid and clicked. The stranger entered, closing the door behind him.

Cedric's cottage was dark and had remained untouched since his death, as Rory and Horace Henshaw were still debating the ownership of the contents. Instead of lighting a candle, the stranger held his hand palm up and brought his fingertips together. He carefully spoke a long, oddly-inflected word, and a tiny spark of luminous blue light appeared in the space between his fingertips. Gently he opened his hand, and as his fingers spread, the ball of spark grew larger and brighter until it was several inches across, hanging in mid-air above his open palm. With a slight motion of his arm he sent the glowing ball drifting through the air until it hovered near the ceiling over Cedric's writing-desk, casting a dim blue light in the room.

Everything remained as it was when Cedric died; papers and books scattered about, dishes waiting to be cleaned near the stove, an old cloak draped over a chair back. The stranger looked about, shuffled through the papers, recognizing several, and found a sealed envelope with a single word written on it in Cedric's spidery script: "Wendolin". The stranger opened the letter, read it, and then put it back in the envelope and hid it away deep in the folds of his cloak. He glanced at the mantle and shelves, noticing Cedric's blanket from Teska. The stranger hesitated, debating whether some action was necessary, and finally concluding it was. He reluctantly uttered a strange spell, one that did not seem agreeable to him, and waved his hands in a sharp, short arc. Little blue flames sprang into being and leapt onto the tabletop, where they sought out certain papers and began to burn them, while they left others untouched and unharmed. Those they burned were consumed completely, burning into thin wisps of delicate smoke and leaving behind no charred remains or ash. The flames split and ran along the table without harming it, some going off to where a thin journal lay, and others up to the mantle over the fireplace where various charms and talismans were to be consumed. Several others shot across the room seeking out their prey. Some flames found none and returned, while others caught on Cedric's blanket from Teska, blazing until every thread of it was gone. At last when all items of magical origin had vanished, the flames ran back together and extinguished themselves in a curling puff of white smoke.

The stranger looked around again, satisfied that everything appeared normal and undisturbed. Nowhere was there any hint of the flames that had run throughout the room. He nodded to himself and withdrew the luminous blue globe, waving it out of existence. The room was dark again, and he went out the door, locking it behind him, leaving the little cottage whose contents were now no more extraordinary than any of the other homes in Hillbrook.

Now that Cedric was gone, the fate of his cottage was the subject of dispute. Just that afternoon, Horace Henshaw had been over to Rory's smithy and the two had had a long argument about it. Horace was sure of his position, and later that evening when he returned home, he checked the deed only to find that Rory was right. The cottage was not mentioned anywhere in the description of the house and farmstead, which of course had been written before the cottage had been built. Bitter and disgusted, Horace was sure he would lose the case, and had brooded over it all evening. Night fell, but he could not sleep, so he sat unmoving in one of the big wooden armchairs across from the fireplace, watching the fire die out. He continued sitting there, mulling over the cottage, occasionally looking out the window at it.

In the night landscape outside, he saw someone entering the cottage, and jumped up from his chair. At first, he thought it was Rory, but the figure was too tall and dressed unlike anyone he knew in Hillbrook. He knew he ought to wake his boys and do something about it, but he sank back into his chair, waiting to see what would happen. Strange blue lights flickered in the windows and he caught a glimpse of fire. *Well let it burn*, he thought, *it ain't mine anyway*, as he wondered what was going on inside. Soon the light disappeared, and the stranger left, without even carrying anything off. A while after the stranger was gone, he went and checked the cottage and saw with disappointment that nothing seemed amiss. Didn't seem like the way Goblins operated, he thought, and who else could it be? He told the story to several people around town, just in case Rory would accuse him of taking something for himself. But it sounded far-fetched, and Horace Henshaw was too well known for telling a tall tale for anyone to take him very seriously.

Talk of the mysterious stranger not only kept Cedric's story alive, it added new speculation as to who Cedric was and with whom he might have been connected. And just as this sort of talk reached its peak several nights later, two Goblin spies broke into Cedric's cottage and ransacked it. This time there was no doubt of it; the place was a mess, footprints encircled the house, and one of Horace's sons had heard noises and had gone outside, only to arrive too late as the goblins ran off into the dark. Whether they had taken anything was hard to determine as no one was familiar with Cedric's things, but the place had been thoroughly searched. Rory and Horace still had not settled their dispute, which had grown worse after two break-ins on the property. Whereas folks had doubted Horace's stories about the first break-in (which Horace claimed was not even technically that, since nothing was broken), the second was clearly the work of Goblin spies. And so, while everyone was shocked that goblins would dare to reveal their presence in the Foothills and feared for their own homes, Horace was glad to have been vindicated and gloating over it.

In the week or so that followed, news of goblins prowling about the Foothills traveled to the rest of the kingdom, and Cedric's story went along with it. Iaven and his friends were having a very light lunch (due to having eaten a late breakfast only a few hours before) in *The Brown Badger*'s main room, when they overheard two travelers talking.

Earlier that day, Iaven and Zammond had told the others how Orven had taken the gem away the night before, and their mood became a subdued and doleful one. After breakfast they all wandered around Old Town, looking in the shops, and returned to *The Brown Badger* for lunch. Zammond felt bad, as if he had failed Iaven. The others felt sorrier for Iaven than for the loss of the gem itself. They were unsure what to say to Iaven, so they said nothing. They all knew how often Iaven and Orven fought, but this seemed beyond brotherly bickering, and Zammond even thought he had sensed something more.

As the dwarves mulled over their food, they sat half-listening to the talk around them, until mention of Hillbrook caught their interest. A trader who had just returned from the Foothills was passing on stories of interest from those parts. Animated and disbelieving at times, he related the story of the death of the old dwarf and the break-ins.

Iaven knew at once that it was about Cedric. Cedric's death had seemed inevitable for years, yet still came as an unexpected shock. Iaven was bitterly sorry he had left Hillbrook. He had missed Cedric's last days, and his burial. Iaven felt as if he had betrayed him. The gem he had lost to Orven —indeed, all the gems and swords— seemed of no value compared to what Cedric had meant to him, and now Cedric was gone. *Why did I leave?* Iaven thought, *Why wasn't I with him until the end?*

Zammond, Wilbur, Hobley, and Tillmore were saddened by Cedric's death, though they were not as close to Cedric as Iaven had been. Morosely, Iaven went back upstairs to their room after they were done eating. The others planned to see the newer areas of Kronivar, and sensed Iaven wanted time alone and wouldn't be coming with them. Iaven told them to go see the city and he'd join them for supper later. They hesitated and finally departed when Iaven insisted he'd be all right and would be resting up in their room until they returned.

Iaven stood upstairs in the dwarves' room, looking out the window at the busy town square. He felt heavy and leaden, and had a sudden urge to return to Hillbrook. He was still tired from the night before in the well, and now all his strength was spent.

Iaven lay on his bed awhile, his anguish deepening as Cedric's death became more real to him. He was tired but could not sleep, so he left the inn and roamed the streets alone, feeling that perhaps he should have gone with his friends. There was no way to find them, so he returned to the inn and sat at a table by the wall in the main common room.

The Dwarven barmaid who had brought them breakfast earlier that day was still serving patrons seated at tables and at the bar. She came and asked Iaven if he wanted anything, and he ordered a glass of beer even though he wasn't really thirsty. She was as cheerful and observant as she had been that morning, her gaze and smile inquiring if Iaven was feeling any better. Iaven recalled having an urge to tell her what had happened, and felt it even more when she spoke to him. He caught himself stealing glances and watching her across the room; her shoulder-length chestnut brown hair, and dark, expressive eyes that made it hard to tear his gaze away. She seemed kind enough to listen to his troubles, and Iaven realized how much he wanted to talk about them. In difficult times Iaven usually went to see Cedric, and the impossibility of it now only made him feel worse.

The barmaid brought Iaven's tankard to his table. "Here you are," she said.

"Do you know—" Iaven paused involuntarily as he met the full scrutiny of her beautiful dark brown eyes, "Are there any carts or traders going south to Hillbrook?"

"That's in the Foothills, isn't it?" She sat down on the edge of the bench opposite Iaven, as if his request was of great importance to her. "There are some going in that direction, I could find out for you... How soon do you need to know?"

"Not for a while, there's no hurry," Iaven said, slightly embarrassed that she had shown such concern. He regretted having bothered her, disrupting her work, all for his own selfish worries. "I might need it later, that's all... I was just wondering how often they went." He was about to shrug off the question as unimportant, but realized he would look even worse, as if he were asking just for the sake of talking to her, which he was.

"I can find out for you tomorrow," she said. She stood, but remained near the table. "Is that where you and your friends are from? You don't seem like you're from around here."

"We don't? No, we're not... We're from Hillbrook," Iaven said, unsure why he was nervous answering the question. He had prolonged their conversation and knew he ought to end it. He was distraught over losing the gem and now Cedric's death, and was just not himself. Iaven paid for the drink and thanked the barmaid.

"You'll be here tomorrow?" she inquired, about to leave.

"Yes, we'll be here a few days," Iaven said, not really having decided it for certain until right at that moment.

Iaven had not considered how long they would stay in Kronivar. At first they had planned to find the gem if they could and leave for the Castle right away. But the city, sprawling and intimidating as it was, fascinated them. And it had comforts they had long been without on the road. Now, after losing the gem and hearing of Cedric's death, Iaven's enthusiasm was gone and a few days' rest sounded like a good thing. He did not look forward to the long road home, and there was still the trip up to the Castle. He wondered for a moment if Zammond and Hobley would take the sword to the Castle for him, but knew they would'nt let him leave them after having come so far. And he was glad they felt that way.

Afternoon passed into evening and soon the others returned and joined Iaven for supper. Iaven hid his sorrow as best he could so as to not trouble anyone, taking part in whatever they talked about or wanted to do. The others spent a good part of the evening telling him about the city and the shipyards, and how they had seen regiments of soldiers practicing around the garrison north of the docks. Iaven found their animated talk soothing and sat back listening to it all, regarding his friends with a renewed sense of his love for them.

The evening went quickly and soon they went upstairs and turned in for the night. The busy day left everyone tired, and one by one Iaven heard them drop off to sleep.

The room was quiet now. Iaven lay in his bed, staring at the ceiling looming over him in the dark. The whole room had the strange and temporary feeling he always experienced away from home. Only his bed at home in Hillbrook was completely comfortable; in other beds he was only a guest. But the bed and room he had always known was his no longer.

Iaven lay alone in the dark. The weight of Cedric's death closed in on him with a terrible, heavy emptiness. A part of his life had been severed; his last link to the farm was gone. And more than that, Cedric had been part of a different age, a time long past, that Iaven could visit as he sat fireside listening to Cedric's stories. Now Cedric had passed into those stories as well. Iaven had known the day would come, but it had been that way for so long that he had gotten used to it. He rolled over in bed, again wishing he had been with Cedric during his final days. He pictured his mother, Rory, and family friends at Cedric's bedside and grave. Iaven shut his eyes, pressing his face into the cold pillow. His mind grew numb, his breathing slowed, and he drifted off into a deep slumber.

Throughout the night Iaven's thoughts merged into hazy, swirling fragments of dreams, chaotic and fleeting images, and passing feelings that were instantly forgotten. An array of soft colors arose, which he came to see as Cedric's favorite blanket, the one from Teska. Iaven tried see if Cedric was under the blanket, but instead found himself examining the image woven into it. The scene grew larger and more distinct, until he realized he was standing in front of the little cottage where Cedric sat on the porch smoking his pipe. The fragrance of lilacs was strong and soothing. Iaven walked across the grass toward the porch and it all seemed unreal. He was back on the farm, but it wasn't the farm; it was Hillbrook, though somehow it wasn't. Everything was eerily empty and quiet. The late afternoon sun hung low, wide and red, about to set, yet he knew that it never would here; it would remain hovering near the horizon, an everlasting twilight. He approached the porch, where Cedric sat slowly rocking, the wood of the chair creaking faintly in the immense silence.

Despite the unreality of the setting, Cedric seemed the same as ever. He nodded at Iaven, drawing on his pipe. Iaven sat down nearby him on the porch. "Cedric," Iaven said, at a loss for words. "I'm sorry."

The old dwarf continued his gentle rocking, amused perhaps, threads of smoke rising from the bowl of his pipe. "Sorry? For what?" He drew on his pipe again. "Ah, not for me! No, no... Not me. Not for what has been... For what wasn't. Aren't you?"

"I don't understand." Iaven looked up at Cedric, who seemed to radiate warmth and joy in the reddish-orange sunset glow. Iaven very much wanted to move closer to him, but somehow simply remained where he was.

"Not for the lost, but for the *loss*..." A long, thin stream of smoke rose from his pipe and dispersed into swirls of turbulence until it was gone. Cedric smiled at Iaven but looked tired. "Where is your brother?" he asked.

"Orven? Who knows... Maybe in the King's army by now." Iaven wasn't even quite sure what he meant, he didn't know if there was an army in this world, a King, or even an Orven. But it didn't seem to matter just then.

"Cedric," Iaven began, unsure what he wanted to say. He was becoming more aware of the dreamlike nature of everything around him. Cedric remained watching him, as if contemplating something.

"Dwell not on either the lost or the loss," Cedric said. "And as for what remains?" Cedric appeared as if he were about to continue, but everything was slipping away. Iaven tried to grasp and hold it steady but as he did it merged into his hazy, overworked thoughts and before he knew it he was awake again.

It was still dark out, so Iaven did not get up. He lay thinking about Cedric's life, wondering what it must have been like for Cedric to return to the world after eighty-three years in the care of the Stone Giants. To find almost all your friends had died and the world you knew had passed on, a stranger in your own land. Apart from retrieving the swords, Cedric never had a chance to visit the Castle again. And to have waited with the swords in Hillbrook for Wendolin to return— Iaven realized, more than he ever had before, just how much Cedric understood and supported his family after his father was gone. He regretted not having thanked Cedric for everything he'd taken for granted, but it was too late.

Iaven fell back to sleep again, and this time slept soundly and deeply until morning came.

The next day Iaven and the others breakfasted around nine o'clock, discussing what they would do that day. Everyone liked the idea of staying in Kronivar an extra day or two. Hobley and Tillmore planned on seeing the New Town Square area, while Wilbur and Zammond wanted to go to the shipyards where the year's last vessels were being finished and put to sea. Iaven was better rested and more at ease, though still lost in thought and easily distracted. They all invited Iaven to go with them and were not too surprised when he later decided to stay around the Old Town area instead.

Alone again, Iaven went back into the main common room. He looked around and inquired whether a certain barmaid would be on duty that day. The bartender, a big heavyset fellow wiping the countertop, nodded with recognition at Iaven's description.

"You mean Rhiane? She'll be working around lunchtime today." He eyed Iaven suspiciously. "Yes, a fine one, isn't she! Hard worker, best of the lot. Best keep to yourself, wouldn't you." Iaven reddened, realizing how many sailors or traders had asked similar kinds of questions, with a far less noble intent. He went and sat at a table near the back wall and decided to wait and not ask any more questions.

Iaven tried to relax. It was still a while before lunch, and only a few men and dwarves were there, meeting for business or just to drink and chat. Sitting alone, Iaven's thoughts drifted toward Cedric again, and how there was no reason to hurry back to Hillbrook, where he would feel Cedric's absence most sharply.

Soon Iaven was dwelling on his losses again, so he searched for distractions to keep him from falling headlong into despair. He listened to the men and dwarves talking at nearby tables, debating how war would affect market prices and trading. Some dwarves criticized King Jordgen for not having acted sooner and for being too indecisive. Others defended the King, while still others complained, saying that Kronivar was now more important than the Castle and ought to be considered as such. Two large longshoremen were arguing with a broad-shouldered dwarf. One of the men declared that Kronivar should be on its own, as there were probably more Men than Dwarves living there. The dwarf shot back that there were more Dwarves, and regardless of that, the King was their sovereign and Kronivar no less a part of Itharia than any other town. This led to further debate and complaints against the King, but it seemed to Iaven that people were anxious about the impending war and wanted an excuse to grumble.

Just as Iaven began thinking about where he might end up if war broke out soon, he noticed Rhiane passing through the room. She looked around and caught his gaze. Iaven tensed as he saw her coming over to his table.

"Some wagons are leaving for the South Road, the day after tomorrow," she told him, "I can tell you where to find them, if you're still interested."

Iaven was unsure what to say. Her glance told him she already knew he wouldn't be leaving yet. "Well, I was thinking of going, but..." Iaven paused, wondering how much he should say, "We have to go up to the Castle first, before we go."

"Joining the troops, then, are you?" Rhiane's tone indicated she found this somewhat unlikely. "Or still deciding what to do?"

Iaven was a bit embarrassed his state of mind was so transparent, even as he felt a little relief. Rhiane's dark brown eyes met his own. She was so willing to listen, the urge to tell her everything rose up in him again. He dropped his gaze to the table. "No, I... it's... a friend of mine died, and—" He stopped as the words stuck in his throat.

"You want to tell me about it?" Rhiane sat lightly on the edge of the bench across from Iaven. Encouraged by the privacy provided by the booth's wooden walls, Iaven almost almost began talking, when he wondered if it was selfish to burden her with it all. Or even, recalling the Splides, if it was safe.

"I'm not on duty yet for a little while," Rhiane told him, sensing his reluctance. "You just seem like something bad's happened to you, and if I can help..."

Under the kindness of her inquisitive gaze, Iaven could resist no longer. He began telling her, slowly at first and in general terms, about Cedric's death and his travels away from home, leaving out any mention of the sword and gems. She even seemed interested in hearing about life in Hillbrook. He wondered why, and then realized that, apart from blatant and unwelcome flirting, most Men and Dwarves in Kronivar probably saw Rhiane only as someone to take their orders or complaints. Perhaps she had sensed something different about Iaven, even found him interesting; or, he thought suddenly, maybe just amusing.

It occurred to him, too, that she was not like any of the barmaids he had ever encountered. She was alert and concerned about him, beyond the attention given a customer in hopes for a tip; she appeared genuinely interested in what he was saying. Rhiane was around his age, intelligent and pretty, and Iaven wondered how it was that she came to work at the inn. He thought of asking, but she encouraged him to continue his story, and so he did, finding great comfort in talking to her.

Much to his amazement, Iaven told her more than he had intended. Trying to describe his situation while avoiding mention of the sword or gems, he realized he had already told her about them, though he had at least left out the history behind them. She listened to it all, nodding and prompting him with questions when he stopped momentarily, showing neither surprise nor disappointment, weighing everything carefully. At last Iaven finished and sat back in the booth.

"Well, that's all very interesting..." Rhiane looked at him, seeing his relief; he had been talking for some time. She stood, hesitating. "I've got to start work right now, but we'll talk more later, especially about your trip to the Castle. You must be thirsty after your long tale, let me get you something on the house."

"Yes, I'd like that, thanks," Iaven said, and watched her walk over to the bar. He wondered how much she really had listened to him, but was thankful all the same for a chance to talk, though he felt ashamed at having gone on at such length. He considered apologizing for it when Rhiane returned with a frothy mug of dark beer.

"Thank you so much," he said, meaning more than just the beer.

"Oh, don't worry about it," she said. "It's interesting to hear how other people live. I've been meaning to see the Foothills for awhile now, but business keeps me here..."

"I'd love to show it to you sometime," Iaven replied, immediately scolding himself for having let the sentiment slip out without thinking.

"I'll remember that," Rhiane said. She was about to add something, when the two longshoremen started shouting for her, banging their empty mugs. She went over to them and Iaven sighed, hoping she'd forget his awkwardness and obvious interest in her.

Zammond noticed Iaven's mood had cleared a little and was glad to see it. Iaven joined them for dinner and an evening stroll around Old Town. While they were all pleased that Iaven had, for the most part, returned to his old self, only Zammond suspected Iaven had become distracted with something else. Since Iaven volunteered nothing, Zammond became all the more curious and determined to find out what it was.

Zammond's suspicions were confirmed the next day when, at lunch, Rhiane came to serve them and introduced herself to the rest of Iaven's friends, whom she seemed to have some idea of already. She talked and joked with them more easily now, telling them about the local establishments and ships coming in and out of port, with many colorful anecdotes. After work she joined them at their table, talking with them late into the evening, long past closing time.

Iaven and his friends stayed on in Kronivar three more days, never at a loss for things to do or see. Their rapport with Rhiane had become relaxed and friendly, and she allayed their uneasiness of the city. She had been working at *The Brown Badger* for almost two years now and knew all of Kronivar quite well. Yet, outgoing as she was, Iaven noticed she spoke little about herself and was even reserved at times, despite being at ease around them.

Over the course of their stay in Kronivar, Iaven thought of Rhiane more and more. Orven's stealing of the gem still rankled and he still mourned Cedric, but whenever anything weighed down Iaven's spirit, he found himself reassured by Rhiane's dark eyes and radiant smile. Amongst food and friends at the *Badger*, Iaven could postpone his uncertain future, like a fire-warmed cabin shutting out a howling blizzard on a dark winter night.

Iaven and his friends continued to pay room and board, their money dwindling away. He knew they would not be able to stay in Kronivar much longer. At the Castle they'd all be expected to join the army, and Iaven dreaded going there, feeling the weight of obligation. During the night, and whenever he was alone, the inevitability of it all gnawed away at him. He would have to say good-bye to Rhiane and leave for the mountains; and then part company with Hobley and Zammond when they joined the troops. Beyond that, he did not know what would happen, and that seemed the most frightening thing of all.

Chapter 13.
In the Shadow of the Storm

By their fifth night at *The Brown Badger* in Kronivar, their money was almost gone. The dwarves gathered for supper in the main common room and Rhiane greeted them and came to take their order.

"Well, tomorrow morning we head for the mountains and the Castle," said Iaven.

"I have a great-uncle who lives at the Castle," Rhiane told them. "I've been thinking of going there for a visit."

"Come with us, then," said Iaven, suddenly in good cheer. "It's not safe to travel alone..." He realized how he sounded. "If you'd like, that is." Nothing he could say now would save him from embarrassment.

"Tomorrow morning..." Rhiane thought it over. "Yes, I could go, but it would have to be early."

"You'll come?" Iaven glanced around. No one seemed to have any objections. "We were going to leave right after breakfast."

Rhiane paused before answering, as if to quiet him down. "I know someone who can take us as far as Greensward," she said, "though we'd have to leave before sunrise." Her voice was quieter now and more serious. Iaven had calmed down and resolved not to show his feelings so easily.

"I suppose we could make it." Iaven watched her without even looking to see if the others agreed to the earlier departure time.

"Alright then, I'll see you downstairs here, before sunrise tomorrow." Rhiane glanced around at all of them, and then left their table.

Iaven wondered what this new turn of events would bring. She wasn't coming for his sake; that seemed impossible. But rather than worry why she was going, he was merely glad she was.

Though they had not objected openly, the other dwarves had mixed feelings about Rhiane joining them. The suddenness of her offer was strange; she'd practically invited herself along, knowing how Iaven would respond. They wondered what Iaven had told Rhiane, recalling how Leland and Lexter had befriended and betrayed them.

"Iaven, do you really think this is a good idea? I mean, considering what happened in Miastolas..." Zammond began.

"She's not like that at all," Iaven snapped at Zammond. "I've talked to her a lot lately—"

"Too much," said Zammond.

"—and I know her a lot better than we knew the Splides. Besides, maybe her great-uncle there can help get us an audience with the King."

"Maybe," said Tillmore, "But who this uncle, and what does he do? He could be cleaning the stables or shackled in the dungeon for all we know."

"Oh, I'm sure it's not like that," Iaven replied. "Besides, there's five of us and only one of her— what could she possibly do?"

"If she were a man I'd agree with you," said Hobley, "but with a woman you never know. It's different."

"Hob, come on..." said Iaven.

"Well, I suppose we have gotten to know her a little, and we do like her, too," Hobley added, "though I still can't help think what nice fellows those Splide brothers seemed to be, at first. And there's just something about her, I don't know how to put it…"

"That she could have had a higher station in life than what she has?" said Tillmore. "Perhaps she's only biding her time, looking for an opportunity."

"Something like that," agreed Hobley.

"If Iaven wants her to come, that's fine with me," added Wilbur. "Maybe we're worrying about nothing."

"I hope you're right," said Tillmore.

That evening they prepared for the next day's early departure, discussing what they knew about Rhiane and finding it hard to substantiate their suspicions. They finally agreed that the arrangement was only temporary. Seeing how meeting Rhiane had consoled Iaven, they would not begrudge him his wish even if it did seem against their better judgment.

The following morning was a cold and brisk one. The dwarves finished packing just as light was breaking in the eastern sky. The inn was empty and quiet downstairs. Rhiane was waiting there, and they all set out together.

The streets were deserted. A dawn chorus of birds chirped exuberantly in a tree. Rhiane led them down a side street, around a corner, and they wound their way towards the southeastern edge of town where she said a wagon would be awaiting them. The path they took seemed indirect to Iaven, and he noticed Rhiane glancing nervously down the streets. Once or twice someone in the distance seemed to notice them, but no one approached them, so Iaven said nothing.

A slow light grew on the eastern horizon. Soon the sky paled and day broke. Iaven hoped the sun's faint warmth would soften the morning chill. The sky was dappled with tufts of white clouds, their edges rimmed with gold and waning purple shadow. Somber contentment settled in as the dwarves realized this would be the last leg of their journey together. Hobley and Zammond were eager to join the King's troops, and the others were anxious to see the Castle although they did not intend to stay. The weather was cooling, and the three of them still had the trip back to Hillbrook which would not be as merry as the trip north had been.

At last they arrived in an alleyway, where a man sat on a hay wagon waiting for them. As they neared he caught sight of Rhiane, nodding to her and surveying the dwarves to see what kind of folk they might be. The driver was a handsome, well-built man, sharp eyes watching from under a strong brow. Dark hair hung to his collar, framing a stern expression. He reigned in the two chestnut mares harnessed to the wagon, both as anxious to leave as he was. Iaven noticed how he scanned the buildings nearby as if to see whether anyone was watching their departure. Rhiane, too, was cautious as they approached.

"Denrolt!" Rhiane said when they were near enough not to have to shout.

"M'lady," Denrolt nodded, "Was it clear when you left?"

"Seemed so," Rhiane answered. "These are the dwarves I told you about. They're coming to the Castle with me, and can be trusted. Two of them are even joining the army."

Denrolt cast an appraising glance at the dwarves, his eyes meeting Hobley's and Zammond's as a momentary glimmer of a smile acknowledged them. Iaven saw how Denrolt knew who was joining without being told, and felt ashamed to be left out of his gaze.

"Climb aboard and let's be off then. People are about, and we must get underway."

Rhiane unhitched the back of the wagon and Iaven and the others climbed on. Rhiane came after them, closing and securing the back railing. They sat back looking out over bundles of hay, Denrolt snapped his whip with a shout, and off they went.

As they rode through town, Iaven was curious as to the need for secrecy. He wondered who the driver was and how Rhiane knew him, and almost said something to Rhiane about it, when Denrolt hollered to the horses and the wagon slowed abruptly.

Near the city limits the road wound past an old outbuilding. As they drew closer, half a dozen men and a few dwarves appeared from behind it and stood blocking the road. Several held axes, one had a pitchfork, and two men were on horseback. They stood in the road unmoving, watching the wagon approach.

Denrolt brought the wagon to a halt a short distance away. "'Morning to you! Aside, good sirs, and let us pass!" he commanded.

The men and dwarves remained in the road, staring with haughty eyes. At last the one with the pitchfork stepped forward menacingly. "Off to the Castle, eh? Didn't think we were on to her? Give her over and we'll let you pass!"

"Stand aside, you brigands!" All pretense of civility had left Denrolt's deep voice. Iaven trembled at the sound, like a sudden boom of thunder from a clear blue sky. Here was no ordinary wagon driver. Near him, Rhiane crouched low in the hay, keenly eyeing the men in the road like a mountain lion ready to pounce. She motioned them all to stay low. Iaven cringed, fearing what lay ahead. He did not turn back to see his friends' reactions, though he could feel their exasperation with him for bringing Rhiane along.

"Found a few others, I see?" said the man with the pitchfork. Iaven peered out between the wooden rails and hay. The group in the road stood tensed, weapons ready. Their measured gazes shifted between Denrolt, the man with the pitchfork, and the wagon. Iaven guessed that they were deciding whether to attack the wagon and if they were outnumbered. He watched them move a few steps closer, their formation tightening into a semi-circle several yards down the road from the wagon.

"I'll not tell you again! Stand aside and be gone!" Denrolt's voice was terrible, firm and unshaken. The dwarves and men hesitated, and only the man with the pitchfork met Denrolt's gaze.

Suddenly Denrolt let out a sharp, abrupt shout that made the men in the road recoil a step. With a crack of the whip he sent the horses at full gallop through the roadblock of men. They whinnied and snorted, plunging forward and receiving ill-timed blows as they passed. Several men and dwarves were knocked to the ground, while others jumped aside in time, the two on horseback forced to sidestep to avoid them.

The wagon rocked and creaked and Iaven thought it would collapse from the strain. Hay fell onto the road and everyone hung on. As they rode out of town, the men ran behind them, shouting, cursing, and brandishing their weapons, finally coming to a halt in the road as the wagon drew farther away.

But the two men on horseback kept up with them. One rode up alongside on the left, his windblown hair and wild grin unnerving Iaven. The man drew a short sword and laughed.

"What other spies have we here?" He sneered and raised his sword arm to strike. Iaven sat up and pulled away from the side of the wagon. The man brought his horse closer, and swung his leg around, stepping onto the railing and into the wagon. Iaven, Zammond, and Wilbur raised their swords. Tillmore wielded his long-bladed knife and Hobley hefted his axe. The man leapt at them and attacked, faster than they expected. He stood tall above them, swaying and keeping his balance, forcing them to remain pressed together. His horse moved away from the wagon as the other rider drew closer.

Iaven and Zammond fought back, but the man held them at bay. Iaven pushed forward on one knee and swung at the man. He took a step back, and they thrust at him again. Their combined forces knocked him backward, and he tumbled over wagon's railing. But even as he fell, they ducked the swipes of the other man on horseback, who had them within reach.

Denrolt drove the horses at a full gallop, but pulling the wagon, they could not outrun the horse and rider. Denrolt drew his sword and held it on his lap, watching the man out of the corner of his eye. Suddenly he yanked the reigns, slowing the horses and wagon. Just as the man on horseback was about to strike again, the wagon pulled back and he was next to Denrolt, who thrust his sword, catching him by surprise. The man swung again but Denrolt's sword caught his and knocked him off his horse.

The riderless horse slowed and fell behind the wagon. Denrolt drove on at full gallop. Once they were a safe distance away, he relaxed the horses' pace. Relieved, Iaven and the others sat back in the wagon.

"A rough ride, m'lady, but all's well!" Denrolt turned and addressed Rhiane, evidently having regained his good humor.

The rest of the morning and afternoon they rode along the West Road past the farmlands and meadows between Kronivar and the crossroads at Greensward. Soon after sunrise they passed fields where flocks of brown, black-necked geese were waking and foraging. By afternoon, the geese were flying high overhead in long, stringy V-formations, honking mournfully as they passed, on their way to warmer lands far away in southern Feäthiadreya. Iaven watched them go and longed to join them.

During the ride Iaven burned with questions for Rhiane, fearing he had assumed too much. He thought it best to wait until after Denrolt left them in

Greensward. Meadowlands flew past, where hundreds of clusters of milkweed pods were breaking open, the soft, white, silky fluff of their seeds borne away on the wind. The day had warmed but clouds persisted, and twice a light drizzle fell on them. Taller and wider expanses of clouds blew in from over the sea and Kronivar. It was quiet now, and Rhiane was riding up front, talking with Denrolt. Tillmore and Wilbur lay napping in the hay. Hobley sat back against the railing, dozing on and off, occasionally interjecting a comment into Iaven and Zammond's conversation. Zammond quietly speculated about their attackers, while Iaven wondered what connection Rhiane had to it all and whether or not it changed what he thought about her.

Just before dusk they arrived in Greensward. Denrolt let them off on the edge of town, wishing them a safe journey. Rhiane invited him to join them for supper, but he politely declined. He had other duties and could not stay, much as he wished he could. Without knowing quite why, Iaven was somehow relieved to see him go.

"Close to suppertime, isn't it?" Iaven remembered the inn where the dwarves had eaten on their way to Kronivar.

"If we keep moving, I think we can make the Gundithe Plateau before nightfall," said Rhiane. Seeing the disgruntled looks on their faces, she adopted a softer tone. "I would love to stay indoors tonight as much as any of you, believe me. But you saw how those men in the road were. I don't know if they'll try following us, but they might. I'd be safer —we'd be safer, up on the plateau. There's a niche carved in the rock there, so we'd be under cover if it rains."

"And just who were those men and dwarves, anyway?" said Zammond, "And who are you, that they'd come after you like that? All this sneaking around!"

"I'll tell you all about it, I promise. Really, I will. It's not at all what you think. But we should leave soon and take our supper with us."

No one liked the prospect of spending the night on the plateau, but they knew Rhiane was right. And they would still be on the road, and far more tired, had she not found them a ride. Each of them knew they ought to help her, even if it meant some discomfort. Stilled by her serious tone and dark, pleading eyes, there was little they could do but acquiesce.

The dwarves looked to Iaven. "All right," he said, "Let's get going."

They came upon *The Crossroads Inn*, and Rhiane agreed to stay for supper if it didn't take long. The dwarves were glad to eat a fine hot meal. Rhiane ordered their provisions for the rest of the journey, paid for them, and packed them herself.

"We might be able to get to the Castle in a day or two if we start from the plateau very early tomorrow morning," Rhiane told them, "Though we'll take extra supplies along, just in case."

"I'll be glad to carry it," Wilbur interjected.

"I'm sure you will," said Tillmore, "Just don't be too quick to lighten it as we go!"

"In case of *what*?" said Zammond, annoyed with Wilbur and Tillmore.

"I take it you've never traveled the mountains?" Rhiane flashed Zammond a knowing look.

They left the inn, heading east to where the mountain road began. Along the way they found good-sized branches for making walking sticks. The ground rose and within the hour they approached the foot of the mountains. There, great pine-covered slopes climbed into the sky. Further in, steep inclines and cliffs rose even higher, and in the haze beyond them rocky summits reached into the clouds. The descending sun cast a golden glow across the wide, broad shoulders of rock and dark expanses of pine. Iaven gazed up at the mountains, their enormous breadth and dizzying heights hinting at wearying days of travel ahead.

The road soon veered off to the north, clinging to the sides of the slopes as it wound its way upward. It was wide enough for two wagons to pass one another and rose gradually, never more than a horse and cart could manage.

"The road curves back and forth, around the slopes," Rhiane explained, leading the way. "But for those on foot there are shorter, steeper paths that cut across and rejoin the roads further up. We can use them and save time, though it's certainly no less of a climb."

They found the paths, wide stairways climbing steeply, hewn from the rock of the slope. Iaven was ready to question Rhiane further, but found himself short of breath as they went up one stairway after another. Once in awhile they rejoined the road again, stopping to rest, breathing hard with pounding hearts.

Their climb went on for a while and Iaven began to feel he would prefer to take the gently sloping road the rest of the way even if it would take longer. But after a while they emerged onto the road, and Rhiane began walking along it.

"Here we are," Rhiane said. "The plateau's just up ahead."

The Gundithe Plateau was a large, crescent-shaped shelf of flat rock, about seventy feet from the mountain wall to the edge at its widest point, and over sixty yards long from where they stood to the far end, where the road resumed its climb. Whether it was a natural formation or had been carved into the mountain as the road was, Iaven could not tell, but the wide flat plain of ground was a welcome sight after so much steep climbing.

During the climb they had faced the mountain, watching their steps, but now they walked on the plateau, gazing out over forests and meadowlands spreading below them to the west. The sun hovered in the thin strip of sky under broad furrows of clouds streaked with soft scarlet and purple. High above the land, the world seemed wider and vaster. Beneath the plateau's edge the road wound back and forth hugging the mountain slopes, each loop further down the mountainside. Lower still and farther away lay the houses and barns of Greensward, like little blocks strewn on a lawn, tiny wisps of smoke trickling from their chimneys. Past Greensward, the West Road disappeared toward the horizon through wide fields and meadows. Surrounding the meadowlands, dense forests spread over the world, Veskwood running to the north and Rundlewood sprawling to the south, both immense and endless, their treetops bright seas of fiery colors. Flocks of geese flew southward, descending with wings spread, gliding down into meadows and fields for the night.

Neither Iaven nor any of his friends had ever been so high above the ground, and they stood staring out over the landscape. Moments later, Rhiane called them over to the mountain wall. There a deep niche had been carved as a shelter area for travelers.

"We'd better get the fire going," said Hobley. The wide red sun sank as they watched, and the wind was growing cold. Hobley, Zammond, and Iaven collected kindling and soon the six of them were seated around a crackling fire just outside the niche in the rock wall.

"First, I want to thank you for letting me come with you," said Rhiane. "I know you're all wondering about me. I would have told you sooner, but I had to be sure I could trust you..."

"Trust *us*?" Zammond interrupted, "We took quite a chance trusting *you*, I'd say!"

"Yes, you did," Rhiane admitted, "And I thank you for that as well. There's unrest in Kronivar these days, as you have seen. Not much out loud and in the open, yet, but it's there, and growing. By some reckonings, Kronivar's got as many Men as Dwarves now, maybe more. Most still recognize the King, but there are discontents. Of course, that, in itself, is nothing new... Long ago, the days under King Varlen were difficult times; the Kingdom was growing to the north and south, and many were leaving the mountains. The Castle had much to oversee, and many demands were made upon it. The Elves and the Goblins had to be dealt with, as well as the Teskans and the building of Teska, and troubles with the Rundlewood Forest Road and the Gnomes. All these things affected the establishment of trade in Kronivar. And then there were the great cave-ins and mining disasters in Bottomcliffe. King Varlen knew they'd have difficulty in fulfilling their usual tribute, but the need for swords, weapons, tools, and such things was especially great. In the long run, everyone fared better, but not all agreed with the Castle's handling of the kingdom's affairs.

"And then there was the war with the Goblins almost a hundred years ago, during the reign of King Orglen. He was killed during the war, and his son Aardgen became king. His reign was a far cry from his father's; he didn't leave the Castle as much, and rarely traveled or visited the cities. Kronivar and the lands around it were growing fast, and many dwarves were leaving the mountains to live there. The King knew little of what was going on there, or so it seemed. He relied on his advisors and lost the hold on the cities that his father had reestablished over the years. So, King Aardgen was loved more by Men than Dwarves, some of whom claimed he had weakened the Kingdom. Many think his death was no accident, and that one of his own advisors was involved.

"Since then, Aardgen's son, King Jordgen, has wielded a stronger hand over the cities, but their resistance is stronger too, especially back when Prastlin was Duke and Lord Governor of Kronivar. Now that Grawson is Duke and the garrison's full there's no more trouble, but the separatists —gangs of renegades like the ones we saw— are gaining support and growing. More and more men from across the sea have settled in Kronivar, and some have joined with the dwarves who think Kronivar should become its own nation-state. Among both Dwarves and Men such unrest is growing."

"And these were the men and dwarves who stopped us?" asked Zammond.

"Yes. Few are so open or daring," Rhiane replied, "But they are becoming bolder, and growing in number. They now hold secret meetings, in houses or cabins on the outskirts of town. Just how many they are, and whether they pose a threat, are some of the things I've been trying to determine."

"So you *are* a spy, then!" said Hobley.

Rhiane smiled. "In a manner of speaking. King Jordgen has many troops stationed in the garrison in Kronivar, but it's at places like the *Badger* that you really hear what's going on. The King wants to avoid war and has been quite cautious, and some feel he's not doing enough to prepare. But anyone who's lived in the Castle knows it's far more complicated than what many of the people —even in Kronivar— realize. So, after much deliberation, my great-uncle and my father and I agreed that I would take a job in Kronivar to find out what I could. It worked well, for some time, but there's been more activity since the threat of war has grown. The danger, of course, was that sooner or later I'd be found out by them."

"So now you're going back to the Castle?" Iaven asked.

"I am," Rhiane said, "and with a good deal to report. The separatists have allies in the Kronivar garrisons, and even in the Castle, keeping a close watch on things. That makes it difficult for us to find out where they are meeting and when. You can see why I couldn't talk about it. If Denrolt heard me telling you anything, he'd reprimand me for it! He's one of the King's best men in Kronivar." Rhiane paused. "That's also why we couldn't stay in Greensward. We're some distance from Kronivar, but it's better to be careful. There's only one other inn besides *The Crossroads*, so we'd be easy to find. Though I doubt they'd bother coming all the way up here on the plateau looking for us."

"I can certainly see why they wouldn't," said Tillmore, pulling his blanket around him as he sat by the fire. The sun had gone down and a cold wind was blowing steadily from the northwest.

"So who is this great-uncle of yours at the Castle? A nobleman, or something?" Wilbur asked, leaning back against the rock.

Rhiane smiled guiltily. "Not exactly," she said, watching their reaction. "My father is Arlen Frosthelm, nephew to King Jordgen. My grandfather, Haden Frosthelm, was Jordgen's younger brother, who died while my father was still young"

Hobley whistled in astonishment. "And those fellows in the road this morning knew that?"

"Not very likely," Rhiane said, "I grew up in the Castle, so they wouldn't know me at all in Kronivar. And, of course, I changed my manner of dress and appearance. Nor would anyone expect to find me at a place like the *Badger*. Still, they must have known I was spying for the Castle, or something like that. I could have been killed if they'd found out sooner, or if I hadn't been as careful."

"So I take it 'Rhiane' is also an assumed name?" Iaven tried not to sound as upset as he was. He wondered if anything he knew about her was true.

"No, it's just a middle name I use sometimes; it's shorter. My first name is Allelia. I have sister, Oellia, and yes, we were named after the Allelia and Oellia of legend from the Old Kingdom. I've gotten so used to 'Rhiane' now, after living in Kronivar, that it'll be a bit of a change to go back to 'Allelia' at the Castle. But you can still call me Rhiane."

All was dark now. Stars winked in the black void between tatters of cloud strewn across the night sky. Wispy veils passed slowly over the full moon. The dwarves continued talking and asking about life in the Castle, as Rhiane told them of banquets, balls, and celebrations to which she had gone; Counts, Dukes, and other nobles and visiting dignitaries she had met; and all the everyday goings-on at the Castle. Iaven listened and spoke very little. He wondered about Rhiane (*Allelia*, he reminded himself) and if her feelings for him had only been feigned in order to find out more about his friends and him. He knew so little about her and was ashamed to have talked about himself so much and so freely. His hopes had been foolish; she'd only been interested in safe passage to the Castle. His joy faded, leaving him cold and tired.

Soon the dwarves turned in to bed. His mind restless and reeling, Iaven volunteered for the first watch of the evening. The others, snug in their blankets, dozed off one by one until all was quiet. The fire had died down and Iaven was cold. He wandered over to the plateau's edge and sat on some low rocks, staring out over the vast expanse of dark landscape shrouded in the sullen glow of moonlight. Gazing down from the plateau, he gradually made out detail in the darkened land, and thought he could see the lights of Greensward. Faint sounds rose from below, the *crack!* of an ax blow, a dog barking, and a wolf howling far away. Across the land, moonlight dimmed and brightened through the passing cloud cover.

"Iaven..." The voice startled him; he had not even heard Rhiane approaching. "May I join you? I haven't been able to sleep."

"What? Sure... me neither," Iaven replied, turning back to the landscape.

Rhiane sat down next to him, and was silent. He could feel her looking at him, and finally gave in and turned to her.

"Iaven, I know what you must think," she began, waiting to see how he felt. "You can see why I had to be careful. But I do really like you, and I meant everything I said. I don't often meet someone like you. Certainly not in Kronivar. And in the Castle... well, it's different there, too. Everyone's caught up in what goes on there. That was another reason I went to live in Kronivar, to get away from it. You can't imagine what it's like growing up in the Castle, so far away up in mountains, spending most of your time there. And I really *would* like to see Hillbrook and the Foothills someday."

"Would you? I wouldn't mind being back there right now myself." Iaven was still upset, but Rhiane sounded sincere. And he had told her too much to be able to hide what he was feeling from her.

Rhiane looked out across the night landscape with Iaven. A cold, damp wind blew on them. "After all those years in the Castle, I wanted to travel, see things, go somewhere," she said.

"My father always encouraged us to travel when we could," Iaven said, "He always told us that he wanted us to have *'a view of the world wider than my own'*. How I would have loved to go traveling with him."

Iaven paused and Rhiane remained quiet, watching and listening. "And now here I am," Iaven continued, "Out in the mountains, on my way to the Castle, the kingdom on the brink of war. And soon I'll be returning to Hillbrook, and learning a new job at the smithy; I don't even know if I'll like it. I doubt it. But I suppose I'll get used to it, at least."

"I know you'll miss Zammond and Hob," Rhiane said, "And I know you don't see yourself joining the army with them —and that's fine," she added. "But aren't you at least a little sad to see your adventures, your travels, coming to an end?"

Iaven considered it. "I am, in a way," he said. "But it'll be nice to be back home, too. Though it won't be quite the same anymore."

"What would you do," Rhiane asked, "if you could do anything you wanted, whatever you chose?"

Iaven was silent and continued looking out over the landscape. He was quiet for so long that Rhiane was about to say something when suddenly he spoke again. "I don't know," he said, "I always figured Orven and I would have the farm, so I never thought about it. I honestly don't know."

"For me it was just the opposite," Rhiane said. "I've always had certain duties, and expectations to live up to. Father always had plans for me, and probably would have married me off to someone by now had I stayed in the Castle. He would never have let me go to Kronivar if Uncle Jordgen hadn't convinced him. I'm not saying I mind Castle life; it's always been good. But it should be my choice, not just what's expected of me."

They sat listening to crickets and owls, feeling the wind on their faces. Iaven tried to imagine what her life must have been like.

"And in the past two years or so that I've lived in Kronivar, I've really come to like it; the sea, the cry of the gulls, the bells, the people coming and going, so many from distant lands. Sometimes when I wasn't working I'd go down to the docks and watch the ships pulling into harbor. One never knew what kinds of strange things they'd bring from afar. Like that clock in the bell tower, in the New Town Square..." She turned to Iaven. "And now I guess that's all over with, at least for some time."

"You could go back after the war, I suppose," said Iaven, "though it wouldn't be the same."

"No," said Rhiane, "and I do miss the Castle sometimes, too. It's been awhile since I've been there and seen everyone."

"At least you have a place to go back to," said Iaven. As they sat on the plateau's edge, Iaven's thoughts returned to Hillbrook. In the quiet, still night, overlooking the darkened land, he could calmly contemplate how his life had changed. He considered going to Cedric's to talk about it and caught himself. Tears rose as Cedric's death hit him full force. He had wanted Cedric to fill his father's role; but in the end he could not. Iaven suddenly realized that he had never cried or mourned his father. For years following his father's disappearance and death, Iaven had refused to give up hope; one mourned only for the dead. Over the years, he had come to accept his father's death, but Cedric had been there to help him. As he stared out into the deep, clouded blackness, he felt terribly alone, and at last his mourning came.

Rhiane sat close to him and said nothing. She put her arms around Iaven as he leaned into her, embracing him and holding him near.

They sat there awhile, until Iaven's tears were spent. Iaven returned Rhiane's embrace. They sat side by side for some time, watching the bright round ball of the full moon passing behind the clouds. At last Rhiane could no longer stay awake. She kissed Iaven goodnight and went over to where the dwarves were sleeping, and woke Wilbur who was scheduled for the next watch.

Iaven stood up and stretched, with a long, relaxing yawn. Rhiane had become dear to him, and he was glad she was along with them. Iaven felt a heavy, soft sleepiness that he had not known for a long time. Wilbur, rubbing his eyes and came over to where Iaven was standing. Stifling a yawn, he assured Iaven that he would stay awake and said good night.

By their campsite, Iaven spread his bedroll on the hard ground, and slept far more soundly than he had in a long time.

The next day dawned cold and damp. Dim veins of sunlight filtered through the leaden, gray canopy of marbled cloud. The dwarves rose early, stiff and unwilling to emerge from their blankets. They ate a meager breakfast and were soon packed and on their way again.

The Mountain Road wound slowly around steep inclines and outcroppings. Footpaths left and rejoined the road, and stone stairs connected loops of the road in places, making their way shorter but steeper. Sometimes they walked on the road, which was easier going than the stairs. A horse and cart heading for Kronivar passed them, the driver smiling at the dwarves laboring uphill.

Above them the clouds thickened into a gray, overcast pall. The dwarves moved sluggishly, dragging their feet and breathing in the moist and heavy air. They leaned on their walking sticks, stopping to rest at every opportunity. By early afternoon they were several mountains into the range, and broad vistas opened before them as the path bent around inclines. Wide basins and valleys spread out below, densely forested, tall pines rising close together. They marveled at the heights they had ascended, looking over precipices down into deep valleys where mists hovered and hung low over the trees. Lengths of road often were visible on the mountainsides ahead of them, reminding them of the wearying miles to go. Far off, faint shapes of rock shoulders and peaks towered into the clouds. Cries of birds echoed off distant mountain walls in the silence.

That afternoon the clouds massed thick and dark, the pale gray sky dimming to twilight. After stopping for a small, cold lunch, the dwarves were drowsy. Only with a great effort did they resume the climb, Rhiane leading the way. They left the road and took a more steeply sloping footpath that zigzagged across an incline. Long series of steps took them higher still, veering away from the road below. A drizzle of rain made them fear the worst. As they went up the steps, great low rumbles of thunder sounded across the valley. A soft, hushing sound broke and drew closer, and soon large cold drops of rain began pelting them faster and faster.

Peals of thunder broke now, gaining in intensity, rippling, rattling, and booming across the heavens. Gradually the rain increased to a heavy downpour, and soon the dwarves' hoods and shoes were soaked and cold. Their heads hung low and they watched as water ran down the steps around their feet. Thunder banged and crackled, sudden and startling in its volume, and sharp, jagged lightning flashed overhead, momentarily lighting the path and rock around them.

"We'll look for shelter as soon as we get back up on the road!" Rhiane shouted down to them, her voice faint and carried away by wind and storm. They continued climbing, but could not increase their pace. The rock was wet and water ran down in widening rivulets until the steps began to resemble a waterfall. Soaked through and through, the dwarves struggled to continue ascending one step after another.

Wilbur had fallen back to the rear of the group and was trying to catch up to them. Instead of watching his step, in his haste he kept looking up to see how far behind he was falling. Suddenly the dwarves heard a shout and scraping behind them. It was Wilbur, sliding down several steps in water and mud. His pack rolled away, picking up speed as it bounded off the stairs, and Wilbur would have followed had he not caught onto the thin branches of a bush by the path. He hung on, trying to regain his footing and shouting for help as rain ran down the rock around him.

The others stopped and turned. They carefully descended the stairs, finding it even more difficult than climbing them had been. At last Wilbur got a better grip, and Hobley gave him his hand and helped him to his feet.

"I'm sorry," Wilbur said, distraught. "I was trying to catch up. I've lost the pack..." He turned and looked down the mountainside but the pack was gone, washed away over the steeper part of the path.

"We've got to keep going," Rhiane yelled from above them, "I can see the road up ahead."

Hobley let Wilbur pass him and together they continued the climb, water running off their hoods. Wilbur gave more apologies on the way up, but no one said anything. At last they stepped up to where the path met the road again.

"We'd better stay on the road now," said Rhiane. Glad to have wider, flatter ground beneath their feet, they trudged up the road as rainwater ran downhill past them in a shallow stream.

They thought the storm would let up but it did not. No matter how the road turned and wound, the wind and rain always seemed to be against them. In the valleys they could see the tops of pine trees swaying as the wind rolled across them. As they came upon a shallow incline rising from the roadside into some cliffs, Hobley glanced up at the mountain.

"Look!" Hobley said, pointing up the slope. "Shelter!" He indicated a rock shelf over an opening into a shallow cave. The climb was slow but not treacherous, and at last they reached the overhang. They entered and found the cave to be cold and damp but drier and enclosed. The dwarves dropped their packs with a slosh in a corner and sat down to rest by the wall. The cave was about fifteen feet across, narrowing into a crevice twenty feet in. It was a shadowy, hard, cold place, normally of little or no interest to travelers, but in the raging storm it almost seemed cozy. Everyone agreed to stay there until the storm subsided. The sky was too gloomy and dark to say how late in the afternoon it was. Tired, they sat glumly, waiting, but the storm showed no sign of abating. Soon it looked as though they would be staying there for the night.

After an hour their stomachs began grumbling and they realized there was nothing left to eat; the rest of their food and other provisions had been washed away with Wilbur's pack. Wilbur began apologizing again, and after that no one had the heart to complain or say anything more about it.

"We wouldn't be able to make a fire anyway," Zammond pointed out, trying to make Wilbur feel better.

"We'll eat well when we get to the Castle tomorrow, don't worry!" Rhiane assured them, though they would have preferred plain food right away rather than wait for the finest of banquets. They were all curious as to what sort of fare was served at the Castle, but no one wanted to talk or think about food and end up even hungrier than they were.

"At least we're warm and dry in here," said Zammond.

"Well, drier, anyway, if not warmer," said Tillmore.

Zammond glanced around at them. Iaven, Rhiane, Hobley, Tillmore, and especially Wilbur looked wet and miserable, and everyone was bored and irritable. Outside the cave entrance, the rain came down as strong as before, now and then pouring even harder for a short time.

"We were fortunate to find this cave, weren't we?" Zammond pointed out.

"True..." said Iaven.

"Looking out at the storm reminds me of that old farm song, the indoors one," Zammond said.

"Not now," said Iaven.

"What song is that?" asked Rhiane.

"Don't encourage him!" Hobley sighed. "He's going to try to cheer us up."

"Well, why not?" Rhiane looked from one to the other, slightly confused.

"Being annoying is one thing," said Tillmore, "Doing so with the best of intentions makes it even worse."

Rhiane looked to Zammond. "I'd like to hear it."

Now Zammond seemed hesitant and looked at the others.

"Oh, go ahead, then," said Tillmore, "Get it over with!"

Zammond cleared his throat, and began singing,

> *When darkening skies with leaden cloud,*
> *Lightning bright and thunder loud,*
> *Drop icy sheets of chilling rain*
> *That spatter on the windowpane,*
> *How nice it is to be indoors!*
> *When lightning cracks and thunder roars,*
> *How nice it is to be indoors!*

When winter winds shriek through the trees,
And all the ponds and puddles freeze,
When sharp cold grips and windows frost
And days grow gray as light is lost,
How nice it is to be indoors!
When gales blow off icy shores
How nice it is to be indoors!

When snow banks cover fallen leaves
And icicles hang from the eaves
I'll hurry home, inside the gates
To where a steaming kettle waits
How nice it is to be indoors!
Let snowstorms wage their wintry wars,
How nice it is to be indoors!

And when my clothes are warm and dried
I'll rest awhile, by fireside
Or on my pillow, tucked in bed,
Beneath a downy quilted spread,
How nice it is to be indoors!
When wind outside my window roars,
How nice it is to be indoors!

So let it rain! Let it snow!
Let it pour! Let it blow!
In blizzards, drizzles, and downpours
How nice it is to be indoors!

After giving in, the dwarves were cheered a little by memories the song evoked. But in the end, thoughts of home, fireside, hot meals, and warm beds only made them more aware of their present misery, and even more homesick than they already were.

Chapter 14.
A Deal Gone Sour

"It would have been better to meet in Bottomcliffe." Lexter was still upset. It was close to nightfall and the Splides' wagon was on the West Road between Greensward and Kronivar. During the last few hours the storm had passed overhead and to the east. They took off their hoods and unbuttoned their coats, wet, cold, and in ill humor.

"Well, I didn't really have a choice," Leland retorted, "Besides, I told you, there were other more important considerations; better things to bargain for, like whether or not we can get them to buy those bucklers and shields from Iaf. So I agreed on Kronivar, as they wanted."

"Easy for *you* to say! *You're* not a wanted man there!" Lexter complained.

"That was years ago!" Leland shrugged it off. "You really think they're still after you? Besides, Kronivar's a big place. And I'm sure old Reuben and his minions have moved on to other business by now."

"That's not what I heard from Harald," said Lexter. "One of the bounty hunters told him there was still a price on my head there."

"There is? How much?"

Lexter hesitated. "Two hundred."

"Only two hundred!" Leland laughed. "Well, I hope your head is worth more than that tonight! I have a hunch the dealing's going to be intense. These fellows *do* mean business... and that's good business for us."

Lexter grunted. "At least we could have met them in a less public place than the *Badger*."

"I told you, we won't be dealing *there*; they want to be sure we're alone. They've likely set the meeting place at the last minute, too, just to be safe. Probably on the outskirts of town somewhere. Precautions! Shows how much they need this deal."

"But how badly do *we* need it?" Lexter replied. "I know, I know... after this we'll be set until spring. Well, I do look forward to that. For once, not having to haul this stuff around in the cold..."

"So where shall we winter this year, then? Back in Tolgard with Linus and Leander? Or in southern Feäthiadreya, around the archipelagoes?"

"Alright, alright!" Lexter pleaded. "Let's get done with it. The sooner we're away from here the better."

And so they drove on to Kronivar.

They arrived in the Old Town neighborhood just as the last of the shops were closing, and pulled into the dooryard of *The Brown Badger* where they secured their horse to a hitching post. The tarp pulled over the crates in the back of the wagon was drenched. They checked to be sure it was still securely bound and left it on in case it rained later. Lexter was pleased at how inconspicuous it looked, considering the crates contained enough weaponry for a small army. After throwing a coin to the yard-boy, who sat watching people's horses while they dined, they went to the side door.

"I see young Eagan's still the yard-boy here," said Lexter, "He was about fourteen when I was last here; how he's grown! I wonder how much the *Badger* has changed."

"Enough for your sake, I hope!" said Leland, "And *you've* gotten bigger around the middle yourself since then; no one would recognize you anyway."

The *Badger* was warm and dry inside. Flames flickered in wall sconces, lighting the dark wood walls. The smell of food and drink mingled with the thick aroma of pipe smoke and the din of longshoremen, shopkeepers, woodsmen, smiths, forgers, and gravers who frequented the place. Although Lexter was hungry and glad to rest, he warily regarded everyone around them, sure he would come across someone who had known him. He and Leland slipped through the common room and took a high-walled booth in the back corner. There they would be out of the way while they waited for Trelt, who was to take them to the meeting. They sat down, and Lexter slid into the far back corner behind the table where he might avoid notice while still keeping an eye on things himself.

"Well, anyone you know?" Leland inquired. "It's been what, almost three years now, hasn't it? All your friends are probably gone, and how many of them lived in Old Town anyway?"

"It's not my *friends* that I'm worried about," said Lexter. He thought for a moment. "On the other hand, if they've fallen on hard times, who knows. It would be an easy two hundred."

Just then Lexter saw a thin, gaunt dwarf with a rather severe expression who emerged from the crowd and came over to their table. At first Lexter thought it was someone who knew him. He wondered what the dwarf wanted, and found he instinctively disliked him.

"Trelt," said Leland, "this is my brother, Lexter."

"Yes, I thought as much." Trelt cast a momentary glance at Lexter, who had been ready to reply to a greeting. "We've been waiting here. The two of you came alone?"

"Of course," said Leland, anxious to get going. Leland knew Trelt would not be given much role in the negotiations and sensed he was trying to make his position as go-between seem as important as he could, lording it over them a little.

"You've brought the entire shipment?" Trelt asked.

"For now. All what was discussed," Leland replied, growing impatient.

While Leland and Trelt went over the inventory and meeting arrangements, Lexter sat back, scanning the patrons of the murky smoke-filled common room. All strangers, he was relieved to find, and all busily engaged in eating, drinking, and spirited conversation. One merchant was talking to a woman with long auburn hair. After a moment she turned and looked in Lexter's direction, and they made eye contact. Lexter had the sudden strange feeling that he knew her, yet he could not quite remember who she was. He felt uneasy, as if the woman was an old flame of his, but there had been too many for him to recall her name. She turned away, and Lexter kept trying to remember, until his thoughts were broken off abruptly.

"—right Lexter?" Leland snapped at him. "Well?"

"Right," said Lexter.

"Then that's settled. We'll have one drink and then get going." Leland sat back and Trelt hailed a barmaid and placed an order. Lexter searched the room again for the woman, but she was gone. At least there hadn't been anyone else, he thought. He was anxious to go now, and it seemed an agonizingly long time before the barmaid returned with their drinks.

The three of them drained their mugs and got up to leave. Trelt left several coins on the table for the drinks, making sure the Splide brothers saw how reluctant he was to do so. As they left the bar, Lexter glanced around again but saw no one he knew.

Outside, night had fallen and a full moon was on the rise behind shreds of dark cloud. Leland untied the horse and climbed onto the bench of the wagon, and Lexter followed him, taking hold of the reins. Trelt climbed up after them and motioned Lexter to slide in closer to Leland. "I'll drive," he commanded. Lexter looked to Leland, who nodded, though Lexter could see in his eyes the same contempt for Trelt that he now felt.

The yard-boy opened the gate for them, smiling and nodding at them as they drove off. Trelt turned south and drove down the street, turning a corner here and there. He said little, and it became obvious the Splides would have to wait to find out where they were going. Lexter looked around to see if anyone was following them, but no one was. It was a cold, damp evening and the streets were deserted apart from lamplighters finishing their evening's work.

Soon they came to the eastern edge of town, where Leland and Lexter had driven in. Trelt took the horse at a quick gallop forward out of town, driving on for a bit. Then, just as suddenly, he reined in the horse and brought it to a stop, turned the wagon around and continued back the way they had come; anyone following behind them would have been in full view. Lexter had used the same trick himself, and was relieved to see the road was empty. Now they drove west again, but instead of entering the city, Trelt turned north and rode down farm roads along the edge of Kronivar. He made several more turns, until they were up in the northern outlying area, where houses were few and far between. Cabins and clapboard houses on stone foundations spread across the land, and beyond them the Veskwood Forest began, a dark wall lining the edge of the fields. They approached a cabin near the woods and Trelt slowed the horse to a trot. All was awash in the full moon's bluish-white glow, and Lexter saw quite clearly that no one was about. At last he could concentrate on the deal at hand.

As they drove around to the back of the cabin and pulled into the dooryard, two men with short swords hanging from their belts stepped out to greet them. Trelt secured the horse to a hitching post, and the two men escorted them inside the cabin.

In the cabin's main room, most of the furniture had been pushed aside along the walls. A great oaken table was set in the middle of the room with chairs around it. Greywood and Aranstone gathered there with a dozen armed men and dwarves, including Olmic.

Aranstone rose as the Splides were ushered in. "Greetings, Leland," he said in a stern but friendly voice. "At last we meet your illustrious brother." Aranstone offered Lexter his hand. "Thon Aranstone, and this is Greywood, my advisor," he said.

Lexter shook his hand, aware of the humor at his expense. Aranstone smiled and bid the Splides to sit at table with them. At a gesture from him, two crystal goblets of wine were poured and set before the Splides.

"We'll not toast the deal until it is done," said Aranstone, returning to his chair behind the table, "Yet we should not be without refreshment in the meantime." The man who had poured the Splides' wine set goblets for Aranstone and Greywood, filling them from the same decanter.

"Thank you," said Leland, "To success for us both!" He raised his glass and drank a sip.

Greywood brought out a list and passed it to Leland. "This is what we agreed upon. And below are a few other items we may be interested in, that you indicated you might have."

Leland took the list and considered it. "We might," he said, "and we have a few other things we thought *you* might be interested in as well..."

Lexter sat back and watched as the dealings began. He put in a word here and there to remind Leland of what they had, or didn't, and other casual comments the real meanings of which only Leland would understand. Some of the Splides' merchandise was less than they made it out to be, and sometimes they would even offer things they did not have but could get quickly, if the need arose.

Leland had always been shrewd at the business end of things, and took charge in most of their dealings. While this was fine with Lexter, he occasionally felt he was playing second fiddle. Even at their age, he was still the younger brother, and sometimes treated as such. But it *was* less work, too, he admitted to himself...

Lyla, thought Lexter, *That was her name; Lyla!* He had finally remembered the name of the auburn-haired woman from the inn. He had known her in Kronivar, but where? He seemed to remember good times with her, yet there was still something that made him uneasy and he had no idea why. Probably because things had turned out badly between them, like most of the women he had known. It had only been three years since he had left Kronivar for good (so he had thought at the time) and so much had happened since then. It all seemed so long ago. Now if only he could remember more about her...

"Lexter? Those broadswords?" Leland interrupted his thoughts.

"Yes, Crowcaw smithy, about a dozen, excellent condition," Lexter chimed in. He knew his attention was slipping, and resolved to be alert to what was going on.

Either something Leland had said was suspect, or Lexter's assertion had not been believed. Greywood eyed them carefully. "Perhaps if we could examine the broadswords in question..." He started to rise.

"Certainly," said Leland. He got up and stood back as Aranstone's men passed through the doorway. Leland followed after them, throwing Lexter an angry glance on their way out.

They went around to the back of the wagon, where Aranstone's men stood waiting for Leland and Lexter to remove the tarp and indicate which crates to take inside. The back corner of the tarp was already undone, and a cord was dangling off the edge of the wagon. One of the men nodded to it. "A bit slipshod..." The man smiled menacingly. But Leland did not rise to the bait.

"My brother can be a little hasty and absent-minded, but you needn't worry," Leland said, chastising Lexter for his earlier inattention. Lexter stood by and said nothing. He and Leland had agreed never to argue in front of people they were negotiating with, so he let it go. He thought he had fastened the tarp down well enough, but he *had* been absent-minded; that much was true. So Leland was right to criticize; more than that, though, and they would have it out later, he thought. But he would pay better attention.

Leland pulled back the tarp and jumped up on the wagon. He moved the needed crates to the edge where the men took them. He and Lexter carried the last two, and they all went back into the cabin.

The three crates with the broadswords were placed on one end of the oak table, the others stacked on the floor. Leland was handed a crowbar and he and Lexter pried the crates open while Aranstone and Greywood watched and sat down again.

Lexter removed one of the crate lids, releasing the strong smell of freshly-hewn pine. Suddenly Lexter remembered. *Lyla and Pitford, of course. How could I forget?* Lyla had been the sister of Robb Pitford, one of the bounty hunters who despised Lexter and had forbid him from seeing his sister. That was before Reuben had put a price on Lexter's head, but Pitford was still dangerous. Lyla didn't care and had encouraged Lexter's advances, always on the sly behind Pitford's back. Once when there was nowhere to run and Lexter was nearly found out, Lyla had hid him in one of the big pine crates near the stockyard. He had sat hunched over in it for several hours, waiting for Pitford and his friends to leave, and the smell of the pine brought it all back. As Lexter finished unpacking the crates and began unwrapping the swords, he smiled to himself recalling all the good times he and Lyla had enjoyed. Too bad she later caught him with Ciandra, he thought; he should have been more careful. That was the last time he had seen Lyla, and she had been quite angry. Lexter wondered if she might still be upset, and supposed she could very well be.

The broadswords were all unpacked now and Aranstone and Greywood were examining them and questioning Leland about them. Lexter was glad Leland was taking care of it all, and found his mind drawn back to thoughts of Lyla. He had the same uneasy feeling again, but now recalling Pitford he knew why. But he and Leland had left soon after he had seen Lyla, so even if she had run off to tell her brother, Pitford would have no way to find them. Of course, Lexter thought, he'd have to tell Leland so they could avoid going back into town; maybe they could go south to Hable or Okiary for the night. If they were careful, that would probably be safe enough, he thought.

More crates were being opened on the table and Lexter's attention snapped back to the dealings, as he tried to pick up what was going on. Leland had removed one of the shields from Iaf and was exaggerating its value. Lexter added a few comments of his own and Leland seemed pleased with them.

During the haggling that followed, Lexter was soon distracted again. He still tried to convince himself that they were safe, since no one had been following them. Under the full moon, the open land around the cabins could be seen plainly. *No one but us on the wagon,* he thought to himself. Suddenly the sight of the tarp's cord hanging loose came back to him. He glanced out the window where the wagon was. *Could she have hid under the tarp?*

He forced himself to concentrate on the dealings, and finally got them to agree on a good price for the broadswords. Next Leland brought out some halberd blades and began talking again, giving Lexter a little more time to think.

No, she couldn't have hidden under the tarp, Lexter thought, *because the yard-boy would have seen her and stopped—* But Lyla and Eagan had been good friends, and Eagen had owed her many favors. Lexter's heart sunk as a sickening cold wave plunged through him. He remembered how Eagen had nodded and smiled at them as they left, a smile that now seemed mischievous. It all made sense; he was sure of it. Raw panic surged within him and he wanted to leave as soon as possible. He was certain she had hid under the tarp and run back. Pitford and his friends were probably already on their way to the cabin.

"Lexter!" Leland raised his voice more than he had wanted, trying to contain his anger. Lexter was shaken and hoped they would attribute his nervousness to Leland.

"Sorry!" he muttered.

Leland looked at him, unable to continue. He turned to Aranstone and Greywood. "Please excuse us a moment."

He got up and pulled Lexter over by the window.

"What is wrong with you tonight?" Leland rasped at him in an angry whisper, "This is one of our biggest deals ever, and you can't keep your mind on it?"

"A woman I saw, at the inn —she knew me— I think she followed us here," Lexter stammered. He glanced out the window again, hoping Leland would catch on and he wouldn't have to explain it all.

"Who? What? That's impossible! What's the matter with you?!" Leland's anger overflowed but he restrained himself since the others were watching.

Across the room, Greywood leaned over and spoke to Aranstone. "What is it with that brother of his? His mind isn't on the dealing as it should be. That's the second time he's looked out the window; is something going on here?"

Aranstone motioned Trelt over to him. "You're certain no one followed you? Just the two of them?"

"I'm sure of it," Trelt asserted. "No one around anywhere; I'd have seen 'em right away." He stood up again and shuffled off with arms folded, annoyed they would doubt his work.

"That may be," said Greywood, "but something's afoot here. I don't like it! We'd best bring the rest of the goods in, right away. Maybe post some of your men outside, too, just in case."

"You really think it necessary?" Aranstone asked. "I agree his brother seems more a fool than what we thought. Still, if Trelt says no one followed them —and I know he can be relied upon in such matters— I would think us safe enough. All the same, the precautions you suggest would cost us little effort."

"Then you are agreed?" Greywood replied. "Have your men bring in the rest of the crates, and post a few outside until we are done."

"Let us continue!" Aranstone stood and commanded in a loud voice, and Leland and Lexter turned sharply and broke off their discussion.

Finished berating Lexter, Leland smiled amiably and led Lexter back to the table. He thought Lexter's suggestion of Lyla's riding along with them a bit preposterous, but not enough that he could entirely dismiss the idea. Now it seemed the sooner they could finish the better, just to be on the safe side. And besides, Lexter certainly wasn't being very helpful. They might not get as much as they could with a few more hours of haggling, but he could always take the loss out of Lexter's share.

"Gentlemen, pardon us for the brief break. My brother has assured me his undivided attention. Let us return to the dealing," Leland noted the others' looks of apprehension, and tried to appear as if everything was fine now.

"We would like to have the rest of the merchandise brought in," said Aranstone.

"Yes, certainly. Not a bad idea." Leland hoped to smooth over their impatience and thought this would placate them and make them more willing to negotiate again.

Aranstone motioned his men out the door and Leland and Lexter followed. Lexter was still smarting from the tongue-lashing and felt that Leland had not let him explain everything.

The full moon was overhead now, lighting the clouds around it, and the backyard was bathed in a pale bluish-white light. Aranstone's men and two of the dwarves went up on the wagon and began unloading the crates. Following them, Lexter and Leland each hoisted a crate off the wagon to take inside. Greywood and Aranstone stepped just outside the threshold, watching the men passing in and out.

One of the men standing on the wagon looked off to the south and jumped down to the ground. There were sounds of voices and then shouting from behind the cabin. An arrow whizzed through the air and stuck vibrating in the wagon near where Lexter and one of Aranstone's men were standing. The shouts grew louder and men were suddenly coming around both sides of the cabin.

"It's a trap! Fend them off!" Greywood tossed bows to the men wearing quivers, and others drew their swords. "And don't let the Splides escape, either!" he shouted after them.

Lexter shoved his crate at one of the men who rushed at him, and turned and ran from the cabin. Leland dropped his crate in the path of one of the men and followed. Men dressed in dark cloaks raced around the cabin on both sides with swords drawn. Two archers on horseback overtook them, one on each side.

Robb Pitford arrived riding a black mare that reared and snorted steam in the cold night air. The sharp ring and clang of metal began as their swords met those of Aranstone's men. Greywood and Aranstone stepped into the cabin and shut the door. Pitford scanned the scene as the fight continued, looking for Lexter. He caught sight of the Splides running off to the north, toward the forest. "After them! I want them *alive!*" he shouted, as the archers rode in broad arcs around the swordfighting and away to the dark forest.

Panting hard, Lexter and Leland saw the horsemen break away from the battle and come after them. "In the woods!" gasped Lexter, "There's nowhere else!" They ran the last ten yards, the horses closing the distance behind them. Arrows bit into trees around them and angry, wild shouts charged the night air.

The deeper the Splides went into the woods the darker it became, and the archers had to dismount to follow them. They dropped their bows by their horses, drew their swords and entered the forest.

Lexter and Leland pushed through the woods, waving their arms to clear away branches that scraped at them. The undergrowth slowed their passage and they were finally able to catch their breath. "If we get in far enough they won't be able to find us!" murmured Lexter. He pushed forward, turning back every now and then to be sure Leland was behind him.

They ran through the dark of the woods awhile, and stopped, breathing hard. They stood motionless, listening if anyone was following them.

"What are we going to do? Our wagon's back there. We never even got our money!" Leland shrieked in a horrified whisper. "They've got everything! Where are we going to go?"

"I don't know," said Lexter, "At least we got out of there with our lives..."

"I heard them!" A shout came from the depths of the forest behind them. Sounds of their pursuers drew nearer.

Lexter and Leland pushed their way deeper into the forest. They kept at it as hard as they could, zigzagging so as to throw off the archers. "I think... they're falling behind... shouldn't be much longer..." Leland rasped.

Lexter kept plowing through the branches barring their way. It was too dark to go as fast as he would have liked, and tree trunks often forced them to change direction. Then, ahead in the forest, Lexter saw a strange, faint, orange glow flickering between the trees. He made his way over to it and soon they stepped out into a small clearing overshadowed by trees. In front of him was what at first looked like a large round rock, but as he drew closer and walked around it, he saw it was a campfire that was carefully shielded on its southern side.

Lexter stopped, standing and staring at it, as Leland came up behind him.

"A campfire?" he said in astonishment, "But who—"

Huge shapes loomed out of the darkness, swiftly moving in around them. Before they were aware of what happened, both Leland and Lexter knew the terror of sharp, cold Goblin blades pressed against the soft skin of their necks.

"*Down on the ground!*" barked a harsh Goblin voice in Tharic heavily accented with Southern Rogglish. Two armed Goblin spies in dark cloaks stared at them with cold eyes set into deep, sagging pouches. One of them grunted and shoved Leland onto the wet, leaf-lined dirt of the forest floor, while the other pushed Lexter down. They set to work binding the Splides' hands behind their backs and tying their legs. Once this was done, the goblins picked them up and laid them off to the side of the fire. The goblins then sat back down by the fire, eating and laughing and talking in Rogglish, of which Leland and Lexter understood very little.

Lexter and Leland's hearts beat hard out of fear, their thoughts heavy with dread. As they lay bound near the fire, their burning lungs and pounding hearts eventually calmed but they were still more miserable and afraid than they had ever been.

Chapter 15.
Fasting and Feasting

On the cold, damp cave floor, no one felt well rested despite the hours they had slept. In the cave's shadowy dimness the dwarves overslept and woke with stomachs empty and growling. Stiff, tired, and grouchy, they said little while getting ready. The sky was a drowsy gray, and it seemed about noon though none could say exactly where the sun was.

"At least it's not raining," noted Hobley.

"Not yet", said Tillmore, glancing warily at the slow-moving cloud cover. The dwarves trudged on, hugging the slopes as the main road wound through the mountains. Lush pine-filled valleys opened into depths obscured by morning mists. In the vast quiet, the rushing of far-off rivers whispered of places unseen. Surrounding all, distant snow-covered slopes and peaks rose into the clouds.

Hours passed. The air was fresh and cold and they breathed in great slow draughts. Apart from his own weariness and hunger, Iaven's thoughts were on the Castle, and at every bend in the road he hoped to see it in the distance.

"So do you think we'll see it today?" Iaven asked Rhiane.

"We're a good part of the way there. We could make it before tonight," she told them.

"If we don't starve first," grumbled Zammond.

"What's it like at the Castle? Do a lot of people still live there?" asked Wilbur.

"Not as many as there were years ago," Rhiane said, "Most would rather live in or around Kronivar. Kronivar may be the center of trade, but the Castle is still the heart of the Kingdom."

"It's a shame it's not closer to Kronivar," said Tillmore.

"Well, the Castle's where Itharia began —the 'New Kingdom', as they once called it," said Rhiane. "In the days of King Taslen II, after leaving their old lands and crossing the desert, the Dwarves came to the mountains and began to build and start their kingdom anew. Long they searched for the right place, climbing peaks and looking out over the land.

"Eventually they came upon a curious mountain that looked as though its peak had been hewn away, and discovered ruins of a foundation built there. Very little was left, only a few courses of large stones. They were enormous and lined the sides of a sunken foundation where some huge edifice must have once stood. Along the northern edge of the plateau, the stones were flush with the sheer mountain walls, rising out of them like teeth.

"Amidst the rubble on the foundation's floor were two huge, heavy stone doors set at an angle into the ground, like the doors of a giant root cellar. They were closed and sealed and no one has ever been able to open them since. The King was wary, but it soon became clear that the place was entirely abandoned, and had been, for some time. Nothing remained of the people who had built there, nor any sign of what had happened to them. All that remained were the foundation and the doors, scored with ancient runes no one could read or decipher.

"The foundation was sound, and the view from the mountain breathtaking, so the Dwarves built their castle there. The plateau was cut into three broad terraces, the foundation upon the highest of them. Castle Frosthelm was built there, and a walled city on the terrace in front of the Castle. Crops were grown on the lowest, broadest terrace and in the valleys around the mountain, where flocks of livestock could graze. Once the Castle was built, the new kingdom flourished and grew, and Itharia was born."

"And you grew up in the Castle?" Zammond asked.

"I did, and I had no idea what life was like elsewhere," Rhiane said. "Year after year, people moved away to Kronivar. Even when I was little, the city around the Castle had shrunken to a village. I was always curious about Kronivar, and how it would be to live there. But I have missed the Castle and I'll be glad to be back."

Despite attempts at distraction, the dwarves' hunger pangs worsened and their pace slackened. Every mile seemed longer than the one before. The day was clearing up, clouds were thinning, and finally glimpses of blue sky cheered them. Angling beams of mid-afternoon gold broke through the clouds and fell into the valleys.

They kept up their pace as best they could. The road wound against much broader mountains now, their peaks higher and steeper and gleaming with snow. Valleys ran wide and deep, and low clouds lingered there, obscuring blankets of pine and winding rivers. The sun was at the dwarves' backs now, heading for the jagged horizon behind them. The air grew colder and the wind was picking up. Rounding the mountain's shoulder, Iaven wondered just how much farther they had to go.

Suddenly the road widened, and on a mountain a mile away rose Castle Frosthelm, broad and majestic, rising from the rock and overlooking the castle terraces. It crowned the plateau, gleaming walls and towers gilded in the golden light of late afternoon. Its cold, hard beauty bespoke of the devotion and skill of the Dwarves of the Old Kingdom. Even from a distance the sheer stone walls, crenellated parapets and balconies, and sleek towers and turrets drew the eye and held one's gaze. Steeples and spires soared into the sky, and standards flapped in the wind. The road brought them around the mountain in a wide curve, keeping the castle in view as they drew closer. Drawn onward by the high walls awash in velvety sunset light and shadow, Iaven found his strength renewed for the last mile's climb.

The central structure of the Castle rose the highest, and from there it angled out in large wings to the east and west, with a thick wall joining their ends, forming an inner ward. In this wall were great gates opening into the city on the terrace below. And the city itself, what remained of it, was also surrounded by a town wall reinforced with guard towers every fifty yards, forming an outer ward. Beyond the town wall, on the lowest and broadest terrace was cultivated land that now lay fallow, and the road led right into it.

The dwarves' pace quickened as they rounded the last curves of the mountainside. The broad road ran along the top of a ridge leading up to Mount

Frosthelm. As they crossed over, they noticed the valleys on both sides were lined with the pitched tents of the Castle forces' encampments. Even Rhiane was surprised at how many there were.

"I wondered how preparations were going," she said, "Uncle —King Jordgen— is set against the idea of war, and would only mobilize an army in the gravest of circumstances."

"Will we get to see the King?" asked Wilbur.

"I don't know," said Rhiane, "I'll see what I can do. I'll ask father about it, but I can't promise anything."

As they approached Mount Frosthelm, the Castle and its terraces loomed larger and larger, towering into the sky. On the open plain of the broadest terrace formations of troops trained as the day came to a close. Targets fixed on hay bales by the wall gave bowmen and archers practice. Others wielded spears or received lessons in swordfighting.

Soon Iaven and his friends climbed a shallow rise and stood at the Western Gate of the town wall. Soldiers standing guard came forward. One muttered something to another, who went off to call their captain, and two drew their swords, startling Iaven by their suddenness.

"Thought you'd return by the Western Gate, did you?" one snapped at Iaven. Brandishing their swords, the guards collected everyone's weapons. Iaven reluctantly handed Halix over to them, confused.

"Wait—what do you mean? We've—" Iaven stammered, looking over to Rhiane, sure she would set things straight. But Rhiane's hood covered her lowered head, and she said nothing.

"You'll have plenty of time to explain later!" growled one of the guards, shoving Iaven through the gate. The other followed behind them, herding Iaven and his friends inside and down a short road toward the Castle gates.

The outer ward's town was the Kingdom's oldest, its half-timbered buildings more ornate, though most were dilapidated or vacant. The stables were in use, and shops and residences were occupied, but only a remnant of the city's glory remained from the days when the Castle, not Kronivar, was Itharia's center of trade. People on the streets watched with curiosity as the small band of dwarves was led away by the guards.

Iaven had no idea what was happening. He wondered about Rhiane again, suddenly feeling very foolish for trusting her. Zammond and Hobley were as stunned as he was. Tillmore's face bore an expression of grave concern and Wilbur looked frightened.

The guards took them around to a smaller gate of the east wing, where an older guard who was their captain was waiting with several others.

"Caught him at the Western Gate," said the guard, as another handed over the weapons. The captain examined everything, taking a special interest in Halix.

"Good work, good work," he grunted, and motioned for the prisoners to be taken away. He watched them closely as they passed.

"Why are you doing this? What have we done?" complained Iaven.

"You need ask?" Anger flared in the captain's eyes. "You've been arrested and charged with disobeying the King and attacking and wounding the King's men."

Iaven was aghast. He looked to Rhiane, but she turned away from them, her hood drawn. Iaven almost said something to her, yet sensed he should not, so he waited.

The guards opened a heavy wooden door and led them down a narrow stone stairway, dimly lit by torches high up on the walls. A short hallway brought them under stone arches and down another narrow dim stairway even colder than the first one had been. Iaven moved along, heavy with dread, trying to make sense of it.

At the bottom of the stairs a long torch-lit hall led away into darkness. They turned a corner and came upon a door of wrought iron bars curled into simple designs. The guards unlocked the massive lock built into the door and had them enter. Inside was another shadowy hallway, with ironwork doors on both sides. A damp, stale smell of wet stone and rusting iron filled the air. The guards unlocked one of the side doors, the hinges screeching in agony as they opened. Here they did not enter, but bade Iaven, Rhiane, and the others to do so.

Once Iaven and the others were inside they shut the ironwork door with a quick screech and locked it again, the bolt clacking into place with frightening finality.

"Please, sirs, we're very hungry," Wilbur cried.

The guards shoved wooden bowls through the bars and laughed. "First time in a dungeon? Of course you'll be fed. Take these now, and we'll be back again in the morning."

As the last guard was leaving, Rhiane stepped up to the ironwork door and spoke. "Please tell Yolias to come," she said, peering out from under her hood.

"Yolias, eh?" The guard sounded surprised to hear the name. "Well, we'll see... Good night!" He grinned, enjoying the looks on their faces, and went out. They heard the outer door shut, the key sending the heavy bolt into place, and footsteps echoing down the hall into silence.

Wilbur sat down with the wooden bowls. Zammond and Hobley joined him, afraid he would take more than his share. Scraps off old bread soaked in the bowls' cloudy water along with a few cold chunks of potato. Despite the poor fare they were thankful and eager to eat. They divided what little there was evenly, and everyone was even hungrier after it was gone. Zammond, Hobley, and Wilbur searched the bowls, hoping to find a scrap more. Tillmore watched them sullenly from alongside the wall.

Iaven sat on the stone bench along the cell wall. He turned to Rhiane, who had removed her hood now.

"Why didn't you say anything at the gate? I mean, if the King is really your great-uncle—"

"He is!" said Rhiane, "I couldn't say anything out there. The guard who pushed you around, he's one of the spies in the Castle. I couldn't risk him seeing me. If they found me out in Kronivar, he might know who I am. We've come this far, and I'm not about to let them stop me here!"

"Well, a lot of good that's done us!" said Iaven.

"We're not in here because of that. He would have acted differently if he *had* seen me," Rhiane replied. "He took enough interest in you, though— what's this charge of attacking and wounding? Is there something *you* haven't told me?" She looked at Iaven and his heart sank at the accusation.

"I have no idea what that's all about," Iaven said, "Maybe they did recognize you, and it was just a ploy to lock us in here." He slumped forward on the bench, head down. After a moment he looked up at Rhiane. "You don't really believe I would do something like that, do you?"

"No," she admitted, watching him as though she were about to say more. She turned back to the gate. "Yolias will come for us, and everything will be alright."

Except for Wilbur's groaning, they sat in silence, too tired to argue or even complain. Terribly weary, Iaven wondered about Rhiane again, wanting very much to believe what she had told him. What worried him the most was that even if Rhiane really was a spy and had deceived them, he still loved her.

Beams of dust-strewn sunlight angled down through the cobwebs in the tiny windows high up on the cell wall. The dwarves awoke to the rattling of keys, the outer door clanking open, and footsteps. A guard began unlocking the ironwork door. Behind him stood an older, distinguished-looking dwarf, half a head taller than any of them and slender of build but very hardy. Silvery hair framed his serious countenance and a short white beard tapered to a point on his dark crimson doublet. Rhiane jumped up when she saw him.

"Yolias!" she exclaimed, "How glad I am to see you!"

Rhiane had explained the night before that Yolias Vierling was one of the King's trusted advisors and closest friends, the Vierling family having served the Frosthelms for many generations. Yolias's duties reached far and wide, from aiding the Castle stewards to leading hunts in nearby valleys and expeditions into the mountains. In his younger days he had been among the first to scale several unexplored mountain peaks, and knew a good deal about the lay of the land. Well respected by all, his advice was often sought as to what might please His Majesty the King.

The guard opened the door and Yolias stepped into the cell. He motioned away the guard who nodded in reply and left them. Yolias smiled at Rhiane. "Well, if it isn't our little Allelia! Whatever are you doing down here?" His attention and scrutiny turned to Iaven and the others. "And who are these friends of yours, if friends they are?"

Sitting down with Yolias, Rhiane related how she had met Iaven, their departure from Kronivar, and their arrest at the gate. Yolias listened, occasionally asking a question and glancing at Iaven, who finally came and sat with them. Iaven was intrigued to hear Yolias speak, recognizing Cedric's accent and manner of speech, the older, more formal style used at the Castle. When Rhiane was done, Iaven told of his journey, how he had come to own Halix, and his intention of giving the sword to the King. Yolias listened well and then, content that he understood the situation, rose again.

"So it was your twin brother," Yolias said, "Yes, the Captain and I saw the sword, and wondered about that."

"Orven and I have been mistaken for each other," Iaven admitted.

"They've even got matching gray cloaks," said Zammond, "But get to know them, and you'll *never* get them mixed up."

"The swords, Halix and Gorflange, are also alike," Iaven turned back to Yolias, "but mine has only one gem in it."

"Yes, we noticed that." Yolias studied Iaven's face.

"But attacking and wounding a Castle guard?" said Iaven. "What exactly happened?"

Yolias hesitated, deciding something, looked to Rhiane, and then back to Iaven. He held the cell door open for them. "We will discuss it over breakfast. But not here. Come, let us prepare more suitable accommodations, and have the table laid for us."

They marched out of the dungeon and down the hall, passing through a large, dark, many-pillared hall with a vaulted ceiling. Their footsteps echoed off into the dark, where the hall vanished beyond the reach of the dim torchlight. They turned a corner again and ascended a wide staircase.

Yolias hailed a servant, gave him directions, and sent him to prepare the room and breakfast. He took the dwarves at a leisurely pace through the Castle halls, upstairs, and even out onto a balcony above the valley behind Mount Frosthelm. Iaven was fascinated with the Castle's many archways, vaulted chambers, pillars, towers, fireplaces, stairways, and halls. Yolias promised them a chance to see more of it that afternoon while he and Rhiane were elsewhere discussing news of Kronivar.

When he thought everything was ready, Yolias brought the dwarves back inside and took them to their room. A chambermaid was finishing the beds, two of which had to be brought in, and extra pillows were also needed. A table in the corner had breakfast for seven laid out, as Yolias had also not yet eaten.

They were in the Castle's west wing, overlooking a valley northwest of the Castle. While Yolias and Rhiane checked on the servants' preparations, Iaven and the others admired the view. Pressing close to the window, they peered out. Distant mountains, gray and purple in the obscuring mists, lay vast and serene in the morning light. The ground fell away below the castle, opening into grassy valleys pitched with soldiers' tents. Beyond the valleys spread hills and steep slopes lined with pine and spruce. Iaven supposed these were the very slopes where the swords had lain undisturbed for so many years after Cedric had hidden them.

Beautiful as the view was, the steaming breakfast drew them back to the table; hot breads and biscuits with fresh butter, eggs and bacon, oats, apples, plums, and pastries, and fruit juices that were a rare treat. Iaven and the others ate and drank, trying hard to not eat too fast and to keep up their manners while Yolias was present.

While they ate, Yolias spoke of Orven's visit to the Castle two days before Iaven's arrival. "According to the guards, your brother and his friends came to the Main Gate of the inner courtyard, demanding an audience, trying to sound as important as possible." Yolias smiled. "Of course he wasn't admitted, so he claimed to have in his possession one of the Lost Swords of the Alliance. The guards laughed in disbelief, but he kept insisting. Even if it was one of the swords, they told him, the King would not grant high rank to such inexperienced swordsmen as he and his friends.

"Orven became irate, and they sent for the Captain of the Guard. Seeing how undisciplined they were, the Captain said they could give over the sword if they wanted, but it was for the King to decide who would wield it and where would be best put to use. He invited them others to join the King's troops with the other new recruits. Orven refused and left in frustration.

"The Captain thought the whole situation somewhat comical," Yolias continued, "When he told me, I was curious and wanted to see for myself, as I knew enough about the swords to recognize them. Orven's party had left the Main Gate, but the guards had seen them go off into town. I sent word to all the guards at the Outer Gates in the town wall to stop them and summon me if dwarves of their description were seen leaving.

"We did not intend to take the sword away from Orven by force; unfortunately he was not as generous as you are, Iaven. And if it was indeed one of the Swords of the Alliance, unlikely as that seemed, we could not afford to lose it. I spoke with the Lieutenant General of the King's Royal Army, explaining the situation. He agreed we could allow Orven the rank of Sergeant, provided he could prove himself and show his mettle. It would have been one way to keep the sword within view, and there was a chance Orven could be persuaded to volunteer to turn it over to us. Or so we hoped.

"Early the next day as Orven's party was leaving through the East Gate in the town wall, the sentries bid them to halt. Orven misunderstood their intention, and he and his friends became surly, and without provocation —so the guards claim— Orven threatened them and kept on walking. As they had not been told to use force, the guards were unsure how far they should go to keep him there. They followed him onto the terrace to where the Ruined East Road begins, and finally Orven drew his sword, challenging and attacking. Once challenges were made, they drew their weapons, hoping to subdue him and bring him back.

"Surprisingly, Orven proved a better swordsman than they'd reckoned. They fought, and Orven wounded one of them. Afterward, Orven and his friends left down the Ruined East Road. I arrived after the encounter, as the wounded guard was being brought back, and they explained the whole situation to me."

"To think Orven could be so bold!" said Iaven. "I mean, we'd always get into fights, but still—"

"He could be mean," said Zammond, "and with the sword, who knows?"

"It does give one a feeling of power," Iaven admitted. "Even I felt that. And Halix only had one gem in it." Iaven recalled wielding Halix against the mountain lion outside Bottomcliffe. "Now that Orven has two, who knows how much more powerful Gorflange has become?"

"I suspected much of Orven's apparent skill was due to the sword," Yolias said. "When the Captain brought Halix to me yesterday, I held it and sensed its power; clearly it is one of the swords as your brother claimed. A shame, though, that we will not have both of them in the service of the King."

"I'm sure Iaven would have liked to present it under better circumstances," Rhiane said.

"Yes, our apologies for mistaking you for Orven." Yolias rose from the table. "Since Orven's party had gone east, we supposed they would soon return. It is strange that Orven's party left by the Ruined East Road, which eventually leads into the desert, rather than the road back to Greensward and Kronivar. And so word was put out to bring them in when they came through again." Yolias smiled. "The guards were somewhat wary when they saw you, and rather surprised at how easily you cooperated with them."

"Well, this breakfast has certainly helped make up for it all," said Iaven, pushing away from the table. "But I'm still surprised about Orven. And now they're off to the east! I wonder why."

"When he comes back through the Castle grounds, we'll have another chance," Yolias said, "Perhaps you will be able to talk some sense into him. In the meantime, we've much to do. I must leave you now, but I'll send someone to show you around the Castle, if you care to see it. Rhiane and I have business to attend to, as I am sure there is much news from Kronivar regarding our discontents there."

"There is," Rhiane agreed. "And I haven't seen father yet, either."

"He's already waiting. We ought to get going." Yolias held the door open.

"We'll see you later, perhaps at dinner. I'll be back as soon as I can," Rhiane told them on the way out. Out in the hall, Yolias stopped to speak to a serving maid who was coming to clean up. She listened, replied and nodded, and went down the hall.

Yolias stepped back inside. "I've sent Elma to find Gwaine, the Steward's son. He'll show you around and answer your questions; that should keep you occupied awhile. I shall try to join you later, as I would like to hear more about your friend Cedric." Yolias turned to Zammond and Hobley. "And tonight we shall also try to find suitable positions in the troops for both of you."

Iaven and the others thanked Yolias for breakfast, the room, and all his help. The door closed and Iaven and his friends were alone again.

"So Orven's left for the desert!" said Iaven, walking over to look out the window. "What's he going to do next?"

"Look for the last gem, I imagine," said Tillmore.

"Well, yes, but what's he willing to do to get it?" wondered Zammond.

"The King must have one here, somewhere," said Iaven, instinctively reaching for Halix, only to find his scabbard empty. As he caught himself he realized how much he missed the sword.

"Well at least Orven didn't get it," said Hobley.

"That must be why he went east," said Iaven, turning from the window. "The fifth gem's nowhere near Kronivar, or in the south; it's either east of the castle, or in the far north somewhere —and I wouldn't want to go up there right now."

"What if he runs into Maëlveronde?," said Hobley. "And Orven won't stop searching, I'll bet."

"I hope not," said Iaven, "He's bold, but he's not stupid. Not *that* stupid, anyway."

"There is a point where boldness becomes stupidity," Tillmore said.

Zammond was about to say something when the door opened. A young dwarf of about their own age came in, golden-haired and dressed in the finery of the Castle. His linen shirt was dyed blue and embroidered about the cuffs and collar with gold and scarlet thread. He looked them all over the moment he entered, making little effort to hide his disdain. "I am Gwaine, son of Erland Clovenstone, High Steward of the Castle. I understand you are guests of Yolias?"

"I'm Iaven. Iaven Ambersheath." Iaven noticed Gwaine glancing at the ornate yet empty scabbard at Iaven's belt, but volunteered no explanation. The other dwarves introduced themselves, Hobley and Zammond telling Gwaine they would be joining the troops, anxious to learn more about how they might serve.

"Excellent. We shall start with the ramparts, then, which give a good view of the grounds," said Gwaine and motioned them to follow.

He led them along a short hallway, down a flight of stairs, to a thick wooden door opening out onto the battlements. They stepped into the cold air and bright sunlight and walked along the town wall. Iaven gazed over the embrasures into the mountain valley falling away to the west. On the other side of the wall were the thatched roofs in the outer ward. Thin wisps of smoke rose from chimneys, amidst the lowing of livestock and the clink of a blacksmith's hammer. Iaven looked down on the buildings from high up on the wall, the overhead angle strange and exciting. Gwaine pointed out smithies, an orchard and vegetable garden, a bakery, a brewhouse and winery, stables, shops, and more.

The town wall took them away from the castle and around the outer ward. The castle rose like a small mountain beyond the half-timbered buildings. Finely cut and mortared stone drew their eyes across walls and up towers.

They passed through several guard towers where the angle of the wall changed direction. Occasionally Gwaine took them up a small, enclosed spiral staircases leading to the towers' tops, where they looked out into the valley or over the castle terraces below, on which squadrons of infantry were practicing drills.

At last the town wall brought them around to the eastern side of the plateau, and then back to the castle's east wing. Passing through another tower, they emerged again on the wall overlooking the inner ward, which was bounded on three sides by the castle and its east and west wings. As the two wings angled out from the castle, the inner ward widened to where the inner wall bounded it on its southern end. Below them, in the center of the wall, was the gatehouse where the main gate opened into the inner ward.

The inner ward was well kept, wide and spacious, with an herb garden, a cistern, benches, and small half-timbered buildings along the walls. The center of the inner ward was open and flagstoned, and Gwaine said that in summer the King addressed audiences there from a balcony. But the northern end of the inner ward was what caught their eyes; centered there was the enormous main entrance to the Castle. An elaborately carven stone arch framed huge double doors of wood and iron. Gwaine explained that beyond them lay the Throne Room Vestibule, and the Throne Room itself, and that this was the entrance used for processions and visiting foreign dignitaries.

They passed through the second story of the gatehouse, where the portcullis was housed, and the great winches and counterweight chains, dark and heavy. They came out of the gatehouse on the other side, went along the rest of the castle wall, and then back into the west wing again.

"As for the Castle itself," said Gwaine, once the heavy wooden door was shut behind them, "In the main part of the castle, between the wings, there's the Throne Room, the Great Hall, map rooms and libraries, chambers of the Royal Family— many important areas; it's the oldest part of the Castle. The east wing and west wing have council chambers, guests' quarters, servants' quarters, an infirmary, lodgings for the Castle Guard and soldiers, and large storerooms below. And below the east wing there's the dungeon, of course; though I'm told you've already seen it."

"I thought we might end with the Throne Room, as it is not in use today; it usually is something visitors want to see." Without waiting for a response, Gwaine led them down a long hall decorated with tapestries, shields, coat-of-arms, and crossed swords mounted high up on the wall. They turned and went down other halls. Various servants and Castle residents passed them, often with curious or suspicious glances. At last they came to the top of a great white and gray marble staircase overlooking a grand hallway.

Gwaine began descending and they followed him. "This is the Grand Staircase of the west wing. There's one just like it on the other side of the Castle, leading up into the east wing."

Two sets of stairs descended from the center of the west wing, one on each side, and then turned and doubled back, forming a great V. Below, where they met, the staircase came forward a flight and then widened out to the sides, each descending step adding a layer in a broadening series of semi-circles spreading down to the main floor. On the ends of the balustrades were large candelabra, twenty-seven candles in each. The sides of the staircase were inlaid with patterns and motifs, and the dwarves barely had time to glance at them all as they passed.

Gwaine led them into the Throne Room by a side door. The room was wide and deep, and along the north wall ran a long, raised dais, carpeted in red. Upon it stood a tall, ornate throne, upholstered with cushions of purple velvet and gilt in gold from top to bottom. Carvings of dragons supported the armrests. On the wall behind the throne hung a large tapestry of the King's insignia, a white dragon against a field of purple. The dragon's design was more detailed than those Iaven had seen on guards' uniforms or on their standards. Flanking the tapestry were wall sconces for torches, and beyond them arched windows overlooking the mountain valley to the north. The windows ran all the way to the far wall on either side, and high above them ran smaller rows of arched windows. Soft afternoon light illuminated the northern side of the room. Reflected highlights glinted on the golden throne as it sat alone in the dark. Other walls had tapestries of portraits and depictions of various scenes from Dwarven history. The darkened hearths of huge fireplaces on the east and west walls faced each other across the room's wide plain of wood parquet tile flooring. Gwaine explained that six years before, two thrones had been on the dais, until Queen Avriana's death.

As Iaven looked at the throne, he heard footsteps entering the hall.

"There you are," Yolias said, "Enjoying the tour, I hope? I shall accompany them now, Gwaine, thank you."

Gwaine chatted a moment with Yolias, and then departed.

"I have good news," Yolias said as Gwaine's footfalls echoed away and the side door closed behind him. "The King was pleased to hear you were returning the sword, and has invited everyone to join us for supper this evening in the Great Hall."

Yolias smiled at their eager anticipation. "Rhiane will be there, too; she wanted me to tell you. It's already late afternoon, and you will need time to prepare for dinner, so was there anything in particular you still want to see? I also have a few questions for you, Iaven, as well."

"Rhiane mentioned something about some doors," Iaven said on the way out, "Old ones, down at the foundations. It sounded interesting."

"The Doors of the Angkhadra?" said Yolias, "She told you about them? Very well, we'll have a quick look at them."

Yolias led them out of the throne room, through a short hall, and down a flight of stairs. Iaven had lost track of where they were in the castle, and as they descended, Iaven learned that beneath the Throne Room were large storerooms and an armory, and beneath that was the wide hall of pillars, the same one he had passed after they had left the dungeon.

It was cooler down in the hall of pillars and quiet as an empty cavern. The hall was wide and dark, the air still, damp, and musty. Iaven thought it smelled very old. They seemed to be the only ones down there; torches were mounted on some of the pillars, but none were lit. Yolias lit one and carried it with them as they went, and widening shadows of pillars trembled and swept across the floor as they walked. The stone pillars, row after row of them, were carved to look like the trunks of mighty trees. Overhead they widened into interlocking carven branches supporting the ceiling in a series of domelike vaults, with pillars at each of their corners. Suddenly a high, broad dome opened above them, and they stepped into a wide, empty circle ringed about by pillars. The round, vaulted ceiling was black and painted with constellations of a starry night sky.

"We are in the center of the Hall of Pillars, also known as The Stone Forest," Yolias told them. "The deepest and oldest part of the Castle, save for what lies below us." Yolias saw they were looking at the stone flooring. Huge flagstones, seven or eight feet across, lined the floor. "These were laid long before the Dwarves arrived here, a part of the foundation our ancestors built upon. But come; we shall see the Doors."

They walked through the Stone Forest to the north. Soon they came upon another open area near the north wall. Yolias took his torch and lit others around them. As the light increased, they came to see to huge slabs of stone lying side by side. Each was about seven feet wide and fourteen feet from top to bottom. They were laid on an angle from the floor, like the doors of a root cellar. But these doors led down into the stone floor and the depths of the mountain itself.

"No one has ever been able to open them, or break through them," said Yolias, "Nor do we know what lies inside. Some say the doors were shut and sealed for a reason; either to keep someone out, or perhaps keep something in." He brought them closer, holding the torch near the doors. Shadows danced on the strange runic inscriptions and in the grooves of their wild yet carefully carved characters. In the center, set in between the edges of the doors, was a flat circular area that overlapped from one door to the other. There, five small round hollowed-out recesses were set in a quincunx pattern, four at the corners of a square with a fifth in the center. An aura of ancient mystery lingered about the doors, as though they hid an old danger still alive in the depths of the mountain.

"Long ago, the Dwarves made a great journey across the desert from the east —whether they were fleeing, or in exile, or looking for new lands, our annals do not record— and they came upon what today we call the Frosthelm Mountains. They followed the remains of roads and trails cut into the stone, and eventually came to this mountain. Here they found the ruins of an ancient people, whom the Elves called the Angkhadra. The ground had been sealed over with layers of thick stone flooring, and the doors set into the ground. Even the Oswai know very little about the Angkhadra, and none can say what happened to them. All that was left were these doors and the ruins of this foundation. That they could quarry and build with stones so large meant they must have been a strong and powerful people. Yet almost nothing remains of them today."

"So no one knows what's down there?" said Iaven, eyeing the doors.

"Did the Angkhadra seal themselves in, escaping an enemy, or did they imprison something down there, and flee?" said Yolias. "We may never know."

"Now that you mention it, I do remember Cedric talking about them. He didn't like them —the doors— but he did find them interesting."

"Which reminds me— I'm interested in hearing more about how you came to know Cedric, and what happened to him during and after the war," Yolias said. "My father, as a boy, knew Cedric well. He would have been very surprised to hear Cedric had outlived him." He paused, looking around at the dwarves' torch-lit faces. "But the dinner hour approaches. We had best get you back to your room and made ready. I've asked the chambermaid to lay out some fresh clothing for you to wear at dinner. Come."

They passed through the Stone Forest. Yolias extinguished the torches, and they followed him back down the hall and up the stairs. On the way, Yolias and Iaven talked more about Cedric, the swords, and Orven. At last they returned to their room, which was now awash with late afternoon sunlight.

"I must go and prepare as well," Yolias said. "Dress, and very shortly a page will come to escort you to the Great Hall for dinner." He closed the door behind him as he left.

Fine clothing had indeed been laid out for them; linen shirts with embroidered trim, light doublets of velvet and brocade, and the finest pants any of them had ever worn. Neither Iaven nor any of his friends were used to dressing up, although Tillmore was slightly more familiar with such garments than the rest of them. They tried on the clothes, enjoying the fresh feel of the fabrics, and at last stood crowded in front of the room's full-length mirror, laughing and looking at themselves in their finery.

"What a sight we are!" Wilbur laughed. "Nobody'd ever recognize us!"

"Doesn't Hob look *noble*!" said Zammond. Hobley, who normally dressed the simplest and plainest, was quite transformed in the fancy clothes. The shirt they had left for him was a bit small, but it was laced in front with a drawstring and eyelets and after he loosened it, the shirt fit fine. Hobley smiled at the dwarves' reflection.

"Hope we can keep them clean at dinner!" he said.

They were still admiring themselves in the mirror when a curt rap sounded at the door, and a page entered. "They are gathering for dinner. If you would follow me, sirs, to the Great Hall."

Walking through the halls in their new clothes, Iaven and his friends felt a bit less out of place. Though eager to attend the dinner, they nervously anticipated the formal surroundings so foreign to them. They came to the Grand Staircase joining the west wing to the rest of the castle, and began ascending.

The Great Hall was in the center of the castle, above the Throne Room. It was the largest hall and often the brightest, grandest place in the Castle. Great wooden beams reached high across the wide, vaulted ceiling hung with chandeliers of lit candles. Balconies and gilt windows lined the walls beneath the beams, with torches set between them. Centered between the doors on the south wall was the Great Fireplace, where large logs blazed in a cavernous hearth. On the north wall, tall ironwork windows overlooked the steep valley and mountain ridges rimmed with scarlet light of the day's close. Beneath arched windows and balconies hung enormous tapestries and shields, coats-of-arms, antlers from hunts, and other decor. Across the floor spread rich, ornate carpets, the finest of these on the King's high table platform. Throughout the room, long oaken tables were being set for dinner. Servants unfolded linen tablecloths and lit candelabra (some made from deer antlers) on the tables. Serving boys and maids passed to and fro, setting out baskets of bread, pouring goblets of water, and laying out glasses, plates, silverware, and rolled napkins. Through side doors Iaven glimpsed huge cauldrons hanging in the kitchen fireplace and smelled many fragrances of food roasting and cooking.

Guests trickled into the Great Hall; noblemen, soldiers and guards, captains, visitors from other kingdoms, Lords and Ladies from northern Itharia, officials from Kronivar, and others. All were well dressed, some in surcoats or tabards emblazoned with the King's insignia. Among them, dressed in velvet and satin, Yolias walked toward Iaven and his friends.

"The clothes fit you well." Yolias guided them to a long table. "Come, here are seats for Castle guests. I will not be joining you here, as my place is at the King's high table—"

"But I'll be joining you!" For a moment Iaven did not even recognize Rhiane. Completely transformed, she stood before them, radiant and smiling. She wore a flowing gown of pale green with gold and white brocade, iridescent chiffon, and lace trim. A string of sky-blue jewels lay across her bosom, and the dark, shining tresses of her hair were embraced in a floral garland, which rose above her earrings of Tigersmilk pearl. Her eyes were bright and clear and sharp and looked kindly at Iaven.

"Rhiane! …I mean, Lady Allelia!" Iaven was stunned by her beauty and at a loss for words, and the others watched in awed surprise as well.

"And look at you!" Rhiane said, laughing. "Very handsome, all of you!"

"The King will be arriving soon so I must leave you," said Yolias. "Earlier today the King spoke of a possible audience after dinner to discuss the swords, so be ready, should His Majesty have time and so desire it. As for now, enjoy the dinner." Yolias nodded and left.

Iaven began telling Rhiane how they liked the Castle, when trumpets sounded and the diners all rose. The double doors of the main entrance opened. "His Majesty, Jordgen Frosthelm, King of Itharia!" announced the Sergeant at Arms. Standard bearers, in satin-lined velvet cloaks with crenellated hoods drawn back, processed in, and following them were members of the royal family, dignitaries, and high officials. King Jordgen walked in front among them, his proud, leonine head held high, gazing forward, stern and solemn. For his advanced age, he still remained vigorous and moved with the grace of a lion. His hair and short, trim beard were white shot through with silver. He scanned the assembled guests, nodding slightly, as he and his party assumed their places at the high table. Grace, led by the King, was said by all. And finally, with a nod from the King, the dinner began. Wooden chairs were drawn as everyone sat down again and began talking, and servers brought out steaming platters.

"Don't you sit at the high table?" Iaven asked Rhiane.

"Sometimes," said Rhiane. "I can whenever I like, but I don't always. I asked father if he minded my joining you and he said it was alright. I don't know if Yolias told you, but tonight is an important dinner, as the King has been entertaining nobles from Kronivar and the north the past few days. Some of them are seated down the table from us."

Iaven looked around at the nobility and other guests. He felt privileged to be present, realizing this would be the brightest, highest point of his adventure, which was almost at an end. Going back would be difficult, he thought. He'd have to say goodbye to his friends and then there'd be the long journey home with Wilbur. They'd be traveling in the opposite direction of everyone leaving for war, and that would look bad. He recalled the evening on the plateau with Rhiane, wondering if he would ever see her again. It all seemed quite impossible now, and he tried not to think about it.

The high table was the first to be served, then the Castle guests, assorted workers and servants, and finally the guards and soldiers. Huge platters and serving bowls passed before the diners, as fragrant aromas intensified their appetites. Fresh loaves arrived hot from the ovens, along with dinner rolls, heavier breads for sandwiches, biscuits, nut breads, and rich black bread. Whipped butter was laid out, along with cheeses, curds, whey, honey, and cream. Soups were ladled steaming into wide bowls, and beers and wines poured into goblets and mugs. A wide assortment of meats filled their trenchers; roast boar, venison, hams, mutton, sides of salt beef, and finely seasoned sausages. Large roast birds like pheasant and goose, and smaller poultry, including turkey, chicken, duck, and partridge, were stewed in gravies and thick sauces, and garnished with parsley and watercress. And there were fish, fresh from mountain streams, grilled, smoked, and battered. Crops from all over the kingdom were present; green beans, cabbages, cranberries, mushrooms, green and red peppers, onions, cucumbers, corn, potatoes, peas in pods, carrots, apples, pears, and more. One could even try various tree-fruits from the distant lands of southern Feäthiadreya.

Serving boys, working at the castle to learn manners and the ways of nobles, took away the dishes as they emptied and replaced them. Just as the dwarves began to feel they couldn't eat any more, desserts began arriving; trays of pastries, pies, creams, sugared candies, cakes, puddings, and sugary marzipan.

While they ate, Iaven observed all assembled there. The King and his folk were engaged in discussions. Rhiane told Iaven about the members of the high table. On the King's right was his son, Prince Varlen, who looked like a younger version of his father, and to the King's left were Rhiane's father and mother, Arlen Frosthelm and his wife Yarra. Near Yolias sat the King's High Steward, Erland Clovenstone, and Lord Kerund and General Knorde of the King's Army, along with several other counselors, military advisors, and friends of the throne. After many names and titles Iaven lost track of who was who and forgot most of it. He was nervous about his possible audience with the King, even though he suspected there wouldn't be time for it. After such a fine, filling meal, a good rest sounded better to him.

Iaven listened as lords and nobles nearby discussed recent events. He heard about various goings-on around the kingdom, opinions and theories (stated as fact) concerning the war, and speculations as to when and how the Goblins might attack, or whether they would attack at all before winter set in. Thankfully, Iaven found little opportunity to say anything, so busy were those around him propounding their ideas and criticizing others.

By the evening's end, Iaven was still sorting out his impressions, trying to get a general sense of the attitudes towards the kingdom and the war. Some called for advancement and attack, moving north and striking before the Goblins made a move, emphasizing the glory of Itharia and its expansion into the north. Another group, opposed to the first, suggested holding back and fortifying the front, hoping to keep the Goblins at bay and avoid war altogether. A third group held that war was inevitable, and that once the Goblins were defeated, advancement into the north would be possible. Yet another group felt that the Dwarves were spread too thin and that the northern lands would fall too easily, but others argued that the Goblins were more interested in Kronivar rather than in the Northern Provinces.

Kronivar's role in the kingdom's future was also hotly debated. One group thought Kronivar had a right to demand separation from the Crown to make a stand on its own, as a state, even if they did not agree that it ought to secede. Another called for the Dwarves to return to the mountains and consolidate the kingdom there, as it had been in days of old. Others thought any sign of insurrection in Kronivar should be met by the Castle and put down with force. It was often implied that a growing number of people throughout the kingdom, even at the Castle, had secretly sided with the Kronivar separatists, the degree of their support ranging from mere sympathizers to revolutionary extremists. Others scoffed at the idea, and were accused of being enchanted with King Jordgen and his ability to keep them out of war. But most seemed to trust the King's judgment (at least when in his presence), or were merely resigned to the current situation.

Having heard so many different sides of the issues, Iaven realized he hadn't really thought much about war, and felt he ought to be doing more for the kingdom. Adrift in all the events and conversations around him, his only hope was that the Dwarves would prevail over the Goblins if, or rather when, it came to war. He still wanted to return to Hillbrook, but now it seemed a selfish and fearful thing to do, and he wondered how he might serve the kingdom. He felt strongly now that he wanted to do something, yet he was never so unsure of what exactly he ought to do.

Chapter 16.
An Evening at the Castle

"Me? Stay at the castle and join the army? I'm sure I wouldn't make a very good soldier." Iaven had known the question would arise sooner or later.

"You could try... Everyone can do something!" Rhiane looked across at Iaven with her dark, expressive eyes, and he wasn't sure if she was amused, disappointed, or debating some unknown scheme in which he was to play a part.

The dinner was winding down. The King and the high table party had been the first to finish and leave, and had been gone a little over an hour now. People were departing, though many still stood around the hall talking or conversing at table with friends they hadn't seen in awhile. Outside the tall, arched windows the sky was black, the stars and moon casting a dim, frosty light on the mountains and valleys.

"Will you refuse the King if he asks you himself?" asked Zammond.

"He'll probably want us all to join," Wilbur lamented. "I should have thought of that when we left." He shook his head. "How I'll hate to turn him down!"

"Then don't!" said Hobley. "I'm sure they could find something even you could do!"

"Thanks for your confidence!" said Wilbur.

As the dwarves talked, Yolias returned and approached their table.

"The King has granted you an audience," he told them. He looked to Iaven. "I told him about you, and he is quite curious to meet you."

Iaven was excited and honored but his heart sank when he thought how he would not meet the King's expectations. Nervousness set in as they left the Great Hall, and he felt as if he were being led to his doom, or at least to a good scolding.

"Don't worry," Rhiane told him, "He's stern, but really very kind."

Iaven assumed the audience would be in the Throne Room, and was surprised when Yolias led them up the staircase into the west wing. They went down a hallway, rounded a corner to the right, then down a vaulted passageway. At last they came to a carved wooden door. Yolias opened it and bid them all to enter.

It was a comfortable room, with a small fire blazing in a fireplace on the wall to their left, fine carpets underfoot, and comfortable well-crafted furniture upholstered with velvet cushions. Along the northern wall were tall windows and glass-paned doors that opened out onto a balcony overlooking the valley behind the Castle. The room was warm and bright with firelight and the glow of candelabra. A large table of mahogany stood on one side of the room, with maps spread out on it and others rolled up and piled off to the side. Behind the table, a dwarf in a blue robe watched them as they entered. His sandy brown hair was slightly tousled, his face long, and his heavy lips were turned down at the corners as if he were contemplating something of great import. Questioning eyes, beneath bushy brows, looked up at them from the maps. Iaven thought he looked like an owl looking down from a tree branch.

Yolias smiled and turned to Iaven. "Iaven, this is Lorrow Ethcairn, scribe and mapmaker to the King."

"Well, Yolias! So these are the fellows, eh?" Ethcairn glowered at them, but his tone sounded friendly enough. Iaven and the others walked over hesitantly, and Rhiane introduced them. "Hillbrook, is it? Come quite a ways, have you. Yes, yes..." He looked down at the map spread out in front of him, and Iaven followed his gaze. The map was much larger and older than any Iaven had ever seen. It was drawn in a fine, spidery hand, the lettering ornate and spiky. There was far more detail here than on the maps Cedric had shown him, and Iaven looked at it, trying to get his bearings, when he heard the door opening behind them.

"Sire." Yolias held the door as the King entered. Iaven and his friends turned from the maps and went over to Yolias and the King. Before Iaven had a chance to bow or make some sign of respect, the King caught his eye and stood appraising him.

"We appreciate your gift of the sword," he said. His gaze was firm and fathomless, betraying nothing of his thought. He lifted a crimson velvet bundle he was carrying, and carefully unwrapped Halix, which winked and shone in the light. "Well done. These swords mean a great deal to the kingdom. A shame your brother did not feel as you did about them." He handled the sword, looking at it again.

Seeing the velvet wrapping, Iaven suddenly remembered he had left Halix's scabbard in their room. "Your Majesty, I'm sorry, I forgot to bring the scabbard..."

The King raised his hand to still Iaven. "Not just yet. There will be time enough for that. Come, let us all sit by the fire." He led them over to the fireplace, as Yolias pulled up more chairs. Ethcairn joined them as well. As they sat down, Rhiane introduced the others in Iaven's party to King Jordgen, and he nodded in turn at each of them. Finally they were all settled in armchairs by the fire.

"Yolias tells me you knew Cedric Redthorn," Jordgen began, "and that it was he who gave you and your brother the swords."

At the King's prompting, Iaven related the story again, with Zammond filling in a few details. The King listened to it all, asking Iaven and Zammond about the Foothills, and of the mood in Hillbrook concerning the war. Iaven told of his travels, how he had heard of Cedric's death, and his experiences in Kronivar (though his description of how Orven had taken his gem at the well was rather sparse). The King listened intently, interjecting a question here and there. At the end of it all, Iaven reaffirmed that his whole purpose was to bring the sword to the castle.

"And now? What will you do?" Jordgen asked.

The dreaded question had come. Iaven hesitated. "Work in my step-father's smithy, back in Hillbrook... helping prepare for the war." Iaven's heart beat hard, his answer sounding vastly inadequate.

"I see," said the King. Lit from the side by the fire, he sat in his armchair looking at Iaven, as if deliberating a verdict from a throne of judgment.

Iaven felt a strong urge to defend his position, but knew whatever he said would only weaken it. He sat nervously, waiting for the King's pronouncement. Iaven had talked at length telling his tale, and now all were silent listening to the crackling of the flames.

At long last the King spoke. "I wonder now, what it was that drew your brother here. As he did not intend to serve, was he drawn by this?" From a pocket he drew out a sparkling, deep blue gem. Firelight glinted on its facets. Iaven drew a quick breath, as did the others.

"It was in among other treasure, tribute paid by one of the northern lords," said Jordgen, "I had Yolias search for it with the sword. To think it was here, perhaps for years. But without the sword, only a wizard might have sensed what it was." He moved the gem near to the hilt of the sword and with a tiny whisper the metalwork leaves rotated to make way for the gem. Jordgen paused, watching them, and then slowly withdrew the gem. The leaves shut. "Ah, the works of Angkelwen, how fine and rare they are! So few remain." He looked up at them. "This sword is nearly a century old, yet it has never held all the gems for which it was made. And it will not be complete until it does."

King Jordgen looked at Iaven and his friends as they sat before him, as if assessing their strengths. "I intend to send out a search party to recover the lost gem; the last remaining one, provided Maëlveronde does not have it as well. I have asked Yolias to lead the party, as it must act quickly and return as soon as possible."

"I'll go!" Zammond declared. "If Yolias will have me."

"I will," said Yolias.

"I'll go, too," said Hobley.

"And so will I,' added Tillmore. Both he and Hobley turned to see if Iaven would volunteer.

Iaven felt the King's gaze, and Rhiane's as well. A part of him slunk back, but he knew it was something he had to do.

"Yes, of course I'll go," said Iaven. Rhiane smiled at him.

"Well, I suppose I'll go then, too," Wilbur said, "Don't want to be left out."

"Wouldn't want to break up the party," said Tillmore.

King Jordgen smiled. "Good, then that is settled. Yolias and I discussed sending out troops, but you know Orven and his friends best. We hope to get to the remaining gem before they do, and you have the best chance of talking Orven into joining us as well. And hopefully you will reach the gem before him, in case he does refuse you." With that, Jordgen brought the gem near the hilt again, the metalwork leaves opened, and he set the blue gem in place.

Everyone sat watching as the King lifted Halix, examining the gems in its hilt, and then raised it up in front of him. He did not swing it about or move it all, but held it steady, its blade bright with firelight. They could see he sensed its power, and in that instant he looked as if he were about to lead armies into battle, consuming his foes like a flash fire sweeping through a dry field. Even in his late seventies King Jordgen his vitality remained, his face shining with valor and strength of will he had possessed since his youth. Then the moment passed and he lowered the sword again.

The King rose from his chair. "Now to determine where the last gem resides." Everyone stood, watching enrapt as he leveled the sword and began to search.

Out beyond the desert's edge, Orven and Max watched as the blue-green light from the sword's pommel dimmed and vanished, leaving them blind in the stark black night. And now more clearly than before they heard the vague, scratching noises of creatures —large ones, it seemed— moving stealthily across the sand in the darkness, not very far from where they were.

"They must have put their gem into Halix," said Orven, his voice tiny and quiet in the surrounding vastness of desert night. With the waning moon blocked by the mountains, the faint pinpoints of starlight made it hard to distinguish what they were seeing from what they were imagining. Orven and Max had left the others camped at the foot of the mountains and walked out into the desert to try to locate the next gem.

Orven moved the sword in a wide arc. As it pointed north, a tiny glow lit the pommel stone. "It must be very far away," said Orven.

"I hope it's not in the desert," Max said, turning away from the cold winds. "Can we head back now?"

"We'd better leave first thing in the morning. I'm sure the King will send someone out after it. Maybe even after us." Orven took one last look and started back to camp, keeping the sword pointed north to give them what little light they could get. In the distance by the mountains, a tiny campfire winked and flickered in the darkness. Orven and Max walked at a steady pace, carefully making their way in the dark around rocks and clumps of spiny plants and thorny bushes littering the desert floor. They did not speak but walked with their swords drawn, tense and listening for the scratching and clicking sounds around them in the blackness. Max tried to keep his eyes on the little light of the faraway campfire, hoping they would never have to go out into the desert again at night.

The sword indicated a gem in a northerly direction, and everyone followed the King out onto the balcony. Cold wind bit at their fire-warmed faces, and in the night sky the mountain peaks were black on black, jagged teeth against the dark horizon.

King Jordgen stood at the end of the balcony, holding the sword up and angling the blade north by northeast. The stone in the pommel glowed its brightest there, a weak glint of blue-green so faint it was almost only imagined. Ethcairn stood by the King with a kind of astrolabe, noting the direction the sword pointed with as much precision as possible.

"Slightly east of north, eight *kiniths*," Ethcairn noted.

The King lowered the sword, watching the dark mountains. Everyone waited, and presently he joined them. "Let us return to the maps," he said.

They went inside and shut the balcony doors, pleased to return to the room's glowing warmth. Ethcairn unrolled a wide map of the northern ranges of the Frosthelm Mountains, from the Castle up to the Arinzei Valley. Many of the mountains were detailed and named along the edges of the range, but most of the interior was unexplored. Ethcairn brought out a compass, triangle, and a fine silver thread with a tiny metal pin bound on one end and began laying out the angle on the map.

"Here *we* are..." Ethcairn gazed down and all eyes followed his finger on the map. "And this is due north," —he laid out the silver thread, keeping one end on the Castle— "Now the gem is angled off eight *kiniths* to the east... there." He moved the top end of the string to the east, changing its angle to match the compass. The silver thread passed through the mountains and into the Arinzei Valley, just above where the mountains' shoulders jutted eastward into the desert before ending at the valley. "It appears to be either around the range's edge, just beyond Mount Harbash, or in the valley. We cannot narrow it down much further at such a distance." His face darkened. "It may even be the gem Maëlveronde has."

"Our lookout towers along the mountainside path report no troops in the valley so far east," Yolias said, "We would not expect Maëlveronde to be there, yet it is possible."

"If the gem appears to move, beware," added Ethcairn.

"From what we know about the swords, this would seem right," Jordgen said, touching the map. He turned to Iaven. "But your brother will also be able to find it. And he has a head start." He looked to Yolias.

"Tomorrow morning it will be three days" said Yolias, "Though he was traveling on the Ruined East Road, toward the desert."

"Which means he probably has reached the desert by now." Ethcairn was repositioning the silver thread. "Assuming a position east of us in the desert, here... he would sense the gem as almost due north of where he is." He moved the thread in the direction Orven's sword would indicate. Everyone watched as he laid the thread across the map. It ran along the edge of the desert and passed right through where Mount Harbash jutted out eastward into the desert near the end of the range. "From where he is, it might appear the gem is in the *Nehncazzariad*." Ethcairn's tone was suddenly grave.

"The burial grounds of King Nehncazzar, whose dynasty ruled the Hill Goblins in ancient times," Yolias explained. "An elaborate tomb of tunnels and antechambers, carved into the southern side of Mount Harbash. A small city grew up around it briefly, for the workers there. The place has been raided and plundered many times since then. During the last war, the Goblins were carrying on a major excavation there, and used the grounds near the tomb as an outpost. It was destroyed by the Elves during their rout after the war. That was where they must have held Cedric and the other prisoners."

Yolias paused. The fire crackled in the silence. "After the war, the Goblins retreated east, to the desert, hoping to get away to the north. The Elves pursued them to the outpost. When they came to clear out the Goblins, many were the atrocities they found there; corpses of tortured prisoners and many on the verge of death. Some prisoners were Elves, comrades of theirs who they now barely recognized. The clearing out of the outpost was among the most brutal events in Elven history, one they regretted deeply soon after, and still do to this day. After the long march through the desert their patience had worn thin and the bitter taste of war had darkened their hearts. Their own ruthlessness surprised them. Few, if any, Goblins escaped their wrath that day, and many Elves were lost to the Goblin resistance before they were wiped out. Horrifying deeds were done there, and evil spirits lingered, seeking revenge. Some Elves went mad, killing themselves and others.

"Even the fires that burned the place could not cleanse it of evil. The Elves left, their hearts heavy with shame. They inscribed warnings there to alert travelers to avoid the place. They took nothing with them, not even the Goblin gold of the outpost or treasure excavated from the King's tomb. Today much of it lies buried in the sand."

"But the dead do not rest there," Jordgen spoke now, "And since the war it has become a dangerous place. Great evils still reside there. Some were disturbed when the tomb was broken into and robbed over the years, and others during and after the war. The Goblins, Dwarves, and Elves all have dead there, deep beneath the drifting sands. Ghosts and demons roam there and have their haunts. They may even inhabit the enkrida, if one believes tales the Oswai tell."

"What are *enkrida*?" Zammond asked.

"Creatures of the desert," Yolias replied, "Crepuscular vermin; they may be likened to spiders or perhaps crabs or scorpions, but longer and much larger — and a far greater danger. Their bodies are hard, shiny, and black; they move about in the dark of night unseen. Their eyes are keen and their claws sharp. They do not abide daylight and hide or burrow deep while the sun shines. They live in holes in the ground, in the desert. Nehncazzar's tomb is said to be overrun by them."

"Except for the enkrida, the tomb has long been abandoned by the living," said Jordgen, "not even the Goblins go near the place. If the gem were there, we would have to consider it lost."

"If any of you no longer wish to go on the journey, I will understand," Yolias said.

"But the gem's *not* there, is it?" asked Iaven, "And we *can* avoid the tomb and the abandoned outpost, can't we?"

"You can, yes," said Ethcairn, "But as you can see, your brother, searching for the gem, will be heading directly into it."

Iaven looked at the silver thread lying across the drawing of Mount Harbash and the inscription of the tomb below it. He was still angry at Orven, yet he could not wish such a fate on his own brother.

They might be able to catch up to Orven's party and warn them, Iaven thought, but Orven was stubborn. He recalled the well in Kronivar, and Orven's fight with the guards at the Castle Gates. Iaven knew how badly Orven wanted a third gem, and the risks he would take to get it. Despite his anger, Iaven worried about what might befall his brother. Iaven knew he had the best chance of talking some sense into Orven, but doubted Orven would listen.

It was also possible they could beat Orven to the gem. Iaven relished the idea of a race with Orven that he had a fair chance of winning. That seemed reason enough to go. Still, concern for his brother welled up in him, almost against his will, along with a sense of obligation to help Orven. If crossing the desert at night was treacherous, Orven might already have encountered trouble, he thought. He wrestled with his feelings and noticed everyone was watching him, waiting for his reaction.

"I must go... I want to go," Iaven said. Zammond and the others agreed, remaining steadfast in their decision to go, despite the risks.

"Very well then." King Jordgen was pleased. "Begin preparations for the journey. Have Clovenstone gather provisions, and set off at daybreak tomorrow. I myself will see you off."

Yolias nodded in acknowledgement. "As you wish it, Sire."

The King bid them all good night and departed. Iaven was still amazed to have spent an evening with their sovereign. Yolias and Ethcairn were busy at the maps, plotting a path through the mountains to save them time. Yolias was familiar with many trails and suggested a shortcut that led off the Ruined East Road. It would take them northeast, bringing them to the desert a good deal north of where the Ruined East Road emerged. He conferred with Ethcairn awhile, and then together they explained the paths to Iaven and his friends.

Soon Ethcairn retired for the evening, wishing them a safe and quick journey. Yolias told Iaven's party they would leave at dawn. The days were growing shorter and every hour of sunlight would be needed for travel. Yolias made sure the dwarves could find the way back to their room and then left them. Zammond, Hobley, Wilbur, and Tillmore were anxious but tired and ready to turn in to bed. Worries lingered in Iaven's mind, and he discussed them with Rhiane by the crumbling embers of the fire.

"I suppose you're not coming with us, are you?" Iaven tried to hide his disappointment.

"I'm needed here," she said, "The fewer you are, the quicker you'll be able to travel. Besides, you'll be back in only a week or two." She held his hand tenderly. "Won't you?"

Zammond and the others saw Iaven was not about to turn in just yet. They expressed how sorry they were that Rhiane wasn't joining them, wished Iaven and Rhiane good night, and left for their room.

Iaven's heart sunk as he pondered the journey ahead and having to leave Rhiane. His feelings for her grew even stronger, and he wondered if his friends suspected just how much he cared about her. It reminded him of an old song from village dances in the Foothills, about the longing to return to a secret love. Iaven felt he understood it better now.

"I really should get to bed," said Iaven, "It's quite late already, and with our early start..."

"I know. And so soon after *our* trip through the mountains, too." Rhiane smiled. "But Yolias will be with you, and no one knows the mountains better. You should have seen him in his younger days." She sighed, looking around the room. "I *have* missed this place..."

"After seeing the Castle today, it's even harder for me to imagine what it must have been like to grow up here," said Iaven.

Rhiane smiled at him. "Ah, the stories I could tell you!"

Iaven and Rhiane talked long into the night.

At the first light in the eastern sky behind the mountains, Yolias came around to wake the dwarves. They got ready, rubbing sleep from their eyes, sluggish with the realization that they would not have nice warm beds to sleep in again for some time. Breakfast was served, and Rhiane joined them as well. Yolias ate heartily and bid them to do the same.

While they ate, the Steward's men brought in leather-bound packs for them. The packs had been carefully assembled; food, flint, rope, a quiver of arrows and a short bow for hunting small game, and whatever else they would need. Yolias checked everything over and seemed pleased.

After breakfast, coats were brought in for Iaven and his friends. The coats were fur-lined and comfortable, yet very practical for hiking. The dwarves donned them, loaded up their packs, and soon Yolias led them down the hall. They descended the Grand Staircase of the west wing and entered the Throne Room where the King waited with Clovenstone to see them off. The sun was appearing over the edge of the mountains, dimly lighting the tall, arched windows. The King and Clovenstone talked with Yolias awhile, and Rhiane said her good-byes to Zammond, Hobley, Wilbur, and Tillmore. Iaven waited for Rhiane, knowing this would be their last moment together, and realized he had not gone a day without seeing Rhiane since they had met in Kronivar.

The King and Yolias gathered the assembled party. "Godspeed you all!" said King Jordgen, "May your journey be swift and may you return in good time with the gem. If your brother can be convinced to come, he shall be pardoned for his offenses. And if not, then so be it. We shall at least have completed Halix." And with that he picked up a velvet bundle on a nearby table and unwrapped Halix. He handed it to Iaven, who graciously took it and returned it to its sheath. "Take good care of it, as you have, Iaven. You will be doing the kingdom a great service here, and it shall not be forgotten." He looked upon them. "You all have my thanks and gratitude. Go now, and may we meet again soon."

Yolias bowed and paid his respect, and the other dwarves did likewise. As they approached the main doors servants opened them wide. Yolias led them through the vestibule and out into the inner ward. The morning air was brisk and chilly. Zammond, Wilbur, Hobley and Tillmore followed close behind Yolias, but Iaven lingered, waiting for a moment alone with Rhiane. She walked with him into the vestibule, where they might be out of sight of those in the Throne Room. As soon they were alone they bid each other good-bye. Rhiane hugged Iaven and looked at him with dark, sweet eyes. "I'll be waiting for you," she said, and kissed him quickly on the mouth. "Hurry back," she whispered, and then disappeared into the Throne Room.

Iaven's friends could not see him, but knew him well enough to guess what was going on.

186

"Now we'll *have* to come back!" Zammond laughed as they waited outside.

"Still think he'll go back to Hillbrook?" Hobley smiled to Wilbur. Wilbur looked away and shrugged, trying not to show his disappointment.

At last Iaven emerged from the doors into the morning light, and they all set off through town, out the East Gate, and across the terraces to where the Ruined East Road began. Iaven said little. He felt a strange mix of exuberance and dread; the first steps of a journey were exciting, yet the weight of it all overshadowed him. He was very glad his friends were with him, and Yolias as well, though his thoughts were with Rhiane. Once again the song about the Secret Love came to him, and floated through his head as they walked,

> In town I have a Secret Love—
> Across the square we'll both make eyes
> And meet each other on the sly
> Though tongues will wag and heads may shake
> I'll bear it all for my love's sake.
>
> And if in town we may not meet—
> I'll meet her in a forest glade
> Where prying eyes cannot invade;
> Till whispered gossip's put to rest,
> There can I woo my lady best.
>
> And if by day we may not meet—
> We'll rendez-vous when evening's nigh,
> Beneath a fading twilight sky,
> And hand in hand watch stars take wing
> Whilst 'round us all is quieting.
>
> And if by dusk we may not meet—
> I'll meet her for a midnight tryst
> By lanterns haloed in the mist
> And gaze upon her in their light
> Until I leave her kissed good night.
>
> And if we may not meet again—
> But separate, and mourn our loss
> On parted paths that never cross,
> I'll still be happy that we met,
> My Secret Love I'll not forget.

The song meant more to Iaven now, though the last verse seemed strangely resonant. Iaven pushed on with renewed spirits, following the winding road around the mountains until they could no longer see the Castle behind them.

Book III: Sand and Shadow

Chapter 17.
Night in the Veskwood Forest

The night was cold and damp, and Urzad grew impatient as he sat wondering when Herog would return. He coiled and uncoiled a piece of twine around his hand as he waited. They had camped in Veskwood long enough, and tonight they would start heading back north. Urzad pulled his dark cloak around him, shifting his position on the log and staring into the dark of the forest. All was quiet except for the rhythmic chirp of crickets, croaking frogs, and the occasional whispered bickering of the goblins' two prisoners. Urzad glanced over to where they lay bound, near the fire, but they had ceased to interest him. They hadn't been much trouble in the past two days, though he knew they might still try something, despite the threats he and Herog had made.

It was time to move on. They had seen what they needed to see. For three days, Urzad and Herog had watched squadrons of Dwarven troops practicing on fields north of the garrison outside of town, soldiers patrolling the forest's edge, and ships arriving in port, no doubt with mercenaries for hire aboard. Kronivar was readying for war; evidence was everywhere. Urzad wondered why King Golhazzar was holding back. General Burzok's marshaled troops lay waiting in the western end of the Arinzei Valley, just beyond sight of Teska's watchtowers, eager to advance. King Golhazzar was biding his time, as reports of spies trickled in from Itharia. What news was he waiting for? Urzad thought they ought to attack now, if they were going to at all. To wait much longer, with winter only a month or so away, was foolish. With every passing day the Dwarves were more prepared, and soon waiting until spring would be more prudent. But the Goblin forces were ready and it seemed there could be no turning back.

Urzad wondered to what extent King Golhazzar's Grand Vizier had a hand in the planning. Rumors claimed the King valued the old man's counsel over that of his Goblin advisors, while others hinted that he was some kind of sorcerer. Apparently, he had come from Phamiar, many years ago. Erog Del-Sorhar, the Chief Spy, now answered directly to him and spoke highly of how he had organized and strengthened the Goblin forces over the years. Urzad grunted as he thought of Del-Sorhar, who was eager for war and angered by his spies' reports when they did not favor it. But Kronivar was now the center and the key to Itharia, he thought, and too well guarded. And without a fleet, the siege of a port city that size was almost impossible. The Goblin armies had been massing now for some time, and even surpassed the number of those marshaled for the Great War almost a century ago, but he still felt that such an attack was not wise. The Goblins could take and hold northern Veskwood, and advance south, although they might just as easily be pushed north again. Yet in the end such things were not his to decide.

He pulled his cloak tighter and sniffed the air for any sign of Herog. Herog agreed with him about the war and Del-Sorhar. The whole situation in Navrogenaya had grown dangerously one-sided. Many Goblins who had spoken against the war had vanished. He had even known one spy who had altered his report to make it more pleasing to Del-Sorhar and his superiors. Urzad was sure that if he could somehow bypass Del-Sorhar and give his report directly to General Burzok himself, the warning would get through and something could be done about it. That would be difficult to do, and risky, as he had already fallen out of favor with Del-Sorhar. Something had to be done, and he and Herog would have plenty of time to talk it over on their way north back to Navrogenaya.

"How long are they going to stay here?" Lexter grunted in a harsh whisper.

Leland and Lexter lay bound, side by side near the fire, stiff from the cold and their inactivity. The Goblins untied each of them once a day to change their ropes, allowing them to stretch and eat a few scraps of leftovers, for which they were grateful.

"At least they haven't killed us!" Leland snapped back.

"Well, why *are* they keeping us alive, then?" Lexter retorted.

They spoke in hushed tones, almost under their breath. Not long after their capture, the Goblins had explained to them in halting Tharic that if either one of them tried to call for help, both would get their throats cut. Leland and Lexter realized that since the Goblins understood more than their native Rogglish, any plans they made could be overheard. The big one sitting on the log didn't appear to be listening to them, but he was not out of earshot, and you could never be sure. Lexter had eavesdropped often enough to know how easy it was.

The first night Lexter and Leland had lain bound in the goblins' camp, trembling, cold and fearful, until they finally dozed off from fatigue. The following morning, finding themselves both alive, they spent most of the time bickering as to whose fault it was they were there. By afternoon both had tired of arguing, although each was ready to start again if provoked. Then a kind of despair set in, as they considered their situation. Everything they had was gone; the crates of weaponry, the horse and wagon, and all the money they were supposed to get from the deal. Even the money and knives they had with them were taken away by the goblins, who seemed pleased with their booty.

That evening and most of the next day, they planned how they might escape, being careful not to mention anything directly when the goblins were nearby. Lexter thought that if they spoke fast and alluded to things that only they knew, the goblins wouldn't be able to follow the conversation. Leland preferred hushed tones and was just as careful. As Lexter suggested ways they might escape, Leland found the flaws in each idea, adding suggestions of his own. Over the last few hours, they had begun formulating a plan.

"So they'll eventually go back north," Lexter whispered, "and we could only try it while we're up and walking."

"They can't get through Teska, they'll have to cross the North Road," said Leland.

"And no one's going to let them through the North Gate."

"Too many guards; even if they had a spy there, which is very unlikely. No, it's got to be something else..."

"A boat, maybe? No, goblins don't use them, and as you said, the Teskans would see them."

"Well, however they're going to get through, we're not going with them. They'll have to come out somewhere, across the road. That'll be our chance. We'll run in different directions, shouting, once we're out of their reach. They'll have to split up to follow us. It's the only way. Once they're apart our chances will improve."

"It depends where we are," said Lexter.

"And how fast can they run?" said Leland, "Can we outrun them, with our arms tied behind our backs?"

"They're big, and I'll bet they're not very fast..."

"We have to be sure! How can we know?" Leland looked at Lexter. "It may just be a chance we'll have to take."

"Even without their packs I doubt they could outrun us. I don't know. But what if we can't get away from them? Or what if we're in swampland, or something like that? Then what?"

"A back full of black arrows, probably. Of course, that could happen any time. But what else can we do? We've got to try. We'll have to use signals. I'll signal you depending on what we should do. We'll have to plan for every contingency."

Lexter looked at Leland. "Well, I suppose we've got nothing better to do tonight..."

For the next hour or so, the Splide brothers worked out their means of their escape. Leland thought of several different plans, and Lexter came to believe that if they worked together they would be able to get away after all. If their timing was good, and it usually was, it seemed possible. Lexter began at last to regain hope. For once in as a long a time as he could remember, he did not mind being the younger brother, as Leland took on his usual role of laying out his plan and telling Lexter what to do. They were working together, as they'd so often done, the planning taking their minds off of their fears and losses. It looked like everything would turn out alright in the end as it always did, no matter what happened to them. Lexter found new appreciation for his brother, something he had not felt in a long time. He listened to Leland, glad to be with him even though he would never admit it.

"...then head for the nearest town. We'll meet at the largest tavern there, if there's more than one," said Leland.

"We'll have no money, but that shouldn't stop us for long," Lexter added.

"No, I've already got a few ideas about that," Leland said. "I'm sure you have some yourself."

Just as they had everything worked out, the goblin seated on the log rose and moments later they heard muted sounds of someone approaching through the forest. They both craned their necks around to see the other goblin approaching.

Herog emerged from the dark, his harsh features lit by the soft glow from the dying fire. "*Gahrek,*" he said. The goblins spoke to each other in Rogglish. "Finished."

"We'll write up the report tomorrow, we must get moving." Urzad motioned to where the packs lay ready to go. He walked over to where Lexter and Leland lay by the remains of the fire. "And then there's these two…" Urzad gazed at them and the Splides grew uneasy.

"One or both?" said Herog.

"Just the bigger one." Urzad handed Herog the long piece of twine he had been playing with earlier. A noose was fashioned on the end of it.

Neither Leland nor Lexter understood much Rogglish and feared the worst when they saw the rope. Herog grabbed their arms, which remained tied behind their backs, and stood them on their feet. The Splides balanced nervously, stiff and aching, their ankles tied together. Lexter shuddered as Herog put the noose over his head and made it snug around his neck.

"Leland!" Lexter groaned, turning to his brother, trembling. Once the noose was in place, Urzad came and took the rope from Herog, who went to get the packs. He brought them over and loaded them onto Lexter's back, between his bound arms. The packs' straps he threw over Lexter's neck, securing them with a short piece of twine. Lexter bowed under the weight, nearly losing his balance. Herog cut the rope binding Lexter's legs so he could walk. The goblins looked at Lexter with his burden, grunting in Rogglish and laughing.

Lexter looked to Leland again. *There's only the two packs*, he thought, *why do I have to haul both of them? Why don't they put one on Leland?* He debated whether to complain aloud but said nothing. It didn't seem fair; Leland always seemed to get the better end of things. He thought of the dealings with Aranstone, the Harvest Festival at Miastolas, and plenty of other times reaching all the way back to when they were kids. Leland always got the best of everything because he was the oldest. *Even the goblins weigh me down instead of Leland*, Lexter thought. It just wasn't fair.

The goblins were bantering again, and the Splides looked at each other, Leland standing bound hand and foot, and Lexter under his load. *We didn't plan for this contingency*, Lexter's gaze accused Leland. Leland stood, looking concerned, even a little sorry for Lexter, and Lexter knew he was considering how they might deal with it and change their plans. Lexter was certain Leland would think of something, but still resented carrying the whole load; he always got all the grunt work.

The goblins finished their discussion. Urzad handed the rope back to Herog, who gave it a good yank to turn Lexter around and point him in the direction they were going. Lexter turned, still cold and stiff, unsteady under the weight. He wondered what they were taking back with them. Lexter stumbled forward, until Herog stopped, waiting for Urzad. With an effort, Lexter turned and looked back to where Leland stood near the glowing remains of the fire. Leland stared back at him, bound and unable to follow. Lexter wondered when they would get a chance to talk together again. The goblins would have several more nights of camping before they reached the northern border.

As they moved away, the campsite, dim in the last of the glowing embers, was becoming swallowed up by the dark surrounding it. The glow lit Leland's face from the side, and Lexter saw him turn his head as Urzad walked up behind him. The goblin drew his knife and reached around Leland, but instead of cutting Leland's ropes he raised it and cut Leland's throat. Leland gasped in pain, and the goblin pushed him down on the ground by the fire. In the shadowy pale light Lexter saw blood seeping from Leland's neck onto the ground, his eyes staring into the blackness. Leland looked up to Lexter from where he lay, and soon was still. The goblin made sure Leland was dead and stamped out the embers. Darkness filled the clearing. Herog yanked the rope cruelly, turning Lexter away from them and into the woods.

Lexter gasped for breath, feeling so weak he could barely stand. Whenever he slowed, the goblin pulled on the rope making him lurch forward the next few steps. Lexter was tired and shivering and too stunned to think. He trudged on through the cold and dark, mud and dried leaves underfoot and branches scraping at his sides, mile after mile the same. Night winds shrilled through the tree branches, rasping through the last of the drying leaf cover, a harsh and empty, lonely sound. More than once that night he thought about just falling to the ground and letting the goblins kill him. There was no hope now; all their plans and contingencies meant nothing. Leland was gone. And Lexter knew that when the goblins were finished with him his life would be over as well.

Chapter 18.
Along the Desert's Edge

The nights were cold and the winds chilling and endless. The days were shorter, the low hills already in the mountains' shadow by late afternoon. Orven's party made their way, rising and falling with the slopes, keeping to the hills at the foot of the mountains, alongside the desert. Often at night the dwarves gazed up into the black sky where myriad hard, white pinpoint stars lay scattered and indifferent. The mountains obscured the sky to their left, and on their right, wide expanses of desert stretched away to merge with the starry darkness. Around them all was vast and silent, a silence they had little urge to break. Looking out over the dark desert plain, the Dwarves imagined their ancestors' journey of long ago. Orven wondered where they had come from and what had driven them from their homeland.

The ground beneath the dwarves' feet sloped uphill and down, but was firm, not sandy, and less barren than the desert beyond it. Occasionally they found traces of a broad, disused road they supposed had been cut and cleared by the Goblins, when their armies had marched south. Most of it was worn away and overgrown, yet now and then they came upon long unbroken stretches of it, wide open and eerily empty in the night.

The hills were safer than the desert, yet the dwarves were still wary as they rounded the top of each hill. The creatures they had glimpsed in the dark came out mainly at night, and had long, clawlike jointed legs extending from hard, black, shiny shells. They seemed aware of the dwarves trespassing through their lands. At night, Orven often sensed movement nearby but saw nothing when he turned to look; nothing he could see, anyway. As long as the dwarves stayed together in the daylight, they felt safe. But when the sun sank behind the mountains the creatures emerged, with dry, whispering, scratching sounds of legs and claws passing over sand and rock. They kept their distance, just beyond the circle of torchlight, watching and biding their time.

For two days the dwarves traveled along the desert's edge, Orven driving them on as many hours as he could. Even with a double watch, nights were uneasy, which meant less sleep for all of them. Orven checked the sword each night and it kept indicating north, the light still very faint and the gem far away. By day they rounded the mountains' shoulders until they grew tired of seeing slopes of rock and low, dry brush and parched grasses. Between the mountains, narrow canyons wound upward into deep valleys, luring them into unseen lands, but Orven kept them moving north. They kept going after the sun had set. Now they were cold and tired, their pace had slowed, and there was little by which they could measure their progress at night.

"Well, Orven, we could set camp any time now, what do you think?" Indignation edged Max's voice.

It was late and Orven knew they would start grumbling aloud if he pushed them much further. He glanced about their surroundings, faint in the starlight. "All right, how's this over here?" Orven led them over to a flat area half-sheltered by shoulders of rock that faced away from the wind. They slung their packs onto the ground. Aaron and Max sat down. Roy unrolled his bedroll nearby. It was Ripley and Orven's turn to gather kindling for the fire, and whatever vittles they could find, so the two of them went off onto a dark brush-strewn slope.

"It's farther than we thought," said Aaron, leaning back against the rock.

"I know… I'd hoped we'd have it by now," said Max.

"I've been thinking," Aaron propped himself up straighter, "We've gone quite far north, and there's still plenty of mountains to go. Not much to eat or drink out here, either. Unless we find more than we have, we may not have enough left to make it all the way back to the Castle."

Max looked at Aaron, considering their situation.

"Nor is the northern border a good place to be these days," Aaron added. "And the gem does seem much farther north than we had guessed."

"Are you suggesting we go back?" Max asked at last.

"Well, we've given it a good try, haven't we? Maybe the gem's out of our reach. If it hasn't been found already. I just don't think Orven has much of a plan any more."

"I've been a bit worried myself," Max admitted. "And hungrier than I'd like. But Orven would never hear of going back."

"We could talk to him. He'd listen to you, I think."

"Maybe," said Max, "but you know how he is."

Roy finished setting up and came over and joined them. "How many more days of this?" he said. "I'd just as soon have stayed at the Castle."

"Orven will have to answer for what happened at the gate," Aaron said. "Of course, we weren't entirely unprovoked, either. But they'd take us back. And it's better than starving out here, or getting caught and dragged off into Goblin country. Or getting killed there."

"If only we knew how much farther the gem was, that'd be different," said Roy, "I'm not eager to go to war, either, but we're no better off out here."

Soon Orven and Ripley returned with armloads of dry twigs and brush. Orven set his on the ground, and Ripley threw his on the pile and knelt down with his flint to start the fire. Bright sparks leapt where the stones struck. Orven stood nearby and sensed Aaron and Max were in the midst of deciding something.

"So how much farther do you think the gem is?" Max asked Orven.

Orven drew his sword and pointed it to the north. A very faint blue-green glow lit his face from the sword's pommel. "Not much closer than last night, we still must be a ways off."

Max tried to read Orven's expression in the dim light. "Just how many more days' walk yet, do you suppose?"

"So what are you saying? That we should turn back, go back to the Castle without the gem?" Orven looked at Max, astonished. He paused a moment, then sheathed Gorflange.

"It is a lot farther than we thought," Aaron pointed out.

"Oh, so this is your idea!" Orven turned to Aaron, angry now with the conspirators. "Trying to convince them to turn around, are you?"

"Well, what, then?" Aaron tensed but replied coolly, hoping to calm Orven and bring him to reason. He drew his knees up in front of him and rested his elbows on them. "You know how our supplies are; we've used up most of what we brought along."

"It's true," said Max, "there's barely enough just to make it back."

"Max, you agree with him?" Orven sounded wounded, and Max struggled with what he had to say.

"We've come out as far as we can... " Max started.

"If we knew how far it was, that'd be one thing," Roy put in, "but we don't know, do we? If we don't find it in the next few days—"

Ripley had got a small flame going and came over by them. "Go back, now? We almost have all three gems for the sword!"

"What good's the sword if we miss the war?" said Roy, "The sooner we get back, the sooner we can join up with the King's troops; isn't that what you want to do?"

Ripley stopped a moment considering this, and Orven jumped in before Ripley could change his mind. "The best thing for us to do is to find that last gem. We've come this far, we can't turn back now!"

"The sword no longer points to the gem at the Castle," Aaron replied. "Assuming that Iaven's given them Halix, the King will certainly send someone out to get the gem. It might not be long before they catch up to us."

"All the more reason for us to try to get to it first. Go back with them, then, if you want; I'm not turning back now!" Orven stood, defiant, his face set and his features edged with firelight. "Besides, you remember what happened at the gate!"

"You were defending yourself," said Ripley, "They shouldn't have attacked us! But you showed them, didn't you?"

"*Attacked*? I wouldn't quite call it that!" Aaron said.

"Listen," said Orven, "we can join the troops at Kronivar or somewhere else. They need everyone they can get."

"That doesn't solve our problem," Aaron continued, "First you said we'd join the army at the Castle, then you wanted to go after the third gem. Now, after the fight at the gate, it'll be that much harder to go back, and we'll still have to go back that way to get through to Kronivar."

Orven was shocked and indignant. "I'm not turning myself over to them. And they're probably not far behind us, either, at the rate we've been going. Once I have the last gem, things will be different. They'll have to let us fight, in Kronivar, or wherever we want!"

"You maybe, but not the rest of us!" Aaron said.

"I'll demand it!" said Orven.

Max turned to Orven. "But what if the gem's too far away? Or over the border, in Navrogenaya?"

"It could be Maëlveronde's gem," said Aaron.

"It can't be," Orven argued, "Why would he be over on the east side of Navrogenaya? There's nothing out there. We don't even know if he's still alive, do we?"

"I suppose not," Roy muttered.

"And anyway, I wouldn't just walk into the valley. But the gem's not that far north; I'm sure of it. We *are* getting closer; we just have a little way to go yet." Orven turned to each of them, their faces dim and serious in the soft wavering firelight. "I'll go on alone if I have to."

Orven looked at them, and they knew he meant it.

"I couldn't let you go off alone like that," said Max.

"So you'll come, then?"

"Well," Max hesitated, "that wasn't what—"

"I'll go with you!" Ripley said. "You can count on me. What else can we do now that we've come so far from Hillbrook, after so long? I want to be there when you find the last gem and put it into the sword! I'll go with you."

There was a pause again as everyone thought it over.

"Well, I'm not in any hurry to go fight in the war," said Roy. "I'll go; I just hope we don't starve or run into goblins."

"We won't!" said Orven. "We'll come right back as soon as we have it. Of course they'll let us through at the Castle; they'll have to."

"I doubt they'll let you off so easily," said Aaron.

"We won't be staying there anyway, just passing through to Kronivar," Orven said, "They'll make me a captain there, with the sword —maybe higher! Remember how surprised they were when I fought the guard off at the gate?" Orven got up and unsheathed Gorflange, for the sheer joy it gave him to wield it, and measured the distance to the gem. He stepped off into the dark to get a better look at the blue-green glow. Ripley got up and joined him.

Aaron watched them go and turned to Max.

"If Orven's going, then I'm going, too," said Max, looking to Aaron somberly. "We really couldn't go back on our own, if the others are going on. We're better off staying together. We've come this far. Wherever it is we go, we go together."

"And die together!" Aaron muttered under his breath as he lay back with a heavy sigh of resignation.

Wrapped tightly in their blankets and huddled against the rock walls, the dwarves slept well. The fire was low and quiet now. A glowing log rolled over with a flash of rising sparks. Aaron broke a stick and tossed the pieces onto the tiny flames. He and Orven were sitting the first watch. Everyone else had dozed off hours ago and Aaron envied them, waiting for his watch to end. He and Orven had not talked much that night. Orven, unable to sit still for long, got up and walked around, staring off into the blackness beyond their camp, sometimes drawing his sword and looking as if he expected something to jump out of the darkness and attack him. Then he'd sheath the sword, pace awhile, and sit down again, deep in thought. More than once Aaron wanted to ask Orven what he was brooding about, but he knew they'd only end up arguing.

Aaron's worries soon gave way to tiredness, and Orven also appeared drowsy. Max was slow to rise when Orven roused him, and Orven was well on his way to deep slumber by the time Max assumed his post. Aaron woke Roy, who reluctantly took over for him. "Sleep well," Roy told him with weary jealousy.

Max and Roy chatted quietly for a while, but soon fell silent. The night was vast and black. They sat with their backs to the rock, listening for the tiniest signs of something approaching. Now and then they started to nod and forced their eyes open.

Max considered anew whether Orven's plan still seemed sound, finding he was less confident about it. He watched Orven sleeping, Orven's tousled blonde hair sticking out from the blanket, his side rising and falling. Max admired Orven's determination even as he was annoyed with his stubbornness. He felt a bit sorry for Orven, who now seemed more concerned about finding the last gem than serving the Kingdom. He had been surprised by Orven's ability to wield Gorflange, which he supposed was due in part to the sword itself. The clash at the Castle gate had been quick and decisive, the guards underestimating Orven. Orven himself had been pleased and somewhat surprised by his success. But Orven had had the upper hand well before he had wounded the guard, and Max thought he had gone too far. They had discussed it during the trip through the mountains, but Orven was unyielding. Ripley agreed with Orven, but Max knew Roy and especially Aaron were as disturbed about it as he was.

Max wondered what they would do. Their plan kept changing, and there wasn't much of one left anymore. As they drew nearer to the Goblin border in the north, their quest seemed all the more foolhardy. But what worried Max the most was Orven himself. Orven had always been bold and stubborn, sure of himself, even prone to getting in trouble; but there was something else now, something more serious than their boyhood pranks and misadventures.

As the ash crumbled and the fire breathed its last, Max sat back, staring out into the dark night. He recalled the goblin in Rundlewood by the river, his stringy black hair and pointed ears spread out on the dried leaves of the forest floor. The goblin lay there helpless as the dwarves looked on, his blood seeping onto the ground as he gasped his last breaths, his eyes bulging in disbelief in the dim light. And then, suddenly, Orven's merciless swift stroke crashing down.

Max longed to be back safe in Hillbrook, away from the war, the Castle, the cities, and the great lonely ranges of mountains. Instead, here they were, far from anything they knew, heading toward enemy lands and unknown dangers. Max yearned for even the most boring, dull days spent in Hillbrook, the kind he had spent waiting and wishing he was elsewhere. Such days were really not so bad after all. Being found by the King's soldiers was their only hope now, he thought. They would certainly fare better with them than with the Goblins or the creatures of the desert.

Suddenly Max came to with a start. The hissing and clicking sounds were very close nearby. He gazed into the darkness. No more than twenty feet away, almost invisible but for the glints of starlight on their shiny black shells, several of the *enkrida*, the size of large dogs, were standing and watching him. They stood motionless, the joints of their legs bent, crablike. In the dark he could not make out their shapes entirely, nor could he tear his eyes away from them for a moment. They whispered together in muted clicking and hissing sounds, and Max wondered if others had been summoned. Max carefully drew his sword and held it on his lap. The fire had almost gone out; he wondered if that was what they were waiting for. Without getting up, and moving as little as he could, he threw some dried grasses onto the embers, hoping to raise a few flames. He continued watching the enkrida, waiting for what seemed like a long time before the grasses finally caught fire. He heaped more on, along with a few twigs, and the light brightened a little. The enkrida backed off a step, and after some raspy whispers among themselves they disappeared back into the darkness. Max sat listening as the scratching and scraping sounds grew fainter until they were gone. He no longer worried about the days and weeks ahead, but found himself counting the long hours remaining until daybreak.

Chapter 19.
By the Falls

The Ruined East Road was a sad place, thought Iaven. After traveling it a whole day and camping, they had risen early to continue their journey. Yolias led them along the lonely, disused road as it wound through the mountains, high above forested valleys and below snow-laden peaks towering into the sky, cold and indifferent. The road was wide and clear, until they came upon a long gap where it had crumbled and been torn out, as if gigantic jaws had gnawed it away. All that remained was a narrow ledge hugging the mountain wall, which the dwarves had to cross carefully in single file. After fifty feet or so the road resumed and they were back on less difficult ground for a few hours, until they came upon another gap in the road. The curves of road were carved from the rock walls and lovingly inscribed with Huskaric runes that told of their making. Occasionally the dwarves even saw reliefs cut into the rock walls, or outcroppings of rocks sculpted into statues. Even where these were damaged or weatherworn, there remained a sense of the builders' care and love of stone in the days of King Taslen II. But after the war with the Goblins, Yolias explained, the road had been made impassable to Goblin chariots and war-wagons that might venture that way again.

"After the war, Orglen's son, Aardgen, became King," Yolias told them, "It was his idea to seal off the Kingdom from attack from the east. Many dwarves disliked the idea of reducing stretches of the road to footpaths, but Aardgen thought it necessary. He said the eastern road was rarely used and the Dwarves would not need a road to the desert. Many dwarves were moving west, to Kronivar, at the time, and the cities were growing in size. Those were not the best years for the Kingdom, under King Aardgen. The Castle loosened its hold on the cities, and it has never been quite the same since. And now we are paying the price."

"And the war?" asked Zammond, "Are we ready for war?"

"More than we were in Orglen's day, though it still may not be enough." Yolias paused. "The Goblins have marshaled still larger forces, and King Golhazzar and General Burzok and their advisors have been planning ahead for some time. King Jordgen is a stronger and wiser ruler than his father was, but it is always harder to tighten the reins after they have been loose for so long."

They walked on in silence awhile, contemplating war and what part they might play in it. Iaven's thoughts turned to events close at hand; Orven, the abandoned outpost, and the gem. He did not think Orven would listen to reason or turn over the sword on his own. Then again, it was difficult to say what condition they would find him in. Iaven's party had received fur-lined coats and supplies from the Castle, while Orven had no such luxuries for his journey. Nor did Orven have any idea of what awaited him at the outpost.

Iaven was both worried about Orven and angry with him. Part of him wanted Orven to get what he deserved and see the look on Orven's face when he realized it was Iaven coming to rescue him. Iaven wondered how close Orven's party was to the outpost and whether Yolias's shortcut would save enough time. As upset as he was with Orven, he did not want to arrive and find him dead.

They walked a few more hours and finally Yolias turned and indicated a rock-strewn slope climbing steeply to their left. "Here we leave the road," he said, "This leads into the way that should take us northeast and out to the desert a good distance north of the road." The dwarves were tired and the prospect of leaving the fairly level road for a climb without any trail was not a welcome one. But it would be worth it, Iaven thought, if it gained them a day or two.

They followed Yolias, ascending in single file, steadying themselves with their hands in the steepest parts. Once they were over, a short and treacherous descent followed, and then another short climb. At last they stopped on a ridge to rest. Yolias pointed to a peak in the distance and said that beyond it the worst would be behind them. Hearts still pounding from the climb, they breathed deeply and pushed on ahead.

They camped that night in a shallow cave, and Yolias sat night watches with them. The following day they rose early and continued on their way. A few times that afternoon Yolias stopped, discerning which way to go. "It has been some time since I came this way," he told them. At last they climbed through a pass and were relieved to reach a long level ridge running alongside the mountain. They felt refreshed, the great efforts of the climb driving all other worries from their minds. They walked along the ridge, the sun lowering into early afternoon, and the sky was clear. The air was cold and brisk, and now that they were back on fairly level ground they were ready to hike until nightfall.

Iaven gazed in wonderment at the mountain passes, the gorges, and high, snow-covered peaks rising in the hazy distance. He breathed easily, feeling loose from the climb, relaxed and lighter on his feet. But his serenity was shaken by what he saw on the ridge across the valley. Three tall, gray figures seemed to be striding across the ridge— but not moving. Looking closer, Iaven realized they were carved in stone, their arms swung out at their sides and their legs frozen in mid-stride. Even at a distance Iaven marveled at their size, guessing them to be around sixteen feet high or so. They were clearly not Dwarven, and seemed to have been placed there deliberately. The sight of them sent an eerie chill through Iaven, as though he were trespassing.

"What are they? Who made them?" Iaven asked.

"They are believed to be the work of the Stone Giants," said Yolias, "What are they? No one knows. Not much is known about the Stone Giants; the Elves and Goblins have some old legends about them, as do our ancestors, but no one has ever seen one. I suppose your friend Cedric came as close to seeing one as anyone has. Here and there we have found their works; I have seen other statues like those. Once I was exploring mountains north of here and came upon a huge arch, cut into the mountainside. It must have been twenty or thirty feet high. A great hallway led inside, but I did not dare venture into it." Yolias smiled at them. "I was young at the time; now in my old age, perhaps I would."

They moved on. Iaven considered the vastness of the mountains, and how little of them had ever been explored, or even mapped. He felt removed from everything else in the world. The few times his thoughts strayed momentarily to the Foothills, the cold, hard beauty of the mountains brought them back, and he was glad to be there.

A short, rocky path took them up into a hidden wooded glen, where a soft rushing sound grew louder. There, amidst pines and rock ledges, a mountain stream fell sparkling from a high wall of rock into a wide pond, from which a river flowed deeper into the glen. The place was quiet and secluded, a few birdcalls echoing over the rushing waters. Yolias led them to a fallen log near the water's edge, where they stopped for a rest. Tillmore collected kindling to prepare their dinner, while Hob brought out a fishing line.

"This place I remember well. A good resting place," said Yolias, relaxing. "No dangers here, at present. But there are plenty where we are headed and enough for our return. And afterward, I take it all of you will be joining the troops?"

Hobley, Tillmore, and Zammond nodded, but Wilbur and Iaven said nothing. Yolias had not yet asked them so directly about their plans, and the question took Iaven by surprise. He suspected Yolias already knew his answer and was just testing him.

"Rhiane wants me to," Iaven began, "I wouldn't make much of a soldier..."

"You can learn." Yolias got up off the log. He motioned Zammond and Iaven over and had them draw their swords. Iaven lifted Halix to meet Zammond's blade. Zammond was smiling, enjoying himself. He swung first, playfully, and Iaven warded off the blow. Tillmore and Wilbur readied the fire, keeping an eye on the swordplay. Hobley fished and watched the lesson with interest.

"First, your stances," said Yolias. "Turn to the side and give your opponent less of a target; there, that's it." Zammond began swinging and thrusting. Iaven fended him off and put it a few thrusts of his own, which Zammond sidestepped. Zammond made a few false moves that Iaven countered, and then suddenly he jumped forward and gleefully whacked Iaven's shoulder with the flat of his blade. Iaven stepped back, a bit alarmed.

"Zammond! That hurt!"

Yolias laughed. "In battle you could have lost an arm! This is mere play-acting. Remember what would be at stake in a war!"

"Come on, Iaven, you're not even trying!" said Zammond.

"Alright!" Iaven lifted his sword again, this time with more resolve.

Zammond danced around, goading Iaven into a better fight. Iaven warded off more of Zammond's thrusts and blows, while Zammond met or deftly avoided Iaven's.

"The hands, watch his hands!" said Yolias. "Lead with the hands, and let the feet follow; otherwise your feet give away your moves. The hand is swifter than the foot; whatever is done with the hand first is true fight."

Zammond moved in a semi-circle around Iaven, looking for an opening. Iaven turned, following him, but at last Zammond caught Iaven after a swing and thrust his sword in, stopping it just as its point pressed into Iaven's shirt.

"Ha! I would have had you there!" Zammond exclaimed.

"Stand in one place and he will find you there, Iaven," Yolias said, "You must keep moving and be nimble on your feet. Stagnant waters do not stay clean."

"Can't be a stick-in-the-mud, Iaven!" taunted Zammond. He laughed, spurring Iaven on. Iaven surprised him with a quick sharp blow that he failed to ward off. Zammond winced and then smiled seeing the others enjoying their roughhousing. "Ho! That's the way!" he shouted, "Come on, you slowpoke!"

Now Iaven, too, was moving about. Sunlight glinted and flashed on their swinging blades. "Strike blows as well as thrusts! Use them together!" Yolias called out his instructions and guided the fight, pointing out each of their failings. Iaven kept moving and began to enjoy the contest. Halix hovered and pivoted in his hand, seeming lighter with the gems than it had been without them. He marveled at the ease with which he could wield it, and knew it was only inexperience that stood in his way. Iaven recalled his skirmish with Lexter in Miastolas, how nervous he had been, fearing for his life, and firmly resolved to learn what he could from Yolias in the short time before the war.

Zammond kept on the offensive. He had a good sense of what Iaven would do, guessing most of his reactions. Iaven righted Halix again and swung. Zammond sidestepped it, nearly tripping over a rock, allowing Iaven a good blow on his shoulder. "Ow! Hey! Iaven, not so hard!"

"You are in danger of losing your balance, Zammond," said Yolias. "And as important, Iaven, is the balance between attack and defense. There, see how swift the change is from one to the other! Good. Now..." Yolias followed them as the fight progressed. Zammond jumped up onto the fallen log and Iaven did likewise. They moved to and fro, their swords clashing and clanging, and Iaven felt the cool spray from the waterfall. He sensed how the sword sometimes seemed to guide or anticipate his actions; he was unsure what was due to the sword or mere luck, but was thrilled all the same to be doing well. Iaven now knew Zammond's style, expecting his attacks, wards, and false moves. Pleased with himself, Iaven found a few more openings. Suddenly, just as Iaven thought he had him, Zammond gripped the log with his feet, gave it a jerk to the side and jumped off. Iaven tipped and fell clumsily into the pond.

Yolias laughed. "You balanced your attacks and defense well, Iaven, but balancing on your feet must come first!" he chided. "There is much you need keep in mind at once, and still much to learn. But that is enough for today, I think."

Zammond sheathed his sword and stepped over to help Iaven to his feet. "Right into the water! Sorry, Iaven." Iaven took Zammond's hand and got up, his clothing soaked. He brushed off a bit of mud. Wilbur, Hobley, and Tillmore applauded the contest. Iaven smiled.

Iaven and Zammond stepped over the log and joined the others over by Hobley, who had a pan of fish simmering over the fire. Wilbur brought out potatoes, bread, and other supplies from the Castle, and they soon had the makings of a good and long-awaited meal before them.

As they sat and ate, Tillmore watched the waterfall glittering in the sunlight, spray hovering around its base. He glanced up into the sky, staring.

"Look! What are those?" said Tillmore.

The others followed his gaze. Two large creatures circled and wheeled in the bright sky. They were much larger than birds, higher up in the sky, and vaguely menacing. They glided on large, leathery, outstretched wings and their long tails ended in arrowhead points.

"Are they dragons?" asked Wilbur.

"No, not dragons," said Yolias, "They are wyverns, distant cousins of the great dragons that once roamed these mountains. Wyverns are much smaller, and only two-legged. They are few in number now and found only in the eastern mountains. The great dragons are no more; their kind flourished ages ago, long before the Dwarves crossed over the desert. The last of them was found in the days of Taslen II, when the Great Dragon Roast was held at the Castle."

"They killed a dragon?" Wilbur said.

"Some wanted people to believe that, but no. They found the dragon lying dead in one of the valleys; it had just died, and was still warm. No one knew how it had died. They cut its tail off and brought it back for a feast. It is said that it took all afternoon just to cut through the tail, and more than a dozen dwarves to carry it back."

"Are they dangerous?" Zammond's eyes were still fixed on the wyverns circling overhead.

"I have seen them twice before in these parts. I do not think they will harm us, but I think it best that we move on." Yolias finished eating and stood. The dwarves refilled their water flasks by the waterfall, with anxious glances above them, while Yolias scanned the valley the glen overlooked. Moments later the dwarves had packed and joined him. "Few are they who venture into these mountains." Yolias looked proudly about them. "I have made some excursions into them, but few stray so far from the roads, especially the Ruined East Road. Who knows what lies out around distant peaks, or in the shadows of Kraz and Karzell? Mapmakers see them in the distance and add them to their maps, but none can claim to know them."

Their march resumed through a narrow pass and zigzagged down rock-strewn slopes. The going was rough and treacherous at times, and the dwarves longed for a level path beneath their feet. Yolias told them remnants of the Goblin road ran alongside the desert and would make for easier traveling.

That day and the next Iaven thought about Halix, determined to learn more from Yolias; if he did join the King's troops, he would likely use a sword other than Halix, and his skill alone would have to suffice. For now, he looked forward to seeing Halix complete with three gems before returning it to the Castle. At times he still thought he might be better off in Hillbrook, but Rhiane expected him to fight and he did not want to disappoint her. He put off deciding what to do because he was becoming sure now of what he should do, whether he wanted to or not.

The day after they stopped by the waterfall, they hiked until they came to a wide, curving slope that began their slow descent. Around early evening it brought them to the last mountain on the eastern edge of the range, and their first view of the Gevhra Desert. As they reached the top of the pass leading down to the hills, the horizon opened wide, spreading far across the plain. Below them a range of low hills ran wider and flatter until they merged into the desert. Low bushes and grasses grew in clumps, thinning farther out until only few shrubs, thorny bushes, and branching grasses dotted the desert sands. Out toward the horizon the dunes were barren and desolate.

Yolias noticed the dwarves' fascination. "Three hundred and sixty-seven years ago, our ancestors came across the Gevhra Desert and settled in the mountains. Why did they come? Some say they were looking for a better life and wanted to start a new kingdom of their own. Others say they were fleeing an enemy, or were exiled and forced out of their homeland. And there are still other claims. The true reasons may never be known. Yet they must have been powerful ones, for the desert is a wide and harsh place, and none have gone back or crossed over it since."

The dwarves stood staring out into the desert, imagining the great crossing, wondering how far it was and what had caused a whole people to make so perilous a journey. It was as if they were looking beyond the edge of the world. After a moment Yolias began the descent and one by one they followed him.

The way down was slower and more difficult than it looked. Several times the ground was too steep and they had to back up and find another way. The sun lowered into the west and the cold shadow of the mountain fell over them. Golden light grazing the desert plain shifted to orange and then darkening red, as the shadows of the range stretched out toward the horizon like a dark tide spilling across the land.

Colder now and tired, the dwarves descended toward the darkening desert plain, and noticed movement here and there in the distance. The faraway creatures were difficult to make out in the gloam, but they appeared to be large, black, and many-legged, moving across the sand. Some emerged from burrows and others came out from behind rocks.

"The enkrida. They come out at night, in the lowlands of the desert," Yolias said. He pointed below them. "That ledge is still well above the road. We will set camp on it for the night. We should be safe enough there."

They climbed down carefully and set up camp. They built a fire for warmth, a small one they crowded around on the narrow ledge. They each had a bite to eat, and then Yolias sat alone for the first watch while everyone tried to get what sleep they could.

Iaven lay awake, gazing up at the bright stars, waning half-moon, and dark shapes of the mountains rising into the night sky. The strenuous climbing and cold air had cleared his mind, leaving him less troubled. Though Orven would not join them, nor hand over Gorflange, they might beat him to the gem. Anger still tempered Iaven's concern for his brother. Still, the incident at the Castle made Iaven wonder about Orven. He sensed the sword's power, even greater now with the second gem in place, so Orven must have felt it as well. Iaven was ready to confront Orven, and if they could reach the gem before Orven did, so much the better.

Iaven pulled his blanket tightly around him as cold gusts buffeted the ledge. He wondered what their lives would have been like if Cedric had never given them the swords but was fast asleep before he realized no answers were forthcoming.

Chapter 20.
The Passage

The rope around Lexter's neck was cold and damp, and his back and legs ached. The goblins' packs weighing him down between his tied arms felt heavier even though they had grown lighter over the past four days. He had walked hunched over for so long he feared he would never be able to straighten up entirely again.

Lexter was weary of breaking a trail through the forest, stumbling over uneven ground, getting scraped by branches and prickly weeds, and the never-ending crunch of dried leaves underfoot. He longed for the rest of the leaves to fall from the trees, making it easier for the goblins to be seen and for him to be rescued. He considered stalling, but whenever he dragged his feet a sharp yank at the rope got him moving again. Sometimes the goblins prodded him along with a stick. Lexter contemplated stopping and collapsing to the ground, but knew he would be killed on the spot once he was no longer useful to them.

Worst of all was being alone. Lexter missed Leland terribly. For days he had clung to the idea that maybe his brother was not dead when the goblins had left him by the campsite. But Lexter had seen him die; they made sure he would see it happen. The memory of it seemed unbearable. Lexter's frustration and anger were cowed by the fear that he would be next. Knowing very little Southern Rogglish, he couldn't try to talk his way out of the situation as he usually did. There was nothing he could do now. Without Leland, he realized, he didn't have a chance.

Growing up, Leland and Lexter had rarely ever been apart. They had traveled together since they'd left Tolgard to see the world and find an easy living. While their two younger brothers, Linus and Leander, were more hard-working and obedient in heeding their father's wishes, Lexter had followed Leland in turning down a life as a cobbler, believing he and Leland could find more lucrative sources of income that didn't require as much work. Some, it turned out, were less than honest, but Leland always had a way of explaining them so they made sense to Lexter. They had never killed anyone, and nobody was forced into making deals with them. And it wasn't their fault if others weren't as clever, Leland used to say. But now Lexter saw that it was Leland's cleverness that had kept them going. Lexter was better at haggling and his intuition was good, but it was always Leland's plans and ideas that got them out of tight spots. Lexter fondly recalled celebrating after deals were made, and the thrill of narrow escapes when things didn't go well. It wasn't just the gold, but the fun of outwitting the other party, who, as Leland often pointed out, would just as soon outsmart them if they could. It was all a game, and they weren't doing too badly at it. They would laugh together, reminiscing and looking forward to more profitable dealings and opportunities. Sometimes they even found legitimate arrangements and did things aboveboard for a while, until something came along that was too tempting to pass up. And whenever Lexter had his doubts, Leland had reasons enough for both of them.

Lexter didn't feel very clever anymore and was upset at how helpless he seemed to be without Leland. Though he had always resented Leland's constant reminders that Lexter was his "little brother", he would have welcomed the most belittling insults just to hear Leland's voice again.

Now and then on his long, forced march with the goblins, Lexter noticed how much he was indulging in self-pity. *But there's no one else to pity me*, he thought. He tried to take hold of himself and plan an escape the way Leland would have. The North Road, that was the key; unless the goblins had a way back through Teska, they'd have to cross the North Road at some point. Without Leland, he would have to hope someone would be passing by and see him with the goblins and come to help. Lexter had been amazed and amused at how willing some people were to help strangers, even people who would never see them again. He and Leland had made good use of such charity many times. He thought of the dwarves they had met on the road to Miastolas, how trusting they were, and how easy it had been for Leland to take the sword from them. He had underestimated them, but that was his own mistake. Yes, the North Road was busier now with preparations for war, and someone would come along in time, he thought. The Dwarves hated the Goblins, so they wouldn't hesitate to help him. It was his only chance.

A few hours before dawn the goblins stopped briefly, allowing Lexter to lie on the ground for a rest. They debated among themselves a moment, then resumed the march, angling off to the right. As they had never left the forest, Lexter was unsure how far north they had traveled. He guessed it was a good distance; they had long since crossed the River Saryl that cut through the Veskwood Forest, though they were still south of where the River Kaihl flowed through Teska. The goblins would likely cross at a place where the forest came close to the road and was out of sight of the northern villages.

Soon the forest thinned and they emerged into wide, grassy fields near the North Road. Lexter was relieved by the change of scenery and the night sky opening above them. He looked around to see where they were, wishing he had paid more attention to maps of Itharia instead of always letting Leland take care of it. The road lay ahead in the dark, a barren strip of land about a hundred yards off. The goblins quickened their pace, scanning the land and sniffing the air for signs of trouble. All was quiet; crickets chirped and wind blew across the fields. On their way through the grasses, the goblins stopped once, crouching low and listening, and then continued and tugged Lexter along again. Lexter looked around anxiously for the same things the goblins did, hoping to hear the creak of a slow-moving cart, footsteps along the road, or a passing traveler on horseback.

The North Road was deserted. Lexter thought he could see the distant, dark shapes of houses, strands of smoke rising from their chimneys, but no one was around anywhere. Shrill panic rose in him. He strained his eyes, certain that someone was coming along the road. But of all the Dwarves and Men, soldiers, farmers, craftsmen, and laborers in Itharia, no one was out that night. The goblins were in plain view and nobody was there to see them.

They came to the road. Gravel crunched beneath their feet, so much louder than the walk through the grass. Lexter slowed his pace but they pulled him onward. A few more strides and they were across the road and in the grassland again. Lexter looked both ways behind him, expecting to see someone arriving at the last minute. No one did. The goblin walking behind Lexter saw him looking around and laughed aloud. He commented to the other one, and they both chuckled hoarsely.

As the road disappeared behind them, Lexter realized his last tie to the Kingdom had been severed. There would be no help from Itharia now. He had taken for granted all the strangers and fellow travelers on the road in the past; indeed, he usually had taken advantage of them as well. He and Leland had what they needed and didn't need anyone else; or so it had seemed. Lexter couldn't quite recall what Leland's reasoning had been on the point, but he remembered he had agreed. It occurred to him that he really liked Itharia and its people, even though he had never really given them much thought.

They passed through fields and over hills, and after while up into a narrow valley, rising slowly into the mountains. The goblins kept going. Under the packs' weight the climb was brutal for Lexter, and he wondered when they would stop to rest. With Itharia behind him and all his hopes gone, death was not just an abstract idea, but an inevitability. And it always was, he realized. He still did not want to die, even if it meant an end to his torment. There were so many things he had not done yet; and, it seemed, so little that he had done. It was not the first time he had despaired about his life, but Leland had always been there to console him and talk him out of his mood. It was no use trying to fool himself anymore; he had little to show for the life he had led. Lexter tried not to think about it, but there was nothing else to think about.

After another hour's hike the goblins were far enough into the mountains to be safe, and they set camp in a sheltered niche under a rock formation. The eastern sky was paling, the mountains' faces growing more visible again. The goblins had Lexter halt and he fell to the ground exhausted. Weak, he gave no resistance as they bound his legs and rebound his arms together behind his back. They laid him on his side facing into the rock wall, and as troubled as his mind was, he dozed off immediately.

Lexter's slumber was short-lived and he was sharply awakened all too soon. The goblins only slept a few hours on an irregular schedule and seemed to need less sleep than Lexter did. Still tired, his mind resumed the review of his life, this time in a groggy despair brought on by prolonged weariness. He was going to die once his role as a packhorse had ended. He wondered where the goblins were going; he knew they were going north back to Navrogenaya, but how? Watchtowers lined the cliffs along the Dwarves' northern border, the mountains forming a high impenetrable wall overlooking the valley. A mountainside path connected the towers, but surely they could not take that. After another full day of slow, northerly travel through the mountains, Lexter still had no idea where they were going and wondered if they did not intend to return to Navrogenaya.

The question of where they were headed provided little distraction as his mind kept returning to his own imminent end. He accepted it, but was still plagued by regrets and thoughts that things might have ended otherwise. He would change his life and live anew, he thought, if given the chance. At least he could see things more clearly now before dying; he knew what he ought to have done and what he had taken for granted. Leland didn't have a chance to realize any of that, Lexter supposed. Lexter sometimes wondered what his brother thought about during the long trips when he drove while Lexter lay asleep in the wagon. He pictured Linus and Leander back home in Tolgard, working with their father, learning the cobbler's trade. He envied them now. Staring down at his own shoes, which were muddied and falling apart, he could almost hear his father's voice chiding him and telling him to bring the shoe-leather and bootblock over to work on a new pair for him.

Near dusk they began descending into a deep valley. They veered off abruptly and made for a low-hanging mountain wall, where a wide gaping hole opened like a frozen yawn. As they approached the cave Lexter suspected this was the end: they had gone out of the way to hide the body of their prisoner, here in this tomb. Lexter felt nauseous and dizzy. Would it be a quick knife to the throat or gut, like Leland? His mind drifted into murky visions of his death. Closer still, and the black maw of the cave grew larger, engulfing them, and they dragged him down a tight tunnel lowering into the earth.

The cave passage widened and narrowed as they went, and was cold, damp, and musty-smelling. The leading goblin lit a torch, which threw a flickering light on the rock a few feet around them. Water dripped onto their heads, and cold puddles soaked Lexter's tired feet. The goblins became more talkative now, their harsh, deep voices echoing down the tunnels. Lexter wondered why they were taking him so far in, fearing the worst.

Torchlight illuminated rock formations as they passed; long, rounded cones of dripping rock, ancient clusters of thin, stone pillars where stalactites and stalagmites had fused, tiny fissures opening into dark spaces, and smooth flows of rock like frozen foam. The goblin in front sometimes laughed and swung his torch for fun, breaking off dozens of little, thin strawlike stalactites from the ceiling. Other passages branched into darkness, but the goblins were very deliberate in their movements and knew where they were going. As his eyes adjusted to the dim light, Lexter noticed the same runic markings carved into the walls or floor at intersections, indicating their direction. Several times they even passed through corridors with rough-hewn walls that looked as if they had been dug out by pick and shovel.

After several hours of musty and constricting tunnels, darkness opened around them and their footsteps echoed strangely off unseen walls. The lead goblin found torches set on the walls and lit them with the one he carried. Lexter began to see they were in a large echo chamber where, to his surprise, they started to set up camp. As the chamber became brighter, Lexter saw stone benches had been hewn from the walls and large wooden chests of provisions lined the back wall. It was a cold, damp and dreary place, and apparently saw frequent use as a waystation in the undermountain passage.

Once again Lexter was shoved to the floor and bound for his night's rest. Suddenly voices and footfalls echoed down the passage and grew stronger as they approached the chamber. The goblins paused, waiting to see who was coming, and tossed a ratty blanket over Lexter to hide him from the newcomers. Lexter's heart leapt with the hope that someone had found them or had even been following them all along. He would have even settled for Elves.

Torchlight appeared in the passage as the sounds grew nearer. Lexter waited anxiously, straining to turn his head and look out of a hole in the blanket. A dozen goblins emerged on the opposite side of the chamber, nodded to the two spies, and joined the campsite. The new arrivals came from the other tunnel, and Lexter noticed that they wore the lacquered wooden armor plates of soldiers. Lexter turned away to the wall, troubled and unsure what to make of it. Raucous laughs and shouts echoed around him in the wavering torchlight as he stared at the dim rock wall inches away from his face. Lexter wished he had bothered to learn more Rogglish as his younger brothers had. The passage, it seemed, was a series of natural caves joined by goblin-hewn tunnels, emerging, he guessed, somewhere in the Arinzei Valley to the north.

The Goblin soldiers struck fear into Lexter, beyond what he was already feeling. The war had always seemed something vague and abstract, like news of distant events or rumors that never came to pass. Impending war meant a greater call for weaponry and better deals for him and Leland; it was one of the reasons they had gotten deeper into the trade. But seeing Goblin soldiers armed and ready for war made him understand what he and Leland had done. There was no denying it; long before their dealings in Kronivar they had known Aranstone's men were not of the King's army but in support of the Kronivar separatists. It hadn't mattered to Leland or to him, since the money was good. Or would have been good, he thought.

More than ever he envied his brothers Linus and Leander and realized they would never even find out how he and Leland had come to their end, or even that they had died. He pictured them at home in Tolgard, working late into the evening, quietly mending shoes and boots, content with a warm home and steady work. He and Leland had hoped to get rich any way they could, even if it hurt the Kingdom. Let the Dwarves sort it all out, they had thought. But now he realized how a civil war, if it amounted to that, might weaken Itharia. If the Dwarven Kingdom fell to Navrogenaya, the Goblins would certainly grow in power. And perhaps Tolgard, on Navrogenaya's western border, would be the next to fall.

Chapter 21.
Ashes and Smoke

Mount Harbash rose in the distance, hazy in the bright afternoon sky. Orven was sure the gem was there; the sword pointed straight to it. Perhaps the gem lay somewhere on the mountainside, or below, lost and buried in the sand. At long last he would soon have it.

After nearly a week of travel in the desert, Orven's party saw the mountain jutting out into the desert and knew they were nearing the Goblin border. Orven thought about what Cedric had told them of the outpost there, and what they might find. The *enkrida* —he remembered Cedric mentioning them now— had kept them all on edge at night, and a week of uneasy sleep had made them all irritable. They tired sooner, yet Orven made them cover as much ground as they could before nightfall. The supplies once intended for their return journey were growing short. Everyone saw the necessity for strict rationing but grumbled about it nonetheless. The gem was much farther away than anyone had supposed, and Orven would not give up his pursuit of it. The others had resigned themselves to that fact, liking it less each day.

The farther north they went, the longer were the unbroken stretches of Goblin road that ran between the low hills at the mountains' feet. As Mount Harbash grew closer, the road ran down from the hills into the desert. Windblown sand engulfed much of the road, choking out thin grasses growing at its edges. Where the ground flattened and the road widened, dozens of carven, gray stone slabs lay scattered in disarray across the barren, sandy ground. The dwarves' pace slowed when they saw the big stones, some leaning over, still planted in the sand. They wandered among them, gingerly touching them and gazing on their ancient, pitted surfaces.

Runes were engraved upon the stones, curious inscriptions of curves, strokes, and accents, etched deep and filled with shadow in the noonday sun. Fine, graceful rows of letters seemed to dance and wave with a strange fey feel to them, while below them a sturdier, solid script bespoke of solemn things. Both languages appeared on all the stones, one below the other. Many stones had fallen over or crumbled. Others were half-buried. Broad fingers of sand drifted up the windward sides of the slanting stones, pulling them into the desert floor and obscuring their etchings.

The dwarves walked warily around the stone slabs, pondering their meaning. Ripley brushed sand off one of them.

"Looks Elvish on top and Old Dwarvish below," Aaron observed.

"Maybe they're tombstones. Cedric said many dwarves and elves died here." But Orven did not believe that any dwarves would bury their countryman on such shifting, sandy ground. He did not like the look of the tablets and thought they boded ill. It occurred to him that they might even be inscribed with warnings. But warnings of what? He wondered if the others felt it, too. "Come on, let's go, it's not far now," he said, hoping to distract them.

They followed the road north, glancing uneasily at the stones and drifts of sand in their path. Further down, ruins of stone buildings lay on both sides of the road, broken walls and the remains of foundations. Corners of masonry stuck up out of the sand like pilings in a tide where the dunes rose and fell. The day was bright and all was quiet around them in the wind's soft howl. Everything was still in the empty vastness of mountain, desert, and sky surrounding them. Seeing the broken walls, they imagined the Goblin army living there before the attack on the castle so long ago.

Soon they neared the foot of Mount Harbash. Remains of stone structures, a small city from the look of it, spread a good way up the side of the mountain to their left, lining the slope with rows of crumbling foundations. Before them, in front of Mount Harbash, a wide semicircle of larger stone structures faced the mountain wall, with a broad, open plaza in the center, all flooded with sand. Ruins ringed the plaza like teeth on a buried jawbone. Some were two and even three stories tall, all weatherworn, dark, and uninviting. Darkness filled the holes and cracks in their walls, black in the bright sunlight. Watchful eyes could peer out from inside without being seen, as the dwarves moved past the buildings.

They entered the semicircular plaza, the back of which was a relief several stories tall, carved into the dark gray and russet wall of Mount Harbash. Deep shadows hung under the outcroppings, hiding from the bright sun overhead. Great ancient stylized figures of Goblins in ceremonial dress were interspersed with trapezoidal and diamond patterns. The figures stood on three narrow, pillared ledges, one above another. Between the figures, each ledge led across the arched entrances of tunnels leading into the mountain. From their portentious and solemn nature, the dwarves guessed them to be tombs of some kind. On the ground below lay large stone doors, thrown down from the ledges after being forced open. The dwarves paused, staring up at the ancient figures and designs. Even in daylight the place cast a dismal mood upon them. The tomb entrances towered above them, rows of frozen, gaping mouths sighing stagnant breath from the dark bowels of the mountain.

After a moment, Orven drew Gorflange, pointing it at the tombs. He cupped his hand around the pommel's stone, looking for the faint glow. "It must be here!" he exclaimed.

"Up there, inside?" said Aaron. "Which one?" He didn't like the dark holes and their guardians and hoped Orven would be quick about finding the gem.

Orven tilted the sword, watching for variations in the pommel stone. But the bright sunlight made reading the tiny glow difficult. "Hard to say. Looks like the top level, maybe... on the left side?" He straightened and sheathed Gorflange. "It's too bright out here; it'll be easier to tell in the dark. Let's go!"

Orven headed for the narrow stairs leading up to the ledges. The others followed, glancing about the plaza and the buildings around it. Everything was quiet and still, and they kept expecting to catch sight of something watching them and pulling away into hiding before they could make out what it was. They saw nothing, yet did not feel any more at ease.

In single file, they climbed all the way to the top level, made their way around an immense carving jutting from the wall, and stopped outside the first tomb entrance. A cold wind was pouring from the mouth of the cavern. Orven stepped inside, disappearing into the dark after only a few feet. Max, right behind him, waited outside. Orven paused in the dark and unsheathed his sword. This time the blue-green glow from the pommel was very visible, but not as bright as it should have been if the gem was very near. But because it was dark and Orven's eyes had not adjusted, and perhaps because he wanted to believe the gem was there, it seemed brighter to him than it really was. "It's close!" he called out. "We're almost there!" After a long pause and a scraping sound, Orven reemerged on the ledge, holding a thick, tapering wooden torch, heavily seamed and charred black on its wide end. "Old torches," said Orven, "On the walls. Maybe some of them will light. Let's set camp for now."

They climbed back down to the sand. In the hour or so that followed, Aaron, Ripley, and Roy went west into the nearest valley in search of firewood and whatever food they could add to their evening rations. Max and Orven stayed behind, setting up camp in the center of the plaza, as far from the tombs and surrounding building as they could. Orven got some flints from his pack and began striking them, trying to light a pile of dried grasses from the sparks. After a few frustrated attempts, the sparks caught and the weeds shriveled in the flames. Orven wet the end of the torch with oil he had found in the tomb and held it close to the small flames, hoping they would take to it. He threw more grasses on the fire and waited. At last the torch was lit. Kicking out the grass fire, Orven watched the licks of flame, protecting them from the wind. "We'll have it by tonight, Max," he said, grinning as he went off to the tomb entrances.

Max watched Orven go, too tired to match his enthusiasm. He hoped they'd get the gem and start back to the Kingdom, maybe even that night; he didn't want to stay in the outpost any longer than necessary. He was hungrier than he liked to be, tired of traveling, and looked forward to returning to the Castle. Orven would have to face the consequences of attacking the guard, but they had no other alternative. Whatever happened at the Castle would still be better than not making it back at all.

Orven ran up the third flight of narrow steps and entered the tomb. His torch was blazing and he lit the few others on the walls that would light. Orven looked around as the cavernous interior came alive with dim, flickering torchlight. Huge, painted murals of Goblin ceremonies lined the walls. Columns of sharp Goblin characters ran down the walls and over wide archways. Passages led deeper into the tombs and down dank stairways. Orven unsheathed Gorflange and pointed it around, until it indicated a passageway on his left. With sword and torch in hand, he passed beneath a heavy, wide arch, where he began lighting torches on the walls of the passageway. It was cold, musty, and damp enough that few of the torches there would light. At last the way was feebly lit by sparse circles of torchlight with darkness in between. Where light revealed the walls, stylized portraits of Goblin leaders stared down with dark solemn eyes painted in heavy lines and now-muted colors. Grim and unwavering was their gaze. The passage itself was long with high, slanted ceiling vaults blackened by smoke and obscured by shadow. Other passages branched off from the main one. Orven thought he heard scratching and scurrying noises down them. He lit as many torches as he could and moved further down the dark corridor.

After passing under several thick, narrowing arches, Orven realized the passage was turning. He could no longer see the sunlit entrance behind him. But he went on. At last he came upon a doorway, two thick stone beams angling upward from the floor, leaning in together until they met, leaving a triangle of darkness between them. Orven hesitated a moment, and then, holding the torch in front of him, he entered.

The room was an antechamber, about fifteen feet on a side, the walls painted with interlocking angular patterns and scenes of burial rituals. Orven was disappointed to see that everything had already been plundered. Piles of rubble lined the corners of the room, and shards of broken pottery lay strewn amongst jagged planks and the inlaid lids of wooden chests. Two pickaxes, a shovel, and some chisels lay on the floor, left there by grave robbers. Nothing of any value remained. Off to the side was another, larger room, but Orven could only look in from the doorway, as it was full of rubble and planks of wood torn from empty, ruined caskets. The ceiling had collapsed, and stone and gravel was piled several feet high in the dark room.

Orven drew Gorflange and moved it about the room, wondering if the gem had been dropped amidst the rubble. When he found the faint green glow, the sword pointed to the back wall of the antechamber. Upset, he moved it again to be sure. *There must be another room, hidden behind the wall*, thought Orven. *Where else can it be? That's why it's still here...* He tried to pinpoint it as best he could and then sheathed Gorflange. Anxiously, he took up one of the pickaxes and began swinging it and chiseling away at the back wall.

Ripley, Roy, and Aaron returned to camp bearing armloads of branches and small logs for the fire. Aaron had also shot a rabbit with his short bow, and all looked forward to some meat for the evening meal. Max had the camp ready, and they piled the firewood in the center and sat down. The sun was lowering into the mountains and shadows already covered the range.

"Where's Orven?" Ripley asked.

"He's been gone awhile, I was just about to go and find out," Max said, nodding towards the tomb. The others looked at the rows of entrances, all dark except for the one on the far left of the top row, where faint orange light flickered. "You start supper and I'll go get him," said Max, standing up. He had a vague apprehension that something had happened to Orven.

Max climbed the three flights of stairs. As he entered the tomb, the dank, smoky smell made him wince. He followed the lit passageway, watching the murals around him and gazing down other darkened passages. Grinding crunches of metal striking stone echoed down the halls. "Orven?" Max called. The grinding crunch stopped.

"Max," said Orven, "Come in here and help me get through."

Max found Orven in the antechamber at the end of the passage. Orven was standing, breathing hard and resting, leaning on his pickaxe. A big gash defaced the mural on the back wall where he had been chiseling it away. "We're so close," said Orven, his eyes wide and wild in the dim torchlight.

"What are you doing? Where's the gem?" asked Max.

"It's in there," Orven said. "The sword points into the wall, there must be a secret room or something back there that no one's ever plundered." He motioned to the other tools on the floor. "Let's break through and we'll have it before supper." He went back to work on the wall.

Max reluctantly took the other pickaxe and joined Orven. He had a nagging feeling that Orven was wrong, and that he would just keep digging into the stone no matter how deep it went. Yet the sword had indicated the gem was in that direction. Something didn't make sense about it, but Max could not put his finger on what it was, so he helped Orven for the moment.

The two pickaxes chopped away at the crumbling stone with a double rhythm, as dust and gravel fell to the floor. After a while, the wall made a hollow sound when they hit it, and then a tiny, dark hole appeared. A rank, stagnant odor wafted out of it.

"We're through!" Orven shouted, chopping faster to widen the hole while Max avoided the exuberant swings of his pickaxe. They worked away at the sides, the hole opening a little with each axe blow, until it was big enough to crawl through. Orven could wait no longer. He threw down his axe and took one of the torches from the wall. Holding it in front of him, he reached into the hole, lighting his way, and then squeezed through, crawling in behind it. Max waited, thinking him somewhat incautious. He heard rubble falling on the floor, and then the light dimmed as Orven stood up inside.

"Max!" Orven's voice was filled with awe. "Come and see this!" Max bent down and peeked inside. Orven stood in the tomb's annex, the orange torchlight casting big, soft, dancing shadows on the walls of the dim room. Around Orven was a stash of Goblin treasure that had been hidden away for centuries. Painted caskets lay beneath ornate carven animal statues with bulging eyes and bared fangs. Boxes of beaten gold inlaid with colored glass and carnelian shone dully in the pale light. Rows of alabaster jars with stoppers lined carved wooden shelves, along with flasks, urns, and vases. Torchlight revealed lamps in lampstands, long pipes of horn and ivory, and rods and canes with heads of sculpted jade. Everything was piled against the walls, leaving only a little space in the center of the room.

As soon as Max saw it was safe, he crawled through the hole and stood beside Orven. Together they dusted off one of the caskets and raised the lid. Inside were dozens of amulets and talismans, and a sheathed dagger of beaten gold, all on a bed of Goblin gold pieces.

"Look at all this, we're rich!" Orven exclaimed. "And ...the gem!" He handed the torch to Max and drew Gorflange, angling it about in the cramped space. As he turned away, the blue-green glow brightened a little. "There, in that corner, I think."

Suddenly they heard scratching sounds on the gravel in the antechamber. Max turned toward the hole and pulled back in horror. The light from the hole was darkened by long black, clawlike legs lined with sharp red ridges like sawblades, bending and reaching into the annex, groping for their prey. The terrifying hiss of whispered clicks and scraping grew louder. Max and Orven swung the torch and Gorflange at the creatures climbing in through the hole. The weak, wavering torchlight outside in the antechamber glinted darkly on crowds of shiny, black, crawling legs rasping and scratching. A foul reek of dried rot and bones choked Orven and Max with its stench. The din of clicking, hissing, and screeching echoed down the halls as the enkrida led their haphazard assault.

With little room to move to defend themselves, Orven and Max were unable to keep the enkrida at bay. Orven stabbed at them as Max pushed the torch towards the hole, trying to keep them out of the annex.

"Ripley! Roy! Aaron! We're trapped!" Orven shouted through the opening, his words drowned in the noise outside.

"We can't hold them off!" said Max, "The torch is burning out!" The thought of fighting the enkrida in total darkness was too horrible to imagine. Within minutes the annex would be overrun and they would be torn apart in the dark.

"Ripley! Roy!" Orven yelled.

"I'll try to block the hole." Holding the torch with one hand, Max found a large gold-plated shield and pushed it over the hole. The enkrida clawed, scraping at the metal, and Orven hacked at the legs reaching around the shield's edges. Orven's heart beat hard as he wielded Gorflange, stabbing into the hole around the shield and slicing at the claws, while Max leaned into the shield, pressing against the shrieking crowd outside. The defense took all their energy, and after using the pickaxes, there was little remaining.

The lick of flame on Max's torch flared, faded, and went out, leaving them entirely in the dark, except for the weak light from the antechamber that bled in around the shield. The foul, stale air weakened and suffocated them. Orven's defense slowed as the waves of enkrida increased. "There's too many..." groaned Max.

"*Orven!*" another voice shouted, faint and somewhere in the hall beyond the antechamber. Orven bent, trying to look out the hole, but he could not see anything.

"Ripley? We're in here! In the hole in the wall! In here!" Orven and Max yelled together until they were hoarse.

No reply came. Orven wondered if Ripley heard them. Perhaps he was overcome by the enkrida as well. Orven and Max still fought them in the dark, tense and straining, dizzy with exhaustion.

At last they heard shouting in the halls, and the clink of metal and the crunch of cracking shells. Shrill, piercing screeches made their skin tingle. The air became warmer, the light coming in around the shield brightened considerably, and the enkrida doubled their efforts.

"Don't come out yet!" Ripley's voice came from the hall. Orven wondered what he was doing. The antechamber was bright with light and alive with scrambling enkrida and loud shrieks and screeching. Orven peeked around the shield and saw masses of fire and burning creatures. Flaming branches and oil had been thrown into the room, landing in the thick of the enkrida. The smell of smoke and the roasted, burning enkrida erupted and Orven pulled back behind the shield, coughing from the stink.

The shrill cries and screeches of burning enkrida rose to a fever pitch and began to die out. Desperate, clawing legs pushed and reached around Max's shield, desperate to get inside, and gradually these, too, subsided. Max felt the shield warming from the heat, and set it aside when it seemed they were safe. Bearing the stink and smoke, Max and Orven watched the fires die down, and crawled out of the hole coughing and gasping.

Smoke hung in the antechamber and the ceiling was blackened with soot. A few torches on the walls still flickered, and tiny fires and glowing embers burned on the floor, among charred remains of enkrida shells and jointed legs. Orven and Max stumbled through the stench, blackened shells cruching underfoot, and out into the hallway where the air was cooler and less stale. Ripley, Roy, and Aaron chopped with their swords at the enkrida that had run to the corners of the room, and crushed broken limbs on the floor that were still twitching. Swords glinting in the sputtering torchlight, they eyed the halls for any other enkrida that might dare to approach.

"Had to burn 'em out," Ripley said. "Sorry it took so long. There were too many of 'em, it was all we could do."

"It was enough!" Orven straightened up, regaining his senses and breathing hard.

The dwarves gathered on the ledge just inside the tomb entrance, overlooking their campsite. The sun had sunk behind the mountains, but Orven and Max were glad to see the glow of twilight in the open sky after being closed in the dark tomb.

"Did you get the gem?" Roy asked, the others also anxious to see it.

"Not yet," said Orven, "There's more in there, too, treasure enough for all of us." He and Max described the contents of the annex. "It's still not dark. If there's enough oil and torches, let's haul it out. We'll pile it by the campfire and go through it there." Orven paused and the others hesitated, weighing thoughts of the hordes of horrible claw-legged creatures against the lure of gold and gemstones. "Aaron, Ripley, and Roy, stand guard in the halls, while Max and I bring everything out, and then together we'll carry it down to the sand." Orven looked at them. "Let's get what we can before dark," he added, hoping to spur them on.

Soon the torches were ready, and they made the halls as bright as they could, hoping to keep the enkrida away. Orven began handing treasure through the hole to Max, while the others stood guard. Each held his sword in one hand and a torch in the other, nervously peering down the hallways into darkness. Now and then they were distracted as Orven or Max came past with an armload of ancient weapons, or caskets of gold pieces and gems, half-empty because of their great weight. The pile at the entrance grew and the light outside faded, and soon Orven reluctantly agreed to stop and leave the rest for the following day.

From the ledge the dwarves all carried the treasure in single file down the narrow flights of stairs. They laid it on a pile near the campfire, which Ripley was tending and feeding. After several trips up and down from the tomb entrances they had brought down a mound of treasure that spread across the sand. As evening fell, they finally ate their evening meal, enjoying Aaron's roast rabbit along with their meager rations.

After dinner they rummaged through the pile, examining everything by firelight. The carven animal statues, frightening in their frozen expressions and strange design, the dwarves rejected and cast aside on the sand. They pulled the stoppers from the alabaster jars, wincing at the pungent odors and stale ointment and perfume. But none of these things interested them as much as the gems and precious metals of the tomb's treasures. Each of the dwarves sifted through handfuls of gemstones and Goblin gold pieces, some of which were round while others were square or hexagonal. They heaped them all near the fire. The gold pieces bore images and inscriptions from the old Goblin Empire of King Nehncazzar's reign. They found pendants and amulets encrusted with jewels and gold, and talismans of striking designs. Some were bizarre and left disturbingly persistent impressions in their minds, so they returned them to their chests and tried not to think of them.

Ripley examined a sheathed dagger and threw it back on the pile. "No swords! I was hoping we might find some better ones."

Orven laughed. "We'll be able to buy the best in the kingdom, for all of us. And armor, too! Whatever we want. Look at all this! We can buy whatever we want and still be rich besides!"

"If only we could trade it for food," Aaron sighed. The others nodded. They were all still hungry and tired of living on limited rations.

Orven ignored Aaron and drew Gorflange, aiming it at the pile of treasure. He moved it about, but the gem in the sword's pommel remained dark. Orven turned and aimed it at the tomb entrances, and a faint glow appeared. He sheathed the sword again. "Still up there!" Anxious disappointment filled his voice. "Well, we didn't get everything. First thing tomorrow, though, we'll have it!"

Secure in their bedrolls and blankets, the dwarves had no trouble dozing off. Above them the stars shed a piercing light and little was left of the waning moon. Orven sat the first watch with Max and envied the others' heavy slumber, their sides rising and falling with deep, slow breaths. They sat glancing around the edges of their camp, into the dark beyond the firelight, where they sometimes glimpsed enkrida moving about in the night. Tiny scratching and hissing sounds crept beneath the wind's dull roar. Crumbling buildings around the plaza gaped at them with darkened holes and empty doorways. From the corners of their eyes in the dimness they could make out leggy, black shapes climbing in and out of them, but the creatures seemed to stay away from the dwarves and the fire. Max wondered if the enkrida that had escaped the fires in the tomb had warned the others, or if they were waiting and biding their time. The dwarves would have to keep the fire going, big and bright, until morning.

From where he sat Orven could see the treasure. His gaze was divided between the murky shadows lining the edges of the plaza and the glinting highlights of the gold and gemstones piled on the sand. As the hours wore on and no enkrida approached, he looked less at the distant gloom and more at the gold nearby. Twice his head bolted back up when he found himself nodding off, and a strange feeling of ease began to settle in. The fire died down, and thin, slow wisps of smoke streamed up from the embers. Orven watched them, his mind playing tricks of distance in the darkness; he would have sworn the tiny threads of smoke were larger, spindly columns of vapor rising from the ruins around the plaza, ghostly tendrils climbing out of crushed and splintered stone around the outpost, spirits of the dead rising like streaming smoke from ashes. Smoke that did not rise into the sky or disperse but hovered low, earthbound, curling and twisting. It surrounded him now, swirling and taunting him, luminous and beguiling. From all sides it converged on their camp, or so it seemed to Orven, and panic gripped him.

"Max," Orven whispered, despising the fear he heard his own voice. Labored breathing behind him meant Max had fallen asleep. He turned away and something kept him from waking Max. Orven couldn't say why, but he wanted to be alone with the diaphanous, unsteady shapes drifting about him. The wind whispered its dreamy, sighing breath, and he strained to hear what it said. Whether or not he was imagining it all no longer seemed to matter. Orven thought of all the Goblin, Dwarven, and Elven soldiers who had been slain here so long ago during the war, and of the runes inscribed on the stones half-buried in the sand. Phantoms lingered, merging and shifting, his eyes drawn to them as often as they were to the fire. His gaze fell again on the heap of gold coins. Orven imagined what he would buy with such wealth; the finest armor and weaponry, banquet tables laden with the richest foods and wines which made his empty stomach growl, and servants bowing and bringing whatever he required of them. The gold shimmered in the firelight, burnished and glistening.

The coins and gold pieces lay in a wide, haphazard pile, strewn through with dark but gleaming gemstones. Orven looked upon the pile as though he were staring down from a great and hazy height on a huge, sprawling, many-terraced castle, which had been built and added onto for centuries, spreading through the valley like a cancer. He sensed a dark power emanating from the castle, one that brought war. Obscure shapes, Goblins perhaps, labored there, toiling under the commands that came from within it. Orven was drawn to it all, picturing himself and his friends in the finest armor, going forth amidst a river of warriors into battle, rising in strength until they vanquished their foe, then dividing the spoils like vultures feeding on carrion. In a dusty old hall, nobles clad in drab garments crowded in a large, vaulted, shadowy sunlit room, and there, parting the throng as they passed, Orven with his friends following behind him strode proudly in gleaming armor, haughtily regarding the nobles and king's men. Orven's eyes were wide with visions of his glory, and he was eager to begin his new life of riches, power, and pride.

From where they lay on the sand, the carved wooden animals glared at him with deep-shadowed snarling faces. The cold wind whistled and voices whispered of all those who stood in his way, trying to stay his hand or take what was his, waiting to tear him down. The frozen snarls mocked his weakness, his lack of resolve and inability to cut away all that was holding him back. The caskets inlaid with jewels stood stolidly on the sands like fortresses rising up to block him, a cluster of alabaster jars like a foreign palace that opposed him. All the treasure that lay around him seemed to glare at him in mockery, doubting he could rise to such a vaunted destiny even with all he was given. Visions of the enkrida attack, the skirmish with the castle guards, the dying Goblin spies, and his capture by the Gnomes crowded his mind, proof of his hesitations and failings. Orven hated their jeering condescension and his heart pounded as he hardened himself, vowing to do whatever was necessary, to crush whomever he had to, and to never falter or doubt himself again. He had Gorflange, two gems, and a third nearby. He had everything he needed; he was sure of himself and worthy of his destiny. He set his hand on Gorflange's hilt; it all seemed so tangible, so close by.

Now it was gold again in his gaze, a pile of coins and gemstones, and he was drawn to dreams of it with sleepy heaviness, glints of failing firelight dancing and seducing him, dimmer now but no less alluring.

"Orven!" Max was shaking him. "Orven! Wake up! The fire's going out! I was dozing too, I admit it! But you were supposed to be watching the fire. Look, it's burnt down to the embers!" Orven came to and saw Max was right. He leaned forward and began blowing, the embers glowing and fading with each breath. "Here, throw these on." Max handed him some dried grasses. "Orven, look!" Max said suddenly in a hushed breath.

The circle of firelight had shrunk and so had the distance of the enkrida circling them. Groups of black, creeping enkrida stalked their camp less than ten yards away now, waiting for the last of the embers to expire. Orven stared into the darkness, much closer to them now, and saw more creatures waiting there.

"Sorry, Max," said Orven, biting his tongue and refusing to apologize any further. "Hand me those branches," he commanded. Orven held the grasses close to an ember, accidentally smothering it. The enkrida crept nearer, less than fifteen feet away, eager for the fire to go out.

Max drew his sword and wondered if he should wake the others for a final battle with the enkrida. "Orven, is it lighting?" His voice crackled with nervous tension. He dared not turn to look at Orven, afraid the enkrida would spring at him from the darkness.

"Wait... wait..." Orven chided, anger in his voice. At last the grasses caught. "There!" The wind gusted, and Orven shielded the new flames. He waited, placing a thin branch onto the fire and watching for it to catch.

"Orven?" Max cried.

"It's going!" Orven said, relieved. He piled a few more sticks onto the fire. The flames began to rise again, and the circle of firelight broadened. Orven grabbed a branch that was burning on one end and stood up, flailing it at the enkrida. "Go on! Leave us!" he growled, waving it at them. For a moment Orven saw the enkrida clearly in the branch's light, and then they backed off into the dark again.

The fire grew and Max calmed and sat down again. "That was close," he said. "Orven, let's leave this place tomorrow."

"Not without the gem," said Orven. He considered telling Max of all he had seen and heard that night, and then thought better of it. "We'll leave when I'm ready."

Max looked at Orven and turned away before Orven met his gaze. He thought Orven was being stubborn, but they'd all had a long day, and both of them were eager for the next watch to take their place. It wouldn't be unusual for Orven to be a bit ornery after all that had happened. Max had heard something else in Orven's voice, though, something that hadn't been there before, and it worried him. He wanted to believe that he was just imagining it, but he knew better.

Chapter 22.
Runes Among the Ruins

In the bright morning light Orven wondered if he had merely dreamt all the things he had seen. Instead of leaving the outpost as quickly as he could, he resolved to stay the night again to find out if his visions would return.

Everyone slept late and the sun was high in the sky when they woke. Orven rose first, eager to get back to work. Max was still asleep but Ripley got up, so Orven bid him to come along.

Ripley understood immediately. "The gem?"

Orven nodded and Ripley bit into their last apple and took it along. Half of it was supposed to have been Aaron's, but Ripley was too exited to care. He and Orven lit torches and climbed the narrow stairs up to the top ledge of tomb entrances.

The interior of the tomb remained dark, since very few torches there would light. They had already replaced some of them with oiled sticks the day before, but the wood burned too fast and was sorely needed for their nightly campfires. They lit what they could and went down the dark hallway, torches and drawn swords in hand. Orven checked for enkrida inside the antechamber.

"It's clear. Stand guard out here while I get the gem, then we'll go," Orven said. Ripley wanted to join him, but Orven held him back. "Don't worry, I won't put the gem in until we're out; everyone else wants to see it, too." Orven entered the antechamber and, after a glance through the hole, ducked into the annex.

Inside, Orven moved the sword around. It pointed to the back wall of the chamber. He dug through some gravel in the corner, finding nothing. It looked as if the sword was pointing into the wall again. "*Another* hidden chamber?" Orven said. He moved the sword and tested the area, with the same result. Frustrated, he sheathed it and went out in the antechamber to get a pickaxe. Shards of the enkrida covered the floor and he shuddered at the sight of them.

"Did you get it?" Ripley asked, looking in at Orven.

"Not yet. Might take awhile, too." Orven went back into the annex. Disappointed, Ripley returned to the hall and waited. Moments later a chopping crunch sounded as the pickaxe began biting away stone inside the annex.

Max awoke, glad to see the sun and bright desert sky. His sleep had been haunted by disturbing dreams and he did not feel rested at all. Aaron and Roy looked dazed, and Max wondered if they had had similar dreams.

"Where's Orven and Ripley?" said Roy. "Up there, I suppose. Hasn't he found the gem yet? I don't care for this place. And there's almost nothing left to eat."

Aaron noticed the apple was gone and knew Ripley had taken it. He took the ration intended for Ripley's lunch. "Treasure enough for whatever we want, yet we'll starve to death out here. Why does he want to look for more? We couldn't even take along a tenth of everything we hauled out."

"He went for the gem," Max said. "Once he's got that, we'll pack up and move on."

"And that, too," Aaron continued. "What makes him think the gem's hidden away in the tomb? The tomb is hundreds of years old. How could the gem be stashed away here, in some sealed chamber, when it's only been lost about a hundred years?"

Max realized what had felt so wrong about digging into the tomb's walls. "You're right," Max said. "After we found the treasure, I didn't think about it anymore. But you're right."

"Shouldn't we go tell him?" said Roy.

Everyone hesitated. Nobody wanted to confront Orven about it, yet it had to be done. "Maybe he'll listen," said Max, unconvincingly. "We've got to try."

They climbed the stairs in single file and entered the tombs, drawing their swords expecting enkrida, and waiting until their eyes adjusted to the dim light. The tunnels seemed empty. A repeated grinding crunch echoed down the passages, just like the day before when Max had found Orven digging into the annex. The sound gave him a strange, uneasy feeling.

They went down the hall. Ripley was standing guard in the narrow, triangular entrance of the antechamber. "What's he doing in there?" said Max.

"Digging, I guess. I don't know," Ripley shrugged.

Moments later Orven came out from the annex into the antechamber. Ripley moved aside and Orven stepped onto the threshold, the thick stone blocks of the doorway angling together over him until they met some fifteen feet above the floor. "Max, it's still further back. Come in and help me."

"Orven," Max sounded almost apologetic. "What... what makes you think it's in there?"

Aaron stepped up. "Orven, these tombs are hundreds of years old."

Orven glanced at Max, and then fixed his glare on Aaron. "Sure they are. So?"

"Well, the gems have been lost only about hundred years, right?" Aaron heard his wavering voice echo down the halls and grew more nervous. "How could they be hidden away in a sealed chamber that no one's ever found? The tomb was closed up long before the gems were made."

Orven stared at Aaron. Too often Aaron asked difficult questions and pointed out holes in their plans. Orven was all worked up from chiseling at the wall, and now they had interrupted him for this. He had given in to Aaron several times, but this was too much. Images of the carved animals' mocking snarls flashed in his mind. No, he would not let them deter him. He was leading them, not Aaron. He thought he had made that clear while they traveled along the mountain's edge, and now here they were, Aaron trying to make a fool out of him. The other dwarves stood in the tunnel, swords drawn, watching for enkrida. All eyes were on Orven as he stood in the doorway.

"We haven't been the only ones in these tombs," Orven began, barely containing his anger. "Grave robbers have been in and out of here. Maybe they left it here, dropped it somewhere. The sword can't be wrong."

"But it couldn't be sealed behind a wall—"

"Oh, and do you know what's back there? How do you know it's sealed off? Maybe there's another tunnel connecting to it, one we haven't found. The sword only points in a straight line. Would you rather we wandered around in these tunnels until we found it?"

Aaron stood speechless. Orven did have a point, although Aaron thought exploration was better than trying to dig through the walls.

"Would we have found all that treasure just wandering around where grave robbers have already been?" Orven continued.

"He's right!" Ripley joined in.

"But it's the gem we came for," said Aaron.

"So you don't want any of the treasure?" Orven's voice boomed down the halls, echoing away behind them.

Aaron fought the urge to argue more; he knew it would come to no good. "Of course I do," he said sheepishly.

A tense silence fell on the dwarves. The torches flickered, underlighting their faces and casting moody, moving shadows on the walls around them. They stood there with swords drawn, as if a fight might break out at any moment. Dark, grim, Goblin portraits on the walls watched them with solemn eyes. Orven stood, pickaxe in hand, framed in the sharp, narrow arch of the doorway. Max looked at Gorflange sheathed at Orven's belt, the metal hilt glinting dully in the torchlight. He wondered if Orven would ever use it on someone he knew.

"Well then," Orven relaxed a little when the moment had passed. "You might give me a hand here, or at least stay out of my way." He glared at them, turned back, and went into the antechamber, leaving them standing in the tunnel.

The rest of that day the dwarves remained edgy and irritable. Orven continued digging in the annex all afternoon, stopping only twice to come out for fresh air on the ledge, where he stood squinting into the sunlight. The others took turns standing guard at the antechamber, and only Ripley appeared to be on good terms with Orven. Mostly they sat by the camp or walked around the outpost, or went off in search of food and firewood. Sometimes they sifted dreamily through the treasure, but no one brought any more of it down that day.

Late that afternoon, Ripley and Roy went off to collect kindling for the fire. They climbed the western slope of the mountain where terraces cut the mountain face into giant steps, each lined with crumbling foundations. Some of them were riddled with the strange runes they had seen earlier. Halfway up the slope they went along a path that ran across the terrace and then down a pass into a small valley. There a long, thin pool was fed from a tiny trickling mountain stream where they could refill their water flasks. Roy stopped beside the stream to get water, and Ripley joined him. Birdcalls sounded far off and a light, cool breeze was blowing. Refreshed to be away from the outpost, Roy sat on a large rock, sipping from his flask. He was still upset with Orven, and with Ripley for having gone along with Orven. Ripley waited impatiently for Roy to get up again, anxious to get the firewood and go back. Roy sat watching him, hoping he would calm down.

Roy and Ripley had known each other a long time and had been very good friends as children. As they grew older they had grown apart but still remained friends. People who didn't know them well found it an unlikely friendship; wild, impulsive Ripley who was always getting in trouble, and quiet, careful Roy, from one of the more respectable families in Hillbrook. Each brought out a different side of the other; Roy had a calming effect on Ripley, and Ripley had convinced Roy to go looking for the gems with Orven. Lately, though, Roy noticed Ripley was spending more time with Orven and agreeing to his schemes no matter what they were. The more encouragement and support Orven had, the wilder his schemes became. And although Roy would not admit it, even to himself, he was a little jealous that Orven was beginning to have more influence over Ripley than he did.

"You don't really want to stay here another day, do you?" Roy asked.

Ripley paced anxiously. "No... I don't, but I want Orven to find the gem."

"Aaron doesn't think it's there, and I think he's right."

"Aaron!" Ripley kicked a small stone into the pool. "Always trying to spoil the fun. Orven's right, if it were up to Aaron, we wouldn't have found the treasure."

"We wouldn't be stuck out here, either. You wouldn't be as hungry, none of us would be."

"Mmmhhh," Ripley grunted. "Orven knows what he's doing. And it would be a lot easier if Max and Aaron didn't doubt him all the time." He turned to Roy. "Are you with them, too, then?"

"Ripley!" Roy chided, "Don't talk like that. We're all together out here, the five of us. And it's not just Orven, either, though sometimes he acts like it's just him." Roy didn't want to get into a fight with Ripley. They were all still upset. He got up and went with Ripley to get the firewood. Roy didn't like the tombs or traveling so near to the Goblin border, and he was tired of going hungry and sleeping outside in the cold. And he especially hated the enkrida threatening the dwarves whenever darkness fell. Treasure or no treasure, he wanted to leave the outpost, and it mattered less and less to him whether or not Orven found the gem.

Orven had chiseled a gash more than a foot deep into the wall, and it was all solid rock. As twilight fell, he reluctantly gave up his efforts, tired and sunk in a foul, frustrated mood. When the other dwarves saw him, their hearts fell. Not just because their tension would be relieved with the finding of the gem, but because no gem meant staying another night at the outpost. They ate a small and stale evening meal, their stomachs groaning for more. No one had much to say. Orven would not give up his quest, and arguing would only bring more strife. Finally the last of the day's light vanished behind the mountains and the sky darkened.

Orven volunteered to take the first watch with Roy, so the others rolled up in blankets and turned in for the night. Roy sat facing one direction, while Orven sat facing the other, both glad that the other said nothing so that there was no obligation to carry on a conversation.

Sitting by the treasure and the fire in the midst of the vast darkness around them, Orven wondered again if his visions of the night would return. At first, he had been terrified of them, but now he felt as if they had spared him, for some reason. These phantoms, or whatever they were, had a purpose for him and were encouraging him. Maybe they had even led him to the treasure. Orven still feared them, but found himself drawn to them, out of curiosity, and from an attraction he could not quite explain. As a child, certain things had fascinated him in the same way: bugs that lived under overturned rocks or were caught struggling in spiders' webs; deep, dark holes and pits in the ground that seemed to go down forever; or the way things burned up when you threw them in the fire. But this was something different. There was a power here, enticing him, offering itself to him, in return for his obedience. He had been chosen; he was sure that what he had seen was for him alone. His vague cravings and raw desire for power and renown were being shaped and forged into a destiny. The night before he had been terrified as the spirits rose; this time he waited and looked for them. And he was not disappointed.

The following day began much as the one before it had. Orven was up early and off to the tombs, while the others awakened later, groggy and irritable, dazed by persistent nightmares. Again, Max had dreamt he was pursued by an unseen force through a dark labyrinth of dim halls and stairways that always spiraled downward into the dark. Orven was somewhere in the labyrinth as well, but Max could not find him, try as he might. Sometimes the floor began to fall away, forcing Max to run to safer ground. Max decided not to discuss his dreams with the others, though they all seemed to have nightmares of their own.

"I can't sleep," Aaron complained. "I don't think I can take another night of this. We've got to do something about Orven."

"We've run out of provisions," Roy added.

Even Ripley seemed quiet and troubled, lacking his usual energy. "I'm tired of this place, too," he admitted.

Max stood and looked up to the tomb entrance. A faint flicker lit the dark opening on the far end. "Let's go talk to him now," Max said. It would be difficult and he wondered what Orven would do. They couldn't just leave him alone in the outpost. Roy and Aaron followed Max's lead. Ripley went with them, to see how things would turn out.

They climbed the narrow stairs and stepped into the tomb entrance. Cold air and the now-familiar musty smell wafted out of the dark passageways. The chopping sound of Orven's pickaxe echoed down the halls. Max stood listening a moment, unwilling to confront Orven. Then, gathering his resolve, he took one of the torches and started down the tunnel.

"Max!" Aaron called suddenly. Max turned back and saw Aaron silhouetted in the sunlit tomb entrance. He was pointing to the mountains. "Look, far away, on the hills; someone's coming!"

Max stood by Aaron, shading his eyes and squinting into the distance. He scanned the range, and found the movement. Several figures were walking close together on the hills by the mountains. It was much too far away to make out who they were, and before Max could count them they went down a slope and disappeared from view. "We'd better tell Orven." He stepped back into the tomb and turned to the others. "We'll *have* to do something now," he said.

Max went in and brought Orven out of the tomb while the others kept watch, trying to locate the figures. "Where are they?" Orven sounded angry, like a landowner who has been told of trespassers. They looked out again at the mountains, but the travelers were still somewhere behind the hills. Aaron indicated to Orven where he had seen them.

"They'll be here in an hour or so," Orven said, "The treasure! We've got to hide it. We can't let them know we're here. Bring it up inside the tomb entrances, hurry!"

The dwarves resented Orven's commanding tone and did not look forward to hauling the treasure back up the stairs, but neither did they want anyone else to find out about it. Ripley, Aaron, and Roy filed down the stairs.

"How many of them were there?" Orven turned to Max when the others were gone.

"Half a dozen, maybe, I couldn't tell," said Max.

"The stairs are narrow enough, we can hold the tombs, if they try to fight. We can take them by surprise. Come on, Max!" Orven sprung into action. "We've got to bring everything up here. Into the dark. We should have enough time, if we hurry!" Orven started across the ledge and Max followed behind him. "If only I had that third gem, Max. We'd be invincible!"

Iaven's party came down the undulating path as it wove between the hills and down to the desert floor. The sun beat cruelly on the sand but the air was brisk and cold. It was the first of November, exactly one month since they had left Hillbrook, Iaven realized. He had not expected to be away for so long, or to travel so far, never imagining he would get to see the desert. He was tired of mountain travel now, and looked forward to returning to the Castle.

"Nehncazzar was King of the Hill Goblins more than five hundred years ago," Yolias explained as they walked. "His tomb city, the *Nehncazzariad*, was among the great Goblin undertakings in the ancient world. Those who built it mourned their King and bitterly hated his successor, whom they blamed for his death. They built the tomb city to remain with King Nehncazzar, and rejected the sovereignty of the new king. Many spent their last years digging tunnels for the King's tomb and tombs of their own nearby."

Soon the descending path widened and the dwarves found themselves surrounded by the stone slabs lying half-buried and jutting out of the sand. They gathered around one of them to take a closer look at the scripts carved into the stone, the dancing, graceful yet fey one above, and the sturdy, solemn one below.

"These stones were erected after the war by the survivors and the prisoners who were rescued," Yolias said. "That's Riaelhaic, inscribed across the top. It's still spoken in parts of southeastern Feäthiadreya. And below is Huskaric, or 'Old Tharic', as you might know it. My grandfather was the last in our family who could speak it. Even in those days it was used only in the Castle. It is somewhat similar to Tharic in sound, once you know how to read it." Yolias fell silent as he began reading the stones.

"What does it say?" Wilbur asked.

Yolias straightened up again, pausing. "They are warnings," he said. He moved to another stone and began reading. The dwarves followed him. "Many died here, both Dwarves and Elves. Some stones tell how they were found and what happened to them."

"Are they buried here?" said Zammond.

"No," said Yolias, "According to the stones, they were buried by their countrymen in a mountain valley near here. The stones were set up to warn any who approached the outpost. Some tell of curses on the place, others of things that were seen there when they were collecting the dead for burial."

"Like what?" asked Iaven, as they moved on to another stone.

"As King Jordgen said, the dead do not rest there. The Goblins committed many atrocities, but both Dwarves and Elves acted in haste and desperation. To this day the Elves still bear the shame of their cruelty during their rout of the Goblins. I hesitate to tell you what is described here. Some of what is written on these stones is even hard for me to believe. Cedric mentioned the prison camp, did he not?"

"Not much. He didn't want to talk about it."

"No, I suppose he wouldn't." Yolias brushed off another stone, reading it silently to himself a moment. "The Goblins were merciless. Cedric was among the few to survive. Much is written about the outpost, but these are firsthand accounts. Some are by prisoners who were rescued, many of whom did not live long enough to return to the Castle. Only a third of the Elves who fought here returned home, and very few Goblins escaped. To those passing through the place now, it would seem to be nothing more than stone and wind and sand, but the engravings tell of wraiths, phantoms, and *hraih* that still dwell in the shade, a far greater danger than the enkrida. We would best turn back the way we came, or pass quickly around it if we must."

"But what about Orven?" Iaven asked. Considering the direction that Halix had indicated that morning, it seemed very likely that Orven had followed Gorflange into the outpost. As upset with Orven as he was, Iaven did not want to lose his brother. "I'm sure he's there. We have to go and look for him."

Yolias nodded. "It would appear so. As the sun shines we will look, but we must leave as soon as we can. Perhaps he only passed through the place."

Despite their questions Yolias was silent and would say no more. They moved stone to stone, as Yolias read more of the engravings. Sometimes he stopped and bowed his head or stood with a pained and sullen look. At one of the stones he stood awhile reading, with Iaven nearby. "My grandfather knew him," Yolias said when he had finished.

Yolias, Iaven, and the others traveled north, and at last came to the ruins of the outpost. All was still and silent, but instead of peace there was a feeling of dread anticipation among them. A cool wind howled through the hollow, broken walls. Harsh, bright midday sun shone on stone and sand, leaving windows and doorways black with shadow. But even in the sunlight a strong presence seemed to oppress their spirits.

At last they came upon the semicircle of ruins around the sandy plaza. They moved to the center of it, where they would be the farthest away from the wall and buildings surrounding them. They dropped their packs and stood right near where Orven's treasure had been piled and the ashes of the campfire lay buried. In front of them the tomb entrances towered up the sheer side of the mountain. Tall, carven Goblin figures stood guard at the entrances glaring down at them, rows of dark holes lining the ledges like mouths frozen in silent screams. But there was no sign of Orven.

Yolias scanned the area. "He may have been here and left. If so, we ought to move on."

Iaven had a strange, sinking feeling, and envisioned Orven and his friends lying among the ruins, dragged off and devoured by the enkrida, their corpses drying and rotting in the sun. The image had come to him unbidden and Iaven shook it out of his head. He could not help imagining that Orven and his friends had already come to a bad end, and that he had arrived too late to do anything about it. He fought against a crushing feeling of despair, and his anger with Orven seemed to grow as well.

"Orven!" cried Iaven. His voice broke the immense silence and echoed far into the hills. He looked around the outpost, hoping for a response. All was quiet. As the silence returned, a weakening panic passed through him again. Iaven looked up and stared at the dark holes of the tomb entrances. He knew they would interest Orven, and wondered what evils Orven might have succumbed to within them.

"Orven!" he called out, his voice aching with desperation. Still there was no response. He forced himself to turn away, hoping to catch some glimpse of Orven's party appearing in the ruins, on the hillsides, or somewhere. But the noonday sun beat down on them, revealing all the emptiness of the ruins around them. "Orven!" Iaven cried one last time, overcome with hopelessness. There was no sign of Orven and his friends anywhere. The echoes of his voice died away into silence and still there was no answer.

As Iaven and his friends entered the bright, sunlit plaza below, Orven pulled back into the shadows just inside the tomb entrance. Sunlight fell onto the ledge and threshold, but Orven pressed back against the cold cavern wall, careful to stay in the dark. He motioned for Max and the others to step back and be quiet. They had just managed to bring up the last of the treasure and pile it inside the cavernous chamber, and all the torches had been put out. Max and Ripley stood guard with swords drawn, should enkrida approach while they waited in the dark. But more often than not their eyes were on Orven pressed against the wall in the shadow, trying to look over the ledge and down into the plaza without being seen.

Orven had expected soldiers from the Castle and looked down now with some surprise. Iaven and his friends stood below on the bright sand in the center of the plaza. An older, taller dwarf was with them, who Orven supposed was leading their expedition from the Castle. Orven stood completely still against the wall and could feel his heart beating. If they started to come up the stairs, he would spring into action and call for the others to defend the ledge. But perhaps they would not come up, he thought.

The older dwarf looked around and said something but Orven could not hear what it was. The others were looking around, too. Orven felt a growing contempt for them. They looked so small and helpless down below in the bright plaza. *Do they really think I'll run out and give myself up so easily?* he thought.

"*Orven!*" he heard Iaven cry. Something in Orven wanted badly to answer and call out, which surprised him. He was able to resist, remaining still and silent. But it continued to tug at Orven, and he could almost picture himself stepping out onto the ledge where they could see him, responding to the call. But he held back.

Suddenly Iaven turned and looked up at the tomb entrances. *Did Iaven see something?* Orven thought. *He couldn't have, could he? Why is he looking up here? Are they going to come up here?* His hand touched Gorflange's hilt protectively. He remained still, and neither did Iaven move.

"*Orven!*" It was as if Orven were hearing Iaven's voice from years ago, when they were children, and Iaven would shout at him in anger after a fight or some mean prank of Orven's. Or like his father's voice, calling him out to work in the morning, or to help with loading the cart for a trip into town. Or his mother's voice, yelling to him to come in for supper. He pictured her at home, standing on the porch, hollering his name until he appeared. Memories of Hillbrook flooded his mind and the urge to answer the voice calling him became very great. He felt his resistance giving in and moved backwards a step along the wall, further into the dark, as if to lessen whatever force was pulling him forward.

"*Orven!*" A hint of futility strained Iaven's voice now, and Orven struggled to keep still along the wall. He was torn between answering and not answering, confused as to why he should feel so compelled to respond. His contempt for Iaven was strong, fueled by his own weakness in resisting the call. He wanted to rush out and start fighting, or throw something down at them, and knew that if they remained down there much longer he might not be able to hold himself back. But with great effort he kept motionless and stayed in the cool shadow of the tomb.

Iaven stood waiting, disappointed. At that moment, he would have gladly fought Orven just to see that he was alive. He wondered if they ought to explore the outpost further, or even look in the tomb itself, though he was afraid of what they might find there.

The other dwarves waited, looking around the plaza. Tillmore's foot struck something buried in the sand. He bent over and picked up a hexagonal gold piece with Goblin inscriptions on it. He handed it to Yolias who looked at it and gave it back to him. Tillmore put it in his pocket.

"They may have dropped it here, or it may have been lost long ago," said Yolias, "Either way, it seems they are not here, so we must move on. Perhaps they realized the gem is not here and are already on their way around the mountain. If that is so, we must make haste."

Yolias shouldered his pack and walked across the plaza to the east and the others followed. Iaven wondered if Yolias was right and Orven would beat them to the gem. He chided himself for worrying about Orven when he was probably long gone and far ahead of them. Of course, on the other side of Mount Harbash was the Goblin border with its own dangers. As they passed the last crumbling building drifted with sand and left the outpost behind them, Iaven resolved that as long as Halix indicated that the gem had not yet been put into Orven's sword he would pursue it and do all he could to get to it before Orven. Iaven pushed onward, picturing his victory in the race to the last gem, but he could not rid himself of the nagging feeling that something terrible had happened to Orven.

Orven watched the sunlit plaza from the dark tomb entrance. Just as he was certain that Iaven's party was going to come up the stairs into the tombs, the older, taller dwarf started leading them out of the outpost. After his initial astonishment at this sudden departure, Orven breathed a sigh of relief and relaxed again. The others standing at the back of the cavern seemed glad as well. As soon as Iaven and his friends were out of sight, Orven moved away from the wall and stood by the treasure piled on the floor. Something bothered him, though.

Aaron and Max went near the ledge to catch a last glimpse of Iaven's party in the distance as they disappeared around an outcropping of rock.

"Where are they going?" said Aaron. "They're headed east. I thought they'd be going back to the Castle."

"Of course!" Orven was on the verge of panic. "They must know the gem's not here. It must be on the other side of the mountain! Quick! We have to leave now. Maybe we can overtake them. We can't let them get to the gem!" He looked down at the pile of treasure, pained that they could not carry it all. "Ripley, Max, everybody— empty your packs and get rid of everything we don't need. We have to take as much of this along as we can. Gemstones and gold, as much as each of us can carry. Hurry!" Orven grabbed his pack and began emptying it out. The others did likewise. Yet as glad as they were to be leaving the tombs, they regretted having to hurry and leave so much of the treasure behind.

Deciding what could be thrown away and what should be kept took longer than they thought. After filling their packs with gems, gold pieces, and other small items, they found them too heavy to haul and had to lighten them again. Orven's anxiety grew and he snapped at them in desperation. Twice they thought they were ready to leave when it was found that the packs were either too full or on the verge of tearing. Finally, they had what they could carry and slung their packs over their shoulders, finding them uncomfortably heavy. They staggered under their weight while descending the narrow staircase down to the sand. As they crossed the plaza their steps were sluggish and seemed to push against the sand. Max wondered if Orven had noticed that their pace would be much slower than Iaven's. He repositioned the pack on his shoulder and realized they would have to march all night if they were to catch up with Iaven's party. He had not slept well in days and just thinking about a long night's march under a heavy burden made him feel weak. But at last they were leaving the tombs, and at the moment that was all he cared about.

Chapter 23.
A Double-Edged Threat of War

A few tiny snowflakes swirled in the gray overcast sky. Rhiane shivered as she stood on a balcony high up on the northern side of the Castle. She looked out over the mountains bearded with mist and knew that somewhere, beyond the horizon and possibly even beyond Kraz and Karzell whose peaks stood above the rest, Iaven and his friends were finally nearing the gem. It was over a week now since their departure and she supposed they would soon begin their return journey. Once they got to Farrenhale, they would ride back by wagon, but it still would be some time before she would see Iaven again.

Rhiane glanced into the valleys below, where the tents of encamped soldiers were scattered. She turned, and with an effort, went back inside the Castle through the glass-paned iron doors. She was in the King's study, where they had put the blue gem into the sword. It was empty now and still in the overcast afternoon light. Rhiane sat down at the table again, sheets of paper and a quill spread before her. Returning to her life at the Castle was not as difficult as she thought it would be, and she found she liked the place better now than when she had left it. After living in Kronivar, the Castle seemed quiet and life seemed slower. Everyone had their place and knew it, and everybody's lives were tightly interwoven. So many people had taken the trouble to welcome her back and were glad to see her again. In every room, the furniture, walls, and familiar smells brought back memories. Her two years in Kronivar were like a long dream from which she had just woken. Rhiane hoped Iaven would consider staying longer at the Castle, and she was surprised she missed Iaven as much as she did. There had been other suitors at the Castle, and more than enough would-be suitors in Kronivar, but none like Iaven. She remembered their talk on the plateau, and the evening before he left, and—

Rhiane put aside her distractions and picked up the quill. She and King Jordgen had gone over all of the separatists' activities and their clandestine forces in Kronivar, and now she was to report her findings at an important council being held that afternoon. There were many things to remember and some were only guesses and vague suspicions, though she had been able to confirm much. She inked her quill and began to write.

Rhiane had completed almost two pages when a knock came and the door opened. Rhiane's elder sister came in, a tall, noble woman in a fine formal gown with a drawn but beautiful face, and long brown hair that fell about her shoulders.

"Allé, it's almost time, aren't you done yet? Father was looking for you," Oellia inquired cheerfully. "Lucky you, getting to sit in with them. Uncle never invites *me* to any war councils."

"You can go in my place," Rhiane said, knowing her sister had no interest whatsoever in them. "I just hope I can remember everything."

Oellia strode to the windows. "Whatever would they do without you, dear Allé..." She turned to look at Rhiane. "Still getting used to 'Allelia' aren't you?

Even father calls you that now. Well, it has been awhile. Do you miss Kronivar at all?"

"Not really," said Rhiane. She liked Kronivar, the huge avenues and crowds milling about, ships coming and going, and the great variety of people and travelers; but the Castle was home.

"I can't imagine going to live there like you did." Oellia shuddered. "And working as a barmaid! The people you'd have to deal with! *Ohh!* Couldn't they have found you something more, well, *noble?*"

"It wasn't at all like you think, 'Elli. Sometimes, maybe, but there were some very nice people there, too. I wouldn't mind going back to the *Badger* for a visit, after the war is over, of course."

"You always were different, dear sister. But from what I hear you won't be going back there any time soon, after the chase they gave you when you left. And what about this Iaven of yours, is he going to fight in the war?"

"He's already gone off into danger, more than your Tomald has seen," Rhiane chided.

"Oh, dear *Toma*, he's off overseeing the smithies in Bottomcliffe, he won't be back until—"

"Allé! We've less than an hour!" Arlen Frosthelm appeared at the doorway and scolded his daughter, and then seeing that she went back to work, he left them.

"Well, I'd better go," Oellia teased, "You poor thing, having to recall your wretched life in that *awful* city!" Oellia smiled good-humoredly and slipped away closing the door behind her.

Soon Rhiane and her father Arlen were on their way to the Great Hall. In one of the main hallways they met a slightly heavyset, middle-aged man dressed in a blue-green doublet and wearing a wide, round hat. His hair and mustache were curled in the current fashion of Tolgard's aristocracy.

"Lady Allelia," he said with a slight but stately bow, "I am pleased to at last make your acquaintance."

"Allé, this is Anrelius Gheel, Ambassador from Tolgard," Arlen told her. "He began his post not long after you left for Kronivar."

Rhiane smiled and nodded. "Welcome, Ambassador."

"Dark times, Arlen. My news is not good," said Ambassador Gheel.

"Better heard now than later," said Arlen. "Dark tidings told late are ill-timed."

At last they entered the Great Hall, where a great oaken conference table was set on the northern side of the room, surrounded by carven chairs cushioned and upholstered in red velvet. King Jordgen stood at the head of the table and motioned for Rhiane to take the seat on his right where Yolias usually sat. Arlen sat next to Rhiane, and the Ambassador took a seat down the table from them. As the other guests came in and took their places, Rhiane noted who else was in attendance. King Jordgen's son, Prince Varlen, sat next to Erland Clovenstone, the Castle Steward, and beyond them were various emissaries bearing tidings from their Dukes, an Elven official from Miastolas, General Knorde from

Farrenhale, and a Teskan official who seemed out of place in the Castle. Rhiane had never been to Teska and had only twice before seen Teskans, as they very rarely came all the way out to the Castle. The Teskan had straight black hair and high cheekbones, keen dark eyes that missed nothing, and the pale olive-green complexion that for Teskans was the glow of health. He was dressed in a thick, woven winter robe that was gray with dark green trim. The Teskan was probably older than he looked, and he said little, choosing instead to watch and listen.

When all were assembled and the customary greetings and salutations made, King Jordgen stood and addressed them. "Dark times have befallen us, and no doubt many of you have ill tidings to bear. Yet speak true and tell all, for hope has not left us. Then may we best decide our course of action."

The King was seated, and reports were heard from the emissaries of the Dukes in the northern and southern provinces, the Foothills, Greensward, and finally Kronivar. Goblin spy activity appeared to have increased, especially in the north, and rumors abounded. Each of the emissaries gave an account of their dukedom's preparations for war and estimates of the numbers of dwarves who had joined the armies encamped in the valleys around the Castle, were garrisoned at Kronivar, or were stationed at the front near Farrenhale and Teska. A scribe at the far end of the table recorded all the proceedings. When these reports were done and everyone sat considering them, the emissaries were led away to their quarters, where they would await the council's decisions and injunctions and return home with them.

Next, Ambassador Gheel gave his report on activities along Tolgard's border with Navrogenaya. "Our relations with Navrogenaya have grown more strained, and our own border guard, stationed at the bridges along the Soskwiteyon River, would be no match for them if they chose to attack us. Some of the bridges have been closed, and there is little trade between us now. The border, though tense, has remained at peace, yet were we to show any sign of favoring Itharia we would certainly risk invasion."

"And these armies, what is known of them?" King Jordgen asked.

"According to various reports their invasion forces include hordes of Goblins, squadrons of Augglins, some grown as big as wild horses or oxen, and even some Trolls from the far northeast. It is difficult to gauge from across the river how many there are of each, but they are very numerous. Recently there have even been rumors of a herd of giant, broadback shaggy Urumak being shepherded and brought down from the Northern Wastes to be trained for war."

"We have heard similar reports from our spies," said General Knorde, "what few have returned." He was a strong, sturdy dwarf with bright eyes, broad shoulders, and a short light brown beard. "Dozens of *Widiwa* families were killed and their homes destroyed in order to obtain these beasts, no doubt."

Rhiane felt her heart sink. Each *Widiwa* family built its home on the back of an *Urumak*, on which they wandered the Northern Wastes. The Urumak were large, gentle creatures, but trained for war, they would be a formidable foe and hasten the Goblin's southward expansion if they attempted an invasion.

"General Knorde, in your opinion, will the Gates hold against an invasion force of that size? And what of Teska?" asked Prince Varlen.

The general looked uncomfortable. "Perhaps. But it may be a question of how long. A greater show of force on our part may keep them at bay. Or an early snowfall could discourage them from starting an attack."

"And why do you think they have held off their attack so long? Surely they must know we were far less prepared only a month ago," said Prince Varlen.

"It may be that they are still readying their troops," said the General, "Were Teska and Farrenhale to fall, they could advance south; and since Gundithe is too narrow and uphill a battle if the plateau is well-guarded, Kronivar would likely be their next goal. Assuming losses at Teska and the lack of a fleet, they would need a large army to attempt to take Kronivar."

"If I may," said Ambassador Gheel, "Some have suggested that they were waiting for the Urumak to arrive, but now that they have, that can no longer be the case, unless there are others still to come."

"Perhaps their spies are aware of our potential renegades in Kronivar, and hope to use our weakness to their advantage," said King Jordgen. "Ships come and go from Kronivar, and traders trade in news as well as goods. They may well have inklings of troubles there. How I would that these renegades would state their case openly. Tergiversators! And yet perhaps they are afraid. My grand-niece, the Lady Allelia, was stationed in Kronivar these past two years, posing as a barmaid, to learn what she might of the separatists." He nodded to Rhiane.

"Although they claim allegiance to the Castle, the separatists are biding their time and growing in number," Rhiane began. Referring to her notes, she described all she had heard, vague suspicions and hunches that had later been confirmed, rumors of suspected leaders, secret meetings, spies stationed at the Castle, and so forth.

"In the event of an invasion during the war, the separatists are maneuvering to have their men in key positions during the defense of Kronivar. They may try to continue to hold these positions afterward, demanding that Kronivar and the surrounding area break away from Itharia and become its own city-state," Rhiane explained. She related how King Jordgen's slow response to the Goblin threat and reluctance to send more troops to the front were often criticized in the common rooms of inns, though it rarely went further than that in the open. As it turned out, the secession movement had many more sympathizers than anyone expected, though most were waiting to see what would happen before taking sides.

"The leaders of the movement remain unknown," Rhiane continued, "Some of the Counts in Kronivar may be involved, though none have openly opposed the Duke as yet. Each Count has a limited number of troops, and there has been talk that some are hiring mercenaries arriving by ship in Kronivar. Such men would be loyal to them but not to the Castle. As the smithies in Kronivar and Bottomcliffe are under close scrutiny by the Castle, weapons for these mercenaries must be purchased by other means. Guards are posted at the docks to watch for Goblin spies and shiploads of weaponry, but some of these guards answer directly to the Counts."

"As Duke of Kronivar, is Grawson dealing with all of this in an adequate fashion?" asked Anrelius Gheel.

Rhiane considered. "So far, but his power depends on the Counts and the King's troops garrisoned there. Some have been assigned to each Count's forces in order to keep a closer watch over them. All claim to fight for the King and Itharia, at the moment." Rhiane straightened up in her chair. "As I've said, many are waiting to see which way the balance will fall before they declare their intentions or act. Of course, if they do, the separatists will want to appear to be the majority. It is often said nowadays that there are as many Men as Dwarves in Kronivar, but most of them, I think, still recognize the King and support the Castle."

"Our efforts in the coming war may regain lost support and help to unify Itharia," Clovenstone said. "But we must send more troops to the front immediately."

King Jordgen nodded slowly. "It would appear so. Yet it seems, strangely, that the Goblins may hold off, perhaps until spring. Kronivar is volatile, and from what we have heard, it may be our greatest concern."

"And if Kronivar *is* attacked and the Castle has too small a hand in its defense, then, too, would the separatist's cause grow in strength," Prince Varlen added.

"May I point out, sire, that troops sent to the front may also serve to quell discontent in Kronivar by showing Itharia to be strong," said Ambassador Gheel.

"Yes, Ambassador, but it may bring us closer to war." Jordgen sounded annoyed. "A build up of armies on one side leads to the building up of the other. The soldiers wait and grow anxious. War is inevitable, yet the Goblins remain at bay. They might well have attacked before Kronivar had fully mobilized, but they did not. Why? In the past month our forces have already increased there; our defense is strong. We have the walls and towers, and a smaller force can easily hold the Gates against a larger force outside them. The Goblins know this and are less likely to attack than before. In a few weeks this unseasonably warm autumn will end and winter will be upon us, and they would be foolish to attempt a winter campaign. If we are careful, we may well stay out of war entirely."

"We all desire peace, your majesty, but even with the onset of winter, they will remain a threat," said General Knorde. "True, I have faith the Gates and Wall will hold, as they have. And adding to our forces now beyond what is necessary may provoke the Goblins to increase their forces rather than decrease them. But war, either now or in spring, is inevitable. Neither side wants to be the first to back down."

"I must agree." Everyone turned to the Teskan official, who had not spoken until then. "Tensions are too great, and would take too long to diminish. '*A fist closes quickly but opens slowly*', as we say. Yet we must hope to avoid war. More at the front will aid the defense, difficult as it is for us all. Still, a shared sacrifice can be a uniting force."

Rhiane understood some of the situation in Teska. Although the Dwarves traded frequently with Teska, there was only one small inn there for foreigners, and visitors were generally not encouraged. The Dwarves who knew the Teskans best were the three hundred or so living in and around Farrenhale, the Dwarves' northernmost village located just south of the Gates. They manned the Gates and towers in peacetime and occasionally visited in Teska as well. Since the threat of war, more and more troops were stationed in the north. Farrenhale had grown fast and was scarcely able to accommodate the increase of dwarves. The Teskans were called upon to help and had done so, and their swamp patrols coordinated with the Dwarven guard at the Gates and watchtowers. The situation became tense but the Teskans tolerated the Dwarves as they always had, finding it necessary to ally with them against the Goblins.

King Jordgen nodded at the Teskan's words. "Wise words, Teska Hunto, you have spoken true." Jordgen smiled. "And yet do you not also have the saying, '*Violence is the refuge of the desperate*'? It is true, I have indeed been cautious, as some say, and there is a point where reluctance becomes mere stubbornness. I am not against the sending of troops; it is more a question of how many."

"Unless our fears concerning Kronivar are unfounded, we will need to send them to both Kronivar and the front. And some for the Gundithe Plateau, of course," said General Knorde.

"With Gundithe and the Ruined East Road secured against attack, we could reduce the troops at the Castle," said Clovenstone.

"True", Arlen Frosthelm added, "If the front is held firmly, Kronivar will not fall, either to the Goblins or the separatists. Each may be hoping to use the other's threat to their advantage."

"We shall send troops to both Kronivar and Farrenhale, then," said the King. "General Knorde and Teska Hunto will precede the troops and arrange a council at the front. I will ask Yolias to stay in Teska, once he arrives there, to integrate the troops we will send with those already present, as well as with the Teskan forces. As some of you may know, Yolias is off on a journey to recover one of the lost gemstones of Aorinthel." Here Jordgen recounted Iaven's visit, with help from Rhiane. The others around the table were impressed to hear of the recovery of the Lost Swords of the Alliance and the news seemed to give them hope. "We may even have *both* of the swords," said Jordgen. "Rather than bring them here, I will have Yolias keep them at the front, and use them to unite our forces with the Teskans; each leader will wield one of the swords in battle. It was for a similar purpose that they were forged, almost a century ago."

"It is good to hear the swords have been found," said the Elven official. "Queen Perla will be glad to hear the front is secure."

Teska Hunto nodded and smiled for the first time that day. "Your majesty honors our people. We shall fight side by side with you."

Others present made declarations of support, and soon talk fell to the preparation of the troops, the numbers to be sent, and who would be in command. Troops would be sent out from the Castle, and at Greensward some would go north to the front while the others would go west to Kronivar. Once

Kronivar was more stable, fresh troops would be sent from the garrison there to hold the Gundithe Plateau. In the event of an invasion and attack on Kronivar, King Jordgen intended to ride out himself, leading the forces at Gundithe and Greensward, to join the battle in Kronivar and cut off any retreat the Goblins might have.

As plans were formed, everyone's spirits rose and soon the council was adjourned. Ambassador Gheel took his leave, and Arlen Frosthelm, Erland Clovenstone, General Knorde, and Teska Hunto talked with King Jordgen awhile concerning troop movements. After they departed, Jordgen called Rhiane and the scribe over to dictate the message that would be sent to Teska for Yolias when he arrived. The message would go by carrier-pigeon that day, and Rhiane offered to take it up to the messaging tower for dispatch. It had occurred to her that she might enclose a short note to Iaven within the small scroll.

The day following the war council saw the final training of new recruits and the mobilizing of the troops. Those encamped in the surrounding valleys folded their tents and ascended to the Castle Plateau where they would spend the night, ready for an early march the next morning. With their packs, blankets, battle armor, and other gear aboard horse-drawn carts, they would reach Greensward in two days' time, if they left early enough. All throughout the Castle's outer ward carts were loaded with stores and provisions, and soldiers gathered into their squadrons, their captains calling them to order. Horses were brushed and their harnesses fitted, and the soundness of the carts checked. The last of the new-forged weapons emerged from the smithies and rang in the mountain air as they were tested.

Clamor and anticipation filled the Castle as well. Brief meetings were held between various commanders and counselors, tracings of maps were made in the Castle Library, and coffers were opened for last-minute expenditures. By nightfall everything had been arranged and readied for the coming morn, and activity in the outer ward died down to a few guards and campfires as the troops turned in to rest for their early start the next day.

Rhiane had spent a very full day helping her father mobilize the forces heading for Kronivar, and she went to bed wearied and tired at the end of it. She tried to sleep and could not. In all likelihood, Iaven, Yolias, and the others would have to remain and fight at the front, and she would not see them until after the war.

Even before the sky began paling behind the mountains, many of the troops were already up and walking around. Some paced nervously, others ate a small breakfast or stood smoking pipes, and a few sat watching the sunrise. All were ready and eager to depart.

On the walls and towers around the Castle, the last watch of the night awaited the end of its shift. Tired as they were, they would not rest before passing through the waking crowd below and bidding their friends farewell. Some envied those going off to Kronivar or the front, while others were content to stay behind. Lots had been drawn and lists made up the evening after the council, and by now everyone was aware of who was going away and who was not. Soon the Castle would be quieter than it had been in months.

Rhiane rose early to watch the troops' departure. In the hall she came upon two young guards chatting on the way to their shift. As they saw her approaching, their conversation broke off abruptly.

"Good morning, M'lady," they nodded and bowed.

"Morning, fellows. Might one of you have the key to the messaging tower? I mean to watch our troops departing," said Rhiane.

"Certainly, M'lady," said one guard, nodding again. They led the way to the door and unlocked it, holding it open as Rhiane thanked them and alighted the spiraling stone stairs.

The guard closed the door behind her and paused, waiting until she had gone up. He turned to his companion. "As I was telling you," he said in a hushed voice, "most of them were sent out with the armies; Elgen and Stavy, too."

"You think they knew about us?" asked the other guard.

"Hard to say. Maybe it was just luck. I've counted, and there's only five of us left, I think."

"More than enough for now, I suppose. Not much to spy on anymore, especially with them sending troops to Kronivar."

"Yes, I don't think they expected the Castle would send so many. I wonder what they'll do about it. I suppose it's out of our hands."

"True... Little remains for us to do here, but let's wait and see what happens. At least we're not off to the front!"

A cold breeze was blowing in through the arched windows when Rhiane arrived at the top of the messaging tower. Pigeons cooed softly and a slight dank smell rose from their cages that the wind did not completely obliterate. The pale pink sunrise lit the tower's top floor, which was a small, round room, some twelve feet in diameter, with windows facing north, south, east, and west. Pigeons strutted in cages on tables along the walls, each cage labeled with the destination to which its pigeons flew. Bags of feed and jugs of water were stored under the tables, and dishes of feed and water lay within the pigeons' reach, just outside the cages.

Rhiane leaned on the sill of the southern window and stared down into Castle's outer ward. The main gates of the Castle opened, commanders shouted orders, and rows of troops began moving out onto the plateau and down the road. Even up in the tower she could hear the slow, solemn rhythm of their march. Soon columns of soldiers filled the road across the ridge leading into the mountains, their ranks broken here and there by slowly moving horse carts loaded with provisions. Rhiane watched the stately procession, wondering how many of those going off to battle would return. Seeing the armies marching out affirmed the inevitability of the war. Up until the day before, Rhiane, like many others, had entertained the hope that war with Navrogenaya could be avoided. Some still maintained it could, but now she saw that such talk was merely to encourage others and no more than wishful thinking. Her thoughts returned to Iaven and Yolias as she wondered if she would ever see them again.

Chapter 24.
Death in the Arinzei Valley

For two days the goblins led Lexter through winding cave systems linked by rough-hewn tunnels. Stiff and weak under his load, Lexter shivered in the chilling dampness. Whenever he fell, the goblins jerked the rope around his neck and whipped or kicked him. Lexter hung on, but knew his days were numbered; when he ceased to be useful they would kill him as they had killed Leland. Escape seemed impossible and he could not have found his way out of the caves anyway.

Resigned to his fate, Lexter's thoughts kept returning to his brothers and elderly parents in Tolgard. Leland's terrible and sudden death and his own impending execution made him wonder how their lives would have been if they had stayed in Tolgard making an honest living. They should never have returned to Kronivar with a price on his head. Or gotten into dealing in weaponry, or made so many enemies over the years… At first it hadn't bothered them at all; whenever they were in trouble or no longer welcome somewhere, they just packed up and moved on until they were forgotten. They had been their own masters, living by their wits, working only when they wanted to —well, that wasn't quite true, making a living was rarely easy, especially when so much of what they did involved speculation. And Lexter was tired of traveling all the time. But they had been many places and seen quite a lot, and he never regretted that.

Once in a while, when they could afford it, Leland and Lexter returned to Tolgard to visit their family and regale them with tales of faraway places. It hadn't always been like that, though. As a young man of twenty-two, Leland had a bitter falling out with their father and Lexter had sided with Leland. Lexter was only eighteen at the time and wished now that he hadn't been so angry with his parents in his late boyhood years. After a particularly bad quarrel with their father, the two brothers had gone off on their own to seek their fortunes, and it was almost five years before they finally agreed to go back for a visit. Everyone was delighted to see them, and even their father gave them a warm welcome. Their overjoyed mother cooked supper for them, insisting they stay at least a week or more. Leland made it clear that they would be off again very soon, as they had some deals in the works, but they enjoyed their stay and the week went by fast. Their father asked how they were doing and where they had been. They told him of work they'd had, loading ships in Kronivar or as hired hands at harvest time, and how they had bought a cart and eventually gotten into trade. They never mentioned their shadier dealings or outright thievery, which had grown over the last few years, but Lexter knew their father suspected something and was disappointed with them.

After that they went back once a year or so, whenever they were passing through Tolgard. Linus and Leander, who were only young children of ten and twelve when Lexter and Leland had left, grew up quickly and were always delighted to see their older brothers. Sometimes they changed so much between visits that they seemed like strangers until Leland and Lexter became reacquainted with them. Once they begged Leland to take them along to "see the world", but Leland just smiled and said they were too young and that he and Lexter had some far-off business that couldn't wait. Their father said nothing, but Lexter knew he was glad to see Leland discouraging them.

Over the years Linus and Leander took on the work of their father's cobbler shop. Still happy to see Lexter and Leland, they no longer desired to travel or go adventuring with their brothers. Lexter was ashamed to think that by now Linus and Leander had guessed how he and Leland made a living. Nothing was ever discussed, and no judgments were made, but he supposed they had some idea. Leland, too, had sensed it, and Lexter wondered if it ever bothered him as well.

With the threat of war hovering over Itharia, business had picked up and they had been busy. They hadn't been back to Tolgard for over three years, and Leland actually looked forward to returning. He had even suggested spending the coming winter there, with the profits from the Aranstone deal. At first Lexter had balked at the idea, but as he thought about it, it appealed to him more and more. They had joked about setting up a shop in Cander, one of Tolgard's port cities, and becoming honest businessman once they had enough saved up and stashed away. In the last month or so, it seemed entirely possible.

Now that Leland was gone, Lexter realized he wasn't so good at business or even much of a thief; most of the big ideas and schemes had all been Leland's. He had often just gone along with them, adding what he could. *Maybe I would have been more honest*, Lexter thought, *if Leland hadn't been so good at what he did...* But there was no use blaming Leland; Lexter made his own decisions, from the time he had first decided to run off with Leland. He had lived an interesting life, he thought. He had regrets, as did anyone out in the world who looked back on what he had done. *And I can still die an honest man*, he thought, *I can decide, right here and now, that that's what I would have been from now on, if I'd only had the chance.*

Oh, it was easy to deceive people, Lexter thought. That fall alone they had cheated some Elves in Iaf who didn't realize it until after they were gone, and men and dwarves at the harvest festival in Miastolas. They even had some tricks planned for the dealings with Aranstone and his men in Kronivar. After so many years, Lexter could almost believe his own lies, which made him sound all the more genuine. He thought they'd never get caught, after so many close escapes and especially after the smooth and easy escapes. But now Lexter really did want to change and wished that he had sooner.

The more Lexter thought about it, the more he liked the idea that he still could at least die an honest man. He managed to convince himself that his death would now be an honorable one, even though the goblins would be the only ones there to see it, and even though no one knew he had changed his mind or his life. But it was important to him, and he held firmly to the idea the way a drowning man clings to the piece of driftwood that keeps him afloat.

Lexter would have been surprised to hear that the passage through the caves and tunnels under the mountains had only taken two days. In the damp, cool darkness underground he had lost all sense of time. The goblins seemed in no hurry and stopped at irregular intervals when the larger of the two wanted to rest or eat, and Lexter never slept comfortably or for long. At last they rounded some bends and came down a straight, narrow tunnel cut from the rock, which ran almost a hundred yards. Suddenly they emerged in what appeared to be a large Goblin hut. The air was fresher, and Lexter heard the faint sound of crickets in the night outside the hut. The goblins stopped there and let Lexter fall to the ground to rest. Instead of hard, wet stone, Lexter landed on a dirt floor. He looked around the hut. Piles of excavated rubble lined the walls. Lexter guessed that the hut had been built at the base of the cliff to hide the tunnel entrance from Itharia's watchtowers on the mountainside path. How long it had taken the Goblins to dig the entrance tunnel and remove the excavated rock he could not say, but he knew they held grudges a good long time.

Lexter shifted himself to get a better look around. A side table ran along the wall, but he could not see what was on it from where he lay. The larger goblin took a wide candle from the table and lit it from the torch, which he snuffed out in the dirt and laid aside.

"*Karza vor ferkrild vo nasrh? Veh ghenar sora ferkrild, ih koszonar narvho shegravolnra hunret!*" the shorter goblin reminded the larger one. Both goblins began speaking Rogglish and Lexter could only wonder what they were saying.

"What should we do with the captive? We weren't supposed to take any captives, and especially not through the undermountain tunnel!" Herog reminded Urzad.

Urzad bristled at the reproach. "We have a long way to go yet, do you want to carry everything?"

Herog ignored him, shaking his head. "You're lucky Hefrad isn't here! Del-Sorhar is keeping an eye on you, why tempt him further? And this idea of going back up to Ordskell... it's too far out of our way!"

"Gherek is leaving Ordskell in a few days and promised to take my report straight to General Burzok himself. Del-Sorhar need never know; we'll write up a favorable report for him. Burzok has to know what's happening in Kronivar, before it's too late."

"I agree; we should have attacked weeks ago. But our forces are still superior, and once we get a stronghold in Itharia, we'll hold it solidly," said Herog.

"What stronghold? If the Dwarves hold the Gundithe Plateau the Castle's out of reach, and Kronivar can't be laid siege to without a fleet, although a month ago we might have taken it without one. The Northern Provinces? Less resistance, yes, but hardly worth taking if we go no farther than that. It's too close to winter for a full-scale campaign. We should wait until spring."

"The Dwarves have mobilized more than expected, but it's still not enough and they know it. They're hoping we'll hold back and wait. Teska could be ours now; by spring it will be too late. What are they waiting for? Burzok would have attacked when the time was right, but King Golhazzar held him back. I've heard his Grand Vizier has something to do with it."

"I've heard the same," said Urzad, "I agree, earlier the time was ripe, when

Kronivar wasn't prepared. Of course, our southern units weren't in place, that's true. Now things have changed, and it's too late. Still, the Dwarves will not attack, and we can afford to bide our time. But Del-Sorhar wants war and suppresses the reports. Burzok must be told about Kronivar."

"And if Del-Sorhar finds out what you're doing, he'll have your head."

Urzad grunted. "Unless Burzok has his first, when they find out what he's been doing."

The goblins had a brief bite to eat and tossed Lexter the scraps. With his hands tied, Lexter had to lean forward and eat them off the ground, and he was ashamed at how willing he was to do so. He had just begun eating when the rope around his neck jerked sharply and he was up and stumbling forward again.

As they left the confines of the hut, the Arinzei Valley opened wide, under the stars. A cold wind was blowing. It was refreshing after being in the caves so long, and the starlight even seemed bright by comparison. The large hut they had emerged from was built at the base of the cliffs, and several others were nearby. From outside, there was no hint of the tunnel entrance at all. The cliffs rose up high on their right, and to the left the valley was open grassland into the far north where the mountains continued, their black shapes hulking on the horizon. Lexter wondered why they were heading east instead of west toward where the armies were, north of Teska. He tried to look around, but they pulled him onward, and he had to keep watching his step over the rugged, uneven ground.

They traveled the rest of the night and stopped at dawn in a shallow cliffside alcove where shoulders of rock shielded them from east and west. Lexter sat up, seeing the valley in the daylight. It was wide and barren, only grasses and shrubs and patches of dried, hard ground where nothing grew. The Goblins had left it uninhabited due to the barren, open ground, and because it was within plain view of the Dwarven watchtowers built along the mountainside path. As the goblins left the rocky alcove, Lexter looked back and saw one of the watchtowers, a tall needle of stone rising from the cliffside, far away and hazy in the morning light. The goblins, he realized, had stayed close to the cliffs so as to remain out of sight as much as possible. At first the sight of the watchtower struck a note of hope in Lexter, but it was so far away and high above them that he soon gave up again.

They traveled all day with only a few brief rests, and the goblins said little and seemed in no mood for talking. Lexter wondered how much further they were going and if his life as a slave would continue somewhere in the north. Yet something assured him that wasn't the case. It was a bright, sunny day and everything seemed quiet and calm, the land so empty it was hard to believe a war was imminent; or, for that matter, his own death. Lexter had never really pictured what his last day would be like. He was amazed at the foolish and irrelevant things that came to mind, as though to distract him. His thoughts jumped from one thing to another almost randomly. The most trivial things held his attention, and unrelated memories, many of which he had thought he had forgotten, flitted through his mind. *What's happening to me?* he thought,

Perhaps I'm going mad. He finally gave himself up to it and let it distract him as best it could.

As the sun went down behind them, the goblins came away from the mountains and angled northeast through the valley. The change of direction made Lexter nervous and all his distractedness left him as he waited for what they would do with him. Visions of Leland dying returned. A wind blew hard and cold as the sun lowered in the west. They had gone a mile or so into the valley, when one of the goblins saw something in the distance.

"*Skog, Urzad! Kor nagtah... Karza ghe nasrho wervrahtai moh, shorgar?*" said the shorter goblin.

They stopped and discussed something, and seemed to agree on some course of action. The larger of the two goblins took hold of Lexter's leash, led him to a big, shallow sinkhole and shoved him to the ground in it. The goblin bent down and roughly tied Lexter's legs together, and then stood up again, watching to see if Lexter was secured.

Lexter's heart was racing. He wondered if they would kill him and leave him laying in the sinkhole. The goblin stood staring down at him, one side of his face lit red by the sinking sun, the other in shadow. He looked at Lexter and then at the other goblin, said something, and walked away.

As they hiked through the valley, Herog wondered how far Urzad intended to go before killing the prisoner. They weren't even supposed to have taken a prisoner; anyone who discovered them in Itharia was supposed to die with the secret. He had to admit it was nice to have a packhorse for the return journey, though he would have left the prisoner dead in the waystation at the tunnel entrance if it were up to him. Suddenly he saw a horse and rider in the distance. "Urzad, look! A border guard... What's he doing all the way out here, I wonder?"

"He hasn't seen us yet."

"We can't let him see the prisoner."

"No. Let's wait until he's gone."

"Look, he's turning..."

Urzad grabbed Lexter's rope and led him over to the sinkhole, shoving him into it with his load.

"I think he's seen us," said Herog. "He's riding this way."

"Let's go to meet him. We'll send him on his way."

Urzad and Herog walked over as the guard rode up and dismounted. Herog recognized him. "Hefrad! What brings you out here?" Nervousness edged Herog's voice.

Hefrad eyed them suspiciously. He was broad of shoulder and half a foot taller than Urzad. His coat of ring mail had a hood of crimson, and his cape was clasped with a silver raven in flight, the insignia of the Royal Border Guard. At his belt hung a long thin sword in a burgundy leather sheath, and in front, angled for the reach of his right hand, a sheathed Goblin *zardaggar*, a broad-bladed triangular dagger with a horizontal grip joined at both ends to the blade.

"I should ask you the same." Hefrad smiled meanly. "You're expected at the front."

"Just some business in Ordskell before we return," Urzad said.

"In Ordskell, eh? Must be of some importance. More than the much-needed reports from Kronivar." He watched their reaction. "Gherek is expecting you."

Urzad looked at Hefrad, trying to remain calm.

"Is he? Well, you can tell him I'm coming!" Urzad remarked.

Hefrad was not amused. He extended a gloved hand. "Your report for Del-Sorhar. I'll do you the favor of taking it to him myself, since you're so busy."

"All in good time!" Urzad showed annoyance but spoke without insolence this time. "I'll take it directly to him myself, as he wants, when we arrive on the front."

"Del-Sorhar would prefer the first draft, not the revised one," Hefrad grew impatient. "Give it to me now. I know you have it. The report."

Urzad and Hefrad locked eyes. Herog waited nervously, unsure whether he might help by interrupting. Hefrad's hand closed on the sheathed zardaggar at his belt. Urzad saw this but his gaze never shifted.

"My loyalty is to Del-Sorhar, not to you," Urzad spoke slowly.

Hefrad laughed and the tension seemed to break. "To Del-Sorhar! Well, won't he be pleased to hear it. And I'm sure the report will contain everything he wants to hear, that'll make him happy, too!"

Hefrad leaned forward, and with a quick, precise swing of his arm, slashed the zardaggar across Urzad's throat. He shook the blade, wiped it off, and sheathed it again. Urzad's hands went to his dagger, but just as he unsheathed it he fell to the ground, choking and rasping. Hefrad watched him fall, and swung a leg over his horse and dismounted. Herog stepped back in panic, fearing he would be next. Hefrad bent over Urzad's motionless body, opened Urzad's coat and reached into the inner pocket. He drew out a rolled-up paper, unrolled it, read a few lines, and then folded it and put it away in his own pocket.

"Gherek said he'd have it on him." Hefrad turned toward Herog, as if to decide his fate.

"I tried to stop him," Herog lied. "He would have sent it to Burzok, it's true. I was going to have him arrested in Ordskell, as soon as we arrived. I thought of going to the front by myself, but it seemed dangerous to let him go like that; I had to keep an eye on him."

Herog felt himself shaking under Hefrad's unwavering gaze. Hefrad's cold smile faded.

"Your service has been without blemish thus far. Del-Sorhar would not be pleased to hear of this. You will not go unpunished, and if there is ever anything more, even the slightest infraction—"

"I understand," said Herog.

Hefrad kept an eye on Herog and slowly mounted the horse. He motioned for Herog to get on behind him, and Herog climbed up obediently.

"I make no promise of leniency," Hefrad said, "You will gladly take whatever sentence you receive."

"Of course," Herog muttered. He glanced back over his shoulder at the empty land and gradually grew more relieved as they rode farther and farther away from the sinkhole where their prisoner lay. Herog briefly thought of mentioning it, and then realized that for the moment, saying nothing was the wisest course of action as far as his own life and future were concerned.

The western light faded and night fell. Crickets began their insistent chirping, and still Lexter lay in the shallow pit in the field. He waited for the goblins to return, wondering if they had set up camp nearby and had simply left him there for the night. Yet their flints, pan, arrows —everything they needed— was still in the pack lying next to him. He strained hard, listening for activity, and could not hear any. At first he assumed they would come back and kill him, as they had threatened to do whenever he tried to loose his bonds or escape. Maybe they were waiting just outside the sinkhole, curious to see what he would do, ready to slaughter him as soon as he broke free. He waited, motionless, to see what would happen. Lexter was not gagged and thought of calling out, but if they really were gone, someone else might hear him and come, and in the valley it was likely to be a goblin.

He slowly realized it didn't matter what he did. They could kill him regardless of what happened. Or maybe he'd live the rest of his life as a slave. He wasn't sure which was worse and was too tired to think about it. Lexter's hands were bound behind his back and he rolled off the arm he had been laying on, feeling pins and needles as blood flowed in it again. He rolled over to his other side and listened.

Hearing nothing, he relaxed, breathing hard and listening. After a while, he carefully sat up, peeking over the edge of the sinkhole. The land around him was dark, no hint of a campfire, no one walking about. Lexter was relieved. He sat up straight now, his back aching and his hands still tied behind him.

He looked at the goblins' pack, the cloth sack he had carried on his back for over a week. He shifted around and kicked at it, trying to dump it out with his feet. The bag was tied on top, with a small opening where it came together. Lexter kicked off one of his shoes, got his toes into the hole, and pulled the bag open. He raised the back end, spilling everything onto the ground. In the dark, Lexter moved close to see what had fallen out and leaned back, kicking things over with his foot. At last he found a small, sheathed knife. He positioned it on the ground with his foot and then turned himself around and groped for it with his hands. Minutes later he had it and cut himself free.

Lexter stretched out his arms and lay back, staring up at the stars, tired and dirty and full of joyous relief. *My days are still numbered*, he thought, *it's just a bigger number than I thought it was*. He lay awhile, thankful and breathing hard, and then sat up to look for goblins. The valley was clear as far as he could see. Lexter looked to the south and saw he was on the valley's eastern end. Far away was the great mountain at the end of the range, and flat lands to the east of it. He decided to head for the mountains and look for a way back into Itharia. Traveling along the bottom of the cliffs was too dangerous; too many Goblin huts. Perhaps he could find a way up to the mountainside path that went past the watchtowers, he thought.

He turned to the goblin pack. It would be several days' walk at least, and he would need to eat. In the pack he found money, knives, and some papers they had taken from him and Leland and stuffed them into his own pockets. The goblins had a bag of nuts, dried flatbread, and long, dark, beanlike roots that he wondered if he could stomach. It was all that was left, so he took them. The goblins had stashed away an extra coat, and Lexter found it fit him. They had not worn it, yet it smelled. Lexter himself had not washed in quite some time, but he still wrinkled his nose at the Goblin scent.

Rummaging through the pack and taking whatever he wanted had a strange effect on Lexter. He was used to going through other people's things and taking what he liked, and it was so natural that he had long since ceased to think about it. But as the habitual nature of his actions brought to mind his old life, he recalled all the promises he had made to himself under the mountain. He had been spared, but would he remain true to them? Strangely, he found he still wanted to be honest. He sat back thinking. Falling back into his old, ingrained habits was the easiest thing to do. Yet maybe he could still live by his wits and be honest, too. No more stealing from others. Of course, the goblin pack was different; he needed the food and coat. Nothing wrong with that. The goblins were gone, they were the enemy, that wasn't really stealing. Lexter was certain he could be a new man, rid of his old habits. He had resolved to do it. Finally Lexter decided that he might as well put everything in the bag and take it along; there might be something he could sell or trade in Teska or Farrenhale.

Lexter stopped again. Why was he making such an effort to justify things to himself? That was another habit that came easily to him; too much so. He and Leland had always found ways to sanction their behavior and quiet any doubts they had. *But this was different, they were going to kill me*, he thought, *It's silly of me to worry about it. Once I'm back safe in Itharia, no more of the old ways. Once I'm back on my feet again, that is. No, no, even before then. I'll be honest even it kills— well, hurts me. No more deceiving, no stealing, no taking advantage of the good-hearted. And manipulating, well, it isn't really lying, is it? No, no, I shouldn't try to justify everything...* Lexter tried to dispel his doubts regarding himself, until he realized they expressed what he honestly thought of himself. *This is going to be harder than I thought...* Lexter packed the bag and slung it over his shoulder. He looked around, climbed out of the ditch, and started walking toward the mountains to the south.

Chapter 25.
The Magpie's Nest

After leaving the outpost, Iaven and his friends pushed onward with renewed urgency, certain that Orven's party was ahead of them and closing in on the gem. Yolias, concerned about goblin activity in the Arinzei Valley, drove the dwarves hard to get around Mount Harbash and up onto the mountainside path. Their climb overlooked the valley, where the desert merged into the grasslands to the west. The sky darkened and they kept a vigilant watch about them during the strenuous ascent. Yolias set a vigorous pace that shamed the younger dwarves into silence and it was all they could do to catch their breath and keep up. Night fell, and still they climbed. Wilbur lagged behind, slowing them down. They stopped to rest a few times, always too short, it seemed. Eager as they were to reach higher and safer ground, they were ready to set camp whenever Yolias let them.

Iaven looked up at the night sky over the valley, where a tiny sliver of moon hovered. The stars were sharp and bright. He remembered wandering alone at night in the fields outside Hillbrook, into the hills, to lie on the grass and stare up at the stars. Endless farm chores made him long to see what lay beyond the Foothills. And now the farm was gone, and the stars reminded him of home.

At last the dwarves found what appeared to be the mountainside path. It was narrow, often treacherous, and much of it could hardly be called a path. Iaven wondered if Yolias was merely trying to encourage them. Whenever they passed close to the cliff's edge they looked into the dark valley, afraid goblins were watching them. None of them liked the prospect of traveling and camping so close to Navrogenaya, even if they were high above it.

"This path goes all the way to Teska?" asked Wilbur.

"It does," Yolias said, "It winds around the mountains' shoulders, following the range to the west. The path was laid out long ago, when the gates and wall were built, to connect the watchtowers and watch over the valley. Since then, the Goblins have moved north of the valley, leaving it barren."

Zammond strained to see ahead of them. "So when will we see the watchtowers?"

"Not for awhile yet. They start by the East Gate, on the westernmost mountain near Teska and there's another every nine or ten miles, until about halfway across the range to Mount Harbash. They keep watch for troop movements and other activity. The Goblins do not like them and have built their own system of huts and waystations along the base of the cliffs, where they are difficult to see from the towers. They have their own border patrol, and occasionally even come up onto the path."

"Is there more than one way up?" Iaven had hoped they were out the Goblins' reach.

"Several, on this end of the range. Around the watchtowers, the mountains are wider and the cliffs sheer and impassable, and the towers guard the path. But not out here. We must be careful. Perhaps that brother of yours has already stirred up trouble!"

"All the same," moaned Wilbur, "we've walked all night and I don't think I can go on anymore. I'm too tired!"

Iaven drew his sword and checked the direction of the gem. "Can't be much farther now. As the crow flies, at least." The stone in the pommel glowed bright and steady in the night, but the path wound wildly as it clung to the mountainside. "It does seem closer than before."

The path ran level for a while, cutting across steep slopes, and then climbed again. At last, high above the valley, it leveled off and led through a sloping pine forest. Streams ran down from the mountains forcing the dwarves to go single file across rocks jutting out from the rushing waters. The path widened and passed a small brook-lined meadow amidst the pines. It was still an hour or two before dawn and the dwarves' pace had become very sluggish, so Yolias suggested setting camp off the path in the meadow. "A very short rest," he warned them. We can get a full night's sleep once we have the gem."

They made sure the place was safe and unpacked. Hobley built a small, shielded fire for warmth, and the others laid out their bedrolls. Zammond finished his and came over by Iaven. "Let's check it again. How close are we?"

Iaven looked at the sword. "It wouldn't be far, if the path took us straight there. But it may be quite a hike yet." The sword's glow told him that Orven had not found the gem yet, but not how close Orven was to finding it.

Yolias joined them. "Though we're near the gem, Orven may be nearer. We ought to continue, even just the three of us. Unburdened, we could travel faster, get the gem, and return. I'd rather not rest until we have it."

"I agree," said Iaven. "But what if we caught up to Orven? We'd be outnumbered."

"If he's gone ahead of us he may not know about the path, and may be traveling the valley instead. The gem seems to be higher up, so he'll have to eventually find a way to reach it. But it may delay him enough to give us an advantage."

"And if he's found the path already?" asked Zammond.

"Then we will have to do our best," said Yolias. He scanned the dark valley. "And Orven is not our only worry out here, either."

Hobley, Tillmore, and Wilbur agreed to the plan and soon Yolias, Iaven, and Zammond were on their way across the mountainside. The path rounded a steep slope dense with pines and curved around the mountain. They expected another deep valley to open, but the way was straighter and less steep than the last pass had been. Pale starlight lit the path, drawing Iaven's eyes along it. His legs were heavy and his feet sore, but he could not bear to lose another gem to Orven. Orven's laugh echoing down the well in Kronivar hardened his resolve with every step he took.

Iaven led them, walking with Halix drawn, lightheaded with tiredness and anxious anticipation. At times the path narrowed, forcing them to go in single file. Often it went straight and took a sudden turn, revealing the way to be longer than it looked, as winding folds took them toward and away from the gem.

The eastern sky paled and birds began calling. The mountains around them grew visible as the veil of darkness thinned. Finally, after many turns of the path, the sword indicated the gem directly ahead. They left the path and came to a small grassy area at the edge of the cliff. There a huge oak tree stretched its branches high and wide, out over the valley. The cliff was a sheer drop of at least a hundred feet, after which it became a pine-covered slope running down into the valley, where a dense morning fog drifted through, obscuring the ground. The tree grew right at the cliff's edge, its roots hanging out of the cliff wall. Iaven moved Halix, and the small green stone in the pommel glowed brightest when the sword pointed forward into the valley. His heart sunk, fearing the gem was below on the valley floor, but as he lowered the sword, the glow diminished slightly. When he raised it again, it brightened.

"It's in the tree!" Iaven moved the sword to pinpoint the gem's location.

They walked to the cliff's edge, looking up at the tree. Despite the clouds, the morning light was now bright enough to see clearly. Iaven swept the sword across the expanse of branches, while Zammond and Yolias gazed up at them. Most of the tree's leaves had fallen, and it was not long before Yolias caught sight of something.

"Look, there, out on that branch, an old bird's nest. It must be in there," Yolias said. Iaven pointed Halix to be certain, then lowered and sheathed it. The nest was set amidst forking branches, overhanging the valley some eight or nine feet out beyond the cliff. Iaven hesitated, wondering if the branch would support his weight.

"Go get it and we'll stand guard!" said Zammond. He and Yolias stood back a bit as Iaven warily climbed up the trunk, gained a foothold, and pulled himself up into the narrow place where the trunk spread out into three big beams.

Zammond and Yolias walked away from the cliff's edge, watching Iaven. "It will hold him, I think," said Yolias. "And now that it is light out, we had better keep an eye on the path, rather than have our backs turned to it." Yolias walked over to the path and Zammond reluctantly joined him.

"We'll be near the path, Iaven," Zammond called as they went, "Hurry, and don't let everyone in the valley see you up there!" Iaven nodded, annoyed at the interruption. He turned back to the branches. Climbing a little further, he found the branch where the nest was. The branch stretched over the valley and hung there, hovering in mid-air. It was thick enough to walk on, but not all the way out to the nest. Iaven climbed further, holding onto branches overhead to steady himself. He took a few steps away from the trunk of the tree, and looking down, saw that he was just over the edge of the cliff. He stepped back again, deciding what to do. A cold gust blew, and the longer and thinner branches creaked and swayed in the wind.

Holding on to smaller limbs above him, Iaven walked out a few steps onto the branch, watching it and trying not to look down beyond it. Fog passing below reminded him of just how high up he was. Iaven placed one foot in front of the other. The branch rose gradually as it went out, and after several more steps Iaven could feel it bending beneath his weight and heard it creaking. Soon the limbs overhead narrowed and came to an end. Iaven backed up a few steps, and lowered himself, gripping the limbs above as long as he could until they bent and he had to let go. He sat down on the branch, straddling it. He crawled forward, careful to feel how it was supporting him.

Iaven was now several feet beyond the edge of the cliff. He turned and looked back, but he could not see Zammond or Yolias. Good, he thought, feeling less nervous now that no one was watching. He slid forward again, concentrating on the branch, but could not help looking into the valley below. He moved forward again. The nest was now less than four feet away. It was an abandoned magpie's nest, a big, woven bowl of small sticks and twigs lined with mud and dried grass. Iaven was not close enough to see what was inside, but he knew the gem must be there. He slid forward again. The branch had thinned and was bending even lower. He dared go no further. Even if the branch didn't break under his weight, it might bend so much that the nest might fall off. Or perhaps not: the nest seemed securely built. Iaven leaned forward until he was lying down and stretched his legs behind him, crossing his heels under the branch. Holding on with one arm, he reached forward with the other, but still fell short of the nest. As he lay on the branch, he noticed his scabbard leaning back on his belt, with Halix ready to fall out of its sheath into the valley. He pulled back and gently eased the scabbard to a safer, upright angle. Iaven reached for the nest again, sliding himself a fraction of an inch forward at a time. The branch creaked and bent lower under his weight. Iaven stopped. If could bring the nest closer to him, he thought, he might be able to reach it.

Iaven carefully drew Halix. He reached forward with it and caught the tip of the blade in the rim of the nest. He tugged at it, but the nest would not move. Iaven pulled a little harder, fearing the nest would loosen and fall off the branch. He moved and tried again, but sent the branch in motion. Iaven pulled back, waiting until the branch was still again. If the nest wouldn't move, maybe he could edge a little closer to it. Carefully, he sheathed Halix. He slid forward a tiny bit, and the branch bent still more. He could see what was in the nest now. There were a few shiny objects the magpie had collected; a Goblin coin, a metal hook, and tucked away inside the dry brown grass lining the nest, the darkly gleaming facets of a gemstone. Iaven drew a quick breath, excited at the sight of the stone. He reached forward again, stretching his arm tight and extending his hand and fingers. The tip of his middle finger grazed the side of the nest. He drew his arm in again. The wind blew, swaying the branch momentarily. The gem was deep enough in the nest that he could risk bending the branch a little more, but soon it would start to give under his weight. Halix hung precariously at his belt, swinging in its scabbard, which he had to keep readjusting. He wished now that he had simply left it on the cliffside.

Iaven lay on the bending branch, his legs wrapped underneath it, his head lower than his feet. He slid forward a tiny bit and reached again. This time his fingers touched the rim of the nest. Suddenly a hearty laugh sounded from the cliff behind him.

"Iaven! What *are* you doing out there?"

Startled, Iaven pulled back onto the branch away from the nest and turned. Orven stood at the edge of the cliff, smiling and watching him.

"So this is how you use Halix, poking at a bird's nest?" Orven laughed. "Oh, I admit you beat me to it. I'm just glad you've gone out there to get it for me!"

"Zammond! Yolias!" Iaven yelled, wondering what had happened to them.

"Don't worry, they're all dead." Orven laughed maliciously. His shirt was cut and slightly bloodied. He held Gorflange before him, dark stains on the blade. "The old fellow, he was the worst. Couldn't catch *him* by surprise! Put up quite a fight, too. But he didn't have one of these." Orven raised Gorflange. "Too bad you didn't let him use Halix!"

Iaven was red and shaking with panic and rage. The branch quivered under him, the pit of his stomach coiled tight, his muscles tensing. He wanted to respond but was too angry to find the words.

"I never thought you'd come so far from home, I'll give you credit for that!" Orven sneered. "And now to find you out here..." Orven laughed again. "No need to panic, brother. Just throw me the gem and I'll let you climb down." He held Gorflange on the ready, waiting for a fight. Iaven tried to stop himself from trembling. He could not believe Orven had killed Zammond and Yolias, yet he was not entirely sure.

Orven watched Iaven closely. "Or don't you even have it yet? I should have known!" Sheathing Gorflange, he walked over to the trunk of the tree, found a foothold and climbed up into the branches.

Iaven stretched out again and thrust his arm toward the nest. The branch bowed lower, swinging, and Iaven held it as tightly as he could. He lunged at the nest and his fingers gripped its rim. He pulled and yanked it free, off the branch. Iaven held the nest firmly in one hand and slid himself back up to the thicker part of the branch. He was sure it would crack this time, bouncing up and down in the wind, with him on it. Iaven tried to turn around on the branch, while keeping the nest from tipping.

Orven climbed up and was standing on the branch by the trunk of the tree, holding on to an overhead limb with his left hand. With his right hand he drew Gorflange and held it out as he advanced.

Iaven managed to turn around. His hand jumped to Halix's hilt, making sure it was still there. Orven carefully advanced, only a few feet away. Iaven held on behind him, holding both branch and nest in his left hand. He drew Halix with his right, positioning himself as well as he could to fend off Orven's attack.

Orven walked a few more steps, the branch straining under the twins' weight. Iaven wondered if Orven even noticed. Orven came at him quickly and Iaven raised Halix fast, catching Orven's blow. Orven stepped back, steadying himself. He swung again and Iaven blocked him and aimed a blow at Orven's feet. Orven pulled away just as Halix swung past. "You've been practicing!" Orven teased, but Iaven knew Orven had been surprised by the defense. Iaven lunged swiftly at Orven. Orven moved back again, but held his ground now.

Iaven straddled a thicker part of the branch and his hold on it was more stable. Keeping his eye on Orven and pointing Halix at him, he let go and brought the nest around to his lap. He set it down and felt inside it for the gem. Orven saw what he was doing and charged him again. Gorflange flew and Iaven crossed blades with Orven, trying to throw him off balance. Hot with fury, Iaven gave no thought to Orven falling to his death into the valley. Iaven put all he had learned from Yolias into his defense, giving Orven more than he expected. Orven lost his mocking tone and said nothing, consumed with anger. Frustration fueled his rage and he swung wildly now, forcing Iaven back out along the branch again. Iaven's hand closed on the gem in the nest, but Orven's onslaught nearly toppled him. He leaned back avoiding a swinging blow, and his left hand thrust out behind him to steady himself on the branch. As he grabbed the branch, the nest fell away turning end over end into the valley. But gripped in between his fingers on the branch, amidst tufts of dried grass, the yellow gem sparkled.

Orven saw the gem in Iaven's hand and forced him further out onto the branch, which bent again under their weight. Iaven held onto the gem and the branch behind him with one hand, wielding Halix with the other. Orven held on and swung Gorflange. The blades clashed and rang, flashing in the morning light. Orven's wild swings and thrusts kept Iaven back, the branch shaking dangerously beneath them as they fought.

Orven slid forward again and suddenly there was a sharp cracking sound that grew louder. Orven pulled back on the branch. Tree bark was sticking up where the branch was cracking. Orven's movement shook the branch, cracking it even more.

Seeing his chance, Iaven slid forward on the branch, gripping it between his knees. With a quick swing of his arm he brought his hand around, shifted the gem from hand to hand, and grabbed the branch in front of him. In his right hand he held the hilt of the sword with three fingers and the gem between his thumb and forefinger. The metalwork leaves around the last empty hole in the hilt sensed the gem and rotated open. But Iaven could not move the gem over to the hole without letting go of the sword.

Orven saw that Iaven had the gem and sword in the same hand. He reached over and swung at Iaven again. Iaven was doing better than he expected, and with three stones to his two, Orven feared he might be beaten. But he still had the upper hand. Orven tried swinging at Iaven, but Iaven warded him off again. Orven stopped and looked at Iaven balancing on the sagging branch and hanging on as he wielded Halix.

"There's nothing you can do, you've lost!" shouted Orven. "Give me the gem, and let's both climb down from here."

Iaven's heart was pounding as he briefly considered what Orven said, but in his anger the thought sickened him. "No! *I* found it, it's *mine!*" He was surprised at the fury in his voice. Iaven wondered again what had happened to his friends, and whether Orven would kill him just to get the gem. But he could not hand it over, he was just too angry. If only he could get the gem into the hilt, if he could just support the sword and move his hand—

Orven brought Gorflange down in front of him, chopping the branch and widening the crack. Iaven screamed. Orven swung again, and the branch splintered and fell beneath Iaven's weight. Iaven hugged the branch, clinging to it with his legs and arms, still gripping the sword and gem in one hand. The branch swung down on its sinews, hanging from the tree. Iaven braced himself as he hit the side of the cliff, the exposed roots poking at him. From above came another cracking sound as Orven struck the branch again.

The branch was long and hung too far below the edge of the cliff for Iaven to climb up onto the grass there. The roots hung out in front of him, within reach, but he clung to the branch with one hand and held the sword and gem in the other. The branch was weakened now and turning on its last few sinews. Iaven looked up and saw Orven raise his blade again.

As Orven brought down the blow that finally severed the branch, Iaven let go of Halix and the yellow gem, grabbed onto the roots, and then let go of the branch, hanging on with both hands. Iaven watched as the sword and gem fell into the valley, vanishing in the fog, the tree branch plunging after them. An angry roar of frustration echoed across the mountain as Orven saw them fall.

Iaven heard Orven climb down from the tree and moments later Orven stood on the cliff above him, looking down over the edge. Orven was furious, trembling with rage, and Iaven wondering if he would start cutting the roots Iaven clung to as well. Orven glared down at him, breathing hard, deciding what to do. Then suddenly he turned away and was gone.

Iaven waited for Orven to leave before trying to pull himself up, and then found he could not. He was still shaking and tried to calm himself. He pulled again, but could not get any higher up the side of the cliff. It wasn't just that he was tired from the fight, the long hike up the mountain, or from not having slept in over a day. The roots hung out from a bulge in the cliff, and as Iaven lay against it, hanging on, he could not get a good foothold underneath it and had no way to push himself back up onto the ledge, hard as he tried.

Iaven yelled again for Zammond and Yolias, but there was no reply. He yelled a few more times, listening to his voice echo, and then stopped, realizing he could be seen and heard in the valley below. Desperation and despair flooded his mind as he held on with all his remaining strength. He waited awhile and called again. Goblins might hear him, but there was nothing else he could do. He struggled, trying to climb and pull himself up higher. Dirt crumbled and fell away, and his legs swung, but he could not get up any higher than he was.

Iaven held on and waited for what seemed like quite a long time. It was a cold November morning and the sky was partly clouded over. Birds chirped and sang, and two landed in the tree above him. Iaven wondered where Zammond and Yolias were. He could not bring himself to believe they were dead, yet now his doubts deepened. He wondered how long it might be before the others at the campsite came looking for him. Unless something had happened to them, he thought suddenly.

Iaven trembled to think Orven would have let him fall into the valley to his death. *Would he really have let me fall?* Iaven was unsure. It was hard to believe Orven would kill anyone, but he did not know what to think anymore. Iaven again attempted to pull himself up, to no avail. He tried to swing a leg sideways up onto the bulge his arms were leaning on, but could not get a foothold on it. He shouted for Zammond and Yolias, though it seemed hopeless.

His arms were tiring and he knew could not hang there much longer. He pulled his hardest, leaning side to side, trying to pull his hips up onto the bulge where the roots were. Reaching up higher, he gripped the roots and pulled, straining his already weary arms. Gradually he rose an inch or so. Again he tried, and gained another inch. He was breathing hard. His head was almost level now with the ground, and he could see the edge of the grass just above him. He struggled and pulled again. Then he stopped, listening, and heard footsteps approaching on the grass.

"Yolias? Zammond?" he inquired tentatively.

"Iaven?" A strange yet eerily familiar voice made him feel uneasy. A figure suddenly appeared above him, extending his hand to pull Iaven up.

Iaven was startled to see it wasn't Yolias or Zammond or any of his other friends. As Iaven was pulled up and set on the cliff's edge he realized with horror, after a moment of recognition, who had found him; it was the thief that had robbed them and fought with him in Miastolas, Lexter Splide.

Book IV: Swamp and Sorrow

Chapter 26.
An Uneasy Alliance

Iaven stood up, still trembling, and stepped back from the cliff's edge. He stared at Lexter, barely recognizing him. Lexter's clothes were muddy and worn, and he looked thinner and almost sickly.

"Lexter?!"

"Iaven? Yes, it's Iaven, isn't it! Whatever are you doing way out here?" Lexter was too happy to see him and Iaven became very suspicious.

Lexter raised his hands pleadingly. "I know what you must think! I only came to help. Please, don't be afraid!"

Iaven tried to fathom his intentions. In his dirty clothes and haggard appearance, he looked like a beggar. Was this some trick? "Where's Leland?" Iaven asked.

"Dead." Lexter seemed genuinely sad, though Iaven expected no less skilled a deception. "And I'm lucky to be alive myself," he added. "You don't believe me?"

"Why should I?" Iaven said. "Why should I believe anything you say, after what you've done?" Iaven saw they were both unarmed. He was glad Lexter had helped him, yet suspected some hidden motive. "And why are you out here? Did you come out here with Orven? Where's Zammond and Yolias?" Iaven stumbled, suddenly realizing how lightheaded, weary, and exhausted he was. He went over to the path, looked around, and saw no one. Lexter followed after him.

"Of course, of course... You're right not to trust me! But much has happened to me, and I've changed. I have! No, no... you won't take my word for it. Alright." Lexter walked a few feet away where there was a large rock, and sat down on it. Iaven felt like going up and down the path looking for Zammond and Yolias, but his tiredness and exhaustion were catching up with him. To keep from collapsing, Iaven sat down, listening to Lexter while keeping his distance.

"It all began in Kronivar..." At first Lexter was not going to mention their dealings, but then he decided not to hold anything back. He described the deal, the surrounding of the house, the chase into the woods, and how the goblins captured them. He spoke rapidly, trying to tie it all together and make sense of it, the memories still fresh enough to pain him. Iaven noted his pauses and the anguish in his voice. His disbelief was strong and he listened hoping to catch Lexter in one of his lies. As Lexter went on, Iaven's disbelief softened a little, and by the time Lexter was done, Iaven was unsure what to believe.

"An undermountain tunnel, leading into the Arinzei Valley? A secret passage?"

"It's true. They meant to kill me too, I'm sure of it. I don't know what happened, they couldn't have just forgotten me. But here I am. It's incredible, but it's all true." Lexter sighed. "Something's got to be done about it; about the tunnel, I mean. I want to help now. I've got nothing left. I want to help and then return to Tolgard after the war is over. I'm not a fighter or anything like that, but whatever I can do, I'll do."

Iaven looked at Lexter and remained silent.

"I told you, I haven't got much —a little food, a few supplies, a few coins— but whatever you need is yours," said Lexter, "I set camp just a little way down the road west of here."

Iaven felt his strength returning. "I've got to find the others." Unlikely as it seemed —especially because Orven had left him alive— Iaven was still unable to completely disbelieve Orven's boasts that they were dead.

Lexter got up, and followed Iaven at a distance like a stray dog looking for a home. He knew Iaven doubted his story, but there was nothing more he could do. Iaven walked ahead, ignoring Lexter. As Lexter fell further behind, he heard something rustling in a thicket off the path. He went and peered into it. "Iaven!" he called, "Zammond's here!"

Zammond was lying face down on the ground, his hands tied behind his back. He was gagged with a burlap strap torn from one of the packs. Lexter drew his knife, knelt down and cut Zammond's bonds and loosened his gag. Zammond startled to see it was Lexter who had released him. As he struggled to his feet, Iaven ran up behind Lexter.

"Iaven! What's he doing here? What's going on?" Zammond scowled at Lexter.

"I don't trust him either. But he did help me, and saw you here before I did." Iaven was greatly relieved.

"Iaven, it was horrible." Zammond rubbed his wrists and brushed himself off. "Yolias and I heard somebody coming. At first, we thought it was goblins, but it was Orven and his friends. Where's Yolias? Did you find him?"

"Not yet," Iaven said.

Lexter jumped up. "I'll go look!" he volunteered, and Iaven stepped aside to let Lexter pass.

Zammond came out onto the path. "Yolias is wounded, I think. He put up quite a fight. Orven and Max were fighting him, and Ripley and Roy came after me." Zammond glanced at the empty scabbard on Iaven's belt. "Orven took it?"

"More or less," Iaven grumbled. "I'll tell you about it later."

Iaven and Zammond went down the path and found Lexter untying Yolias. Yolias was surprised to see Lexter, and even more incredulous when the dwarves explained who Lexter was and what had happened in Miastolas.

"It's all in the past, now, I've changed," Lexter insisted. He started to repeat his story again, when Yolias silenced him.

"Let us gather the others and then we will hear you out and decide for ourselves." Yolias spoke sternly but not unkindly to Lexter, and Lexter became quiet and did as Yolias bid him.

"You're badly cut." Zammond noticed the blood on Yolias' left leg.

"We should tie it, to keep the bleeding down," Lexter suggested. Yolias nodded and Lexter bent to work.

"A scrape from Gorflange, but it did not bite bone," Yolias told them. "Nor were they spared my blade. A few scratches and they were flailing like madmen."

"So that's what happened." Iaven remembered Orven's bloodstained shirt. Lexter finished and helped Yolias to his feet.

"I can walk," Yolias said, waving off their concern. "A little more slowly perhaps, but I am fine. We almost stopped them, Iaven, we hoped you would get the gem before Orven found you."

They traveled back along the mountainside path more easily than they had the night before, though slower due to Yolias' injury. It took them awhile to return to their campsite. Tillmore, Hobley, and Wilbur were there, bound hand and foot. Yolias had Lexter untie them, while Iaven and Zammond examined the ransacked camp. Hobley and the others were just as surprised and distrustful of Lexter, who was deferential and apologetic; gone was the cocky self-assuredness they remembered so well.

At last they sat in a semicircle, with Yolias perched on a rock and Lexter sitting before them, ready to tell his story.

"Not long after you left, Orven and his friends arrived," Tillmore told Iaven, "I woke the others, but it was too late. I didn't think they'd attack us like that, all five of them on us at once. Well, Orven was the main one, of course. Before we knew it, they collected all our weapons and tied us up. We put up a fight, but they had us almost two to one. Then they went through our packs and took what was left of the food, fighting over it and eating it as they found it. They were starved, I'll bet. We wouldn't tell them where you were, and finally they left down the path."

"You can have what little food I've got," Lexter piped in. Yolias glanced at him and he stopped.

"Yes, we may need it. We will consider your offer," Yolias said.

"I can see what they meant about Orven at the Castle," Hobley said, "He's become meaner, alright. Max and Aaron almost seemed embarrassed about it, but went along with it. The others were just hungry more than anything else."

"They were all ornery and took it out on us. They were even kind of rough with each other," Tillmore said, "On edge and bickering about what to do and how to do it."

"We were mostly worried about the three of you," Wilbur added.

"They caught up, but we heard them coming," said Zammond. "Yolias fought off three of them, you should have seen it! Rip and Roy were on me, and I did what I could, but we were outnumbered. And Orven had Gorflange, too, of course."

"Orven is raw and untrained in fight," said Yolias, "but he has good instincts, and the sword heightened his abilities considerably. Were it not for his friends, his lack of technique might have done him in, but he held his own quite well." He saw them looking at the bloodied rag tied around his leg. "Yet were Gorflange wielded in more experienced hands, I might have been slain. As it was, I was fortunate, and I could have beaten him alone. Orven knew it, and once I was bound he might have done more, but his friends held him off."

The dwarves marveled and agreed that Orven had gotten worse. Iaven told them of the tree and the magpie's nest, and how he had almost reached the gem when Orven came upon him. He described the fight in the tree as they listened and asked for details of the fight and Orven's reactions. Everyone felt the loss of the sword and gems.

"So you really thought Orven killed us?" asked Hobley.

Iaven shrugged. "Well, I wasn't sure, I didn't want to believe it..." Iaven was ashamed he could think such a thing about his brother, and even more for the hate that had darkened his own heart at the time.

"Would he really have let you fall from the cliff?" said Wilbur.

"I don't know... but you should have heard him yell when I dropped the sword and gem!"

Zammond brightened. "What are we waiting for? Let's get back there and down the cliff somehow, maybe we can still find it! No, I know, Orven's probably gone down and found it already."

"If there's anything I might do to help..." Lexter put in tentatively.

"We're lucky we got the sword back the last time we met you!" Zammond snapped.

"Zammond! A quick tongue and hot temper make poor companions. We will hear what he has to say, at least." Yolias shifted on the rock and turned to Lexter, "Tell us, then, why we should trust you or let you travel with us."

"It's all true, what they've told you about me. I won't deny it. I've been a scoundrel! But now I want to help. Well, anyway, after I was released from Miastolas, I met my brother in Bottomcliffe, and from there we went to Kronivar..." Lexter related again what he had told Iaven, answering questions and describing things in even greater detail this time. Yolias stopped him, asking pointed questions as though testing him, and others that related to the dealings with Aranstone and his men. Lexter was unable to answer some of them, and Yolias nodded and let him go on. When the undermountain passage was described, there were more questions. Yolias tried to determine the location of the passage entrance, but Lexter was not sure how far they had traveled, or which watchtower he had seen in the distance. Everyone remained quiet as Lexter told of the promises he had made to himself and how he still meant to keep them. He pleaded with them, wondering whether they believed him or not.

"Quite a story," Zammond said skeptically.

"That's how it happened." Lexter sounded pained. "I answered Iaven's cry for help. It's a risk for anyone to stay out here, I could have just continued on to Teska, but I didn't. And there's no other reason for me to be out here, either." He leaned back. "Well, I've told you all I can, I can't prove it to you any more than that. If you want to leave me here, or throw me off the cliff, there isn't much I can do about it."

The dwarves debated whether to give Lexter the benefit of the doubt. He had lost the brashness they'd seen in Miastolas, and even seemed on the verge of tears when speaking of Leland's death. What convinced them the most was how thin and pale he looked and his humbled manner. There was still the possibility that it was all an elaborate scheme, but their hearts told them otherwise. Even Zammond felt sorry for Lexter, though he decided to continue voicing disbelief simply because he didn't want Lexter to think they trusted him.

Yolias was silent a moment, watching Lexter. The dwarves looked to Yolias, awaiting his verdict. "If you mean to help Itharia, you can travel with us as far as Farrenhale. You may be useful there in the preparations for war. Your news of the passage will be a great help; perhaps you can aid us in locating it."

"I'll do my best, sir," said Lexter.

Yolias got up. "It's a long way to Teska, and we'd best get underway. Morning is already spent, and the days are growing short."

In a little less than an hour they made their way to the clearing where the oak overhung the valley, and Hobley, Tillmore, and Wilbur wanted to have a look at it. Yolias sat down on the rock near the path, and changed the rag tied around his leg.

The dwarves crept to the edge of the cliff and looked into the valley. The fog was lifting, and most of the trees were visible on the sloping ground far below.

"Iaven, look!" Zammond indicated movement in the valley. Five figures prowled about, vague shapes walking purposefully through the fog, searching the ground. "There, with the sword drawn, it's Orven!"

A jolt of anger pounded Iaven's heart, and for a moment he felt like taking the large rock by the path and rolling it down onto the dwarves below. "Have they got it yet?"

"Looks like they're still searching." Zammond knelt down and laid on the edge of the cliff so he could look over the edge without being seen, and Iaven joined him. Zammond found a stone nearby and threw it down at Orven's party, laughing and pulling back out of sight as he did so.

Zammond's stone glanced off a rock, startling Orven. He looked up to the cliff's edge, but could see no one there. He turned back to Gorflange again, and the small blue-green stone set in the pommel glowed steadily as he moved the sword about trying to locate the gem.

"I've found Halix," Max called from a short distance away near the base of the cliff. The others came over to see the sword as Max brought it to Orven. "The gem can't be far away."

"It's not," said Orven, distracted with his task. Max started searching with Halix as Orven walked past him. Orven smiled as the glow increased. He swept across the hillside, his glance jumping from the sword to the ground and back. Finally he caught sight of something in the grass. "Here it is!"

Orven picked up the yellow gem. It sparkled in his hand, its rich, golden facets oddly cold and precise. Everyone gathered around watching Orven, and he held the gem up for them to see. Orven raised Gorflange and moved the gem near to the hilt. The tiny metalwork leaves around the last empty hole slid open with a whisper. Orven slowly drew the gem away and they closed again. He brought the gem closer and watched them open again, amused.

Orven looked up at his friends. "This is it, the moment we've waited for. Gorflange is complete!" He placed the gem into the sword and the leaves closed, holding it firmly in place. Orven held the sword aloft in victory. Immediately he noticed Gorflange was even lighter than before and power seemed to course through it. Flames of confidence and surety shot through him like wildfire, making him feel stronger and taller. He lowered Gorflange and noticed the others staring at him. "All the gems! And both swords!"

Everyone cheered. "Remember, we're all taking turns carrying Halix," Ripley reminded Max. "I get it when we get to Teska."

"I know, I know, don't worry!" said Max, annoyed.

"... All of the *lost* gems," Aaron corrected Orven.

"What?" said Orven.

"You said we have all the gems; we have all the *lost* gems," said Aaron. "We haven't got the red gem; that must be the one Maëlveronde has."

"*Has* or *had*?" Orven said, lifting the sword and leveling it. He moved the sword to and fro, until he found a faint glow in the pommel's gemstone. "It's somewhere northwest of us, far away." He gave them a wild look, grinning. "What do you think, should we go after it? We've got both swords! We could complete Halix!"

The others looked at Orven hoping he wasn't serious. "Well, who knows? Maybe Maëlveronde's lost the gem," said Orven, "He's probably dead, for all we know. All right, then, let's find a way back up to the path."

The dwarves picked up their packs, which were still heavy with treasure from the tomb. Everyone was tired of hauling them, but no one wanted to reduce their share. They had already reluctantly lightened their packs to catch up to Iaven's party and were not willing to part with more. Each shouldering his load with a grunt, they made their way down the slope.

Iaven and Zammond watched the tiny figures as they went downhill and off to the west. "Looks like they've got everything," said Zammond. He pulled back from the cliff edge and they walked over to where the others were resting.

"Orven's party must be on their way to Teska, said Zammond. "If we hurry, we might catch up to them before they get there!"

"And then what would we do?" asked Tillmore. "We're unarmed. We'll be lucky if we get to Teska without encountering any goblins along the way."

"Let's not forget that Yolias is wounded," said Hobley, "He hasn't complained, but I'm sure the going will be harder for him."

Yolias smiled and stood. "I'll have time enough to heal in Farrenhale and Teska. Once we get there, we can have Orven arrested, provided he is still there when we arrive."

"And if they're gone by then?" asked Wilbur.

"One of us has got to get there ahead of them, and keep them there, somehow, until the rest arrive," said Tillmore.

"How would you do that?" Hobley said. "They'd catch on right away to what you were doing. They know Yolias now, too. Lexter's the only one they wouldn't know."

"Me?" Lexter sounded nervous, "You want me to go?"

"I don't trust him!" said Zammond. "How do we know he won't just steal the swords and run off with them?"

"I wouldn't do that!" said Lexter, offended.

"We're not asking him to steal anything," Yolias said. "It may be all we can do. Well, Lexter, here's a chance to prove your loyalty to Itharia, and make up for past misdeeds. All you have to do is get them to stay in either Farrenhale or Teska, until we arrive. Can you do that much?"

"What should I tell them?" asked Lexter.

"I'm sure you'll think of something," said Zammond.

"And you will need to help locate the undermountain passage. Even a tiny hole can let in enough water to sink a ship," said Yolias. "For now, all you need to do is keep Orven's party from leaving."

"How will you be able to find us?" asked Lexter.

"Orven will likely want to see Teska, and the city has only one inn where foreigners can stay," said Yolias, "So you should have no trouble getting him to go there. The bridge is the only way into and out of the city, apart from boats. It should be easy to keep track of him. We will find you there. You had better be on your way though; you will need to arrive before Orven and wait for him. And you will need to wash up and clean your clothes; you will not detain them long as a beggar!"

"Yes sir, I will!" Lexter nodded. "I'll see you in Teska, then. I won't let you down!" He got up and soon disappeared down the path.

"I hope he can be trusted," said Zammond, "I've got my doubts."

"As do I," Yolias said. "Yet if he is a changed man as he says, this much he can do. News of the undermountain passage will aid us greatly. Perhaps even before it is too late. We will alert all the watchtowers as we pass them and have them begin a search. And Lexter may remember more on his way back."

As Yolias began hiking again they all saw his wounded leg was stiff. He noticed their concern. "I can walk. Slower, but we can still make good time. We have a few days' travels ahead of us. We should come upon the last of the watchtowers some time tomorrow or the day after. But we have been up all night and must rest."

The morning was overcast and gray, and no one found it difficult to sleep. In a few hours they awoke, still groggy yet determined to walk until dark when they would set camp for the night. The dwarves packed and were off along the road, this time at a much less strenuous pace. When the path brought them close to the edge, Iaven gazed down into the Arinzei Valley. Thin fog still veiled the ground there, as well as any goblins that might be patrolling the base of the cliffs. Several times Iaven's hand unconsciously touched the top of his scabbard, expecting Halix to be there, only to find it wasn't.

Chapter 27.
A New-Found Friend

With five gems and both Halix and Gorflange, Orven and his friends strode along with ebullient spirits. Orven was still amazed at how close Iaven had come to getting the gem and how hard he had fought. Orven was always willing to be a little more savage or cruel, whatever it took to win, but this time Iaven had kept up with him and he admired that. He wondered how the fight would have gone if they'd had equal footing on solid ground, each with two gems in his sword. Now he would never know. He was glad to have both swords nonetheless.

Orven and Max led the dwarves up the slope to the mountainside path, the same slope Lexter had climbed the night before. Their packs weighed them down but no one dared to complain. Whenever they wearied of carrying their treasure, thoughts of spending it made them bear it farther. Orven kept telling them it would only be a few more days on foot. In Farrenhale they would buy new clothes, armor, and a horse cart, and then ride down to Kronivar to join the troops. After the war they would use their remaining wealth to buy adjacent fiefs on the outskirts of Kronivar and make their estates there.

For the next three days they traveled west along the mountainside path, planning their lives after the war, and how they would fight during the war, earning honors and names for themselves. "There's five of us and only two swords, but we'll always fight together!" Orven promised them. The others were content to be a part of it all, though they wondered what Orven would have done without the swords.

At last they came upon the easternmost watchtower and stopped to talk with the guards and see if they might buy some supplies there. The dwarves stationed in the tower were surprised to see Goblin gold, but were happy to hear of the looting of the Goblin tomb, though Orven deliberately left vague the details of its location. After a brief exchange they were off again, eager to reach Farrenhale.

Three more days of travel along the mountainside path took them past more watchtowers, and finally to the Mountain Gate. It was late afternoon when they arrived. The narrow footpath suddenly ended at a high stone wall built between the mountain and a watchtower rising from the cliff's edge. The gate's doors were two stories tall and built of heavy wooden beams bound with a grid of thick iron bars. Dwarven guards passed to and fro along the parapet atop the gate, and two stood watching in wonderment as Orven's party approached.

"Ho there, friends, from where do you come?" one called down.

"Adventurers, returning to the Kingdom!" Orven called back.

The guards looked at each other. The one in charge nodded to the other and disappeared behind the wall. Moments later a heavy beam was drawn back and the huge doors creaked opened a crack to admit Orven's party. They filed through and the door was closed, three dwarves thrusting the beam back into place. Their captain came down a narrow staircase and over by them. Captain

Torben Holgen was a stout and sturdy dwarf, round-faced with an unruly fringe of orange beard.

"Adventurers, eh? Where have you been, and how have you fared? Have you any news that may aid us?" asked the Captain. "Good tidings can be a greater treasure than gold." He could not help noticing the ornate swords that Orven and Max wore.

"Gold and gems are all we have," said Orven, tossing the Captain a gold piece. "No tidings, good or bad. We tried to avoid the Goblins as well as we could."

"I should not doubt you did," said the Captain, distracted now with the image on the coin. "Nehncazzar! Old treasure, friends, but gold all the same. And where did you find it?" He tossed it back to Orven, wondering if it had been intended as a bribe.

"Loot stashed away in a hidden cave," Orven lied. "But it's too dangerous to stay out there now. We've come to buy new armor and goods!"

"Well done, then. We could use more of your sort here."

Orven smiled and nodded as he turned to go. He could sense the Captain's curiosity and knew they ought to leave. The Captain stood watching as they went down the path, unsure what to make of the 'adventurers' and their treasure.

The East Gate, or Mountain Gate as it was sometimes called, was high up the cliffside, and the road descending from it wove back and forth until it brought them down out of the mountains. Below them to the south lay the rooftops of Farrenhale, and north of the town dozens of pitched tents lined the meadow where Dwarven troops were encamped. Beyond the tents were the North Gate and the Wall, which ran down from the mountain and to the west to where it ended at a watchtower rising out of the swamp. And out past the watchtower, at the end of a long plank bridge extending over the waters, they could make out the vague shapes of Teska amidst the distant haze.

Orven led the way down the slope, following the scent of food cooking on wood fires until they found supper at the edge of the Dwarven camp. They ate hungrily and spoke little, ordering whatever they wanted and spending extravagantly. Farrenhale was very small, its houses spread far apart except for a cluster of buildings at the center of town, where an inn and a few shops were. These were unusually busy as soldiers passed through the streets going to and from the encampment. Orven was determined to find out what was happening in the kingdom, and after dinner he and the others made their way toward the North Gate.

"We could stay here and fight," said Ripley, "Or are you still set on going to Kronivar?" Ripley had Halix now, and laid his hand on its hilt at his side. He had bought a scabbard to fit its blade.

"I don't know," said Orven, glancing around the camp. It was getting dark already and fog was thickening about them. "We should join the main units, but maybe they'll be coming up here anyway."

From where they stood all the way out to the wall and towers, tents sheltered troops and supplies, and campfires burned with dwarves ringed around them for warmth. Near the swamps, cold, damp drafts drifted in from the west. Heavy mists hung throughout the camp, dulling the firelight and the dwarves' spirits. Some dwarves were cooking over fires or dividing rations and eating, while others sat talking or sharpening their swords, knives, and other weaponry. A few bursts of laughter and lighthearted chitchat lightened the mood, but most were somber and anxious, tired of waiting and eager to be sent into battle or sent home if the Goblins backed down. Many had been waiting there for weeks, the weather continuing to cool as winter drew near. Recently they had received word that more troops were on their way from the Castle, and this raised their spirits, even as it verified the likelihood of war, which seemed inevitable now to all but a few of them.

Orven and the others walked through the camp, the weight of the solemn mood descending on them. Beyond the camp, watchtowers rose from great expanses of the wall. Where the North Road ran into Navrogenaya, the broad massive, double doors of the North Gate stood between two large towers, four times the width of the Mountain Gate. Orven looked at the wall, which marked the northern border of Itharia, and thought about the Goblin armies camped just out of sight on the other side. He imagined them storming the wall with siege towers and battering rams. Or perhaps their catapults and trebuchets would rain of boulders down on the encampment. Orven craved an enemy he could confront with Gorflange on the field of battle. He was certain now that he wanted to go to Kronivar instead of waiting here for the Goblins to attack. He was willing to fight at the front but the decisive battles were sure to be in Kronivar, and the greatest glory would be there. At least those were the reasons he gave himself.

They decided to stay the night and begin the journey south in the morning. With a horse and cart, they would reach Kronivar in a matter of days. The inn at Farrenhale was small and without vacancies, so Orven suggested they buy new clothing, weapons, and armor and camp with the troops so as to learn what news they could regarding war preparations around the Kingdom. At one end of the camp the clank of hammered metal told of blacksmiths working over small brick furnaces. Newly-forged swords, shields, halberds, and other weaponry were laid on the ground or hung up to cool. Other dwarves stood nearby, haggling prices and examining hilts and blades. Aaron found a new short sword, and Roy picked up a long-bladed broadsword, hefting it around from hand to hand.

"That's too long for your height, friend. Try this one." The voice, with a slight foreign accent, spoke from behind Roy and he turned. The stranger handed him a shorter broadsword, which was indeed much easier to wield. The stranger smiled. "A longer sword may keep the enemy further away, but not for long if you can't parry well with it." All five dwarves were looking at the stranger now, a man of nearly forty with a fringe of graying beard, dressed in a dark green cloak, black trousers, and boots. "And those blades have a good, sharp edge, but they're also more brittle." He nodded at a sword Roy was holding. "Your first time buying new weapons? It is for quite a few dwarves these days. Though you two seem to have found quite a bargain." He eyed Gorflange and Halix on the dwarves' belts.

"And you?" Orven asked the man. "A long-handled knife is all you carry?"

"At the moment," said the man. He extended his hand to Orven. "Lexter Splide, at your service. I deal in weaponry, and whatever I can do to help you in your choosing—"

"Are these yours, here?" asked Max.

"No," said Lexter, "I'm merely browsing, like you. Ah, here; this one would suit you—?"

"Roy... Roy Goldbeard." Roy shook Lexter's outstretched hand.

"Yes, well, Roy, this one has a much stronger blade. And feel how the hilt is wrapped. The grip is much better."

Roy held the sword and it was just as Lexter said.

"Do you know anything about armor? We are in need of some, if you know anything about it and are willing to help," said Orven.

"Oh, certainly," said Lexter. "Right this way..." Lexter led them over to a tent where armor fittings were being done. After their initial apprehension had passed, the dwarves began talking more with Lexter, getting his opinion on helmets, aventails, different weaves of ring mail, and other things. Lexter was sorry he had spent so much on new clothes that he only had enough left to buy a long-handled knife instead of a sword. But they didn't seem to think much of it and probably thought he had more stashed away nearby. Lexter told them of various types of weapons he had sold, and even began to enjoy dispensing advice, which he rarely ever got to do when Leland was handling things. He was eager to be useful to them and surprised at how happy he was to simply help them without expecting pay or anything in return. Best of all, he thought, he could even brag without lying. When it came time to buy, he did the haggling for them and saw with great delight how impressed and pleased they were with him. Later Orven even gave him a few extra gold pieces and a small gemstone from his pack. Now it was only a matter of keeping them there until Iaven got to Teska. They had nearly finished buying everything they needed, and Lexter was sure he could find other topics of interest to them.

"Thank you, Lexter, you've been a great help!" said Max.

"How fortunate we are to find someone with your experience," Roy added.

"Lots of trade going on of late, with the war and all," Lexter said, reminiscing freely now, "Had quite a deal going in Kronivar not too long ago."

"Kronivar?" Orven sounded interested. "You know anyone there, troop leaders, or anything like that? We're going there, and we might get better positions if we knew who to ask."

"Well, yes…" Lexter hesitated, "There was... uh, Thon Aranstone, and his advisor, Greywood..." It was a stretch, but it was true. "They were buying a whole cartload."

The dwarves were intrigued. "You could introduce us, couldn't you?" Orven said. "Maybe they could use a few captains..."

Lexter smiled, amused by Orven's naïve ambition. "Well, they're down in Kronivar, and it's really too far—"

"Join us," said Ripley. "We're leaving tomorrow morning, aren't we?" He looked to Orven.

"Of course," said Orven. He turned to Lexter. "Will you do it? Take us to them?"

"Later, maybe, there's no hurry," said Lexter. "I just got here yesterday. Have you seen Teska yet?"

"No, we weren't planning to, either," Orven said.

"Oh, well, as long as you're up here, you should stay an extra day at least. It's quite something to see." Lexter had only been there a few times, years ago, and tried to think of what he could say about it. The dwarves gazed toward the swamp, but at that distance, with night having fallen, all they could see were torches and firelit windows glowing in the mists.

"All built on poles over the swamp," said Orven doubtfully.

"Oh, it's plenty sturdy, it's enormous," said Lexter, "It's the Teskans' largest city. The Dwarves helped set up the foundational platforms when they built the Wall and Gates. It's been built upon and added to for quite some time. Beautifully made, and worth seeing." Lexter looked to see if they were interested. Aaron and Roy clearly were. Ripley seemed apprehensive, and Max was waiting to see if Orven wanted to go.

"It'll take us a while to get to Kronivar, even with a cart," Orven mused. "I don't think we can wait around—"

"That's true," said Lexter, "you won't have time to train with all the other new recruits—"

"Oh, I'm not worried about that," Orven sounded offended. "Surely they'll make me a captain when they see what I can do." He patted Gorflange's hilt. "Besides, your friends there can get us in, can't they?"

"Of course," Lexter said, feeling a tinge of guilt at the half-truth.

"We could use a bit of a rest anyway," Max put in. "I wouldn't mind seeing Teska myself, after all I've heard about it."

"I'd like to see it, too. One day won't matter much," Aaron added.

Orven hesitated. "Alright, we'll stay. Just a day, though." They passed into the encampment and strolled about until they found a fire with only a few soldiers around it. Orven asked if he and his friends could join them and they nodded. Soon they were all seated by the fire, the soldiers discussing news from the rest of the kingdom and the readying for war.

"They say troops are coming from the Castle," said a young dwarf named Rolen. "Once they get here, the front will be more secure. We can hold the Wall and Gates with a small force, but I'll feel better with them here."

"Me, too," agreed his friend, who had introduced himself as Orty. "Though I've heard rumors about the Goblin forces." He shrugged. "Still, General Knorde sounded hopeful, and the troops are on the way..." His tone revealed that he did not share the General's hopes. "What about you, whose command are you under?"

Orven explained how they were on their way to Kronivar and what they intended to do there. Hearing their plans told to strangers, especially encamped soldiers, Max wondered if perhaps they, too, should stay at the front. The soldiers listened and nodded, but gave no sign of what they thought.

"We've never been to Kronivar, though we've heard about it. We're both from Halloway, and this is the farthest we've ever traveled. So you've been to Kronivar?" said Rolen.

"Well, a day or so," said Orven, unwilling to say any more.

"Not even that," said Aaron, still upset that they had left so quickly. "We arrived in the evening and left the next morning."

"My brother and I used to live there," said Lexter, and they turned to him. He smiled and began regaling them with tales of his life in Kronivar, and Orven and his friends asked questions and listened just as attentively as the soldiers. Lexter was careful, however, to leave out any details that might contradict or conflict with the image of himself he wanted to cultivate with the dwarves.

They talked a good long time, until it was very late and the dwarves were dozing off, interested as they were. At last they bid each other good night and rolled up in their blankets near the fire. For once Orven and his friends could all sleep at the same time without need of a watch. Only Rolen stayed awake, relaxing and throwing small twigs onto the fire. Lexter watched the dwarves sleeping, content with his day's work. They would stay now, and hopefully Iaven and Yolias would arrive soon. How they enjoyed hearing about Kronivar, he thought. Initially Orven and his friends had struck Lexter as more worldly and less gullible than Iaven's party had been, but now he could see they were really about the same. The two young dwarves from Halloway were even younger and had seen far less. Lexter suddenly felt old and aware of how much of his life was already over. And what had he to show for it? Well, he thought, I'm a new man now.

So you've been telling yourself these last few days, another part of him said. He had stretched the truth perhaps, but he hadn't really lied, had he? *At least be honest with yourself, if no one else: you've been deceiving them right along with your promises of Kronivar*. Deceived them, or merely allowed them to jump to the wrong conclusions? It wasn't quite the same thing, was it?

As he watched the dwarves sleeping, the urge came over him to steal the swords and run away. Earlier, they had let him hold Gorflange, and when he had to hand it back it was almost too much to bear, especially after having had Halix a short time in Miastolas. And now both swords were within his reach, and with gems in them as well.

Despite all the soldiers walking around the camp, he could do it; making an excuse would be easy. The dwarves' packs lay nearby, and he knew they were loaded with gold and gems. He had watched them and his thief's instincts had come into play from the moment he saw them. Where they had gotten it all from he had no idea; they probably had stolen it themselves. He'd always had fewer qualms about stealing if what he was taking was already stolen goods. A handful of gold or gems from their packs would set him up nicely, and they wouldn't even notice it was gone if he took a little from each pack; they all had more thn enough.

Lexter watched Rolen sitting by the fire. Was his presence the only thing keeping Lexter honest, this young dwarf by the fire? Lexter knew he could simply claim some of the treasure was his, and the young dwarf would believe him completely.

"Seeing Teska tomorrow?" Rolen asked, turning to Lexter. Lexter's train of thought broke off, and a part of him was glad it did before it had gone too far.

"Yes, if that's what they want." Lexter realized how tired he was and no longer felt like talking. "I suppose I should get some rest, too."

"Well, good night then, Mr. Splide."

Lexter pulled the blanket around him and lay down. *Mr. Splide*, he thought, touched by the respect shown him by the young dwarf. He suddenly wanted to be worthy of that respect, and was ashamed of what he had been thinking only moments ago. *I hope Iaven and Yolias get here soon*, Lexter thought. *I've done my job and kept them here, and tomorrow we're seeing Teska and I don't know how much longer I can get them to stay. They're eager to leave but I'll do what I can.* He honestly hoped he wouldn't have to lie to them anymore.

They all woke cold and stiff. Mists rolling in from the swamps wet their faces and blankets. The fog was densest at dawn, and beyond thirty feet in any direction everything vanished into the thick, paling whiteness. Apart from a few shrill bird cries over the swamp, all was quiet. Lexter felt heavy and groggy, but at least he was well fed and nicely clothed, and wasn't tied up. He had dreamed that the goblins had him again and were taking him north.

Lexter wiped his face, squinted at the diffuse morning light, and sat up. He tried to stretch and his back hurt him. Around the camp, soldiers were up already, cooking breakfast and beginning their daily routine. Rolen and another soldier had hen's eggs sizzling in small skillet, and shared a few with Aaron and Roy. Amazingly, the faint scent of fresh bread lingered in the damp air. A short distance away, dim in the fog, a baker's cart had come up from Farrenhale. Soldiers ringed about it, eager and hungry. One of the dwarves returning came their way, and Lexter watched Orven emerge from the fog with small loaves in his hands. He tossed one to Aaron and another to Lexter.

"Max come back?" Orven asked.

"Not yet," Aaron said, tearing open the hot bread and biting into it.

Orven smiled to Lexter. "Max is buying a cart. Hard to find one these days, but we can afford it."

"But when we go to Teska—" Lexter began.

"We're getting an early start to get to Kronivar as soon as we can. After hearing your stories last night... Well, I got up this morning, really looking forward to going there. The others felt the same. So we'll leave right away. And you didn't really want to stay here at the front, did you?"

Lexter rubbed the sleep from his eyes, panicked. "But... there's someone I have to see in Teska first." *If Iaven and Yolias even get here today*, Lexter thought. "I can't just leave right away without—"

"Well, you can stay and join us later, then. We'll ask around, join Aranstone and his company, and you can find us when you arrive."

"It'd be better if I went with you," Lexter muttered, "I mean, we could all leave together tomorrow—" He bit into his bread, trying to seem calm and unflustered.

Max returned and shouldered his pack. "It's on the edge of town, an old cart, but enough to get us there. Ripley and I checked the horse over, she'll do."

"Let's go, then!" Orven ate the last of his loaf, chewing it as he spoke. He started walking with Max. Aaron and Roy quickly rolled up their packs and followed, and Lexter picked up his belongings and scurried after them. *Better to keep an eye on them than lose them*, he thought, *I may yet think of some way to get them back to Teska...* There was no time to go to Teska and leave a message for Yolias and Iaven, and waiting for them empty-handed was out of the question. Lexter caught up to Orven's party and walked along with them.

"What about your meeting?" said Orven, a bit surprised to see Lexter.

Lexter shrugged. "Ah, the more I thought about it, the more I could see the deal would fall through. This'll be much more interesting."

"Well, glad you could come along, then," said Orven, giving Lexter a rough, friendly slap on the back.

Lexter nodded, feigning offhandedness. As they walked, he glanced at the beautifully wrought hilts of the swords on Ripley and Orven's belts. *It's the swords they wanted, isn't it?* he thought, *That's why they sent me, that's what they wanted back. Well, all is not lost yet...*

Chapter 28.
Fog over the Swamp

As the mountainside path rose higher over the Arinzei Valley, Iaven's party felt more secure. The first week of November was overcast, the mornings foggy, gray, and heavy with cold dew. Other years had seen frost by then, but the chill dampness was no less easy to bear. Yolias promised them the watchtowers would provide warmer, drier refuge for the nights ahead.

For the first few days after Lexter left them their mood had been a foul one. Iaven was quiet and sullen, often walking ahead or behind everyone by himself. The others let him be and blamed themselves for Orven's ambush. Iaven assured them it was not their fault; no one could have known where Orven's party was. And they still hoped Lexter would help them, however unlikely it seemed.

Iaven could not help mulling over the fight with Orven, and what he could or should have done. Orven had changed somehow, Iaven reflected. He wondered whether Orven really would have let him fall into the valley. It was altogether different from their encounter at the well in Kronivar; he had never seen Orven like this. But Iaven was also ashamed at the depths of his own anger and the moment when he would have been glad to see Orven panic and fall. Only Orven could make him that angry.

If they failed to recover the sword there were other consequences as well. The King would pass judgment on Iaven for having lost both the sword and the gems. The loss was sure to have a great effect on the war. And then there was Rhiane. His disgrace was too great for him to face her; she would have nothing to do with him now. She had helped convince the King to send Iaven on this errand, and he had failed. Iaven wondered if Rhiane had come with him to the Castle only to avoid travelling alone. The more he thought about it, the more he chided himself for ever having believed otherwise.

Joining the troops seemed the only way to redeem himself. He was less resistant to the idea now that life seemed so burdensome. He had learned a good deal from Yolias and thought he could be useful at the front. That's all there was, unless they managed to get the sword back; but how could they depend on Lexter, who only a month ago had stolen the sword himself?

For Zammond, worse than losing the sword and gems was the effect it had on Iaven. He gave what comfort he could, careful not to bother Iaven. Yolias remained solemn and guarded in his speech, revealing little of what he thought of it all. His injured leg pained him, yet he still set a quick pace for everyone despite his wound.

By the third day of their hike, the dwarves had grown so quiet and their mood so somber that Yolias took pity on them and began to tell them about Teska, to ease their troubled minds and prepare them for where they were heading. Teska, he explained, was the largest of eleven tribal pole-villages built out over the swamps where they were safe from the marauding goblins who often hunted the Teskans. When Itharia grew to include the Veskwood Forest, the Teskans —or rather, the *naquihlaaw-ithwatiila*, "people of the waters", as they called themselves— seemed natural allies in holding the northern border against the Goblins. The Teskans would patrol the swamps, while the Dwarves would defend the land and mountains. Farrenhale was established as Itharia's northernmost outpost and had frequent trade with Teska. The Teskans were a quiet, thoughtful people, slim of build, with straight, jet-black hair, high cheekbones, and a pale olive-green cast to their complexion that for them was the glow of health. Their patriarchs and matriarchs headed each of the eleven tribes and intermarriage between villages was common. They built of wood, rope, stick, and plank, and only certain tools, such as firebowls, axes, chisels, and flints, were of stone. The inn in Teska, which had no name, was a small one. Teska was the only village that allowed foreigners, and only a few at that. Iaven and the others listened with curiosity and questions, wondering how well they would be able to sleep in a wooden structure built on poles over the water.

In the late afternoon the path wound past an outcropping, hugging the cliffs around to the next shoulder of rock. In the distance on the mountain's edge, where the road disappeared around the corner, was the easternmost watchtower. It was built into the rock where the mountain jutted into the valley, and the path led under a gated arch in the pass between the tower and the mountain wall. The watchtower rose several stories above the path, a gray pillar topped with a crenellated parapet and conical roof, all silhouetted with the mountain against the reddening sky. The sight of Dwarven stone brought them great relief. With a goal in sight, their steps lightened.

They reached the watchtower by sunset and were let in by two Dwarven guards. The tower's furnishings were sparse and plain, but it was safer and more comfortable than the mountainside had been. The guards let them replenish their supplies and were concerned to see the travelers were unarmed. Yolias assured the guards they would find arms at Farrenhale and gave no further explanation despite their curiosity. While Iaven and the others were getting ready for bed, Yolias asked about Goblin activity and told the guards about the undermountain passage. At last he joined the others, finding them all sound asleep.

In the morning they woke well-rested to the best breakfast they had had since leaving the Castle. Soon they bid the guards farewell and continued west along the path. The watchtowers were set apart so that from the top of each one the next could just barely be seen in the distance. But the path wove in and out around the mountains, and it took much longer than expected to get from one watchtower to the next. The dwarves found them to be about half a day's walk apart; they would pass one about midday and stay overnight at the next one. They walked all that day and the next, twice passing guards going the other way on their rotation of shifts. Their spirits lifted as their thoughts went on ahead of them, and the following day in the early afternoon, they came at last within sight of the Mountain Gate.

"Ho, what's this, yet more travelers!" said Captain Torben Holgen of the Gate Guard, gazing down from the parapet at the approaching dwarves. "First the Tolgarder, escaped from the Goblins, then a party of Dwarves yesterday, and now more of them... and there's Yolias with them!" He motioned to a guard standing nearby. "Timald, fetch the message for Yolias Vierling, the one sent by the King. And you below, open the Gate for them!" He hurried down the stairs to meet his returning countrymen.

The heavy beam was drawn back with a low rumble. The gate opened and the dwarves entered, and soon it was closed and bolted again behind them.

"Yolias Vierling! A long time since you favored us with a visit. We had word of your coming; a message from the King arrived for you. But come inside, we have a roast on the fire!"

Yolias smiled for the first time in many days at the captain's warm greeting. "We shall, Torben. And it has indeed been awhile since my duties brought me this way. Tell me, when did the message arrive?" While Yolias and Captain Holgen talked, they all went into a common room at the base of the tower where mutton was roasting. Introductions were made and benches were brought out for everyone. All were encouraged to hear that Orven had come only the day before, and that Lexter had arrived before him. The meal was served and they ate heartily, and afterwards lingered in the glow and warmth of the fire, hearing what news they could of the Kingdom. Yolias spoke of the undermountain tunnel and Captain Holgen sent word to General Knorde and promised that search parties would be sent out to find the passage.

Soon after, Timald returned with the small sealed scroll sent to Farrenhale by messenger-bird. Yolias anxiously read its contents, his face betraying none of his reaction. Captain Holgen sat watching him, and finally Yolias looked up.

"The King tells of troops dispatched for Farrenhale. They should arrive any day now. He has asked me to remain here and help unite our forces with the Teskans, for the defense of the border. There will be a council in Teska, and I have been asked to report at it," said Yolias. "From this, then, I understand there have been some difficulties?"

"Oh, there's been tension," said Captain Holgen, "but the Teskans are generally cooperative. They can see it's for their own good as well, I think. They've doubled the number of boats out on patrol, and even the *nasauri* riders are armed. They'll be the greatest help in the event of an attack. But yes, us and them, we don't always agree, and we've had rough spots to smooth out." The Captain smiled. "I'm glad you're here, Yolias. Teskans who've met you always have good things to say. I'm sure you're the best choice the King could have made. And here you are already!"

"I'll do what I can," Yolias sounded thoughtful. A sealed slip of paper was tucked into the scroll, and Yolias handed it to Iaven. "It appears a young lady at the Castle has included a note for Iaven within my letter."

Iaven snatched the note, glanced at his name written on it in Rhiane's handwriting, and tucked it away into his pocket without looking at it. "I'll read it later," he announced nonchalantly. What ever it was, he had no desire to answer the curious and inquiring gazes around the table.

The Captain laughed. "A stowaway note, eh? Well, we won't pry. Now then, Yolias, where will you be staying in Farrenhale?"

"With the council approaching, the King has arranged accommodations at the inn in Teska." Yolias got up to go and the dwarves followed his lead. "We had best be off, then, for tonight. It was good seeing you again, Torben!"

"Likewise, old friend." Captain Holgen stood to see them off. "It is even rumored that you are bringing with you the means to unite the Dwarves and Teskans in battle." An encouraging pause followed as the Captain waited for Yolias to clarify what the rumored means might be.

"We shall see, Torben, we shall see," said Yolias.

On their way down the mountain into Farrenhale, Yolias was quiet and his mirth was gone. The dwarves followed him silently.

"The swords?" Iaven asked, "Is that what he meant?"

Yolias nodded. "The King has assumed our success, and has ordered the swords be put into use at the front. General Knorde and Teska Humber are to lead the defense with them, uniting our forces." He glanced at the darkening sky. "Of course, they will still do so with or without the swords. We must find Lexter and Orven soon. A bad report at the council would not be good for morale. We must win the Teskans' trust. And bolster our own troops' confidence."

The sun was descending into the swamps ahead of them as they passed through the camp. Zammond asked if they would stop for weapons, but finding Orven in Teska was of first importance and Yolias indicated that he would attend to their needs afterward.

"We won't have to fight Orven ourselves," Yolias explained. "We'll bring guards along with us to the inn, and others will be at the bridge entrance just in case. Orven will not be able to leave Teska. We have charges enough to hold him in Farrenhale. But even if we regain Halix, there still is the question of Gorflange, which is rightfully his." Yolias turned to Iaven. "You know your brother the best. Would he relinquish it for use in the war if we forgave the charges against him? Better that we all fight together than with one another."

Iaven was still angry with Orven and hated the thought of dropping any of the charges. "He might," Iaven said, "if there's no other way. He'd have to be forced to do it."

"Let's hope Lexter is reliable," said Zammond, "or it won't matter much about Orven."

As it grew dark, Iaven remembered the note in his pocket and brought it out while there was still enough light to read. It was a small piece of paper and the note was short:

Dear Iaven,

I know the swords will be staying at the front, and we have you to thank for them. We are sure to hold the border. After everything is over, we hope to see you again here. I will be awaiting your return.

Allelia (Rhiane)

Iaven thrust the note back into his pocket. Instead of cheering him it made him feel worse. The disappointing news would reach the Castle long before his return there. Perhaps it would be best not to go back at all. Unrealistic hopes of regaining the swords rose again and he tried to quash them. Iaven hurried along with the others, struggling to remain calm.

Tendrils of smoke rose from the Dwarven encampment. Yolias led them around the tents and through scents of firewood and food, and sounds of soldiers' conversations. The last glow of sunlight faded, and campfires lit the land. In the west, faint and flaring lamps were visible in the mists of Teska across the water. At the campground's edge they crossed the North Road. On their right the enormous North Gate rose in the wall between two broad watchtowers. The wall ran into the swamp, ending at a watchtower taller than the others. Firelight filled the towers' small windows and dwarves moved along the top of the wall.

A path veering west off the North Road took them between tall wooden posts bound with thick rope, where the wide plank bridge to Teska stretched over the water. Yolias's footsteps became audible as he walked onto the wooden planks, and Iaven and the others reluctantly followed. Between the planks they caught thin glimpses of black water below them. The bridge, though wide and sturdy, swayed a little and made them uneasy. Fog hung low and thick across the swamp and the air was still, the water dark and quiet. Now and then a muted *plop* of a fish sent rings of soft undulations over the surface. *Hoo, hoo, hoo-HOOoo-aw!* cried a barred owl from a tree somewhere. To the north a few shadowy boats patrolled the swamps, and strange, long-necked, two-legged beasts with thick waving tails waded through the water with riders saddled on their sloping backs. These, Yolias told them, were *nasauri*, great water-beasts introduced from northern Phamiar and raised and bred by the Teskans. The dwarves strained their eyes to see them, but they were too far off in the fog and darkness.

As they crossed the plank bridge, other night sounds of the swamp broke softly around them: the high-pitched *quawk* of the night-heron and an occasional, unnerving *oo-AH-hoo! kee-a-ree! kee-a-ree!* of a far-off loon. But long gone were the choruses of peepers and frogs that had lulled summer nights to sleep.

Ahead of them, Teska grew more visible. Wide wooden platforms, set at varying heights, rose on poles and piles from the water. Wooden buildings, many with walls and woven partitions adorned with bunched and bundled sticks, rose two and three stories high, a few to four stories. Narrow rope-and-plank bridges hung zigzagging between them, passing over and under each other. High balconies protruded over the water, and here and there spaces opened around huge trees growing in the swamp. Clusters of huts and houses crowded the platforms, and many had ropes and rope ladders hanging down to moored boats below the city. Windows flickered with lamplight and smoke rose from spindle-like chimneys atop conical roofs. Narrow avenues ran between the buildings, turning this way and that. Yolias led the dwarves into the city, and while they looked around he spoke with the Bridge Guards. Iaven gazed at the layers of huts and houses. Teska was enormous and yet had a closed and tightly interwoven feeling to it. A few Teskans passed on the walkways above like phantoms, looking down curiously at the dwarves standing in the torchlight at the bridge entrance. Iaven felt as though they were trespassing there.

Yolias finished talking with the guards and led Iaven and his friends into town. They walked down narrow avenues, passing lit doorways where woven reed baskets hung, and heard the shuffling of looms working behind curtained windows. Teskans passed them along the way, some nodding curtly while others gazed at them warily. Most of the men were tall with straight dark hair and dark eyes, and many of the women had ornately braided hair. No one spoke to the dwarves or welcomed them, but neither were they ignored or mistreated; they were a curiosity to be politely endured.

"Yolias," said Zammond, "aren't we taking guards along with us, to arrest Orven at the inn?"

"Dwarves come and go, but the Bridge Guards saw no one of Orven's description, either today or yesterday," Yolias replied, "It does not seem we will find them here. Still, they may be on their way over, or Lexter may have left us a note."

Following Yolias, the dwarves threaded their way through the streets and at last came to the inn. Long dark rafters arched over the vaulted space of the common room, and wicker chairs ringed tabletops of thin crisscrossing wooden slats. A few patrons, all foreigners, were dining in the back. In the center, wood and charcoal burned in a wide stone firebowl, heating the room. Thin white threads of smoke rose into a flue overhead. Doorways lined the common room's walls, and beyond them stairways angled higher and lower to rooms that had been built and attached to the inn over the years. On the back wall hung a huge tapestry of the Teskan insignia, a white, eleven-pointed star on a field of green. Each of the points curved in a broad, shallow arc, with a small white circle near the end of each point. From a side entrance, an old Teskan, his graying hair bound in a queue, stepped forward to receive the guests. He smiled, heightening thin wrinkles at the corners of his eyes as he surveyed the dwarves, perhaps with some amusement.

"You, eh, 'Yolias Vierling'?" His Tharic was thickly accented in a strange, fluid way Iaven had never heard before. "Room is waiting, two rooms, hall takes you there." He motioned them to a doorway in the back.

"*Prenthii*, Teska Tedemu," Yolias nodded graciously. "Have you seen a Tolgarder by the name of Lexter Splide, or received any messages from him?"

Tedemu looked warily at Yolias. "No messages, no such man," he said.

"*Prenthii*," said Yolias and sent the dwarves before him to their rooms. They went single file down the hall and descended a few steps to two rooms across the hall from each other. Each room was small and square in shape, with one bed along each wall and a firebowl set on a low stand in the center of the room. The bowl was filled with hot, glowing coals from the large firebowl in the common room, emanating a welcome warmth.

"Beds under a roof, at last!" said Wilbur. The quarters were spare and cramped but no one complained. Hobley, Tillmore, and Wilbur took one room, while Yolias, Iaven, and Zammond took the other, and they laid their packs on the empty bed in each.

"Neither Lexter nor Orven has been here," said Yolias. "They may be late in coming, though I doubt they will come at all. As the council is tomorrow, we will wait a day, but I have little hope of seeing them."

"We should never have trusted Lexter," said Zammond.

"Should they arrive, the Bridge Guards will hold them and alert us," Yolias said. "As it is not late yet, I have people to talk to concerning the council. Walk about and see Teska if you wish, but do not stray too far from the inn, and do not wander into the back reaches where the elders live. Remember, we are guests here."

Yolias left, and Hobley and Tillmore decided to go and have a look around. Wilbur yawned and lay down on his bed. "I'll stay here, in case we hear anything," he said, though no excuse was necessary.

"Well?" Zammond turned to Iaven.

"Of course," said Iaven, and soon they were off exploring the narrow streets of Teska.

The new moon was only five days old, a thin waxing crescent in the black sky between the roofs and suspended walkways of Teska. Iaven and Zammond went up one avenue and down another, gazing all around them. Long lanterns hung near intersections revealed brief glimpses of the cautious expressions of Teskans passing them in the streets. A quiet unease, heightened by the fog, hung over the city. Iaven began to feel homesick and a bit sad. Neither he nor Zammond said much, as if they did not want to disturb the stillness there. The city filled the night around them; long angling walkways creaking in the wind, candlelight dancing behind curtained windows in walls fashioned from poles, beams, and woven matting bound together, places that smelled of fish and cooked vegetables, and sticks tied together into lattices and frameworks for purposes neither of them could fathom. They felt out of place and everything was too crowded and close, as though it were closing in around them. At times it even felt like they were being followed. They wandered nervously across walkways that swayed under their weight and found themselves rising one or two levels above the streets. The planks creaked often under foot, and the dwarves longed for the surety of stone or solid ground.

Soon they realized they did not know the way down to the street level, much less back to the inn. They turned in and out of dead ends, and at last shyly asked a passing Teskan who directed them down to the street, though they were now in a different section of town.

"We'll just ask someone else where the inn is, when it's time to go back," Zammond assured Iaven. They made their way down a passage between two buildings, and emerged on a deck overlooking the swamps, relieved to be in the open again. They came to the edge and leaned on the railing there, looking out across the dark waters.

"So Lexter deserted us," said Zammond, "You know, I actually was beginning to think maybe he *had* changed."

"I almost thought so, too," said Iaven. His hopes had been much higher than he was willing to admit.

They were quiet again for a while. In the distance vague shapes of boatmen and *nasauri* moved in the night, obscured in the drifting fog. Straight ahead, even farther away, Iaven thought he saw lights in the hazy darkness. Soon Zammond was looking at them, too.

"What do you suppose it is?" said Zammond. "They aren't moving."

"They're too high off the water to be boats, I think," said Iaven. "Maybe it's another city?"

"It is indeed." They started as a voice sounded behind them. It was an old voice, a soft, velvet growl, stern but not unkind. "Each of the eleven tribes has a city on the waters. We call them 'Teskans', but Teska is only the largest of the eleven tribes." They turned and saw the stranger was neither Teskan nor Dwarven. He was a tall, old man with a long white beard flowing down the front of his dark cloak. His hood was thrown back, his white hair flowing into it. Fine wrinkles defined the features of his face, yet his keen blue eyes remained undimmed by age. Frightened by his quiet and sudden appearance, the dwarves pressed their backs against the railing. With a creeping sense of fear, Iaven realized that, deliberately or not, the stranger stood blocking the narrow passageway and he and Zammond were cornered there.

"Eleven tribes?" Zammond tried his best to sound casual.

"Each tribe has its own pole-village. Teska is the largest, and the next largest is Chisk, and then Neffa, Thesa, Hassa, Misket, Oska, Hutha, Guffet, Thuft, and Utha. But only Teska allows visitors," said the old man. "Though visitors usually do not enter *this* part of town," he added with a note of reproach.

"We're sorry," said Iaven, "We were trying to get back to the inn."

The old man smiled and their tension eased a little. "I am a visitor here myself, and an old friend of the Teskans," he said. "But you are here for the first time, are you not? Mr. . . . . *Ambersheath*, of Hillbrook, I think?"

The dwarves froze, unsure who the old man was and what he was after. Iaven instinctively reached for the hilt of his sword and was again reminded that their weapons were gone.

"Or should I say, Mr. *Empty-sheath*?" said the old man, eyeing Halix's scabbard. "Though I trust Cedric passed the swords on to dwarves worthy of their care."

"And how do you know Cedric?" Zammond asked, astonished and fearful.

The old man waited before responding. In his eyes it seemed judgment was being passed on Iaven and Zammond. After a tense moment it appeared to have come out in their favor.

"I am Wendolin, of the Oswai. I know Cedric has told you about me..." He stood before them, seeming taller now, and imposing. Even in his old age he had remained a formidable figure. He paused and smiled at the dwarves. "And *he* has told me a bit about *you* as well." He brought an envelope out of the folds of his cloak and held it up for them to see.

"What did he say?" said Zammond.

"And how can we be sure that you really *are* Wendolin?" Iaven added. "Anyone could have found the letter."

The old man laughed. "Good! Good, you are right in asking! I am glad to see Cedric did not choose fools. I have proofs enough, but first, will you not introduce yourselves, so I may know to whom I am speaking?"

"I'm Iaven, Iaven Ambersheath."

"I'm Zammond Brockleberry." Zammond hesitated. "Now, ah, sir, if you would let us see this letter—"

Wendolin held it up but did not offer it to them. "It was written after you left Hillbrook and left for me in his cottage." He handed the letter to Iaven. "Would that I have come sooner and spoken with Cedric before he died; but I was too late."

Iaven and Zammond opened the letter, and Iaven recognized Cedric's thin, spidery handwriting. Together, Iaven and Zammond read:

Wendolin,

> *I have waited faithfully for thirteen years now, and I leave you this letter in the event that I will not be around for your return. Nor can I be certain you will return. It did not seem wise or safe to leave the swords hidden here during the war, so I have given them over into the keeping of two young dwarves who are very dear to me, Iaven and Orven Ambersheath. I have told them of the swords and gems, and of you. They will see to it that the swords will be put to use defending Itharia in the war. You will no doubt find them both in service to the King.*

> *As for me, my years draw to a close, many though they have been. How I hoped I would see you and talk to you once more before I die. That meeting will need wait for the World Beyond. Look after the twins when you find them, and you will gain two fine friends as I have. Take what you would from my cottage, too, if anything remains.*

Cedric

Wendolin watched them as they read and took the letter back when they were satisfied. "It was foolish for him to leave such a note behind, for it might have fallen into other hands, but I was glad to receive it all the same." He stared at Iaven and Zammond, assessing them. "I admit I was surprised to find you here, in Teska. It was the scabbard that caught my eye; it has been some time since I have last seen the swords. Of course, in Hillbrook it was also easy enough to get descriptions of you and your brother. And so, Iaven, I take it you are here, in service to the King, as Cedric says?"

"I suppose so." Iaven realized he sounded uncertain. "Not enlisted, yet, but yes, I am."

"Begging your pardon," Zammond said, "but have you anything besides the letter? For all we know, Maëlveronde could have found the letter, and claimed just as much as you have."

"Quite true," Wendolin smiled again. "Very true, yes. But Maëlveronde never knew Cedric, and I knew him well." Wendolin went on to describe Cedric, his mannerisms and ways, how he smiled and gestured with his pipe, his laugh and favorite sayings, and a wealth of other details. Through his words an image of Cedric arose in the dwarves' eyes, an impression so strong he seemed present among them. Iaven longed to see Cedric again, and his remorse at Cedric's passing was renewed afresh. A tinge of his homesickness returned.

"All right, I believe you," said Zammond, missing Cedric as well.

Wendolin turned and went down the passageway. "I am going back to the inn myself, in case you have lost your way."

Iaven and Zammond looked at each other, and followed, walking fast to keep up with Wendolin's strides.

"So are you here for the council as well?" Iaven asked.

Wendolin gave Iaven a sharp glance but kept walking. "And how do *you* know about the council?"

"We came here with Yolias Vierling, and he—"

"Yolias!" Wendolin sounded cheered. "It has been some time since I have seen him. Is he well?"

"Apart from an injured leg, he seems to be fine," Zammond offered.

"An injured leg, you say? Well, there's sure to be a story behind that."

Iaven and Zammond exchanged a glance of agreement that Yolias could tell the story later. Iaven wondered what Wendolin would do when he found they had lost the sword and gems; he had no idea what to expect from a wizard. They moved through the streets, sometimes in single file, and Wendolin led them back. The way was shorter than they expected, and soon they arrived at the inn.

Hobley, Tillmore, and Wilbur sat around a table near the central firebowl, and were surprised to see the doorway darkened by the tall, daunting figure accompanying Iaven and Zammond. They were frightened a moment until they saw all was well. In answer to their awe and curiosity, Iaven introduced Wendolin to his friends, who gave him a warm welcome.

Yolias was sitting at one of the back tables talking with representatives. Disturbed by the commotion, he recognized Wendolin and came over by them. "Wendolin! Nine years has it been since we have seen you last! They said you were here, but I was loath to believe it."

"Old friend! Yes, much have I to tell you," Wendolin greeted him, "Come, before the evening is spent." And together they went off to a corner table to talk, the innkeeper hurrying over to bring them something to drink.

Toward the front of the common room Iaven and Zammond settled in with Hobley, Tillmore, and Wilbur.

"Just like Cedric described him!" said Wilbur. "Did either of you see— did he, you know, use his powers, or anything?"

Iaven and Zammond told them how they met Wendolin. "A letter from Cedric," said Tillmore, "So he's been to Hillbrook. Must have frightened old Henshaw, I'll bet!"

"So you didn't tell him about the swords yet?" said Hobley, "By the way, Yolias said they wanted you to sit in on the council tomorrow, to talk about the swords and gems and Orven."

"They do?" Iaven had been curious about the council, but now that he was going to be reporting at it, he no longer wanted to go. Most of all, he had no desire whatsoever to describe his failures in front of high-ranking Teskan and Dwarven officials, and now Wendolin as well. "Are you sure he wants me to go? I mean, Yolias knows everything that happened."

"Maybe they just want someone there to blame," Tillmore joked.

"Just think, getting to sit in on a war council, in Teska!" Hobley beamed, envious of Iaven. "You're quite a lucky fellow, Iaven!"

Iaven slumped back in his chair. "Yes, it seems I just have all the luck, don't I?"

Chapter 29.
The Council of Teska

By morning the fog had crystallized into the first snow of the season, which melted as soon as it touched anything. All was quiet around Teska as light crept up behind the mountains. Hobley and Wilbur slept soundly, wrapped tightly in their blankets. Tillmore lay still, eyes open, listening to the gentle ebb and flow of his friends' slumber, and the faint sounds of water below the inn. The room's stone firebowl had cooled but embers remained. Tillmore sunk into a grim mood as he thought about being at the Goblin front. He had left Hillbrook with no intention of fighting in the war; yet now he could not imagine returning home without doing his part. And the thought of actual hand-to-hand combat frightened him terribly. He looked out the window and supposed they would move to the encampment at Farrenhale and wait there until the Goblins stormed the gates.

Across the hall Iaven woke slowly, unwilling to leave the blanket's warmth. Finally, he and Zammond rose and went to the inn's common room for breakfast. Men from Tolgard and dwarves from Itharia were dining, delegates and officials who had come to Teska for the council. Yolias sat with a dwarf in military garb whom Iaven later learned was General Knorde. Iaven and Zammond ate at a table near the warmth emanating from the large central firebowl. Servers came and went from an adjoining room, smells of food escaping the doorway curtain as they passed. In the kitchen, cooks made breakfast, distilled the day's water, and gathered ingredients for dinner.

Later Hobley, Tillmore, and Wilbur joined Iaven and Zammond, and Yolias came and sat with them, to go over what Iaven would be reporting at the council. After breakfast, Wendolin came to their table. He asked about Cedric's last days, the swords, and what Halix was like with the gems in it. Though eager to answer Wendolin's questions, Iaven was still bashful under the old wizard's scrutiny. Yolias had explained to Wendolin all that had happened, and Iaven was afraid Wendolin would be angry with his failings.

Soon Zammond, Hobley, Tillmore, and Wilbur went off to Farrenhale for the afternoon to find weapons for themselves and Iaven. They would also watch for any sign or news of Lexter and Orven. Iaven stayed behind to get ready for the council.

Around noon it was time to go. Iaven left the inn with Yolias and Wendolin. The council was being held on the northern end of Teska, in a large meeting-hall where elders of the eleven tribes met once a month to discuss intertribal matters. To Iaven's relief, he learned that the council would be held in Tharic, since so few foreigners spoke *Riiwa*, the Teskan language.

The fog had lifted, and Iaven looked out across the water. Many tall silver maples, cottonwoods, and black willows grew in the swamp. Large trees also rose up within Teska, between platforms, with houses and bridges built around them. Water lapped against the poles beneath them, a constant reminder that they were not on dry land.

The streets of Teska awoke as Teskans began their day's labors. A Teskan man tended a vine with his young daughter who bore a strong resemblance to him. Both turned to watch the dwarves pass, a grim look on the girl's face aging her beyond her years. Though wary of visitors, the Teskans were polite and always gave the dwarves right of way. Iaven greeted some of them but wondered how much Tharic the Teskans understood. Wendolin spoke several times to passing Teskans and seemed conversant in their language.

"General Knorde says a search for the undermountain passage has begun," said Yolias, "And the towers are keeping track of the comings and goings of Goblins in the valley."

"The valley is long, but the passage cannot be too far to the east," said Wendolin, "Nor can it be too close to the Gates. A difficult search, and one fraught with peril. The Goblins will soon realize that we know of it."

"When they find out, it may force them to act," said Yolias. "We should be ready for them. We received word yesterday that the Castle troops are encamped at Greensward and will begin the march north today."

"Time grows short and fewer paths lay open to us," said Wendolin.

As they neared northern the edge of the city, Iaven looked over the swamp. Fifty yards out, Teskan barks and gondolas patrolled the waters. A few nasauri waded by in the distance, riders saddled on their sloping backs. Reins ran along the beasts' long, arching necks to tapering lizard-like heads, their snuffling snouts tasting the air for any sign of goblins. Another hundred yards beyond the swamp's far shore, dark plumes of smoke rose from Goblin camps hidden behind the hills. A single wooden tower stood there to watch over Teska.

Iaven, Wendolin, and Yolias approached a railed balcony over the water. Wendolin paused to let Iaven watch the nasauri. "It has not been a good year for the *naquisauri*, the keepers of the nasauri," Wendolin said, "Spring brought a large crop of eggs, but many of the young died during the summer."

Yolias looked to the west and they followed his gaze. Some distance away, poles and buildings of a neighboring village rose from the swamp, and still another far beyond it in the haze. On nearer waters, several gondolas were heading for Teska. In each stood gondoliers poling their boats, and older Teskans sitting solemnly in furs and woven robes.

"The tribal elders are arriving," said Yolias. He and Wendolin left the balcony and Iaven followed. They went over a bridge and came to the meeting-hall. Guards greeted them at the threshold. The hall was large and broad, its ceiling raftered with curving beams of dark wood. Woven tapestries covered the side walls, their colors dimmed in the overcast gloom. On the northern wall a wide window made of many small, rectangular panes overlooked the water. Outside, boats were lining up to moor at landings beneath the hall.

In the middle of the room a large round table encircled a huge stone firebowl set into its center, its rim flush with the tabletop. Heaps of glowing embers radiated warmth, along with smaller firebowls in the room's corners. Attendants removed ash and added hot coals in preparation for the meeting. A dozen wooden armchairs surrounded the table, and rows of chairs lined the back walls. The Teskan elders of the other villages had insisted on sitting there so their foreign guests could sit at the table, and also so they could watch them.

As they entered the room, two Teskan elders approached. *"Athiiwa,* welcome, Wendolin, Yolias, and Mr. Ambersheath." Teska Humber was tall, broad-shouldered and virile, his silvering black hair pulled back and bound at the back of his neck, while Teska Sauntu was thinner and shorter. Both wore gray cloaks of a thick woven fabric lined with fur. Their movements were unhurried, slow and confident like lions. On Teska Humber's shoulder a small, bright green six-legged lizard regarded Iaven nervously.

"Athiiwata, Teska Humber, Teska Sauntu," Wendolin replied. Iaven nodded, following their lead. Humber set the lizard on the wall's rough surface, and Iaven watched it run up the wall and into a small hutch built into the upper corner of the room.

"Wendolin, we are glad to have you over our waters again," said Teska Humber. "Your presence here brightens a dark hour. Too long gone were you in years past."

"Too long indeed," Wendolin nodded, "But fonder is the return."

"And our Dwarven friends, welcome." Humber turned to Yolias and Iaven, well aware of their reluctance to leave solid ground and appreciating their willingness to endure the discomfort. "We are grateful to have you here. Please, sit where you will."

Yolias and Wendolin sat together, facing across the table toward the window, and Iaven was allowed the other seat next to Wendolin. Iaven looked around, worrying about his report, and tried to be calm. From the overcast sky a soft light bled into the room leaving the side walls in shadow. In front of them, the soothing warmth of the large firebowl spread across the table. Yet a shred of Iaven's trepidation remained, as he watched curling threads of smoke rise from the hidden Goblin camps across the water.

Young solemn-faced attendants brought out wooden goblets of reed-wine and placed them in front of the guests. Iaven found it stronger than he expected, yet still smooth and delightful. As he set the goblet down, he noticed a ring of small characters inscribed around its rim.

"Sishi noa taa-reska," said Wendolin, "It is a toast, meaning 'To see all without malice'; a reminder to those who would confuse defense with vengeance."

As they waited, others arrived and took their places; Teska Hunto, General Knorde, Ambassador Gheel of Tolgard, representatives from Kronivar, the Foothills, and the northern and southern provinces, and a tall, stern Elven emissary, distant and aloof, who said little. Teskan elders from other pole-villages entered and sat down, talking among themselves and greeting the foreign guests. Some were surprised to see Wendolin there, though they did not show it openly.

When all were seated, Teska Humber stood and welcomed his guests and countrymen. He began with news from Teska and the reports of swamp patrols. Elders from other villages added what their patrols had seen or heard. Yolias announced the discovery of the Goblins' undermountain passage, and he and General Knorde assured everyone that its entrance would soon be found.

More reports from the front were given, and Iaven was dismayed to hear that the encampment of Goblin troops was already larger than expected, with more arriving each day. Ambassador Gheel reported what was known in Tolgard regarding the encampments, repeating what he had said at the King's council. General Knorde and Teska Hunto summarized what had been discussed at the Castle, of the Augglins, Trolls, and the herd of shaggy Urumak brought down from the Northern Wastes. Someone said that spies had seen the Urumak being fitted with war-towers. The integration of the Castle troops into the front was also debated. Gradually Iaven formed an understanding of what was going on, and the weight of the impending war oppressed him. He saw how the threat of the Kronivar separatists weakened the kingdom and wondered how numerous they were.

The Teskans had many questions and began a long discussion regarding the separatists. They were concerned that Grawson, the Duke of Kronivar, would not be able to command the full support of his Counts. Others questioned how united the Men and Dwarves would be if Kronivar were attacked. Despite the Teskans' alliance with the Dwarves, they had many reservations. Later, in a hushed whisper during a break, Wendolin explained to Iaven that since the building of the Wall and watchtowers, the Teskans feared Farrenhale would grow too large and threaten their way of life. Around the time of the building of the Wall, Teska had been a small pole-village similar in size to the other ten tribes' villages, which were farther out into the swamps. The Dwarves, wanting a stronger defense over the water, had volunteered to help build great wooden platforms and pillars, greatly enlarging Teska. Though wary at first, the Teskans had agreed. Over the years, Teska had limited trade with the Dwarves, allowing infrequent visits. The Goblins, long-time enemies of the Teskans, saw alliance with the Dwarves as further insult. The pole-village of Teska grew, and soon in the eyes of Dwarves, Men, and Goblins, 'Teska' came to stand for all eleven tribes of the *naquihlaaw-ithwatiila*. Some complained that Teska had grown too large, upsetting the balance between tribes. And so, even though the Teskans cooperated with the Dwarves and would stand beside them in war, an undercurrent of mild resentment and hesitation remained.

"Once the war is past, we will reconsider Farrenhale's role and all agreements pertaining to trade," General Knorde assured them. "Our allies are always rewarded."

"It is well and good that we defend our peoples together," said Teska Hunto, smiling, "Yet even gifts can disturb peace and make the eye hungry. Music, beautiful as it may be, cannot serve the same purpose as silence."

General Knorde considered a moment and then said nothing. Humber and Sauntu seemed pleased with this response. After a quiet moment had passed, another elder spoke from along the wall. "As for the uniting of our forces at the front, we have heard rumors of the finding of the Dwarven Swords of the Alliance from the Great Goblin War of our grandfathers' days."

"They have been found," all eyes turned to Yolias as he spoke, "and are within our grasp, though not yet grasped and raised for war."

"We know very little of them," said the elder, indicating with a slight nod that Yolias should relate the story of the swords. Others along the wall assented. Yolias glanced to Wendolin, who rose at his place and began the tale.

"In the days when Rauwi sang and Thu poled the waters, Aorinthel built a tower on an island in the Silver Sea..." Iaven listened as Wendolin told the story of the swords and gems that Cedric had told the twins. The hall was silent as Wendolin's voice carried them back into the past, through the war and imprisonment of Maëlveronde, the discovery of his escape, and finally Wendolin's meeting with Cedric in Teska. As the tale drew on, Iaven realized he would be asked to continue it, and grew nervous as Wendolin finished.

"As it turned out, Cedric settled in the Foothills, in the town of Hillbrook," said Wendolin, "He lived with the Ambersheath family and worked on their farm. Shortly before his death, he entrusted the swords to the Ambersheath twins, Iaven and Orven." Wendolin laid a hand on Iaven's shoulder and bid him to rise. "And here with us is one of the twins, Iaven Ambersheath." Wendolin took his seat again and the room fell silent as everyone's gaze came to rest on Iaven.

"My brother and I had very different ideas of what we would do with Cedric's gift..." Iaven began. All the night before, Iaven had lain in bed thinking of how he would tell his story. He was ashamed now of how reluctant he had been to leave Hillbrook and search for the gems. Yolias had agreed he could leave out many embarrassing details unimportant to the council, and Iaven was also relieved that Zammond would not be there to mention them.

Iaven told his part of the story as well as he could, with Yolias adding comments and clarifications, until at last he came to the battle with Orven on the tree overhanging the Arinzei Valley. When Iaven finished, he expected there to be questions and perhaps criticism of what he had done. Instead, there was only quiet consideration. Iaven felt the weight of the silence settle on him like a dread sentence and sat down again.

"At least the swords remain in Dwarven hands," said General Knorde, his voice heavy with veiled disappointment. "And we may yet obtain them for service at the front. It is believed that your brother and his friends will be joining the troops in Kronivar, then?"

"I doubt he would return to the Castle after what happened there," said Iaven, "and my friends are looking for him in Farrenhale, should he have decided to stay here."

"And there is still no sign of the thief whose help you enlisted?" General Knorde looked skeptically at Iaven and Yolias.

"Doubt my decision if you will; and it is true that ill may come of it," said Yolias, "yet perhaps our trust was not unfounded. We had reason to believe, and there was no other hope."

"A far-fetched hope is little more than nothing. Still, even a situation deemed hopeless can be misjudged," said General Knorde. "Would that you had gone to Hillbrook sooner, Master Wendolin, we might have the swords here now."

"The swords, perhaps, but not the gems," said Wendolin. "From the time I learned of Cedric's death and found his cottage until now, I could not have collected the gems as these twins have done. Indeed, it would have been a long search in the Foothills for Cedric had word of his death and great old age not traveled in the gossip between villages. Nor was I the only one looking for him."

"Others knew of him, and the swords?" said the General.

"After his return from the abode of the Stone Giants, Cedric told me of the Goblin captors who fell with him," said Wendolin, "If Cedric survived, it seemed to me that they might have as well. The Stone Giants would tend them all alike. And finding themselves alive after so long, they might wonder if Cedric was still alive.

"At the time when I met Cedric here, I was occupied with other duties, and could not go with him for the swords. I instructed him to find the swords, and settle in obscurity far in the south, in the Foothills, until such time as I could come for them."

"Could they not have been given over to the King?" asked Yolias.

"Aardgen was king in those days, and I did not trust him, for reasons of my own," Wendolin gazed at Yolias, who seemed to understand. "I did not even know if Cedric would be able to find the swords again after so long, but he had to try. Cedric left, and his visit with me did not go unnoticed. There was a young Eloswai, thought to be a protégé and close friend of Maëlveronde's, who was also in Teska: Zhindarren, or *Jhin-dahrin*, as he is known in Phamiar. He traveled much in the north in those days, on errands for the Eloswai, sometimes disappearing for months at a time. I was certain he knew the whereabouts of Maëlveronde. And now we were both in Teska, and he knew I was waiting for him to leave, to follow his trail. Whether he guessed who Cedric was or not, I do not know. I decided to leave and draw him away, to give Cedric a chance to escape. Outside of Teska, I waited to see what he would do, and others were watching the boats beneath the city as well. Several days passed. I was due in Tolgard, but the opportunity to find Maëlveronde was too great to forego. At last Zhindarren left for the north and I followed him.

"He traveled along the sea and wandered west on the edge of Tolgard, and then up into Phamiar. Gradually he became aware of my pursuit, and led me north, to Ghutsho Rhobi. There did we play as cat and mouse, around the domes and spires and through the pillared porticos, courtyards, and canals of that great city. Many days passed. He was determined to lose me and could not go to meet with Maëlveronde until he had done so. And yet he must have managed to send him some message in the mean time.

"At long last he led me high up and out onto the long lip of balcony extending around the great dome of Sora Khoti, high up, overlooking the river valley. And there he sprung his trap. He turned and confronted me. 'Enough of such chasing!' he said, 'Is it Maëlveronde you seek? Behold!' I turned, and there, coming around the dome behind me, was Maëlveronde himself. I was trapped between them on the balcony, and it was a long way down to the ground. We stood there, around the dome, the wind whipping at our hair and cloaks. Maëlveronde had grown much older, as had I, yet though my hair had all gone white, his was still jet-black. I sensed his powers were well beyond what they had been. Outnumbered two to one, I dared not challenge him. He seemed to be amused to see me.

"'So, Wendolin, at last you have found me,' he said. 'Though it has taken longer than I would have thought. Now that you have, what will you do?' I was resolved not to give up without a fight, yet they had chosen the setting well and there was no means of escape. Turning to fight either one of them meant turning my back to the other, and there was nowhere to flee. Maëlveronde could see I realized this, and laughed.

"We stood there awhile longer, the wind around us brisk and cold. Maëlveronde raised his right hand toward me, and there on the back of it was a large, ruby-red gem, set into a wide gold ring. I recognized it as one of Aorinthel's gems. 'Not all of them were lost,' he said, and as I gazed at it he reached over and placed his hand on my shoulder. At the touch, my shoulder grew cold as ice, all its warmth drained away. My knees weakened, and my heart slowed as the coldness spread and gripped it. By some black art was the gem's power twisted and put to this use, I thought. I fought it as long as I could and began to feel faint. I collapsed on the balcony as all went dark and knew no more."

Wendolin paused a moment and all in the room were quiet. Wind whistled outside the window, shrill and hollow. Wavering heat rose from the table's firebowl. "At the first sign of faintness, I realized in a flash I had been going about it all wrong," Wendolin began again, "As long as I appeared to resist, Maëlveronde would continue his attack, and I would soon be helpless, or perhaps even dead. Only by feigning a collapse would he be satisfied and pull back. I was certain he did not want to kill me; he would have done so earlier, and quicker. My only way out, then, was to appear to give in."

"*Nareskii taa-vesh kanniwe fentha-i, bo kawi taa-vesh poniwe fentha-i,*" Teska Humber nodded approvingly, "Enemies doubt their opponent's strengths, but rarely doubt their opponent's weaknesses." The elders along the wall quietly agreed in low, praising tones.

Wendolin glanced to the elders and resumed. "My insight almost came too late, however. I was sufficiently weakened that things did go dark for a short time. Slowly I became aware of being carried, and of descending a staircase. Soon we left the city in the back of a cart. Both Maëlveronde and Zhindarren sat around me, so I dared not open my eyes. I had to be patient that a better opportunity would come. My strength had greatly ebbed and was slow in returning; the coldness lessened very gradually, and fortunately our trip was a long one.

"At last we stopped and I was unloaded and carried again. I glimpsed where I was being taken; an old abandoned tower near the mountains. I realized then that Maëlveronde intended to imprison me there. They carried me inside and down a long flight of stairs and laid me on the floor. I waited until they had gone. Cold and stiff, I tried to move. I rose and went up the stairs, and heard the heavy door closing. They meant to seal me inside, alive, just as Maëlveronde had been imprisoned; but without food, and awaiting a long, agonizing death. With all my power I commanded the door to remain open and rushed through it. I caught them off their guard, but the advantage was only momentary. We fought at first, but as I had grown in my arts in the years since our last meeting, so had Maëlveronde. He had the gem and Zhindarren at his side, while I was far from recovered from the ills he had inflicted upon me. At last I escaped and fled to the mountains, hoping to gain time and find some advantage there, and Maëlveronde and Zhindarren followed.

"I led them into the valley and up through the mountain passes, taking the higher road and hoping to find some vantage point where I might turn on them. They pursued me and did not weary. At last I emerged on a precipice overlooking a valley through which a mighty river coursed, its sound rising up to where I stood. There was nowhere to go, so I made my stand. I kept them at bay, but could not withstand their combined efforts. With no other choice, I leapt from the cliff and fell into the river below. I was swept away in its torrents, and I was so spent that it was all I could do to stay afloat as the current bore me downstream.

"Sometime later the river let out into a lake. There I drifted in tranquil waters. Fishermen from a mountain village pulled me into their boat and took me ashore. Thrice had I been wounded and weakened, at the dome, the tower, and the clifftop, and so near death was I from my ordeal that they took pity on me and brought me back to their village and into their care.

"Long time was I in recovering and slow to mend. My hosts were gracious ones and I did what I could to help them in return. At first I feared Maëlveronde would find me and come for me, or send Zhindarren; but apparently my whereabouts remained unknown. I considered what I had learned from the encounter; my guess about Zhindarren working with Maëlveronde had proven true, and I knew for certain now that Maëlveronde had the red gem and carried it with him. I knew something of both of their powers now, and they had learned as much about me. Yet Maëlveronde's purpose was still obscure to me, and it had always seemed strange that he should so readily give up his study of the Angkhadra to pursue the gems.

"At long last my health was restored, and I thanked my hosts who I had come to know well. I went south, then east, and returned to Teska. From there I sent a message by carrier-bird to Castle Frosthelm. I planned to stop there on my way back to Arthel Hall, which lies near the mountains out to the east of Feäthiadreya. I also sent a message to Arthel Hall, announcing my return and giving a cursory description of the misadventure that had waylaid me, though I mentioned neither swords nor gems. I would only make a full report after I had arrived in person. From there, I planned to go to the Foothills and find Cedric and the swords.

"During my stay at Castle Frosthelm, I spent time in the Dwarven archives, to find what I could about Aorinthel, since the Dwarves had built for him. I doubted there would be much of use, though; Aorinthel's writings and journals were locked away in Arthel Hall, and as he refused to side with either the Oswai or Eloswai, neither side could lay claim to his belongings. Nor would one side let the other look through them, for fear some advantage would be gained. And so the debate continues and his writings remain locked away.

"As I pondered these things at the Castle, I also remembered Maëlveronde's interest in the Angkhadra, and began reading the lore and legends of what was known or guessed about them. I wandered the Stone Forest beneath the Castle, and while looking at the doors there, a peculiar idea struck me. Centered between the great Doors of the Angkhadra is a round flat stone, flush with the Doors themselves, in which there are five shallow holes, set in a quincunx pattern. Some claim it is a kind of keyhole, yet no keys were ever found. As I looked at them, I realized that the holes were the same size as the gems; as I looked closer, I became sure of it. Either the Angkhadra had somehow foreseen the gems long ago, or perhaps Maëlveronde had influenced the shaping of the gems while he was apprenticed to Aorinthel. In any case, Maëlveronde had never given up his interest in the Angkhadra; the gems served only to further it. They may well be the keys that could unlock the Doors of the Angkhadra and whatever lies beyond them.

"My work was interrupted by an urgent message sent from Arthel Hall. I was directed not to return but to go north again. I was to investigate certain policy changes in Navrogenaya, and had to leave immediately."

"Could you not have taken one of the swords along, and searched for Maëlveronde in the north?" asked Ambassador Gheel.

"It occurred to me," said Wendolin, "but I would have had to search the Foothills for Cedric, whom I had told to lie low, and that would have taken more time than I could spare without appearing to be on another errand. Even if I had the swords, the other gems, which were lost, could have waylaid and misdirected me, when it was Maëlveronde I sought. And if Maëlveronde discovered I was searching for him, he could have laid a trap for me. So I went north again, hoping my chance would come soon after, and Cedric and the swords would remain safe.

"Had I gone into Navrogenaya openly as an Oswai, I would have received a warm welcome and comfortable accommodations, but I would have learned little of what was going on there and much would have been hidden from me. Instead, I went into Tolgard, reacquainting myself with the language there, as well as Rogglish, which I would soon need. I took on the guise of an old Tolgarder, a woodcutter, dressed in old clothes. I cut my hair and shaved my beard, changing my appearance until none could recognize me, and it was in this fashion that I made my way into Navrogenaya.

"I wandered west and near Ordskell allowed myself to be captured as a spy. There were no charges they could prove, but all foreigners in the area were suspect. I was taken to the dungeons of Nirogenvah Castle, the Goblins' huge, sprawling edifice that has spread through the valley like a plague. I was taken to a small, high-ceilinged cell deep within this wild, haphazard labyrinth, and even if they hadn't locked me in, retracing my steps would have been difficult. Of course, my powers could effect an escape, provided I could find my way out.

But I had to limit the use of my craft; any hint of magic seen by the guards would be suspect and give me away. Only when I had achieved my goal would I be able to return to my former ways and escape would not be too difficult.

"Not long after my arrival I was forgotten about and treated like any other prisoner. Sometimes I was called upon for forced labor, though as an old man I was not considered to be very useful to them. I talked with the guards occasionally, and eavesdropped on many others who did not think a Tolgarder could understand their tongue. Gradually, on my brief sojourns outside of my cell, I learned some of the layout of that part of the Castle and heard many of the rumors and happenings among the Goblins. The guards spoke freely, criticizing their leaders when no one of import was within earshot, and I learned a great deal. There was much talk about King Golhazzar, Del-Sorhar the Chief Spy, and the Grand Vizier who over the years had risen in power until he was practically second in command to the King. It was said by some, though always in hushed tones, that he now exerted a great influence over the King. And strangely enough, it was even rumored that he was not a Goblin.

"I also found that the changes in policy that Arthel Hall had wanted me to investigate had come after the appearance of two old goblins who supposedly claimed to have fought in the Great Goblin War of almost a century ago. I realized then that these were the Goblins who had fallen into the valley with Cedric; the Stone Giants had healed and released them as well. Could the change of policy right after their appearance have been a coincidence? I thought not, and after finding out what I could, I concluded that the Grand Vizier was none other than Maëlveronde himself."

As Wendolin paused, the room filled with appreciative silence. "So you are saying that Maëlveronde is behind the war, and his main goal is to recover the gems and open the Doors of the Angkhadra with them?" asked General Knorde.

"Whether the idea of war was Maëlveronde's or not, I do not know. But he would certainly use it to his own purposes," Wendolin replied. "If Maëlveronde knew about the goblins who had returned after a long absence, they may have told him about Cedric having fallen as well. They may have guessed Cedric to be alive and knew he could find the Lost Swords of the Alliance, as they are now called. Zhindarren had seen me talking to an old dwarf in Teska around the same time, and he may have mentioned it to Maëlveronde. While imprisoned, I was not sure how much they knew, but I had learned enough and thought it was time to return to Itharia.

"But my escape would be much more difficult now that I knew Maëlveronde resided at Nirogenvah Castle. All wizards, be they Oswai or Eloswai, can sense the use of another's magic in their vicinity. I had sensed the use of it myself several times in the Castle, but thought others had come from Arthel Hall to investigate openly, to distract the Goblins. Now I knew it was Maëlveronde, and I cursed the few times I had used my powers right after my arrival. Nothing had come of it and I had not been found out, so perhaps he had been gone at the time; still, I could no longer take any chances. I could not rely on my powers at all now. If I did, Maëlveronde would find me out and there would be no escape. Without my powers, I was like any other prisoner, and escape would be very difficult."

"This, then, accounts for your long absence," said Teska Hunto, "It seems your patience has served you well. We wondered if we would ever see you again."

"I wondered that myself," said Wendolin. "Nine years was I imprisoned there, until at last, as troops began massing in the east, Maëlveronde spent more time away from the Castle, and although I could never be certain of his coming and going, I had to make my best guess and take a chance. Even if he was there, I thought I might be able to elude him, though not without much difficulty. Whatever the outcome may be, I thought, I could wait no longer.

"I freely exercised my powers for the first time in years, and carefully worked my way out of the Castle. Ordskell had grown during the time of my confinement and I had to find other routes out of the area. I went north and slowly made my way across Navrogenaya to Tolgard. From there I went south and took a boat in to Teska. I learned of all the news I had missed and realized how urgent my task had now grown. I sent a message to Arthel Hall, explaining my absence. In their reply I learned that Zhindarren had been missing for almost five years, his whereabouts unknown; and he had stolen some of Maëlveronde's early writings and journals and taken them with him. I made my way south to the Foothills and began my search for Cedric. It was slow going, until news reached me of the death of a very old dwarf, whose age was disbelieved and said to be a great exaggeration.

"At last I found Cedric's cottage. The swords were gone, and a letter was left for me, which I took. Various papers and items I had entrusted to him had to be destroyed, and when I left, nothing remained to give any indication that Cedric had known me. His leaving a letter for me was most foolish and dangerous; yet without it, I would have been entirely in the dark as to what had happened to the swords. I traveled north, looking for any sign of the twins or the swords themselves. Thinking the swords would likely be employed at the front, I returned here, and later, to my surprise, came across our Mr. Ambersheath and his friends." Wendolin turned to Iaven as his tale ended.

"Would that you could have arrived in Hillbrook sooner and claimed the swords!" said General Knorde.

"So I thought at first, but no," Wendolin said, "As I said earlier, collecting the gems by myself would have taken far longer than what the Ambersheath twins were able to do, working in tandem. Now, with the gems in place in the swords, as they were meant to be, we can employ them at the front, and we will be able to use them to find Maëlveronde."

"Once we retrieve them," General Knorde added. "I have great faith in you, Wendolin, and your ability to recover the swords." Others nodded and voiced agreement, and after a moment everyone fell quiet again. General Knorde motioned to a small, wiry Teskan who had slipped into the room and sat down during Wendolin's tale. He was dressed in a shabby, dirty dun-colored cloak and looked as if he had been crawling through fields and mud. As he stood to speak,

General Knorde introduced him. "Teska Kulthi is one of our finest spies, and has just returned from the northern shore."

After an uncertain nod to General Knorde, Teska Kulthi began speaking rapidly, all in Teskan. Humber, Sauntu, and Hunto listened around the table, as did the elders in the back of the room. At last when Kulthi had finished, all eyes around table turned to Teska Humber as he translated what had been said.

"The shaggy Urumak have arrived, and he has seen them being trained for war. The Trolls have returned north, for reasons unknown, but more Goblin troops have taken the high road and are coming over from Ordskell. King Golhazzar's Grand Vizier is said to be with them." Teska Humber then translated the spy's detailed and lengthy description of the layout of the Goblin camp. Iaven was amazed that Humber was able to remember everything from one hearing, and listened to as much as he could.

Gradually Iaven's mind drifted through all he had heard. It was late afternoon now, and the long day, Iaven's tiredness, and the strangeness of the place, with its different foods and suspension over the water, finally took their toll. Iaven found himself stifling yawns and taking a long time to blink. He tried to stay awake and look alert, but his mind wandered as the council went on. Representatives from Kronivar led a discussion of Kronivar's role in the defense, as well as the unrest there. Assurances were given, and questions answered, yet apprehensions lingered. Elven representatives spoke, reminding the Dwarves of their alliance, and Iaven found them too formal, long-winded, and often condescending. They seemed to doubt the Dwarves' ability to defend the front and stave off the Goblin's attacks. The Elves' comments engendered more debate, and Ambassador Gheel and others added their views. Plans of defense, counterattack, fortification, and troop positions were made and criticized. As the discussion continued, more candles were brought in and lit while dusk fell outside.

As the windows darkened and the room brightened with candlelight, Iaven sat up, more rested and attentive now, after having given in to his drowsiness awhile. The talk had now turned to Teska's future. Yolias and General Knorde guaranteed that Itharia would renew its friendship with Teska and reconsider old trade agreements, and promises were made that all treaties would be more favorable toward Teska after the war. Iaven wondered how well the old ones had been kept. For now, they would fight together under Dwarven leadership, hopefully united by the Swords of the Alliance, which their leaders would wield together in battle. Yolias would stay and help integrate the troops, while Wendolin would go with Iaven and his friends to Kronivar, to find Orven and the swords. When accords were reached and agreed upon, everyone relaxed and conversations broke out across the room. The firebowls' coals were replenished and tables were brought in for those seated along the walls. Servers laid place settings and refilled goblets from long, hollow reeds that tapered to a narrow lip.

When dinner was ready, Teskan women with braided hair proudly brought in steaming dishes and wicker baskets filled with hot disks of bread. Iaven devoured the bread, which had a sweet herbal flavor, and cautiously tried the thick, speckled green soup placed in front of him. The main dish consisted of a small, dark-olive sea creature, which looked more like an oval-shaped eel than a fish. Its long, wide fins, extending from the top and bottom of its body, had been spread carefully across the plate. Alongside it lay bulbous vegetables of various earth tones, their long, thin tube-like stems braided together. Tucked beneath them were rounded leaves diced into a mush with a strong, tart aroma. Everything was beautifully arranged on the plate, yet Iaven stared at it contemplating whether or not to eat it. Wendolin looked askance at him, and the unspoken command was enough for Iaven. He picked up his utensils and gingerly tried a few nibbles. Despite his hunger, Iaven ate slowly, taking in one new taste at a time. Feeling it was a part of his duty, he cut up and ate the sea creature, which he later learned was a cooked *hoori*. But try as he might, he could not bring himself to eat the fins.

While Iaven ate, Wendolin explained how difficult it was for the Teskans to engage in war. "What about their land?" Iaven asked, "The swamp, I mean. They want to protect their borders, don't they?"

"They do not claim territory as Dwarves or Goblins do," said Wendolin, "For them, land is not something that can be owned. And as for borders, they have a saying, '*The line that includes also excludes.*' It is others who have drawn lines on maps around them, lines that enclose less and less, tightening around them like a noose."

"The Goblins are doing that?" asked Iaven.

"Both the Goblins and the Dwarves," said Wendolin. "Though the Dwarves are slowly coming to realize it. This alliance is a delicate one, but good will come of it, I think."

"I doubt Orven would hand over the swords even if he knew about all of this," said Iaven. "There's not much I can do about it. You might have to take the swords from him by force."

"Certainly I could, if it came to that," said Wendolin, "but you may be able to get him to understand and give them over willingly. The Goblins likely have spies after the swords, and there is also Maëlveronde and Zhindarren to consider. Orven must be warned of the dangers and the need. Despite his impetuousness, he may yet listen to reason."

"But not to me," Iaven said. "I'll do my best. I just hope we can reach him in time."

Supper ended with the room awash in the warm murmur of conversation. Servers removed the dishes and cleaned the tables, and a band of Teskan musicians appeared and set up along the eastern wall, facing the company. All nine wore elaborately woven robes depicting scenes from their family histories. One had a long, many-holed reed flute, while another had a pan flute of short reeds and straws bound together in rows. The other musicians had curved wooden horns, hide-covered drums, and stringed instruments made from carved gourds with long necks. Soon everyone sat down again, each chair angled to view the musicians, and conversation ceased in anticipation of music and song. Teska Humber gave the signal and the musicians bowed and began playing.

At first, Iaven found the music strange and discordant. It rose and fell, rhythms undergirding melodies woven together in fugues and changing in unpredictable ways that in retrospect seemed inevitable. As he listened he began to understand it better and came to like it. And just as he thought he could predict where a song was going to go, it would end and another more complex one would begin. After several songs, the musician who carried no instrument stepped forward and began singing. His voice rose over the music, riding it like a boat on rolling waves. Even though Iaven did not understand a word of Teskan, he listened intently to the singer's voice aching with sadness and longing, moved by what he heard.

Several song cycles followed with short breaks in between, and toward the end of the evening Teska Humber announced that a song had been translated into Tharic for their guests. Wendolin leaned over and whispered to Iaven, "It is a song about a father and son going into the mountains to carve firebowls; the boy is about twelve years old or so, and it is the first time he has ever gone ashore. It was written hundreds of years ago, around the time when the Dwarves first came here, and Goblins lived in the mountains then." Wendolin straightened up again as the song began. Iaven relaxed and gave it his full attention, drifting along with the music and the singer's clear, smooth voice.

> As rings extend forever
> From stones thrown in the water,
> So tales I am telling
> Pass on to son and daughter
> Like threads, run interweaving,
> In tandem, crossing never,
> Though tides of time be swelling
> And memory's light be fading,
> Still lives are interleaving
> Throughout the ancient dwelling
> Where boatsmen's poles are wading.
>
> In times before the Drifting
> With autumn's shadow falling,
> A saffron morn was dawning
> As geese above were calling.
> Young Vethu and his father
> Awoke as dreams were lifting
> Arising early, yawning,
> Descending, boating, rowing,
> Without a care or bother,
> Up to the reedy awning
> Where solid ground was growing.
>
> Ashore they soon were strolling
> The hardened land, distressing,

Unyielding, immobile,
On Vethu's feet was pressing.
Flat plains gave way to steeping
The mountains skyward rolling,
Magnificent and noble,
The backbones of the world
Where firebowls lay sleeping
Down deep in stones immobile,
Still covered and uncurled.

High up within the mountains,
Through many valleys treading,
Young Vethu realizing
How wide the world was spreading
Up slopes the trails rise on
Past hidden springs and fountains
Deep distance hypnotizing
Long ranges still extending
And out at the horizon
More distant peaks arising
Old mountain lands unending.

They reached the stony summit
Where firebowls are fashioned;
At last their work commences
And carries on impassioned.
Emerging from a boulder,
Their bowl is chiseled from it,
As hand on hammer tenses.
They work long in the clearing
As twilight skies grow colder
Until his father senses
The hairy strangers nearing.

His father signs "There's trouble"
"Be silent, hide from dangers!"
So Vethu, he obeys him,
And then he sees the strangers,
But cannot comprehend them.
They pass close through the rubble
These foreigners amaze him
And give him strange ideas.
Though Vethu would befriend them,
His father's hand now stays him
"They'll kill us if they see us."

In hiding, they lie waiting
Young Vethu's heart is beating
And tense with fear he's straining
The strangers soon retreating,
At last their terror pales.
Of kingdoms, warring, hating,
His father is explaining,
And Vethu listens, learning.
Descending mountain trails,
They walk as light is waning
And homeward are returning.

Down slopes where trees grow taller
They bring their firebowl, and
Across the water, glowing,
Beyond the stretch of lowland,
The water village rises,
But now it seems much smaller.
His father starts the rowing
As Vethu keeps on thinking,
"So small!" he realizes,
His fears and worries growing
And sense of safety shrinking.

No longer carefree playing,
Young Vethu's heartstrings tauter,
He looks ashore now dreading
What lies across the water.
New strands of life he's braiding,
As older ways are fraying.
New weaves of life he's threading,
And old threads he must sever.
His childhood gone and fading
Like widening ripples spreading
Whose rings extend forever.

The music continued awhile after the lyrics, and then slowed and came to an end. Iaven sat back, the song still echoing through his mind. It was late now and strangely he no longer felt tired. Instead, his mind was all a blur, with thoughts of the Goblins and the impending war, of finding Orven and the swords, and of where he would end up serving. And he thought of Rhiane and whether he would see her again, or if she would even want to see him. It overwhelmed him, along with the shame of having stood before everyone to describe his failures and the losing of the sword. He wanted to hope without doubt and put the past out of mind, but found he was unable to do either.

After the musicians had been thanked and congratulated, everyone resumed their conversations, bidding each other farewell. Iaven sat next to Wendolin and guessed they were waiting for Yolias. Many who were leaving came to say good-bye to Wendolin. They often nodded politely at Iaven, and he returned the greeting. Iaven saw no judgment in any of the Teskans' eyes, yet his heart was heavy, and he felt relieved when the last of the elders had departed.

"How fond I am of the flute and stringed *kaluwi*," Wendolin said, watching the last musician leaving. "Nowhere is there such a sound to rend the soul."

"Yes," said Iaven, "I was just thinking about that song."

"It is often said that the 'hairy strangers' of the song were Goblins," Wendolin explained, "but some say it was the Dwarves, with their long beards. No one knows for certain. It is a good reminder, and well chosen."

Iaven was quiet a moment, considering. "I'm glad you're coming with us to Kronivar," he said. "It's too bad Yolias has to stay here. Are we waiting for him?"

"I told him we would return later. We have one errand yet tonight. I thought you might want to come with me."

"Where are we going?" Iaven had no idea what it was, yet strangely he very much wanted to do it.

Wendolin lowered his voice slightly, as if an eavesdropper were near. "To see Teska Ahna, the Silkspinner."

Iaven nodded. "Cedric told us about her. And her loom that could foretell what may happen."

"Then you know why we must go to her now," said Wendolin.

Chapter 30.
Silkspinner

After a good meal and evening of song, even Wendolin found it difficult to leave the warm, bright meeting-hall and bundle up into the cold night outside. Long after the visiting elders had departed and the foreign guests had returned to the inn or to Farrenhale, Wendolin still lingered, talking with Teska Humber and Teska Sauntu over a last goblet of reed-wine. Iaven sat comfortably nearby, eager to ask Wendolin more about the old Teskan woman known as Silkspinner. At last Wendolin rose and Iaven put on his coat, they made their farewells, and emerged into the chilling November night air.

It was very late and most of Teska's narrow walkways were empty. Wendolin led Iaven to the platform overlooking the water where they had stood that morning watching the elders arrive. Wendolin leaned on the railing, gazing northward into the darkness. Smoke rose from the distant Goblin watchtower, barely visible against the black night sky. Iaven stood next to Wendolin and realized they were waiting for something.

"So this Teska Ahna is still alive?" asked Iaven.

"She is the eldest of the Teskans and matriarch of Teska," said Wendolin, "and highly regarded by all the tribes. As for her loom— It is she who does the weaving, but it is a loom unlike any other."

"Because she weaves pictures of what will happen?" asked Iaven.

"Pictures of what *may* happen," Wendolin corrected him. "No one knows what *will* happen, not for certain."

Iaven looked out over the railing. He thought he could make out a *nasauri* wading by in the distance. "It's too bad they didn't have a loom like that at the castle, before we left. They will think me quite a failure, losing the sword, and so close to Farrenhale and Teska. I'm glad the meeting's over, though I really enjoyed the dinner and the songs —especially the songs," Iaven said, recalling the dark green fins he had left on his plate.

"You did what you could." Wendolin turned to Iaven. "Do you think me a failure for not stopping Maëlveronde?"

Iaven recoiled. "No, no, of course not," he said in a small voice.

"Each of us has something which we are called upon to do," said Wendolin, facing the dark again, "And whether or not we can do it, we can try, and keep trying. We cannot always be successful, but we can always be faithful to what we must do."

They were quiet then, listening to the night. A *plop* sounded and spreading ripples appeared where an unseen fish had surfaced. Iaven gazed at the water beneath them, mysterious and black as onyx. The suspension over the water on poles still made him nervous and he looked forward to having solid ground beneath his feet again. Long, rippling waves rolled out from underneath the platform, and Iaven heard the sound of a boatsman poling the waters. Wendolin straightened up. "He's here," he said, "He will take us to Silkspinner."

They left the railing and Wendolin led Iaven down a staircase of narrow plank steps. The stairs were steep and Iaven clung to the rope handrails on both sides as he descended. Below, they went along a short plank walk and stepped into the gondola waiting for them. A tall, lanky Teskan stood leaning on his pole, using it to steady the gondola as Wendolin and Iaven climbed into it. They were close to the water's surface now, the fluid motion of the boat making Iaven uneasy. "*Athiiwa*, Wendolin," said the boatsman, "Humber said you would be visiting my Grandmother."

"I hope you do not mind my friend Iaven coming along," said Wendolin. He turned to Iaven. "Iaven, this is Teska Letha, grandson of Teska Ahna." He looked back to Letha as the Teskan began pushing the boat away from the walkway. "And how is she these days? It has been some time since my last visit."

Letha laughed. "Sixteen grandchildren, nine great-grandchildren, and one great-great grandchild. She is weak on her feet now and rarely leaves her rooms. But her fingers are nimble as ever, and still she works her weavings."

They were adrift on the water now, traveling underneath the city itself. Thick poles and pilings rose up around them supporting the wide plank and beam platforms that formed a low, dark ceiling overhead. Small boats, mainly punts and coracles, were moored to the poles, and rope ladders hung down by them. All was dark, except where lamplight fell from openings where narrow stairways or ladders led up to the city. On the beams overhead hanging lanterns revealed the well-traveled waterways beneath the city, leaving the rest in darkness. Lantern light gradually lit, fell upon, and then silhouetted Letha and Wendolin as they passed beneath each one. All was quiet in the cold damp air, except for the soft poling of the boat and the occasional creaking of wood and planks overhead.

As they turned various corners and went around thicker poles, the moored boats drifted by in their pools of dim light. Fish swam in fenced areas sunk into the water, and water plants grew in other ones. At last they came to an open area beneath a wide square of night sky opening above them. Letha poled the boat to a stop as Iaven watched the ceremony taking place around the open square above the water. Several Teskans stood on the platforms' edge, holding ropes and slowly lowering a wrapped, oblong bundle into the water. The Teskans averted their gazes, and none would look at the bundle. A chorus of low chanting rolled down from above, and Letha quietly joined in with them, his eyes downcast.

Wendolin leaned closer to Iaven. "Look away, Iaven; at Teskan funerals, no one looks directly at the body of the dead as a sign of respect. They believe it is only a husk now, for whoever inhabited it has passed into the next world. Some look away, and some skyward, but it is not proper to stare at the body itself."

Iaven dropped his gaze and listened to the chanting, which continued for several minutes. The body sank into the depths, the singing above growing fainter as the Teskan procession drew away and was gone. Letha began poling again, steering them around the burial waters and deeper through the waterways under the city.

"Kitiia died yesterday," Letha told them, "Two sons of hers died at Goblin hands, and she was never the same since."

The boat passed beneath the city and no one said anything for a while. Soon they came to the older section of the city, and Letha slowed and began to moor the boat. Near the pilings in the water around them, bundles of flax and jute were retting in low, fenced areas. Letha gave his hand and helped Iaven and Wendolin onto a low plank walkway and climbed the narrow steps at the end of it. They emerged on a small wooden patio open to the sky. A tree grew up through a hole in the platform, and the patio zigzagged toward the city, rooms and doors opening onto it from both sides. Letha waited for Wendolin, and together they led Iaven into one of the houses there.

They passed behind a thick, heavy doorway curtain and entered the warmth of the candlelit room. A firebowl gave off its heat there, and two older Teskan women working at spinning wheels looked up at them, greeting Letha and his guests. Wendolin greeted them in Teskan and Iaven nodded cordially. He glanced around the place, breathing in the heavy scents of fiber and dye. Piles of folded tapestries and blankets lay on short benches along the wall. Down the hall, doorways opened into other rooms where the breaking, scutching, and hackling of flax went on, and others where baskets of raw wool and goat's hair were being carded and spun into yarn. As it was late many rooms were dark, only a few Teskans remaining to tidy up after the day's work.

Letha led them into a large, high-ceilinged room lit by clusters of candles in sconces and candlesticks on corner tables. Woven tapestries of detailed imagery hung on all the walls, and on the floor large racks held spools of thread and yarn of every color. In the center of the room was a large, old loom, six feet tall and just as wide. Warp threads angled down to the beam in front of the bench, where an ancient Teskan woman sat. She was small and frail, with finely wrinkled skin and high cheekbones, her white hair pulled back and held in place with crisscrossing rings of loose fabric. She wore garments of gray and forest green and was wrapped snugly in a knitted white shawl which enveloped most of her tiny body. She stopped what she was doing and turned slightly when Letha and his guests entered. A Teskan boy helping her at the loom also looked up.

"*Athiiwata, suati,*" Letha said, exchanging a warm greeting with his grandmother, who spoke in a quiet voice that he leaned over to hear. He listened a moment, responded, and listened again. At last he straightened and addressed Wendolin and Iaven. "She welcomes both of you, and wishes you well." The Teskan boy stepped forward from his place at the loom by his great-grandmother. "*Thiiwa, su Letha. Kavitha vos?*" He nodded deferentially to Letha and then turned to Wendolin and Iaven. "Greetings, friends. She has been expecting you. She began this weaving earlier today in anticipation of your visit, Master Wendolin."

"*Prenthii, suati Ahna,*" said Wendolin.

"My nephew, Teska Kiuwaa." Letha set his hand on the boy's shoulder.

Kiuwaa turned to Letha again and his face became grave. "Uncle, the *liwe* tapestry from this morning, the one she was finishing, is complete. We waited all evening for you to come and see it."

"In time, Kiu. Go lay it out for us, and then come right back and help *suati* with her work." The boy went off into the next room, and Letha turned again to his guests. "Kiu was eager to meet you when he heard an *Oswai* was coming, but he knows the importance of his work."

Teska Ahna spoke in her thin voice and Letha leaned down to listen. He conversed with her briefly in Teskan, and Iaven saw her point with a long thin finger to the back room where Kiuwaa had gone. As Letha listened he became more concerned. At last he stood up again. "She is glad you are here, Wendolin, as the weaving of this morning disturbed her greatly. We will see it presently."

"When she weaves, does she know what she is going to weave?" asked Iaven.

"She knows what color thread or yarn to choose while weaving," said Letha, "and which heddles to thread on which harness, and the order of weft threads, but she does not know what it means, or what the result will be."

"She cannot weave this way on any other loom, nor can anyone else weave as she does on this loom," said Wendolin. "And there is no other loom like it."

The loom was far more complex and intricate than any Iaven had ever seen. A series of treadles ran below the bench, weighted with blocks of wood so that the slightest touch of Ahna's feet would move them. Each treadle controlled a harness holding a row of heddles through which the warp threads ran. Instead of closed loops, the heddles were of a spiral design, allowing them to be unthreaded and rethreaded easily for every pass of the shuttle during weaving. Several dozen shuttles with thread of different colors hung within reach from a rack on a side beam. Wendolin was explaining the workings of the loom to Iaven, when Kiuwaa returned to help his great-grandmother. He indicated to Letha that all was ready.

Letha spoke again to his grandmother, gave her a brief hug, and led Wendolin to the back room. Kiuwaa stood ready by the loom as Teska Ahna turned back to the weaving and sat as though meditating. She slowly began working again, picking up where she had left off. Her pace increased and Iaven was amazed at how swiftly she moved. The shuttles flew back and forth through the sheds as the treadles and beater clacked in rhythm. Kiuwaa assisted, knowing what was needed without being asked. He reloaded shuttles and made sure all ran smoothly. Teska Ahna seemed in a trance as she wove, her eyes reflecting a cold, dreamlike distance, her movements fast, fluid, and without hesitation. Something strange and otherworldly lit her face. Iaven wanted to tear his gaze away, yet found he could not. Her long, sinewy fingers sent the shuttles to and fro, bending like spider's legs dancing as she plucked the warp threads in and out of heddles like a harpist. Kiuwaa watched her, timing the swing of the beater in between her moves to press the weft threads into place onto the finished tapestry curling tightly on the cloth beam.

Letha and Wendolin were waiting in the back room, so with an effort Iaven pulled himself away. As he left, he glanced at the wall behind him where an array of woven tapestries were hung. All were images, of varying weave and detail. They depicted scenes of Teska and the other villages, towns or forests in Itharia, and places in Tolgard or Navrogenaya. One showed a busy Goblin marketplace, behind which a great entourage was arriving over a hill in the distance. In another, dwarves picnicked on a wide green tree-lined lawn in front of an arch-like building supported by pillars shaped like long thin teeth, while a man in a three-cornered hat stood nearby holding a staff. A third featured three goblins in a field, one lying on the ground, one standing, and one on horseback looking down at them. As he was about to leave, one weaving caught Iaven's eye. Two dwarves stood looking off to the left, in front of some kind of wooden railing. Beyond them was what looked like a dark expanse of sea, a crescent moon in the sky casting a faint path of moonlight on the water. The weave was fine enough and the image of the dwarves large enough that he thought he could recognize them. Iaven was still standing there when Wendolin stepped out of the back room.

"I know them," Iaven said, "That's Roy Goldbeard and Aaron Spurro, they're friends of Orven's." Wendolin looked at the weaving. "They're by the sea, and appear to be aboard a ship. Do you suppose they did go to Kronivar?" asked Iaven.

"They may not be there yet," said Wendolin, "The moon above them is a waxing crescent, in first quarter; about three days from now. We will leave early tomorrow and ride for Kronivar, and perhaps we shall find them."

"But why would they be aboard a ship?" said Iaven.

"We wondered what that one meant," said Letha, joining them. "She made it over a week ago. We often do not recognize what is seen in the images. But the one she finished this morning, which I have just shown you, is all too clear in meaning."

"Perhaps," said Wendolin, "or maybe it is only a warning of what *may* come to pass." He motioned to Iaven to follow them.

They went into the back room and Letha drew a thick curtain across the doorway, muting the sound of the loom. There, a large weaving spread across a wide table. Dark greens, blues, and blacks blazed with streaks of yellow and orange. It was an image of Teska at night, its houses and walkways burning in a raging fire. Some buildings consumed in the blaze were collapsing. Figures of Teskans, dark against the flames, hurried across the scene.

"The burning of Teska," said Letha resignedly, "This is what awaits us when the Goblins attack."

"It has not yet happened," Wendolin chided, a note of reproach in his voice. "And may not; the bridge can be cut during an attack, and the Goblins might be held back. Let us take it as a warning and redouble our efforts. We cannot give up or assume defeat before anything has happened."

"So you have said many times, but still my heart is heavier now," said Letha.

"Would you let a heavy heart slow your hands and feet, and allow the image to come true? Better that the loom be destroyed and thrown into the swamp, if so! We are fortunate the weaving was finished too late to be shown at the Council this afternoon, for there would have been great dismay and dampening of spirit." Wendolin paused. "Still, Humber and Sauntu should be told of it, though I pray they do not lose hope."

Teska Letha said nothing but seemed deep in thought, perhaps fighting off despair. He looked up again after a moment. "*Suati* has been long at work on her weaving, she began the present one soon after this one was finished. Will you and Iaven not stay awhile, to see it completed? Perhaps it will bring us hope."

"We will," said Wendolin.

Iaven and Wendolin sat in the back room with Letha, who offered them something to drink, grateful they could stay. Iaven's thoughts returned often to the Council, and he supposed Wendolin's did as well. Now and then they examined the weaving showing the burning of Teska. Looking closely at the tapestry, Iaven saw only strands of colored yarn of crisscrossing over and under each other; but from farther away they formed a picture of Teska. He had stared with the same fascination at the image on Cedric's blanket, and wondered if the image of Teska would prove just as true.

The night grew late. Iaven, stifling a yawn, was about to ask Wendolin if they could go back to the inn, when the muffled sound of the loom slowed and came to a stop. Letha rose anxiously, pushing the doorway curtain aside. Iaven and Wendolin joined him. In the other room, Kiuwaa was detaching and tying off the warp threads, while Teska Ahna sat directing him with frail gestures and tired eyes. Satisfied that Kiuwaa could finish the edge of the tapestry, Ahna nodded and Letha helped his grandmother up from the bench and across the room to her small bedchamber down the hall. When they were gone, Iaven watched as Kiuwaa carefully removed the finished weaving from the cloth beam. Wendolin stood looking at the tapestries hung on the walls around them.

Letha returned and came to help Kiuwaa. He nodded to Wendolin, who led Iaven into the back room, bringing more candles from around the loom. Letha and Kiuwaa carried in the rolled-up weaving and set it on the table on top of the other one. They unrolled it and stood in silence, examining the image in the flickering candlelight.

"This is below Castle Frosthelm," said Wendolin. The weaving showed the inside of a great hall, with many staggered rows of pillars stretching back into darkness, their capitals carved to resemble spreading tree branches. Iaven recognized it as the Hall of Pillars, the Stone Forest, where he had seen the Doors of the Angkhadra. Two figures were in an open area ringed about by pillars. On the left stood a tall, angular figure in black, a long dark cloak hanging from his shoulders and a sword held on the ready in his hand. He stood over the second figure, a dwarf lying prone on the ground like one defeated in battle or perhaps even dead. Iaven noticed with growing horror that it looked rather like Orven. He wondered if that were possible. Iaven saw Letha glancing curiously at him and realized with a start that it could be himself just as well. A sickening fear crept through him.

Wendolin indicated the figure robed in black. "Maëlveronde."

"The dwarf on the ground, is that me?" Iaven said in a small voice.

Wendolin did not respond immediately. "Either you or Orven, as you look alike; it is difficult to say." Wendolin pointed to a shape on the ground near the fallen dwarf. "But look, over here on the floor." The fallen dwarf's hand was reaching out as if he had dropped something, and a short distance away lay a sword. Although it was at an angle, three dots of color were visible in the hilt.

Iaven bent closer and saw the dots were green, violet, and yellow. "Gorflange," said Iaven, "Orven stole the violet and yellow gems from me, and he must have found the green one before that."

"Look, in Maëlveronde's hand," said Wendolin. The dark figure held a sword, and although his hand was on the hilt, the sword was similar to the other in size and shape and Iaven recognized the Tigersmilk pearls on the ends of the cross.

"Halix! Maëlveronde must have taken it from them, somehow," said Iaven, "And he has the last gem, doesn't he? Do you think Orven will die, or is he already dead?"

"Iaven!" Wendolin growled. "Do not talk like that! Remember what I have been saying about these weavings! Even if they *can* come about, we can still change the events they show. Perhaps we have been given this weaving as a warning, so that we may do so."

Letha looked down at the image as though it were something that had already occurred. "What worries me is that if Maëlveronde is in Castle Frosthelm, as you say, then perhaps Kronivar has already fallen," said Letha, "and Teska before that... Unless the swords can be recovered."

"We should not rely too much on either the weavings or the swords," said Wendolin, "Nor count as certainties things that remain to be seen. Teska has withstood the Goblins for some time now, and it falls to us to see it remains standing, with or without the swords." As if to put the idea of defeat out of their minds, Wendolin rolled up the tapestry. Yet even as he did so, revealed beneath it was the image of the burning of Teska.

Letha paused a moment, and seemed to gain some resolve. "Let us put these weavings to good use then. I will show them to Humber and Sauntu, and we will all redouble our efforts to keep them from coming about." He reached to take the weaving from Wendolin.

"*Prenthii*, Teska Letha," said Wendolin, handing him the tapestry.

As Letha rowed them back to the inn, Iaven noticed that it had become colder outside, and even darker, he thought, if that were possible. Letha took them on a different route beneath the city and let them off at a small platform and staircase that led back up into the warmth of the inn. Iaven was tired and ready to sleep, yet the woven images remained in his mind.

Wendolin bid Iaven good night and Iaven slipped into his own room, where Yolias and Zammond were fast asleep. A good, dry heat emanated from the firebowl, which was still hot to the touch. Iaven came to his bed and stopped. Lying there was a sword Hobley had bought for him in Farrenhale to fill his empty scabbard. He picked it up and it seemed dead and heavy in his hands compared to Halix. It was well-used and rather plain —dull-looking, really— and seemed like it would take a great effort to wield. Iaven realized how much he had come to like Halix and even depend on it. With Halix, there had been a chance he might become a capable swordsman with practice; now it no longer seemed so. Iaven reminded himself that Halix wasn't really his, it belonged to the King, and he felt strange that he had become so attached to it.

Iaven sheathed the sword, which did not quite fit as well as it should. He took off his scabbard and laid it on the empty bed with the packs, and then climbed into bed, resting his face on the cold pillow and wrapping himself in his blankets. He lay there, looking at the rim of the firebowl in the dark. The wavering heat rising from it made the back wall appear to shimmer. And moments later he was fast asleep.

In the morning Wendolin came around to wake them for their early start. Yolias was gone to secure the horse and cart, which would be waiting for them where the bridge from Teska reached the shore. The dwarves grumbled and rubbed their eyes, even though they all looked forward to returning to solid ground again. They packed their things, ate a small breakfast in the inn's common room, and said good-bye to Yolias when he returned. He urged them onward and told them to hurry back, and Iaven felt particularly encouraged by his words.

The light was growing stronger over the mountains as they left, and the good hard ground beneath their feet made the dwarves feel like walking, which they would have insisted on doing had they not been in a hurry. Wendolin took the reins and Iaven joined him up front, while the others climbed in the back, returning to the general laziness that had been disrupted by their wake-up call. Overhead, a dozen geese flew south honking, late-starting stragglers waylaid or lingering.

Now that they were in daylight and back on land, and partly because they were leaving the front, Iaven was confident that with Wendolin's help they would find Orven. The plain sword in Iaven's scabbard now seemed only temporary, instead of a replacement.

Soon they passed the Dwarven encampment, awake now and bustling with activity. Since he had a good reason for going to Kronivar, Iaven did not feel guilty about leaving the front. In some ways he even looked forward to returning to it, and that surprised him.

The camp passed out of view and Iaven's thoughts turned inward to their late-night visit and the weavings. A question occurred to him that he had overlooked due to his tiredness.

"Wendolin, how many of Silkspinner's weavings have you seen?" Iaven inquired.

"Quite a few, in my years. Why do you ask?"

"You said that what the weavings show doesn't always happen."

"They show what *can* happen, but not necessarily what *will*, yes," said Wendolin. "The Teskans are often too eager to believe in them, even when they bode ill. Especially then, sometimes."

"Well, if that's true," said Iaven, "Then how can we be sure that Orven will be in Kronivar, or aboard a ship there? The weaving showed them aboard a ship, but what if it's wrong?"

Wendolin cast a keen glance at Iaven. "It's at least a good place to start. And, yes, the weavings *can* be right, and frequently are."

Iaven was silent awhile, but could not resist asking one more question. "Of all of Silkspinner's weavings you have ever seen, how many of them did *not* come true?"

Wendolin did not look at him this time, and was silent for so long that Iaven was about to speak again when he finally answered.

"As far as I know, they all came true," said Wendolin, turning to Iaven, "But that does not mean we will give up hope!"

Chapter 31.
Liar, Thief, and Spy

"So then we rigged the crossbow, carefully shut the door, and ran off before they knew we were gone. Leland said even if the trap didn't get Fogarr, he'd have quite a time trying to dismantle it." Lexter laughed, pleased at how attentive his audience was. Max, Roy, Aaron, and Ripley leaned against the sides of the cart as they rode, listening to Lexter's stories. Two days on the road, and they still hadn't tired of his tales. Lexter was happy to be needed again and glad to oblige them. He enjoyed their company and was unsure what to do now. They were not returning to Teska and he certainly didn't want to go to Kronivar with them, unless they could see him safely aboard a ship bound for Tolgard. That had become his new hope and plan; he was sorry he had been unable to help Iaven's party, but he had tried his best and nothing more could be done. Lexter had already told Orven's party all he knew about Aranstone and Greywood, and hoped they would let him part ways before they went to meet Aranstone in Kronivar. It would be a delicate situation, but Lexter was certain he'd find some way to deal with it before then.

"So what happened to old Fogarr?" asked Max.

"We never heard," said Lexter, "Though there was another time before that, when Leland and I got him in trouble with the Duke..." Lexter shifted his legs and piled more hay behind him, making himself more comfortable as he began relating yet another escapade.

Orven sat at the reins and had no trouble hearing Lexter's stories, but he'd had quite enough of them. At first Orven was glad Lexter had joined their party; they'd bought the best weapons and chain mail they could find, and thanks to Lexter's haggling, paid as little as possible for them. Lexter knew plenty of people in Kronivar, particularly Aranstone and Greywood, but he couldn't always answer Orven's questions about them. After while it seemed all he had left were guesses and unimportant details. His stories amused the dwarves, but included nothing that would be of use to them in Kronivar. Only Orven seemed to notice this, though; the rest had taken to Lexter, enrapt by his adventures, which Orven was sure were exaggerated. Even Ripley had warmed to him; there was something of the rascal in Lexter that he admired. Orven was annoyed that Ripley wanted to sit in back with Lexter instead of riding up front with him. Like everything else, Orven had made a point of making it *his* decision that Lexter would join their group, and now he was beginning to regret it. They had everything they needed to know about Kronivar and were unlikely to get anything more. It was even possible, Orven thought with horror, that once they got to Kronivar, Lexter would himself join with Aranstone, claim credit for finding the dwarves, and become a captain with the dwarves under his command. No, Orven decided, he could not let it come to that.

Orven hid his growing dislike of Lexter. Lexter had become too much a part of their group to be simply kicked out of it, but it was still several days' ride to get to Kronivar, and things could change before then.

That evening the dwarves camped in a field off the North Road, behind a low hill where they would be out of the wind. Orven took the first watch of the night by himself, and the other dwarves were soon dozing around the fire. Lexter lay awake, but as Orven seemed withdrawn and moody, Lexter said nothing. He noticed how quiet Orven had been on the road, and suspected Orven was jealous of the attention he had been getting lately. *I'd better be more careful*, Lexter thought.

Lexter lay pondering what he now thought of as his "new" life, following his reprieve from death at Goblin hands and his loss of Leland. He missed Leland terribly and did not want to be alone. He wasn't used to it; it frightened him. For a long time, Leland had been his only source of solace, and, he supposed, he had been Leland's. He would go back to Tolgard now, for good, difficult as that might be at first. He remembered their last visit. They had cut short their stay with excuses to avoid seeing successful friends of theirs who were happy with their families (and in a few cases, grandchildren), ashamed at their lack of any lasting accomplishments. Leland had been especially bitter and said he would never go back, though Lexter didn't think he really meant it.

But returning to Tolgard was the best thing to do. Itharia was under the shadow of war, and that was another reason why he didn't want to be alone. He was a foreigner, and a hunted one as far as Kronivar was concerned. Orven's party seemed the answer to his troubles; perhaps when he left them they would reward him for his help, seeing him safely off on a northbound ship. Yes, he thought, that would be nice; unless Orven wanted him to introduce them to Aranstone and Greywood before they would let him go.

From what little Iaven had told him about Orven, Lexter had not looked forward to meeting Orven and trying to keep him in Teska; but he'd come to like Orven's party quite well. He was the center of their attention, whereas Iaven's party had treated him with doubt and contempt. Orven's party had more money, too, and were easier to manipulate since they trusted him now, even though they knew so little about him. Yet Lexter found he did not want to manipulate them or abuse the trust they had invested in him. This feeling was rather strange to him, and he was proud of it. He would resist falling back to his old ways, he thought. He liked Orven's party and decided he would not be a spy for Iaven's party. Then again, Iaven and Yolias had not asked him to be a spy, nor even to steal the swords, only to keep Orven in Teska. And he had been sincere in his promises to them, even if his attempts had failed.

Now he'd have to figure out what to do about Kronivar. Although he hadn't lied outright to Orven's party, he had misled them into thinking that he knew Aranstone and Greywood in a much different way than he did. They'd soon find out how wrong they were; he just couldn't be around when they did. Getting them to give him enough for passage on a ship to Tolgard and let him go as soon as they got to Kronivar would be very difficult. Maybe it would take one last lie. Lexter cringed at the thought; it was still so easy to justify things to himself. It was a trick he had learned from Leland. Yet what if he couldn't get home to Tolgard *without* lying? Would he risk giving that up, considering how often he'd lied before, and for so much less?

Lexter let out a sigh on the cold, hard ground. *I really want to change*, he thought, *why is it so, so hard?* Once he was home in Tolgard it would be easier; until then it would be a great struggle. Maybe it always would be, or at least for a while. Or perhaps he just couldn't do it. It all depended, he supposed, on whether or not he *wanted* to, and he decided that he did. At least at that moment.

Lexter watched Orven sitting near the campfire, poking the logs with a stick. Several times Orven looked over to him, and then seeing he was still awake, looked away again. He said nothing and Lexter sensed his anger. *I must be more careful*, Lexter thought, almost feeling sorry for Orven, *I've taken their attention away from him, and he needs it. He's a lot like Iaven, maybe more than he realizes.* Lexter thought about the twins and how similar they were, and his own brothers, and gradually his thoughts slowed down until he dozed off.

When Lexter woke it was still dark out. Apart from the hushed hum of field crickets, all was quiet. He glanced around the camp to see who was awake on watch, realizing with a jolt he was the only one. It was Roy's turn, but Roy had lain back and fallen asleep. Knowing from experience how the woods and roads of northern Itharia were not safe, Lexter sat up, wondering if he should wake Roy. He made a move to get up, and looked over to where Orven was sleeping. Dull sparkles of firelight on metal caught his eye. Orven's sheathed sword lay right by his blanket within easy reach. Next to him Max slept soundly, his sword laid close nearby as well.

Halix and Gorflange, Lexter thought, *the Lost Swords of the Alliance, right there for the taking*. A palpable thrill tingled through him. This was the greatest opportunity he had ever been offered. Take the swords and walk away, just like that. Simple, without risk, and too good to pass up. They were his.

Lexter crept over by Orven. He knelt down, listening to Orven's deep breathing, half-expecting Orven would wake and wonder what he was doing. Lexter carefully placed his hand around the hilt of the sword, his heart leaping at the touch of the fine, cold metal. A soft metallic whisper rang as he gently drew Gorflange from it sheath. Lexter sat back and raised the sword in his hand, its lightness and balance surprising him. He had examined hundreds of swords and had wielded a few, but now even the best of them were little more than metal sticks compared to this one. Lexter understood why Orven had fought Iaven for the sword and gems. He moved the sword through the cold night air, their tiny campfire flashing in the blade.

Glancing guiltily around the campsite, Lexter was sure someone was awake and watching him. But no one was; all were sound asleep. He could take the swords and all their gold, or even kill them as they slept. Just like that, he would be rich; far better off than he and Leland had ever been. *You've done it, Lexter,* he imagined Leland telling him, *in less than two weeks you've gone from being a wretched Goblin slave with nothing to a rich man!* A nervous laugh escaped from Lexter, startling him in the silence. He glanced at the dwarves again and saw all was still. *And these dwarves*, Leland's voice continued, *they think themselves such warriors, but look at them now, snoring away, while anyone could walk by their camp and take everything.*

Lexter looked at the dwarves' young faces, so peaceful while they slept. Something about them softened him. Of course he would never *kill* them, he had never killed anyone in his life— *Not that you're aware of*, he thought suddenly, *you rigged that crossbow and knew Fogarr would open the door, standing right in front of it...* Lexter had a sinking feeling. The crossbow had been Leland's idea, and he had gone along with it. *Excuses,* the inner voice snapped, *you thought it was a great idea, you were even envious that Leland thought of it before you did*. True, but nothing could be done about it now. Perhaps he *had* helped cause someone's death; it still wasn't like murdering them outright. *No, it's all the same outcome,* the voice said, *just easier to excuse, isn't it?*

He looked at the dwarves again and sighed. He had no intention of harming them. He would just take the swords and go, along with enough gold for passage to Tolgard. He looked down the dwarves and then at Orven sleeping, only a few feet away. *They trust me*, Lexter thought. He looked at the sword in his hand again, a pang of passion still burning. Lexter slowly exhaled, realizing what a temptation the swords were. He had always been aware of temptations; he was just not used to resisting them. He lowered the sword and looked around again at the sleeping dwarves. He almost wished someone would stir and force him to put the sword away and go back to sleep, but they all lay heavy and still.

Lexter lowered the sword onto his lap. What if he took the swords for some other, unselfish reason? If only Yolias had told him to retrieve the swords. But could he take them back to the front once he had them, or would he just keep them? That was probably why he wasn't asked him to steal them, he reflected. Maybe they actually believed he was trying to give up stealing, trusting him as they did. Lexter wished he had left Iaven's party a note in Teska. It looked bad, like he'd simply run away. Now he could return with the swords and prove them wrong. Lexter looked at the sword in his hand. The swords were important to Itharia, but could the kingdom really fall without them? That seemed unlikely; could two swords really make such a difference? *Itharia probably won't fall*, he thought . . . *but I might, if I take them*. If he took them now, never again could he promise himself anything, or hope that he could change. Yet force of habit urged him to be practical and take the swords while he could before it was too late.

Lexter grunted and slid Gorflange back into its sheath. For a moment he held the hilt, and then finally let go and withdrew his hand. Slowly he got up and walked over to where he had been sitting. He was about to wake Roy, but seeing how soundly Roy was sleeping, he decided to sit the watch himself. His mind was too alert now to sleep anyway, he thought, so he might as well. That would show them how much their trust in him was warranted.

Lexter shivered and sat listening to the crickets, thinking about the swords, the dwarves, and Kronivar. It occurred to him that he had helped both Iaven's and Orven's parties without having done anything underhanded, and despite this they still found him useful and were thankful for his help. He was proud to have resisted stealing the swords, and glad he was not as weak-willed as he had feared. And yet, another part of him deeply regretted having passed up the greatest opportunity of his life.

Roy stirred and shook himself awake, realizing he had fallen asleep on his watch. He looked around and was surprised to see Lexter sitting near the fire.

"I must have dozed off," said Roy, "Not too long, I hope."

"I don't know," said Lexter, "I got up just a little while ago myself, couldn't sleep. I saw you were asleep, so I sat the watch myself."

"Thanks, Lexter." Roy moved over to the fire as Lexter went back to his bedroll. Instinctively, Roy glanced around the camp, particularly at Orven's and Max's swords. Everything was in order and undisturbed, and he was ashamed to have thought badly of Lexter, even momentarily. "You know, Lexter," Roy said, "I'm glad you joined us in Farrenhale. It's been nice having you along."

"I've enjoyed it as well," said Lexter, and smiled.

"Thanks for sitting the watch for me, too. Don't tell Orven about it, alright?" said Roy.

"No, of course not, don't worry," said Lexter, rolling over. "Good night!" And feeling reassured that he had indeed made the right decision, Lexter's mind troubled him no more and he was soon asleep.

The following morning they rose late, several hours past sunrise. Ripley built a small fire over which Aaron cooked breakfast for everyone. The evening before, they had stopped at a small farm off the road and bought some bread, eggs, milk, and whatever else they could get. And it was, Lexter reminded them, still about two or three days' ride to Greensward.

"If we don't keep stopping so often," said Orven.

"We haven't let the horse rest enough," said Aaron.

"If he dies, we'll buy another one," Orven said sharply, "We've got the money."

"It won't be easy to find one anymore," said Aaron, "We were lucky to get one in Farrenhale."

"And we paid dearly enough for him, too," said Max.

"We can sell him again when we get to Kronivar," said Orven, "And I'd like to get there as fast as we can."

"Orven," Aaron spoke hesitantly, "it'll only take us longer to get there if we have to find another horse."

"You've never had a horse of your own before—" Max added.

"My Dad had one, you remember," snapped Orven, growing impatient, "and I went on trips with him..."

"Yes, but that was different," said Max, "He was never in such a hurry. And he was careful about stopping often, as far as I can remember."

"What does Lexter think?" said Roy.

Aaron turned toward Lexter, "You've owned horses, haven't you?"

"Well, yes, my brother and I did." Lexter was pleased to give his opinion. "And Aaron's right, we—"

"It isn't a matter of letting Lexter settle it!" Orven was angry now. "It's my decision, isn't it?" He glared at Lexter. "You should just be glad we took you along with us! You've been eating our food, costing us plenty—"

"Orven—" said Max.

"And as if that weren't enough..." Orven looked around at them, "He's a *thief*!"

"Well, he's told us all about that already," said Ripley.

"I mean, he's stolen from *us*," said Orven.

Lexter was so taken aback that Orven's accusation hit him like a punch in the stomach. "I—I've done nothing, what—what are you talking about?"

Max and the others were stunned by Orven's accusation.

"Orven, how can you say that?" said Max, "We haven't had—"

"This morning I was looking for my dagger," said Orven, walking over to where Lexter sat by his pack. "The gold dagger with the jeweled sheath, the one we found in tomb. And it was gone! I don't think any of you would have stolen it, so it must have been Lexter."

"Never, I—I didn't take anything!" Lexter muttered. "I—Why do you say—"

Orven knelt and snatched Lexter's pack away from him. He opened a pocket on the outside of the pack, and pulled out the gold dagger he had just described. "I knew it!" Orven roared, holding it up for them to see.

The other dwarves stared at the dagger in Orven's hand. They liked Lexter and could not bring themselves to believe that he had stolen from them, especially since he had been with them awhile now. And something seemed strange about the suddenness of Orven's accusation.

"When could he have taken it?" said Max, "And why?" While buying weapons in Farrenhale they had let Lexter choose a nice sword for himself, so Max thought it odd that Lexter would steal a small dagger.

"When we were asleep," said Orven, "It wouldn't have been hard to do."

"But we always had a watch," said Max, "We would have seen him do it."

Roy was stung with guilt. He wondered if Lexter really had taken anything, but he remembered looking around the camp and seeing nothing amiss. And for some reason he just didn't believe Lexter had done it; he could have taken better things than the dagger, and even run off the same night. But Roy wasn't about to let Orven know he had fallen asleep, so he said nothing.

"It would have been easy enough to do when someone wasn't looking," said Orven, growing upset with the others' defense of Lexter.

"If you didn't see him take it," said Aaron, "then how did you know exactly where it was? You seemed to know right where it was in his pack—"

"A lucky guess!" Orven was furious now, his face flushed red, and he turned on Aaron. "Why do you insist on defending him?!" He looked to each of the dwarves to see who would meet his gaze. "All of you! How can you take his side? You can see he's a *thief*!"

Lexter was so shocked, his mind reeling, that he was not sure what to say. He was not used to being falsely accused of anything; normally any accusations brought against him were true. And when he was guilty, he knew it in advance and had alibis and excuses ready. But now he was innocent, the false charges were a complete surprise, and there wasn't much he could say in his own defense.

Lexter remembered Orven's furtive glances the night before; now his motive was clear. Lexter cursed himself for having charmed attention away from Orven. *I should have been deferential and supported him more*, Lexter thought, *I overdid it this time. What can I tell them now? The sooner I say something the better. I don't want to sound guilty... What can I say? I've got no defense, I haven't stolen anything, I've been helpful to them, I've gone out of my way—*

"I've—Orven," said Lexter, getting Orven's attention and realizing how fearful he sounded. "I—I didn't take it, why would I—" Lexter was startled at the abrupt way Orven turned to him. A strange new expression lit Orven's face as though Lexter's denial had added some further insult.

Orven looked to the others and pointed accusingly at Lexter. "Did you hear that? Did you hear what he just said?" he shouted.

"What?" Max was confused. "He didn't say any—"

"Right when he started to talk!" Orven smiled vindictively now, as if he had just been given proof of Lexter's thievery. "Didn't you hear him? He said 'Iav— Orven'! He slipped and almost called me *Iaven*! And we haven't told him about Iaven at all, have we; we've been too busy listening to all his stories, his *lies*... No wonder he knew how to approach us, what to say, how to respond! He knew who we were all along; he's been spying on us for Iaven and the King!"

All the dwarves were staring at Lexter now, and he could see their disbelief turning into disappointment. "No, no, I—I was going to say—" said Lexter, his voice trembling with fear and trailing off into a whimper as he forgot what he was going to say. They waited for his response, but he couldn't think of anything coherent. "I didn't— I'm not—"

Lexter knew that whatever he said would not be believed, not even the truth, and anyway, the truth was that he *did* know Iaven. Lexter was about to speak when Ripley jumped forward and drew his sword, ready to swing it at Lexter. Ripley had listened to all that was said, and when Orven was convinced, so was he. Lexter stepped back, throwing a glance at his own sword, which lay sheathed on the ground a few feet away, out of reach.

"And to think I even liked you!" said Ripley, anger masking the hurt in his voice. He waved his sword at Lexter, forcing him to step back. Orven came over to them as Ripley backed Lexter into a rocky field nearby. There they knocked Lexter to the ground and beat him up, to keep him from even thinking about following them. Lexter knew he was outnumbered and gave in, hoping they would leave him be. Orven vented his anger, doing most of the beating, while Ripley landed punches in between. The thought of killing Lexter flitted through Orven's mind, but passed as his anger began abating. Lexter wasn't a goblin, after all, and he had been useful, even if he was a spy. He even thought it was quite a shame about Lexter, as he was the kind of man Orven would have had liked to have under his command. Had Lexter not had any ties to Iaven or the King, Orven might have let him stay in their party and only beat him up as a warning. But he didn't trust Lexter now. Lexter was more cunning than Orven liked, and too popular. They had what they needed to know about Kronivar and could do without him.

Lexter lay on the cold ground, dirtied and curled in pain. Ripley gave him a few last kicks and watched him lying there holding his side.

"All right, let's pack up and go." Orven felt a great sense of relief and wanted to leave as soon as possible, before Max or Aaron started feeling sorry for Lexter. It was annoying how unwilling they could be to acknowledge their own best interests, he thought. Silently, they began packing and loading up the cart, and even Ripley was quieter than usual after a fight. Orven was glad to see that no one tried to argue with him, and he gloated on how right he had been about Lexter's being a "spy" and a "thief", quite forgetting that he himself had planted the dagger in Lexter's pack. He could see the others believed him now, or at least hoped they did. A few miles down the road and it wouldn't matter any more, he thought.

Lexter lay on the ground for almost an hour after the dwarves were gone, waiting for his pain to subside. He rolled over and pain shot up his leg. Ripley had kicked his shins and stomped on his left ankle, which felt sprained when he tried moving his foot.

Dusted with dirt and grit, Lexter shivered and groaned as he lay on the hard mud. He had nothing and no one again, and felt anew the sharp pain of Leland's loss. He cursed himself for not having taken the swords while he could, but was not entirely sincere in his regret. *Well*, he thought, *at least nothing's broken, and I'm not in Goblin country this time. And they didn't take my coat. I won't have to worry about Kronivar, either.* Lexter didn't know what to do next and didn't feel much like doing anything.

Morning wore on. At last Lexter rolled over and tried sitting up. He grunted as all his pains flared up again. He sat up anyway. Besides the sprain, his foot had fallen asleep and he winced at the sudden feeling of pins and needles in it. Lexter looked over to where their camp had been. He didn't think they had left anything for him —certainly not the sword they had bought him— and then noticed his pack laying on the ground. Max or Roy had probably insisted they leave it behind, though there was nothing of value in it anyway. Lexter looked the other way, across the fields toward the Veskwood Forest, and saw a small farmstead several hundred yards away.

Lexter summoned what little strength remained and tried to stand. His sides still hurt from the pummeling, and pain shot up from his ankle when he tried to walk. He hobbled over to his pack and sat down again. He was hungry and found he had nothing to eat. Pushing himself up, he stood, balancing most of his weight on his right leg. There was nothing nearby from which he could fashion a walking stick, but a few trees grew near the farmstead, where he intended to go anyway, so painfully, step by step, he started heading in that direction.

In the next hour Lexter stopped to rest several times and only covered half the distance to the farmstead. He began to wonder if he'd reach it by nightfall. Before him was a barn, a few outbuildings, and a small farmhouse. As he sat watching, a farmer emerged from the house, looked in his direction, and went into the barn. Moments later he was carrying a pitchfork, tines up, and walking over to Lexter.

"Ho, there! Who goes on my land?" he yelled.

Lexter remained sitting, watching the farmer approach and assessing him as he could. He was a lean old dwarf, in overalls and a thick heavy shirt. His scraggly gray beard hid a hard mouth, his lips pressed together and curled down at the ends, and dark eyes peered out from under a brow clenched in annoyance at his trespasser.

Lexter waited until he came closer so he could explain without shouting.

"Who are you and what are you doing here?" As the farmer drew near his expression softened a little when he saw how muddy and beaten Lexter was. He slowed his pace, curious as to why Lexter sat on the ground and made no effort to run away.

"Lexter Splide, sir. A traveler from Tolgard. Asking your pardon, sir, as I've been falsely accused and beaten, quite badly…" Lexter indicated his injuries and explained his situation. The farmer listened without saying much or changing expression, and Lexter had no idea whether the old dwarf believed him or not, or what he would do about it. The farmer nodded with neither pity nor sympathy in his gaze, only a tired sense of duty. "Alright," he nodded sternly, "we'll have to take ya in."

He lowered the pitchfork, turned around, and walked back to the barn. Lexter wondered if the farmer expected him to get up and follow, even after he had told him about the sprained ankle. Moments later the farmer returned with a wooden wheelbarrow. He set it down near Lexter, who thanked him several times while pulling himself up into it. Without a word, the old farmer picked up the wheelbarrow handles with less difficulty than Lexter would have guessed and began pushing Lexter towards the farmhouse. The farmer moved at a steady pace, taking the most direct route rather than the smoothest one. Lexter rumbled and bounced, feeling every jolt in his spine. Lexter could have been a big sack of potatoes from the way the farmer was hauling him, but he bit back his complaints and was glad to have help.

As they neared the little farmhouse, Lexter longed for the warmth of a fire and a good meal, and wished he had some way to repay the old farmer. But instead of going to the house, the farmer steered him into the barn.

"We'll putcha up in the barn, you can set on the hay here, you'd best stay off that foot tonight," he said, dumping Lexter on some hay by the wall. "Supper's at dusk, we'll bring a dish out t'ya."

The afternoon passed quietly. Lexter dozed awhile, finding the hay softer and less cold than the ground had been. He watched the shadow of the barn stretch farther and farther across the dooryard, until it merged into the darkening gloam around it. His stomach growled and dusk seemed interminably slow and long, until at last the farmhouse door opened and the farmer's wife, a short, cheerful lady, emerged with a cup and steaming plate. There was a small chunk of beef with gravy, potatoes, and corn, and a cup of cider to wash it down. Lexter thanked her and chatted with her, finding her more talkative than her husband. Her name was Essie Thelred and Lexter learned that she and her husband Arl had two sons, Mern and Thom, who had gone off to the Castle to join the King's troops, and a daughter, Vell, who was married and expecting, and lived on a farm only a mile away. When Lexter was done eating, he thanked her again, and she took the dishes and returned to the farmhouse.

Lexter half expected Arl Thelred would come out sometime that evening, to see how he was doing, but the old farmer never did. The sky darkened to black, and the windows in the farmhouse were lit into the evening, making Lexter wish he could join his hosts indoors. He slept awhile and woke later to find the barn doors had been shut. He woke several times that night, finding the hay to be not quite as uncomfortable as he thought it would be, and noticed he had already grown accustomed to the musty smell of the old barn.

A rooster crowed as dawn broke. Lexter awoke cold and stiff. He rolled over to find his pain had dulled a good deal. Even his ankle hurt less. Outside the barn he heard sounds of the morning's work beginning. Cows lowed and Lexter guessed they were being milked, and later he heard the old farmer cussing when he found his chicken coop broken into and a chicken missing. The sun still had not appeared above the mountains to the east when the barn door was unlatched and opened. Mrs. Thelred greeted Lexter and brought him a small breakfast of fresh eggs, milk, and bread.

"And how are you, this morning?" she asked.

"Better," Lexter said weakly.

"If you need to stay another day, I think it would be alright with Arl," she said.

"Thank you," said Lexter, eager for the breakfast.

A few minutes later he finished and returned the plate, with many thanks. Mrs. Thelred left and Lexter lay back on the hay, finding thinking much easier now that he had eaten something. He stretched his legs and moved his left ankle, standing up to see how it would take his weight. He could walk slowly, but only with pain. *Better to stay off it*, Lexter thought, settling down into the hay again.

Lexter looked around the barn. Two long sawblades hung on the wall and several sacks of feed sat beneath them. A spare horse's harness lay in the corner, near a plow. Bales of hay lined the wall. The whole place was modest and run-down, but had a calm to it that Lexter liked. After all the ill treatment of late from the Goblins and both Ambersheaths, he did not want to leave the Thelreds' hospitality too soon. It was this feeling more than the injury that allowed Lexter to accept their charity and remain there another day.

Lexter considered what he ought to do next. He couldn't go to Kronivar, but saw he could be useful in Farrenhale. It was a chance to earn his passage back to Tolgard. He was in no hurry now, and Farrenhale was several days' walk north, so he would get what rest he could.

Lexter relaxed and drifted off to sleep now and then throughout the afternoon, his awareness sharpening and fading like light on a meadow when clouds pass before the sun. He felt heavy and lazy, and considered staying a third day if they let him. No, he thought, he could not take advantage of the Thelreds; they had been kind, and he barely needed to stay a second night much less a third. He would have to leave the next day.

That night Lexter woke several times and found it difficult to get back to sleep. He had slept too much during the day and was not tired. He lay listening to the crickets, crows, and night sounds around the farm. The barn was at the back of the farmstead, near where the woods began, and now and then Lexter thought he heard rustling sounds outside. Deer maybe, or other animals foraging. Or perhaps hungry Goblin spies had broken into the farmer's chicken coop the night before. Lexter looked at the big wooden barn doors with the crack of night sky between them and felt less safe. He wished Leland was there with him, and realized that Leland's corpse was still lying on the ground somewhere, slowly decaying in the very same forest that began outside. Lexter shuddered and longed for morning to come. He resolved to leave after breakfast and walk as far north as he could that day.

When Mrs. Thelred woke him for breakfast, Lexter was surprised to find he had slept through the rooster's crowing. He talked with her, and Arl Thelred came by to see his progress. Lexter got up and walked around, and said he'd be leaving that morning. His ankle still hurt a great deal, but he smiled and hid his pain, moving around briskly to show them he was all right so they wouldn't worry about him.

The Thelreds were glad to hear Lexter was doing well. Lexter thanked his hosts, realizing that it had been a long time since he had thanked anyone so sincerely. After exchanging goodbyes, Lexter shouldered his pack and was off down path leading to the road. He kept his pace up in case they were watching him, until he was far enough away from the farmstead. His sides and back still ached but the swelling in his ankle had gone down. As long as he wouldn't have to run, he could continue walking and stopping to rest and not do too badly.

It was a cold, crisp, mid-November morning. The sun was out and the North Road was empty. As he walked, Lexter's thoughts turned to Farrenhale and Teska. By now Yolias must have passed on his news about the undermountain passage; the Dwarves might have even found it already. There really wasn't much else he could offer them, apart from helping to fight against the Goblins, and he was no soldier. Maybe he could help with armor fittings and taking care of swords and other weaponry, if they'd trust him. There'd be plenty of menial jobs, of course, and Lexter had not changed so much that he did not immediately balk at the idea. *It would be a waste not to put my cleverness to better use than that*, he thought, convinced that his avoidance of menial tasks would be most beneficial to the Dwarves. But he wanted to do something; of that much he was sure. He wanted to be useful to *someone*.

With frequent rest and a slower pace, Lexter was able to continue walking for most of the day. The sun passed overhead, shedding a faint warmth, until it slipped behind clouds. The sky grew overcast and a slow dusk set in, the air growing damp and cold. Lexter pulled his coat around him and looked for somewhere to stay the night.

Soon everything grew dim in the murky blue-gray dusk. There were no buildings or even farmsteads as far as Lexter could see. The road ahead went over a shallow hill, the incline reminding him of how tired he was. His ankle was feeling sore again, too. At the top of the hill, he looked out over the land but still there was little to be seen. A horse and cart were approaching in the distance, and Lexter hoped the driver would tell him what lay ahead, and how much farther he had to go.

As the cart drew closer, Lexter saw the driver was an old man with a long beard who was too tall to be a dwarf. With him was a dwarf, and others rode in the back. Lexter was about to hail them when the dwarf in the front seat turned and shouted something to the others. The cart came to a halt and the dwarf jumped down and ran to Lexter. Before Lexter realized what was happening, the dwarf had shoved him to the ground and jumped on top of him.

"Where are they, you *thief!*" shouted the dwarf.

"Wha—who—*Zammond!*" said Lexter when he got his breath back. "Ow! Stop, stop!"

"Zammond! That's enough!" The old man had come down from the cart and stood near where Lexter lay on the ground.

"It *is* him, I was right!" said Zammond. "Where are they, where are the swords?"

"I don't have them— I never had them!" cried Lexter, "I couldn't get Orven to stay in Teska, so I went along with them when they left, I thought maybe—"

"Liar!" Zammond growled.

By now the others had joined them. "Zammond, let go of him, let him speak!" said Wendolin. Zammond obliged and released Lexter, who sat looking at them, and at Wendolin in particular. Lexter hastily explained what had happened, and after a brief hesitation, told them how he could have stolen the swords but did not.

"They were *both* right there and you didn't take them?!" Zammond sat back in utter shock. "To think we could have had them both!"

"I just... couldn't bring myself to do it," Lexter apologized, "I didn't—"

"Well that was a fine time to change your mind about it!" snapped Zammond.

"Yolias did not ask him to steal the swords, Zammond," said Wendolin. "Only to bring Orven to Teska, or at least keep him in Farrenhale a day or two," he turned to Lexter, "which apparently was *still* too much to ask!"

Lexter collapsed, exhausted with grief and on the verge of tears. "I tried! I tried, but they were too excited about going to Kronivar! And believe me, I didn't want to go there!" He left out that it was his talk of Kronivar that had encouraged them to go there in the first place.

"Well, now we're all on our way to Kronivar," snapped Zammond. "All because of you."

"You are?" Lexter looked distraught.

Wendolin considered Lexter sternly. "If you could not keep Orven in Farrenhale you ought to have stayed there yourself. You could have helped search for the undermountain passage. We must get you back there as quickly as possible." Wendolin motioned the dwarves to step back, and Lexter got up wearily, brushing himself off.

"You mean we're going *back* to Farrenhale?" Iaven asked, while the others grumbled. The day before, their horse, which Wendolin had complained was long in tooth (and had been all they could get on short notice), collapsed and died, and they had spent almost the entire day trying to find another horse they might buy or borrow. The delay and inconvenience had put them all in a dour, irritable mood, and was partly responsible for Zammond's ferocity with Lexter. The thought of having to go all the way back to Farrenhale was unbearable to them.

"Not us, just Lexter," Wendolin said, "The King's troops should be camped at Halloway tonight, a few hours' ride south of here. They will take him to Farrenhale, or send him there with their herald. But we must ride; we have wasted enough time as it is." Wendolin led them all back to the cart. He had Lexter sit up front with him, which Lexter reluctantly did, and soon they were riding south again, into the night.

As they rode, Lexter told Wendolin all that had happened with Orven's party and what they intended to do in Kronivar. This led into a discussion of what Lexter knew about Aranstone, Greywood, and the Kronivar separatists, which Wendolin was interested in hearing. Lexter was glad to be able to talk and help, hoping it would lessen their anger with him. He still was intimidated by the old wizard, who interrogated him, prompting him along, and would not allow another moment to be wasted.

Crowded in the back of the cart, the dwarves longed for the day's travels to end. They had wearied of the cart's motion and looked forward to warming themselves around a campfire.

"If only he could have kept Orven in Farrenhale," said Zammond, not caring if Lexter heard him. "We wouldn't be out here."

Iaven was angry with Lexter for failing him, mainly because Lexter's success would have lessened his own failure. "Well, I suppose it's no different than expected," said Iaven, "I didn't think we'd see him again anyway."

"It's a shame we had to," said Zammond, "Unless he can be of use in Farrenhale. Maybe they'll put him to work there."

"What he says could be true enough, knowing Orven," said Hobley. "I think we ought to give Lexter a chance. And you know how stubborn Orven can be."

"True or not, it isn't much help." Zammond leaned back.

"If he knows anything useful, Wendolin will get it out of him," said Tillmore.

Iaven sat and let his anger disperse into the cold night around them. They were all recovering from a foul mood and there was no point in arguing, and thoughts of his own failings kept him from saying anything more about Lexter.

After Lexter finished answering questions they rode on in a sleepy but irritable silence the rest of the way. When at last the bonfires and tents of the King's troops near Halloway became visible in the darkness ahead, Iaven sighed with relief. Drawing closer, they saw tents with their flaps tied open, smoking campfires with soldiers walking past them, horses tethered, and carts being unloaded, and the bright bobbing points of torches moving about. After three lonely days on the road the busy camp was a welcome sight.

As they pulled up, soldiers approached, and Wendolin explained their errand and inquired as to what lodgings they might have for the night. When all was set, the dwarves shouldered their packs and climbed down, happy to be on their feet again. A soldier unhitched the horse, took the reins, and led the horse away to rest while two others stood talking with Wendolin and Lexter. When they left, Wendolin came over by the dwarves.

"We will stay in a tent on the edge of the camp, over yonder," Wendolin pointed toward the back of the camp, on the side near the mountains. "It is all they can spare, but it will do. Go toward the back and ask for a Captain Gallorne; they say he'll find us a tent. I will join you later, as I have to arrange the ride for Lexter, and learn what news there is from the Castle." And with a last sharp glance to make sure they were awake and heard him, Wendolin departed.

Iaven led the way through the camp, eager to find their tent, drop off his pack, and warm himself by the fire awhile before turning in to bed. Throughout the camp soldiers were walking around, eating together around the fires, talking, laughing, and telling stories by firelight. Several smoked pipes, and others played games with dice. The mood was one of good cheer, unlike the tense and wary feeling of the Farrenhale encampment. Iaven felt reassured the Dwarves would hold the Goblins at bay and was even less anxious about returning to the front once they had found Orven in Kronivar.

"Iaven? Iaven Ambersheath?"

Iaven turned, unable to identify the vaguely familiar voice. A young soldier around Iaven's age came up to him. In the bright firelight Iaven saw it was Daglind Ell, an acquaintance of his from Hillbrook.

"Where'd you come from? I didn't even know you were with us!" Daglind smiled. He was tall and boyish looking, with sandy brown hair, a youthful version of his father Dorand. "Hey, Hobley, Zammond..." he nodded to them.

"We just got here," said Iaven, "We're looking for Captain Gallorne—"

"Oh, I know where he is, follow me." Daglind led them through the camp. He kept pace with Iaven and turned to him again.

"So who's your Captain, are all five of you in the same company?" said Daglind.

"Well, no..." Iaven admitted, "We've just come down from Teska and are on our way to Kronivar—"

"Kronivar?" Daglind was surprised. "Farrenhale's the place to go. The King's sent troops to Kronivar, we just parted company with them four days ago near Greensward. Why didn't you just stay in Farrenhale?"

"It's a long story," said Iaven, hoping to sound too weary to answer any more questions. "We've been asked to recover some... weapons… in Kronivar. Important things." He thought of mentioning the Lost Swords of the Alliance, but knew it would only lead to more explaining. "I *am* going back to Farrenhale, as soon as I can, too," he added.

"In Kronivar, huh?" Daglind eyed Iaven suspiciously. "Why don't they just send someone up from there instead?"

"I wish they could," said Iaven. "But, well—"

"Seems a funny time to be traveling south." Daglind's voice was edged with disbelief and reproach. "Unless you really don't— Oh, there he is... Captain Gallorne!" He waved to an older dwarf nearing them. "These fellows were looking for you."

"Are they now?" Captain Gallorne was a stern-eyed, broad-shouldered dwarf with a curly beard and a smile that was as much of a threat as a welcome. "Well, the more the merrier, eh?"

"They'll only be staying the night, from the sound of it." Daglind nodded to Iaven. "Well, good luck in Kronivar!" he said, and went back the way they had come. Iaven wanted to tell him that he'd see him again later at the front, but Daglind was gone.

Captain Gallorne led them to their tent at the edge of the camp and found out who they were and when they had come. "So Wendolin is with you?" said Gallorne. "I shall have to hear more of your errand. Well, good evening to you all."

Iaven went inside the tent and unrolled his blanket. He was cold, and yet after meeting Daglind he no longer felt like going out and talking around the bonfires. He suddenly was even more tired than when they had entered the camp. The other dwarves dropped their packs and left, disappointed that Iaven was staying behind.

Iaven lay lost in thought a while and decided to turn in early. Some time later Wendolin peeked in where he lay and seemed in much better spirits.

"They'll take Lexter north when they leave tomorrow," Wendolin said, "And they've promised to take us to Kronivar by horseback. We'll make up for lost time, at least. Good night, now, and be ready to leave early tomorrow!"

After Wendolin had gone, Iaven lay down again, staring up at the poles that gave the tent its shape. He mulled over all the dwarves going to the front, and Hillbrook, and of the bad impression he had given Daglind. Back in Hillbrook, after the war, word was sure to get around, and people would wonder about him. Iaven rolled over and tried to sleep. *Let them talk*, he thought, *I've been faithful to what I have to do, even if they don't understand.* Iaven tried not to bother about their gossip and disapproval. Then he thought of Rhiane, with a pang of regret; *her* opinion mattered to him. But there was no point in worrying about either Rhiane or Hillbrook, or anything else, for that matter, until after the war.

Chapter 32.
Aboard the *Riantar*

"So we *are* going to *The Brown Badger*, then?" Aaron inquired. While Iaven and his friends were riding to Halloway, Orven's party was passing the outlying farmsteads around Kronivar. Talk of Lexter had died down after they had left him by the roadside two days earlier, but he was still in everyone's thoughts.

"We might as well," said Orven, sounding doubtful. "We're supposed to ask for a 'Trelt' there, who can take us to Aranstone."

"If Lexter was lying, he may have lied about them, too," said Aaron, "He may not know anyone in Kronivar. He just knew we wanted to hear about it."

"I don't think he made up all his stories," said Max. "Oh, no doubt he embellished them, but he seemed to know a lot about the place."

"He did help us in Farrenhale," Roy added, "At least he did that much. And if he lied about Kronivar, well, we're no worse off than if we hadn't met him."

"True," said Orven, "Well, we'll give it a try anyway."

"So what will we do if we don't find them?" said Aaron.

"I don't know," said Orven, "Maybe see what it's like at the garrison." Orven was most upset by his doubts regarding Lexter's story because it meant losing his shortcut to a good position among the troops. He and his friends deserved special treatment and privileges because of the swords, and he was simply not willing to start at the bottom like everyone else. If the captains failed to recognize that, he wasn't sure what he would do. And after his altercation at the Castle gate, the thought of having to go to the garrisons was not easy to bear.

Soon they rode into Old Town and pulled into the dooryard of *The Brown Badger*. The inn was busier than usual, the common rooms full and bustling with people. The King's troops had arrived a couple days earlier and were now spending their evenings around town. The air was close and loud with shouts in the *Badger*'s main common room, the mood so festive it was hard to believe Kronivar was readying for war. Orven and the others filed through the crowd and stood awhile, until they saw some dwarves leaving and took their booth along the wall just in time before others reached it.

When everyone was seated, Orven stood up again. "Get me a beer when our barmaid comes," he said. "I'll go ask about Trelt." And he merged back into the crowd.

"I still can't believe it about Lexter," Roy said. "Could Orven have been right about him?"

"I don't know," said Max. "It was odd how quickly Orven found that dagger. I suppose there's no point wondering about it now. I'm just worried that wherever we go Orven won't be happy. I would have gladly joined the soldiers at the Castle. Let's hope he likes it here enough."

"Yes," said Roy, "unless we really can get better positions here. After Orven's fight at the Castle, he has little choice, anyway."

"Even Farrenhale would have been fine," said Ripley, "I wonder if we'll be sent back there. I'm tired of all this traveling around."

"Me, too," said Max, "Maybe we ought to insist on staying here, even if Orven changes his mind again." The others nodded.

The barmaid came around and took their order, and afterward they sat awhile listening to the tumult of voices around them.

"Well, whatever happens, I just hope we all come out of it all right," said Max. "And we still have a plenty of treasure left. Enough to settle us nicely in Hillbrook, certainly."

"Orven thinks we ought to settle in Kronivar," said Aaron, "But I know what you mean; I miss home, too, and I'll probably go back. Oh, here's Orven..." They looked up and watched as Orven threaded his way through the crowd until he sat down again at their table. He looked glum and disappointed.

"We're out of luck. The bartender said he'd never heard of any 'Trelt'," Orven said.

"Are you sure you asked the right one?" said Max.

"Hurd Purrlow, and he was just as Lexter described him," said Orven, "At least he got that right." Orven pounded a fist on the table. "Why did we trust him? We should have never gotten our hopes up."

"So the garrison's our next stop?" asked Aaron.

Orven shot Aaron a cold glance and looked down again. "We'll take a look at it, but... I don't know..."

"Orven," said Max, "we can't expect to become captains right away, can we? Even if we have to start out like everyone else, well, that's not so bad. We can work our way up, too, right?"

Orven looked up at Max. "We shouldn't have to, Max. I was hoping we wouldn't have to."

During a rare pause in the evening's business, Hurd Purrlow stepped into a back room to refill a few jugs. A few candles burned on a small table, and several dwarves sat talking there among the barrels.

"Someone was looking for you, Trelt," said the bartender.

Trelt looked up irritably. "Who was it?"

Purrlow shook his head. "Dunno. Some dwarves, never seen 'em before."

Trelt set down his glass and got up, disliking the disturbance but curious, nonetheless. "Point them out to me."

Soon Trelt was making his way through the crowded room, careful to stay off to the side and go around the long way, in case they knew what he looked like. At last he stood a few feet away from Orven's booth, with his back turned. He scanned the room, pretending to be looking for someone, but kept his ear facing the dwarves.

"Well maybe it was poor judgment on our part," said Orven. "but we've talked about Lexter long enough. So let's just forget about him, all right? We planned on coming here anyway..."

"We were," said Aaron, "but we never decided what we would do—" Aaron stopped suddenly as they noticed a thin dwarf standing by their table watching them.

"I am Trelt. I am told you were looking for me."

There was a surprised pause as they realized Lexter was right, and then Roy and Ripley slid around to the back of the booth, making room for Trelt to sit on the edge of the bench. With obvious hesitation, Trelt sat down with them, across the table from Orven.

"We are interested in joining with Aranstone and Greywood," said Orven, feeling uneasy under Trelt's unwavering gaze.

"Are you?" said Trelt. He supposed Lexter could have hired assassins to pretend they wanted to join Aranstone, but these dwarves were so naïve and unpolished that he dismissed the idea. Still, he thought, something would have to be done with them; he had no idea how much Lexter had told them. "I can take you to them tonight." He glanced around at them. "How many are you?"

"Just the five of us," said Orven, suddenly feeling he had answered too easily.

Trelt continued eyeing them. "You mentioned Lexter Splide. How do you know him?" Trelt watched for their immediate reaction.

Seeing that what Lexter had told them was true, Orven's hopes began rising again. "He did ...business with us," said Orven. He realized he was not quite sure how Lexter had known Aranstone and the others.

"Did he? And how is he doing these days?" Again, Trelt watched Orven's reaction.

"He's . . . fine, we parted company on the North Road," said Orven.

"Didn't care to come along and see us again, did he?"

Orven shrugged. "Had other business, I suppose."

"*Other business*, yes..." said Trelt. "Well, it'll just be the five of you, then. Are you ready to leave now?" Just then the barmaid arrived carrying five mugs. Orven generously handed her more than enough coins. "And one for our friend here," he told her, indicating Trelt. Trelt was not pleased, but said nothing. He sat back, making a great effort to be patient. He motioned to the barmaid, told her something, and she nodded and left.

A moment later the barmaid brought Trelt's beer, and two of the dwarves who had been sitting in the back room with Trelt came and stood near their table. Trelt emptied his mug quickly. "We had best leave now," he said.

Orven nodded and everyone hurried and finished their drinks, Aaron taking the longest. Soon they rose from the table and followed the two dwarves, while Trelt came behind them, the swords at Orven's and Max's belts catching his eye.

Outside, dusk had already deepened into night, the days having grown short. Once they were all in the dooryard, Orven led them to the cart and climbed up in front. Trelt motioned for Orven to move over and climbed up and took the reins. Orven slid down the bench, thinking Trelt rather brazen to not let him drive his own cart.

They drove through Kronivar, taking what seemed to be a secretive and very indirect route. Orven sensed something not quite aboveboard, but waited to see what would happen.

At last they arrived at the docks. Trelt brought the horse to a halt and tethered it there. Large merchant ships lay at anchor out in the bay, and nearby a few small piers reached over the dark waters. Trelt led them down one of the piers, though Orven saw no boat at the end of it. He exchanged an anxious glance with Max, and followed. At the pier's end, low in the water, a small rowboat was moored. Trelt climbed down and sat in the bow, the two dwarves with him settling into the stern. Two planks seats were left in between for Orven and his friends, as well as the oars; they were expected to do the rowing. Orven was reluctant to get in the boat and wondered what they were getting themselves into.

Orven hesitated. "Where are we going?" He looked down at the rowboat rocking gently in the black waters. "I've never rowed a boat before," he said.

"You'll do fine. Climb in!" Trelt grumbled, growing impatient again.

Orven was ashamed to appear afraid and stepped into the boat, raising his arms as it swayed with his weight. He gripped the sides and carefully sat down. Max and the others followed apprehensively, wary of the unstable and now-crowded boat. At last Trelt untied them and pushed off from the pier. He watched as Orven and Max fitted the oars into the oarlocks and tried rowing. It took a few minutes before they had the motion and rhythm they needed. When Trelt was satisfied they drifted out farther into the bay.

"We are going to the *Riantar*," said Trelt, indicating a large merchant vessel anchored out in the bay. "There you will meet Aranstone and Greywood, as you desire."

While rowing, Orven again wondered what they were getting involved in. The secrecy intrigued him, but he did not like going offshore, unable to return if they changed their mind. Only the rowing gave Orven a slight sense of control and kept his panic from surfacing.

"These are the King's troops we'll be joining, aren't they?" asked Orven.

Trelt smiled in the dark. "The Castle troops are in the garrison, if that's what you mean. But they aren't the only ones defending Kronivar. Grawson is Duke of Kronivar and the surrounding area, and each of his five Counts raises their own troops as well. Most are from their own counties, but occasionally some are . . . hired from other lands."

"You mean mercenaries?" said Max.

"If you like," said Trelt, "or, 'soldiers for hire', if you prefer. It's all for the defense of the Kingdom." He smiled again and the dwarves in the stern seemed more jovial as well.

"I see," said Orven, wondering now if joining the Castle troops in Kronivar would have been better. Yet here he might have a better chance of becoming a captain or higher; it was worth a try, anyway, he thought.

As they approached, the *Riantar* towered over them, a great two-masted merchant ship, its sails furled on the yardarms for the night. The crescent moon cast a thin light on the black rigging hanging from the masts. Woodcarvings framed windows in the hull, lantern light glowing within them. The main deck was lined with wooden railings, beyond which crowds of men and dwarves swarmed on deck, shouting and cheering as though a fight were in progress.

The rowboat came alongside the ship, bumping against the great wooden hull bowing up over them. Orven and Max did as Trelt directed them. Men leaned over the railing, laughing down at them. A gate swung open and a rope ladder fell down the side of the ship. The dwarves maneuvered the rowboat under the end of the ladder, and moored the rowboat to the ship. Trelt stood and pulled himself up the ladder, while the other two dwarves stayed behind to see Orven and his friends up to the deck. Orven, feeling he ought to lead, stepped forward first. He moved cautiously, grasping the ladder anxiously as the rowboat rocked under the shifting load. More laughter erupted from the men above on deck. Angry and ashamed of his nervousness, Orven gripped the rungs of the rope ladder tightly, afraid to let go of one until he held the one above it. As he neared the top, one of the men grabbed his hand, pulling him aboard. Orven nodded in thanks and turned away, trying to regain his composure. Behind him, Max and the others were helped aboard.

Around a hundred men were on deck and a few dozen dwarves as well. A series of fights, or rather contests, were going on, the recruits proving their mettle to justify a higher wage or position. Orven felt the scrutiny of the crowd, regarding the newcomers with suspicion, amusement, and open contempt. Scraggly beards lined scarred and sunburned faces leering at them in the half-light; soldiers of fortune, adventurers, fugitives, deserters, and untrained roughhousers, a wild and curious bunch seduced by fortune and a chance to fight. Orven felt out of place, straining to appear as confidently at ease as everyone else. Max was wary and wondered if Orven felt as he did. Roy and Aaron stood against the railing, already regretting having come and hoping they would not be asked to fight. Ripley looked around wide-eyed, excited to finally be joining some kind of troops, though they were different then he expected, and he was disappointed that the men outnumbered the dwarves.

Looking around, Orven saw three men watching over everything from atop the forecastle. One, in uniform, he guessed to be the ship's Captain. Next to him stood a dark-haired, broad-shouldered man in a long brown cloak, and a tall, older man with a long gray beard in a coat of dark crimson. Trelt climbed the forecastle's stairs and told them of the newcomers. As he spoke, he pointed to Orven's party and they turned to regard the dwarves below on deck.

"They spoke of Lexter Splide?" Aranstone was amazed. "It is good you brought them here. They may be untrained and of little use to us, but we shall test them and see." Aranstone turned back to see the results of the two fights below on deck.

"You are right about the swords, Trelt," said Greywood, "rather ornate for dwarves such as these. We shall see what they are about."

"When these fights are over, bring them out and match them with Faltusk and Harrel, and have the two with the jeweled swords go first," Aranstone told Trelt.

Greywood laid a hand on Aranstone's shoulder to stop him. "No, have Khale and Pyrwoed test them, and let Faltusk and Harrel test the others."

Aranstone turned in surprise. "Khale and Pyrwoed? The newcomers wouldn't stand a chance, they could even be killed if they are not careful."

"Perhaps," said Greywood. "That would be unfortunate. But so would letting them go. Either they will prove themselves useful, or the swords will be put to better use in more skilled hands. At any rate we will not have to worry about what Lexter may or may not have told them. Do not think it cruel, for they have come here on their own and must be tested like everyone else."

"They need not defeat our best fighters to be considered acceptable. Still, if they own swords such as those, they may be more than they appear." Aranstone turned back to Trelt who was awaiting his word. "Let it be done as he says."

"Bring their swords up here to us, if they fail," Greywood added.

Below on deck, Orven and Max watched the two swordfights going on. Had they not been told otherwise, they would have thought it a fight to the death. Aranstone's men were better dressed, had finer weapons, and were winning in both cases. Their opponents were big fellows who lacked the speed and poise of Aranstone's men, and their moves grew more desperate as they saw they were losing. The swordsmen leapt about, angling around the main mast while narrowly avoiding the capstan and windlass. Often the crowd pulled back from them as they veered about the deck.

One of Aranstone's men found an opening and surprised his opponent, knocking him to the deck and wrenching the sword from his hand. The big fellow was panting hard, and raised his hand in deference to the victor. The audience's attention shifted immediately to the other fight, which was less even and ended in a clear victory for Aranstone's man. Orven watched both fights, his heart beating hard, knowing his turn would come. He bit back his fear, readying himself for the inevitable, and saw worry and concern welling in his friends' eyes.

"It's just a test," Orven whispered to Max.

"They seem pretty serious to me," said Max. "Even with our swords... Orven, we just don't have that kind of experience!"

Aaron and Roy pressed their backs against the wooden railing. Aaron looked down into the black waters, wanting nothing more than to be back on dry land. He knew Roy felt as he did, even if he wouldn't admit it. Maybe they could decline and be let go; they'd be accepted at the garrison. There was no reason they couldn't join the Castle troops instead. Ripley, on the other hand, enjoyed watching the fight. He was a little wary, but thought Orven was right, it was only a test; they just wanted to see what he could do.

"Good work, men," Aranstone addressed the two losing swordsmen who turned to him as they got up off the deck. "A good effort. Yet we cannot afford to hire all. You may join us," he indicated the big fellow who had fought reasonably well. Then, to the other, he added, "And we wish you a fine voyage home." The second man shook his head in anger and cursed, humiliated, and two guards escorted the man below deck. The other was brought over to a scribe, who recorded his name and the terms of his employment.

"You see?" said Orven, "They took him on even though he was beaten. They just want good fighters."

"I didn't think the other one did all that badly!" said Max. "I just hope I do as well."

"You've got Halix!" said Orven, "What are you worried about?"

"These men aren't from Kronivar," said Roy. "Do you think they'll just let us go, if we don't make it?"

"It'll be worse if we don't fight," said Aaron. "And maybe not that much better if we do. We should have never come out here."

"No," Roy agreed.

Trelt came around and took the names of Orven and his friends and brought the list up to Aranstone. Greywood looked over and glanced at it.

"We are not quite done yet for tonight," Aranstone spoke to the crowd, "Our newcomers are Dwarves of Itharia, come to fight for their King." Some jeers and laughter erupted from the audience as if this were a joke. "We will put all five to the test. Ripley Ironshard, you will fight Faltusk. Roy Goldbeard, you will fight Harrel. And Aaron Spurro—" Aranstone looked down at Aaron who was visibly nervous even from where Aranstone stood on the forecastle, "you will be matched with Arehon. . . . And as for Maxmire Huffe and Orven Ambersheath, you will fight Khale and Pyrwoed."

There was a gleeful gasp from some of the onlookers and anticipatory applause. The crowd backed up against the sterncastle to make room for all the fights and looked around eagerly to where Khale and Pyrwoed were standing. Max had a sudden sinking feeling and turned to Orven. "Sounds like we're getting quite a challenge."

"Let's hope we're up to it," said Orven. He let out a nervous sigh and unsheathed Gorflange as Max drew Halix.

"To give them room, we will test Ripley, Roy, and Aaron first, and then Max and Orven afterward," Aranstone announced. There were sounds of playful disappointment from the crowd, but they soon became quiet as the fighters spread out across the deck in front of the forecastle. The three pairs of opponents stood facing one another, their bodies turned to the side and sword arms raised, their eyes locked on each other waiting for the signal from Aranstone. A hush fell over the crowd.

Aranstone paused, watching them and letting tension mount. "Begin!" he shouted.

Yells and cheers went up from the crowd as the fighters began stalking each other in broad arcs. Soon swords clanged and flashed in the lantern light. On the deck's starboard side, with his back to the forecastle, Aaron watched his opponent closely, trying to keep from being distracted by the crowd. He fended off a few blows, but kept backing up and moving to the side, avoiding instead of attacking. Arehon saw this and became more aggressive. He was a man of small build, with a young-looking face that belied his ferociousness. Aaron knew what was happening and attempted an attack, but was too tentative in his movements. He tried to hold his own and ward off Arehon, hoping it would be enough for acceptance.

Cold metal blades clanked and rang in the damp night air, rising above the din of the onlookers. An agile clomp of feet sounded as the fighters danced about the wooden deck. Roy was caught between the other two matches, moving around and trying to gauge Harrel's weaknesses. Roy eluded his opponent's sword as well as he could, dashing in with a jab or a blow where he thought his guard was lowered. Harrel fended him off each time, but Roy kept looking for an opportunity. He felt constrained by Aaron's and Ripley's fights and worried about getting hit, all while keeping his eye on Harrel. Roy was nervous and told himself it was all just a test, not a life-and-death battle, and hoped Harrel would remember that as well.

On the port side of the ship, Ripley and Faltusk attracted the most attention from the crowd. Ripley shouted and whooped and taunted Faltusk, who was growing annoyed with his antics. Ripley swung wide and wild, lunging and jumping about, his energy all he had to make up for his lack of discipline. That he often did not do what was safest, best, or even wise, gave Ripley an unpredictable quality that Faltusk disliked, but he knew that as soon as Ripley tired he would be lost. Several times Ripley came dangerously close to Roy and Harrel, distracting both of them.

Orven and Max stood at the front of the crowd watching the fights and measuring up Khale and Pyrwoed, who stood on deck in front of the forecastle. As the sword fighting continued, Greywood motioned Trelt over and spoke to him. Trelt nodded and descended the stairs to the main deck. He walked over to Khale and Pyrwoed and spoke to them. They listened and looked disbelievingly to Greywood and then back to Trelt. One of them asked him something, and Trelt shook his head. They nodded reluctantly and returned their attention to the fights as Trelt went back up to the foredeck.

"What was *that* all about?" said Max, but Orven was too caught up in the fight, cheering Ripley on. Max was about to say something again when a shout rose from the onlookers on the starboard side. Aaron had fallen to deck, the sword knocked out of his hand. Arehon stood above Aaron, holding his sword over him. Aaron got up slowly and Arehon motioned him over to the railing, where they both stood watching the other fights.

When Ripley saw that Aaron had fallen, he used the brief moment of distraction and dashed clear around Roy and across the deck toward the forecastle, to get a new angle on Faltusk. Faltusk side-stepped around Harrel and engaged Ripley again. Loud shouts seemed to confirm the crowd's approval of Ripley's unorthodox fighting style.

Roy was tiring and knew Harrel was more than his match. Roy's movements were too awkward, cost him too much energy, and Harrel usually expected them. As he lost confidence, Roy became bolder in his moves, and during a backswing Harrel smiled and jumped in, swinging his sword right at Roy's head. At the last moment he turned the blade so that only its flat side hit Roy instead of the edge, smacking Roy on the ear. Roy's heart leapt and he lost his balance in a flash of panic. The crowd jeered as he fell to the deck, and bright orange motes swam before his eyes. Dizzily he got up, and followed Harrel to the deck's railing.

Ripley had the whole deck now, and was still dancing madly about. All eyes were on him and he, too, was tiring and slowing down, more hesitant and less sure of his moves, deciding where to spend his waning energy. Faltusk eyed Ripley closely. He had things well in hand and was merely waiting for an opportunity. Ripley flailed about, but saw he was outmatched. He swung and his sword rang as Faltusk's met it in counterparry. Ripley pulled back and took a wide step, turning so as to swing around at Faltusk from the other side. Deftly, Faltusk leaned back slightly, extending his leg, and hooked his foot on Ripley's as he turned. Ripley lost his balance and fell to the deck. Even as he landed, Faltusk was already standing over him, his blade inches away from Ripley's face. Frustrated and panting hard, Ripley knew he was beaten and relaxed.

"Unfair!" shouted Orven, "He tripped him!" Orven was upset by Aaron's and Roy's losses and expected them, but he was hoping Ripley would win, and for a while it had seemed possible. "Unfair!" Orven cried, and began walking out onto the deck with Gorflange. Max followed behind him, to urge him to not interfere, but looked as if he were coming to help Orven. Immediately sensing danger, Khale and Pyrwoed sprang forward to meet them, separating them and engaging them without warning.

This unexpected and abrupt start of the next two contests excited the crowd as nothing had before and they glanced up to see if Aranstone would stop it. But Aranstone stood and nodded, and they cheered all the louder. Ripley crawled off to the side near Roy, not wanting to miss a bit of Orven's fight, and Faltusk moved over by the railing, having completely forgotten about Ripley as the next two battles began.

Orven's fight occupied the starboard side of the deck, and Max's the port side. Khale and Pyrwoed were in peak form, sharp as hawks. The four swordsmen's movements were tense with restrained energy, careful and calculating. Their blades clashed less often, but their swings and blows were well-placed and cleverly done. Sometimes after a quiet moment a burst of fighting would erupt, setting the crowd ablaze with excitement.

At first Max was hesitant in wielding his sword and doubted his own ability, but he found Halix light in his hand and incredibly deft. He thrilled at its touch and how well he was doing, and his confidence grew quickly. With Halix his movements seemed faster and easier, allowing him to hold his own against Pyrwoed. He admired Pyrwoed's style and tried to predict his moves. Max was often wrong, but learning fast. Pyrwoed was more aggressive, forcing Max back several times, and it took all Max's effort just to keep up with him.

Orven was initially frightened by Khale's confidence and how swift and sure his movements were. He realized that Khale had initially underestimated him, but Khale's surprise soon passed and his attack grew even more formidable as he understood Orven better. Yet Orven was pleased with himself and had never felt more at ease with Gorflange. He had fought the goblins with one gem in it, and fought the Castle guard and Iaven with two gems in it, but now with all three gems the sword felt amazingly light, its movements smooth and effortless. He seemed to know what he had to do to keep pace with Khale. It was as if he could think faster, or as though all around him had slowed, and he was able to anticipate Khale's moves and react to them as needed. He even was able to sense openings and weaknesses, though he rarely made the best use of them. Orven's amazement and enthusiasm, combined with his awe for Gorflange, distracted him, and at last Khale swung and nicked him in the shoulder.

The lanterns hung on deck tilted in a cold wind and their light flickered. Orven had stepped back as Khale had swung, and his wound would have been much deeper had he not done so. Suddenly Orven saw anger and fire flaring in Khale's eyes, his pride as one of Aranstone's best men, and his determination to bring Orven down in front of the crowd. Everyone saw the injury and a hushed expectation fell on the crowd. Even Max stole a glance at Orven to see what had happened. Khale renewed his attack, changing his direction and tactics constantly. Orven began backing up and stepping to the side, and then realized this was just what Khale wanted. Orven was being backed into Max and Pyrwoed's fight. He tried to angle away from it, but Khale caught him, forcing him closer towards them. Orven's attention was divided between Khale and Pyrwoed now and he strained to keep an eye on both of them. Unable to move out of the way, he had to swing and deflect Pyrwoed's sword. Khale used the opening to swing at Orven but Max caught his blade in time. The four fighters shifted around, and for a moment Orven and Max had exchanged opponents. The crowd of onlookers howled and roared now, arms waving, barely able to contain themselves.

Khale and Pyrwoed moved across the deck in opposite directions, drawing Orven and Max apart. Orven recoiled and Khale leapt at him, brandishing his sword. Afraid he would be attacked as Khale passed, Max swung at Khale. Khale reacted immediately and Max's attention was diverted. Pyrwoed landed a blow that caught Max as he pulled away and he fell to the deck. Pyrwoed jumped forward as Max fell, looking as though he would strike Max again. Orven screamed in anger and dashed at Pyrwoed and Khale, taking them both on. They pressed him back and Orven began fending them both off. The crowd grew louder still, cheering for Orven. Men climbed the rigging and lined the top of the sterncastle, all straining for a better view of the fight. Aaron, Roy, and Ripley had forgotten about their own losses and trembled as they watched Orven.

Orven was red with rage, wielding Gorflange fast and fierce, but with both Khale and Pyrwoed circling him it was only a matter of time before they cut him down. Orven swung in tight, controlled arcs, fending blows and attacking in the same move. Gorflange whirled clanging into one blade, angling and slicing through the air just in time to stop the other, and then back again. Orven's muscles tensed and ached. The crowd's roar rose, almost drowning out the constant ringing of blades, until a loud shout was heard.

"Enough!" Aranstone's voice thundered out over the din of the crowd. "Enough! Khale, Pyrwoed, pull back! He has proven himself." Greywood shot Aranstone a cold glance, which Aranstone returned. Aranstone turned to the crowd, raising his arms for silence. "Orven has done well—" Here the crowd cheered so loudly that Aranstone was momentarily drowned out. He paused, waiting for the sound to subside. "Orven has done well, and so has Max. We will take them on." Another cheer went up. Aranstone raised a hand to the crowd and gradually they quieted again. "Ripley has also shown himself to be quite a fighter," —here there was some cheering and laughing— "Untrained, yes, but certainly a raw talent. With guidance, he will grow in skill." Ripley was cheered again, and some men nearby congratulated him and slapped him hard on the back.

Aranstone looked around and became more solemn in tone. "As for Aaron and Roy, however, we will not be taking either of them on." Even at this there was some clapping from the mercenaries. Max, still recovering, stood up, shocked at the announcement.

Trelt stepped closer to Greywood. "You're not going to just let them go, are you?"

"You know what to do. Take them back to shore by boat, and when you are out of the sight of the ship, deal with them then," Greywood replied, keeping his words too low for Aranstone to overhear.

Below on deck, Orven stepped forward and looked up to the forecastle, and the crowd quieted again. "Lord Aranstone," Orven said, "my friends and I come here together. We have come a long way, and through much. We have always fought side by side; take us all on together, sir. All of us or none of us!"

The mercenaries liked Orven's attitude and applauded him, admiring his loyalty to his friends. They looked to Aranstone on the forecastle, curious what he would do with these brazen young dwarves. Seeing Aranstone was considering his reply, they grew quiet again and waited.

The night wind blew through everyone's hair and across their faces. Aranstone stood back a few feet from the railing, thinking. He did not want to appear to be giving in to the crowd's demands, but he was amused by Orven's boldness and agreed with his sentiment.

"He has won the crowd's favor," Aranstone said quietly to Greywood. "I have a mind to grant him what he asks." He glanced at Greywood. "You were right about the swords."

Greywood leaned close to Aranstone. "We'll want to keep an eye on Orven, that's certain. We could make him a captain, —a minor one, of course— put his friends under him, along with a few of my men who will win his trust and keep a close watch on him."

"Yes," said Aranstone, considering, "he'll have his friends and a few men besides. Not too many, though. He has their respect, but he will have to prove himself a good leader."

"True," said Greywood, "I wonder how well he or his friend would do without those swords. Or what Khale or Pyrwoed could do with them."

"Orven and Max did well enough," said Aranstone. "And we cannot give their swords to others now."

"No," said Greywood, "which is why we must keep them both within our reach."

Aranstone considered a moment longer and then strode back to the railing. "We will take all of you on," he told Orven. "Your friends will be your responsibility and under your command, along with a few other men. We have decided to offer you a position as a captain." The crowd voiced its enthusiastic approval, and Orven raised his sword and accepted. Men and dwarves came forward and surrounded Orven, congratulating him and slapping his back and shoulders. Orven was simply overwhelmed by it all. The raucous sound and the press of the crowd on all sides were almost too much to bear. He turned looking for Max and the others, but they were unable to get through to him. Orven had never had such a reception and was pleased and a bit frightened all at once.

Soon all the mercenaries were milling about on the main deck. Now that the testing and hiring was done for the evening, Aranstone's men opened barrels of wine and mead. Mugs and tankards were passed around, and the noisy celebration continued.

Aranstone gazed at the boisterous crowd below on deck. "I hope they will prove ready when the day comes to make our stand. The time for training is short."

"Whether well-trained, seasoned soldiers or untried roughhousers, all will add to our number," said Greywood.

"They shall," said Aranstone, "though an army's size is no assurance of victory."

"True," said Greywood, "Unless Orming can convince Abern and Sherleaf to join us, that may be our only hope."

Lanterns lit the *Riantar*'s decks long into the night. From the shore the sounds of merriment were muted and the lighted deck much fainter, though the dark shape of the ship stood out in the moonlit bay beyond the docks of Kronivar. A short distance into the city, Count Orming stood on the uppermost balcony of his mansion overlooking the Silver Sea. His long face tapered into a small but firm jaw, and his lips curled in an austere expression as he contemplated the evening's events. The lights aboard the *Riantar* were barely visible at that distance, but he was well aware of what was taking place there. Of his three generals, he trusted Aranstone the most, though Orming was still doubtful and eager to hear of the outcome of the hirings. So, too, were Counts Abern and Sherleaf, who favored the idea of Kronivar as its own nation-state but were unwilling to back him. They had been on the verge of doing so, until the King's troops had arrived, adding to those in the garrison.

Along with the troops, the King's orders concerning the final deployments for the defense of Kronivar had also been sent by courier. They were delivered directly to Grawson, the Duke of Kronivar, and all were awaiting his commands. It was expected that some of the garrisoned troops would be sent to hold the Gundithe Plateau overlooking Greensward, both to guard the Mountain Road and Castle from attack, as well as to act as a rear guard should the Goblins attempt to take Kronivar. As yet, none had been sent, though it seemed likely they would be very soon.

A servant tentatively leaned out the balcony door behind Orming. "Counts Abern and Sherleaf have arrived, my lord."

"Show them up," said Orming.

The servant withdrew, and after a minute or two, Abern and Sherleaf came out onto the balcony, still wearing their brocaded coats.

"Lovely evening, isn't it?" Count Abern was a short robust man, powerfully built, with a jolly but wry expression. Behind him Count Sherleaf stood, taller, leaner, and somewhat more solemn, his arms folded and his long, red face ashen in the dark of the balcony.

Orming turned to them as Sherleaf shut the door behind him. "I hope so, but I'll wait to hear from the *Riantar* before saying for certain. Any word from Grawson?"

"None," said Sherleaf, "Either the King told him to wait, or has allowed him to make certain decisions regarding the defense of Kronivar, and he's still deciding."

"Or both," said Orming, "Grawson may be biding his time. With Raymin and Mothmoon behind him, and the garrison, he can afford to wait." He watched the other two Counts for their reaction. "Unless both of you are with me." As it lay within his dukedom, Grawson had command of the garrisoned troops, and the other two Counts, Raymin and Mothmoon, were also loyal to the King. If Abern and Sherleaf joined Orming, and some of the garrisoned troops were sent to hold the Gundithe Plateau, the balance would be tipped in their favor, and the three Counts would probably have enough of an army to take control of Kronivar.

"We are," said Abern, though unconvincingly, "provided all is in our favor. It seemed so until the troops arrived; but now the garrison's overflowing. Nearly all the King's troops are at the front or stationed here."

"There would have been more at the front and fewer here had the King less suspicion regarding Kronivar," said Sherleaf with a hint of reproach, "I wonder how much he knows about your doings, Orming."

"Difficult to say. Very little, I should think; and yet the King has his misgivings, I am sure," said Orming. So far none of the Counts had openly opposed either Grawson or the Castle, but rumors of separatist activity still circulated. Orming suspected that the King had some idea of what might be happening, but so far it had been made to look a few pockets of insurgents rather than an organized movement, and certainly nothing that could be linked to one of the Counts. A few Castle spies had been rooted out and caught, although one had gotten away. "And yet soon, with enough men behind us and the right moment at hand, none of that will matter any more," said Orming, as much to himself as to Abern and Sherleaf.

"But do we have enough men?" asked Abern.

Orming looked out to the *Riantar* again and the others followed his gaze. "Almost," he said, "and after tonight, . . . we should."

Chapter 33.
Thunder in the Valley

All was quiet and still in the Arinzei Valley. Darkness was abating in the eastern sky. Two Dwarven soldiers, Tímald and Rolen, surveyed the valley and stayed low behind an outcropping of rock.

Rolen glanced to the east. "We ought to go back, Tímald. It's already light out, and we're too far from the path."

Tímald's unwavering gaze remained on two Goblin huts along the cliff wall. "We should have a look in those first," he said, "then we'll go."

"Let's look now, then; we've waited long enough." For nearly an hour they had watched for any activity or reason to believe the huts were not abandoned. There was no smoke or sign of a fire, no movement or sound. And yet they had to be sure before they could chance a look inside the huts.

Tímald slipped around the outcropping and crept toward the closer of the two huts. Rolen followed silently behind him. At last they reached the threshold, and seeing the hut was empty, they entered. Cold, damp air blew out at them like a sigh of dread. Both dwarves gasped at the wide, deep darkness at the back of the hut. "The passage," Tímald whispered. They stepped aside to let in more light, and saw the passage was cut into the rock wall of the cliff and extended deep into the mountain. They stared into its depths, steeling their stomachs against the rank goblin smell wafting out of it.

"Good. Let's go now." Rolen was tense and anxious. Dawn broke and a thin pink glow spilled across the valley and into the hut, the doorway of which was angled to the east to avoid the gaze of the far-off Dwarven watchtower. Rolen motioned Tímald aside.

"Look, on the ground," said Rolen. On the hut's mud floor, in front of the passage, the faint light revealed dozens of goblin footprints overlapping. All pointed into the undermountain passage. "More than a few spies. Looks like a small army passed through here."

Tímald knelt and looked closely at the footprints. A slight amount of water had collected in them. "Two or three days old, I'd reckon." As he looked, the footprints grew dark as the doorway light was blocked. A low, laughing growl came from outside. Tímald looked up as the goblin's broadsword smote Rolen, dropping him to the ground. Tímald fell back, the goblin came at him, and there was no escape.

The encampment near Halloway was still in the mountains' shadow as dawn neared. Dew beaded on the grass. A solitary crow's cawing echoed in the lonely sky. On the north side of camp, Daglind Ell sat watch with Mischief, a frolicsome beagle traveling with the troops who had become something of a mascot. Another soldier, whom Daglind did not know, stood guard on the southern side of the camp and was slowly pacing about in the distance. Daglind sat on a barrel at the edge of camp, eager to be relieved and get some rest before they struck camp and moved north again. Mischief had woken only an hour earlier, lively as ever.

Daglind glanced around, not expecting much. There was little to worry about while they were still so far south, but in two days or so they'd arrive at Farrenhale. He sensed the tension growing among the troops as they neared the front. They were eager to do their duty and return home. Some wanted to prove they were heroes, while others merely wanted to show they weren't cowards. Daglind wasn't sure where he fell; he thought he was brave but had his doubts. *At least I'm not running away from the front like that Iaven Ambersheath*, he thought.

He turned quickly at a low rustling sound, and then calmed again, chiding himself for being so jumpy. *And we're not even at the front yet*, he thought. He hoped the Goblins would withdraw; winter was not far away. *If we can hold out a few more weeks, maybe there won't be a war*, thought Daglind. But he could not quite believe that.

Mischief began yelping again, startling Daglind. The frisky dog stood at the camp's edge, barking at a bush. "Quiet, Mischief! How aptly named you are. Quiet, now, or you'll wake the camp!" But the dog went on growling. Daglind got off the barrel. He glanced across the camp. The other guard was gone. He turned to the dog. "What is it, boy, what do you smell?"

Daglind jumped as Mischief gave a shrill yelp and spun onto the ground. A black arrow stuck out from the little dog's side. A huge shape sprang up from behind the bush. "Goblins!" Daglind shouted. He ducked as a black arrow cut through the air. He tried shouting again, a hoarse gasp escaping as an arrow caught him in the neck. Something struck the back of his head, knocking him to the ground.

Goblins emerged from behind bushes and out of tall grasses on the slopes. Throughout the night they had quietly advanced, surrounding the encampment in an ever-tightening circle hidden from view. Now they came forth pulling bows on all sides of the camp. Dwarves sounded the alarm, but those leaving their tents too hastily found themselves in the range of sharp-eyed goblin archers. Goblins swinging firebrands ran into the camp, torching the tents to flush out the dwarves. Those who fled met goblins with broadswords.

As the dwarves awoke, many were slain. The dwarves' numbers dwindled and their advantage was lost. Bodies lay scattered and smoke billowed up from the burning tents. Cries of anger, pain, and confusion went up all around as they desperately tried to coordinate their efforts. Some escaped and began a counterattack, and several goblins were felled. Others were unprepared and panicked. Gradually captains pulled their troops together, but losses were mounting too fast.

Stiff and groggy, Lexter woke alone in his tent to shouts and clashes of metal. He crawled to the edge of the flap and peeked out. Seeing goblins, he pulled back, though the smell of burning canvas told him he would not be safe there for long. He wondered where so many goblins had come from, and then remembered the undermountain passage. He cursed himself at not having acted quicker in Farrenhale, ashamed to have even considered withholding his knowledge of the passage until they had met his demands. *It's all my fault*, he thought, *why didn't I stay in Farrenhale and help them find the tunnel? Now it's too late...*

Lexter smelt smoke nearby and a darkening patch appeared at the back of his tent as it began burning. He looked outside as cautiously as he could. Heat grew at the back of the tent as the flames engulfed it. Lexter stepped outside into the chaos, trying to think as fast as he could. He quickly lost hope.

His mind cleared as he cast his fears aside. For the first time in a long while he felt good about himself. He was sad his time had come —the second time, he reminded himself— but he no longer felt he had lived in vain. His thoughts broke off abruptly as the roar of battle intensified and the tent behind him collapsed. His mind, so used to scheming, was still searching for a way out; yet he had been in enough difficult situations in his life to recognize that there was no way he could escape the camp without being seen by the goblins. *They won't be taking prisoners this time*, he thought. *Well, at least I can now die an honest man.* He had helped the dwarves and resisted stealing the swords; it had been his final test to prove his good intentions. His promises had been kept, and he had made good on the chance he had been given. He had the satisfaction of knowing he had done all he could. In a moment that left him profoundly surprised, he found himself finally at peace.

Iaven woke to harsh shouts and clashes outside as Wendolin came in. "Draw your swords and take what you can," Wendolin commanded. The other dwarves were sitting up, their hair tousled, pulling on their coats and hurrying to bind up their belonging. Oil splashed their tent, and it darkened and began burning as fire spread across it. Wendolin stood at the back of the tent, his sword drawn. He slashed an opening, drew the fabric aside, and saw the way was clear. He stepped out, urging Iaven and the others to come.

Outside they moved in a tight group away from the edge of camp. Wendolin shot a glance about, quickly assessing their grim situation. "To the mountains!" he shouted, and Iaven and his friends obeyed. Around them many were leaving the burning camp and calls went out for the dwarves to regroup in the mountains and take on the Goblins from higher ground. Some dwarves turned and fought their pursuers, trying to hold them back. Many met their death amidst the chaos. It was hard to say who was outnumbered now, but the Goblins clearly had the advantage. Retreating and regrouping seemed the Dwarves' only hope. Fires burned and smoke rose from the camp. The Goblins combed the camp and the last of the remaining troops were slain. Dozens of dwarves lay dead and scattered across the battlefield that morning, many having died to allow others a chance to escape. And among them lay Lexter's fallen body, his hand still grasping the black goblin arrow jutting out from his neck.

Iaven and the others made for the low hills. Wendolin led them on a zigzag course, to throw off their pursuers. The land rose beneath them and they looked for a way to the east. Soon they lost track of all other dwarves. Wendolin guided them toward a pass that opened as they rounded the hillside. Once they were high enough, they would move north and find other dwarves who had escaped.

Suddenly, near the steep rise leading into the pass, four goblins came over a hill to the north of them and moved to cut them off.

"Quick! Up the slope!" Wendolin let the dwarves by him, Iaven and Zammond leading the way. The dwarves slipped past to higher ground, but turned sharply as they heard the clang of swords clashing. Wendolin's blade swung to ward off goblins and he held them at bay, edging past them. The dwarves turned back but Wendolin shouted, "Run! Go now!" They obeyed reluctantly, fearing Wendolin would sacrifice himself for their sake. Wendolin dodged the goblins' blows, and with a strange, fluid gesture, a small host of bright, crimson balls of light appeared floating in the air behind his sweeping forearm. They glowed, translucent, swarming about the goblins who swung and swatted them anxiously, afraid of touching them. Those hit by blades burst with flashes of red light in their faces.

Meanwhile Wendolin came up the slope shouting at the dwarves. "Turn around and watch where you are going! What are you looking at? They are meant to distract the goblins, not you!" he roared. "Hurry, you slowpokes! They will be after us again!"

The goblins continued their pursuit. Wendolin and the dwarves left the valley and climbed, hoping to find higher ground they could defend. The lay of the land forced them south, and soon they gave up hope of rejoining other dwarves from the encampment. At last, with Wendolin's guidance, Iaven's party eluded the goblins, but Wendolin would not let them stop until they found a safe haven.

"They will want us to think we have lost them. They are a tenacious lot and will be tracking us, you can be sure of it. We must keep moving and choose our way carefully, avoiding blind alleys and backtracking, or they might find us," Wendolin told them. "I suspect few dwarves escaped this morning."

"What are we going to do now?" asked Iaven, "I suppose going back is out of the question."

"Yes," Wendolin said, "we cannot go back. We must make for the Castle now, and ride to Kronivar from there."

"The Castle?" Zammond said, "That's rather far, isn't it? Do you really know the way through all these mountains?"

"No," Wendolin admitted, "but if we continue to the southeast, we will eventually come upon the mountain road that runs between the Castle and Greensward. Once we do, we'll have to find a way up to it, and go from there. We have little choice now; our wagon is gone, and the North Road will be treacherous with goblins about. Let us hope word of them reaches Farrenhale in time. A difficult journey awaits us. Nor have the goblins given up on us yet."

They climbed higher and higher, looking for places they might traverse on foot. The paths they took meandered and rarely ran straight, but the passing sun helped them keep their route in a roughly southerly direction. Their pace slowed, and still there was no sign of goblins.

As the sun began descending, they searched for a place to spend the night.

Zammond and Hobley collected what sparse branches and brush could be found for a fire. A wide, deep valley opened before them and they went single file along a ledge, nervously regarding the steep drop only a few feet to their left. Snowflakes drifted in the air now and a cold wind blew. At last they came to a cave opening onto the ledge, about ten feet across and dark and dank inside. With a nod from Wendolin the dwarves filed into the cave. Ten yards in, near the back of the cave, water dripped from the ceiling into a small shallow pool, and a narrow crevice opened high up into the ceiling of the cave. The ground beneath the crevice seemed the best place for the fire, so Hobley and Zammond piled the wood there and set to work with the flints. Tillmore and Wilbur found a dry spot along the wall and set all the packs there.

"It's either this or nothing, I suppose," said Wilbur. He looked out the cave at the sunlight fading on the mountains across the valley as the shadows of the range crept up them. A low rumble like thunder boomed in the valley.

"Sounds like a storm," said Tillmore, "I thought the skies were clear."

"They were," said Hobley. "Maybe a storm's blowing in."

Hobley walked to the cave entrance and stood on the ledge. Zammond set down the flints and joined him. "The sky *is* clear," he said. Soft and faint, the low rumble sounded again.

"It sounds like it's coming from below, down in the valley," said Zammond. He and Hobley approached the cliff's edge, trying to peer as far down the steep drop as they could. Wendolin came to the cave entrance. The rumble sounded again, low and long like a great trembling, so quiet that they strained to hear it.

"Echoes in the valley," Wendolin explained. "In the old days, the Dwarves thought it to be the slumber of dragons." Zammond and Hobley stood staring into the valley, listening to hear the rumble again, trying to imagine a dragon down there somewhere.

"That must have kept them from wandering out too far in the mountains," said Hobley. He turned his head to better hear the rumble, and something down the cliff path caught his eye. Goblins were rounding a shoulder further down the mountain. They saw Hobley and Zammond and their pace quickened.

"Four goblins," Hobley shouted, "They've seen us!"

Zammond and Hobley stepped back into the cave. The dwarves drew their swords and Wendolin unsheathed his as well.

"We'll hold the mouth of the cave against them," said Wendolin. "They'll have their backs to the drop into the valley. We'll force them to the edge." They assembled near the cave entrance, finding their footing and looking for the thinnest part of the ledge where they might push the goblins over. "They'll try to force their way in. Stand back and get them to come in front of the mouth of the cave, away from the cliff wall. It's our best chance." The dwarves pulled back over the threshold and waited tensely, hoping to surprise the goblins. Soon they heard the goblins' heavy tread and the *shing!* of swords unsheathing.

The goblins expected to find the dwarves ready. They moved across the entrance, sure of themselves despite the risk. Metal rang as blades clashed. Iaven tried to stay calm and wished he had Halix; the sword from Farrenhale seemed heavy and dead by comparison. He concentrated hard, recalling all that Yolias had taught him. Zammond, too, was holding his own. Wendolin wielded his sword in swift, efficient strokes that the goblins struggled to avoid. Hobley, Tillmore, and Wilbur held two goblins at bay, trying to shove them back. The goblins stood firm, shouting, snarling, and pushing their way inside. The noise intensified and echoed into the valley. The low rumble sounded again, louder than before, but the goblins refused to be distracted by it.

The tight quarters made fighting difficult for both sides, and the goblins renewed their efforts, realizing they had underestimated the young dwarves and the old man. A loud, rolling boom sounded in the valley now, a long, slow growl, loud enough to be heard over the fighting. The goblins appeared wary but kept their eyes on their opponents. The dwarves and Wendolin were clearly tiring and the goblins would soon break through into the cave. A great, long roar went up from the valley, frightening in its intensity and strength, and the air stirred. An ancient, musty odor rose on the wind, faint but unmistakable, as though a long-sealed tomb had exhaled centuries-old stale breath. The goblins pushed even harder now to gain entry, as the dwarves' resistance weakened.

The air roiled, a rank wind gusted their faces, and the sound of great wings moving beat the mountainside. The ground trembled beneath their feet. The goblins were visibly unnerved as the sounds grew louder. Suddenly the dwarves saw a great and terrible head and long neck rising, and wide, leathery wings large as a ship's sails moving through the air. Awestruck, they caught a terrifying glimpse of great curving teeth and narrowing eyes as the dragon rose into the sky, its russet armor of hardened scales catching the fading sunlight. Its tail was thicker than a hundred-year oak and ended in an arrowhead point that sliced through the air as it writhed like a serpent. The dragon rose heavenward, a grim force of nature disturbing all in its wake.

Iaven stood gazing at it, petrified. Yet as it slowly ascended into the dusky sky, his terror lessened, becoming a strange sadness as he watched it fly away. Iaven sensed what he was seeing had outlived its time, something ancient lingering long after its age had ended.

The goblins could not help but turn to steal a glimpse of the dragon, and when they turned back Wendolin's hands were raised to their faces, palms open wide, and a great flash of bright white light struck them at close range. Overhead, the dragon let out a thunderous roar that rolled and echoed across the valley. The flash blinded both goblins and under the dwarves' pressure they stumbled back and fell over the edge of the cliff into the abyss.

But the goblins at the sides of the cave entrance were better positioned and less distracted. Tillmore jumped forward, catching one of them off guard. He thrust and dealt a mortal blow, but left an opening momentarily. The goblin's blade swung hard, cutting Tillmore deeply near his waist. Tillmore fell back onto the cave floor, while the goblin he had struck staggered backwards a step. The goblin fended off a blow from Hobley and toppled over the edge, his yowl trailing away behind him as he fell.

The last remaining goblin retreated down the path to safety, hoping one of the dwarves would come face him alone. When no one came after him, he turned and fled, cursing them.

Hobley watched to be sure the goblin was gone for good, while Iaven and Zammond searched the sky for any sign of the dragon. Iaven wished Yolias had been there to see the dragon, remembering the wyverns they had seen. Back in the cave, they found Tillmore laying on the floor bleeding, trying to sit up, and Hobley went over to help him. To their horror, Wendolin was lying on his back after having collapsed to the floor, exhausted. At first they thought he was wounded, yet he did not appear to be.

Wilbur knelt down by Wendolin. Wendolin's brows rose suddenly and his penetrating eyes held Wilbur in their gaze. "Fear not! I am not dead yet!" he said. Yet he lay still and made no effort to get up. "Don't worry about me!" He slowly turned onto his side. "I am not wounded. But Tillmore is; quite badly, I think. Hurry and tend to him!" Even from the ground, Wendolin's commands carried an urgent authority that made Iaven respond immediately.

"The wound is deep," said Hobley, looking up at Iaven. The gash was worse than they had expected, and they bound up the wound as best they could, until the bleeding stopped.

Iaven knelt by Tillmore, trembling at the sight of all the blood on his clothes. "Tillmore..." Iaven was not sure what to say.

"He got me," Tillmore muttered, "But I got him first, didn't I?"

"Don't try to talk, just rest," said Hobley, "They're gone now."

Tillmore nodded, seeing how stern and solemn Iaven and Hobley were. He couldn't quite see his wound and the looks on their faces scared him.

Hobley and Iaven carried Tillmore over by the cave wall, where Zammond and Wilbur unrolled blankets and made a soft bedding for him. Tillmore looked pale and faint and groaned as they lifted him. They had him lie back and rest, and he did not find sleep difficult.

Iaven went over by Wendolin. Zammond had pulled him over to the opposite cave wall and helped him sit up. They put their coats behind Wendolin's back to cushion him. After Tillmore was asleep, Hobley joined them.

"So an Old One still lives in these valleys!" said Wendolin. "How fortunate we were to see it, though we could have paid dearly for the glimpse, as the goblins did. Doubly fortunate, then, are we, to see it and live. For many have thought their kind long gone."

Though his voice was strong, Wendolin moved very little, and suddenly seemed old and frail to Iaven. Finding the Wendolin lying on the ground had almost been as much of a shock as the dragon had been.

"Are you surprised to find me so weakened?" Wendolin looked at them, seeing their concern and distress. "Powers such as you have seen exact their price on those who would use them. I must recover now. And our climb through the mountains today was a strenuous one. I am still, after all, a very old man."

They sat talking and gradually the dwarves grew more at ease, seeing that Wendolin, though exhausted, was still in good spirits. The sky outside the cave was black now and sprinkled with white pinpoints of stars.

"We should keep a watch tonight," Wendolin reminded them, "We must be careful. The goblin who fled may return. And he may not be alone."

"I'll sit the first watch," Iaven volunteered, hoping to talk with Wendolin awhile. The others were too tired to argue, and soon Iaven and Wendolin sat alone amidst the low murmur of the dwarves' slumber.

Iaven pulled his blanket around his shoulders and sat back against the cave wall next to Wendolin. He looked over at the dark cave entrance filled with night sky. He needed only to watch the entrance, though if the goblin returned he would have to act very quickly. He hoped he would be quick enough.

Iaven relaxed again, trying to stay warm. Now that he could talk alone with Wendolin, he did not know where to begin. So much was swarming through his head. The massacre of the dwarves at Halloway meant that the war had begun. He dwelt on that dark thought for some time in silence.

In time his mind drifted to other things; Wendolin's deeds, Tillmore's wounding, the dragon, the goblin who escaped, and the mountainous journey ahead of them. And, of course, there was still Orven, the swords, and Rhiane; Iaven suddenly did not want to go to the Castle or face Rhiane until he had Halix back.

And Iaven was surprised how well he had fought without Halix. He had always assumed it was the sword, but realized now how much he had learned from Yolias. He hoped the dwarves had regrouped and defeated the Goblins, though it seemed unlikely. His own troubles seemed insignificant compared to the massacre at Halloway.

"If only we'd learned of the undermountain passage sooner," Iaven said.

"Yes," said Wendolin, "I was hoping to speak to Lexter again this morning. There was something else in what he told me that struck me as strange, or rather, as familiar; it reminded me of something—" Wendolin could not recall it and shook his head wearily. "It will come to me later; the goblins have put it out of my mind."

"So what will happen now?" asked Iaven, "Will the Goblins go on to Farrenhale? Or has the war has already started there?" He shifted around, pulling his blanket tighter. "Either way, it seems we can't do much until we get to Kronivar." He turned to Wendolin. "How long until we get to the Castle?"

"I do not know," said Wendolin. "I have not traveled these mountains and there is only the sun to guide us and keep us moving southward and to the east. The way will be hard, but we do not have much of a choice."

Iaven was silent awhile. "I suppose it may not even matter one way or the other, by the time we get there," he said. He wondered if the goblin who had fled would return with others. "If we even get there at all."

"Iaven!" Wendolin chided, "Do not say such things! That is just what the Goblins want you to think. Those without hope are already defeated. Never believe evil to be more powerful than good." Wendolin's voice still held its authority, but was labored and weary now. Iaven's heart sunk to hear it.

"But why does it seem so, sometimes?" asked Iaven.

"Evil must appear powerful, if it is to draw anyone," said Wendolin, "Evil desires nothing more than to draw others into itself. That is why we cannot respond to it in kind. If it seems stronger at times, that is only part of its illusion and its power over those who give in to fear and despair. But in the end, it is not so."

"Then why would anyone choose it?" asked Iaven.

"Some choose evil because it looks stronger or seems an easier course to follow; but it is self-destructive and its promises false and deceptive," said Wendolin. "Many are seduced into believing when much is promised them, even if they must ignore the truth to do so. But truth remains when all lies have burned away.

"Long ago, there was an order of Oswai whose aged leader, Menferius, died suddenly. A young, scholarly Oswai, Preoziansfera, was called upon to succeed him. Those were difficult times, and so it was with great reluctance that he accepted the mantle of authority.

"When Preoziansfera became head of his order, many paths lay open to him, some darker than others. Some courses of action and alliances would have strengthened the order, but at too great a cost. He pondered long over the future of the Oswai, and one night a dream came to him. There were many orbs, of some pure and clear material, like water or glass, and light shined through them. Over time, some became clouded and obscured, and light did not pass through them as easily as before. These absorbed the light and gave off heat. Thinking to grow in power this way, some orbs darkened even more, and gave off an even greater heat. A few darkened entirely, hoping to become so hot that they might glow and give off their own light. For a time, these orbs held sway. But at last the Great Light came, a strong, bright light surpassing all others, a light which left nothing hidden.

"The Great Light passed freely through those orbs that had remained pure and clear, leaving them shining and unharmed. Those orbs that had clouded a little —and there were very few that had not clouded at all— burned inside until the light had cleansed them and they were clear and pure again. But those that had darkened, and were black and opaque, blazed and burned up entirely, and were destroyed. When only the clear orbs remained, and all were cleansed and pure, they all shined with the light that passed through them, reflecting each other in all their shining surfaces. Thus do we say, *Truth, like fire, illuminates and purifies.*"

Iaven sat listening in silence. The fire at the back of the cave was low now, and all was quiet. "Yes," he said finally, "I think I see what you mean. Orven and I would get in fights all the time when were young. He was always willing to be meaner, and he usually won. Sometimes I wanted to act like him and beat him, no matter what it took, but something always held me back. I never understood what it was. I wondered, too, if Orven ever felt it. Maybe he did but he ignored it. Whenever he wanted something, he always had to have his way." Iaven was quiet a moment. "On the other hand, I know what that's like, too, I guess; I just wanted different things. Orven was right about the farm and Cedric, and I didn't want to admit it. *'You're both stubborn, especially with each other!'* Cedric used to say. He was right, and knew us both very well."

"And you and Orven know each other well, better than anyone else," said Wendolin.

The image of Maëlveronde wielding Halix and standing over Orven's fallen body flashed through Iaven's mind. "We do," he admitted, "and I hope it won't be too late for Orven. Oh, I know, what's pictured in the weaving may not happen, but I'm still worried about him, angry as I am. If only we had brought that tapestry along, perhaps I could have shown it to him and convinced him."

"We will do what we can," said Wendolin, "however small our deeds may seem to us. But I must rest now, and for some time, I think. Good night!"

"Good night," Iaven said. He wanted to talk more, but let Wendolin rest.

Iaven sat on the cave floor, looking out the cave entrance into the night sky, still thinking about the massacre at Halloway and all the dead there. Without Wendolin they would not have escaped. There was nothing they could do now except get to the Castle.

Iaven could not help thinking how things could have been different. Had he not lost Halix, Lexter could have stayed in Farrenhale and the tunnel might have been found in time. Or what if he had left Hillbrook sooner, or gone into the outpost caves to look for Orven? What if he had arrived later and found Orven on the tree branch? Would he have climbed up and fought for the gem? Could he have left Orven hanging as Orven had left him? His heart pounded just thinking about it. He and Orven had always been alike. Each stood his ground, refusing to budge. Iaven's anger rose again as he imagined himself fighting Orven.

Strong feelings and desires moved him. He imagined keeping to himself on the farm, never leaving Hillbrook or letting the outside world intrude upon his cares. He knew people like that and realized how important his father's travels and Cedric's tales were in making him think about the rest of the world.

Iaven again recalled the dead on the fields near Halloway. He himself had done so little, and only with great reluctance. His hesitance disturbed him. Iaven vowed to change.

He glanced out of the cave at the night sky. Perhaps the goblin had gone north and would not come back. He got up and walked over to the cave entrance to look out into the valley. Everything was quiet outside. The dragon, too, was gone, and Iaven found himself hoping it would return.

The following morning the dwarves woke late. Daylight spread over the mountains and crept thinly across the cave floor. Wilbur finished the night's last watch, glad to have company as the others woke. Only Tillmore and Wendolin remained asleep.

"Should we eat here, or look for something along the way?" said Zammond.

"Let's wait and see how Tillmore is," said Hobley. "What do you think, Iaven?"

"We'll let him rest for now," said Iaven.

"I'm awake," Tillmore's feeble voice came from the side of the cave where he lay. The others went over and sat down beside him, surprised at how pale and haggard he was.

"You look terrible!" said Wilbur, "Uh, I mean, not so well..."

Tillmore smiled weakly. "I *do* look terrible, don't I? I feel terrible. I slept in fits and starts. I—" Tillmore coughed. "—my side's in pain, but I think it stopped bleeding."

"No, no, don't move, I'll look," Hobley offered. The wound had clotted over, but Tillmore's clothes and blanket were soaked with blood. "You'd better stay put, it could reopen if you move around."

"We'll have to stay here another day," said Iaven.

"Not if you carry me," Tillmore suggested. "I wouldn't want to hold everyone up."

"We'll wait for now," Iaven said, "We'll ask Wendolin, too." Wendolin was still fast asleep.

Hobley and Zammond went out for brush to rebuild the fire, while Wilbur and Iaven searched everyone's packs for what little food was left. When all had returned, a meager breakfast was soon underway.

"You did well yesterday." Hobley smiled at Tillmore. "We all did. We're lucky Yolias taught us what he did. Who knows what would have happened otherwise?"

"I'd like to learn more," said Zammond. "And I must admit Iaven did pretty good without Halix!"

Iaven shrugged. "I didn't do too bad, I guess. But I'm really not cut out for sword-fighting."

"Yolias thought you were picking it up quite well," said Zammond.

"He did?" Iaven was surprised. "He said that? Well, I just hope there won't be any more goblins on the way."

"Nobody out there, from what we could tell," said Hobley, "They must have all went north."

"Then we should move on." Tillmore's voice betrayed the fervor of his words. "Make a litter of blankets and carry me, and I'll walk as soon as I can."

"We don't want you to get worse," said Iaven, "but Wendolin might be able to help—"

"Should I wake him? He's usually up before we are," said Zammond. He sat down by Wendolin. Gingerly he touched the old wizard's shoulder to rouse him. He watched a moment, and gently felt the side of Wendolin's face. "Iaven," said Zammond, "He's cold. Do you think— is he dead?"

They gathered around Wendolin. He was cold to the touch, but not stiff like a corpse. To their relief, he still seemed alive, though his breathing was slower and shallower than that of sleep; it was like a great tide ebbing and flowing that could slowly draw away and not return. Wendolin was not gone, but he had retreated to somewhere deep within and they were not sure he would reemerge.

"He's alive," said Iaven, "but there's nothing more we can do."

"So what do we do now?" Hobley asked quietly.

They all looked to Iaven for the decision, and he considered their situation. The four of them could carry Tillmore and Wendolin, but the mountains were too treacherous, they wouldn't have a trail, and there was no telling who or what they might encounter on the way. Staying would be dangerous, though defending the cave entrance would be easier than holding off an attack in the open. And Tillmore and Wendolin would be able to rest.

"We'll have to stay another day," Iaven concluded. The others nodded in agreement and set to work making the cave as comfortable as they could, tending the fire and moving Tillmore and Wendolin closer for warmth. The day was overcast and a light, icy rain fell. The wind howled softly at the mouth of the cave, chilling them. Cold air, damp stone, and concern for their friends kept their spirits subdued, and the day seemed to drag on interminably.

Iaven knew he had made the right decision and found himself dwelling on other decisions he would soon have to make. He had no idea how many days it would take to get to the Castle or how far they would have to go out of their way to get there. Their supplies were limited and he thought they might be better off down in the valley near a stream. At any rate, they could not stay in the cave much longer.

"Maybe I won't make it, Iaven," Tillmore said weakly. He had always enjoyed good health and found his affliction difficult to bear.

"Don't say that, you'll pull through," Iaven told him, trying to believe it himself. "We'll get you to the Castle."

"What do you think will happen with Wendolin?" asked Tillmore. He glanced past the fire to where Wendolin lay.

"I don't know," said Iaven, "He's about the same as he was this morning. At least he's not wounded."

"As far as we know," said Tillmore.

The afternoon passed laboriously, and as evening drew on their mood grew heavier. Light faded from the cave as the sun passed overhead, and the air grew colder. A drizzle of rain fell which was close to turning to snow. Even Zammond's heart was heavy. At first, he had paced restlessly, in and out of the cave. Now he sat leaning on the cave wall, staring out into the valley.

"I used to think Zammond's singing and whistling all the time was annoying, but this is worse," Tillmore told Iaven. Tillmore seemed in better spirits than any of them, and Iaven hoped this was a good sign. He did not think he could take another long day of inactivity like they had just endured.

The dwarves prepared for bed, morose and ornery, and found sleep difficult. Everyone had been eager to go out for firewood just to have something to do. At last they had enough for a nice-sized fire the entire night, and the added heat and warmth was welcomed by all.

Iaven sat the first watch again. Without Wendolin to talk to, it seemed the longest and loneliest he had ever sat. He even wished Lexter was with them. No matter how bad their situation seemed, images of the dead of the Halloway encampment reminded him of how fortunate they were.

With nothing to do, Iaven's mind wandered and he made little effort to rein it in. He kept checking the night sky to see if enough time had passed to wake Hobley for the next watch and go to bed. The night seemed sluggish and frozen in place, the constellations barely inching their way across the sky. At last he decided it was time, or close enough, and woke Hobley. Iaven stretched out near the fire, his blankets tight around him, and was asleep before he knew it.

But Iaven's sleep was uneasy, his mind wild and restless, unable to settle on anything for long. His thoughts churned in an inky turmoil of disturbing imagery. He was moving through blackness, a murky, damp, cool darkness that bloomed and billowed in front of his eyes as he tried to see through it. Iaven advanced slowly. Faint flickers of pale firelight moved behind columns of stone around him in the dark. He walked toward the light, where torches burned on a few of the pillars.

As he moved across the floor, either the light brightened or his eyes adjusted, and he could see the pillars of stone stretching far away into darkness on all sides. Overhead each widened into a carved canopy of interlocking tree branches, wild, tangled and intertwined, like piles of curling snakes slithering in the flickering shadows. *I'm in the Stone Forest under the Castle*, Iaven thought with a shiver, reminded of the weaving's image.

He walked a few more paces, sensing he was not alone; Orven and Maëlveronde were down there as well, somewhere. He did not see or hear anyone, but the place seemed alive around him, as if he were in a real forest, or as though the stones themselves were living, far more ancient than trees and aware of his presence. He resisted looking up at the serpentine branches covering the ceiling, afraid they would unwind and lower, grasping at him. The torches were strangely bright yet unable to dispel the darkness around them. Iaven walked faster now, worried he was not alone. The place seemed vast and endless. He thought of calling out to Orven but fear held him back. Perhaps somewhere nearby, Maëlveronde was already standing bent over Orven's lifeless body, Orven's sword fallen away on the floor, out of reach. Iaven badly wanted to go and help Orven even though it was too late. A sense of doom and defeat swept through him like a cold draft. Iaven shuddered.

Further along, he approached a wall of some sort, as his vision swam again in the dark. The air turned colder and fresher, and the floor was wood instead of stone. Reaching out to touch the wall, he found it was also made of wood. Iaven found a door, and after a moment's hesitation, he opened it. A cool, moist breeze struck him as he walked out onto on a wooden platform under a black night sky. A soft murmuring roar like a slow slumbering breath swelled nearby. A huge, thick mast rose a short distance away, and wooden railings; he was on the deck of a ship. Iaven walked and stood at the railing, watching and listening to the vast expanse of endless sea spread across the night. Starlight glittered serenely on the waves. He had never been on a ship before and a strange apprehension filled him, even as the slow undulations of the sea calmed him. Grim melancholy overcame him; he knew, somehow, that he was on board the *Yoner*.

He glanced around the deck. Further down the railing, a dwarf in his late forties stood with his back turned, looking out to sea. Iaven's heart leapt as he recognized his father.

Iaven tried to cry out, but only managed an agonized whisper. He walked over to where his father stood, happy and anxious, sensing how fragile the moment was and how easily it could vanish. When he was only a few feet away, Hagen Ambersheath turned and smiled at him.

"Iaven," Hagen said.

Iaven had so many questions he wanted to ask, yet he just stood there, unable to speak. His father was exactly as Iaven remembered and looked gently upon his son now. Iaven wondered if his father felt the same sense of doom that he did aboard the ship. But Hagen's eyes were steady and caring, as though he knew what was troubling Iaven. Together they stood at the railing looking out to sea.

"Yes," said Hagen, "It is a risk, going off to sea, but so is staying behind. Either you risk losing what you have or you risk losing opportunities."

"I... I know," Iaven said. He wanted to talk but was quiet now. He looked with love at his father.

"You remember Uncle Dalen?" Hagen smiled at the memory. "He liked to ask older people, 'Which do you regret more, things you did, or things you didn't do?'" Hagen laughed. "Maybe you were too young to remember him."

"I remember," Iaven said. He wanted to say so much he hardly knew where to begin. He again recalled overhearing his father talking to his mother the night before he left, *"You'll be fine. So will the twins. Iaven will be fine."* Iaven gripped the railing tight as emotion welled up in him at the unwarranted concern. There was no need to worry about him any more than Orven. Iaven wanted to tell his father all he had done and seen, and prove he could do anything Orven could.

Hagen's voice broke into Iaven's thoughts. "Have you seen the forecastle? Come on, let's go up there." Hagen led Iaven across the deck and they climbed the stairs. Behind them the sails billowed in the wind, the wood of the ship creaking below them. As they crossed the ship's bow, Iaven looked around and back over the deck. They seemed to be the only ones aboard. Even the large ship's wheel, its spokes ending in wooden handles around the wheel's rim, remained unmanned.

They walked to the front of the narrowing bow and stood at the railing, gazing out to where they were heading. The ship cut through the water, gaining speed. Wind gusted their faces. Ahead, the Silver Sea reached out to the horizon where stars hovered over the water. A dark shape appeared there and grew steadily. Iaven saw it was an island and grew uneasy and fearful at the sight of it.

"Looks like we're in for some rough sailing," Hagen said. Nearing the island, Iaven saw the waters ahead were caught in great swirling maelstroms drifting around the island. Whole stretches of sea were pulled violently into the torrents of each whirlpool and funneled away into the abyss at the eye. The *Yoner* was heading right into them. They were much closer now and Iaven could hear the sea roaring. Panic seeped like a black liquid into his heart.

"Can't we stop, or turn back..." Iaven's voice trailed off as he grasped for words.

"You can't stop a ship, but at least you can steer," his father said.

Iaven wanted to turn to his father but the maelstrom held his gaze. His eye was drawn around it as the swirling dark waters grew closer and closer. And looming beyond them was Aorinthel's Island, where Maëlveronde awaited them. Iaven wondered if Maëlveronde could see them from the tower, or if he was somehow drawing them to himself.

Iaven finally turned back to his father, glad he was there, wishing he could freeze that moment in time. Yet it was already fading. He tried to hold onto it longer, and then relented and gently let it go.

Iaven stared into the darkness. His eyes were open now, and he was staring up into the uneven recesses of the cave's ceiling. It was still night. He looked across the cave floor to where the others slept, and where Wendolin lay. Iaven thought about the dream, realizing Maëlveronde had escaped from the island long before the *Yoner* had sailed, long before he was even born. But there were other dangers to face and decisions to make. His friends expected it of him, and he would not disappoint them. As soon as Tillmore could walk they would carry Wendolin and head for the Castle. If they came across goblins, or the dragon, or anything else, they'd do what they could and it would have to be enough.

Iaven rolled over on the hard, cold stone floor, not minding it as much now. He breathed in deep and was soon sleeping soundly again.

Chapter 34.
Fire and Darkness

Night had fallen. A few snowflakes drifted in the cold air. Yolias walked along the wooden balcony overlooking the swamp, still unaccustomed to the wood creaking beneath his feet despite all the time he had spent in Teska. The snow reminded him of the Castle and he longed to return home. Even lodgings near Farrenhale on solid ground would have been better, he thought, but his duties lay in Teska. When the sun rose again, it would be five days since Wendolin and Iaven had left Teska. He wondered if they had reached Kronivar yet.

The last few days had been long and tense. The mood had grown edgy and irritable, weary of waiting for the Goblins to move. There was still no sign of the Dwarven troops coming up from Greensward, though Yolias supposed they would arrive the following day or the day after. The watchtowers of the Gate reported increased activity among the Goblins, and more seemed to be arriving every day. Tensions were deepening between the Teskans and the Dwarves, though all remained civil, mainly due to their separation over water and on dry land.

Yolias noticed a Teskan flag hanging nearby on a wall, shadowy under the eaves; a white star of eleven crescent-like points on a field of green, representing the eleven tribes of Teska. He wondered what support they would get from the other villages. Chisk and Neffa had sent boatloads of warriors and the smaller villages had sent a few token tribesmen, but Teska would have to bear the brunt of the attack. Although the tribes were bound by blood and would fight together, Yolias often sensed that the other villages felt it was Teska, not them, who owed a debt to the Dwarves for the city's rebuilding, a debt they thought should never have been accepted.

Above them the moon was bright, only four days from waxing full. Yolias looked out over the swamp and could just barely see the lights and dark shape of Chisk on the far waters. Out several hundred feet from Teska, a *nasauri* and rider on patrol waded past. If not for the war, Yolias thought, it was a beautiful, quiet November evening.

His calm was broken by the sound of feet running up behind him on the plank walkway. "*Su* Yolias, please come! Hurry!" said a young boy's voice.

"Kiuwaa, what is the matter?" Yolias turned to face the youth as he approached.

Teska Kiuwaa stopped before him, out of breath. "Her weaving, sir. She has just begun another, but already it bodes ill."

Yolias studied the boy's face in the dim light. Kiuwaa was not easily excited, and it was strange for him not to wait until a weaving was finished. Kiuwaa had also heard Wendolin's warning that the weavings were not be to be taken as certainties, but the Teskans were prone to fatalism, especially under the shadow of war.

"Let us go to her then," Yolias said.

They made their way through the village and Kiuwaa let them in. All was dark and quiet in the hall, and they could hear the loom clacking rhythmically. At the sound of their entry, Teska Ahna broke from her trance and the loom slowed to a stop. She sat a moment and then turned to see them.

"*Suati*, I brought *su* Yolias to see the weaving," Kiuwaa explained.

"*Athiiwata, suati*," Yolias nodded, "Kiuwaa thought it of grave importance, so I came."

Teska Ahna listened to Yolias and replied in a reedy whisper of a voice. Kiuwaa leaned forward to hear, and then straightened again. "She says needs a short rest, but will finish the weaving as soon as she can." Kiuwaa helped her to her room. The weaving had only been begun earlier that evening, and the colorful, tightly-packed weft threads revealed the top of an image emerging from the loom. Yolias leaned in for a closer look.

"I recognized the rafters," said Kiuwaa, pointing to the partially-woven image, "and when I saw the loom, I knew for certain." The weaving depicted the room they stood in, including the top beam of the loom itself. But sections of the ceiling burned with yellow and orange, consumed by fire, and a long wooden rafter angled down from the ceiling where it had fallen in, breaking the top beam of the loom in two.

Yolias bent toward the weaving and touched it, studying it closely. "Kiu, bring me the candle over there."

Kiuwaa obeyed and handed Yolias the candle. Yolias held it close and in the light he was able to see more detail, though it was limited by the weave. Within the picture, angled on the loom's broken beam, hung a weaving. Yolias looked closely at the woven fibers, noting their colors and patterns. Tiny bits of yellow and orange combined with browns, beiges, forest greens, and darker colors. Yolias examined them awhile and then, to Kiuwaa's surprise, he stepped back and looked at the entire loom at a distance of a few feet.

"The image on the broken loom in the picture appears to be the very one she is weaving now," Yolias said.

Kiuwaa looked at Yolias. "A picture of the weaving appears in itself?" He studied the weaving again.

"If the image is to come true, it will do so before the weaving is removed from the loom," Yolias said. "We may have little time to prepare. The Goblins have keen eyes in the dark, and long have I suspected they would move at night." He hurried out into the hall and Kiuwaa followed behind him.

"I must warn the village. We may have to cut the bridge. As Wendolin says, the image may not come true, but we must take it as a warning. Go and warn others!" said Yolias as he left down the hall, "And don't let *suati* finish that weaving!"

Yolias strode through Teska, alerting the Teskans to be ready for an attack. They nodded as he passed and set to the task. Word spread and horns sounded. Teskan men and boys strung their bows, and women and children began dousing houses on the city's perimeter to lessen the threat of fire. Yolias made his way to the city's eastern edge. Messengers would have to be sent into the Dwarven camp and Farrenhale, and signals could be sent from the city's towers overlooking the water.

A distant horn blared in warning. Yolias paused on a railed balcony overhanging the swamp. Across the water, the Dwarven camp was still and quiet. Less than a mile south of the camp stood Farrenhale, the village's small houses and barns barely visible now in the dark. As Yolias watched, the horn sounded again, the call coming clearly from Farrenhale. Out of the corner of his eye he caught sight of movement approaching up the North Road, obscured by the forest's edge. The rumble of hoofbeats and wheels grew steadily, and shouts went up from the Dwarven camp.

The riders and carts finally reached the camp and continued up the road at full speed. Over two dozen horses and a cartload of foot soldiers went past in a blur, but even at that distance Yolias knew them to be Goblins. He left the railing and hurried to the bridge towers.

Dwarves sounded the alarm as the goblins rode past the encampment. Several goblins fired flaming arrows into the air, and moments later beyond the wall flaming arrows shot skyward from the Goblin watchtower in reply. Burning arrows flew over the camp and set one of the Dwarves' tents ablaze. Shouts went up on all sides. Panic spread and tore frightened dwarves from their slumber.

The goblins on horseback rode up to the Wall, reined, and drew up with their backs to the Gates, fighting off the surprised Dwarven guards. The shock and unexpectedness of the Goblins' appearance inside the camp took the Dwarves aback. The cartload of archers and foot soldiers pulled up at the Gate and swung the balance there in the Goblins' favor. Goblin archers and swordsman set up a perimeter, while others began drawing back the huge bolts that locked the Gates.

Cries and shouts echoed through the Dwarven camp and Teska. "Cut the bridge!" cried those in the Bridgehouse. Soon great loops of rope were loosened and unbound, and the entire length of the wooden plank bridge dropped with a rolling *plop* into the swamp and began sinking. Hastily-written warnings were sent by bird to Kronivar, the Castle, and Miastolas, but keen-eyed Goblin archers stationed south of the swamp shot them all down as soon as they left Teska. Only a single horse and rider from Farrenhale would succeed in escaping with the news.

Loud shouts and desperate yells went up among Dwarven troops near the Wall and on top of it. Just outside the Gates a massive army of Goblins was forming like a deluge behind a dam. Great battering rams were pushed up to the Wall. Goblin catapults and trebuchets swung, and boulders flew over the wall and into the Dwarves' camp. Ladders were raised and goblins climbed the walls. Captain Torben Holgen led the defense and Goblins fell, but more began climbing. Fear spread over the dwarves on the wall. Guards dumped burning quicklime from the Gatehouse onto the attackers. Swords clashed where goblins had successfully scaled the wall. Dwarves fought and slew the invaders, and some were pulled or thrown from the walls. Rocks crushed and stone crumbled.

The Dwarves' battle rage grew as more joined the defense of the Gates. Wheeled assault towers rolled up to the wall and goblins leapt from planks onto the parapets. Blades rang and darkened with blood.

The last Goblin spies inside the Gate were cut down, but the bolts had been thrown and the Gates swung open. Soon the Goblins controlled the whole area around the Wall. A host of them poured through and were met by the Dwarves. Those who fought on top of the wall felt it tremble beneath their feet with thrusts of the battering ram. The Gates were pulled down, their great iron hinges screeching under the strain. One gate hung at an angle, its upper hinge torn away from the wall.

Above the gateway the parapets were broken, and swinging rams began to break down the walls surrounding the Gates. Hordes of goblins poured in beneath the gateway arch. A war-wagon came through and released a herd of tarred and burning swine. Squealing and grunting, they ran spreading fire, panic, and terror throughout the Dwarven camp.

Passage through the Gates cleared momentarily as booming, grinding crunches sent huge blocks of shattered masonry tumbling onto the road. Soon the entire Gatehouse collapsed. Shock struck dwarves who could not believe what they were seeing. After a few more blows of the battering rams, the breach in the wall began to widen. Goblins shot black arrows at the dwarves remaining atop the crumbling walls and swarmed over the rubble onto Dwarven ground. Captain Holgen felt the bite of Goblin arrows and toppled from the wall, only to be stabbed and skewered by Goblins on the ground.

As the gatehouse debris was pushed aside, the entire Dwarven encampment sank into horror and chaos. Fear broke Dwarven chains of command and some dwarves panicked and fled. The Goblins rolled in huge wheeled crossbows shooting bolts of red-hot iron. Black arrows flew through the night air. Everywhere dwarves and goblins clashed in combat, firelight flashing off helmets and mail, shields and blades. Hasty and confused battles erupted on all sides, the skills of many reduced to instinct and blind luck.

The breach in the wall was now twice as wide as the Gates had been. As the next wave of goblins came through, whole bands of chained augglins were brought to the front lines, starved and angry. They were huge, oversize grotesque versions of the Goblins, some big as oxen, bloated with thick muscle scarred by many whips. Mindlessly hollow eyes stared from faces deformed from generations of inbreeding for strength and size. Most dwarves had never seen augglins and found them frightening to behold. The larger ones needed six Goblin masters to hold them in check until they were unleashed on the Dwarves. One goblin at the chains showed momentary fear and was crushed by the augglin he had tried to control, despite the whips of the other five. The Dwarves continued to fight, though in terror and desperation many began to lose heart.

Squadrons of Goblin infantry marched through the ruins of the wall, carrying tall flags and banners bearing the insignia of Navrogenaya, a black raven on a field of red standing in profile with wings raised. Standards flapped in the wind. Beyond the troops large, striding shapes approached through the smoky gloom, weakly illuminated by the torches and fires of the night. These were the broadbacked Urumak, beasts of rumor among the Dwarves, for none there had ever seen one. They were huge, larger than elephants, covered in thick, shaggy brown fur. They stood on legs tall as a house and were ten to fifteen feet across from shoulder to shoulder. At the end of their long necks were large heads, shaped like neither elephant nor horse but something in between, with short, broad tusks protruding forward from a large lower jaw. Even in the half-light they fascinated and terrified the Dwarves.

The Urumak walked slowly with enormous strides of their armored legs. Apart from their bony spines, each of their backs was broad and flat enough to carry an entire *Widiwa* family and their *irlpiri*-style house built to fit comfortably over the great beast like an enormous saddle. These houses had been removed and destroyed, and the Goblins had refitted the Urumak with small war-towers, which swayed slightly as the Urumak walked. All that remained of the *Widiwa* were the drivers, tiny dark-skinned men who were larger than Gnomes but smaller than Teskans. One rode poised on the end of each Urumak's neck at the base of its skull, gently guiding and whispering to the enormous creature, both of them forced into service by the Goblins. Every driver had a metal collar attached to steering chains that ran up into the war-tower on the animal's back.

From atop a lookout tower in Teska, Yolias and Teska Humber saw the Urumak advancing through the broken wall. Yolias knew the *Widiwa* drivers' families were held in captivity to force them into submission. "Without the drivers, the Goblins may lose control of the Urumak," said Yolias.

Humber shook his head slowly. "That may be; but our men will be hesitant to fire upon them. The *Widiwa* have suffered much at the Goblins' hands as have we, and their families continue to suffer."

"Their families may have already been killed," said Yolias, "and if they do not die now, they will be slain during the war."

"Likely enough, I agree," said Humber, "but they will not be slain by Teskans."

As each Urumak passed through the ruins of the crumbling wall, a hail of arrows rained down from its swaying Goblin war-tower. Some dwarves brought out a captured wheeled crossbow to fire bolts at the eyes of the Urumak. Others hurled stones with slings or shot arrows of their own. Five more Urumak came through the gap in the wall, and several were wading through the swamp, their Goblin masters firing upon Teska.

While Humber and Yolias coordinated the city's defense, Teska Sauntu rode a *nasauri* and led the other riders in defense of the swamp. The *nasauri* were quicker and nimbler than the lumbering Urumak, dashing close around their legs, where the aim was more difficult from the war-towers. Riders tried to wound the Urumaks' great legs to slow them down, or cut the ropes and bands that bound the towers to their backs. Some launched arrows into the towers, Goblin cries revealing they had hit their marks. But many riders were also hit and fell into the swamp, losing their mounts. Two riderless *nasauri* ran grunting past an Urumak, which reared up at them, toppling its war-tower backwards into the water. The falling tower tugged at the chain around the *Widíwa* driver's neck, pulling him down and drowning him in the swamp.

The Urumak advanced on both the northern and eastern sides of Teska, as the Goblins redoubled their attack. From land, catapults fired burning tar-covered boulders overhead into the city. Dozens of fire-tipped black arrows flew from the far shores and the war-towers of the Urumak, leaving smoke trails hanging in the air behind them. All of Teska was joined in the battle around the city. Sharpened spears flew back at the Goblins, and long-necked catapults hurled stone spikes at the invaders. Bows and crossbows sent a hail of arrows, bolts, and poisoned darts over the swamp. Shouts and cries echoed across the water. Though many of the Goblins' firebrands were successfully extinguished, fires burned throughout the city. Suspended walkways weakened and collapsed. The air throughout Teska was thick with the smell of burning wood and rope.

Urumak from the eastern and northern shores led the attack on Teska, spreading the Teskans across two sides of the city while fires ravaged it from within. At last the Urumak reached the city and began landing troops upon its boardwalks. Goblins drew their zardaggers and jagged blades in anticipation of the hand-to-hand fighting which they relished. Teskan captains shouted and swords and spears were taken into hand for close combat. Although the Dwarves had supplied the Teskans with a fair number of swords, many of the Teskans still preferred their own spears, darts, and slings. Men trained in the old ways whirled and swung long *taro* poles, impaling their enemies at nine feet or at least driving them off platforms and into the swamp below.

The Teskans held the Goblins at bay for some time, but all saw that Teska was lost. All that remained was to keep the Goblins occupied for as long as they could while the women and children were evacuated to Chisk and the other villages. Much of the city was burning now, and little else could be done. On the eastern side of the city, Teska Letha stood holding his *taro* pole at the ready. Teska Kiuwaa stood beside him with bow and quiver. Letha turned to his nephew.

"Kiu, go now and take *suati* over to Chisk. I will meet you there if I can," said Letha.

"But Uncle—"

"Go now! There is nothing more you can do here. The boat is waiting, and it will be dangerous under the city. We cannot wait any longer. Go now, and hurry! *Ruathta!*" Letha barked the last word, and Kiuwaa jumped to obey. Letha watched him hurry off into the city, where so many fires lit his way.

Letha turned back sharply, the sound of Goblin feet clomping on wood catching his attention. With a swing of his broadsword, the approaching goblin chopped away the remains of a charred railing and leapt onto the far end of the platform Letha stood upon. Letha poised his *taro* pole, keeping the end of it in motion, ready for the attack. The goblin advanced warily, his eyes darting between Letha and the pole's spike-ringed sharpened point. Closing in, he swung his sword at the pole as Letha had hoped, and when the goblin's arm moved out Letha deftly thrust a well-placed jab that grazed the goblin's face, barely missing his eye.

The move startled the goblin and his anger flared. Letha backed up, hoping to lead the goblin onto a walkway above the city where an advantage might be had. The goblin followed, afraid of losing his prey. He swung his sword in two short arcs, more carefully now, trying to catch the pole with his blade. But Letha spun the pole around his sword arm, knocking against the flat of the blade and nicking the goblin's sword arm with the pole's tip. The goblin grunted, barking something in Rogglish, then came on as Letha maneuvered him up onto the walkway. Letha stopped and the goblin came at him.

Suddenly Letha lunged forward, whirling the stick into a sharp blow on the side of the head and neck, tiny spikes biting the goblin's flesh. The goblin roared and the fight erupted. The goblin slashed hash marks into the pole, but Letha matched his pace and kept drawing blood with the pole end. At last the goblin hacked off the end of the pole. Letha swung it around, expertly hitting and changing direction as the goblin tried to stop him, and caught the goblin off guard. The moment the goblin lost his balance, Letha nudged the pole and sent him tumbling off the walkway and into a burning ruin below.

Letha drew in the pole but caught sight of another goblin watching from the street. The Goblin grimaced up at him with a bow in his hand, and Letha felt the black feather-tipped shaft bite into his side. Another from an unseen assailant pierced him in the neck, and a third in his thigh brought him down. But as he lay in pain dying amidst the sound of curdled Goblin laughter, he was consoled by the thought of Kiuwaa and Ahna on their way to Chisk.

Teska Ahna sat at her bench, her spidery fingers plucking the heddles, the loom clacking rapidly in her hands and feet. Her eyes were distant, caught in a trance, and her mind swam feverishly as she worked to finish the weaving. Until he had gone to join in the defense of the city, Kiuwaa had gently kept her from completing the weaving and had even wanted to remove it from the loom unfinished. But never in all her years did she begin a weaving she did not complete. She wanted more than ever to finish this one to see if she was in it, sitting at the bench, or lying dead across it, and to discover what fate lay in store for the room.

Usually the events depicted in her weavings did not interest her. She rarely left her rooms in Teska and had no idea which, if any, of the images woven on the loom came true, or what they meant; those were the concerns of others. Unless the pictures were of Teska, she recognized few of them, and they mattered little to her once they were off her loom. But this one was different; though her eyesight was failing her, she recognized her room, and Kiuwaa and Yolias had confirmed that it was. The idea that the loom would be broken horrified her; she was certain that if she could complete the weaving and begin another, nothing would happen. Her hands ached but she would not feel pain until she was done. The shuttle flew back and forth, the shed opening and closing around it, the sound and movement and rhythm of the loom comforting her like nothing else could.

"*Suati!* What are you doing?" Kiuwaa ran into the room, out of breath, and gently tried to pry his great-grandmother's hands from the loom. "No more, *suati*. The city is burning. We must go. Uncle Letha will meet us in Chisk. Please," he pleaded, meeting with resistance. He started at a loud, muted crash somewhere outside, and thought he could hear the low husky roar of fire now. He smelled a smoky odor of wood and looked up. The ceiling was darkening on the eastern side of the room, and a hole fringed with fire began opening above.

Teska Ahna sensed herself coming back as the trance loosened its hold. She wanted to pretend it hadn't, she wanted to ignore Kiuwaa, feeling a sharp moment of anger at his interference. Never had he interrupted her work like that. But her resolve softened as the trance left her.

"We have to go now, *suati*," Kiuwaa implored. He bent over and put one arm behind Ahna's frail back, and with the other lifted her small bony legs from the bench. She gave in and let go, her hands pulling out of the threads and heddles and dropping onto her lap as Kiuwaa carried her out of the room. The hallway outside was silent and deserted, and behind them a loud thud with a cracking sound made the floor tremble beneath his feet. He remembered the unfinished weaving and pictured the fallen rafter lying across the broken beam of the loom. Kiuwaa suddenly had a strong urge to run back and peek inside to see if it was exactly like in the weaving. He resisted, the fragile weight of the body in his arms reminding him of his duty.

Kiuwaa emerged onto the zigzagging patio outside, now lit the brightest it had ever been in the depths of night. Fires burned all around the city, and they had grown much worse than when he had left Letha. One of the walkways into town was no longer usable, and Kiuwaa was glad it was not far to the boat. Carefully he held his great-grandmother and turned sideways, gingerly feeling his way down the narrow staircase leading below the city where the boat was moored. Hurried as he was, he stopped on every step with both feet, unwilling to risk losing his balance. The weight in his arms seemed heavier now, but he did not have much farther to go. Looking down, he was comforted by the sight of the boat moored and rocking on passing waves. A hanging lantern cast a flickering glow nearby. At last he stepped down from the bottom step onto the platform, and walked over and laid his great-grandmother in the prow of the boat. Kiuwaa stood and looked around, loud splashes echoing beneath the city. Here and there into the distance, beams and floorboards were collapsing into the water and flaming rafters were falling into the swamp, as more holes opened into the burning city.

Kiuwaa climbed into the stern, took the rowing pole and untied the boat. He pushed them away from the platform and into the water lanes beneath the city. It was not far to the western edge of the city, and beyond that Chisk was less than a mile away.

Suddenly a log splintered and fell burning into the water with a shower of cinders, some falling into the boat. Kiuwaa quickly wet his fingers and extinguished them. Until they were clear of the city, burning wood could fall on them at any time, he realized. Carefully Kiuwaa stood, balancing himself, then pushed his weight into pole and sent them moving forward.

Kiuwaa glanced at his great-grandmother. She looked relaxed in the prow of the boat. Now and then her face would brighten momentarily as the light of burning timbers fell around them. She laid there, eyes half open in the weak light, and he wondered what she was thinking, or if she was as anxious as he was. At least they were on their way to Chisk. He hoped Letha would be waiting for them there. As they passed some pilings on the way, Kiuwaa noticed bales of flax and jute soaking in the water. It seemed sad to him that these bundles would never be spun into fiber, and that all the work that had gone into collecting and bundling them had been for naught. Kiuwaa's attention suddenly jumped to the bow as another long beam, charred and still burning, fell into the water right ahead of them. Large pieces of wood fell along with it, some big enough to float and remain on fire. As they drew close to the boat, he quickly angled their course to the north.

In the dark beneath the city, the falling beams disoriented Kiuwaa, and for a moment he was not sure which way to go. Further away, between the pilings, he caught glimpses of other boats escaping under the city. He panicked a moment, but followed their movement and regained his bearings. Soon he saw a dark blue rectangle of moonlit swamp, slightly brighter than the fire-lit darkness around it. He pushed hard to keep their boat moving, watching ahead for anything that might fall into their path. Although it was visible, the edge of the city approached with a maddening slowness. The air was thick with smoke and cinders, and creaks and thuds in the wooden planks just above his head kept him on edge.

All at once a loud breaking boom followed by splashes sounded, and he shook, rocking the boat. He looked behind them where a huge section of platform had fallen, beams angling down into the water, flames running up and down their length. The boat moved forward as he looked and suddenly a splintered plank fell directly on top of them. Kiuwaa reached out his hands instinctively, burning them on the hot wood, and shoved the plank aside into the water. He pushed against the pole, soothing his blistering hands with the feel of it.

When they emerged from under the city and the night sky opened above them, Kiuwaa breathed in the cold night air and gave a sigh of relief. He pushed the boat out further, and saw the lights of Chisk in the distance. A few boatsmen were out in front of the city, and several small boats from Teska were on their way there already. Chisk was Teska's nearest neighbor, and had sent more warriors than any of the other villages. The Goblins were only interested in Teska because of the Dwarves, and Kiuwaa was sure they would be safe in Chisk.

As they floated away from Teska, Kiuwaa looked down at his great-grandmother lying serenely in the prow of the boat in the moonlight, frail and little. He was suddenly struck with a profound love for her, and thankfulness for Letha's insistence, glad that *suati* would be with them in Chisk. He looked forward to when they would all be together again.

Kiuwaa felt something fly past close by him and shrieked aloud as his great-grandmother was struck with two black arrows in quick succession. Standing on a balcony overlooking the water, two Goblin archers laughed and shot three more arrows into Kiuwaa, who slumped forward onto Teska Ahna in the boat. The overzealous goblins shot several more black shafts into each of them, oblivious of the need to conserve arrows and pleased to have found such easy and unsuspecting targets.

Goblin archers fired upon other boats leaving Teska during the evacuation. Many escaped, and boats from Chisk came out to meet them. In Teska, amidst fire, smoke, and collapsing buildings, battles raged throughout the city as the Teskans made their last stand. Goblin troops were still arriving by Urumak on the edges of city, and began to outnumber the Teskans there. An Urumak with wooly gray-brown fur, larger than the others, strode powerfully through the swamp. The war-tower on its back was three stories high, and more ornately carved and painted than the other war-towers. Dark green zigzag patterns framed the sills of small arched windows and alternating crescents cut into the walls provided ventilation. Red velvet lined the inside walls of the uppermost floor, where a solitary figure sat watching the burning of Teska from his high vantage point.

Yanks of the chain around his neck alerted the *Widiwa* driver that the Goblins wanted to pull up alongside the city. He steered the slow-moving Urumak into position, until its legs and side rubbed against the wooden platform. When the great beast came to a halt, a door opened in the side of the war-tower. Goblins dismounted, drawing their swords as soon as they stood firm on the platform. The last to climb down was Erog Del-Sorhar, Chief Spy of Navrogenaya, a tall, lean Goblin with muscular legs, long fingers, and sharp fiery eyes that slid to and fro, quickly assessing the situation at Teska. The goblins with him were his hand-picked trusted men, and they stood in a semi-circle looking up to the doorway of the war-tower. After a moment, a tall, dark-robed figure appeared there and stepped outside and down onto the platform. He wore a long black coat but no hat, and his dark hair whipped in the wind like black fire. Del-Sorhar stepped forward to greet the Grand Vizier, bowing slightly and grinning slyly. "Lord Maëlveronde, I present you the city of Teska."

"I am sure the King will be pleased," said Maëlveronde, returning his gaze. The other goblins looked on. There was, among them, a fascination with King Golhazzar's Grand Vizier, the old man with the strange foreign name who had risen in the ranks to become a confidant of the King. They were always nervous around him and rumor had it that he was a sorcerer of some kind. Maëlveronde glanced around at them, but they were afraid to meet his gaze. He was an old man, over two hundred years by some accounts, his hawk-like features lined with age, yet still he was feared throughout Navrogenaya, his name rarely spoken aloud. The corners of his mouth turned down now into his short black beard that tapered to a point, and his cold eyes fixed them with a sharp glance that seemed to pierce their inner being and divine all their secret vices. He turned back to Del-Sorhar. "They know what to search for. Send them out, and we will follow."

Del-Sorhar turned and with a shout sent his goblins off through Teska. Then he and Maëlveronde strode through the burning city at a more leisurely pace, examining all the damage and enjoying the warmth of the fires. Most of the Teskans were gone already, but Del-Sorhar walked with his sword drawn, crossing blades and dispatching several Teskans along the way. Twice, hidden Teskan archers shot arrows at them, but Maëlveronde merely raised his hand, palm out, deflecting the arrows in other directions without touching them.

Teska was nearly deserted now and some of the fires were dying out. Empty spaces opened where buildings had stood and walkways had hung only hours before. Down the streets that remained, missing planks and holes revealed the debris-strewn waters below the city. Plumes of smoke rose on all sides. Del-Sorhar's goblins had spread out and passed through Teska, flanked by the last blazing beams and charred rafters of collapsing buildings. Foot soldiers bearing standards of the black raven on red marched across the city. Behind a post, Yolias waited and caught one goblin by surprise. In minutes Yolias had the goblin at a disadvantage and backed him into a fire. Soon his body rolled into the swamp.

Alone again, Yolias moved warily through the city. He had killed several goblins already, but the gash in his leg from his fight with Orven was paining him again. It had grown worse of late and Yolias tried to ignore it. Once in awhile it flared up causing him to limp, and there was little he could do about it. But soon he would rejoin the Dwarven troops on shore. He hoped they had fared better than the Teskans.

Yolias raised his sword as a goblin approached. This one was different, he thought, readying himself for the challenge. The goblin saw him and laughed haughtily.

"A dwarf, stranded out over the water!" Del-Sorhar taunted. "It'll be a watery grave for you, then!" He swung his sword, and Yolias met Del-Sorhar's blade with his own. Each expected an inferior opponent but quickly sensed the other's skills, delighted to find a more than worthy adversary.

Yolias and Del-Sorhar were evenly matched. Their swings and parries and counterparries were swift and sure, their blades biting into each other with such ferocity that sparks flew from them. They moved nimbly across the wooden platforms, stepping over holes and around jagged planks and fiery beams, without losing sight of each other. Yolias knew several Goblin fighting styles, but Del-Sorhar was a master of the sword as well and kept Yolias guessing. Yolias led Del-Sorhar through the skeletal frame of a charred and still-burning building. Del-Sorhar sidestepped out of the trap and swung his sword, splintering a support beam, releasing a frame of blackened rafters. The falling firewood grazed Yolias's arm and shoulder as he pulled away. He lunged around, forcing Del-Sorhar to step back. The goblin stumbled but caught himself in time.

The fight went on, with neither Yolias nor Del-Sorhar able to get a clear advantage. Both had fought long that day, but the challenge of a close fight fueled the intensity of their combat. Now they were high up on a platform over the city, where a tower had been reduced to a haphazard pile of broken planks and beams underfoot. Del-Sorhar's size kept him from being as nimble as Yolias, and he began to regret moving onto the high platform. More than once he had to glance away from Yolias to be sure of his footing. At last Yolias caught him off balance and swung his sword, catching Del-Sorhar's blade and knocking it from his hand as the goblin fell backward onto a woodpile. The sword flew across the wood and dropped over the edge of the platform.

Del-Sorhar stared in shock, for such a thing had never happened to him before. Yolias stood over him, victorious, and raised his sword for a final blow. As Yolias stepped forward and put his weight on his left leg, he cringed as pain flared in the wound from Orven, causing him to waver. Del-Sorhar, already in motion, grabbed a wooden beam and swung it hard, hitting Yolias on the side of the head. Yolias fell to the ground still grasping his sword. Del-Sorhar sprang up and hit Yolias again before he could react, then stomped his sword arm and brought the beam down on Yolias so hard that it cracked. After wresting the sword away from Yoilas, Del-Sorhar turned it on him and with several thrusts broke through his chain mail, stabbing him deep in the chest. Yolias lay on the ground as he bled, staring up at Del-Sorhar standing over him. He saw his sword in the goblin's hand, his own blood running down the blade.

A dark figure in a long black coat stepped up onto the platform behind Del-Sorhar. "Well done," he said. Del-Sorhar turned and moved aside. Maëlveronde reached out to examine the sword, and Del-Sorhar handed it to him. As Maëlveronde took it, Yolias saw a deep red gem sparkle in a ring on his hand. Maëlveronde returned the sword to Del-Sorhar, disappointed. "Not what I had hoped, but it will still make a fine trophy for you," said Maëlveronde.

As the lifeblood flowed from his veins, Yolias weakened, lightheaded and aching. His vision swam and all grew hazy. He saw Del-Sorhar raise his sword, felt a sharp explosion of pain as it fell, and then was gone.

Teska burned, and the glow of the fires on the swamp gradually diminished. On the eastern shore, dwarves lay strewn about the ground, and Goblins pillaged the deserted buildings of Farrenhale. Others strode through the ruins of the Dwarven encampment, plundering and slaying dwarves who had fallen but were not yet dead.

Bonfires lit the cluttered camp and goblins ringed around them, resting, talking, shouting, and laughing. Limbs of the Augglins killed in battle were skewered and roasting on spits, the flesh on them dripping and blackening as the goblins licked their lips. The Goblins toasted large mugs, singing loud, harsh war-songs, and their deep voices shook the night air as they sang.

Striking is the sight
Of lightning slicing night!
Our mighty swords shine brightly
As we put our foes to flight!

Thrilling is the feel
Of cold and cruel steel!

Blades drawn, we come to conquer
And in battle show our zeal!

Acrid is the smell
Of battles waging well!
Dispatching foes in kingdoms
Where our fathers once did dwell!

Raucous is the sound
Of victors gathered round!
Whose bold, courageous efforts
Now triumphantly are crowned!

Bitter is the taste
Of honor that's disgraced!
Let us reclaim the mountains
Our ancestors embraced!

As the night wore on and morning drew near, goblins heaped booty on the ground and piled it into carts, and distributed stores of food from Farrenhale. Shifts of goblins slept while others remained busy. Some tended to the shaggy Urumak, cleaning and resting them for the great march south. Throughout the goblin camp ran a rush of exhilaration and victory, and a growing hunger for further advancement into Itharia.

On the eastern shore of the swamp, Maëlveronde stood surveying the last fires burning in Teska. On his arm he bore a hawk, which he spoke to tenderly and then raised and released into the sky, where it went forth to do his bidding. He watched as it flew away, dark brown against a black sky paling to the east.

Del-Sorhar and several of his men approached Maëlveronde along the shore. They had just returned from plundering Teska and two of them carried a large, bent bundle.

"Lord Maëlveronde, the loom you spoke of was destroyed in the attack," said Del-Sorhar, "But we found these and rescued them from the fire." He gestured to the men who unrolled the large bolt of thick cloth they carried. It was a sheaf of weavings, each a colorful tapestry. The two goblins held them out for Maëlveronde to see, tilting them towards the light of the fires from across the swamp, while a third held up a lantern. Maëlveronde considered them carefully.

The first tapestry was of the burning of Teska, and the tapestry itself was burnt on one side. The next showed a scene in Teska or one of the other poled cities of the swamp, and the one after that had a landscape scene of picnickers in front of Glanting Hall in Tolgard. Another depicted streets in Navrogenaya where goblins shopped and traded. The next few images likewise contained nothing of real import, but the last one Maëlveronde took and examined closely. It was the image of himself in the Stone Forest beneath Castle Frosthelm, holding a sword and leaning over the body of a fallen dwarf whose sword lay out of reach a few feet away. Maëlveronde considered the image in silence.

Del-Sorhar nodded at the image. "We thought it a good omen," he added, disappointed that Maëlveronde's reaction had not been more enthusiastic.

"There is no guarantee that what these weavings show will come true," Maëlveronde replied, still absorbed with the details of the image. "Though it is useful to consider them. It is a shame the loom was destroyed." He handed the weaving back to them. "It bodes well, but we must be cautious. The Teskans will have certainly shown this image to the Dwarves. And so we will not rely on it or put our faith in it," Maëlveronde said. A faint smile flickered on his face in the dim light. "But perhaps our enemies will."

Book V: Sieges and Sorcery

Chapter 35.
A Change of Plans

The day dawned cool and bright in Kronivar, and a great mass of supply carts moved amidst hundreds of men and dwarves marching through the New Town Square. That morning, while goblins pillaged the smoking remains of Teska and Farrenhale, Kronivar's streets were full of troop activity. Though news of the burning of Teska would not reach Kronivar for several days, word of the battle of Halloway had arrived in late afternoon of the previous day and spread fast, upsetting everyone greatly. That evening Grawson, the Duke of Kronivar, had convened the Counts and laid out his plans for the defense of the city. The garrisoned troops were mobilized and the watch around the city's perimeter was doubled. And now nearly half of Count Orming's troops, under the command of General Thon Aranstone, were being sent out to hold the Gundithe Plateau above Greensward.

Two figures stood shadowed under the eaves on a balcony overlooking the New Town Square, watching Aranstone and his men marching down the street. Count Raymin was a man of medium build and strong but delicate features, while Count Mothmoon was a tall, long-limbed, pale and distant figure, his long gray beard parted in two prongs. Both regarded Aranstone's troops leaving with amusement and relief.

"Brinksmanship, it was, sending Orming's troops off to Gundithe with so little warning. News of the attack couldn't have come at a better time," said Count Mothmoon.

"I heard Orming was furious afterward," said Raymin, "I was amazed at his restraint when Grawson laid out his plans."

Count Mothmoon nodded without turning to Raymin. "And to think Grawson briefly considered sending the garrisoned troops to hold the plateau…"

Raymin turned to Mothmoon. "Well, it *was* what the King ordered. I wonder what will happen now when the King finds out Orming's troops have been sent instead of his own. It may go badly for Grawson."

"I doubt it; the Castle knows Kronivar's importance, even as they envy it. Sending Orming's troops and keeping the garrisoned troops strengthens the King's hand here and weakens Orming's. Were the King more directly involved, he would certainly have welcomed Grawson's shrewd move," said Mothmoon.

"Perhaps, yes… though as Grawson noted when we spoke alone, nothing in the castle spies' reports could be tied directly to any of the Counts, not even to Orming." Raymin glanced at Mothmoon. "But he also told me that just yesterday he received an anonymous note from someone on the insides of Orming's schemings; proof was even sent. Aranstone and his advisor Greywood were named as not to be trusted." Raymin turned to Mothmoon and smiled. "You know nothing of the note? I thought one of your men had sent it."

Mothmoon's solemn features registered mild surprise. "Mine? Not mine; I thought yours had. Has Grawson faced Orming with it yet?"

"No, but he won't need to now, with Orming's men reduced." He watched as the last of Aranstone's troops passed below them. "Sending Orming's men was the wisest course, and with the proof he has, he could explain the decision easily enough, should the King take him to task for it."

"And what of Abern and Sherleaf?" asked Mothmoon.

"Perhaps it will finally discourage those fence-sitters from siding with Orming," Raymin said, glancing sidelong at Mothmoon.

Aranstone rode near the front of the troops, with Greywood's steed at his side. Their entire company was in a quiet, foul mood that morning, having voiced their protests the night before and again right after waking. Aranstone contained his outrage, but his edginess and short temper revealed how close to the surface it lay. Greywood spoke with Aranstone, calming him, and whatever resentment he felt remained hidden behind his steel-gray eyes. As they passed out of Kronivar and through the outlying farmlands, they became somber and thoughtful.

"It's too sudden, sending us out like this," Aranstone said, "They must have found out something."

"It is the King's doing, of that we can be certain," said Greywood. "Perhaps the King included a spy's report with his orders. It could have been that castle spy posing as a barmaid, who escaped."

"No, that was almost a month ago," said Aranstone, "If that were the case, they would have acted sooner."

"Unless Grawson was biding his time, waiting for the right opportunity. He wouldn't have dared it before the garrison was full," said Greywood.

"And now an unpleasant duty awaits us at the end of a long march," Aranstone said. "And there will be little for us to do on the plateau. We did not hire men to wait, and they are already growing restless." Aranstone shook his reins a little. "At our captains' meeting tonight we shall see what can be done for morale. Which reminds me, how is Orven doing, and those men you put under him?"

"They will keep an eye on him," said Greywood. "Orven enjoys being in command and it is obvious he has never done so before." Greywood smiled slightly. "They bristle at his arrogance, unearned as it is, but with their help he is learning how things are done and what he needs to know. And he is willing to learn, so they tell me, albeit in his own stubborn way."

"And his loyalties?" asked Aranstone.

Greywood shook his head. "We need not worry. They say he spoke ill of the Castle and a visit there that went badly. He even fought the Castle guards, and they turned him and his friends away. That's what brought him to Kronivar, evidently. I talked to Orven myself last night, briefly, and it was as they said."

Aranstone looked at Greywood. "And did Orven or any of his friends ever say where those two swords of theirs came from?"

"Apparently not," Greywood returned his gaze. "Though, of course, what concerns us more is where they will end up."

Further back in the throng marched Orven and his friends, disappointed to be leaving the comforts and excitement of Kronivar so soon. Over the past three days they had met a good many of Aranstone's troops, strange foreigners and dwarves quite different from those of the Foothills. Aaron and Roy found the mercenaries intimidating, though they tried not to show it and were glad everyone was on the same side. Orven and his friends better understood what was expected of them, and were falling into the rhythms of life in Aranstone's camp. Relishing his new position as captain, Orven spent his time meeting people, learning what he could, and doing his best to try and impress others. Max, Aaron, and Roy were happy for him, though they all thought it had gone to his head. At Aranstone's orders, two mercenaries, known as Rafnel and Strable, and Haidren Elkherd, a dwarf from Kronivar, had been added to Orven's command. Max and the others welcomed them, although they had liked it better when it was just Orven and themselves, and no outsiders. But Orven wanted more men under his command and was glad to have them.

"Though I would have expected more than just three," Orven complained to Max as they walked along now. The others were farther behind in the crowd, so they could talk freely. "All these men, hundreds of them, and only nine captains. And yet I have so few under my command. Some of the other captains have squadrons that have more men than I do. It just isn't fair!"

"Well, Orven, you've just started out, maybe they'll give you more later," said Max.

"I hope so," said Orven, "I've done all I can so far, I think I've proven myself."

"Proven yourself? How? We haven't seen any battle yet," said Max. "We may not, either, up on the plateau, unless the Goblins get through Teska and Farrenhale, and even then, we're really just keeping them from entering the mountains. Not that I mind that —not seeing battle, I mean. Maybe we'll attack them from behind when they march on Kronivar. I just wish we were through camping outdoors. It's getting too cold, and it'll be even colder up in the mountains."

"Yes, I wonder what this is all about," said Orven, "No one seems to have expected it. Or to like it. There's been grumbling about the King among the troops."

"I've heard it, too," said Max, wondering how Aranstone felt about it.

"Greywood asked me what I thought of it, and I told him all about our visit to the Castle," said Orven.

"Oh, Orven, you shouldn't have done that, he might not—"

"No, not at all," Orven waved it off, "He seemed amused by the story. Said it was just what he expected of the Castle, how they never could see the value of dwarves from other parts. Or the importance of anything beyond the Castle. He said King Jordgen won't admit that Kronivar has become the heart of the Kingdom now."

"Well, I don't know about that," said Max, "But I'm not looking forward to sitting up on the plateau for who knows how long..."

"The worst of it," said Orven, "is that we won't get a chance to do much of anything there. All the glory that will be had will be either in Kronivar, or maybe even only at the front, if the Goblins are kept at bay."

"Let's hope they are," said Max. "And anyway, we *could* have stayed in Farrenhale, too, you know."

"True, true," said Orven, "I'm not complaining. I think we did the right thing; I can just feel it. There's more opportunity for us here with Aranstone. Maybe you're right, maybe they want to see how I'll do with a few men before they give me more. Well, they'll see..." Orven's sternness and self-importance made Max smile to himself. He was pleased to see Orven so happy, yet he wondered if Orven was aware of how much the past three days had changed him.

"Just don't get any more arrogant than you already are," said Max, worried that Orven might not take it in the friendly way it was intended.

Orven flashed a sharp look at Max that quickly faded into a bemused smile. "If you don't seem confident, they aren't going to trust you." There was an edge to his words. "They *asked* me to be a captain, I didn't ask them." He nodded to Halix on Max's belt. "You might have tried to become one yourself, or at least asked about it. You didn't do too bad that night against Pyrwoed, you know."

Max nodded, though he knew it was mainly due to the sword that he had done as well as he did. He even thought he could lead a squadron; yet somehow, he did not feel the desire to do so. After the fights aboard the *Riantar*, he had found favor among the troops, though nothing like Orven's popularity. Orven had also suggested that Max could now carry Halix as his own, rather than taking turns with the others. Aaron and Roy had given in without much argument, but Ripley had been quite upset, until Max and Orven calmed him down, saying he could use it now and then occasionally, though neither really promised him anything.

"Well, if they ask me, maybe I'll consider it," said Max, knowing full well they wouldn't ask him.

"You don't have to," said Orven, "but don't begrudge it to me, then, either."

They walked in silence for a while until Max was sure that Orven wasn't upset with him. "And if they hadn't asked you," he said finally, "you would have demanded they make you a captain anyway, wouldn't you?"

"Of course," said Orven.

Aranstone's company traveled east all that day and the next, taking turns marching and riding in the extra wagons that weren't loaded down with supplies. On the second day, the few rest stops they took were brief, as they wanted to reach the Gundithe Plateau before nightfall. The sun passed overhead without warming the brisk air. As the troops approached Greensward, it lowered into the west, stretching their shadows in front of them and bathing the mountains in a reddish-purple glow. By dusk the company began climbing the wide road snaking back and forth across the slope leading up to the plateau. It was the most demanding part of their journey, and came at the end of a long day. Only weariness kept their tempers from flaring. Even their grumblings against the Castle settled into a silent festering and there was very little talking amongst them. The sinking sun and darkening sky further burdened their spirits, and the thought of camping on the cold rock shelf of the plateau offered little comfort.

The climb seemed interminably long, the road reversing and winding farther upward just as they hoped it had reached the plateau. Eventually as the stars appeared overhead, the road turned and widened and finally they arrived. Aranstone had his tent and campsite set up on a rise at the back of the plateau, while everyone else spread out in groups across the wide rock shelf. The captains had their squadron leaders keep everyone together, and Orven's group of eight sat ringed about a small campfire near the end of the plateau, not far from their tent at the edge of the semicircle. Soon everyone was settled, and dinner rations were sent around, as well as the schedule of watches for the night.

"Quite a view from here," said Rafnel, looking out over the land.

"Neither of us have ever been anywhere in Itharia, outside of Kronivar," explained Strable.

"Yes, it is something, isn't it?" said Orven. The last time he had passed through he had been in too much of a hurry to get to the Castle to appreciate the view. Now he looked out into the vast starred darkness and saw that the plateau did indeed command a wide, broad vista, beginning with the small village of Greensward far below them. Somehow looking down on everything from above lifted his spirits a little.

Orven turned back to his men. That was how he had begun thinking of them since he was put in command. He had attempted to get to know the three newcomers better in the last few days, and was pleased with them. Blanes Rafnel and Anrelius Strable were both from Tolgard and had known each other there before they had set sail on the *Riantar*. They were, Orven guessed, only a few years older than him, yet they were very knowledgeable in the ways of the world and what they jokingly referred to as the 'mercenary arts'. Orven was intrigued by the idea that they would fight for Itharia for money, though they did talk about settling in Kronivar if all went well for them.

"Of course, there wasn't much reason for us to travel outside of Kronivar," said Strable, "and foreigners are not too well-thought of in some parts, or so I've heard."

Rafnel nodded. "It is different there from the rest of Itharia; in Kronivar, I mean. All the trading going on, and people from all around the Silver Sea coming there... What about you Orven, are you going to settle there after the war?"

"Possibly," said Orven, as uncertain as he was hopeful.

"I've lived in Kronivar my whole life," said Haidren. Haidren Elkherd, Orven had learned, was the son of a Dwarven shop owner struggling to stay in business in the far corner of the Old Town Square. Haidren had grown up seeing his father's difficulties and listening to his cursing, and decided, much to his father's chagrin, to try his hand at something else. Orven was surprised he was in favor of Kronivar becoming a separate nation-state even though he was a Dwarf. "We'd be better off on our own," Haidren said, "We could keep all the tribute going to the Castle, and it would be good for business all around. Not under Grawson, perhaps, but there are others."

"You forget it's the King who helped Kronivar grow and encouraged the trade there," said Max, "A lot of the tribute paid goes back into building the city." Max remembered his father and his uncle discussing royal tribute and was happy to be able to add something to the discussion.

"And if it weren't for King Orglen a hundred years ago, it'd be in Goblin hands now," said Aaron.

"Well, neither the Goblins nor the Dwarves are a sailing people," said Rafnel, "but of course we prefer the Dwarves, given the choice..."

"And it *has* taken Tolgarders, Ellurians, and traders from Phamiar and elsewhere to make it what it is," said Strable. "You know, I've heard there'll soon be as many Men as Dwarves in Kronivar, if things continue as they have."

"So they claim," said Haidren, "though no one's made a fair count of them lately—"

"Someone was saying that Aranstone is one-quarter Dwarven," Orven said, hoping to divert the topic to safer ground.

"It's true," said Rafnel, smiling. "He's done quite well for a mixed-breed, wouldn't you say?"

Orven stared at Rafnel, unsure if his comment was intended as a compliment or an insult to the Dwarves.

"We wouldn't be here if it weren't for him and Greywood," Strable added, "Aranstone really does have the respect and the confidence of the men. Joining him was the best of all the opportunities we've ever had." He looked knowingly at Rafnel, who returned his gaze, and then back at Orven. "And Greywood, too. Orming's fortunate to have both of them."

"Though he might have put them —and us— to better use, rather than allowing us to be sent out up here, in the cold," said Rafnel.

"I think we can all agree with that," said Orven.

Just then Harrel walked by their campsite and nodded to Orven. "Captain's meeting tonight, Orven. They've got supper for us, too. You didn't forget, did you?"

"No, no," Orven said, jumping up to follow Harrel. "All right, Max, like I said before, you're in charge while I'm gone." And with that he turned and left with Harrel.

Max shook his head. "I wish he wouldn't do that."

Rafnel seemed amused. "He enjoys his command, doesn't he?"

"Too much," said Max.

"At least they probably won't promote him any further," said Aaron.

"Yes, that's rather unlikely, isn't it?" Strable smiled, a gleam of firelight reflecting in his eyes.

Orven and Harrel made their way through the crowd settling in on the plateau, towards Aranstone's tent, which stood upon a wide slab of rock near the cliff wall. A bright fire burned there, and Orven saw Aranstone and Greywood sitting around it with others. As Orven and Harrel took their places, they received their portions of the roast that Aranstone and Greywood shared with the captains.

As they ate, Orven looked around at the other captains. He had heard much about Khale, Pyrwoed, Faltusk, and Harrel over the last few days, and he especially admired Khale and Pyrwoed for their skills and style of command. Orven realized that had he known more about them that first night on the *Riantar*, he would have been too intimidated to fight them. But now they were all friends, and he hoped to get to know them better. Neither Khale nor Pyrwoed were from Itharia, and he still had not learned where they were from. Harrel was a Dwarf, and Faltusk was only half-Dwarven, or at least that was what he had heard. Orven felt more comfortable around them, and they seemed more disposed to talking to him. Olmic was a Dwarf, and the oldest of all the captains. Orven had seen very little of him and had met him only briefly. The other three captains, a dwarf named Sparlow and two men named Hult and Wortle, Orven did not know at all, and even now they seemed aloof, with an air of seriousness Orven decided to emulate.

As they finished eating, the small talk between the captains died down, and their attention fell to Aranstone and Greywood as the meeting began. Aranstone looked at all of them, the whites of his eyes bright in his tanned face. "So here we sit here on the plateau, banished as it were; mere sentries waiting for the Goblins' approach and little more than a deterrent to deflect them into Kronivar. Many of your men are in a foul mood and lookout duty is all we can offer them."

"They grow restless," offered Faltusk, "Especially since it is uncertain how long we shall have to remain here." The others nodded, adding their own observations. It was harder to lead without clear goals for the men, and there was general agreement that morale was already a problem and would worsen as the days passed.

"No doubt Count Orming considers his gold ill-spent, and Grawson knows more than he is letting on," said Aranstone.

Greywood nodded. "Grawson would have backed down, if Orming had stood up to him. Abern and Sherleaf might even have joined Orming, but there will be little hope of alliance now after such a show of weakness. Orming wants much but risks too little." He turned to Aranstone. "Were you in his position, I am sure you would have won the other Counts over to your side, perhaps even Grawson as well."

Aranstone seemed uncomfortable at the compliment and shrugged slightly. "Grawson is weak but shrewd. Orming could topple him, but, as you say, he pulls back too often. If the yoke is to be thrown off and Kronivar is to become a free state, we must act; yet he continues to waver. And now it would seem our chance is past."

They were all quiet a moment in the crackle and warmth of the fire, as gloom settled over them. Greywood, however, looked hopeful. "Is it though? Perhaps we can give Orming the push that would set him firmly on the course, forcing his hand and setting things in motion."

Aranstone grunted. "Sitting up here in the mountains while Kronivar readies itself? How, then? Return to Kronivar? But they would surely have advance word of our return, and the King has too many troops garrisoned there."

A silent moment passed, the captains looking into the fire and nodding in agreement.

"Too many indeed," said Greywood. "And many more at the front. So many, in fact, that we could lay siege to Castle Frosthelm."

The captains glanced up in surprise, as Aranstone stared at Greywood, trying to read his intent. Greywood held his gaze, waiting for a reply.

The fire snapped and the tension grew, until finally Aranstone's sternness broke with a sudden sharp laugh. "A good jest, my friend, but this is hardly the time for joking."

Greywood paused but did not smile, and they saw he was serious. "You do not agree? Whether we fight the King's forces in Kronivar or at the Castle is it not to the same end? Certainly, it would be a show of strength, and an unexpected one. They would take our demands more seriously and be forced to listen. Kronivar has long been the heart of Itharia, though the King is loath to acknowledge it. He has brought this on himself, ignoring the situation in Kronivar for too long, just as he put off preparations for war. If Itharia and Kronivar are to be allies, they should be as equals: each its own nation. That is all I would ask. A siege would best show how weak the Castle has become. They would have to listen to our demands. And the longer such negotiations take, and the longer we can hold out, the more it will upset the balance of power in Kronivar in our favor."

Aranstone was quiet now, considering. The captains all watched eagerly, enjoying the exchange and waiting for Aranstone's reply.

"Even if a siege was successful, I doubt the King would give in so easily," said Aranstone.

"True, he could resist, even as a hostage," said Greywood, "but once we had control of the messaging tower, he would be cut off from Kronivar. And we could issue an ultimatum or whatever reports we wanted; that would certainly be unsettling. Of course, Grawson could send troops up from Kronivar, but they would take a while to get to the Castle and sending them would lessen his strength in Kronivar as well." Greywood paused. "In the end, it may not even matter whether the King gives in; it will be out of his hands."

Aranstone studied Greywood, weighing all he had said. The fire leapt and snapped, throwing large, shifting shadows on the rock wall behind them. Orven was shocked and fascinated by the idea of a siege, and noticed the other captains were intrigued as well, though the Dwarven ones appeared more wary of it.

"I agree, it would help us, were it possible to do as you say," Aranstone said, "But to try to lay siege to the Castle..."

"It may not be as impossible as you think," said Greywood, "As I've said, most of the King's army is away at the front or garrisoned in Kronivar—"

"We have many men, but not enough," said Aranstone, "Yes, most troops have left the Castle, but a good number are still encamped in the valleys around Mount Frosthelm, armed and ready to leave at a moment's notice, their supply wagons loaded and waiting in the castle's outer ward. According to the figures from our castle spies —what few remain— their number in the valley is still far greater than ours here."

"I have seen the figures," Greywood said.

"And even if that were not the case," Aranstone continued, "there is still the Castle itself. Its walls are well fortified and can be held by a few against an army of many. We would have no hope against it."

"Quite true," Greywood admitted, "if we were trying to take the Castle by force from without. But we need not take it by force. We are friend, not foe; or so the Castle thinks. Not the King, perhaps, but by the time he learns of our arrival it will be too late. The guards will let us in readily enough, and we still have five spies within the castle, several of whom are in the guard, and they can help arrange things to our benefit. We can send a messenger ahead of us to the Castle to alert them of our plans and assure that our arrival does not cause too much suspicion too soon."

"Go on," said Aranstone.

Greywood leaned forward, pleased at how attentive they were. "Once we're inside the outer ward of the Castle, we position our men along the wall of the outer ward, especially where it joins the east and west wings of the Castle. At a given signal, we all act together and overtake the unsuspecting guards there. We would effectively cut the wall off from the Castle. Once we have the outer ward, the inner ward will not be difficult to take, and we can station men at all the entrances to the Castle, working our way in. Most of the guard is stationed on the wall of the outer ward, so we should have less trouble once it is in our grasp. Of course, our surprise will be short-lived, and we will not go unopposed; the troops encamped in the valleys around the Castle are sure to come to the Castle's aid. But as you pointed out, a small army can hold the fortified walls securely against many. And so we shall."

Aranstone nodded. "And we would have their supply wagons in the outer ward as well."

"Exactly," said Greywood, "and while the outer wall is held, our remaining men will lay siege to the Castle itself, confining its occupants as tightly as possible, until they accept our terms. Again, we are not undertaking a coup, but rather a show of force to encourage the Castle to submit to a treaty acknowledging Kronivar as a separate state, and for the withdrawal of the King's troops from the garrison."

"It will all depend on how quickly we can secure the outer ward," said Pyrwoed, "our actions will have to be well-coordinated."

"Yes," said Greywood, "we shall have to plan carefully." He stood and reached into the tent, bringing out a large map, and then sat down again and unrolled it. "Though most of our spies were found out, a few skilled ones remain. This map indicates how the wall is fortified, as well as the guard rotations."

"It seems you have given it much thought," said Aranstone, settling back after glancing over the map. He could see the captains were, for the most part, very much in favor of the plan. "Yet there may be some among our troops who will not agree to this; some who may even become a danger to us if they learn of it."

The other captains voiced agreement. "I know of several among my own men," said Olmic, "Dwarves supporting the King, loyal to a fault."

"I have some like that as well," Harrel added.

Greywood raised his hands to quell their unrest. "We will need to leave an occupying force behind us to hold the plateau, or rather, appear to hold it, so that no one will suspect our plans from afar, especially in Kronivar. I suggest each of you make a list as to who you feel should be left behind. We will give them an excuse for our departure; perhaps the King has armaments or supplies that are to be brought back to the plateau. Or maybe he distrusts our mercenary friends and requires an audience with them, to test their loyalty—"

Khale laughed. "And perhaps he has sent a list, indicating who he trusts and who can be left behind on the plateau, while the rest of us go grumbling off on a trip to the Castle." The other captains laughed, suggesting how the announcement could be worded.

"Yes," said Greywood, "whatever the case, few will desire more hiking through the mountains. Once we have separated out those who might betray us, we can reveal our plan to the rest on our way to the Castle. I suggest we decide now who will be with us and who will not, and then discuss how to employ everyone when we get to the Castle." He looked to Aranstone. "With your leave, of course, General."

Aranstone nodded. "Let us see how many will join us." He motioned for the captains to begin drawing up lists and they set to work among themselves. He turned to Greywood then. "It will be difficult, but I see it is possible, as you say. We have much to work out tonight. I still have my doubts."

"I am sure you do. And that is good, for we must plan for every contingency. But think what it will mean for you when we succeed. You will be known as the one who made Kronivar a free state."

"Perhaps," Aranstone said stolidly, though Greywood could see the idea appealed to him. "Now let me see that map again..."

For the next hour or so the captains discussed who could be trusted and who couldn't, and what part they hoped to play in the siege. Greywood talked with each of them in turn, fielding objections and working with them as they developed their plans. An air of enthusiasm animated them now, for the first time since their assignment to the plateau.

The captains drew up lists which were collected and examined. Aranstone and Greywood paged through them, nodding and giving their opinions on the men they knew. Patient and nervous, Orven waited, still readjusting to the changed plans. A siege was a bold move, and he was skeptical, yet the other captains were in favor of it and Orven did not want to appear unconfident in front of them. Things were quite different from what he had expected when he had first joined Aranstone's party, but he was determined to stay in control of his fate. And he still felt as though he had to prove himself and justify his rank of captain. Well, he would, he thought, idly fingering Gorflange's hilt.

Greywood finished paging through the lists and looked up. "Orven, you haven't turned in a list," he said.

"No," said Orven, "I have few men and know them well enough. They will all be with us." Orven straightened his posture, as though it would help him remain firm and resolute.

"You're certain of this?" said Aranstone.

"Yes," said Orven. They had given him very few men, and he simply could not afford to lose even one of them. He wondered if that was part of their plan: weed out his men, gradually stripping away what little power he had, until finally he would be asked to relinquish the swords. No, he decided, he would keep all his men, whatever it took. He knew Aaron, Roy, and Max would not want any part of a siege of the Castle. But they were under his command now. And, he thought, in the long run it would be for their own good; once they all had fine estates around Kronivar, they'd laugh at their reluctance and thank Orven for his leadership in their younger days. Nor would they find out about the siege until they were already on their way to the Castle. They would know better than try to turn back or go against the crowd. "My men are behind me, you have nothing to worry about."

Aranstone and Greywood looked at Orven. "Very well," Aranstone said. Greywood seemed to accept Aranstone's decision, and so they turned to other things. Over the next few hours plans were drawn up, and the squadrons' positions and roles were decided, the captains making suggestions and discussing who might be stationed where. At last when their plans were finalized, a messenger was appointed who would precede them to the Castle, supposedly bringing news from Greensward. The fires had burned low now, and the plateau was darker as the captains returned to their tents.

"We will get an early start tomorrow," Greywood told them as the meeting ended, "and in the evening announce the plan to those joining us. You are their leaders, and soon you will be the founders of a new nation. One that will grow and flourish, until your names are known in all the kingdoms around the Silver Sea." The captains responded with exclamations of agreement, reassuring Orven that he was doing the best thing, not only for himself but for his friends as well.

Walking back to his campsite, Orven imagined himself as an old and venerable leader of the people, standing on the main balcony of his mansion, hailed by cheering citizens below, an enormous crowd stretching beyond his statue in the town square. Orven smiled at his friends as he approached their fire. Once he was in power, Max would be his main general and second-in-command, while Ripley would be his sergeant-at-arms. He pictured Roy as his treasurer and steward, and Aaron as his trusted advisor. Yes, Orven thought, he could begin as a Lord, and as the nation grew, perhaps he would eventually have his own province.

Orven sat down at the campsite and everyone began asking him about the captains' meeting. He told them how they would be leaving for the Castle the next day while others stayed behind. Orven found he was a bit nervous as he told them, wondering how they would take it. Rafnel and Strable complained and Haidren was indignant, but Orven was surprised at how hurt his friends seemed.

"We were named on the King's list?" said Max, "I can see questioning the loyalty of the merce—of the foreigners, but to question the loyalty of Dwarves..."

"They don't even know us!" said Ripley.

Orven shrugged. "Well, considering how things went when we visited the Castle—"

"That's true," said Roy, "but how would they have known us? We never gave them our names. How could we be on the list?" The others considered this and nodded.

"Well, we are," Orven snapped. He realized he had not thought out his version of the excuse very well and worried they would continue pursuing their questions. "And anyway, I have my orders."

"But we couldn't have been—" Max began.

"Max!" Orven was nervous now and fought to control himself. He lowered his voice, and groped for some way to end the conversation. "Look, I'm only telling you what they said... I—I don't know how they—"

"It must have been Iaven," Aaron spoke suddenly. "He came to the Castle after us, he could have told them all about us and given them our names."

"Yes, that's it," said Orven, greatly relieved. For once Aaron had helped him instead of pointing out the faults in his plans. "It must have been Iaven. He's right."

"Hmmm…" Max nodded and they all seemed satisfied with the explanation.

"Well, it's late and we're getting an early start tomorrow," said Orven. He started preparing his bedroll, hoping they would follow his lead. "We've all had a long day. Good night!"

Everyone bade Orven good night and went to bed. They had enjoyed their time around the campfire but the prospect of another two days' hike through the mountains dampened their spirits and they felt heavy and tired and ready for sleep.

In the cold and sluggish dawn Aranstone's men woke to the now-familiar horn-call that began every morning on the road. The plateau was still in the mountains' shadow, the sky lightening and birds calling. Dwarves and Men shuffled about the crowded camp, partaking of the morning meal rations and preparing for the march through the mountains. Tents were struck and wagons loaded. A small group of dwarves and a few men from Kronivar were separated out from the troops to hold the plateau until the others returned. A dwarf under Olmic's command, Loarn Erdrock, was made a captain and left in command of the Plateau. Aranstone and Greywood arranged the watch and had the remaining campsites and tents moved to the plateau's outer edge, to give the impression of a large army guarding the plateau. Other campfires across the plateau would also be lit to add more rising plumes of smoke. When everything met their satisfaction and everyone was ready to go, Aranstone mounted his horse and led his company into the mountains.

Orven was not looking forward to the hike and on top of that he had to contend with his friends' complaints. He needed more men under his command, he thought, for Max and the others to take him seriously. If things went well during the siege, he hoped Aranstone would add to his command. Orven glanced around at his friends, talking with them during the morning's march. He knew they would need convincing once the siege plans were revealed, and dreaded facing the objections Max and Aaron were sure to have. Orven even wondered if he should have given Halix to Ripley instead. But Ripley needed no convincing, and Max did, so he would let Max have the sword for now. Orven looked at his friends, feeling a pang of guilt for having deceived them. He reasoned that it was only temporary; they would find out soon enough why they were going to the Castle. And, he reminded himself, they would thank him in the long run. Would they really be as bothered by it as he expected? Maybe he was worrying too much. He supposed he could tell them anytime, even now, but it would be best to wait and let Greywood describe the plan.

Orven walked along the Mountain Road, his friends close by him. His *best* friends, he realized. They would back him up; he could trust them. All would be fine. Still, something bothered him, as much as he tried to ignore it. *Everything will have to be fine*, he thought, imagining how it would reflect on him as a captain if anyone refused to follow orders and jeopardized their plans. Not only that, but the captains would have to do something with whoever wanted to turn back. He shuddered to think what. Certainly Max and the others would understand that much. *We couldn't turn back now even if I wanted to*, Orven thought with some relief. And, oddly enough, it also frightened him.

Chapter 36.
Dusk and Twilight

"The pain's gone down some." Tillmore offered Iaven a feeble smile as they sat there alone. "Quite a bit, actually. I do feel somewhat better today. Maybe we could go this afternoon."

"Good. Rest now, and we'll see how you feel when the others get back." Iaven patted Tillmore's hand as he knelt by his bedside. Though still drained and pale, Tillmore seemed to be regaining his old self again. Three nights of sleeping on the cold cave floor had made everyone stiff and irritable, but Tillmore had not complained. On the second night Hobley gave Tillmore his bedroll to put beneath his own to make it softer. "You're laying there all day," Hobley told him, "And I haven't been getting much sleep in here anyway." They all wondered whether Tillmore would pull through as each day dragged on, and were restless and anxious to get moving again.

Iaven sat back, watching Tillmore. "It'll be good to move on again. I'll be glad when we reach the Castle. But we'll leave only when you're better." So strong was Iaven's desire to leave that he eagerly believed Tillmore felt as good as he claimed he did.

Tillmore looked at Iaven. "I'm glad we learned what we did from Yolias. I didn't even realize how much I learned until those Goblins attacked us. And I never properly thanked Yolias, either. I will, when we see him again after the war."

"Yes, I was thinking the same thing," said Iaven.

"Thanks to Wendolin, too... How is he doing?" asked Tillmore.

"I don't know." Iaven glanced over to where Wendolin lay. Unlike Tillmore, the old wizard's condition had not changed at all. He remained in a deep sleep, his breathing so slow and shallow they could barely tell he was alive. Iaven hoped someone at the Castle could help him. Once Tillmore recovered they would have to carry Wendolin on a litter and make their way as best they could. The Goblins hadn't returned, and they could not wait any longer. Iaven often looked up into the sky half-expecting to see the dragon circling overhead, but the valley was quiet and they appeared to be alone.

"It'll be slow going to have to carry him, but there isn't much else we can do," Iaven said. "He doesn't seem to have gotten any worse, at least."

"Then let's go this afternoon," said Tillmore, "I'm as tired of this place as anyone. The walk might do me good." As he tried to sit up, a bolt of pain shot through him and he lay down again.

"Not yet," said Iaven, "Rest now, and wait." Iaven glanced over to where Wendolin lay. The old wizard looked gray and cold in the pale morning light.

Iaven walked to the mouth of the cave and stood looking out into the valley. Zammond, Hobley, and Wilbur had gone off to look for food and collect firewood, even though it was still quite early. Everyone was eager to do such mundane tasks, so much had their restlessness grown. And in all of them, even Zammond, the mixture of boredom and anxiety had begun to ferment into a kind of despair. They dwelled upon the attack at Halloway and what it meant, and the thought of all the dead burdened their spirits.

The enemy had entered the kingdom. Perhaps more goblins were along the North Road, or already in Kronivar. It was possible that goblins had come upon Orven's party on the road and had killed them and taken the swords. A cold shiver ran through Iaven at the thought. As angry as he was with him, he could not bear the thought of losing his brother.

Iaven bowed his head. He was ashamed how all his squabbling with Orven had been on his mind while dwarves were dying and Itharia was under attack. At war now, he thought. He pictured Hillbrook overrun with Goblins; families fleeing through the fields, houses burning, Goblins swarming over the bridges. Not only in Hillbrook, but everywhere around the Foothills. If Kronivar fell it would only be a matter of time.

Iaven's reverie broke as he heard Zammond coming up the path. He looked around and realized he had been sitting there over an hour. The sun was overhead, and daylight no longer angled into the cave. Zammond climbed the path and Hobley came into view, with Wilbur panting behind them.

"Well?" said Zammond as soon as he was in earshot of Iaven.

Iaven waited until Zammond was closer so he wouldn't have to shout. "He's resting now. He said he might be well enough to go later."

"Good!" Zammond tossed Iaven a clump of red-orange berries. "Found 'em hanging on tree, further down. Thought they might be good to eat." Hobley and Wilbur passed by Zammond and went into the cave. "We refilled the water, but didn't find much else."

Iaven was about to taste the berries, but stopped. "You're sure they're alright? We won't get sick?"

Zammond laughed. "We decided to see what you thought, first. Go ahead and try them if you want!"

"Zammond!" Iaven threw the berries back at him. "Try them yourself if you want to find out—"

"*Iaven!*" Hobley's voice broke from the depths of the cave with a strange, desperate sound that startled and frightened them. Iaven went in and Zammond followed.

Hobley knelt over Tillmore's body. "Iaven," he whispered hoarsely, "he's dead..."

Wilbur sat sullenly off to the side, and Iaven and Zammond approached and knelt down by Hobley. Tillmore lay still in the gloom, glassy eyes staring into the dark recesses of rock overhead. "He's cold," said Hobley, "His hand is cold." Hobley placed Tillmore's hand gently back at his side, as if trying to not disturb him. He passed his hand over Tillmore's face to close his eyes, touching him as little as possible, and then moved back, looking at his friend.

The dwarves sat awhile in silence, feeling small and ashamed to be alive in the presence of their dead friend. They felt helpless knowing nothing could be done. Hobley sat with his shoulders slumped forward, by his friend's side. In the dusky gloom the dwarves solemnly averted their faces, and now and then a restrained sob or sniffle broke the silence and was quickly stifled.

"Goodbye, dear friend," Hobley managed in a pained whisper, though he had more he wanted to say. Again the terrible weight of the Goblin attack and a heavy weariness engulfed them. They continued sitting there, unable to move and not knowing what to do next, until finally Iaven stood. "We should bury him," he said, and the others nodded and rose.

There was nowhere to dig a grave on the mountainside, nor did they have the means to do so. In the end they decided they would carefully cover Tillmore with stones and entomb him there in the cave, where he had spent his last three days. The afternoon had faded now and they lit a small fire at the back of the cave, but the firelight failed to dispel the gloom. They placed Tillmore along the back wall of the cave, and in somber procession brought stones and placed them around and on top of him, passing silently in and out of the cave as they went. At last when Tillmore was covered they sat down to rest.

"It's my fault he's here," said Hobley suddenly. "He came along because of me. He was afraid of what might happen to me. I never really thanked him for that."

"I think he knows," said Iaven.

The conversation waned. Each of them seemed about to speak but waiting until someone else did so. None of them wanted to stay in the cave another night, so finally Iaven suggested they make their way down into the next valley to camp, even if it meant a few hours' hike in the dark. It was two nights before the full moon, enough light to see where they were going. The others readily agreed and soon they packed up to leave.

Wendolin still lay by the cave wall where he had been the last few days, and they unrolled some blankets, making a litter, and lifted him onto it. He was lighter than they expected, and this worried them. Every time they checked they thought they would find him dead; it seemed only a matter of time. Yet his long, slow, deep slumber continued unchanged, neither worsening nor improving.

At last each said his final goodbye to Tillmore and placed one more stone upon his tomb at the back of the cave. Iaven and Wilbur each carried two packs, while Hobley and Zammond took the ends of Wendolin's litter and hoisted them onto their shoulders, making a kind of hammock in which the wizard lay. The night was clear and the moon was bright. Iaven lead the way and Wilbur followed, and they made their way in single file down the sloping mountainside path.

As they walked their thoughts turned to Tillmore, and after while they began talking, recalling stories, memories, and happy times from years past. To be moving again after camping in the cave for so long also helped to ease their spirits and dispel their restlessness. The moon drifted through the night sky as they slowly descended into the valley ahead. Cold winds howled and blew. Soon they made for the valley floor where they might be shielded from the harsher gusts. Twice they stopped to rest and trade the carrying of packs for the bearing of Wendolin, and all could not help but wonder what would become of him.

For two more days they labored over mountain passes and through valleys, moving in a southerly direction as best they could. Wendolin remained unchanged, and they carried him unfailingly. Their pace was slow and they seemed to tire sooner. Even Zammond was subdued. Many quiet hours passed with thoughts of their dead friend, the attack at Halloway, and unspoken worries that tormented them. The valley floor was not much warmer than the mountain ridges, and only a few hours after noon the sun sank behind the mountains again.

As evening of the second day settled over the ranges, Iaven looked for shelter for the night. The nearly full moon bathed the valley in a pale silver glow, frosting the edges of rocks and trees. Near the valley floor they found a cleft protected by two angling rock walls, as good a place as any to set camp. They were pleased to have grass underfoot again. Wood was more plentiful, so they soon had a fire burning. They laid Wendolin near the fire to warm him, as they had every night, and set their bedrolls between the walls and the fire. With Tillmore gone, it fell to Iaven to sit the first and the last watch of the night. It was late now, and the moon had already traversed a third of the sky, so with little conversation they went to sleep, leaving Iaven alone with his thoughts in the cold November air.

Iaven sat idly poking at the fire with a stick, watching sparks swirl up with the smoke. He leaned back against the rock and gazed up at the stars, feeling oddly detached from everything. In light of the attack on Halloway and Tillmore's death, so many things seemed less important than they had. Worries of Hillbrook life were gone; any life there after the war would be enough to please him now. He felt ready to confront Orven and looked forward to doing so. The others had looked to Iaven to lead them over the last few days, and he had done well. He had even faced goblins, and had fought them without Halix.

Thinking more about Orven, Iaven began to see just how often he had stepped on Iaven's confidence to further his own. But there had been something else in Orven's manner when they had fought in the tree overhanging the valley. Orven had been surprised, and despite his snide remarks he had shown a kind of respect for Iaven, unlike anything Iaven had seen before. Orven had fought harder, but had struggled more this time. Had they been on even ground, perhaps Iaven could have bested Orven. Yet now, strangely, that didn't matter much to him. He just hoped Orven was still alive, and that they would both make it through the war and return home.

Before long, they would arrive at the Castle, and new worries were starting to present themselves. Wendolin had said they would travel south until they met the Mountain Road going to the Castle, but most of it was high up and would be difficult to get to, if they could get to it at all. He recalled looking out the Castle's northern windows at the sheer drops into the valley below. Wherever they went, a long climb awaited them. Yet soldiers had been bivouacked in the valleys around the Castle, so there were paths up to the Castle Plateau. But they might veer too far east, missing the Castle altogether, and become lost. He would have to try to keep their course due south as best he could. It concerned him yet he was calm about it; he felt he could do it. Only now was not the time to delve into such things, for he wanted to be able to fall asleep quickly when his watch ended.

The night wore on. Iaven sat back listening to night sounds, from the reassuringly familiar rhythmic whirr of crickets nearby to the long, lonely moon-howls of far-off wolves echoing through the mountains. His mind still swarmed with thoughts of what could happen and what he should do, and he gave up trying to ignore them. As he weighed them and picked them apart, he grew more confident that he was doing the right thing. And finally, when Zammond woke to take the next watch, Iaven rolled up in his blanket by the fire and fell right to sleep.

Although the shifting night sky and full moon told him otherwise, it seemed very little time had passed when a bleary-eyed Wilbur shook Iaven awake for the last watch of the night. Iaven rose and stretched, shivering and warming his hands by the fire. At the edge of camp he propped himself up against the slightly warmed rock where Wilbur had been sitting.

Iaven was more rested now and not as anxious as he had been earlier. He took a deep breath of cold night air and slowly let it out. Under the starry night sky, the mountains were removed and indifferent to the worlds of Dwarves, Elves, Men, and Goblins. Even the war was small by comparison; the mountains stood, broad and still, unchanging as kingdoms rose, fell, and were forgotten. It was foolish to think anyone could lay claim to them, yet until then he had always thought of them as somehow belonging to the Dwarves.

A small rustling sound nearby dispersed Iaven's thoughts. He sat up, realizing how distracted he had become. At first he feared goblins had found them, then he glanced around the camp and realized Wendolin was moving. The old wizard uttered a dry cough and began bending his stiffened limbs. Iaven went over by him.

"Wendolin!" He tried to keep his voice down so as not to wake the others. "Wendolin, are you alright?"

"Eh?" Wendolin shielded his eyes from the fire until they adjusted. He grunted as he stretched and sat up, his movements paining him. "Water," he said, his voice a dry rasp. Iaven brought him a flask. Wendolin drank heartily, water running down his beard. When he had finished, he wiped his mouth and nodded, handing the flask back to Iaven.

"I suppose you must be hungry, too. I'll see what we've got left." Iaven rummaged through a pack and found the remains of some trout they had caught in a mountain stream, a bit of cheese, and some dried, crumbling bread from Halloway. "It isn't much, but it's been five days since we—"

"Five days?" asked Wendolin, astonished. He considered and leaned back against the rock in resignation. Iaven gave him the food and Wendolin took a few small bites and mouthfuls of water. "I am getting too old for adventures such as this." He shifted around to sit more comfortably, aches slowing his movement. "I have never been in an *erasnii* for more than a day. Nor do I feel as rested and healed as I used to when awakening from them. I am old," he said, as though admitting it for the first time. "You must have been worried about me! I did not think it would take so long. I will be alright, though it will be some time before I recover fully. How is Tillmore faring?"

Iaven described Tillmore's last days, and Wendolin listened and offered his sympathy. "He will be numbered among those who died in the war," said Wendolin, "and honored with them throughout the kingdom."

"That seems little consolation," said Iaven.

"Yes," said Wendolin, "What things are worth a life? Only other lives."

"He was only a year older than me," said Iaven.

Wendolin nodded. "And many die who are younger still. But a life's worth is not measured by its length."

"I've tried to do my part," said Iaven, "though I've lost the sword and three of the gems —four, if you include the one in the well in Kronivar."

Wendolin smiled kindly at Iaven. "Have you forgotten what Cedric told you? During the war, I lost *both* swords, and afterwards, *all* of the gems."

"But not by accident," Iaven said.

"No, not at first, but in the end it was," said Wendolin. "I had thought that after the war, Cedric and I would recover the swords. But he was gone for many years. And I went to seek Aorinthel when there was no word from him. On the island I tried to keep Maëlveronde from getting the gems, and then lost them to his hawks!"

"And if you hadn't lost them? What would have become of them?"

"It is difficult to say," said Wendolin, "My old master, Gromindral, could have done much good with the gems. Had Aorinthel lived, we might have learned much more about them. While we were apprenticed to Aorinthel, Maëlveronde and I discovered that the gems were more powerful and varied in their abilities then either the Oswai or Eloswai suspected. Of course, Aorinthel revealed very little to them, knowing how easily the gems could upset the balance in power between them. And he said little to us, until he came to trust us and let us aid him in his tasks. I suppose it was around this time when Maëlveronde began to covet the gems for himself."

"It must have been hard, sending them off with the ravens from the tower like you did," said Iaven.

"It was," said Wendolin, "but there was no other way. A clear and difficult decision is easier to decide than a murky one. Too many paths to choose from can slow you down more than an obstacle in your path."

"How did the split between the Oswai and Eloswai come about?" asked Iaven.

"Long ago, before I was born," said Wendolin, "When Aorinthel was young, barely past his twentieth year or so, the debates began, cordially enough at first, but gaining in intensity. The Oswai had long been humble scholars, sojourning in other lands and returning to Arthel Hall with news and word of new discoveries. During their travels, they would visit Kings and Queens and other rulers who sought their counsel. In return, these rulers often sent gifts or aid to the Oswai, and that was how Arthel Hall was built. Over the years, the libraries in Arthel Hall grew quite large, and the Oswai were held in high regard. Emissaries came from other countries seeking their advice and aid. And the Oswai's help was given freely with no return demanded or expected.

"Eventually the Oswai acted as advisors in more than a dozen kingdoms around the Silver Sea. After while, some Oswai thought they were entitled to something in exchange for their help, which could be withheld whenever demands were not met. These Oswai, who would one day become the Eloswai, wanted the Oswai to withdraw from other lands and release their knowledge only at a great price, so they might profit more from it. They thought themselves the wisest, supposing they knew what was best for other lands. They wanted to have a hand in reshaping kingdoms, not through gentle advice and guidance but by command and decree. Some even dreamed of establishing their own kingdom, through which they would rule and oversee other kingdoms. Those espousing such views were small in number, and they had little effect initially, but the debates continued.

"Now the number of Oswai had always been small, with no more than a few hundred even at their peak. Arthel Hall was remote, built on the northeastern edge of Feäthiadreya, and under the protection of the Elves. The Oswai had neither land nor an army, and their only power was that of influence, which they had so far been careful to not abuse. And so they remained as they were, though a rift was beginning to open.

"Decades passed, and the Eloswai's ideas persisted. Many Eloswai traveled less, and some remained cloistered in Arthel Hall. They became more secretive, no longer as open to sharing their findings as the other Oswai were. The Oswai bristled at the uncooperative attitude of the Eloswai, and began withholding their own news and findings, demanding a fair exchange between the two sides. Gradually the rift widened. Differences of opinion came to color all work and collaborative efforts and were divisive during council meetings.

"Through private conversations and personal influence, other Oswai came to join the Eloswai. Since they traveled less, their numbers grew in Arthel Hall, so the Oswai began to travel less as well. Around this time that the name "Eloswai" came into being, to separate them from the true Oswai. Some, like Aorinthel, tried to stay neutral, and there were a few —wanderers, mostly— who refused to formally join either side, and became rejected by both. But they are no more."

"And you were always an Oswai?" Iaven asked.

"I was raised by them," Wendolin replied, "I cannot even remember a time when I was not one. An Oswai must begin learning when he is very young, if he is to learn at all."

"Why?" asked Iaven.

"There is much to learn, but one must be of the right mind. And an unformed mind is easier to form." Wendolin reached down and picked up a small round stone. He held up his left hand and placed the stone in the center of his open palm. "This was one of the very first things I learned as a child." Wendolin held his hand steady, then slowly drew it downward, careful not to disturb the stone. Instead of falling with his hand, the stone remained where it was, hanging in mid-air. It wobbled a little as a breeze gusted it. Iaven stared at it amazed, watching it float in the air, defying his understanding. All of a sudden Wendolin snatched it away and threw it to Iaven. "Now you try it."

Iaven took the stone and placed it on his hand as Wendolin had, holding it up in the air. Slowly he brought his hand down, but the stone came down with it, just as he thought it would. He tried again, feeling discouraged and a bit foolish. "I can't do it," he said.

"Of course you can't," Wendolin replied, catching the stone as Iaven tossed it back. "From little on you learned it was not possible. But I grew up among the Oswai where greater deeds than that were common sights; it was all I knew, and how I learned." Wendolin held up the stone. "This stone is but a pebble. Yet Gromindral's master once told him that if one was of the right mind, one could uproot an entire mountain and plunge it into the Silver Sea; but I have yet to meet anyone of such ability. At any rate, that is why only the very young can be trained. And perhaps why our number is dwindling."

"I wish I could have learned things like that," said Iaven.

"Do you? But you have learned many other things, useful things. You have enjoyed things that I never had. Only later did I learn what it cost to be raised the way I was, and of all the sacrifices required of an Oswai." Wendolin was silent a moment. "Do not wish for it, Iaven. '*Better to be a good man than a great man*', as the Teskans say. My life has been a lonely one: full of solitary travels, disappointments, dangers, wandering, and waiting. And as my own powers have grown, so have those of my adversaries. It is the only life I have known, but I would not wish it on anyone."

As Wendolin rested, Iaven was quiet, considering what he had said. Dawn was breaking in the east behind the mountains, edging them with the faintest trace of blue.

Zammond yawned where he lay and rubbed his eyes. He blinked hard in disbelief. "Wendolin? It is! And I thought I was hearing voices!" He sat up, pulling his blanket around his shoulders, and came and sat near them. "Are you alright now?" he asked Wendolin.

"I will be," said Wendolin, "It will take time. Too much, I fear."

"But you'll be able to fight Maëlveronde, if it comes to that, right?" asked Zammond.

"Let us hope it will not come to that," said Wendolin, "Or if it must, not for a long, long while. I will take some time to recover, and even then, facing Maëlveronde would be a thing to dread. Still, we each must do what we can, as I was telling Iaven."

"Yes, Iaven, what *are* you going to do?" Zammond taunted.

Iaven shook his head. "I just wish I was able to do more, that's all..."

"And who are you to judge the size of your deeds?" said Wendolin, "Can you see all they bring about, or will bring about? We call those deeds 'small' whose consequences are unseen, and do so at our own peril. And when we think our deeds do not affect others, how much easier it is to justify our misdeeds. By such little steps, do we begin down a darkening path." Wendolin's expression softened. "No, Iaven, do not wish for more power. Wish instead to use wisely what power you have, for you may one day find you had more than you knew."

Iaven nodded. He found himself thinking of his encounter with Orven. "I wonder if Orven found anything at the desert outpost," said Iaven. "Do you think it could have changed him?"

"It would depend on what was in his heart when he came there," said Wendolin, "Despite all the evils that reside in the outpost, all they had to work with is what was already within Orven."

Iaven recalled his fight with Orven. The fire crackled and snapped in the silence. Zammond joined them and leaned back against the rock, looking eagerly to Wendolin.

"If you and Maëlveronde were both raised in Arthel Hall, how did he become evil?" asked Zammond.

Wendolin considered long before giving his answer. "Of what he did in the years following his escape from Aorinthel's island, I cannot say," he began. "But as a young apprentice he did have a certain curiosity and a fascination with sorcery and conjuring, though such things were forbidden by the Oswai and even by most of the Eloswai. He was not allowed to pursue his interest in them, but he had a great capacity for exploring and learning on his own."

"But for Maëlveronde it must have been more than simple curiosity," said Zammond.

"Sometimes curiosity is enough to keep a thing in mind, until temptation gains a foothold," said Wendolin, "Without guidance, desire for knowledge can develop into desire for power. Many seek power with realizing the temptations that accompany it. As the Teskans say, '*The brighter the light, the darker the shadows.*' Even after years of study, such desire may not abate. On the contrary, it often grows; for too easily can the learned man find ways to justify his desires and misdeeds to himself. Supposing himself wise enough to resist temptation, he will allow himself another step closer, thinking he is safe."

Wendolin paused a moment, gazing into the dark, and then resumed. "It is like someone approaching a deep abyss. He who stands on the edge of a steep cliff peering down into the valley will eventually think about jumping. To see deeper into the abyss, he will approach closer and closer to the cliff's edge. And the closer he stands to the edge, the smaller is the step that could take him over it."

Iaven and Zammond understood. At times while traveling in the mountains, they had both stood looking down from the edge of a cliff, imagining the drop and feeling the strange pull it exerted on them. Zammond threw stones over the edge just to see them fall and grow smaller and smaller until he could no longer follow them. And sometimes Iaven would look down, amazed that he was just one step away from falling to his death. It drew him and frightened him until at last he stepped backwards to safety before losing his balance.

"Yes," said Iaven, "I think I know what you mean."

The sky had paled considerably, and birds were taking up their morning songs. Hobley and Wilbur stirred and rose, expressing their relief to see Wendolin awake and breakfasting. Soon they all joined in, passing around the morning's rations and contributing food for Wendolin's recovery. They talked about everything he had missed in the last few days, and were more encouraged about returning to the Castle. Wendolin seemed mildly amused and embarrassed that they had had to carry him the last two days.

After breakfast they packed up again, and soon they were hiking through the valley alongside a mountain stream. Without roads or paths, the going was slow. They all took up walking sticks and pushed onward, looking about and wondering if they were the first dwarves to have ever seen that particular valley.

By noon their exuberance had waned, and they trudged along wearily. The day was now as warm as it would get; a brisk mid-November day, bright and cold, that reddened their cheeks and chilled the backs of their necks. Their passage was slow, and they longed for a good clear and level road. "Maybe if we take our time the war will be over and we won't have to go to Kronivar at all," Wilbur grumbled. "I suppose they wouldn't really miss us, would they?"

"No more than they will miss you in Oakitsburrow!" Wendolin snapped. "Wilbur, have you not been listening? How you wallow in pessimism! Do not be so proud as to suppose you can see all that your life touches. Consider the Teskans' outlook. They see each life as a thread running through a great tapestry: sometimes as a part of an image, and sometimes hidden below other threads. A single thread may cross thousands of other threads, and when examined closely, its purpose may seem unclear. But when the weaving is complete and one steps back from it, a greater picture emerges, an image to which every thread has contributed."

Iaven thought of the tapestry he had seen in Teska. "I just hope the 'greater picture' looks nothing like the weaving of Orven and Maëlveronde."

"Then we must get to the Castle as quickly as we can and not spend any more time whining or complaining," said Wendolin, and there was very little of either after that.

Chapter 37.
An Enemy Within

King Jordgen stood on a balcony of Castle Frosthelm's western wing watching the encampment in the valley, where the last gray tendrils of smoke from extinguished campfires rose in the morning sun. Soldiers were moving about the camp. Jordgen looked for his son, Prince Varlen, under whose command they would march for the Gundithe Plateau. Tents were struck as the remaining troops were mobilizing. Supply wagons were packed and waiting in the Castle's outer ward, ready for the Mountain Road. The troops were restless and their spirits had risen now that new orders called them to duty. Word of Farrenhale's fall and the burning of Teska shocked them like shadowy cold hands gripping their hearts. Anger spread like wildfire, and many swore vengeance, while others were bowed by the responsibility that now fell to them. Their worst fears had been confirmed, and rest and return home seemed further away than ever.

Along with his men, the King shared the anxious relief that comes after a grim period of dreading. He looked toward the rising sun. Less than four days ago the unsettling news had come of the attack at Halloway, after which he had immediately sent an occupying force from Kronivar to the plateau. And then just last night news of the burning of Teska arrived, and he cursed that it had taken so long to reach them. He blamed the Teskans. It was now four days since Teska and Farrenhale had fallen. The Goblin army would already have advanced a good distance down the South Road, and would probably reach Greensward in a day or two. From there, on their way to Kronivar, they would have to turn their backs on Greensward, risking an attack from behind, and they would certainly have a rear guard ready. The encampment on the Gundithe Plateau would keep them from entering the mountains but it would not deter them from marching on Kronivar. Unless the Castle troops could get to Gundithe in time; and Varlen had assured him that they could.

A knock sounded at the door to the hall. King Jordgen turned away from the balcony and stepped indoors. "Enter!" he called. The heavy wooden door swung open and Erland Clovenstone, the Castle's High Steward, came in. Behind him, a young messenger dwarf named Laren stood waiting outside the door, should the King wish to send back a reply.

"News from Kronivar." Clovenstone handed a large scroll to the King, the size of which told him it had come to them by rider and not by bird.

"Come Erland, sit down," said Jordgen as he took the scroll. Clovenstone nodded to the messenger in the hall who bowed and closed the door. Alone now, Jordgen and Clovenstone sat in upholstered wooden armchairs near the hearth.

"Grawson's sent a company of Orming's men to Gundithe," said Clovenstone as the King glanced at the scroll. "He's explained it all in there. It seems a sound decision, under the circumstances. And he has enclosed a mysterious letter he received, which was sent with proof of Orming's treachery: a note to Aranstone, in Orming's own hand." He was quiet as the King sat reading the letters and note.

"Mmmph," Jordgen grunted, still considering. "Perhaps... Too often he takes the initiative only when it suits him. It rids him of a problem he ought to have taken care of some time ago. We may find it more difficult to coordinate the troops at Gundithe now."

"True, but if it strengthens Kronivar, it will be worthwhile. It was fortunate he received the letter in time to act," said Clovenstone, "Kronivar will be more stable now."

"Yes," said the King, begrudging the admission. He set the note and letters down and sat back in the chair. "Considering the turns of events, there would have been little time for him to decide. Perhaps he has done well. I, too, would like to feel that Kronivar is secure, but after Halloway and Teska... Acknowledge what he has done and tell him Castle troops are on their way to Gundithe."

"Yes, sire," Clovenstone rose and Jordgen walked him to the door. Outside, the messenger was waiting patiently. Clovenstone was about to depart with him, when the young dwarf turned anxiously to the King and bowed. "Begging your leave, Majesty, Bolren said I should tell you, they have seen a hawk lingering about the messaging tower these last few days. He thought it a bad omen."

"Superstition!" King Jordgen growled, "He who grows anxious sees portents everywhere."

Speechless and humbled, the messenger bowed low and accompanied Clovenstone down the hall.

Jordgen closed the door and was alone again. He regretted having responded so harshly. In the last few weeks he had succumbed to the same grim foreboding as everyone else. And Jordgen knew that had the report been of a good omen, he would have been all too ready to believe in it.

The winds on the mountain paths were much colder, and the situation more grim than the first time Orven and his friends had journeyed to the Castle. Aranstone's party moved in a dense, narrow stream along the winding Mountain Road, hardened to the weather and the strenuous march. Along the way, Max walked with Orven, Rafnel, and Strable. He looked around for Aaron, wanting to talk with him, but Aaron had fallen back somewhere behind them.

Max was silent and brooding. The night before, at camp, Greywood and Aranstone had revealed their plans for a siege of the Castle. To Max's surprise this had been received by the gathering with some enthusiasm. Later, when he had a chance to talk with Aaron, they remembered how Aranstone had selected men from each of the companies to hold the plateau, rather than having an entire company stationed there. And Max knew Orven well enough to know he had probably refused to leave anyone behind.

Hearing the roar of the crowd after Greywood's announcement, Max had been afraid to say anything against the siege plans and noticed that Aaron and Roy likewise were quiet and stunned by the news. Ripley didn't seem to mind, though he still was surprised. Orven apparently had known all along, and that bothered Max. He wanted to confront Orven, but the tight quarters along the mountain path made it hard to talk without being overheard. Of the others under

Orven's command, Rafnel, Strable, and Haidren, it seemed one or more of them were always around Orven, making it impossible to get a word in private with him without looking suspicious. Nor did they seem to trust Max and Aaron as they trusted Ripley; Max wondered if they already suspected how he felt. Now as they walked, Max listened as Orven discussed the siege with Rafnel and Strable.

"I still don't like the idea of attacking the Castle," said Max, immediately feeling Rafnel's gaze fall on him. "It's too well-fortified," he added.

"Max, as I've said, we're not *attacking* the Castle, it's just a show of force," said Orven. "Kind of like holding someone's arm behind their back, instead of landing punches on them. We're not *against* the King, we're just helping Kronivar. And Kronivar will help us when we're done; handsomely, I expect. The siege will pressure the King into signing a treaty and agreeing to Kronivar's independence after the war. That's better than Kronivar having to fight against the Castle later, isn't it?"

"But why not fight together now against the Goblins, and then discuss it peacefully after the war?" said Max.

"It's like Greywood said," Orven replied, "'*If you want to shape iron, strike while the iron is hot; for as it cools it hardens and becomes inflexible.*' We have an advantage now over the King, one we won't have again after the war. This is the best time to act; he'll have to agree to it. And then, when he does, Kronivar and Itharia will fight together against the Goblins, but as Allies."

"And if the King doesn't give in?" asked Max.

"He'll have to," said Orven, "sooner or later. He'll see we mean business. But it'll be a peaceful siege, they haven't asked us to kill anyone."

Rafnel laughed. "Of course, if we have to in self-defense, we will, but only if they attack us first."

Max turned away, looking down the road. Rafnel continued watching him, and Strable was now as well. "If we're all going to profit from this, we'll all have to work for it. Don't you agree?"

Max met his gaze, but said nothing. Orven laughed. "Well, let's not worry about that. And anyway, they haven't exactly given us the most prestigious position during the siege, either. It's just guarding some staircase in the Castle. I said we could do more; '*You don't have enough men*,' they told me. 'And whose fault is that?' I almost said. But it'll have to do, for now. Funny, isn't it, you'd think they'd want the swords right there in the thick of it, but maybe things will change once we get to the Castle."

"So tell me again what this plan is and where we are in it?" said Max, hoping to change the subject and lessen the tension.

"Aranstone's spy went on ahead of us," Orven began, "he's probably in the Castle already. He'll make sure what few spies we have in the Castle will be on guard duty when we arrive. Two at the front gate, one each where the walls join the Castle on each side, and one in the messaging tower, which we'll need to take control of right away. Once we're in, we hold the wall and secure the entrances to the Castle. When those are secure, we'll force those inside into the east wing and hold them there. That way we'll have the storerooms under the west wing and the supply wagons in the outer ward, and the King and his men will have neither."

"And the troops in the valley won't be able to help them once we have the wall and gates," added Strable. "If we can secure them before they're aware of what we're doing."

"Anyway, once everything's in place, our job is to hold the main staircase joining the east wing to the rest of the Castle," said Orven, his voice tinged with disappointment.

"But it *is* a very important position," offered Rafnel, and he and Orven and Strable began discussing strategy again. Max had tired of it and slowed his pace until he was walking a few strides behind them. He saw Aaron several yards back and went over to walk with him.

"Have you seen the way they hover about Orven? It seems they're always around him," Max told Aaron in hushed tones, "It's as though they were told to keep an eye on Orven, instead of the other way around."

"Or on all of us," said Aaron. "Or maybe it's the swords they're supposed to look after. That's what I'm worried about."

"Well, I don't know how much longer I'll have Halix," said Max, resting his hand on its hilt, "Orven knows I don't like the idea of the siege. And he's been talking about letting Ripley carry Halix, but hasn't had me give it over to him yet. So I haven't pressed the matter too much."

"There isn't much we can do at the moment," Aaron agreed. He glanced around and lowered his voice even more, "When we get to the Castle, maybe there'll be some way to go and join the King there. And he could certainly make use of the swords —or even just one of them."

"I've been thinking the same thing," Max said, "And I know Roy will join us. But Orven has to come with us. We can't just leave him with *them*."

Aaron nodded and was silent. "True," he said after a moment, "He doesn't even realize what's going on. But what if Orven won't join us? You know how he is. And I agree we can't just go without him."

"It's hard enough just to try to talk to him in private," said Max, "seeing as—"

"Fellows," Haidren Elkherd walked up between them, greeting them with a friendly clap on their shoulders, a hint of menace in the gesture. "How are you faring? We should be arriving very soon." He smiled at them. "Are you ready to do your part in our undertaking?"

Max and Aaron glanced at each other. "As ready as we'll ever be," said Aaron truthfully.

The Mountain Road wound around the slopes, rising and falling, never more than a horse and cart could manage. Near the vanguard Aranstone and Greywood rode side by side. Aranstone hoped Greywood was right about reaching the Castle around noon. The wind was cold and strong, and snow had blown in it before sunrise. Their troops had been hiking for most of the morning and a good part of the night before as well, taking advantage of the full moon. Tension in the party was growing as they expected the Castle to appear in the distance every time the road wound around a mountain. Aranstone sensed the men were ready for what lay ahead. Greywood assured him that all would be arranged by the Castle spies. And so the morning wore on, long and winding stretches of road opening before them, bringing them eastward even as they veered north or south.

At last the road rose, rounding a curving wall of rock, and Mount Frosthelm emerged before them in the distance. The noonday sun lit the castle's huge gray towers rising behind the high, crenellated walls of the outer ward. Flags fluttered at the tops of spires. Aranstone realized it had been awhile since his last visit there, the enormity of the Castle reminding him of the impossibility of what they were trying to do. Yet Greywood's plans seemed sound enough, and the men were committed to them.

Enthusiastic shouts erupted behind Aranstone. As the men saw the Castle their eyes flared with hungry looks. Aranstone noticed Greywood was relaxed but focused and regained his confidence in their plan. He looked back to the Castle again. Guards walking along the top of the outer wall had stopped, aware of the party approaching and trying to see who they were.

Aranstone and Greywood rode at the front of the company, leading them across the castle terrace and up to the wide center gates, which were open. Loaded supply wagons waited within, lining both sides of the way leading to the main gate of the inner ward. As Aranstone approached, the gate guards hailed him apprehensively.

"General Thon Aranstone, under Count Orming of Kronivar," Aranstone told them.

"We come at the request of the King," Greywood added.

At this some of the gate guards glanced at one another with suspicion.

"Yes, of course," said one of the guards, a dwarf named Haren whom Aranstone recognized.

"I was not told of this," said Jorwoll, the guard in charge, with a hard look at Haren.

"They were not expected until tomorrow," Haren replied coolly.

"It is true," Greywood said. "With the full moon we were able to march at night and arrive sooner. I am sure the King will be pleased."

Jorwoll watched the old man as he spoke, weighing his words. Behind Aranstone, more and more men were massing, waiting to enter the gates. Even at a glance Jorwoll could see there were more Men than Dwarves, and something about them made him uneasy. He sent one of the guards to tell the King, and then turned back, examining the growing crowd, but without any indication that he was going to admit them.

"We have marched a long way," Greywood continued, "And we should prepare for our audience with the King."

Jorwoll looked at Greywood impassively. Even though the men pressed in now around Greywood and Aranstone, almost to the threshold of the gate, there was silence. "Of course," Jorwoll said.

"Surely they can wait inside, out of the wind," Haren said. Jorwoll glared at him and glanced around at the other guards. He stood silent for a moment and then relented. "Very well," he said, standing aside and nodding to the other guards.

"Thank you," said Greywood, riding in as though he was angry that he had to ask for what was his right. Aranstone rode in with him, and behind them the men began flooding through the gates into the outer ward. Aranstone and Greywood rode slowly down the center aisle between the loaded wagons, toward the main gates of the inner ward, which lay open. Men marched behind them, while others began to congregate in groups moving to the left and right of the central gate. The guards watched them warily as they poured in, more numerous than they expected and less than half of them Dwarves. Greywood and Aranstone had almost reached the inner ward when they turned to watch the men entering the Castle. Greywood removed a small ram's horn and held it on his lap.

Inside the gates, Aranstone's men assembled themselves in large groups on either side and a small group filled the central aisle between the wagons, Orven's party among them. The guards grew more anxious now, holding their spears as if they expected something to happen. Only Haren, and a few others, seemed at ease.

The guard Jorwoll had sent away was returning now, moving along the wall with a sense of urgency. Greywood saw him and gripped the horn. He glanced at Aranstone, who nodded. Greywood lifted the horn and sounded his signal. At once all the men moved to their stations, no longer a milling crowd. The men at the gate drew their swords on the guards, and those who resisted were wounded or slain. Others moved around the gatehouse and up the staircases inside, weapons drawn and ready to take control. Men shouted orders and blades rang as swords crossed. The gatehouse guards clashed with the men coming up the stairs. Others tried to lower the portcullis but Aranstone's spy drew his sword and held them back. By the time he was slain, mercenaries had filled the gatehouse and gained control.

Cries and shouted orders went out along the wall. On both ends of the outer ward the gates were shut and barred and each portcullis dropped. Once they were secured, men ran along the wall to join the battle at the center gatehouse. In the outer ward Aranstone's men swarmed to the entrances of the east and west wings of the Castle. The King's guards held them off and some of the doors were barred. At other doors the guards were too late, and fights broke out over the thresholds as Aranstone's men tried to force their way inside the Castle.

During the entire attack Orven's men acted as a rear-guard for Khale's company, fighting off Castle troops. Orven wielded Gorflange with relish, feeling the strain of dividing his attention between fighting and shouting orders to his men. While concentrating on Gorflange, he had the sharp clarity of mind he always felt while using the sword, as if all else around him had slowed down. But now he was continually glancing about in the chaos to make sure all was going well and nervous because of it.

Max wielded Halix and felt the sword's power. He had grave misgivings about fighting the King's men, and all his moves were defensive ones. "*Traitors!*" shouted the Castle guards. The word struck Max like a blow and his heart shriveled with shame and guilt. Yet he still had to defend himself, or he and the others would be killed. Frustrated and angry, he wanted to pull back but was concerned about Orven and Ripley who needed his help. And the three mercenaries under Orven's command were also watching him. Strable had even gone so far as to suggest that Orven give Halix to Ripley instead. Orven, however, said they would continue the rotation of the sword between Max and Ripley as he had promised.

Roy and Aaron reluctantly obeyed Orven's orders, seeing the need for defending themselves despite feeling like traitors. Guilt and simple fear held them back as they looked for a way out. Rafnel and Strable yelled at them, though it was clear they couldn't do much better than they already were.

At last, Pyrwoed's men gained control of the central gatehouse. Aranstone's men filled the outer ward, closing the gate and lowering the portcullis. The guards on the wall attacked them. Swords flashed in the cold sunlight and the wind whipped around them as they fought. The King's guards held their ground, but Aranstone's men outnumbered them and pushed them back.

Outside on the castle terrace, troops from the valley came in answer to the alarms sounded. They found all the castle gates shut against them, the King's guards unable to hold either the east or west gatehouse long enough to unbar the doors and raise the portcullis. Suddenly a hail of arrows flew from the arrow loops in the central gatehouse, hitting soldiers on the terrace. Archers emerged along the wall, forcing the King's troops to draw back.

Amidst the fighting, Aranstone and Greywood led a charge into the inner ward, followed by Khale's and Orven's companies. Guards tried to drop the portcullis to close off the inner ward but found it sabotaged by Aranstone's spies. Khale's men wedged boards in the threshold to keep the portcullis from being lowered. Further in, beneath the arching gateway, guards began closing the heavy wooden doors. Khale led the charge and his men leapt ahead and forced the doors open. More of Khale's men joined them and at last they broke into the inner ward of the Castle.

The inner ward filled quickly and arrows rained down upon the intruders, who expected them and had their shields raised. Some fired back, though the King's guards had a clear advantage. Aranstone's men came along the wall, fighting the guards and forcing their way into the inner ward's gatehouse. Fewer arrows fell, and finally ceased as the gatehouse of the inner ward was taken.

With Aranstone's company dominating the outer wall, more of the other captains' men joined in the fight alongside Orven's and Khale's men, and the Castle guards were subdued. Aranstone's men now held the entire wall surrounding the outer ward, and after one last struggle, the inner ward was theirs as well. Battle continued at the Castle entrances and more men joined their fellows there. A huge throng massed at the thresholds leading into the east wing, and an even larger number pressed around the west wing entrances. In a few places they forced their way inside. Elsewhere the King's men gained the upper hand and doors were shut, Aranstone's men raging against them.

Disturbed and shaken, King Jordgen strode through the halls of the Castle's west wing. Soldiers came and went, delivering reports and receiving orders. Weaponry and supplies were redirected. Shouts and the clanging of swords echoed down the halls. The King passed through the frenzied activity around him, his troubled thought broken only when he paused to listen to a guard or give a command. Outrage at Aranstone's audacity tore at his calm, adding to the burdens of war already laid on his shoulders.

King Jordgen looked up as his nephew Arlen approached. Together they left the hall and entered a room on the northern side of the Castle.

"We're holding them off at the Castle entrances, but we haven't enough men to do it for long," Arlen said, closing the door behind him. "It's the worst outside the west wing. They've gained footholds into the halls, and they already have the messaging tower."

"They mean to flush us into the east wing," said Jordgen, "That much is clear. They know of the west wing storerooms." Jordgen walked to the window and Arlen joined him.

"Without the men in the valley, we won't have enough to hold both wings," said the King, "and with the outer wall held against them, Varlen is cut off." Jordgen thought sullenly about the supply wagons in the outer ward that were now all in Aranstone's hands. He turned away from the window. "Our only hope is to give up the east wing for now and concentrate on securing the west wing. With the storerooms, we will be able to hold out for some time. That may let us regain the messaging tower and one of the gates in the outer wall." Jordgen's face bore the weight and gravity of his kingship. "Bring them over from the east wing and secure the west staircase and entrances. And have everyone prepare for siege."

Arlen left down the hall toward the east wing of the Castle. A safe withdrawal from the east wing would be difficult, and he began mulling it over in his thoughts.

"Father—" Rhiane was striding next to him, matching his haste. "With seven or eight men I think we can bring in Varlen and troops in from the valley," she began. Arlen stopped suddenly, listening. Rhiane led him aside out of the hall traffic. "Do you remember Iaven telling us how Wendolin sent Cedric to hide the swords?"

Arlen was ready to rebuke Rhiane for not coming to the point when he saw what she was driving at. He smiled at his daughter. "Yes, of course! It must be done right away." He stopped a guard passing in the hallway. "Give her a half dozen men from downstairs, and get her whatever she needs." The startled guard went with Rhiane, while Arlen hurried down the hall again. *That's my daughter*, Arlen thought proudly, which seemed to excuse the fact that he hadn't had the idea first.

Khale's company had endured a difficult struggle to take control of the inner ward. At last it was theirs, though all the Castle doors were shut against them. Once the rear-guard was no longer needed, Orven and the others came in to look around. The Castle bounded the inner ward on three sides, the west wing to the left and the east wing to the right. There was a cistern, some benches, small, half-timbered buildings built at the corners and sides, and a small garden plot, now empty, near the west wing wall. The center of the ward was open and flagstoned. Directly ahead to the north, under the wide, carven stone arch, the massive double doors of wood and iron barred the main entrance to the Castle. Now that they had the inner ward, nothing remained for them to do but guard the great doors so that none might leave by them.

Orven was still recovering from the shock and strain of battle, and doing his best to hide it. Ripley, tired and still nervy, chatted with Khale's men. Max, Roy, and Aaron were relieved that the King's men had gone inside and that the doors were shut, though they could still hear the fighting going on elsewhere.

The outer ward was quieter now. Aranstones's men walked along the walls, surveying the damage from above. Many of the half-timbered buildings had broken windows and doors wrenched off their hinges. Supply wagons were ransacked, and the captains had them wheeled over to a corner where they could be rationed out slowly. The streets of the outer ward were strewn with debris, and bodies of Aranstone's men and the Castle guard lay scattered across the flagstones. The wounded were sitting up or crawling, and they were taken into the gatehouses. Max looked at it all with great shame. He renewed his resolve to side with the King as soon as he could get away, and wondered if he would do so without Orven. Yet something warned him against leaving Orven with Aranstone's men, convincing him to wait.

Max walked over to where Orven and Ripley were talking with Rafnel and Strable, and Aaron and Roy joined them as well. During the heat of battle Ripley had slain a Castle guard, and he was unusually quiet as he thought about it now.

"You did fine," Strable told Ripley, "we all did."

"A lot of our men were slain, too," said Rafnel. "We ourselves could have been, easily enough." He gave Ripley a slap on the back. "He's become quite a soldier," Rafnel smiled at Orven. "And think what he could do wielding Halix," Rafnel said, with a piercing glance at Max. "Holding this place against closed doors will give us some respite, but it's far from over yet. Taking the west wing will be difficult, and we'll need every last man, until we can shut them up in the east wing and begin the siege."

"And it's going to take more than merely defensive maneuvers," said Strable, eyeing Max, Aaron, and Roy with menace in his stare.

The afternoon wore on. The sky clouded over and snow whirled in the air. The battle in the west wing ended in deadlock. Khale left a squadron of his men and took the rest over to the east wing where Aranstone's men had fought their way inside at several entrances, and gradually the sound of battle died down as the men pushed their way into the east wing.

The mood throughout the inner ward grew more relaxed, and Orven's men and Khale's men discussed what should be done next. The boisterous conversation was suddenly halted when a low rumbling and a big *thunk* boomed from the huge central doors under the arch. Inside, the enormous beams were being drawn back. All eyes turned towards the doors. Another *thunk* sounded, and then a clattering of bolts and a shuddering groan as the doors opened. A multitude of metallic whispers chilled the air as Khale's and Orven's men drew their swords. Those in front raised their shields cautiously, expecting archers to clear the way as soon as a crack opened between the doors. Tense, they all waited. The doors swung wider and light fell into the Throne Room vestibule. The leader of a small host of warriors stepped forward, and to everyone's relief it was Khale, announcing that the east wing was theirs. Cheers went up in the inner ward and the crowd poured into the Castle to get out of the cold.

Khale received many congratulations as the men passed him, but he was not elated about the capture of the east wing. "Now their hold on the west wing is solid," Khale explained to Orven, "With the extra men, they've retaken everything on the lower floors, and we've lost what we had in the west wing, except the messaging tower. An hour from now Aranstone is having a meeting of all the captains, to change our strategy and reassign everyone as needed."

"At least we have the east wing," Orven said.

Khale nodded. "We do, but we'll have the dungeons below us now instead of the storerooms. Without them, we'll have less food and water than we had planned. And they will have more."

"We've still succeeded and have them under siege," said Orven.

"Yes," Khale admitted, "But it will be much longer than we expected."

Clouds obscured the sun's descent into the west and Iaven braced himself for another cold night. Snow was in the air, and even in the valleys the winds were shrill and sharp. The four dwarves and the old wizard labored over the steep and uneven land. Wendolin had kept them moving in a southerly direction and seemed to have a general idea of where they were. Few were the reassurances he gave the dwarves, yet they gladly put their trust in him.

"Look," Zammond pointed, "Between those peaks, over there."

Iaven almost didn't look up. Too many times over the past two days, Zammond had thought he had seen the top of Castle Frosthelm emerging from behind a mountain. But this time, far away in the graying gloom, Iaven could make out a tiny flag fluttering upon a small, conical rooftop. "Yes, I see it," Iaven said, surprised and greatly relieved. The others saw it now as well.

But as they approached the peak in front of them rose and the spire was hidden from view. They felt lost again, and as the valley angled east they became afraid they would veer too far off course. At last they came upon a turn and a steady uphill climb over a broad pass. They ascended, the land opened beneath them, and the Castle came into view again. Now the way was downhill, and the valley ahead wound around the next peak and joined one of the valleys Mount Frosthelm overlooked.

As they entered the valley the Castle disappeared again and reappeared later as they came around the mountain's high shoulders. Castle Frosthelm was less than a mile away. Viewed from behind, the Castle was high and inaccessible, rising flush out of the steep rock walls that climbed over a hundred feet from where the ground sloped more gently into the valley. Drawing closer, they saw what looked like three strings of climbers moving slowly up the rock wall like lines of ants following a trail.

"They're going up ropes, into the Castle," said Hobley, "Soldiers, it looks like. Are they training for a climb?"

Wendolin peered into the distance and said nothing, his brow furrowed with concern. They pressed forward, eager to get to the Castle after so many days in the mountains, and watched the soldiers climbing up the rock and castle wall until they were taken in through the windows high overhead. Some soldiers in the valley noticed Wendolin and the dwarves and drew their swords, ready to fight. The soldiers looked at them with amazement, calling for them to halt when they came within earshot. Wendolin told Iaven and his friends not to draw their swords and to do as the soldiers said.

"We come to the King from Teska," Wendolin announced as soldiers approached them. Their captain, an older dwarf with a graying beard and bright blue eyes stepped forward. "Can it be?" he said, "Wendolin? We have long thought you dead!"

"Not yet, but near enough," said Wendolin, "Narrowly did we escape the attack on the encampment near Halloway, and we have traveled the mountains since then. We must see the King," he glanced at the dwarves going up the ropes, "if all is not already lost."

"The Castle is under siege," said the captain, "the outer wall and gates are held against us. I do not know more than that at the moment, but come and join us. The help of a wizard is sure to tip the scales in our favor."

Wendolin and the dwarves followed the captain, walking with his men up the slope to where the others were. "I shall do what I can," said Wendolin, "but I have been ill of late and it shall be some time before my full powers are regained."

"Even so," said the captain, "you are awake and sound of mind, and that will no doubt prove as useful to us as any magic."

They walked amid the tall pines and climbed the slope. Where the rock rose steeply, soldiers waited as others pulled themselves up the ropes. Iaven looked up the cliffs, the Castle tantalizingly high above them. The rock wall rose into the sky with just a slight slant away from the vertical, and beyond that the Castle wall went straight up for several stories. Soldiers climbed the ropes and into the windows of the west wing, as great masses of pearled clouds drifted far overhead. Just gazing up at it all gave Iaven vertigo, and he braced himself for the climb. He could see that his friends dreaded it as much as he did.

Wilbur stared skyward and whistled. "Well, I guess there's no other way in. I'll try to not look down!"

Soon the last few soldiers hoisted themselves up the ropes and walked up the dark rock walls, and it was Iaven's turn. The captain had offered to go last to see that everyone made it all right, and Wendolin was to go right before him. Zammond and Hob went over to one of the other ropes and started climbing. Iaven and Wilbur stood looking up their rope. "You go first," said Wilbur, "I don't want to slow you down."

Iaven made sure his sword and pack were secured and then gripped the rope with both hands. He pulled himself up, finding it harder than the soldiers had made it look. His first few steps were awkward and tentative, until he found his footing against the wall and positioned his arms so as to move hand over hand along its length. Iaven gradually found the rhythm he needed to keep going, and he concentrated on the wall in front of him as the captain had suggested. The slant of the rock wall took some of his weight off his hands, but they were already red and raw by the time he was halfway up.

Iaven looked across to the other rope. Zammond was about ten feet above where he was, enjoying the climb. Below him Hobley was moving more slowly, and he nodded and smiled when he saw Iaven looking their way. Forty feet or so up the rock wall, Iaven looked down and saw Wilbur lumbering up the wall. He was already panting, and was too absorbed to notice Iaven watching him. Far below him, Wendolin was starting up the wall, the captain waiting on the ground behind him. Iaven looked up and resumed climbing. The Castle still seemed a good distance away, and at the top of the rope two soldiers were finishing their climb up the Castle wall. As each made it to the window, arms reached out and pulled them inside the Castle.

The wind blew sharp and cold and daylight was waning, the overcast sky slowing the onset of dusk. Although Iaven's attention stayed focused on his climb, he wondered what was going on inside the Castle. Tired and weary, he recalled the warmth and comforts the Castle had provided earlier, realizing things would be quite different this time. But whatever the Castle had to offer would be better than the cold, hard solitude of the mountains.

Iaven finally reached the top of the cliffs. There the large stone blocks of the castle walls rose from the dark rock of the mountain as though they had grown out of it. The first few rows were much broader and older than the rest of the Castle, and Iaven recognized them as the foundations laid by the Angkhadra. While he hung on, resting before beginning the climb straight up the Castle wall, he chanced to look down beneath him and shuddered. The drop was over a hundred feet and the land below was obscured in darkness now, like a yawning abyss waiting for him to fall into it. The wind gusted against Iaven and he tightened his grip on the rope. Some twenty or thirty feet below him Wilbur labored up out of the dusk, and just beyond him Iaven could make out the shapes of Wendolin and the Dwarven captain. Iaven looked up again, and the courses of stone leading to the lighted windows of the Castle did not seem as far away. Soldiers leaned out the window, watching and urging him on. He pulled on the rope, balancing his feet against the wall to keep from swinging.

As he climbed, Iaven's arms ached terribly, his hands were cold, raw, and numb, and it was with great relief that he finally felt the soldiers grab hold of him and drag him in through the window. The room they were in was a part of the Castle living quarters. The furniture was pushed aside to make way for the soldiers, and the rope's end was tied to the legs of a heavy wooden bedframe, which was further braced and weighted down to keep it in place. Iaven remembered that Zammond and Hobley had gone up before him, and were probably in the room next door. He stretched, feeling better but ashamed of how exhausted he had appeared in front of the soldiers.

Iaven went out. Soldiers were passing to and fro in the hallway. Further down the hall he heard Zammond and Hobley, and saw they were talking with Rhiane. Iaven's heart sank when he saw her. Since his stay in Teska, he was sure he had given up hope that Rhiane had any interest in him. But seeing her now his feelings for her returned afresh, stronger than before, and he realized he had never given up hope, foolish as that seemed to him. The weight of his failure crushed him, and he dreaded facing Rhiane more than he dreaded facing the King. Iaven was about to turn and go the other way down the hall, when the three of them called out and came over by him.

"What a hike, eh?" said Zammond cheerfully, "And we've landed right in the middle of things, from what Rhiane tells us."

"It is quite a surprise to see all of you like this," said Rhiane, turning to Iaven. Iaven looked into her dark eyes, the frenzy of activity in the hall outside his notice as he tried to fathom her feelings. Zammond and Hobley had already talked to her, and he sensed deep disappointment in her gaze. Iaven wanted to say something to Rhiane, to explain it all. "Yes," he said, still trying to find the words.

The moment passed. "I'm glad you're all here. They'll need you downstairs," Rhiane said, "I've got to go now, I'll see you all later tonight. And I'm very sorry to hear about Tillmore."

And she was gone again. Iaven watched her go, sure that she was no more interested in him than any of the others. Just then Wilbur emerged into the hall, breathing hard and rubbing his sore hands. "Iaven! Iaven, I made it! I did it! That was so— Iaven? What's the matter?"

"They need us to go help down in the storerooms," Hobley told Wilbur.

"She has a lot to do," said Zammond, clapping Iaven on the shoulder. "Really, Iaven. She just didn't have time to talk just now." They turned a corner and began descending wide stone stairs. "Don't worry, Iaven, she did ask about you. I think she still likes you!"

Iaven looked exasperatedly at Zammond, who smiled back at him. "Hob and I filled her in on all the news, but that was all the time she could spare... You really should have climbed the other rope!"

Iaven, Zammond, Wilbur, and Hobley labored into the night, working in a storeroom below the west wing where rations were being divided and distributed. Sounds of battle continued down the halls, until soldiers from the valley helped tip the scales in the Castle's favor. Aranstone brought in men from the outer wall to try to gain an advantage, but the Dwarves held their ground. Aranstone's men were finally pushed out of the west wing, the doors shut firmly against them. Some claimed that had the troops been brought in sooner, they might have also held the Throne Room, the Great Hall, and perhaps the entire central part of the Castle. Now it was a question of how they would regain lost ground.

Soon the Dwarves secured the west wing at all points, the last of the battles wound down into the evening, and the siege began. Some soldiers went down the ropes into the valley again, with orders to go and summon troops from Kronivar. As they reached the bottom of the ropes, they were met with a hail of arrows from Aranstone's archers stationed in the valley, and only one of the King's men was able to elude them in the dark.

Night fell and the cold deepened. Shrill winds encircled the Castle peak and snow beat upon the windowpanes like diamond dust. Aranstone's men huddled in shifts stationed outside the west wing doors and in the gatehouses along the outer wall. Those who were off-duty were housed in the east wing, where they kept warm while awaiting the change of shifts. Word quickly spread amongst the men that a siege of possibly several weeks could be expected, which made their victory seem a bitter and hollow one. Yet they had faith that Aranstone and Greywood would find a way to pressure the King into agreeing to their demands before troops from Kronivar intervened. As Greywood had told them, it was the imminent Goblin attack more than the siege itself that would finally cause the King to concede. This comforted them, until it was later learned that the King had rejected Aranstone's first attempt at a parley.

"Well," said Max, "it may be a dull duty, but at least we're indoors." To accommodate the change of plans, Orven and his men had been stationed at the top of the huge staircase outside the Great Hall, by a door that led to one of the upper floors of the west wing. The door was shut fast against them, and they made their camp on the landing right in front of it. Although they were to guard the door and keep the King's men inside, it felt instead as if they had been shut out and trapped outside the door, and it did not look like anyone would be leaving or entering by it.

Max was glad the fighting was over, and saw the others shared his relief. Still, the prospect of spending days, perhaps even weeks, guarding a door did not please him. They were also expected to man the post continuously, since it was an enviable indoor position and because Orven's party had too few men to have rotating shifts. Their rations were brought to them at intervals, and one or two of them could leave for short periods of time, but for the most part they would have to remain at the door, holding the landing in case the King's men should attempt to retake it from inside. Since the door opened outward onto the landing, they barred it with a beam that Aranstone had sent up to them, and the rest of their time was spent watching and waiting.

"It is a strategic point to hold," said Orven, repeating what Greywood had told him, finding it difficult to believe himself. "But I was hoping we'd have a more important position," he admitted.

"It's only temporary, and it isn't so bad," said Rafnel, "It's fine for now, as far as I'm concerned. We should rest while we can. I wouldn't doubt Aranstone's looking for a way to shorten the siege."

"Yes," Strable said smiling, "and you can be sure they won't leave Halix and Gorflange out of the action."

"I hope not," said Orven, not noticing that Strable had referred only to the swords.

By nightfall the Castle had quieted down considerably. Aranstone, garbed in a long, brown, fur-lined cloak, made the rounds along the outer wall and Castle entrances, encouraging the men and learning what casualties had been incurred. As he paced in the cold air through the outer ward, the thought of a long siege lay heavy upon him, as did the hopes of his men that he would find a way to force the King to concede. The unexpected loss of the west wing had hurt them, and now the King refused to parley. Other means of pressure would have to be found. Alone in the dark and cold, doubts crept into Aranstone's mind, and he began to question Greywood's plans. He had not seen his chief advisor in the last hour or so, and suddenly found himself in need of Greywood's reassurances.

Aranstone returned to the east wing, but Greywood was not to be found there. Someone thought he had gone out along the wall. Aranstone passed through the gatehouses, but Greywood was not among them. Finally, he looked up at the messaging tower and, nodding to the guard posted there, entered the door leading into it.

He climbed the winding steps inside the tower, cold air spiraling down the stairs around him. The room at the top of the tower was dark and lit by starlight alone, yet something told him to keep going. At last he reached the top. A lingering aroma told him the room's candle had only recently been extinguished. And there, framed in an arched window, Greywood stood staring out into the starry night sky.

"I've been looking all over for you!" A slight note of reproach edged Aranstone's voice. "What are you doing up here?"

Greywood withdrew from his thoughts and turned to Aranstone, ignoring his tone. "Enjoying the view. And our victory. Let us return, then." He moved past Aranstone and went down the stairs.

Aranstone stood, watching him go, his instincts forming a vague suspicion. For a moment he wondered idly if Greywood had come up here to send a message, then dismissed the idea. He looked around the room, relieved to find everything was in order. All the messenger-birds were still in their cages and none were missing.

And the sky was empty, except for a hawk flying off to the north.

Chapter 38.
The Shadow Lengthens

By the light of the moon the hawk flew out over the mountains, veering northwest now, eager to return to its master. Wings outstretched, it rode the snow-strewn gusts high above the mountains. Miles of dark, spreading ranges passed below, the vast wintry silence broken only by the roar of the wind and an occasional wolf-howl from the valley depths.

Eventually the mountains gave way to lower hills, then meadows and forest. The hawk scanned the ground for the great entourage it had left several days earlier. The North Road was a narrow, barren ribbon running north-south through the moon-washed landscape, and the hawk followed it. It was long deserted at this late hour, and further along, fires dotted some of the farms off the roadside. Seeing these, the hawk circled in a wide sweeping arc and flew south, searching the land.

At last a twinkling, bobbing stream of torches grew visible on the dark road below. The hawk dropped lower and flew toward it. A huge caravan, wider than the road, was moving south. Lanterns swung and torches burned in the dark, as columns of firelit figures marched in the night. In the center of the throng, lines of great shaggy broadbacked Urumak walked in pairs, shoulder to shoulder. Those in front pulled supply wagons and troop wagons, while those in the rear, walking single file, carried war-towers on their backs. Companies of Goblin infantry marched in front of the Urumak, and horsemen rode on both sides of the columns. Squadrons of chained Augglins made up the vanguard and rear guard, and some pulled carts and wagons as well. Smoke and noise rose from the horde, and the hawk heard the snuffle and grunts of their beasts as he flew lower and sought the painted war-tower wherein his master awaited him.

Circling the war-towers, the hawk found the one with the familiar crescents and zigzag patterns on it and perched on a narrow windowsill there. A black-gloved wrist extended to receive the bird and drew it inside. Maëlveronde stroked the hawk, whispering to it, and removed the tiny scroll attached to its leg. He unrolled it and read Zhindarren's report, which pleased him. Their timing had been close, but all was well. He filed the report away in a thin, oblong, painted wooden box and placed it alongside some leather-bound volumes. Maëlveronde sat back in his chair, feeling the gentle sway of the Urumak's movement. Soon he would tell Del-Sorhar and General Burzok, and word would spread among the troops, providing just the encouragement they needed after a long, cold march of several days.

The Goblin army marched for Greensward now, making good time. Morale was high and their mood was a hungry and raucous one. Since the ravaging of Teska and Farrenhale, they had moved south unopposed, pillaging farms and villages along the road in the northern provinces as needed. No one in the rear guard even noticed the small, wary company of Dwarven soldiers following the great Goblin throng at a distance and keeping out of sight.

The company consisted of survivors from the Battle of Farrenhale and those who had escaped the attack on the encampment near Halloway. They had regrouped under Captain Gallorne, and for the last few days had been trailing the Goblins, passing through the destruction left in their wake along the North Road. Around two dozen of them moved along cautiously like hunted animals, to learn what they could of the Goblin army. They were too few to fight, yet all wore helmets and chain mail, even the Tolgarder who looked curiously out of place in Dwarven armor.

When the smoke had cleared after the attack at Halloway, the rising sun revealed a land strewn with charred canvas, burnt wood, and other debris, as well as the dead of both Goblin and Dwarven troops. And among the bodies lay Lexter Splide, his hand still grasping the black goblin arrow jutting out from his neck. Only after all was quiet a good long time did he even loosen his grip on the arrow. He had broken the tip off the arrow and held it close to his neck, hoping the angle of it looked believable. The goblins were searching the camp, slaying whatever wounded they found, but they didn't waste any time on the dead. Lexter had lain there, breathing as shallowly as he could until he nearly fainted. At last the goblins were gone, on horses stolen from the dwarves, away to the north somewhere. Or so it had sounded. Lexter lay face down and was afraid to get up and look around, in case any goblins had stayed behind. Finally, he shifted his head to one side to get a better look around the camp, and saw he was alone. He dropped the arrow and found his hands were shaking. He got to his feet and was barely able to stand, so great was the nervous tension strung throughout his body. Lexter cried aloud at the sight of all the carnage that lay about him, startling himself. He looked around, and no goblins were in sight, only those killed in battle. Yet nowhere seemed safe now. Gradually his shaking came under control, relief easing through him along with profound sorrow for all the dead that lay across the battlefield. Alone, he cried.

Lexter tried to calm himself, and searched the camp to see if Iaven and the others had been slain. Their tent lay in a pile of burnt wood and canvas. Seeing all the dead sickened him; many lay as they had fallen, bent in agony, blood darkening their clothes and the ground beneath them. Hands still gripped weapons, and strained and distorted faces stared with blank eyes. He could not meet their gaze.

Several times Lexter was startled by a noise behind him, only to find it was a bird or squirrel. He realized how tense and nervous he was. All was quiet, yet Lexter still felt a rising, naked panic and vulnerability, as though a black arrow would soon fly out at him from somewhere to make up for his escape. He had lost the protection of the Dwarven camp, and was alone again and unarmed. Looking around the camp he found a helmet on the ground, near one of the larger dwarves who had fallen. Lexter picked it up, and tried it on. It fit him, and as he spread the attached aventail over the back of his neck and shoulders, he felt a little safer.

He adjusted the helmet and left it on and began to search for a coat of ring mail that would fit him. Lexter cringed at having to touch and move the corpses. Sometimes as he moved a body he would make eye contact, and have to turn away, unable to do anything for a moment. Finally Lexter found a coat of ring mail that fit. Some were damaged, and many were too small or too short, but a larger dwarf had been putting on his mail when the goblins had burst into his tent and stabbed him. He had only put one arm in the coat before they had found him, and had fallen with it half on. Several metal rings were stained with blood, but the coat was intact and large enough. Lexter scrubbed the metal and could not get it entirely clean, but he took it anyway.

Next he looked for a good sword and scabbard. He was not used to wearing either helmet or mail, and was still adjusting to the added weight. He had learned a good deal about mail and other types of armor along with Leland, yet neither of them had ever fought in it or worn it for any length of time. He appreciated now how difficult it was, and had greater respect for those dwarves who seemed to wear it effortlessly.

Lexter was examining a sword and scabbard when he heard the sound of people nearby. One called out to him. He stood up and looked around. Three villagers, a farmer and two of his sons, were walking over from Halloway, cautiously approaching. Others waited further back, afraid to come closer. The three glanced away behind Lexter, and he turned to look as well. Two Dwarven soldiers were returning from the hills and hailing him now. Lexter realized that they thought he was a fellow soldier.

"Any others?" the soldiers asked Lexter.

"Just me," Lexter replied, as they walked up to him.

"A Tolgarder, from the sound of it," said one, surprised. "You were with us here, last night?"

"I was," said Lexter, deciding it best to let them make their own assumptions beyond that.

"Well, good to see you all the same," said the other dwarf.

"Pardon me," the farmer from Halloway stepped closer, fearful of interrupting anything. He had sent his two sons back to the village. "We will help you all we can." The farmer regarded the bloodied field with shock and sorrow.

"Thank you," said the first dwarf. He turned back to Lexter. "Captain Gallorne is in the hills, seeking dwarves who escaped the attack. It seems he's the only captain who survived. He said we'll regroup here and then head up to Farrenhale to join the others, as planned."

"Yes, of course," said Lexter, though it was the last thing he wanted to do. He wanted to go to Kronivar instead, where he could slip away and find passage home to Tolgard. But he knew he would end up going with them to Farrenhale because he didn't want to travel alone and also because it was what he *ought* to do. Though he doubted he could be of much help at the front, he owed it to the Dwarves to do whatever he could. And maybe they would help send him home afterward, too, he hoped.

The day passed quietly, and Captain Gallorne returned before dusk with a few other dwarves. Several were wounded and were taken to Halloway to recover. Those who could continued to search the hills until night fell. Lexter went with them, and they found two more wounded and carried them back to the village. By the day's end they were bivouacked among the farmhouses of Halloway, eighteen soldiers in all, six of them wounded and laid up.

While the grief-stricken village settled into an uneasy slumber, Lexter sat up with Captain Gallorne. Gallorne had assigned Lexter to the same house as himself, and Lexter wondered if his motive was suspicion or mere curiosity. He supposed it was a bit of both. They sat near the fireplace, tending to a wounded dwarf laid out on the family's wooden table and covered with a spare blanket. Soon they had done all they could. Once the dwarf was asleep, Lexter and Gallorne sat back near the fire, keeping warm and trying to rest. Both watched the shallow breathing of their wounded compatriot.

"I don't even know his name," Gallorne said. "He wasn't under my command."

It was some time before either of them was able to sleep, so they sat there, tired and somber, and said very little. The questions Lexter expected never came. As he considered the day's events, Lexter felt ashamed at how much he had worried about himself in light of all that had happened. He realized how selfish he was, and worse, how typical it was of him. Faces of dead dwarves on the battlefield were etched in his mind, staring out at him fresh in memory. Somehow he found himself thinking of all the people he had cheated, stolen from, or injured in any way. Such thoughts burdened him, weighing his heart with guilt, but he did not resist them; instead he tried to remember all he could. He felt very low and terrible, wondering how he had fooled himself into thinking he was somehow better than those he had cheated. He had deserved to die on the battlefield that morning, but here he was, not even wounded, wearing the armor of others who had died in his place. And the survivors had taken him in without hesitation. Lexter suddenly had the urge to tell Gallorne who he was and confess everything, but the Captain was asleep already and snoring. Lexter breathed deeply, and decided he wanted to go back to Farrenhale, even though he dreaded it. As he sat pondering why this might be, his thoughts loosened and diverged until he slept soundly.

Lexter awoke to sunlight and birdsong, and for a moment the attack and its aftermath seemed like a bad dream. The weather was sunny and cold, and the grimness of their situation quickly returned. Captain Gallorne went out to check on the other soldiers, while Lexter tended to the wounded dwarf. He was awake now and told Lexter his name was Thaern.

Lexter and the others spent the day tending to the wounded in Halloway. With the help of the villagers they collected the dead on the battlefield and heaped them all into a mass grave they covered with a mound of dirt. The goblin bodies they piled and burned. The work was cold and tiring and the mood quiet and sullen. A light, icy rain fell on them. In the evening they learned that four of the wounded soldiers were improving, while the other two had worsened and looked as though they would not recover. Lexter began to appreciate Gallorne's leadership and was glad to serve under him.

Although only a dozen troops were ready for active duty, Gallorne was still eager to get to Farrenhale and join the army there. The following morning he gathered the soldiers together. One of the wounded had died during the night, and they buried him in the field near the mound. Two were back on their feet and joined them, while the others would remain in the villagers' care until the troops returned from Farrenhale. The soldiers packed the provisions they were offered, thanked the people of Halloway, and made their way up the North Road.

Captain Gallorne's company, little more than a squadron now, marched up the North Road keeping watch over the fields on either side of the road. Although Gallorne suspected the goblins had all gone north, there was always the chance a few spies were lingering. The day right after the battle, Gallorne and two others had ambushed and killed a goblin who had been returning from the mountains. So they kept an eye open on all sides, and three of them kept a bow and arrow in hand should any goblins appear.

After an uneventful afternoon on the road, their tension eased, though they still remained wary. That trouble was afoot was certain. They all wondered if the troops at the front would discover the goblins coming before any damage was done. Such speculation occupied their minds for many hours on the road. Lexter recalled all he had seen in Farrenhale, wondering how secure it really was.

As evening fell, Captain Gallorne found them lodgings for the night in a barn at a roadside farm, and Lexter was reminded of his stay with the Thelreds. The people of the northern provinces tended to keep to themselves but were willing to help the soldiers when needed. Sometimes their children came to get a cautious look at the soldiers, peeking around doorframes or from behind their parents. Lexter was moved by the fascination and admiration in their eyes and wanted very much to meet their expectations. Since his decision to stay with the troops, Lexter had come to feel a part of them and no longer like an imposter who would eventually be found out.

"I cannot help but be curious how a Tolgarder comes to fight for our King, and in Dwarven armor at that." Gaern Loriver, brother of the wounded dwarf Lexter had tended in Halloway, sat the double watch with Lexter and regarded him with interest. The rest of the soldiers were asleep around the barn, laying in the hay and bundled in coats and spare blankets. All was dark and quiet.

"Well, I've lived and worked in Itharia for some time," Lexter began. The temptation of an easy lie was great and Lexter could think of a dozen of them. But he resolved to stay as near the truth as possible. "It seemed the thing to do. And this—" Lexter indicated his armor, "I didn't have any of my own, and there was an extra helmet that fit..."

"I see." Gaern was amused. "Most foreigners seem to have joined the troops in Kronivar. It's safer than the front, and the accommodations are better. And they're really just protecting their best interests there. But you... It's rather rare to see a foreigner going to the front."

Lexter shrugged. "Oh, I'm not the only one. There's a few from Kronivar there already, and—"

"You've been up there?" Gaern sounded impressed and suspicious. "What were you doing up there? How long ago was this?"

"Well, I was... meeting some friends, actually. Dwarves. And I sort of got involved in things. And being around the soldiers, well, I thought about how Itharia's been like a home these past few years..." Lexter waited for Gaern to draw his own conclusions and hoped to change the subject before he was asked anything too specific. Even a goblin making a sudden disturbance outside the barn would have been welcome at that moment.

"Remarkable! Quite commendable," said Gaern, fascinated. "It's an honor to have you with us."

"Oh, well... thank you." Lexter said sheepishly. He had been tempted to tell Gaern everything and then thought better of it. "But you know, I'm not much of a soldier, I'm so new to it all. If I knew better what was expected—"

As Lexter supposed, Gaern was eager to talk and instruct Lexter in the ways of the King's troops and soldiering in general. All Gaern's suspicions ceased when it was clear that Lexter was a willing audience. Lexter spent the rest of the watch learning more than he had desired to, but he was thankful for Gaern's acceptance of him and tried to be as attentive as he could.

The next day they set out again, and Lexter felt more a part of the Dwarven troops than ever, despite lingering feelings that he was somehow deceiving them about his intent. He wondered if perhaps he had really meant some of the things he had told Gaern. It was somewhat unnerving to think that he might be changing his mind about certain things and only realizing it later.

Gallorne's company had been marching a few hours when they encountered a horse-drawn cart approaching at great speed. Gallorne signaled for his company to stop and move off of the road. They strained to see who the driver and riders were, readying bows and swords. The cart slowed and came to a halt. It was loaded with Dwarven soldiers, all of whom looked haggard and despondent. Lexter sensed something was amiss and fear rose in the pit of his stomach.

"Farrenhale's fallen," shouted the cart driver, a mailed dwarf with dinted helm and battle-stained doublet. "Return to your troops, and ready them for battle. There is little time."

"It is too late," said Gallorne, "we are all that remain of them. The Goblins surrounded the camp at Halloway and burned it down."

The cart driver was hit hard by the news and a wave of dread passed over all the riders. "Then Kronivar is our only hope." He paused, biting back despair. "We have far to go. Climb on, and let us make haste." More than a dozen dwarves lined the back of the cart, leaving barely any room for Gallorne's troops. They climbed in, the Farrenhale troops pressing closer together. The cart creaked under the added weight as the horse strained to get them moving again.

Lexter had never been comfortable in close quarters with strangers and found the crowding unbearable. Worse, some of the Farrenhale troops glared at him as though he were some spy or imposter that Gallorne's troops had failed to notice. He ignored them as best he could, looking away, but felt their questioning gazes and distrust all the same.

They had gone only a few miles, at a greatly slowed pace, when the cart finally gave way with a loud *cracking* that ended with a wheel splintering and an axle breaking, spilling the overcrowded dwarves onto the road. Curses and grunts of disgust erupted, and it was a while before the grumbling died down. Captain Gallorne discovered that he was the highest-ranking of all the dwarves present and took charge of the situation. There were no objections from the Farrenhale troops, who were tired and demoralized by their losses and defeat. A Captain to serve under was a welcome addition to their disorganized and battle-weary band.

With the Farrenhale troops joining them, Lexter felt out of place all over again. But Gallorne's men had good things to say about Lexter, and over the next few days the Farrenhale dwarves came to accept him. Everyone regrouped into squadrons of six or seven, and Captain Gallorne assured them that in the villages ahead they would find another cart to speed their journey.

And so they marched down the North Road. They were cold and tired, but marched as long as they could into the evening. Captain Gallorne led the company along with the cart driver, Eron Silvernail, who walked their horse. Lexter and Gaern had fallen to the back of the group and tried to keep pace with everyone.

"I've ridden a horse now and then," said Lexter, as he and Gaern discussed differences between Dwarves and the Men of Kronivar. "And there's even some dwarves there who ride them, I've seen it. Not many, though."

"I've heard that. Must be the half-breeds," said Gaern, "—No offense meant, of course!"

"None taken," said Lexter, who had heard enough of such talk that he had come to expect it. "It could be useful at a time like this. We could send someone off on Silvernail's horse to find us a cart or wagon... Though I'm not volunteering; I never did enough riding to get used to it."

Gaern stopped in the road, pausing. "Do you hear that?"

"What?" Lexter stopped and listened. Ahead of them, the clomp of marching dwarves continued as it had all day. But behind them was a quiet and growing marching sound mingled with the faint clip-clop of hooves. The land to the north was dark now, and far away clusters of tiny lights bobbed on the road.

"More men from Farrenhale?" said Lexter, but he knew it wasn't.

"We'd better tell the others right away," said Gaern.

Lexter and Gaern ran to catch up to the troops and spread word that goblins were coming. Gallorne led everyone off the road, through the fields, and into the cover of the woods. There they crouched low, watching and hoping to remain unseen. "Lexter, Gaern, come with me!" Gallorne whispered, motioning them forward.

The three of them crept into the field and found a low rise in the land where clumps of dried grasses stood. They kept down, out of sight, peering through the weeds to the road. "We'll find out what we can," said Gallorne. "We should get a good idea of their number, and what armaments they have."

They waited and the noise of the Goblin army grew louder, unmistakable now. Lexter began to make out a huge procession approaching. A growing terror overtook him as they neared.

From where he lay Lexter could see only dark overlapping shapes, lit by swaying points of torchlight and tiny lanterns hanging higher up and farther back in the throng. They grew closer, only a hundred yards away. The rise Gallorne had chosen was some twenty or thirty feet from the road, and Lexter was already nervous that it was too close and that they would be seen. He held as still as he could, his heart pounding and his breathing tense and shallow.

The caravan advanced. At less than fifty yards, Lexter could smell the smoke from their torches and hear the murmur of Goblin voices. The smell of the Goblins made Lexter nauseous, reminding him of the dank cave tunnels. At the front of the horde were wide, ambling shapes, followed by Goblin infantry, their boots falling in unison. Lexter had heard about the Augglins but had never seen one. Chained and held in check by armored goblins, they were the vanguard; huge, broad-shouldered muscle-bound shapes harnessed to supply wagons. As they passed Lexter saw big hulking creatures piled in the first rows of wagons pulled by augglins.

"More augglins," Gallorne whispered to them. The noise level was high enough that they could talk quietly without being heard. "They keep the others drugged until they need them. They'll exchange them with the ones pulling the carts when they tire out." The next rows of wagons held sacks, crates, and other supplies. Goblin horsemen rode past and infantry marched behind the carts. Row upon row went by, and the mixed stench became almost too much for Lexter.

More infantry passed and kept coming and Lexter lost count of the rows. The caravan was so wide that many marched alongside the road, and Lexter kept worrying that someone would stop and sniff him out. Next came horse-drawn wagons with walled sides, heaped with some dark material. "Feed for the Urumak, it looks like," Gallorne said, "They can feed them on the move that way." Rows of great shaggy Urumak followed, and Lexter was fascinated by the huge, striding beasts. The torches of passing horsemen lit their wooly gray-brown fur, massive legs swinging forward, broad heads bobbing on their long necks as they walked. Lexter strained to see the tiny dark-skinned men riding near the heads of the great beasts, and saw chains extending from the men's necks up to railed wooden platforms atop the Urumak. There a good many Goblins rode, some climbing up or down rope ladders that hung on the great beasts' sides. Some Urumak pulled enormous wagons and wheeled war-towers, while two rows of them had long loads of thick poles and dark lumber strapped and hanging beneath them.

"Look at that," Gallorne whispered with astonishment. "Battering rams and ladders, big ones. As though Kronivar were a walled city. Very strange..."

Lexter and Gaern stared in wonderment as more pairs of Urumak went by. The last few had tall, ornately carven war-towers built upon their backs, which were lit from within. Something about them disquieted Lexter. More Goblin infantry followed, row upon row, and horsemen rode along either side of them. Finally, after the last row of infantry, came a rear guard of chained augglins and their masters, keeping watch lest anyone try to attack the army from behind. And, Lexter realized, they were probably useful in keeping the Goblin infantry moving along as well.

Finally, the last of the caravan was receding into the distance. The clamor died down and soon Lexter and the dwarves were alone again. They relaxed and breathed easier now, still unnerved by the Goblins' passing.

Gaern was staring off to the south. "What're they doing?"

Lexter and Gallorne turned to look. Down the road, the lights of the Goblin throng could be seen. Several torches, carried by horsemen, moved off the road into a nearby farm. They reappeared, carrying things, and another led an extra horse out from the farm. Light glowed inside the barn there, and minutes later its roof was engulfed in flames.

"Looting and burning," said Gallorne. "Taking whatever they need along the way." Gallorne stood and the three of them returned to the troops waiting in the forest. "What bothers me most, though, is why they didn't leave the ladders and battering rams in Farrenhale," said Gallorne.

"The garrison in Kronivar has a wall around it," Gaern pointed out.

"True," said Gallorne, "but it's on the far edge of the city, and the walls are not as high as their ladders were long."

Gallorne gathered the troops from the forest and soon they were all back on the road, looking for a place to camp for the night. The passing of the Goblin army had left them anxious and full of dread.

"We must try to keep up with them for now," Gallorne told them, "They are sure to pillage Greensward and replenish their stores before making the final run for Kronivar. As they do, we may be able to cut through lower Veskwood and get to Kronivar before they do. Otherwise we will join the rear guard from Gundithe after the Goblins turn toward Kronivar."

"Surely the Goblins won't be able to take Kronivar," suggested one of the dwarves.

Gallorne nodded sadly. "Many said the same of the Wall and Gates at Farrenhale."

For the next two days, Gallorne's troops moved south, through the destruction and burnt fields in the Goblins' wake. Some villages and farms went untouched while others were left in ruin. Chicken coops and barns were burned to the ground and livestock stolen or slaughtered. Horses were not to be found on any of the ransacked farms. At last they found a wagon, hitched Silvernail's horse to it, and added a second horse given to them in one of the villages where they stayed overnight. Some villagers had seen the Goblins passing in the distance, and Gallorne learned of their progress. At a good pace, it seemed the dwarves might be able to catch up to the Goblins, pass them around the outskirts of Greensward, and reach Kronivar before them. Lexter was wearied by the relentless pace, meager rations, and the pall of dread he had endured the last few days, but he did all he could to help speed Gallorne's company along.

Now and then they stopped at farms or villages to find sustenance, and soon it was Lexter's turn to join the search. He and Gaern and two others disembarked and strode across the fields. As they neared the outbuildings of a farm, it became clear that the Goblins had already raided the place. They called out, but there was no answer. The destruction was less than usual, as though the Goblins had been in hurry. The chicken coop behind the barn was broken into and lay empty. The ground was full of hoofprints from the Goblins' horses. Lexter looked around in shock as he recognized the Thelreds' farm.

"Look… In here—" cried Gaern. Lexter followed them into the barn. There Arl Thelred and another dwarf lay twisted on the hay-strewn floor, slain by goblins. Pitchforks lay nearby and there were signs of a fight. After a brief search, the dwarves took a bag of feed for the horses and left. Lexter lingered a moment, pained by the sight of the dead farmer, and then joined the others in the dooryard.

The farmhouse had been broken into, and the dwarves went inside. Lexter had not been invited into the farmhouse when he had been there before and felt strange entering it now. The others stopped on the way in, and Lexter soon saw why. Mrs. Thelred lay slumped in a pool of blood on the floor where the Goblins had left her, next to the body of her daughter. The dwarves paused in solemn respect for the dead. In silence, they examined the kitchen. The hearth was dark and the room cold. Cabinet doors were left wide open, revealing the ransacked pantry. Flour was spilled and jam oozed from a broken jar on the floor. Curving shards of broken pottery littered the countertops. An apple with large, fearsome bites bitten out of it lay in a corner. The table had been set for dinner and scant remains of food dirtied the serving bowls, thrown aside after the Goblins had eaten. Tears filled Lexter's eyes as he looked upon the old woman who had been so kind to him.

Everyone stopped and listened when a faint cry came from the back rooms of the house. Lexter was nearest the hall and cautiously went down it. There, in one of the bedrooms, a bundle lay in a woven basket. Lexter moved closer and heard the sound again. "It's a baby," he said. "There's a baby in here!"

Either the Goblins had not known about the baby or they had not cared. Gently, Lexter lifted the baby from the basket and stared sadly at the infant. The baby made weak, whimpering cries and his eyes were dull. "He's cold," said Lexter, "he's been lying here in the cold."

"He doesn't have the strength to cry any more," said Gaern, watching the infant. "It may be too late. There isn't much we can do."

"We have to bring him with us," said Lexter, "We can leave him with someone in one of the villages." No one objected, so Lexter wrapped the baby in a blanket, and followed the others outside.

On their way back to the cart, Lexter thought what a strange sight he was; a Tolgarder dressed in Dwarven armor carrying a baby in his arms. The dwarves in the cart looked at Lexter as if to say it was useless to bring the dying baby with them. Lexter ignored them and pressed the baby to his chest, trying to keep it warm. The cart started with a jolt and soon the clip-clop of the horses' hooves was with them again.

Lexter looked down at the baby as they rode. In its small, round face he could just barely make out the faintest traces of the Thelred features. The baby was limp and had no struggle left in him. He looked up at Lexter with forlorn eyes as though he knew he was not to be long in the world. "How far to the next village?" Lexter asked Gallorne.

"Another half an hour, maybe" said Gallorne. "We'll find someone to care for the child."

Lexter tried to be patient as the day wore on, gray and dim. The cart seemed too slow, and he kept looking ahead for the next village or farm. The baby's condition did not improve, and Lexter cradled it and held it close. It no longer made any sound and its eyes were half-closed. A short time later it lay lifeless in Lexter's arms.

They stopped briefly to bury the baby. That night as they traveled Lexter was silent. He could not sleep and envied the slumbering dwarves around him in the cart. Lexter's mind was restless and too tired to concentrate on anything for long. He could still see the baby's round face and cold eyes, the Thelreds lying dead, and the massacre at Halloway. Everything numbed within him, and he drifted through the night, the wind chilling his skin his only comfort. The full moon cast a cold light on the landscape around them. It felt as though it were all already a distant memory. Lexter stared out at the dark fields passing by, at the road ahead and behind them, and the night sky lined with silvery clouds lit with moonglow. Nothing else would hold his mind for long.

Three days after the Goblin army had passed them, Gallorne and his troops reached Greensward in the evening. Even though he had spent most of the time riding in the wagon, Lexter was worn and tired and feared things would not go well. He leaned against the side of the wagon, his mind wandering, when Silvernail startled him with a yell. "Greensward ahead! Wake Gallorne! It looks bad..."

Lexter sat up and strained to see what lay ahead. From afar he saw fires burning and furls of smoke rising into the night sky. Livestock ran loose and he heard echoes of distant screaming in the town. In the center of it all, laboring in the cold moonlight, he recognized the dark shapes of the Goblin caravan moving down to where the North Road crossed the roads to the mountains and Kronivar.

"Silvernail!" Gallorne cried, "Head to the right, we'll drive around beyond the outskirts of town, over the fields, and onto the Kronivar road."

Immediately Silvernail pulled the reigns. The wagon veered to the right and jerked forward as he whipped the horses into a fast gallop. The dwarves at the back of the wagon almost fell out and hung on tight as they rode past the outlying farms of Greensward.

Lexter turned to watch Greensward. Most of the buildings huddled together near where the roads crossed, and Goblin horsemen were swarming through the streets. Some buildings blazed, and further out the huge wooden frame of an unfinished barn was burning and collapsing. Several horsemen rode around the edge of the city and caught sight of the dwarves.

"They've seen us!" Lexter yelled. "They're coming!"

With some difficulty in the tight quarters the dwarves and Lexter drew their swords and held them out the sides of the wagon on the ready. Silvernail urged his horses on to their fastest gallop, but the Goblin riders caught up with them. The goblins spread out around the wagon, two riding on either side, swords swinging. Their faces were fierce and dark against the pale silver clouds of the night sky. They were well-armored, long-armed and swift, and the din of metal was fast and sharp. One of the dwarves tumbled from the wagon and was lost. Another nicked the shank of one of the Goblins' horses, and its rider fell back out of reach. The dwarves held off the other goblins but their strength was waning, and the goblins were fresh and mean and expert with the sword. Lexter feared they were lost when a shrill whistle sounded and the Goblin riders pulled up and withdrew, heading back to the crossroads.

The dwarves were relieved but thought it strange. "Why have they turned back?" said Gallorne. "They would not let us go without good reason. Surely they do not want Kronivar warned of their coming?" Gallorne gazed intently behind them as the wagon rode westward. "Unless..." Gallorne turned and shouted to Silvernail. "Turn us around, and take us off the road!" Groans and angry objections rose from all the dwarves. "We must be sure of them before we go to Kronivar," Gallorne explained.

The wagon lurched around as Silvernail brought it off the road and to a stop. "They will not bother to come after us, if I am right," said Gallorne.

"And if you are wrong?" snapped one of the dwarves.

Gallorne ignored him. "Look, there, at the crossroads..." Far away the shapes of the Urumak could be seen in the failing light. The great caravan was massing at the crossroads, and those in the vanguard were turning, though it was difficult to see. Lexter strained his eyes and some of the figures appeared to be receding. "They're turning towards the mountains!" he cried.

"Ridiculous!" shouted one of the soldiers. "Gundithe is secure. Look!" High above the crossroads, tents lined the wide shelf rounding the front of the mountain and smoke rose from campfires all the way across the plateau. "The pass up to Gundithe is narrow and easily held and defended. Their numbers would scarce help them to take it."

"Unless there is some other devilry afoot," said Gallorne.

"Like that of Halloway? But there's no reaching the plateau unseen, only the road," said Gaern.

"No, not an ambush," said Gallorne, "Yet what exactly, I cannot say. They carry ladders and battering rams, which would serve them better at the Castle than at Kronivar. Still, a siege of the Castle would be difficult and the time is not right. No, it all bodes ill."

"Shall we wait, then, and see if the plateau is taken?" asked Silvernail.

"They would not attempt it unless they had some hidden advantage; that much is certain," said Gallorne, "Take Feren with you, and make haste for Kronivar. We will remain here. Go now, and Godspeed!"

The horses were unharnessed, and soon Silvernail and Feren were riding away in a swift gallop. Lexter, Gallorne, and the rest watched them go and moved to set camp in the edge of the woods where they might watch the plateau unseen.

"I don't understand,' said Lexter, "If they're planning to lay siege to the Castle, why now? It's almost winter!"

"If they succeed in capturing it, we'll have no chance of getting it back before winter starts," Gallorne said, "But that's only if they capture it quickly, and the Castle's too well-defended for that. Even with what they have."

"Unless something strange is going on there as well," said Lexter.

"Yes," said Gallorne, "that's what I'm afraid of."

Chapter 39.
Hearts Laid Bare

King Jordgen sat next to Wendolin's sickbed in the narrow, high-ceilinged upstairs room set aside for Wendolin's recovery. Late morning light angled down into the room, slow dust motes glowing in its soft beam. Jordgen sat listening as Wendolin told of the journey from Teska, the Goblins, and the attack on Halloway. The King saw the toll it had taken on the old wizard, amazed at how gaunt and frail he looked. Yet even more disturbing was the news he brought.

"But can the word of a thief be trusted?" asked Jordgen.

"He had no reason to lie about it. His descriptions were vivid, and held together when I cross-questioned him," said Wendolin. "It was only later, in the mountains, when I was going over what he had said, that it occurred to me that Lexter's description of Greywood could very well fit Zhindarren; his looks, as well as his manner and way of speaking. I assumed Zhindarren would be accompanying Maëlveronde, and apparently Greywood has been in Itharia for some time. But Maëlveronde's plans reach over many years, so it is indeed possible."

"And Greywood, this Zhindarren, he is here now, with Aranstone?" said Jordgen.

"He is lying low, I think, keeping his powers hidden and identity secret. I doubt even Aranstone knows."

"All the better to cloud Aranstone's mind," said Jordgen. "So the siege, then, may be part of some larger plan of Maëlveronde's." Jordgen let rumble a dread-laden sigh. "Eloswai!" he grunted with contempt. He looked fondly to Wendolin. "On you rest our hopes of staving them off, Master Wendolin. How it pains me to see you like this, old friend."

"I will recover in time." Wendolin sighed. "But too slowly, I'm afraid."

Jordgen nodded. "We may have less time than I supposed," said Jordgen. "With the troops brought in from the valley, our stores will not last as long. Even with strict rationing, Varlen says we cannot hold out much longer than a week. Confound that Aranstone, the traitor!" Jordgen growled. "Twice have I refused him parley. I know well what he is after, and he will not get it. And now we see what is behind his treachery."

"He should be told about Zhindarren," said Wendolin, "Arrange a parley with him alone, and things may be different. When he understands the situation, he may relent. It may even be that the siege was not his own idea."

Jordgen sat considering what Wendolin said. "Perhaps," he said, "but we will parley only on my terms and after he asks again. There'll be no sign of giving in on our part." Jordgen's expression lightened. "And they will ask again. There is little else they can do. The troops remain deadlocked, and the west wing is secure. With you here, I am certain we will regain the upper hand. How glad I was to hear you had come."

"I am an old man and not as hale as I was in the days when your father was King," said Wendolin, touched by the concern in Jordgen's eyes. "Nor do I think I shall need more than a week to recover. Yet much may happen by then."

"Good," said Jordgen, getting up from the chair. "Perhaps it will even be less than a week. We shall hold steadfast until then. Rest now, old friend." Having found the reassurance he needed regarding the wizard's condition, Jordgen wished Wendolin well and departed.

When Iaven saw the guard posted outside Wendolin's door, he knew King Jordgen was visiting and kept his distance. He knew he ought to beg the King's pardon for having failed his quest, but continued to put off doing so, fearing the King's wrath. Wendolin had assured him he would not be punished, but he still did not relish the thought of appearing before the King. Zammond told him he had nothing to worry about, as long as the separatists held the east wing where the dungeons were.

Iaven came back later and, seeing the guard was gone, went in to see Wendolin. At first he was surprised Wendolin was laid up again so soon, but now in the morning light he saw the strain in the old wizard's face. Iaven realized Wendolin had undertaken the journey through the mountains without being fully recovered and it had cost him greatly. Wendolin smiled at Iaven and motioned for him to come and sit down.

"So are they keeping the four of you busy downstairs?" asked Wendolin.

"Busy enough," said Iaven, "There's the dividing and doling out of the rations from the stores, the readying of lodgings for the soldiers in various halls, shifts of guard duty at all the doors, which Zammond and I are supposed to join tonight... And all on very little rest after yesterday's hike and climb."

"Well, that should keep you from being idle," said Wendolin, "I would rather be up and about, too, but recovery is work enough for me now. I may have to face Zhindarren soon."

"Zhindarren?" said Iaven, "He's here?"

"Do you remember when I said there was something strange in what Lexter said? It was his description of Greywood. I am quite certain now that Greywood is Zhindarren. He is here with Aranstone. And he is sure to be in league with Maëlveronde."

"Will you be ready to deal with him?" Iaven's worry bled through his words.

"I do not know," said Wendolin, "Zhindarren is much younger than me, but his skill is great, from what little I know of him. Fortunately, he does not know I am here, and some advantage may be gained from that. But first we must weather this siege and break it. The Castle troops outnumber those of Aranstone, and they know it. And as long as they keep us shut inside, they can use our numbers against us."

"As I understand it, Prince Varlen has plans to break through their defenses and retake the messaging tower, in the next day or two," said Iaven. He rose from the chair. "And I should be getting back. I just wanted to see how you were doing. The others were wondering, too." Iaven paused, turning back. "We were also curious what the King might have said about our return, if anything."

"So that is the reason for your visit! He did not say much about it, and he has many other concerns at the moment. I know he was bitterly disappointed, and rightfully so. Others in his household seem to be of a like mind. But King Jordgen is wise and just, and slow to anger if not swift to forgive. Apparently Yolias sent a report from Teska, and had kind things to say about you and your friends, including that there was hope of recovering the swords. Our arrival put an end to those hopes only yesterday, and at a time when the swords are sorely needed."

"And Rhiane?" Iaven asked, "He didn't say anything about her or what she thought, did he?"

"No," said Wendolin, "you will have to find that out for yourself. And now you must return to your duties and I must rest, though I would rather it were the other way around. For work is as good a balm as any for the troubled mind, while too much inactivity can leave it even more restless."

Iaven left Wendolin and returned to the halls below where furniture was being moved and lodgings arranged for soldiers brought in from the valley. He had been at work all night and had come to know his way around the Castle's west wing. Iaven hurried down the hall to get back to preparing beds for some of the wounded. Soldiers who fought or stood guard during the night before were being sent to rest while others took their place. Iaven had been kept so busy with various tasks that he now looked forward to his evening guard duty with Zammond.

The siege continued into the long, gray, wintry afternoon and activity in the Castle finally settled into a routine. Only a day had passed since the siege had begun, yet it seemed more like a week. By late afternoon Iaven was exhausted, and as his chores slowed his tired mind kept returning to Rhiane and what he would say to her. In the end he decided he would be brief and not try to make excuses or exonerate himself. Thoughts of the siege and the war made his own troubles seem small and trivial, and he would not give them mind. He could not change how Rhiane felt; nor the King, for that matter. He had won their trust by bringing them the sword and gem, and then lost it along with everything else. He had raised their hopes and dashed them. That his hopes regarding Rhiane should now be dashed seemed only fair. He had put off seeing Rhiane all day, as he had the King; but better to see her and be done with it, he thought. Still, he found himself avoiding the places he thought she might be.

As dusk fell, gloom seeped into the corners of rooms and candles were lit. Many had grown low from burning all of the night before, and had to be replaced. Iaven dug out the stumps of wax and clumps that had dripped down candlesticks and put them all in a wooden bucket, to be melted down and reused in the molds. Counting, he found a dozen new ones were needed, and left for the workroom where candles and soap were made.

The workroom was long and narrow and smelt of tallow and wax. Candle molds lined the side wall, and bundles of wicks lay on a table nearby. Pairs of newly-molded candles hung by their uncut wicks on rows of wooden pegs. A single window on the far wall revealed the graying sky, bathing the room in a fading paleness that chilled Iaven's spirits.

Iaven set down the bucket of wax stumps. He stood in front of the wall where the new candles hung, counting out what he needed. Reaching for them, he was startled by a soft voice behind him.

"Take the beeswax ones, they burn brighter than tallow," said Rhiane.

Iaven turned to Rhiane, nervously alert in her sudden presence. Dim, dusky light from the window fell upon her and she carried a single lit candle as well. The candle's glow warmed the side of her face and her eyes were dark and deep, a tiny point of flame reflected in each. Soft flickering highlights glimmered on the tresses of her dark hair. She watched him intently, her expression difficult to fathom. Iaven had long considered what he would say, but none of it felt right. He froze now as she stood before him, expecting the worst.

"Iaven," she said, "I've been meaning to talk to you."

Iaven's eyes met hers. "I'm sure you've heard by now that we didn't get the sword or gem back," said Iaven. "And how we lost everything. I've failed you. I should have let someone else go after Orven. I did all I could."

Rhiane nodded. "I know you did. Yolias spoke well of you when he wrote us from Teska. And you did beat Orven to the gem, after all."

"Well, yes, but he took it away from me just as he did in Kronivar," said Iaven.

"So you got to both of them before he did," Rhiane pointed out. "Do you realize that? Out of the five gems, you got to four of them before Orven did."

Iaven paused. "I suppose that's true." He had never thought of it that way. "But he did take two of them away from me."

"Would you have done the same to him, if he had got there first?" Rhiane asked.

"No," said Iaven, stopping to wonder why this might be so.

"And why not?" Rhiane asked, her eyebrows raised slightly.

"Well," said Iaven, thinking it over, "It wouldn't be fair. It wouldn't be right, if he was the one who got there first."

"And so you would be more concerned about that than with getting the gems for yourself?" She seemed to be goading him now.

Iaven felt a bit upset and wondered what she was getting at. He didn't like where her questions were leading and feared she would not like his answers. "I suppose I wouldn't... I know they were important, but... it wouldn't be right to steal them from him, even if I was going to make better use of them." Iaven was more confident now. If all Rhiane cared about was the gems, then maybe he had been wrong about her. "So, no; I wouldn't. It wouldn't be fair."

"Of course not," Rhiane smiled. Much to Iaven's surprise, she leaned forward and gave him a quick little kiss. "And that's why I love you, Iaven. You want to do what's fair and good. And you're kind-hearted. Yolias even told us how you went out of your way to look for Orven in the tombs, even though it was dangerous."

"Well," Iaven was stunned by the praise from Yolias and especially the kiss, "I guess I was worried about Orven... I mean, he is my brother after all. We've always fought, but... you know, brothers do that. Especially twins. And I am still mad at him... —Did you say you loved me?"

Rhiane laughed and set her candle on the table. "I did. Oh, I thought about it for quite awhile. Ever since that night on the plateau. And later, when you left the Castle, I missed you. I had plenty of time to ask myself why." She hugged Iaven. "Well now I know." She smiled and looked into his eyes. "True, when we heard from Yolias I was saddened by what happened, and I knew you must have felt badly about it."

"I have been meaning to see King Jordgen about it," said Iaven.

Rhiane smiled slyly. "It's a good thing you weren't here when the news came," she said, "He's gotten a little better about it since then. Let me talk to him some more first, and then we'll both go to him together."

"All right," said Iaven reluctantly. His eyes met Rhiane's again. "I'm just glad you're not upset with me. I really didn't know what you would think..."

"Did you suppose it would change the way I felt about you? If anything, Yolias convinced me that I was right about you. He seems to like you, too."

"Now if only the King did," said Iaven.

"Well, I'll see what I can do." Rhiane let go of Iaven's shoulders and her hands slid down to hold Iaven's. "Of course, it would have been much easier if you had both swords and all the gems," she teased. "And the siege only makes matters worse. Which reminds me, we should be getting back to our duties." She let go of Iaven's hands and picked up her candle. "I'm glad you're here, Iaven. We'll have more time alone after all this is over. And don't forget you promised to show me around the Foothills."

"I will," Iaven said as he watched Rhiane leaving. Knowing she really did care about him, he suddenly felt relieved and buoyant of spirit despite thoughts of the siege and worries that threatened to weigh him down.

Long hours of night passed, and Iaven and Zammond's guard duty was tense but uneventful. Both Aranstone's men and those of the King were deadlocked at all the doors around the west wing, and none came or went by them. The following day the sky remained overcast and the siege continued. Already some cast a nervous eye on cistern and larder. Water was conserved, and rations carefully measured and distributed. Belts were tightened. Prince Varlen's attempt to retake the messaging tower failed when Aranstone added more men to the guard there. And Aranstone's assault on the storerooms was likewise repelled by the King's men. Wounded returned from both sides until the fighting died down again.

The overcast day dragged on and passed with agonizingly slowness into night just as sleep only gradually overtakes a restless and troubled mind. At last evening fell upon Castle Frosthelm and a light snow blew in the air. Zhindarren stood at the parapet atop the wall around the outer ward, near the central gatehouse, enjoying the cold wind and black sky. He looked to the west. The dark mountains filled his view, rising up to blot out the stars. Faint detail could be seen on their slopes in the light of the waning moon. Zhindarren lowered his gaze to the Mountain Road, where a solitary figure approached the Castle. As it crossed the Castle plateau, Zhindarren wondered if this was the news he had been anticipating. The soldier made his way up the Castle terraces and came toward the central gate. Zhindarren watched him awhile and then turned from the parapet, rounded the gatehouse, and hurried down the stairs. At the bottom he was greeted by the guards posted there.

"Master Greywood," said one, "a messenger from Gundithe has arrived."

"Let him in," said Greywood.

The bolt was drawn back and the gate opened. The young dwarf, still in awe of the Castle, which he had never seen before, was out of breath from his hike and surprised to see Greywood. He nodded respectfully. "Bole Tarshin, under Captain Erdrock's command," he introduced himself, "I have a message for General Aranstone."

"Come in, Bole" said Greywood, "Follow me." Greywood led Bole out of the cold and into one of the small buildings in the outer ward. The place had been used as quarters for stable hands and was sparsely furnished. A bright fire in a small hearth warmed the room. "Sit down, you have traveled far," Greywood invited him. When he was sure they were alone he turned again to the young dwarf. "Now, what tidings do you bring?"

Bole looked up from where he sat, unsure of himself. "Captain Erdrock said I should tell General Aranstone directly—"

"That is quite alright," said Greywood, "At the moment, General Aranstone is an honored guest in the King's chambers. But if it is important, I could take the news in to him there.'

"Well," Bole began hesitantly, "All right. Soon after you left, we had word of defeat in Farrenhale and Teska. Captain Erdrock expected you would hear of it from the King and be sent right back. Then, two nights ago, from the plateau, we saw the Goblin army advancing down the North Road. As soon Captain Erdrock saw them, he sent me into the mountains. He hoped I would find you on your way back." Bole looked troubled that things had not turned out as expected.

"Yes, we have heard of what happened at Farrenhale," Greywood assured him, "and we have been waylaid here awhile. But the Castle troops will be joining us as we return. I will give General Aranstone your message, and we will surely depart as soon as possible. Rest a moment now and have a bit of supper, and then you must hurry back to Gundithe, to let them know we are coming."

Bole listened eagerly to Greywood, disappointed to have to hurry back, but finding comfort in Greywood's words and tone all the same.

"And not a word to anyone else here," said Greywood. "General Aranstone should be the first to know, and we wouldn't want to cause a panic."

"No, of course not," Bole agreed.

Greywood saw to it that Bole had a filling though hasty meal, and then took him back to the gate to send him off. "Now hurry back!" Greywood told Bole outside the gate, "Tell Erdrock we are coming, have them wait for us in Greensward. The Goblins may reach Kronivar by the time we catch up with them, but we will have twice the rear guard to attack with than we would have had otherwise. Go!"

Bole nodded and without another word was off across the Castle plateau. Several minutes later he merged into the moonlit darkness of the Mountain Road. Zhindarren stood watching him go, sad to have to send so young a fellow into the hands of the oncoming Goblins.

Night settled around the Castle, deep and dark. A cold, heavy dampness gave the wind its teeth. Aranstone made the evening rounds, inspecting the guard with a word of discipline or encouragement where needed. No activity was reported at any of the doors, nor any new development or weakness on the part of the King's troops that they might exploit. Instead of being pleased that the siege had stabilized, Aranstone was concerned that he had made no progress towards the forging of a treaty. The longer they waited the less likely it seemed.

Aranstone walked along the walls and came to the inner ward, greeted his men, and entered the Castle there. He passed through the vestibule of the Great Hall and came to the west staircase. He climbed the stairs, listening to the voices of Orven's party on the landing above, where the soothing glow of torchlight shuddered on the walls and ceiling. As he approached, they noticed him coming and fell silent. Orven and Rafnel, who were standing guard at the door, straightened up and their pallid torchlit faces strained to look alert. Max and Haidren sat back on a pile of straw near the thick stone balustrades, and Aaron sat contemplatively with his back to the wall, his arms resting on his bent knees. Orven and his friends looked nervously at Aranstone as though he had come to reprimand them.

"Good evening," Aranstone greeted them. "All has been quiet here?"

"It has," Orven replied, "They've kept the door barred against us, but they're still there, all the same." Orven felt it was the Captain's job to assess the situation and report, even though there was almost nothing to say.

Aranstone nodded. "A long dull day for us all, but a restful one."

"Quite dull," Rafnel replied. "But Strable, Roy, and Ripley are due to relieve us soon." His eyes darted to Max and Haidren who would stand guard at the door next. "*Some* of us, anyway," he smiled.

"How goes the siege?" asked Aaron from along the wall. All eyes turned to him as he spoke, and then to Aranstone for his reply.

"Much as yesterday," said Aranstone, "Nothing lost, nothing gained. Hopefully we will not keep you idle too much longer. We shall see what the morrow brings. Stay vigilant for now." Aranstone's gaze looked hard and serious in the torchlight, but his words were calm and kind. He surveyed them a moment longer and turned to depart. "Good night, then, and keep alert! Remember, your post is envied by many who must spend the night outdoors."

The dwarves and Rafnel all bid Aranstone good night and listened as his steps receded down the stairs until he was gone. Gradually their conversation picked up again.

"It's true, you know, what he says," said Rafnel, "Imagine if we had to stand guard on the wall, or by the doors out in the cold, huddled around a little fire."

"Aranstone must like us," said Aaron.

"Oh, it wasn't him," Rafnel said, "Greywood got it for us. '*Nice and quiet, away from everyone else*', he said. A strategic position that a small group can hold. Dull, certainly, but at least it's out of the wind, if not the cold."

"And away from the action, too," Orven added, unconsciously fingering the metal of Gorflange's hilt.

After speaking with Orven's party, Aranstone went downstairs to check on the men stationed on the ground floor. From there he passed through the darkened Throne Room, on his way to the east wing for the night. He had intended to simply walk across to the lit doorway on the far side, but the Throne Room's vast, dark emptiness slowed his steps, its immense stillness and cavernlike silence drawing him into a thoughtful state. Bluish-white light of the moon, now three days past full, frosted the parquet wood floor on the northern end of the room where diamond-paned windows overlooked the valley. Aranstone walked over to them, glancing about the room. At the center of the back wall between the rows of arched windows stood a dais with a single throne, its gilt gold arms, carved dragons, and tall, elegant back awash in the cold moonlight. The throne seemed ancient and vacant, as though its King had died in ages past and had long been forgotten. Somehow the sight of it made Aranstone uneasy.

Aranstone stood at the windows, his breath fogging the glass only inches away, and looked down into the valley. The mountains' folds grew darker farther down where the moonlight was occluded, merging into a sea of blackness. Somewhere down there, four of his guards kept watch on the Castle windows above, making sure no one was lowered into the valley. Twice they had fired arrows at dwarves who were quickly drawn back up again. He knew his men dreaded guard duty in the valley more than any of the other posts, and had Greywood set up a rotation so no one would have to do it more than what was fair. Aranstone preferred action or negotiation to waiting, and found the siege as draining as anyone else. He contemplated other courses of action, his mind roaming in the quiet, sifting the possibilities. They could not negotiate so long as Jordgen refused him an audience. Absently he looked across the Throne Room; the dark tapestries lining the walls in shadow, the throne, and the huge banner with Frosthelm insignia, the white dragon on a field of purple. His gaze fell on the empty throne again, and he wondered if the siege had gone too far, if they had been too zealous and overplayed their hand.

Aranstone turned back and looked out the window, towards the men he could not see below. He thought of the nighttime guard duties he had stood as a young man, envying the indoor positions of his captain and others of superior office. He imagined what it would be like on guard duty again, cold and bored in the dark, but able to sleep soundly when the time came. Lately his nights were full of decisions and pacing, second-guessing and contemplation, and at best he slept briefly and fitfully until new problems required his consideration. Such was the command he had longed for in his youth.

A door creaked open. Aranstone recognized Greywood's silhouette in the lighted doorway. Greywood closed the door behind him and came across the dark plain of parquet tile flooring, his steps echoing across the room.

"I see we are both in need of quiet," Greywood spoke when he was only a few paces away.

"Yes." Aranstone turned his attention to the valley again.

Greywood joined him there in the silence. Together they stood at the arched windows, their features rimmed in the blue silver of the moon, looking out into the dark valleys.

"Many years ago, the Goblins fought the Dwarves, but they could not take Castle Frosthelm," said Greywood, "How they longed to see this view."

Aranstone's features hardened slightly as he glanced at Greywood. "We did not come here for the view, nor to take the Castle," said Aranstone. He gazed into the valley. "Nor is the siege going as I had hoped. I intend to ask for parley again tomorrow."

"So soon?" Greywood barely restrained a chiding tone. "The King refused you the night the siege began, and again the morning following, and already you think of asking a third time!" Greywood bristled. He walked away from the windows and then turned to Aranstone. "We did not come here as beggars! We came for a show of strength, and this is a sign of weakness. They should be asking us for terms."

"Their position is stronger than you expected," said Aranstone. "They will not ask."

"Fight them then. They will weaken. Khale and Pyrwoed say that with the west wing storerooms they may hold out longer than we had planned. We must act before the Gundithe troops are recalled to Kronivar. Once we succeed and send word to Orming, our support in Kronivar will grow, when it is realized what we have achieved."

Aranstone considered what Greywood said in thoughtful silence. Greywood continued, "When Abern and Sherleaf join Orming, Kronivar will be ours, and the people will hail your return. Perhaps they will even call to make you a king."

"A king?" said Aranstone, "I would have Kronivar be its own master and a land unto itself, but I do not seek kingship of it."

"But who better for the throne? ...Orming? No; nor any of the other counts..." Greywood indicated the empty throne, inviting Aranstone into it. "Come now, sit down here, and see how it suits you."

Aranstone remained impassive. "No. I will not sit in it. I did not come here to usurp the throne," he said, anger creeping into his tone.

Greywood stared at Aranstone and his eyes gleamed in the darkness. "As you wish," he relented. He stepped forward into the moonlight. "But the men grow restless with this stalemate. They are willing to fight and look to you to lead them."

Aranstone met Greywood's gaze unwaveringly. "There has been more bloodshed than I bargained for. We will wait. In two days' time, I will ask a third and final time for parley. If they refuse, I will consider what you say. But for now, we will wait." And after one last look at Greywood he turned and strode across the empty throne room and out into the torchlit hallway of the east wing.

Zhindarren watched Aranstone leave. *Only two days*, he thought, *hopefully that will be enough time.*

In another part of the Castle, Iaven and Rhiane climbed a winding tower staircase, on their way to King Jordgen's study. It was the King's favorite room in the west wing and, since the siege began, the place where he held all his audiences and meetings. Iaven remembered it as the room where they had put the blue gem into Halix and determined the location of the remaining lost gem. He had been nervous during his first audience with the King and was even more anxious now.

"We don't have to see him tonight," Rhiane reminded Iaven.

"I should have gone to him when we first arrived here," said Iaven, "I've waited too long as it is, and he may even think worse of me because of it."

"Well at least let me find out what mood he's in first," said Rhiane. "He was supposed to meet again tonight with Varlen, Clovenstone, and my father. If there's bad news at the meeting I think we should wait until tomorrow, if not later."

"If you say so." But Iaven had resolved to see the King that night even if Rhiane wasn't with him, so much did he want to put an end to his waiting. While working during the siege he had decided to join the King's troops and go where they sent him, continuing his service to the King for as long as he was needed.

As they rounded the top of the stairway and walked down the hall, Iaven grew tense. Soon they came to the vaulted passageway leading to the King's study and saw the carved wooden door at the end of it was closed.

"They're in there," said Rhiane. "We'll have to wait. If you still want to."

"I do," said Iaven, and so they sat down in the hall on a wooden bench facing the passageway. As they waited, Iaven looked around. He had seen very little of the floor they were on, for it was the one on which the royal family and all those of Frosthelm descent lived, as well as the Castle Steward's family. After all the hurry and bustle of the Castle's lower levels, the quiet made him uneasy. The waiting seemed interminable. He let his eyes wander, but they always returned to the carved wooden door at the end of the passageway.

At last the door opened. Prince Varlen emerged, followed by Arlen Frosthelm and Erland Clovenstone. Rhiane got up and talked to her father, who stopped as the others passed by. He listened to her, glancing once over to Iaven. Iaven could not read his expression and wondered if he was doing the right thing, and then quickly assured himself that he was.

Rhiane came back as Arlen left down the hall. "Neither bad news nor good news," she said, "They discussed moving some of the stores upstairs. And there may be longer hours and smaller rations, as might be expected." She looked at

Iaven intently. "So it may not be the best time, but it probably won't be any better later."

"We might as well," said Iaven, starting down the short passageway.

Rhiane got ahead of him and motioned for him to stay a pace or two behind her. She walked down the hall and peeked into the study. "Uncle Jordgen?" she inquired sweetly and carefully.

"Allelia. Come in." Iaven heard the King answer in a tired and reassuring tone. The room was aglow in the soft light of a candelabra, and Iaven heard the low crackle of a fire dying in the hearth. He felt his heart beating and worried that his voice would leave him when he tried to speak, so he cleared his throat and took a deep breath.

"Uncle Jordgen, Iaven wanted to talk to you." Rhiane turned as Iaven stepped into the room without waiting for Rhiane's signal. As King Jordgen's gaze fell upon Iaven his features seemed to harden. Iaven could almost feel his restrained disappointment.

"I— Your Majesty…" Iaven bowed, ashamed to have forgotten his manners for even a moment. "I come to ask your pardon for losing the sword, and to offer my service, whatever is needed of me, for as long as you may need it." No sooner had he said this than he realized how inadequate it sounded. Certainly the King would not want his service after he had lost the sword. Everyone in the Castle was working hard during the siege, and here he was wasting time making pledges, promising to do what was already his duty.

King Jordgen sat in his armchair, his face stern, a regal and inscrutable air about him. "And the gem," he said after a moment, "You lost the blue gem as well as the sword."

Iaven could not bear the King's gaze any longer and wanted to look away. He took a moment to steady his nerves. "They were both my responsibility, yes. I have no excuses. And I know we could have found the last gem sooner if we hadn't stopped at the tombs—"

"They did reach the gem before—" Rhiane tried to interrupt.

"—but I had to see if Orven was in danger," said Iaven, "I couldn't just leave him there if he was." He was silent a moment. "I suppose I would do it again, if I had to."

The King listened to Iaven and nodded slightly, as though in agreement with Iaven's answer.

"Please, Uncle Jordgen," Rhiane pleaded, moving a step nearer, "Yolias said Iaven tried—"

"Yes, I know," said the King, his tone more kind toward his great-niece. He looked at Iaven a moment. "I had hoped we would have both swords, and all of the lost gems. We gambled what we had and lost. The swords were dearly needed, and there was little else we could do." He stopped and waited to see if Iaven would reply. Iaven looked up and met the King's gaze, but kept silent. This seemed to please the King. "Yet Yolias did commend you in what he wrote," the King continued, "He even said you were learning the sword, and doing well." King Jordgen spoke as though the compliment had taken some effort. "And you can be sure we will make good use of you here during the siege."

"I'll do whatever's needed, even fight on the front lines, if I have to," Iaven promised.

"He's been working ever since they brought Wendolin here," Rhiane added, hoping Wendolin's arrival would be another point in Iaven's favor. Iaven realized what Rhiane was doing and his heart leapt to see how she strove to reconcile him with the King. With her help, perhaps in time he could even begin to regain the King's favor.

"Since Wendolin brought *them* here," the King corrected her. He eased back in his chair a bit and his manner softened a little. "How good it is to see Wendolin after so long, and at such a time as we need him. I have little hope that he will recover in time to aid us, but we shall see." The King turned to Iaven again. "Wendolin, too, has spoken well of you. Let us hope his words prove true as these next few weeks test your mettle and show us what you are made of."

"Thank you, sire," Iaven managed in a humble voice. He felt the King had accepted his pledge and was eager now for Rhiane to let the audience end so he could return downstairs.

"I met many dwarves in Kronivar, but never one like Iaven," said Rhiane.

King Jordgen noted the way Rhiane's eyes sparkled and the little smile that flashed as she glanced at Iaven. A look of concern overtook his face and his expression hardened again as he regarded Rhiane and Iaven. Granting Iaven pardon was one thing, but this was quite another.

"And likewise, he has never met anyone like you," King Jordgen added brusquely. "I hope he understands what befits someone of your station."

"Uncle Jordgen—" Rhiane's voice was pained as she suddenly understood what King Jordgen meant.

"He was given a chance," said the King. "And we shall not punish him for failing. I'm sure he understands the situation." He flashed a gaze of cold scrutiny at Iaven.

The King's words struck Iaven like an iron rod. All he had feared before talking to Rhiane returned. He had expected such an outcome, though he had thought it would be Rhiane who would reject him. It had happened so suddenly that he could not think of anything to say in his defense, but he met the King's gaze without averting his eyes.

Rhiane took a step forward. "Tomald was not of one of the Old Families when Oell—"

King Jordgen raised his hand to quell Rhiane's pleas. "Allelia, please, you know well enough those were different circumstances."

"But father said—"

"Enough!" the King said sharply. "It is out of the question. Do not argue with me any further!" He rose from his chair and strode across to the windows to indicate the audience was over. Rhiane's shoulders dropped in disappointment and frustration as she bit back a reply. King Jordgen turned toward them again. "You have not changed, Allelia, and your time away has only made you more headstrong."

The King's words were interrupted by shouts from outside, down in the valley behind the Castle. King Jordgen went over to the glass doors, opened them, and stepped out onto the balcony. The candles in the room flickered as a gust of cold air blew indoors. Rhiane and Iaven followed King Jordgen to the balcony.

Another shout arose, along with the clink of metal and sounds of a scuffle. From the balcony, even with the moonlight, it was difficult to make out the shapes moving in the dark far below them. "Goblins!" one of Aranstone's men cried.

"Goblins?" said the King, "From where have they come?" As they watched, more dark shapes came around from the west and Aranstone's men were outnumbered. Swords clashed, shouts echoed, and soon all was silent again. Suddenly a black arrow flew up and hit the wall near the balcony. Iaven, Rhiane, and the King went back inside and locked the glass doors.

No sooner had they reentered than a loud knock sounded and a messenger burst inside, out of breath. He bowed low to the King. "Your Majesty, Goblins are marching on the Castle plateau."

King Jordgen strode across the room and Iaven and Rhiane hurried behind him. The messenger stood aside deferentially as they passed. King Jordgen went down the hall and through the Castle, into a room overlooking the inner and outer wards. Erland Clovenstone stood there at an open window. He had put out the candles and was watching the wards below. "I had the guard doubled at all the doors as soon as I heard," he told the King solemnly. "Aranstone won't be able to hold the outer ward."

Iaven and Rhiane joined the King at the window. Even from their high vantage point Iaven could hear the stomp of hundreds of marching boots and the shouts of Aranstone's men. Several stories below, the walls of the inner and outer wards were bustling with activity. Beyond the outer wall, the Castle Plateau was darkening as hordes of black shapes poured onto it from the Mountain Road. A sea of torches bobbed and flickered as the massive crowd advanced, the pungent smell of their smoke rising on the wind. Standards flapped in the moonlight bearing the Goblin insignia of a black raven with its wings upraised on a field of red. Farther down the road were more war-wagons, and further still the huge striding shapes of the Urumak moving in single file amidst the infantry, a good distance between each one.

Guards running along the wall called out the alarm and others from the east wing came to join them. The Goblin army spread across and up the terraces of the Castle plateau. While the assembly was still marching in, ladders were raised to the walls and battering rams were hung from rows of frames and positioned at the gates. The Goblins were clearly aware that the wall had insufficient men to defend it and they moved fast, confident in their attack. Arrows hissed through the air. Aranstone's men managed to force Goblins off the wall and several ladders were thrown to the ground, but for every one that fell another two or three went up unchallenged. Soon the Goblins overcame the outer wall and forced open the center gates. As Goblins poured into the outer ward, shouts went out that Aranstone was recalling everyone to the east wing, which they would try to hold. Some were slain as they fled. Swords crossed, clashing and clanging. Soldiers dropped the portcullis of the inner ward. Doors slammed. With help from the east wing, Aranstone's men held the inner ward. Black arrows bit into wood and nicked stone. Those who were too late fell outside the threshold. Some groups banded together and fought their way to the east wing where they were taken inside. Arrows flew at the Goblins from the upper stories of the Castle. Gangs of Aranstone's men resisted the Goblins in the outer ward, but they were outnumbered and losing ground.

While goblins flowed into the outer ward of the Castle, the remainder of the army marched onto the plateau. Six great, shaggy Urumak came along the turns of the road and onto the broad terraces. Wide berths were made for them as they arrived. Maëlveronde rode at the back of the throng, watching the procession from his war-tower atop an Urumak, pleased with the Goblins' progress. The outer wall was already overrun, and under General Burzok's command morale was high even after the last few days' grueling trek through the mountains.

As he rode, Maëlveronde looked out his window at Castle Frosthelm. He felt a certain thrill at the sight of the great stone edifice, its walls and towers rising into the night sky, washed in silver-gray moonlight and full of lighted windows and activity. It had been some time since he had last been to the Castle and he was greatly anticipating his return. Somewhere in the east wing, Zhindarren awaited him and would have everything ready. And if Zhindarren was right, all of Aorinthel's gemstones were there now, all but his own— he looked at the red gem on his ring, its large, dark, ruby facets sparkling dully in the dim light. For the first time in many years he found it difficult to remain patient.

High up in the Castle Steward's rooms, Iaven, Rhiane, Erland Clovenstone, and King Jordgen watched in rapt horror and dread as Goblins filled the outer ward. Iaven roiled with feelings of anger, frustration, and fear, wondering what they would do, and what could be done.

"From the look of it, they mean to rest after taking the outer ward, and weaken us with a few more days of siege," said Clovenstone. He sadly eyed the Dwarves' supply wagons down in the outer ward, now in Goblin hands. "And they can afford to, if they left Gundithe secured."

"They must have gone through Greensward at least two days ago," said King Jordgen, "Forces from Kronivar will certainly be on their way. But even if they're able to retake the plateau, by the time they get here they will find the walls held against them."

Clovenstone nodded. "The Goblins cannot afford too long a siege. And if Wendolin is right, they may know we have already spent several days under siege. They may be counting on it."

"Aranstone is sure to agree to our terms," said the King. "If he and any of his men remain. And he must be told about Zhindarren." King Jordgen moved away from the window and the others followed. He spoke to Clovenstone as they left. "Keep the guard doubled, and post more archers at the windows. We may need to move more of the stores as well."

"Yes, sire. Consider it done." Clovenstone closed the door and went the other way down the hall. Iaven and Rhiane followed the King toward the tower stairs.

"Tell your father I want to see him early tomorrow morning," the King said to Rhiane, "Once we have the east wing back we will have to rework our plans. I'll be with Varlen this evening."

"I'll let him know, sire," Rhiane nodded and hurried down the stairs.

When Rhiane was gone, Jordgen turned to Iaven as they parted at the stairs. "So you'll 'fight on the front lines', will you? Well, Iaven, it seems you'll soon have a chance to do just that."

Chapter 40.
An Uphill Battle

Lexter marched up the winding road, surrounded by the regular tromp of boots. Now that they were finally making their way up to the Gundithe Plateau, the thrill of fear shook him. He fought to control it and forge it into a desire to fight. Lexter exchanged a quick glance with Gaern, marching nearby, and felt encouraged.

Word of the Goblins had reached Kronivar, and troops were sent to Greensward the day after Gundithe had been taken. The Kronivar troops had arrived in the evening, setting camp on the edge of town, their spirits sobered by the fallen, blackened timbers and scattered remains of the looting. To keep the balance of power in Kronivar, companies came from each of the five Counts, all under the command of General Doalm Thundrum who led troops from the Royal Garrison as well. The General's camp was encircled by the five camps of the Counts' companies, each with their Colonels who conferred with and answered to General Thundrum. Captain Gallorne and his men received supplies and a campsite between the Sherleaf and Mothmoon camps, and Gallorne was to answer directly to Thundrum.

As part of a large force, Lexter felt more secure. Each of the five camps tended to keep to themselves, and their underlying mood was one of grim anticipation. Eyes and conversations turned often toward the Goblin camp atop the Gundithe Plateau. Fires could be seen, along with the tops of conical tents, and dark figures moved along the plateau's edge. Further back in the camp, rising above the rest, stood the tall hulking shape of an Urumak, visible in the firelight yet shadowy and indistinct. Rumors spread through the camps regarding the Urumak and the huge, chained augglins the townspeople had seen. Dread gnawed the troops' morale, as many came to believe an attack on the plateau was doomed to fail.

Gallorne's men mingled with those in Sherleaf's camp, describing what they had seen of the Goblins' forces up close, and what might be expected of them. Lexter found himself the object of much curiosity. "A Tolgarder in the King's troops, fitted with Dwarven helm and mail! How did this come to be?" they asked. Lexter related his story briefly, leaving out all mention of the twins and highlighting his encounters with the Goblins. Some disbelieved him, others were inspired, but most were amused regardless of what they thought of him. "If a Tolgarder's not afraid of the Goblins, why should we be?" said some. "True enough!" Lexter admitted, glad to raise morale even at his own expense.

And now the Dwarves were climbing the sloping road in the bright morning sunlight loathed by dark-adapted Goblin eyes. As they approached the stretch of road directly beneath the plateau and within bowshot of it, their progress slowed as they readied themselves. Higher up the road lay the bodies of Captain Erdrock and his men, severed and thrown down from the plateau by the Goblins. The carnage angered and sickened the Dwarves, leaving them shaken. Above on the plateau the Goblins moved into position, eager to crush the assault as soon as the Dwarves were within range.

To get to the plateau, the Dwarves had to travel across the winding road beneath the great ledge of rock, exposed to the plateau's defenders. A row of soldiers went out first, bearing great shields overhead side by side, like half a tunnel wall. Rocks hailed down upon them with a terrifying rumble. Once the shield-bearers were in place, archers moved in and began shooting through the gaps between the shields to clear the goblins from the plateau's edge. Goblin archers returned fire, aiming at gaps between shields. Other soldiers, including Lexter, moved quickly behind the shield-bearers and archers. They followed the second group of shield-bearers and archers who were already advancing across the sweep of road curving up to join the plateau. Lexter's nerves were all afire and he regretted taking a position so far in front. Flattery and praise had gone to his head, he had promised too much, and now he was sorry. He winced as rocks thundered down on the shields overhead. Passing beneath the shield cover, he caught glimpses of the road above them. Dwarven arrows found their mark and a goblin fell from the ledge, crashing down onto the raised shields and knocking dwarves to the ground. The line was disrupted and rocks clanged on Dwarven helms as they stabbed the body and rolled it down the slope. Above on the ledge the Goblins pushed steaming cauldrons to the edge and dumped them over the side. Boiling oil and pitch hissed and sizzled and ran down the shields. Archers were burned. Endless hails of rocks beat upon the upraised shields, the dwarves beneath buckling from the impacts.

The first waves of dwarves reached the plateau and the Goblins met them in force. Big, hulking, chained augglins, starved and ferocious, stood at the fore. Beady eyes blazing as they growled, the augglins swung hammers wildly at the dwarves with no regard for themselves. The dwarves' swords flashed and cut the augglins' thick callous-hardened arms, the wounds only enraging them further. Their chains were given slack and they lunged at the dwarves, crushing those in front and pushing others over the slope's edge.

Lexter had made it to the bend in the road when torches flew down, igniting the oil and pitch still dripping from the shields and pooling on the ground. Fire rose and spread rapidly. Shouts erupted and the rows of shields faltered, becoming unstable. More dwarves fell and the line halted. Horns sounded the call for retreat.

Those on the road turned back. Lexter felt panic rising as he saw the road behind him clogged with a crowd of soldiers. The dwarves in the road held up the shields and waited until the slow-moving troops had passed behind them. Lexter impatiently followed, rocks denting and thumping against the shields only inches away. At last he reached the next turn where the retreat was moving faster, and soon he was out of the Goblins' range. From high on the plateau, laughing, taunting shouts and sounds of victory echoed off the mountain wall.

An evening defeat leaves soldiers little time to dwell on their failings before sleep overtakes them. But defeat in the morning or early afternoon leaves much time for brooding, the bright light of day offering no relief from the ruin and sorrows that remain. As the wounded were tended and the dead buried, the encampment's mood went from solemn to somber. A meeting of Colonels was called in General Thundrum's tent, and Gallorne attended as well, expecting it would run most of the afternoon and maybe into evening. The retaking of the Gundithe Plateau now seemed impossibly difficult, and some said that by the time they broke through, the Castle would already be lost. Others thought that returning to Kronivar seemed the best course. None looked forward to what lay ahead.

Lexter sat with Gaern by the remains of their campfire. It was cold and sunny, and there was little to do but wait. Most of the dwarves and men around the camp rested or slept or sat talking and gambling. Some went into Greensward in search of supplies and others went off in groups to hunt. Gaern sat listlessly, tired and morose, too drained for conversation. Lexter was cold sitting in one place and his mind too active for sleeping, so he got up and wandered off through the encampment.

Lexter walked around the perimeter of the five camps, finding the same mood in all of them. Whenever he stopped and chatted with the men, their reaction to him was similar to what it had been in Sherleaf's camp. Such was the extent of their curiosity that Lexter himself began to wonder why a Tolgarder would join the King's troops. Aware of how he raised morale, however slightly, he continued his tour of the camps.

"By the horns of the moon, if it isn't Lexter Splide!" called a familiar voice.

Lexter was immediately apprehensive. People recognizing him usually meant some kind of threat or danger would follow, and he had the urge to look for cover. But times had changed, and he was wearing chain mail, so biting back his reluctance he turned around, already guessing who it was.

"Robb Pitford!" said Lexter, feigning pleasant surprise. "What brings you out here? Not me, I hope."

But Pitford's joy seemed genuine. "No, but I'm glad I came," he smiled, eyeing Lexter's Dwarven armor, "as this is indeed a sight worth traveling to see. You must be desperate for a hiding place!"

Lexter grunted, about to move on.

"I suppose you haven't heard," said Pitford, "Old Reuben died a while ago, almost a year now. I left him sometime before that, to go work for a Captain of Count Raymin's."

"So there isn't a price on my head anymore? And there hasn't been for some time?" said Lexter.

"Nope." Pitford laughed. "Ain't worth anything now! And it was never more than a hundred or so; and not for very long, either."

"Leland told me it was up to two hundred." Lexter sounded hurt.

"Two hundred? That would've been a grand waste of money! No, the last price that I heard, right before Reuben died, was around forty, or maybe fifty when he was particularly upset."

"Forty or fifty!" Lexter said in wonder, almost hearing Leland laughing at the figures.

"And I tried to tell you about it, too, but you ran off with Leland. How is he these days, by the way?" asked Pitford.

"When did you try to tell me?" said Lexter.

"After that deal you were making, out by the woods, you know, the one we interrupted. Like I said, I've been working for Count Raymin, rooting out separatist activity. When Eagen saw you at the *Badger*, Lyla went in to be sure. We knew something was going on, and figured it was separatists if they had to buy from you and Leland. We never did find out who was behind it all; the leaders hid in the cabin and we were outnumbered. And later the cabin was abandoned."

"Well it sure seemed as though you were out to kill us," said Lexter.

Pitford laughed. "I was trying to save you both! My archers are good shots, but I told 'em I wanted you alive. With you and Leland as witnesses, we could have rooted out whoever was behind it all. And they would have killed you themselves anyway, most likely, if you'd have stayed."

"Then I suppose it wouldn't have made much difference," said Lexter sadly.

"What do you mean?" asked Pitford.

"We were captured by goblins," said Lexter, "They killed Leland."

Pitford grew serious. "I've very sorry to hear it."

They were silent a moment, Leland's death paining Lexter anew. He realized Leland had already been gone a month, and was still amazed at the strange turns his life had taken since then.

Pitford looked up again. "And how did you escape?"

They sat down, and Lexter found himself recounting the entire story since he and Leland had been captured by the goblins. Pitford nodded and listened, and Lexter was glad to be with someone he had known on and off for some time. As Lexter grew comfortable talking, he even described his change of heart, his doubts, and all that had gone through his mind. Several times he wondered if perhaps he was saying too much, but Pitford was so interested and sympathetic that he kept going. When at last Lexter finished and sat back, Pitford remained quiet and Lexter could see he was touched by all he had heard.

"Well, Lexter, I don't know what to say," said Pitford, "I can understand why you'd want to help the Dwarves."

A dread fell upon Lexter. "And yet I wonder now if I've done more harm than good."

"How do you mean?" Pitford asked.

"I just thought of it," said Lexter, "You told me that Aranstone and his men were sent from Kronivar to hold the Plateau. Well, I talked to Orven and his friends as if I knew Aranstone, and they were eager to join with him when they got to Kronivar. Suppose they did? Maybe they were on the plateau when the goblins attacked, and now the swords, the Lost Swords of the Alliance, are in Goblin hands. All because of me!"

Pitford thought a moment. "We don't know that for certain," he said. He paused, trying to think of something reassuring to say, but couldn't help wondering if Lexter was right.

Everyone stirred and shouts announced the Colonels' return. All were eager to hear the new plans.

Lexter looked at Pitford and stood. "I guess I'd better get going," he said.

Pitford rose and shook Lexter's hand. "Let's meet again sometime, after the war is over," he offered, "You won't have to worry about coming to Kronivar any more."

Lexter nodded. "I'd like that," he said, "All right. We will." He wanted to add, *if we both survive*, but thought better of it.

Lexter arrived back at Gallorne's campsite just as everyone was gathering to hear the news from General Thundrum's meeting. The dwarves and Lexter sat around the ash-filled firepit at the center of their camp, and Gallorne sat across from them. It was mid-afternoon and the sun was starting its descent. The dwarves were more awake now and less grim. Gallorne surveyed them silently with a stoic expression, and whether the news was good or bad none could say.

"We will make another attempt to retake the plateau tomorrow morning," Gallorne began, "The occupying force on Gundithe was greater than expected. We don't know what losses they incurred when they took the plateau, or how many went east to the Castle, but they left behind more than we expected. We've also gathered reports from Greensward of what looting went on and what was taken." Gallorne gave a summary of the townspeople's experiences, and how their estimates of the Goblin army's size compared with what he'd seen on the road. The Goblins had stolen the largest cauldrons they could find, and had slaughtered and taken a good amount of livestock, presumably for the augglins.

"How will this help us?" said a voice from the back. "We know there are more of them, but we still know little about their camp. A second attack is as doomed to fail as the first."

Others began agreeing and Gallorne raised a hand for silence. "We will soon have some idea of their camp's layout," said Gallorne. "Some townspeople told us of a narrow pass through the valley next to a small creek flowing out from the mountains. Higher up, it angles near a series of slopes at the top of which is the Mountain Road. The way is hazardous and rocky, and the slopes up to the Mountain Road are steep."

Gallorne watched the dwarves, gauging their reaction. "It is much too narrow and difficult to send a fighting force of any size," he said, anticipating their next question. "And there's always the danger of being seen by the Goblins. Especially coming up the slopes."

"Of what use is it then?" asked one of the dwarves.

"We plan to send a small party, no more than three or four, up to the Mountain Road this way. The road winds past once, high above the plateau, before it curves back on the way down where it rejoins the plateau. If you look up the cliff wall from the plateau," —Gallorne pointed and the dwarves followed his gaze to the mountain— "there's a slight edge of rock where the road goes past." Lexter saw the cliff wall rising behind the Goblin army, and found the slight break, barely visible, where the road ran. On either side it wound away until it was out of view. It was so far away that Lexter wondered if he was seeing it or just imagining he was.

"From that vantage point, we will be able to see how the Goblin camp is laid out along the plateau, and make a rough count of what they have. This will give us a sense of what to expect and how to prepare for the attack tomorrow morning."

"Tomorrow morning?" said one dwarf, "That doesn't leave much time. And what if they change the arrangement?"

"The group will have to leave before this evening, and someone will remain there until tomorrow, to give us a signal to back down should anything change," said Gallorne. "I myself have volunteered to lead the group. We'll need at least two more to go."

All were quiet as the dwarves considered what Gallorne had said and the dangers involved.

"I'll go," Lexter offered. Muted laughter erupted from some of the younger dwarves who thought Lexter too old for such hiking and climbing. Lexter himself would have agreed, but in the last month he had thinned down and done a great deal of walking and felt better than he had in a long time. Still, he thought, there was always the chance he didn't really know what he was getting into.

"We have proof enough of your bravery from this morning's attack, Lexter," said Gallorne, "You don't need to volunteer for this as well."

"Not at all," said Lexter, "I relish the challenge, and you know I'm very observant." Sneaking around the mountainside sounded a lot better to Lexter than joining the crowd for another attack on the plateau. He recalled being stuck in the retreating crowd and his mind was made up. "I've done my fair share of spying and sneaking around and it's just the thing for me," he added mysteriously.

Gallorne had always wondered about Lexter's past, and this seemed to confirm his suspicions. At the same time, he believed what Lexter said. "All right then, you may join me."

"I'll come, too," said Gaern. "If you'll have me."

"I will." Gallorne smiled. "Then it is done. Get ready while I go tell the General. Meet me at his tent as soon as you can, and we'll leave from there."

A short while later Lexter and Gaern stood outside General Thundrum's tent, waiting for Gallorne to emerge. Dusk was nearing, and Lexter was eager to get underway for the going would be more difficult in the dark of night. As Lexter and Gaern stood talking, a merry voice rang out behind them.

"Aha, Lexter! I knew you were going!" Pitford called as he approached them, pleased at Lexter's expression of surprise. "When I heard the nature of the mission and who was leading it, I knew you'd offer to go," he said to Lexter, "Especially considering the alternative. So, I thought, why don't I join them as well?"

"Didn't want to go into battle, eh?" said Lexter.

"No more than you," said Pitford. He smiled and nodded at Lexter's armor. "You're not taking that helmet along, are you?"

"Well, yes, why not?" said Lexter.

"The moon's only four days past full," said Pitford, "We can't have it shining in the moonlight. The Goblins' eyes are keen in the dark, and it's a greater risk to wear the helmet than to go without it."

Lexter removed the helmet and looked at it in his hands, as though he were loath to part with it. "I suppose it is. It is a bit heavy, and I'd just as well have the wind in my hair."

"And anyway, you never wore a helmet in Kronivar, either, even with a price on your head," said Pitford. "How fortunate that you and Leland were good at fleeing!"

Gaern looked on in wonder and questions arose in his eyes. Pitford laughed at his curiosity. "Oh, he's not told you, I see! Well, there'll be time enough in the valley tonight."

Lexter threw a daggered glance at Pitford, which made Gaern wonder all the more. Moments later Gallorne stepped out of the General's tent, helmet in hand, with a small pack slung over his shoulder. He eyed the three of them standing there. "You must be the one from Raymin's camp," said Gallorne, "Glad to have you along."

"I wouldn't miss it," said Pitford cheerfully.

"We must travel as light as possible," said Gallorne. "We'll leave our armor here, though we'll take provisions for the climb. We'll need to move as quickly as we can."

As Gallorne turned to lead them through the camp, Lexter exchanged knowing glances with Pitford, sensing the hike through the valley would not be as quiet as he had hoped.

Gallorne, Lexter, Gaern, and Pitford began down the trail into the mountains, the setting sun casting growing shadows before them. They descended into the pass, where the air was colder and the gloom deepening. Gallorne led the way and kept glancing above to their right, to see if they could be seen from the plateau. Surrounded by dark mountains with the camp far behind them, they lost the urge to banter and kept their eyes on the ground ahead. After a few hours' march they passed into the mountains where they would no longer be visible and felt a sense of relief. Pale silver moonlight edged everything around them. Wolves' howls echoed, long and soulful, dispelling what little peace Lexter hoped they might have. Already he was tired, and steep slopes still lay ahead. Lexter kept reminding himself why he had volunteered and hoped he was right.

Gallorne watched the sky and thought they were making good time, but was still wary of stopping for long. The trail had risen a good distance from the valley, and at last found the slope that was supposed to lead up to the Mountain Road. Wearily they made for it, eager to reach the level road where they might rest.

The climb was difficult and they took their time. Their eyes, accustomed to the moonglow, gazed around the quiet mountainside. Lexter was struck anew by the beauty and vastness of the mountains, even in the dark. He understood why the Dwarves loved the mountains so. Lexter's silent appreciation and prolonged efforts calmed his nerves, and he stood breathing deeply when at last he climbed up onto the Mountain Road. The others joined him, resting and looking out into the starry night skies, feeling a little closer to them.

"Still a ways to go, but it's all by road," Gallorne said after a brief respite. "You can rest when we get there. Remember, I still have to make the journey back to Greensward before morning." The thought of having to go back right away, even though most of it was downhill, made the others glad to have watch duty instead and they walked down the road without complaint.

Feeling more at ease, they began to chat a little as they walked, and Lexter explained more of his background to Gaern and Gallorne. Pitford listened and explained what Lexter had been like in the 'old days', often puncturing Lexter's stories with embarrassing details. Though neither of the dwarves said anything in judgment of him, Lexter felt ashamed of his past and hoped they would not think too differently of him now.

"Well, well," Gallorne said when Lexter had finished, "Seems I'm not the only one with wild days in my youth. Yet here we are. Perhaps we wouldn't be able to do what we must now if it weren't for those days. Which is not to say I have no regrets; but one can always make the best of what one has become." He stopped just as they hoped he would reveal more of his past. After a moment Gallorne smiled and turned to Lexter. "And I am glad you have come to realize your love for our country."

"And my own," said Lexter, "Never have I missed Tolgard so much. I couldn't even tell you why, entirely. Leland and I left when I was young and I never really even got to see much of it."

"Tolgard has been careful in dealing with the Goblins," said Gallorne. "The Soskwiteyon River is all that stands between Tolgard and Navrogenaya, and the border is long. I do not blame your countrymen for staying neutral," Gallorne glanced at Lexter, "But neutrality can turn into compromise, or worse, complicity."

Lexter wanted to say something in Tolgard's defense but realized he knew nothing of the prevailing mood there.

"But *you've* got the right idea, Lexter," Gallorne's tone was kinder, "What you do for Itharia, you do for Tolgard as well."

"Aw, you almost make him sound noble!" Pitford groaned, "He was just trying to save his own skin, even if it took Dwarven armor to do it!"

Soon the road turned and an expanse of night sky opened before them. They slowed their pace and grew quiet, for ahead of them lay the long curving ledge of rock overlooking the Gundithe plateau. Here the road hugged the mountain's shoulder, beginning its downward slope as it doubled back into the mountains, turned, and eventually led back onto the plateau below them. Carefully they approached the edge, Gallorne in the lead. They knelt down and crawled forward to look out over the plateau. With fear and wonder they spied upon the Goblin camp, adjusting to the strange overhead point of view. A hundred feet or so below them the wide crescent of the plateau spread around the mountain, the rising air thick with smoke and the smell of roasting meat. From above, the conical tents appeared as rough circles or octagons, and Goblins could be seen leaving and entering them. Cauldrons and firepots lined the plateau's edge and small boulders lay nearby, ready to be dropped over the side. In the midst of it all, chained and hitched to a supply wagon, stood a great, shaggy Urumak, its head rising above the busy camp.

"Not as many as we thought, but they're well-fortified," Gallorne said in hushed tones. "On both sides, too." Both ends of the great crescent where the road led onto the plateau were lined with rows of chained augglins standing or sitting shoulder-to-shoulder, impenetrable walls of hide and hard muscle. Goblins were removing charred livestock carcasses from spits and throwing them to the augglins for their dinner. The augglins fought over them and growled, tearing them apart and devouring them, much to the goblins' amusement. Lexter noticed that the goblins deliberately threw the meat where it was most likely to be fought over, so much were they entertained.

"The attack will be difficult," said Gallorne, "The camp is arranged well, but they are weaker on the inside along the wall. It also looks as though they have little or no burning tar or oil left to pour on us; that'll be useful in forming our plan of attack. And knowing the layout of the camp, we'll be able to put our archers to better use. Their position is good, but their quarters are rather tight."

"That could be used against them quite well," said Gaern.

Gallorne and the others drew back from the ledge and sat by the sloping rock wall behind them. "Maybe," Gallorne said, "but only if we can reach the plateau. General Thundrum is quite a strategist, and with the camp layout, I think we can break through. I've got to get back down to Greensward as quick as I can to give them more time to plan."

"And if the Goblins change their camp in the meantime, what then? They may be expecting another attack tomorrow morning," asked Gaern.

Gallorne indicated the horn Gaern carried. "Sound the call of retreat. Though I doubt we will need it; there's little they can do that they haven't done already. Also, during our attack, you three can help us with some well-timed arrows or rocks from above. Wait until the attack is underway, and then be on the lookout should they send anyone after you." Gallorne got up to leave.

"Godspeed you, and may your return journey be safe," said Gaern.

"As well as your stay up here. If we succeed and the Goblins retreat, you will have to have to be very careful." Gallorne nodded to them and departed.

"And if they don't succeed?" said Lexter, when Gallorne was gone. "Then what?"

Pitford looked sternly at Lexter a moment and shrugged. "Then all is lost."

The three of them slept fitfully, each waking and doing the watch awhile until one of the others could not sleep. The road was hard and cold, with nothing to shield them from strong winds that kept blowing. The only distraction they had from the elements was the Goblin camp. By night the Goblins seemed especially fierce and invincible, even from their vantage point high above the plateau. Noise from the Goblin camp echoed off the mountain wall, late into the night. Smoke smelling of burnt wood and grease crept up the mountainside, seeping into their sleep and poisoning their dreams. The night was endless and interminable, and Lexter lost track of how many times he dozed and woke.

At last the night broke and a glow appeared beyond the mountains to the east. Gaern awoke, groggy, only to find both Lexter and Pitford asleep. He nudged Lexter in the side with his foot. "Awake! Awake!" he cried, "It was *your* watch!"

"My watch?" Lexter grunted as he rubbed his eyes and shoved Gaern's foot away. "It wasn't my watch. I was up most of the night!" Lexter sat up, stiff and cold. He saw Pitford sleeping nearby and woke him with a kick.

"You could have let him sleep," said Gaern.

"If I have to get up we might as well all get up," said Lexter. "He's done more sleeping than both of us put together, I'll bet."

Soon they were ready and lying prone at the roadside, peering down at the Goblin camp. They could see everything below clearly in the morning light, but they could be more easily seen as well. The Goblin camp was quieter now, fires were still burning, and guards were walking around. Several stood looking down the mountain towards Greensward, where the Dwarves' five-spoked encampment could be seen on the outskirts of town. Or what was left of the town; from here they could see just how badly burnt and ravaged Greensward was.

Lexter, Pitford, and Gaern watched the Dwarves' camp as well, wondering if that morning's attack would fare any better than the first one had. Gaern pulled back and stood. "Well," he said, "We've no food left, so I'll see if I can fill our flasks at least; water's better than nothing."

Gaern collected their flasks and left. Lexter and Pitford resumed their watch. Time passed slowly. The sun climbed into the sky, and it would not be long until the Dwarves began their ascent to the plateau. There was no hope of a surprise attack, and Lexter wondered whether their chances were any better with the knowledge Gallorne brought them. Lexter considered what it would be like to watch a defeat from above, feeling a bit of a coward for wanting to avoid fighting. He looked at Pitford, curious if similar thoughts were running through his head.

"Look at those beasts down there," said Pitford, indicating the augglins below. "If only *we* could have slept so well. I guess that's one advantage of being mindless, eh? They'll be all rested for the attack, at least."

Lexter looked at the rows of sleeping augglins at the back end of the plateau, their sides rising and falling. "I can't say I envy them," said Lexter, remembering his own bondage in Goblin hands. He looked at Pitford, wondering if he had any pity at all for the Augglins. "You've never been up close to a goblin or augglin, have you?" Lexter said.

"No," said Pitford, "and you didn't exactly go near them willingly either."

"Well, now's your chance," Lexter nodded towards the plateau and smiled. "Go down there while they're sleeping. I dare you... just go down there, right next to one, and come back."

Pitford looked at Lexter, annoyed. "You go down there, if you think it's so

444

safe. You're the one who used to be a thief!" He raised an eyebrow. "And anyway, that's nothing compared to everything you claim to have done in the past few weeks, if you weren't exaggerating it all."

"So you're afraid to go, then?" said Lexter.

"You're just as afraid as I am," said Pitford. He was upset that Lexter refused to be baited and believed his story even more now as a result. He looked back down to the plateau. "Sure, I'll go if you'll go, but you won't, so what difference does it make?"

"Robb, Robb, you're getting old and too respectable..." Lexter sighed. He pulled back from the edge and got up to walk around. "Well, that's alright. I guess a steady job will do that to you."

"You ain't so young yourself anymore," Pitford snapped. "And as for a steady job—" But Lexter was gone already. "Hasn't changed," Pitford muttered.

But Pitford knew Lexter had changed; it was obvious. He was envious of Lexter, for he had hoped to change himself, now that his youth was gone. And although he wouldn't admit it to Lexter, he did want to become more respectable. Lexter's story inspired him and shamed him into trying harder. Pitford was lost in thought until a few steps sounded behind him.

"Filled them all up," said Gaern, holding up the water flasks. "Where's Lexter?"

"Lexter?" Pitford suddenly knew. He craned his neck to see the road leading down to the plateau, and sure enough, Lexter was on his way down. Pitford swore under his breath, pulled back, and got up. Gaern looked alarmed and Pitford motioned him over to the edge.

Looking down, Gaern was startled when Lexter came into view, sneaking along the curving road. He shook his head. *Whatever was Lexter doing?* he wondered. He turned back but it was too late; Pitford had already gone after Lexter. *Well,* he thought to himself, *that's what they get for sending Men instead of Dwarves!*

Gaern turned back to the plateau, and motion further down the mountain caught his attention. The Kronivar troops were already on their way to the mountain path, and Goblin activity below was starting to pick up in anticipation of the attack.

Pitford ran as quietly as he could to catch up to Lexter, and stopped him just as they neared the last turn in the road. "What're you doing? Get back here!" Pitford roared in a whisper.

"I had an idea," Lexter said, "but I have to check something first." He continued walking down the road.

"Wait!" Pitford followed after, trying to reason with him.

They came to the turn in the road, crouching low, and peered around the corner. Only a few yards away were the augglins. Even lying on their sides, sleeping, their bodies were still more than four or five feet high. A heavy pungent stench filled the air, making Pitford cringe. A row of augglins lay close together, across the road from side to side, and another row slept behind them. Their massive chests heaved up and down like enormous bellows, their breathing low and labored like long, patient growls. Lexter and Pitford were still and silent in awe, taking in the strange and terrifying sight up close. Then, much to his horror, Pitford watched as Lexter crawled out to where the augglins lay. Nervously, he followed suit and came up alongside Lexter, hoping he could talk Lexter out of whatever he was thinking of doing.

"Very clever," Lexter whispered, pointing, "They're chained arm to arm, with chains long enough to fight but not enough to turn around easily. And the control chains are almost like reins. Handy, too, for when they have to sedate them."

"And look at these links," Pitford noted with surprise, indicating the chains on their arms, "They're only held together with a simple bolt! You could slide it right out, just like that. No locks or anything."

"All the easier to move them around when they have to," said Lexter in a harsh whisper.

"If the augglins had even half a flea's brain they could pull out the bolts and go free," said Pitford, "But of course they don't."

Lexter moved even closer to one of the sleeping augglins. "Then I suppose we'll have to help them." He bent down and there was a slow rasp of metal as he pulled out one of the bolts.

Pitford tensed with panic. "Lexter!" he hissed in a loud whisper, "What are you doing, are you crazy?! Put that back!"

Lexter smiled and bent to pull another bolt. "Come on, Robb, they're sound asleep! At least for a few more minutes..."

Pitford suddenly understood what Lexter was doing. "Lexter... Alright, but we'd better be quiet and quick." He gingerly crept forward and gently pulled a bolt. Lexter had three of them already and was pulling a fourth. Pitford pulled another, and a third, and looked up.

"What are you doing? Lexter!" Pitford stared in horror as Lexter, still crouching down, stepped over the chains and pulled a bolt in the second row of augglins. "Enough, Lexter! And stay low! If the Goblins see us..."

Lexter raised a finger to his lips to shush Pitford. He pulled another bolt and stepped back over the chains, still bending over. "We need a few more on that side, and then we'll go." As he crept over with Pitford, one of the bolts fell from his hand and landed with a clang on the ground.

Pitford and Lexter froze, watching the augglins. They went on sleeping as if nothing had happened. "They must be heavy sleepers," said Pitford, "But still, Lexter, be more careful, at least for my sake!"

Gaern stood frozen, watching in horror as Lexter and Pitford crept around the augglins. He knew something would happen and wished they would leave and come back up the road. Activity in the Goblin camp caught his eye; he noticed the Goblins moving the Urumak to the back of the camp and more Goblins shifting to the front where the attack would take place. Cauldrons were brought out from tents and placed on fires. Had they underestimated how much tar and pitch the Goblins had left? And now as Gaern watched, further down the mountain the Kronivar troops were already advancing up the winding road on the lower slopes. He wondered if the changes in the Goblin camp were substantial enough to warrant calling off the attack. And then there was Lexter and Pitford; if he sounded the horn loud enough for the Kronivar troops to hear, the augglins would awaken and Lexter and Pitford wouldn't stand a chance of escaping them.

Gaern stared down at Lexter and Pitford and wanted to scream out to them to return. His gaze shifted again to the Kronivar troops climbing the last slope, readying for the attack. The Goblins were waiting for them, and several motioned for the extra cauldrons to be brought over. Gaern nervously fingered the horn hanging around his neck, and looked down at Lexter and Pitford, who were still sneaking around the sleeping augglins. He put the horn to his lips and drew a deep breath, watching and hoping Lexter and Pitford would leave just as he did so, but still they remained lingering about the augglins.

Lexter crept around the corner up the road, with Pitford right behind him. Suddenly Goblin shouts and whip cracks snapped behind them. Lexter and Pitford broke into a run, not looking back until they had gone far enough up the road. Goblins whipped the augglins to wake them for battle, but finding themselves unfettered, the augglins turned on their masters. One caught a goblin's whip arm, twisting its owner to the ground and crushing him. Stunned, the goblins fought to regain control of the loose augglins, unprepared for an enemy within their camp. Other goblins came to assist as anguished shrieks echoed from goblins in the augglins' grasp.

Confusion and distraction spread swiftly through the Goblin camp and the front lines faltered. The dwarves in the vanguard leapt to the advantage and gained ground, finally reaching the plateau under a hail of rocks. As a few loose augglins were subdued and killed, the remaining ones grew more vicious, and even those on the front lines seemed to lose interest in the Dwarves and gave out long guttural shouts. Swords clashed, and bolts and arrows flew. Torches smashed into shields and helms. In the back of the Goblin camp one of the cauldrons tipped over and burned the leg of the Urumak, who was already spooked by the augglins running wild. The Urumak began rearing up and braying loudly, frightening all augglins, goblins, and dwarves who beheld it.

Havoc engulfed the Goblin camp as it strove to fight off the Dwarves while trying to contain the augglins and the Urumak. After breaking through and establishing a foothold on the edge of the plateau, the Dwarven troops advanced slowly and held their ground while the chaos played itself out. Goblins and augglins fell over the plateau's edge and blood spattered the ground and cliff wall. Hot tar and oil ran and dripped from the ledge. Gradually the Dwarven forces pressed forward and more reached the plateau. With steady effort, the Goblin front broke and General Thundrum's Dwarven forces began to retake the plateau. Once they were outnumbered, some goblins fled up the road into the mountains. In a panic, the Urumak slipped in the oil and fell over the plateau's edge, dragging goblins and augglins along with it and crushing dwarves on the road below. The Urumak landed on its side and let out a loud, deep, curdling roar of pain and bewilderment, flailing its legs as it tried to stand. Dwarves were thrown back and knocked off their feet. The Urumak struggled on the road's edge and toppled down to the next pass of road across the slope where the last of the troops were passing.

Gallorne and Silvernail pulled back into the dwarves behind them as the huge beast fell, the stench and panic overwhelming them. The Urumak's huge legs, like the boles of great trees, still kicked about aimlessly, but the beast was stunned and dazed. Dwarves on both sides of it approached with swords drawn, swinging and stabbing at the Urumak and jumping out of the way. None of the dwarves had been so close to such a creature, and even as they swung at it out of fear they gazed on it in wonder and pitied the great beast. The Urumak's tortured grunts and braying howls of pain chilled the dwarves, until at last the huge beast lay still.

The Urumak lay blocking most of the road. There was only a small gap between it and the cliff wall, which the dwarves began squeezing through in single file, the heat and smell of the beast near suffocating. Gallorne stepped through quickly, Silvernail right behind him.

"A few more of those piled in the road, and we'd never get to the plateau," said Silvernail.

They climbed the road as it wound its way up to the plateau, dodging weapons, rocks, and bodies falling over the plateau's edge. They reached the plateau and joined in the fighting as others arrived behind them. The Dwarves had all but regained the plateau, and now only a rearguard of goblins remained to give the others time to retreat into the mountains. These fought tenaciously and were eventually overcome, though not without the loss of more dwarves.

When the noise and frenzy finally died down, the wounded were tended to, and orders went out for the dismantling of the encampment by Greensward. It was still before noon, and General Thundrum wanted to get as far into the mountains as they could before nightfall. Gallorne wandered the ruins of the Goblins' campsite on the plateau, aiding wounded dwarves wherever it was needed. Many times he glanced up to the bend of the road high above them, where he had left Gaern, Lexter, and Pitford. Silvernail and Feren had gone to search for them. Gallorne wondered whether the three lookouts had anything to do with the disturbance in the Goblin camp. He suspected they did, and hoped they had survived the Goblins' retreat.

A call for ropes went out in the camp, and Gallorne saw Feren returning. Gallorne went over to talk to him as others brought a coil of rope.

"We heard them arguing," said Feren, as he and Gallorne climbed the road from the plateau. "They slid down a long slope off the road, where the Goblins wouldn't see them. Once the Goblins had passed, they couldn't get a foothold to climb back up." Gallorne rounded turns in the climbing road, until Feren stopped and threw the rope down the sloping wall. Dwarves pulled up Lexter and Pitford, who were grateful and relieved.

"I still say it was a bad idea," Pitford complained.

"Well, it saved us in the end, didn't it?" Lexter snapped.

"We were lucky to stop sliding when we did; I didn't think we would at all," said Pitford, "We would have been dead all the same, and without a chance to take a few Goblins with us!"

"Yes, and here we are," said Lexter.

"No thanks to you! It was all luck."

"It was my idea!"

"You could have picked a slope that wasn't so steep—"

"They would have seen us," Lexter shot back.

Gallorne clapped them both on the back. "Good to see you're both doing well. We're striking camp and hauling it into the mountains, and need every hand we can get."

As they walked back to the plateau, Lexter and Pitford told Gallorne how they had unbolted the augglins, each giving their own story and taking credit for what they could. Gallorne was glad to have them back and listened patiently. They were still discussing what had happened when Silvernail returned.

"We found Gaern," he told them. "Goblins must have been returning from the Castle siege, messengers, perhaps. The arrows were in his back; he probably never heard them coming. He still gripped the horn, as though he were about to use it."

They all were quiet at the news and found a place to sit down. Moments passed as they remembered their friend. Lexter suddenly became despondent. "If only we hadn't gone down to the plateau," he said, "He might still be with us."

"Hard to say," said Pitford, his tone softened, "We don't know how many goblins there were. They could have found all of us."

"I'll bet there was only one or two," said Lexter.

"If you hadn't gone down, our attack might have failed," Gallorne pointed out. "Or at the very least, the cost would have been much greater." Gallorne glanced around the plateau at the wounded and the dead. "You yourselves could well have been among the dead, daring what you did."

"We nearly were, thanks to Lexter!" Pitford looked at Lexter. "And it's probably thanks to him that we weren't, too."

"Or if Gaern had come with us—" Lexter began.

"We cannot alter what is past," said Gallorne, "Nor can we foresee all. So let us not be blinded to what little we can foresee by such musings." He got up again, gazing toward Greensward where the camp was being struck. "We must look ahead now, not behind. We have much to do and a long way to go yet. Our most difficult task still lies ahead of us. Regaining the plateau will mean little if the Castle is lost."

By late afternoon the entire company was making its way through the mountains in a long mass that snaked down the road. The victory at the plateau had been a hard one and their pace was slow. None were eager for what lay ahead, yet no one was willing to turn back. For a while they traveled unhindered, with no sign of the Goblins. Around dusk, however, the vanguard stopped and the forced halt passed down through the company, along with reports of what had been encountered.

Where the road curved around a steep outcropping of rock they found a dead Urumak slumped across the road, blocking the way. The huge beast was emaciated, scores of maggots squirming in its dried and matted fur. Large sections of its side had been cut away and butchered for food once it was no longer capable of pulling its burdens. Piled on top of it and behind it to make the way impassable were dozens of augglin carcasses, all branded and scarred with scores of whip marks. Many were dismembered, and others still chained together, making them difficult to move without cutting them up further. Burnt limbs and bones littered the pile and the road.

It took more than two hours to clear the road so that carts could pass. Even in the cold November air the smell of rot and decay was strong enough to turn stomachs. Worse of all was the feeling that this was only the first of many such obstacles that lay ahead. Those toward the back of the company stood or sat on the cold stone waiting for the delay to end, and all wondered how long it would take to get to the Castle and what they would find once they got there.

Chapter 41.
Between Hammer and Anvil

Aranstone stood at the parapet on one of the east wing's tower balconies. Cold wind blew around him and the warmth of the late morning sun was faint. It was already the last week of November, and the third day of the Goblins' siege. Winter was in the air, and he did not think the Goblins would wait much longer before attacking the weakened Castle. His men, too, sensed the vice-like grip of the Goblin siege tightening around them as they awaited his command. Greywood seemed the least daunted of all his men, and while his advisor's calm gave him confidence, something about it made him uneasy as well. Greywood was late in answering Aranstone's summons that morning, and he wondered if the delay was deliberate. As Aranstone thought about it, it seemed a breach had opened between him and Greywood, and that disturbed him. And now he would have to leave Greywood in charge along with Khale and Pyrwoed while he went to speak with the King.

At last Aranstone heard Greywood come up the stairs behind him. He glanced at the old man impatiently and then back down into the valley. "I have decided to accept the King's terms. We will parley this afternoon."

Aranstone expected objection and argument, but Greywood was strangely quiet. "As you wish. If you feel there is no other course of action."

Aranstone had deliberated for most of the day following the Goblins' arrival. By evening he had decided that two days was too long a time to wait before asking for parley again, despite what he had told Greywood. He had sent word to the King and was told that the King would grant him an audience, but only under certain conditions. They would meet in the King's study in the west wing, not in the Throne Room as Aranstone had asked. Only one aide was to accompany him, and they were both to come unarmed. Greywood was not invited. Aranstone seemed put at a disadvantage but the King would hear of no other terms.

Greywood had mocked the terms and called them an insult. "You see how they fear my counsel!" he had said. "You have been too eager to parley, and now they will allow you to come groveling alone before them. I warned you not to ask again so soon."

And so Aranstone waited, still debating what to do. Greywood said the King would change his mind but Aranstone was not so sure. On the second day of the siege Aranstone had been kept busy reordering the guard rotations and settling complaints of unequal treatment and other squabbles that arose. Every dispute between companies led by different Captains had to be brought to either him or Greywood to be settled. When it was found that someone had been stealing from the rations, accusations flew, and guards had to be posted at the storerooms, upsetting the rotations. By the day's end Aranstone was in a foul mood and had made up his mind to parley the very next day, bitter as the terms seemed to him.

"Go then," Greywood said now, "But do not let him suppose his hand to be stronger than ours. It may seem so at first, as they have more stores and can hold out longer. And troops from Kronivar may be on their way by now. But they have not yet arrived, and may be held back. Even a short delay could be enough to give the Goblins an upper hand."

Aranstone turned to Greywood. "And should they gain the upper hand we would certainly die as well."

"Not at all," said Greywood. "The Goblins have no interest in us; they have come here to take the Castle. If we were to surrender the east wing to them, they would surely let us walk out unharmed." He watched Aranstone's reaction. "I am certain I could arrange it."

Aranstone was silent, taken aback by the idea. He saw that it was possible and had a strange feeling of surety that Greywood actually could arrange it for them. They could all leave, without any loss of life or even fighting. And his desire to return home to Kronivar was great.

A gust of wind blew around Aranstone as he paused in thought, the quiet of the mountains enormous and deafening after the noise and argument within the Castle. Greywood stood near him, awaiting his reply.

"I could not allow the Castle to fall to the Goblins," Aranstone said simply.

Greywood shrugged. "Just as I thought. Then we remain between hammer and anvil, beaten by the Goblins or bent and forged into footmen for the King. Go, then, and ask for terms."

Resentment welled up in Aranstone and threatened to burst upon Greywood, but he held it in check. He moved brusquely past Greywood, who stepped aside in time, and went down the stairs into the Castle.

The afternoon sky was overcast and a pale, sleepy light bled into the halls as Aranstone and his aide were led to the King's chamber for the parley. He had chosen Ered, a young dwarf from among Olmic's men, a move calculated to remind the King that there were dwarves under his command and that Aranstone himself was a quarter Dwarven. He even felt shame that the siege, meant to be a show of force, had gotten so far out of hand, beyond what he had thought it would be. But, as Greywood had said, much of it had been in defense against the King's men, even if his Captains were a bit overzealous at times.

At last the Castle guards stopped near the short, vaulted passageway leading to the King's chamber, and indicated that Aranstone and Ered should enter. Upon Aranstone's arrival the murmur of conversation in the room ceased as attention shifted to him. Two armchairs had been placed near the center of the room toward the entrance for him and his aide. No one stood as Aranstone entered, and a quiet tension filled the air. A fire crackled in the hearth along the wall. Aranstone recognized most of those in attendance. The King sat in his armchair, in the place of importance, and next to him sat Prince Varlen on one side and Erland Clovenstone the Castle Steward on the other. An old man with a long white beard sat next to Clovenstone whom Aranstone did not know. He seemed very old, yet his eyes were curiously clear and alert. Next to Varlen was his cousin Arlen Frosthelm, and next to Arlen sat a young female dwarf who looked vaguely familiar to Aranstone. After a moment he realized he had seen her somewhere in Kronivar, and gradually remembered it was at *The Brown*

Badger. He thought she must be the castle spy who had escaped, and he wondered what she knew of their doings and why she was at the parley. It did not seem a good sign.

"Sire," Aranstone acknowledged the King with a polite nod but did not bow. After a moment he and Ered sat down. Although the King's study was well kept up, here and there effects of the siege were visible; candles burned low that had not been replaced, smaller rations of firewood, and a pot of tiny violets by the window that looked dry. But for the most part, the west wing seemed better off than the Castle's east wing.

"It is good you have come," said the King, with a hint of encouragement. "May our time here prove fruitful. We have much to discuss." Indignation edged the King's words despite his apparent good will.

As the parley began, Prince Varlen introduced the common problem of the Goblin siege, and the King asked Aranstone for news of the inner ward and the defense of the east wing. At first there was only an exchange of information, sometimes reluctantly. As both sides grew more at ease, talk flowed more readily and soon the parley was underway, though tension remained regarding the negotiations to come.

Rhiane sat listening as the parley proceeded, absorbed in what was being said, yet still anxious about her role as Aranstone's accuser when the time came to discuss separatist activity in Kronivar. As interested as she was, from time to time she became distracted. Three days had passed since she and Iaven had had their audience in this very room, and the King's words still rankled. More important things lay before her now, and she would keep her mind on them. But thoughts of Iaven and her love for him kept returning. It seemed unfair that she could not choose whom she wished. What had particularly irked her was that Oellia had taken the King's side when they had talked the next day, even though her own husband Tomald had not been nobility...

Rhiane caught herself getting distracted. For now, it would have to wait. She would talk to King Jordgen again after the war; perhaps he was right about her being more headstrong after living away in Kronivar. But she loved Iaven despite what the King thought of him, and regardless of whether or not he performed heroic feats during the war.

With an effort Rhiane brought her attention back to the parley. Aranstone was stating his case and his intentions. He explained the situation in Kronivar, listing perceived injustices and justifying various separatist activities. Aranstone began to see some of the faults of his cause more clearly, or at least the manner in which it had been defended, as he came to understand the King's situation. The King listened patiently and countered with lists and justifications of his own, though he conceded a few points as well. Several times he turned to Rhiane for verification and explanation of events that she had seen or heard about. Aranstone stared at her, silent and stolid, with an unreadable expression on his face whenever she spoke. The King and Rhiane talked of spies, conspiracies, threats and disturbances, smuggling, vandalism and destruction of property, and even murder. For several years, spies' reports had helped the Castle keep the separatists at bay, allowing the King's troops to stop them here and there. But there was never enough to trace their roots back to the Counts or even their Generals, and so the activity continued and grew. It had been Rhiane, at the *Badger*, who had managed to connect many loose strands and threads and uncover the forming conspiracies.

At last the King finished and became silent. Aranstone sat still awhile, weighing all he had heard. "In their zeal, men often overstep the bounds set for them, going beyond what they are called upon to do," Aranstone began, "And leaders must take responsibility for the discipline of their followers, if they truly lead them. We always wanted what was best for Kronivar, even when our means were less than noble. I admit that other courses of action could have been taken at times —*should* have been taken. Yet quenching fires is far more difficult than starting them, especially when they light easily and spread quickly."

"It is true that some of these 'fires' began before your time," said Prince Varlen, "but many were mere flames or smoldering wicks, until they were fanned and fueled."

"We worked to unite discontents and add them to our cause," Aranstone admitted, "but not all misdeeds are our doing. Many things you have spoken of —threats, murders, the burning of property— were neither commanded nor incited by me." Aranstone had been shocked by some of the things he had heard and found little he could say in response. More and more he realized how much he had come to rely on Greywood for quick rejoinders and the reasoning behind his deeds and those of his men. Now his answers came slower, his conviction wavered, and as past justifications dissolved his wrongs became clearer to him.

"Do you doubt our words?" asked the King, barely concealing his anger. "We know who did these deeds and why." King Jordgen glanced at Rhiane, which she took as a signal to speak, until the King spoke again. "Do you dare deny your role in all of this?"

"I do not deny my role in it," Aranstone stated firmly, almost angrily. "Not at all. But I did not give the orders for some of these deeds attributed to my men."

"Others may have given them in your name," said the King, calmer now after Aranstone's admission. "For example, this advisor of yours, Greywood— from where did he come? How long have you known him?"

This turn of questioning took Aranstone aback. "I have known him for years. He came from the north, I think; Tolgard or Phamiar or elsewhere, I do not recall." Although his answer was calm, Aranstone realized he did not know much about Greywood's past. In the years he had known him, however, he had come to rely on Greywood's advice, and Greywood's planning and cunning had done much to advance the separatists' cause. Yet Aranstone could recall times when Greywood had issued orders on his behalf, without leave to do so. On those occasions things had turned out well, but he wondered now if there were other orders he did not know of.

The King turned to Wendolin, who spoke now. "Greywood is none other than Zhindarren, an Eloswai; what you would call a wizard or sorcerer," he began. "He is in league with Maëlveronde, who has the ear of King Golhazzar, and has become his Grand Vizier. He has played you into the hands of the Goblins; first by ceding the Gundithe plateau, and then through your siege."

Aranstone was momentarily stunned, as though this was a ruse to test his gullibility. He grunted to make it clear that he had taken offense and turned to the King. "As the parley has gone well thus far, I shall pardon this old man's words," he said. "But do not think you can so easily drive a wedge between my advisor and me. He has served me well and his advice has been sound. Nor have I ever seen him engaging in magic or wielding such powers; and surely he would have done so if he were a sorcerer."

"A whispered word in the ear of power can be stronger than an incantation," said Wendolin. "He has chosen to lay low and go unnoticed. He may have lived in Kronivar for some time; Maëlveronde is very patient and his plans and deeds span many years. Zhindarren no doubt established himself as 'Greywood' long before you met him; he has gone by other names as well."

Aranstone looked at Wendolin with veiled contempt. "He has been with me for some time, old man. He has had no dealings with the Goblins."

"Has he?" said Wendolin, "He has not been to the north, perhaps, but you must be aware of the Goblin spies in the forests around Kronivar. They could have brought and delivered messages for him. And was it not at Greywood's suggestion that you purchased a house in northern Kronivar by the forest's edge for your secret meetings and deal-making?"

Aranstone remembered how Greywood had shown him the house but refused to admit that Wendolin's guess had been correct. Angrily he turned to the King, pausing a moment to regain control of his temper. "You suppose too much. If Greywood is a sorcerer, produce the proof. Otherwise end this charade before it sours the parley."

"I fear we have too little," said King Jordgen. He turned to Wendolin, who nodded his head.

"Alas, we have no proof or evidence to show you," Wendolin said, "It is true, you have only our word to go by. But at least consider what we have said. Zhindarren has already done his work, but you may yet see him for what he is."

Without answering Wendolin, Aranstone turned to the King. "Let us return to the matters at hand."

Talk then returned to the Goblins' siege and the defense of the Castle. King Jordgen claimed the west wing contained enough stores to last until the Kronivar troops arrived, though none could say when that would be. Certainly, Kronivar would have reacted to the Goblins' march into the mountains by now, he suggested, although the plateau would have to be retaken. Yet there was also the grim suggestion that the Goblins had utterly destroyed sections of the Mountain Road, making it impassable, so certain were they of their victory.

"It is a terrible thing to consider, but quite possible," Prince Varlen admitted. "Burzok is not beyond doing so. Eliminating all possibility of retreat would give the Goblin troops great incentive to succeed in taking the Castle."

"Destroying the Mountain Road would take time," said Clovenstone. "They would not be able to do much in their haste. Still, there are other things they could do."

"The Kronivar troops could arrive and find the Castle held against them," said the King, "That would be a worse trap than any they might encounter along the road. That would weaken Kronivar as well, which may even be part of their plan."

"In any event, we must hold the Castle as long as we can," said Varlen. "We cannot waste what we have by fighting each other."

"I agree," said Aranstone. He had seen how low his stores in the east wing were running. Only a few of his men knew as well, though rumors and complaints were spreading despite the trust Aranstone inspired.

"From what you have said, Aranstone, your forces are mostly in the east wing, and you may not have enough to continue to hold the center and the inner ward once the Goblins begin their attack," said Clovenstone. "Once the Goblins take those, any collaboration between us becomes impossible. Surely breaking us in two will be the first stage of their attack."

"True," said Aranstone, "Though the inner ward can be held with fewer men."

"But for how long?" said Varlen, "Have you enough to stand guard day and night?"

"For a while, with difficulty," Aranstone admitted. He thought about what Greywood said about the Goblins allowing all his men to walk out unharmed. He was certain Greywood could arrange it, just as he had claimed. There was no other way, Aranstone thought; either collaborate with the Castle forces or walk out and risk losing the Castle to the Goblins. Although he did not like King Jordgen, he saw the need for the Castle; a Goblin stronghold in the Mountains was too great a risk for Kronivar. Aranstone felt the need for Greywood's advice, and again felt anger at his being barred from the parley. Still, it was clear to him what had to be done.

"Then let us defend the inner ward together," said Varlen.

Aranstone turned back to the King. He paused, assessing the situation, and then spoke. "If we agree to cooperate in the defense of the Castle, including the east wing, will you agree to grant amnesty to all my men after the war, and allow us to return to Kronivar unhindered?"

At this the King turned to Prince Varlen and the two conferred privately. Aranstone guessed that amnesty had already been discussed among the King's advisors before the parley, and from what he knew of them, the King had probably been reluctant until Varlen had convinced him it was necessary.

"Amnesty would be granted to all but Greywood," said the King finally.

As the subject of Greywood surfaced again, all grew quiet.

"Either grant amnesty to all, or to none," said Aranstone, "I will not leave any of my men behind." He met King Jordgen's gaze. "Surely you can understand that."

Another silent pause swelled, and the King sat unmoving. He glanced to Wendolin and then back to Aranstone. None could say what his decision would be.

"My terms stand," said Aranstone. He leaned back and waited.

The King sat watching Aranstone, gauging his resolve. "Very well," said the King, his voice tinged with begrudging acceptance. "Amnesty will be granted to all, including Greywood."

The tension lessened, even as unease regarding Greywood remained, and gradually progress was made. Aranstone agreed to send word of the truce to Khale and Pyrwoed immediately so all would hear of it while the parley continued and defense plans were made. Rhiane brought a small writing table over and Aranstone began the notes to his captains. Ered wondered how they would be received when he delivered them.

"I hope we can be assured of your men's full cooperation," said the King as he watched Aranstone.

"They will follow my command," said Aranstone, mildly offended at the King's condescending doubt. "Have we not aided the Castle before? Recall that it was your own decree, Sire, which removed us from Kronivar and stationed us on the plateau to defend the Mountain Road."

King Jordgen was taken aback. "That was not my decree, but Grawson's," said the King, "He did so on his own, to protect the balance of power in Kronivar."

"Grawson?" Aranstone looked up, surprised.

The King looked to Varlen for the letter, which Varlen produced from a side table. "Grawson received a letter and a note," said the King. "He sent it here afterward to justify what he had done. It speaks of Orming's treachery, and names you and Greywood as not to be trusted. A note to you in Orming's own hand was sent along with the letter as proof. We had thought to use it here if you denied our charges."

"May I see it?" Aranstone was clearly shaken by the news. He reached for the letter and the King handed it to him.

King Jordgen watched as Aranstone sat reading. "It would seem not all your men were loyal to Orming," he said.

Aranstone examined the note from Orming, trying to remember when and even if he had seen it. He then turned to the letter and read it. As he did, he noted the writing, and how the 'Gr' in 'Grawson' looked familiar, finally realizing with horror that the handwriting was Greywood's. He barely managed to restrain his reaction and sat staring at the paper. There was no question about it; Greywood had deceived and betrayed him.

"It would seem not," Aranstone replied coldly, hiding his reaction. He handed the letter back to Varlen. With an effort, Aranstone calmly finished the notes to Khale and Pyrwoed. He debated adding something about Greywood but decided to wait and handle it himself. The irritation with Greywood he had felt of late had fermented into anger, and he was eager to confront Greywood and deal with him as soon as the parley was over.

When the notes were finished, Ered, Aranstone's aide, left to deliver them to the captains. Aranstone sat back, his mind whirling, his staid countenance betraying none of his turmoil. The King, Prince Varlen, Clovenstone, and the others continued as before, and Aranstone was soon engaged in discussing plans for the Castle defense. Recovering from the shock, he found himself more alert and quick-thinking than he had been in weeks. He still refused to believe Greywood was some kind of wizard or sorcerer, but here was the suggestion that he was a traitor, and to Aranstone there was no worse accusation.

Thin smoke trails curled and rose sluggishly from hanging incense burners, and candle flames flickered in the dimness of Maëlveronde's tent. Cold night winds howled outside, their sounds muted, while the air in the tent was still. Near the candles three leather-bound books were piled; a large red volume, a smaller green one on top of it, and an even smaller black one on top of them. The clasps of all three books were locked shut, their leathery covers glinting dully in the wavering candlelight. The floor of the tent was carpeted with furred pelts, and metal lampstands stood on carved wooden tables. Heat rose from a large firebowl plundered from Teska. Within the richly-appointed tent interior, Maëlveronde and Zhindarren sat resting in dark wooden armchairs. They had talked long and eagerly, as old friends do who have not seen each other in awhile, and now they were silent.

Their long-awaited time had come. The mood within the Castle had changed. After Khale and Pyrwoed had read Aranstone's notes, word of the truce had spread through the east wing and inner ward. The captains feared it would be difficult to convince the men to cooperate with the Castle guard whom they had until now been besieging, and some doubted whether the King's men would follow the truce once the doors to the west wing were opened. On both sides those who had fought bitterly were now reluctant and resentful. Others were relieved the truce had come before the Goblins attacked. Most understood the need for cooperation, so long as their roles and duties were clearly defined. Among the King's men, the issue of amnesty was hotly debated. Aranstone's men were glad to hear of it, but worried the King would not keep his word after the war. Still, the siege and dwindling supplies left no other alternatives.

Zhindarren had cursed silently upon hearing of the truce and slipped away unseen to the lower levels of the east wing. There he walked the halls through the dungeon, and left by a stair leading up to the outer ward. The heavy door there was barred solidly and no guard was posted there. In the outer ward, he turned himself over to the Goblin soldiers and told them to take him to the Grand Vizier. They brought him to Maëlveronde's tent, where his old friend and mentor awaited him. And now they sat, still basking in the warmth of long and satisfying conversation, tense in eager anticipation of what was to come.

Maëlveronde stirred. "Soon," he said quietly, his voice low and soothing, "soon shall the Doors be opened. I will have General Burzok begin the attack. Let us go now into the Stone Forest."

"I will send for the swords and bring them down to you," said Zhindarren.

They relaxed there awhile yet, enjoying the quiet stillness of the night. Candlelight played softly on their faces, the flames trembling in the slightest movements of air. The calm lingered a moment longer, like a pleasant aroma.

At last they roused themselves and stood, and Zhindarren followed Maëlveronde out of the tent. As they passed through the Goblin camp in the outer ward, Maëlveronde sent his message to General Burzok, and excitement grew among the Goblins as word spread that the attack was about to begin. Zhindarren led the way back to the door in the east wing that went down to the dungeon, and many Goblin guards stared in awe and wonderment to see the Grand Vizier pass by, led by an old man. Those who saw them entering the Castle were surprised and curious as to what was happening and grew in confidence that soon the Castle would be theirs.

As the evening wore on, the mood in the King's chamber calmed but remained intense. Ered returned and reported the captains' acceptance of Aranstone's plans. King Jordgen, Prince Varlen, Erland Clovenstone, Arlen Frosthelm, and Aranstone worked out the final details of the Castle defense, and all were pleased at the progress made. Earlier Rhiane had taken Wendolin back to one of the sickrooms, where he would be under Oellia's care. She had talked awhile with her sister, and with her niece and nephews who were playing happily and seemed to be faring well despite the siege. Now she returned and found the parley nearing its end.

"Together, my men should be able to hold the east wing," Aranstone assured them again. "With the inner ward secure, we will be able to push out into the outer ward. I am sure they understand the need to cooperate."

"There were difficulties between Teska and Farrenhale,' said Prince Varlen, "and they fell. May we fare better."

"In the last great war, our alliance with the Elves brought us victory, even though all did not always go smoothly," Clovenstone reminded them.

"Yes," said the King, "Swords were made to help forge the alliance, but they were lost before they could be put to use."

"I have heard of these 'Lost Swords of the Alliance', as they are sometimes called," said Aranstone, "Then they are not simply legend or rumor?"

"Near enough," said the King, "They were never completed; the gems housed in their hilts never arrived, and the swords went into hiding when all looked bleak. We thought they were forever lost; and then they were found. We had hoped to use them at Farrenhale and Teska, but now they are lost again." He looked grimly at the gathering. "It is even possible that they have already fallen into Goblin hands."

Aranstone thought about the two ornate swords that Orven had and wondered if they might be used in a similar fashion, perhaps by himself and the King. He supposed that such a generous offer might begin to atone for his misdeeds, and perhaps even help him win the King's favor which would be of use to Kronivar after the war. They had agreed to discuss the situation in Kronivar further, and Aranstone was determined now to do what he could to create favorable conditions for negotiations.

"We have ornate swords that might be used to similar purpose," Aranstone said. "They are stationed at the top of the grand staircase leading into the west wing."

"Send for them," said King Jordgen, pleased at Aranstone's offer. "We should begin redeploying the men right away."

Aranstone turned to his aide. "Ered, bring Orven here with both swords, and have him send his men over to Olmic, in the east wing."

Ered nodded and left the room.

Rhiane turned to Aranstone, suddenly very curious. "Do you mean Orven Ambersheath?"

Aranstone was startled and wondered just how much Rhiane knew of his doings. "Yes," he admitted, "Orven Ambersheath. Did you know him in Kronivar?"

"No," she said, "but I have heard of him." Rhiane looked at the King, wondering if she should not have said anything. She could tell the King was anxious to see the swords, but as he said nothing, neither did she.

"I see," said Aranstone, sensing there was more left unsaid. "Well, at any rate, he shall soon be here, and you can talk to him yourself."

"Still no word; I wonder if we should go?" said Orven. He and his friends along with Rafnel and Strable still sat guard at the wide double doors at the top of the stairway. Orven was tired of such dull duty and the others were weary of it as well. "If there's really a truce, they don't need us here, do they? Maybe they want us somewhere else now."

"Well, you're a Captain," Max reminded him, "The other Captains won't tell you what to do. Aranstone's at a parley; maybe Greywood has orders for us. Or you could just decide on something yourself."

"Maybe I should find out from Khale or Pyrwoed where we're needed the most," said Orven, "they seem to know."

Just then they heard someone coming up the stairs. Orven turned, and saw it was Trelt, who lately had been acting as a messenger between Aranstone and Greywood and the Captains. Orven still disliked Trelt, and guessed the feeling was mutual.

"Orven," Trelt said when he was near enough, "Greywood wants the swords sent to the front." He eyed Gorflange on Orven's belt, and then looked around. "Where's the other one?"

"Ripley has it," said Orven, unwilling to volunteer anything beyond what was necessary.

"And where is Ripley?" Trelt sounded annoyed at Orven's reticence.

"He went to relieve himself," Orven said, hoping Trelt would regret asking. "We'll leave as soon as he gets back. You can tell Greywood we're coming."

Trelt glared at Orven, taking the hint to leave and irked that Orven would not come with him right away. "Don't take too long in coming," he said, trying to sound threatening even though they all knew there was nothing he could do about it. He turned and went down the stairs again.

Orven sighed when Trelt was gone. "Well, it looks like Ripley and I will be busy after all. ...Where is Ripley anyway? He can't be taking this long."

"He probably got distracted again," said Roy. "He's been more jittery than usual. He can't sit up here for more than half an hour without getting up to walk around somewhere."

"They should have stationed him on the wall," said Aaron. He yawned. "I'm bored, too, but at least it's warmer in here."

"Well, we may not be up here much longer. I'll find out if they want us over there, and then send word," said Orven.

"Just don't send Trelt," said Roy.

"Agreed," Orven paused, looking over the railing and growing impatient. "Where is that Ripley?" He started down the stairs. "I'll look for him on the way to the east wing. If he comes back, send him over there."

"I will," said Max. "And don't forget about us waiting over here, either."

"It won't be long," said Orven, already halfway down the first flight of stairs.

Maëlveronde walked slowly through the Stone Forest. The air was cold and damp, and all was quiet. Around him rows of the tall, stone pillars carved to resemble tree trunks stretched off into the dark, out of his circle of torchlight. Here and there he lit torches ensconced on the pillars, until the place was aglow with flickering light and shadow. High overhead the pillars widened into soot-blackened capitals designed to look like spreading branches and leaves that met and filled the vaulted ceilings. Maëlveronde made his way through the hall, stopping in the central chamber, an open circular space twenty feet across and ringed about by pillars. He lit torches all around the circle and gazed above into the round dome, where a night sky with constellations was painted. It had been quite some time since he was last in the Stone Forest, and the pleasure of past visits returned to him now. He paused looking at the constellations in the dome, little painted stars that were only seen by firelight.

After a moment he moved on through the Forest again, lighting torches and working his way north, to the wide area along the back wall where the Doors of the Angkhadra sloped up out of the floor. There he lit all the torches he could find, until the stone doors were well lit and their engravings filled with shadow. He set the torch aside and looked upon the doors. Eager anticipation thrilled through him and he had to calm himself to keep from trembling.

Maëlveronde set down the folded cloth bundle he had been carrying and walked up the incline of the doors, kneeling down in the center, near the quincunx of indentations set in the central circle that overlapped both doors. He ran his hand gently over the circle, caressing the indentations, his breathing deeper and slower now.

He raised his left hand in front of him, and the large red gem on his ring sparkled in the firelight from all sides. He whispered a word of release, and the ring's setting opened like a claw, freeing the red gem. He took the gem and placed it in the central indentation in the quincunx, where it fit snugly inside the rock as though the indentation had been cut to fit the gem. Maëlveronde smiled and removed the gem, putting it back in his ring. He could barely wait for Zhindarren to bring the other gems and wondered what was keeping him. Maëlveronde stood again, gazing down at the inscriptions on the doors he had studied over so many years. He had come to believe that he had a good idea of what lay behind them, and tonight, finally, he would find out if he was right.

Maëlveronde heard footsteps echo somewhere far off in the hall. He walked down the gently sloping doors and onto the floor again. *At last*, he thought, as he passed into the Stone Forest, listening to the wandering footsteps as they drew closer.

"Orven must have found him," said Roy, "otherwise Ripley would have been back by now."

"I hope so," said Max, "I'm about ready to go looking for him myself."

Suddenly a *thunk* and the sound of a big bolt being drawn back made them jump. After a moment's pause one of the big wooden doors they were guarding began to swing open. Rafnel and Strable seemed mildly amused, while Roy and Aaron looked in surprise to Max.

"Well, there's a truce now, so I suppose it's alright," said Max, shrugging.

The door opened and a young dwarf, whom they had seen with Aranstone, stepped out. "Where is Orven?" said Ered, "Aranstone wants him to come and bring both swords to the parley, while the rest of you are to be stationed in the east wing, under Captain Olmic's command, until Orven returns."

"Looks like Greywood beat him to it," said Max, "He just called the swords to the front, and that's where Orven and Ripley took them."

"They went to Greywood?" said Ered, alarmed.

"Yes," said Max, curious now. "Why? What happened?"

Ered stood still a moment, thinking hard. "Go to the east wing and send Orven and the swords back here as soon as you can, Aranstone's orders. Tell Greywood that General Aranstone commands it, if he resists."

"Resists?" said Aaron, puzzled. "Why would he resist?"

"Go now," said Ered with great urgency. "I'll return and tell them." And with that he slipped inside the door again, and guards on the other side pulled it shut.

"What was all that about, I wonder?" said Max. The dwarves and Rafnel and Strable got up and began down the stairs. "Well, at least we won't have to sit around here any longer! A change will do us good."

"Unless it gets us killed," said Aaron.

At the parley, Ered reported what had happened to Orven and the swords.

"Greywood!" exclaimed the King. He turned angrily to Aranstone. "Do you believe us now, do you see how this sorcerer has deceived you?"

Aranstone ignored the King's tone. "Sorcerer or not, he is a traitor, and that is enough for me." He rose from his chair. "I will go and deal with Greywood myself."

"You will need help," said the King. "If you will not believe what we have said, you do so at your own peril. Do not endanger our swords as well!"

Aranstone caught how King Jordgen had said "our swords" and wondered anew if Orven's swords were indeed the very swords of which they had just spoken. If so, more was at stake, and recovering them would mean a greater bargaining chip for Kronivar after the war. "Very well," he conceded, looking to the group, "who will come with me?"

As the King and Prince Varlen conferred, a desperate knock at the door startled them. A page opened it and stepped into the room bowing before anyone bid him enter.

"Begging your Majesty's pardon," he began, nearly out of breath, "but the Goblins have begun their attack on the Castle."

The King rose from his chair. "We must go now. Varlen, see to it that the inner ward is secured with Castle troops and Aranstone's men redeployed to the east wing as soon as possible without losing our hold of the west wing. Make haste, lest the east wing be lost. Erland, assign guards to accompany Aranstone, and see to it that stores be moved to the east wing as needed."

The King's chamber was suddenly astir again as each left to fulfill the King's orders. King Jordgen left with Varlen to oversee the Castle's defense, and Arlen and Rhiane were the last to leave.

"Go and tell Wendolin what has happened, see what he can suggest, if anything," Arlen told his daughter as he departed down the hall.

Rhiane hurried downstairs, on her way to the back room where Wendolin lay. Thoughts of the swords, Zhindarren, and Orven filled her restless mind. *If only Iaven had stopped Orven in the mountains*, she thought, knowing she should not dwell on it now, and wanting badly to believe that it did not change what she felt about Iaven.

Orven walked all the way to the latrine and back to the west staircase, and still there was no sign of Ripley. He looked around, trying to imagine where Ripley would go, and descended a flight of stairs into a dimly lit hall. Orven stopped when he noticed the hilt of his sword. The small blue-green stone set into the pommel was glowing, and at once he drew the sword and moved it to see where the glow was the strongest.

"Maëlveronde," Orven muttered quietly to himself. *Was that possible?* he thought, *Maëlveronde, here in the Castle?* But they could not be certain Maëlveronde still had the last gem, after so many years; he could have died and someone else might have it. Yet Orven felt almost instinctively that it was Maëlveronde, unlikely though it seemed to him.

Suddenly Orven realized that what had just happened to him could have happened to Ripley. Halix still had one stone missing, and Ripley would have gone after it without a second thought.

Ripley! Orven thought, *I've got to find him before he finds Maëlveronde...* Orven tried to determine which way to go. The lowest level was dark and the guards were gone. He lifted Gorflange and pointing it east he saw the blue-green light shine the strongest. Farther down the hall, the entrance to the Stone Forest loomed in the dark ahead of him. Unexpected firelight glowed within it. He leveled Gorflange to be sure of the direction. The blue-green glow grew stronger still, lighting his face and making him blink in the dimness. Then, all at once, the light winked out entirely, leaving him in the dark.

It took Orven a moment to realize what had happened. At first, he thought the direction had changed; but the light would glow no more, regardless of where he pointed the sword. *The gem must have been put into the sword*, he thought. But Ripley could not have simply found the gem lying around by itself; something must have happened. Orven felt a sickening panic rising within him and fought to keep it under control. He gripped Gorflange's hilt, and with sword drawn, walked cautiously into the Stone Forest.

Chapter 42.
In the Stone Forest

Smoke, flame, and the shouts of angry Goblins, Dwarves, and Men filled the night air around the Castle. Fiery missiles flew into the inner ward, and archers shot from the walls. Despite the truce, Aranstone's men were loath to hand the inner ward over to the King's guard, but they knew they would not be able to hold it much longer. The east wing was likewise in danger of falling to the Goblins. Ladders and grappling hooks assaulted the outer walls and Goblins swarmed like flies on a carcass. Anguished cries went up amidst the hiss of arrows and terrible rumbling thuds of battering rams pounding the gates of the inner ward. Even the sobering cold November mountain air could not dispel the nauseating swirl of noise, smoke, and chaos filling the Castle's walls and wards.

King Jordgen led the defense of the west wing, which the Castle Guard held firmly, for all had been readied there during Aranstone's siege. The messaging tower was theirs again, and the Dwarves worked to regain the western run of the outer wall, which was needed for the retaking of the outer ward. Fighting atop the wall was bitter and harsh and no progress was made. Some wondered if they would be able to hold out against the Goblins until Kronivar troops arrived.

The Goblin army's main forces, led by General Burzok, pushed into the inner ward to break the castle defense in half. Battering rams lunged at the gates and portcullises, and bands of augglins clamored nearby waiting to pour inside. Thick iron pegs and hooks dug into the masonry of the inner ward, and goblins and augglins climbed up them onto the wall. Prince Varlen's men gradually took over the defense from Aranstone's men as they went to hold the east wing. Supplies were moved into the Castle, and stores transferred between the Castle wings. A rain of rocks and arrows fell from above making even the simplest tasks treacherous. Aranstone's men and the Castle troops worked together as lingering resentment gave to way to begrudging cooperation and they all saw the loss of hope in each other's eyes.

Many thought it was already too late. At several entrances the Goblins had broken through and were fighting their way inside. After three days of siege, the Goblins were rested and eager for shelter and warmer quarters. Their morale was high and recent victories gave their deeds a strong-willed surety. Erog Del-Sorhar, Chief Spy of the Goblins, oversaw the attack inside the east wing. His cunning and decisiveness assured their success, provided the Goblins could gain enough ground quickly and hold it. Aranstone's men rushed in from the inner ward but were only able to stem the tide, barely keeping the Goblins from advancing any further. Amidst the torch-lit halls and stairways, goblins fought dwarves and men, grunts and taunts echoing with the clang of swords and fearsome roaring of augglins. Thanks to Zhindarren, the Goblins knew exactly where Aranstone's stores were kept and fought their way toward them.

Max and Roy were stationed on the ground floor with Aranstone's men. The company fought to keep the Goblins out of the large audience chambers and push them back down the hall, where two large augglins stood in the vanguard holding the doorway. Aranstone's cohort had succeeded in killing one of the augglins, though it had taken over a dozen men and three had been lost in the effort. Roy was gripped by mortal terror at the sight of the augglins and weakened by their foul smell, but he refused to let his fear master him. Max thought they were spread too thin to hold the east wing and gave his all in the defense. At last, more of Aranstone's men arrived, relieving those in the front line and assuring their hold on the hall.

"Well, I guess we're fighting to defend the Castle after all," said Max.

"I hope we're not too late," said Roy.

"Don't talk like that," said Max, though he felt the same. "We've got to keep trying. We're all on the same side now."

"I just wish Ripley and Orven were here, too," said Roy. They had left Aaron working in the inner ward on their way to the east wing, but still had no idea where Orven and Ripley were.

"We'll find them," Max said, "They're probably busy with goblins somewhere around here."

Just then Greywood entered the hall, his movements quick and impatient. Anger flared in his eyes, and in his wrath he seemed more than just an old gray-bearded man. He stood before them suddenly, and they feared him. "Where's Orven?" he demanded. "Why has he not come?"

"He said he was coming here," said Max, wondering why Greywood was so concerned about Orven. "We haven't seen him. He could be anywhere in the east wing, I suppose."

Greywood impaled them with an angry gaze a moment longer, as though expecting them to confess or deciding their fate if they didn't. Then he turned abruptly and left them.

"Do you think Orven's in trouble?" said Roy once Greywood was gone.

"Wouldn't surprise me," said Max. Down the hall, the crash of swords and shouts grew again as the Goblins began another charge. "Right now, we have troubles enough of our own."

Orven approached the archway that led into the Stone Forest. In the flickering orange firelight, the pillars carved to look like the trunks of trees seemed ancient yet alive. Orven moved slower now, finding himself hesitant to enter. *Ripley*, he thought again, *I have to find Ripley...* Orven pushed himself to move forward. His steps were sluggish as he entered the Stone Forest, and finally he stopped.

Orven stood still listening. All was quiet within, except the sounds of air moving and the slow burning of torches ensconced on the pillars. Orven wanted to call to Ripley but was afraid to make a sound. He stood there awhile, fear holding him back. He tightened his grip Gorflange's hilt, hoping it would bolster his confidence as it had in the past. With a great effort he walked in, passing between the pillars.

Inside the Stone Forest only a few scattered torches were lit, casting small circles of firelight with darkness in between them. Widening shadows wavered behind torchlit pillars, stretching and merging into the surrounding dark. The air was damp and cold. Orven walked carefully and lightly, trying to make as little sound as possible. He passed from light to dark and into light again, casting furtive glances all around him. There seemed to be no one there. He moved on, following the path of torchlight, wondering if Ripley had done the same. A wide, well-lit central chamber opened before him, but he was afraid to enter it. He walked around it, cautiously looking in. All remained silent.

He wandered until he came to the eastern end of the Stone Forest, near the entrance to the dungeons. Orven wondered if Ripley had gone inside. He walked further and saw a dark heap on the floor near the wall. A single torch burned nearby, and as he moved closer it looked like a blanket or cloth spread on top of something. He knelt down and drew it back. Ripley lay slain beneath it.

Orven pulled back in horror. "*Ripley!*" he shouted, agonized, his voice catching in his throat in terror as he heard it echo through the Stone Forest. He pulled the blanket away and saw Halix was missing. He looked around for it, but it was gone.

Then his gaze fell upon the cloth that had covered Ripley. It was not a blanket at all, but something like a tapestry. He took it and straightened it out, the firelight revealing an image woven into it.

Orven sat frozen in fear. The image was of the Stone Forest, where a tall black-caped figure holding a sword stood poised over a fallen dwarf. Even in the faint light, Orven recognized the sword in the figure's hand, and the one on the floor just out of the dwarf's reach. As his mind clouded with raw, black panic he recognized the fallen dwarf as himself.

His hands trembling, Orven dropped the tapestry. He tried to fathom what it meant and how it had come to be, certain now that he was not alone in the Stone Forest. He stood up, searching around him. He knew he must have been heard; he had been expected, in fact, and allowed to come to the body and the tapestry. He went along the eastern wall in the dark until he came to the dungeon entrance, but even before he came to it he knew it would be locked. The only way out was through the Stone Forest. He walked a few steps back into it, and heard other footsteps approaching.

"*Orven!*" called a low, menacing but soothing voice, and Orven found himself having to resist answering it. He whirled around and caught sight of a black-clad shape moving between the pillars toward him. Maëlveronde wielded Halix in his hand, and it now held all three gems. He stood at the end of a short corridor formed by pillars, a dark figure silhouetted against the torchlight. The light was weak but Orven could still make out Maëlveronde's short black beard rimming his face and the whites of his eyes glowering beneath his brow.

As Orven saw the sword in Maëlveronde's hand he remembered the one in his own and raised it higher. It burned with power in his grip, but the metal was cold in his clammy palm. He realized his arm was shaking.

Maëlveronde seemed amused. He had relished the idea of a swordfight ever since Zhindarren had told him about Orven. "Well, Orven? Care to avenge your friend?" he said in a calm, cold voice sheathed with venom.

Orven was so frightened he could not move or speak, his fear growing as Maëlveronde slowly moved closer. He even debated whether he ought to drop the sword and run, when Maëlveronde sprang forward and swung at him. Orven reacted on instinct, raising the sword and barely fending off Maëlveronde's blow. He stepped back nervously and delivered a blow of his own, but Maëlveronde caught it and laughed at him. Orven tried again, his fear and humiliation flashing into raw anger as thoughts of Ripley returned. Orven raised Gorflange high and fought back, his thrusts poorly aimed but vigorous and wild.

Maëlveronde met each blow with a quickness and force that surprised Orven, who suddenly realized Gorflange gave him no advantage over Halix. Orven fought back hard, already giving in to despair. Fear made him unable to concentrate or think clearly. Orven felt the same sense of speed that Gorflange always gave him, but Maëlveronde moved even faster. Flames on the torches around them flickered slowly as they fought and moved between the pillars. Orven tried every feint and attack he knew and still Maëlveronde anticipated his moves and kept the upper hand. The swords clashed and sparks sprang from the blades. Orven sensed Maëlveronde was only toying with him, and saw his youthful strength and anger were no match for a lifetime of skill and guiles. He began to tire, his moves all defensive ones now, and found himself falling back as Maëlveronde advanced.

Orven pulled back and ran between the pillars into the dark, hoping to get away from Maëlveronde and out of the Stone Forest altogether. But during the fight he had lost his sense of direction and he ran deeper into the Forest instead of out of it. Pressed against the back of a pillar, Orven stood still, hiding and listening as he tried to calm his breathing. He heard Maëlveronde's footsteps, slow and deliberate, their echoes making it difficult to know exactly where he was. Orven waited and listened and knew he would not be able to hide for long.

Rhiane hurried through the halls to the back room where Wendolin lay. The room was bright with candlelight and filled with the high, spirited voices of children at play. Oellia's little boys, Hamet and Horlen, wore large, folded paper hats and were sparring with big, wooden toy swords. The boys were cheerful and rambunctious, blissfully oblivious to the war going on outside. But Oellia, drawn and anxious, looked to Rhiane now for more news of the parley, and joined her at Wendolin's bedside.

Rhiane told Wendolin of the end of the parley and how Orven and the swords had been sent to Greywood at the front. When she was done, she sat back with Oellia, waiting to see what Wendolin might suggest, since he was in no condition to go into battle himself.

Wendolin sat pondering what she had said. "The swords were taken to the front? They were called for, but did they arrive there?"

"I suppose so, but I don't know for certain," said Rhiane. "If they fell into the hands of the enemy, surely the enemy would flaunt them, and likewise if Aranstone and the King have them, everyone would soon hear of it."

"Find out," said Wendolin, "Quickly. And send Iaven to me."

"Iaven?" said Rhiane. She nodded and got up to go. "As you wish. I know where he's stationed."

"I thought you might," said Wendolin.

Deep in the Stone Forest Orven moved from pillar to pillar, straining to hear Maëlveronde's footsteps. All was silent, and that scared Orven even more. He fought to master his fear and glanced out from behind a pillar. Seeing nothing, he slid over to the next one. A short distance away he saw a brighter space where the pillars seemed to cease. With slow and quiet movements, he made his way over to it.

Orven hoped he had found the way out, but his heart sank when he saw he was somewhere else instead. Great, thick slabs of stone angled up out of the floor, inscribed with lettering he did not recognize. He stepped out from the pillars to get a better look at them. They looked like doors, larger than any he had ever seen, and he wondered where they led.

Suddenly Orven caught sight of something out of the corner of his eye. Maëlveronde stood off to his right, ten feet away. Orven heard a sharp laugh, but the sound, or perhaps its echo, seemed to come from his left. He turned and there was another figure of Maëlveronde standing a few yards in the other direction. Orven froze in fear and tried to run back into the Forest the way he had come, but stopped as a third figure of Maëlveronde appeared at the edge of the Forest. Yet another such phantom appeared behind Orven, all four of them circling him now, swords on the ready and moving in step, identical in appearance and movement. Unsure which one was the real Maëlveronde, Orven turned frantically, afraid to let any of them out of his sight. Another laugh echoed as the four figures stalked around Orven.

Orven's bloodlust for battle drained away and he realized his folly. He looked around nervously, seeing he was surrounded.

"Do you want to see the doors opened?" Maëlveronde taunted. "Foolish dwarf! Drop your sword and I may let you live! I will have it in the end, one way or another." The voice circled him and Orven tried to follow it. The figures moved closer as the circle tightened. Orven sensed Maëlveronde was about to strike and raw fear rose like bile within him.

Orven raised Gorflange in defense, watching the figures of Maëlveronde, trying to determine which one was real. They all looked exactly alike. Orven could wait no longer, and with a loud cry he plunged forward behind Gorflange at the figure blocking the way into the Stone Forest. Orven half-expected to feel the return blow of Maëlveronde's sword, but instead he plowed through the phantom as it dispersed like black fog. Orven kept going, turning this way and that around the pillars, losing his way, and he could hear Maëlveronde's footfalls somewhere behind him. Afraid of falling into another trap or dead end, he found another hiding place in the dark and stood as quietly as he could, trying to think. He heard nothing more, though he knew Maëlveronde was still on the move.

Orven's heart pounded hard and felt like it would burst. Panting harshly, he tried to control his breathing before it gave him away. He looked around in the dark, still unsure of the way out. And wherever it was, Maëlveronde might be already waiting there and watching for him. Orven suddenly felt very small and helpless, and wondered why he had ever thought so highly of himself. But it was too late now to dwell on such things, he realized. Once his breathing calmed he began moving again, stiff and cautious, pillar to pillar, expecting Maëlveronde around every corner with the cold, shining blade of Halix ready to cut him down.

Iaven arrived in the sickroom still wondering why Rhiane had sent for him. There, Wendolin rested on his bed and Oellia watched her children playing. Seeing such a happy domestic scene amidst the war made Iaven long for Hillbrook. The Goblin encroachment had made him feel he would never see it again.

Iaven came by the wizard's bedside. "Wendolin, are you feeling any better? Rhiane says Maëlveronde is here with the Goblins. Will you help us fight against him?"

"Perhaps," said Wendolin, "As I can; confined to my bed here. I am an old man, Iaven, and I mend slowly. In time I may recover fully, though it will not be soon."

Rhiane returned, and it was clear from her pace that other tasks awaited her. "No sign of the swords or of Orven, as far as I could find," she told Wendolin. She looked to Iaven, and there was love where their eyes met. "Come back down as soon as you can," she told him, "We're trying to retake the outer wall, and Varlen will need as many there as can be found."

"I will," said Iaven. Rhiane smiled at him and left, and Iaven resolved to prove his worth to Varlen and the King.

"It may be as I feared," said Wendolin. "Orven has gone missing, as have the swords. No one has had any news regarding them." He shifted about slightly, silently enduring a momentary flaring of pain. "And I have sensed Maëlveronde using his powers, far below us and to the east; inside the Castle, I think."

Iaven grew solemn. "The Stone Forest," he said, recalling the tapestry from Teska.

"Yes," said Wendolin, "Orven and his friends were stationed by the doors at the top of the Grand Staircase leading into the west wing. The same stairs lead down below, and it is quite possible Orven may have gone down there. I fear he has. The other sword may have been taken down there as well."

"Then the tapestry has come true."

"It may and it may not," Wendolin chided, "We may be given to see these events to stop them from happening. Do you understand? Let us prevent them if we can."

"What can we do? Can you help us?" asked Iaven. "If you can't fight Maëlveronde—"

"You must go in my stead," said Wendolin, watching Iaven.

Iaven was stunned and thought Wendolin was joking, but saw he was not. He began to wonder if perhaps Wendolin was more ill than anyone had supposed.

"Not to fight Maëlveronde, but to help Orven escape," said Wendolin. "It will be dangerous, of course. There is not much else we can do. Otherwise both

Orven and the swords will be lost. You do want to save him, don't you?"

"Of course," said Iaven. He was still angry with Orven and would be for some time, but they were brothers and Iaven could not imagine losing him. "What do you want me to do?"

"Our only hope of subduing Maëlveronde is to take him by surprise in an ambush; and even if it succeeds many soldiers' lives will surely be lost. But we must try. I have already asked Oellia to arrange it in the halls below the west wing. You must go in and lure Maëlveronde out of the Stone Forest and away from Orven. That is all, and it is quite enough," said Wendolin.

Iaven did not like the sound of Wendolin's plan, but saw there was nothing else they could do. "So it has to be me," he said, "Orven and I look alike, but how can we know what he was wearing?"

"We can put the weaving to our own use," said Wendolin, "Do you remember it?"

Iaven nodded. The image was burned into his mind. "He was wearing his gray cloak. I have one just like it."

"And a pale shirt and pants of dark brown," said Wendolin. He motioned to Oellia to bring the clothes over. "I have not been lying here idle. These are as close as we could find; they will have to do. The Stone Forest is dark, and Maëlveronde will not be expecting more than one Orven, at any rate. Now there's just one more thing we need. Give me your sword."

Iaven drew his sword and handed it to Wendolin. The old wizard looked at it, measuring the blade, and frowned. "Too long," he said, setting it aside. "You have the right scabbard on your belt, but you'll need a sword like Gorflange. Which gems did Orven have in it?"

Iaven recalled the image again. "Green, purple, and yellow," he said, "In that order."

"Good," said Wendolin. He sat up and glanced about the room. Oellia came to see what he needed. "Swords," Wendolin said, "are there any other swords in here?"

Oellia brought over one that had been leaning by the wall. "Allé left it here for me, should I need it, will it do?" she said.

Wendolin looked at it and handed it back. "Also too long," he said sadly. He looked over where the children were playing. "Hamet!" he called, and the boy ran over to him. "There's a fine young fellow," Wendolin smiled, "May I see that a moment?" Hamet gave Wendolin the wooden sword he had been playing with. Wendolin seemed pleased. "I think this will do," he said.

"A *wooden* sword?" Iaven objected.

"Wait!" Wendolin commanded, and all were silent. He focused his attention on the sword in his hand and drew his free hand up and down in the air near it, whispering incantations in some ancient tongue. As Iaven watched, the wood began to shine and appear silvery, and forms and shapes became distinct on the hilt, until he saw they were vines and leaves. And in dark holes amidst the leaves, three gems slowly grew visible.

Oellia gasped and Hamet clapped his hands with joy. Iaven watched in rapt amazement, until Wendolin finished and turned to him. "Well, Iaven, what do you think? I helped design them originally, but it has been many years since I last saw them. Does it look right?"

"Close enough," said Iaven, still dumbfounded. The sword was vague in places and lacking fine detail that could only be seen up close, but for the most part it was convincing. "Those leaves there were a little more curved, maybe, otherwise it looks fine."

Wendolin motioned with a whispered word once more and the leaves adjusted themselves. "There," he said, "Maëlveronde will never suspect."

Seeing the sword gave Iaven confidence but as soon as he held it his mood sank again. The hilt was wood in his hand, with none of the heft or weight of a real sword. "It still feels like a wooden sword," Iaven complained.

"It still *is* a wooden sword," said Wendolin, "Do you think I can turn wood into steel? It is only an illusion, nothing more."

"What good will that do me?" said Iaven.

"Remember, you are not going in there to *fight* Maëlveronde, only to lure him out of the Stone Forest," said Wendolin. "Do not get too near him! We only want him to follow you to the west wing. You must be very careful. And do not take too long, either."

Iaven changed his clothes and put on his gray cloak. He kept looking at the sword, amazed at how it felt like wood but looked like steel. Suddenly he looked to Wendolin anxiously. "If wizards can sense each other's use of magic, won't he know it's an illusion?"

"He has been exercising his own powers of late, I can feel it even now," said Wendolin. "As long as he does so, he will not notice it. Still, there is a risk. That is also why you cannot take too long. And why we must hurry. You have all that you need; leave now. The ambush will be waiting." Wendolin looked at Iaven and Oellia. "*Go!*" he commanded, and they obeyed.

As they emerged into the dark hallway at the bottom of the stairs on the lowest level, Oellia laid a hand on Iaven's shoulder, and he turned to see a darkened corridor into the west wing where soldiers were gathering quietly with swords drawn and bows on the ready. "We'll be waiting for you," she whispered, and for a moment she reminded him so much of her sister that Iaven felt a great pang of desire for Rhiane. "Don't take too long," Oellia told him. And with one last look she turned and hurried down the corridor. Iaven glanced around making sure he knew where to lead Maëlveronde, and then walked alone toward the Stone Forest.

Iaven approached the entrance where the pale orange glow of torchlight flickered within. The air was humid, with a slight chill. It was quiet inside, and that made him uneasy. He stopped momentarily and had to force himself to enter. He hoped to come across Orven early on, so he wouldn't have to go anywhere near Maëlveronde. It would probably not be as simple as that, Iaven thought, hoping it wasn't merely a fool's errand ending in death.

Iaven passed through the arch into the forest of pillars, his pace slowing as he thought about why he had come. Not because Wendolin had told him to, or because he loved Rhiane, or to prove something to the King or even to himself:

it was for Orven that he was here. Iaven was still angry with his brother and did not know what he would say when he found him. He was still upset and would have it all out with Orven once they were safe. And if Orven was stubborn and refused to leave the Stone Forest? Iaven had not considered that possibility, and decided he would force Orven to leave, whatever it took. And so he continued walking amidst the pillars, the faltering torchlight, and the smell of smoke and cold, damp stone.

Iaven still did not see anyone, but sensed a presence there. He tingled with nervous energy. Slowly, he made his way toward the open area under the central vault. The scene from the weaving took place there, and he had a strong, sickening feeling he would arrive just in time to see it happening and become Maëlveronde's next victim. *It doesn't have to come true*, he reminded himself, and resisted believing it.

Ahead lay the torchlit central vault. Iaven's view between the pillars widened and he saw it was empty. He was so sure he would find someone there that he now had no idea where to go next. He stepped out into the open circle, looking around, hoping he might hear something. It was brighter there, and the torches ringing the circle made the dimness of the Forest beyond it appear even darker. Here he would be seen; that was why he had come, but now he wished he had stayed out of the open. Staring into Forest, Iaven heard something stir. The tall, black-garbed figure of Maëlveronde stepped from the dark into the circle. With a jolt of recognition Iaven saw Halix in his hand. He gasped and wondered if he was too late. Iaven turned to run when he noticed three more black figures of Maëlveronde surrounding him at the circle's edge, all posed alike and moving identically, each wielding another Halix. Iaven whirled around in shock, raising his sword half-heartedly as he searched for an escape.

Maëlveronde laughed softly and stepped forward, closing the circle around Iaven more tightly. Iaven brandished the wooden sword, hoping it would buy him time to think. He watched the figures, trying to discern what was real, and as he did they began circling him. Iaven took his chances; only one Maëlveronde was real. He raised his sword and lunged at one of the figures, realizing only too late its solidity. Maëlveronde swung Halix, catching the blade of the wooden sword and knocking it from Iaven's hand, and on the downswing Halix's tip tore across Iaven's chest. It might have killed Iaven had he not lost his balance and fallen backward, the wooden sword flying out of his hand and onto the floor with a clatter.

Iaven collapsed to the ground, pain burning across the left side of his chest. The cold stone floor pressed against his head and his body ached. His mind swam with fright and shock. Blackness crept in from the edges and he fought it back as he could.

Maëlveronde walked up to where Iaven lay on the floor, the circle of phantoms likewise closing in tighter. It had been too easy, he thought; Orven had so quickly lost his nerve and given up. Maëlveronde looked at the body at his feet. Halix wavered in his hand. He expected Orven would be defeated, and that Gorflange would be his. But something was wrong, and Maëlveronde could not decide what it was. The dwarf was the same; there was the scabbard on his belt. He glanced to where the sword lay on the floor. After years of planning and waiting, here at last was Gorflange, three gems glinting in the hilt; all the gems were his now. And yet— Maëlveronde leaned forward slightly, staring at the sword where it had landed with a clatter. *With a clatter*, Maëlveronde realized, a *clatter*, not a *clang*; the sound of wood, not metal. Suspecting a trick of some kind, he reduced his magic to nothing, the phantoms dispersing and fading away. Now he saw it clearly; the sword was nothing more than illusion and wood. It looked just like Gorflange, and only one wizard knew the swords' design so well. Fury rose within him. "*Wendolin!*" he uttered with malice under his breath.

Maëlveronde's anger flashed and erupted. Suddenly a shout echoed behind him. The shock of a sharp, searing, raging pain exploding in his side was worse than anything he had felt in many, many years.

Orven could not believe what he was seeeing. He had been hiding in the dark of the Stone Forest, watching the open circle under the vaulted ceiling. Orven hoped Maëlveronde would pass through, revealing where he was going, so Orven could slip away and escape. But Maëlveronde had not come. And then, amazingly, Iaven had stepped into the circle, carrying what appeared to be one of the swords. Orven was shocked. *He'll get himself killed*, Orven thought, *What is he doing?* And that sword— where did Iaven get it from, and what good would it do him? It looked like Gorflange, but had to be just an ordinary sword, he thought. It made no sense, and something about it made him very apprehensive.

Iaven stood there, looking around, and Orven almost called out to him. He was about to when Maëlveronde appeared. As he did, Orven's view of Iaven darkened, obscured momentarily by one of the phantoms appearing. Iaven gasped and was clearly at a loss for what to do. Orven watched as Iaven tried keeping Maëlveronde back and then and saw the other figures. As Iaven raised his sword, Orven felt a sorrow and concern for his brother that surprised him. It was as though he were seeing himself in danger. Orven watched Iaven, unsure what to do, the phantoms passing and blocking his view as they circled Iaven while he frantically looked for an escape.

With a low, quiet, satisfied laugh, Maëlveronde suddenly closed the circle, the figures moving faster. Iaven was panicking now and Orven wanted badly to help his brother, ashamed that his fear of Maëlveronde kept him from moving. Then Iaven lunged with the sword, trying to escape, and Maëlveronde swung at him. Orven watched in horror as Iaven fell, the sword knocked from his hand. The figures of Maëlveronde stopped pacing and stood, heads bent, staring down where Iaven lay. Together they all stepped in closer like vultures ready to scavenge a dying animal. Then, to Orven's wonderment, three began to fade and disappear, like smoke clouds shaken by a gust of wind.

Maëlveronde stood alone now, poised over Iaven's fallen body, and Orven realized he was seeing the image from the tapestry. All at once his fears left him and he understood its meaning. He gripped Gorflange, crept stealthily around the pillars, and dashed out into the torchlit circle behind Maëlveronde. With a shout Orven raised Gorflange in both hands and with all his strength charged at Maëlveronde.

The blade caught Maëlveronde in the side and arched him back in sudden agony. Most bitter for him was the torment of having been tricked. He had been caught off guard, and pain blurred his vision as he whirled in an instant of raw, uncontrolled rage, catching Gorflange with Halix's blade. Maëlveronde angled and lashed out at Orven, slashing him just above the waist. Orven cried out and stumbled backwards, dizzy with the blast of pain. He pulled back, moving around the circle's edge and trying to stay out of Maëlveronde's reach.

Iaven stirred and managed to get up. He picked up the wooden sword again, hoping to distract Maëlveronde and give Orven another chance. Maëlveronde reacted quickly and soon Iaven and Orven were evading Maëlveronde, pulling away in fright and hiding behind pillars at the circle's edge.

Wounded and pained, Maëlveronde was still poised and ready to strike, keeping an eye on both of them. Twice Maëlveronde sprang and crossed swords with Orven. With his free hand he sent a dazzling red disc of fire screaming toward Iaven, who ducked behind a pillar as it struck stone and exploded. The twins trembled with fear as they moved around the circle, changing direction often to escape Maëlveronde. They tried to confuse Maëlveronde as to who had Gorflange, but they were wounded in different places and their torn and blood-stained clothing no longer matched.

Iaven and Orven eluded Maëlveronde, dashing one way and then the other. Maëlveronde raised his hand and a blaze of blue fire shot forth and burned a pillar as Orven jumped out of the way in time. Iaven reversed direction and passed Orven going the other way around the circle, behind a pillar. As Orven moved close by Iaven in the dark, he snatched the wooden sword and gave Iaven Gorflange. Iaven's and Orven's eyes met, a knowing look passing between the twins. Maëlveronde whirled and found Orven again and swung at him, Orven pulling back just in time. From the opposite side, Iaven jumped forward and thrust Gorflange at Maëlveronde, wounding him at the hip. Taken by surprise, Maëlveronde spun, reversing his swing in midair and slashing hard across Iaven's shoulder. Iaven staggered and fell to the ground, the sword hitting the floor and sliding out of Iaven's hand. As Maëlveronde stepped forward to strike again, Orven saw a split-second chance and took it even though he knew it might get him killed. He leaped past Maëlveronde, swinging at him hard with the wooden sword, hoping to knock him off balance. Maëlveronde reversed his swing again and scratched Orven, who fell back to the edge of the circle, his heart pounding hard, sharp pains throbbing, and his breath coming in short, quick gasps.

Lying on the floor, Iaven reached toward where Gorflange lay, his blood darkening the stone floor beneath him. The sword was only inches away, but Iaven was dizzy with pain and could not reach it. Orven ran past, deftly replacing Gorflange with the wooden sword. With Gorflange in hand, a little of his confidence returned though his fear had not abated.

Maëlveronde saw that Orven had exchanged swords and drew himself up again, watching as Orven moved side to side with desperate movements like a panicked, hunted animal. Maëlveronde moved to the circle's edge, goading Orven into the center. As Orven unwittingly stepped forward the three phantoms reappeared throughout the vault, surrounding Orven as they moved. At first Orven was afraid, thinking he would lose Maëlveronde, but the phantoms stood tall, unbowed and unbent; for Maëlveronde in his pride could not imagine himself wounded. Seeing the difference, Orven avoided Maëlveronde, waiting for an opening. When the moment came, Orven swung and dealt another strong blow that cut Maëlveronde even as he countered it skillfully.

Maëlveronde reacted instantly once Orven was in reach. With a sudden, sharp swing, he sliced Orven's hand, knocking Gorflange from it. The sword flew across the circle, landing a few feet away from where Iaven lay. Yet Maëlveronde had not counted on Orven's quick response; he was forced to step back, and lost his balance. The phantoms faded, and as Orven pulled back in horror holding his gashed and bleeding hand, Maëlveronde toppled onto the ground, grunting in anger and dropping Halix as he did so.

Orven dove to recover Halix and rolled aside with it just as Maëlveronde sent a shock of blue fire at him. Orven dodged as the brunt of it passed, charring the floor, but the edge of it grazed his side, sending a bolt of pain through him. Maëlveronde was back on his feet and Orven pulled away, afraid to rush him again.

Black dread gnawing his heart, Orven nervously stood his ground, moving back and forth, knowing Maëlveronde would strike. Behind Maëlveronde, on the ground, Orven saw that Iaven had reached the wooden sword and was using it to pull Gorflange over to him. Iaven's recovery gave Orven hope, and he jumped around wildly, trying to distract Maëlveronde and give Iaven time.

Orven tried to keep moving but his pain was worsening. Maëlveronde saw Orven was slowing down and watched him keenly, waiting to strike. Orven tried his best to steady his nerves and resist succumbing to his growing fear. He did his best to keep Maëlveronde turned away from Iaven as much as he could.

Maëlveronde glowered at Orven, enjoying the taste of Orven's fear. He uttered a sharp curse and raised his hand, sending out a wave of force that pushed Orven back. But Maëlveronde did not risk putting all his power into it, and Orven only stumbled.

Suddenly Maëlveronde turned, and Iaven stood behind him, sword in hand. Iaven and Orven began moving around the edge of the circle, weaving in and out of the pillars, both evading Maëlveronde, nervously holding their swords at the ready. Maëlveronde watched the twins, amused they would dare to withstand him. He no longer had a sword but was certain he would soon have both. The dwarves had wounded him several times and he throbbed with great pain. Only his great discipline allowed him to clear the haze of pain and remain focused. The twins were wounded as well and were tiring fast. Maëlveronde sensed that even in his weakened state he would outlast them easily. The intensity of his wounds warned him not to expend his full powers in an attack; regaining a sword was the best course. And that would not be difficult, Maëlveronde thought. Orven's brother was the more fearful of the two; he had already fallen twice. Now he would fall a third time, losing his sword, and with it Maëlveronde would cut Orven down and kill them both.

Orven strained with fatigue, trying to ignore his deepening pain and keep his mind on the fight. He was pleased to be using the swords together with Iaven against a common foe. This was the way it was meant to be, he thought; it was what he had envisioned and hoped for when Cedric had given them the swords. He kept a close watch on Maëlveronde, now and then exchanging troubled looks with Iaven across the circle. Orven was very glad Iaven was there. Even if they both died, it would at least be fighting for the kingdom, together as brothers. Orven found himself appreciating and even liking his brother for the first time in a long while.

But Iaven was wounded and tired, too, and more nervous and fearful. Orven knew Maëlveronde had noticed it as well. He considered charging Maëlveronde, even though it would mean his own death, if it gave Iaven a chance to run away. He would shout to Iaven as he charged, telling him to run, hoping Iaven would understand what he was doing. But would Iaven? Iaven would try to save him and end up dying as well. It seemed inevitable now, Orven thought, his despair growing.

Maëlveronde saw the twins' confidence waning, especially Iaven's, and was amused to see them realizing their foolishness and petty airs. Orven was wounded worse than Iaven, but was a better fighter, and less easy a target. Maëlveronde heard Iaven breathing hard and saw Iaven's sword arm shaking. Iaven was clearly losing hope; perhaps he even suspected that he would be attacked first.

With a suddenness that surprised the twins, Maëlveronde turned his fury on Iaven and with both hands raised sent out a white pulse that threw Iaven to the ground trembling, the sword loosed from his hand. Orven dashed forward to defend Iaven, and as he approached Maëlveronde raised his hand at his side and turned to Orven with a look of cold arrogance and calculated fury. The sword Iaven had dropped leapt off the floor and flew into Maëlveronde's outstretched hand.

As Iaven's sword rose from the ground and flew through the air, Orven recoiled and his heart was like ice, his confidence shattered at the suddenness of it all. Maëlveronde had a sword again and Iaven was out of the fight. Orven felt weak and ready to collapse. He steeled himself and raised Halix, lunging forward at Maëlveronde and putting his full force into the charge. With only a split second to act before Maëlveronde had the sword, Orven knew he would be killed, but there was no other way to give Iaven a chance to escape. Orven's fear left him as he accepted his fate and rushed at Maëlveronde, Halix's shining blade extended before him. Out of the corner of his eye he saw the sword flying into Maëlveronde's hand and tensed for the deathblow that was to come.

But as soon as the sword was in Maëlveronde's grip, the old wizard's expression turned to bitter rage and agony. Maëlveronde groaned aloud in anger as his hand closed around the hilt of the wooden sword.

Admiring Iaven's shrewdness, Orven thrust Halix into Maëlveronde, shoving him to the ground. As he fell, Maëlveronde dropped the wooden sword and expended the last of his energy in an attack on Orven. He raised his hands to touch Orven, and a pale, flaring pulse beat against Orven, drawing the heat and life from his body and leaving him stiff and cold. Suddenly the freezing numbness was torn to shreds as dazzling, hooked streaks of red fire zigzagged and pierced Orven. He screamed and shook violently, falling to the ground writhing in searing pain, holding onto Halix even as he felt his grip loosening.

The attack left Maëlveronde weakened; he had lost a great deal of blood. From where he lay dying on the cold stone floor, he could see Gorflange lying near the edge of the circle, where it had been within his reach the whole time. The sword's blade was bright with torchlight, the gems glinting within the hilt as if to mock him. Maëlveronde stared at the sword and gems and suffered to think they were so close. He had been patient; he had worked hard and waited long. He had given up much in his life in order to obtain them. He could not bear the sight of them any longer and turned away.

Maëlveronde lay on his back and above him spread the round vaulted ceiling with its painted night sky full of constellations. As he lay gazing up at them, he recalled learning them in his childhood. The pain of his wounds dulled his senses and memories flooded his mind now; he was no longer an old man dying in the Stone Forest but a young boy on some grassy hilltop, watching the stars and dreaming of the future. Gone was the defeat and humiliation he had suffered, his years in Nirogenvah Castle, and even his studies of the Angkhadra and the gems. The constellations, he reflected, were what had first led him to study the Angkhadra. Maëlveronde closed his eyes and saw the night sky in all its brilliant clarity, as he remembered it, and he rested and did not open his eyes again.

Orven lay exhausted, his breathing heavy and labored. His blood stained his clothes and the floor all around him. He wanted to see if Iaven was still alive, but was too tired to raise his head off the floor. "Iaven?" he managed, his voice weak and strained. With a painful effort he rolled over and looked across the floor, and saw Iaven lying on his side, his back to Orven, unmoving. "Iaven?" Orven's head slumped on the floor as he wondered if Iaven was dead.

Fatigue kept Orven from holding any thoughts for long. His body ached all over as he felt the pain of his wounds more now. His hand was bleeding, and the entire lower front of his shirt, torn where Maëlveronde had cut him open, was soaked in blood. Orven closed his eyes and tried not to move. He hoped Iaven was not dead and was doing better than he was. Whether or not he would live to find out he could not say.

Blinking his eyes, Iaven was starting to be able to see again, after Maëlveronde's pulse of white fire had blinded him. His body still trembled and tingled from the shock. Wounds on his shoulder and chest pained him more now, growing intense, and he lay still. He had heard Orven scream and feared the worst. Footsteps came from the southern end of the Stone Forest, and Iaven heard Oellia's voice mingled with those of the soldiers. Iaven called out and soon the soldiers were ringed about the open area, standing torchlit in all the spaces between the pillars. Others stepped forward and thrust spears into Maëlveronde's body to be certain he was dead.

The captains took Halix and Gorflange into battle to give them to the King. Soldiers lifted up Maëlveronde's body on the points of spears so it could be taken and shown to the enemy. Iaven and Orven were both laid on stretchers and carried upstairs into the west wing to one of the sickrooms. Oellia walked near Iaven's stretcher, her expression one of grief and anguish. Iaven felt sorry for her and wanted to tell her they would be alright, even though he wasn't so sure of it himself. Finally he managed a weak smile at Oellia.

Oellia's distress seemed to ease a little. "You poor thing," she said to Iaven, "Nearly got yourself killed. Rest, and we'll take care of you now. And you had better pull through, or Allé and I will be very upset."

Chapter 43.
A Final Farewell

The onslaught continued through the darkest hours of night. The inner ward remained under heavy attack and Aaron wished he was with Max and Roy. He had been asked to help momentarily in the inner ward, and as one task led to another he ended up staying there. Now he was busy moving the wounded into the Throne Room vestibule, and when that was full, into the Throne Room. Dozens of dwarves and men lay there, groaning in agony. Blood soaked the blankets beneath them. Some writhed in pain, straining to endure gashes and open wounds, while others lay silent and unmoving with dulled, unblinking eyes. Aaron wanted to comfort them, but there were too many and he felt nauseous and dizzy and overwhelmed by it all. As the attack increased the inner ward became even more hazardous. A wounded dwarf he was lifting on a stretcher was hit with an arrow and killed right before his eyes. As the number of wounded increased, more dwarves were assigned to help move them; some of them would die as well. Suddenly, amidst the dim torchlight of the Throne Room vestibule, Aaron saw a familiar and unexpected face.

"Wilbur!" Aaron called.

Wilbur looked up, unsure of how to respond at first, until Aaron greeted him. "Wilbur, it's good to see you!" Aaron was genuinely pleased. "I was worried you were all in Farrenhale during the attack. How long have you been here? Where's Iaven?"

Wilbur was wary at first, but saw Aaron meant well. "We were with the troops near Halloway when they were attacked," Wilbur said. "I don't think very many survived." Wilbur's thoughts drifted, cold and numb, in the smoky torchlit space around them. He moved toward the door and Aaron went with him. Together they carried in more wounded, concentrating on what they had to do and talking in between tasks in the vestibule.

"Wilbur, I'm sorry about what happened in the mountains, you know, our ambush," Aaron apologized. "I—we shouldn't have gone along with it. Orven got us all excited, and well... I—there's really no excuse..." He wanted to say more but was exhausted and drained.

"It's behind us now," said Wilbur. His initial resentment eased, and standing among all the wounded he could hardly refuse to forgive Aaron. "We can talk about it later. We've got work to do right now."

Aaron followed Wilbur out of the vestibule, recognizing in Wilbur the same grim determination he had to haul as many to safety as possible. They worked awhile, putting themselves at risk to move the wounded. Aaron followed Wilbur's lead and found he had a new respect for him.

"I really do feel bad about what we did," Aaron repeated later, still unsure what to say. "How is everyone doing?"

"Tillmore was killed by goblins," Wilbur said solemnly.

Aaron was shocked and humbled. "I'm sorry to hear that," he said in a small voice. He looked down and became quiet.

When Wilbur was done with the wounded dwarf he was tending he came over by Aaron. He saw how guilty Aaron felt for the ambush and the part he had played in Orven's schemes. He supposed the others felt the same way, maybe even Orven had regrets. Surrounded by the dying and wounded, Wilbur saw Orven and his friends without malice, even though he was still upset with them. "Where is Orven?" he asked Aaron.

"Orven? I don't know," said Aaron. "He and Ripley had the swords, and we don't know where they went." It occurred to him that they might have fallen into Goblin hands, but he didn't dare say it. He looked around, trying to stifle the thought. Wilbur got up and went toward the doors again. Aaron rose and followed, ready to resume their work.

Outside there was considerable noise and consternation, and Wilbur and Aaron stopped and looked up. On the wall around the inner ward a band of soldiers walked close together carrying torches and tall spears. They carried a long shape like a body, blacker than the night sky, impaled and hoisted high on the ends of the spears.

"*Behold your Grand Vizier!*" the soldiers shouted to the Goblins as they moved along the wall. Many of the Goblins recognized Maëlveronde, for he had allowed his reputation to grow until he was greatly feared and respected among them. Rumors had it that he was a powerful sorcerer of some kind, and seeing him dead was quite a blow to their morale. None had expected the Grand Vizier to fall in battle; for many it was the first inkling that defeat was possible. But General Burzok still rode tall on his steed Gantyad, commanding the Goblin forces and maintaining their hold on the outer ward. The sight of the portly general helped calm the unrest caused by Maëlveronde's corpse, and Burzok's presence in the outer ward raised morale there. Yet he himself was unnerved by the sight of Maëlveronde's corpse and could not imagine how the Dwarves had come by it. He did not let his concern show and reminded his Captains that success was still in their hands. Privately he would acknowledge that he had had differences of opinion with the Grand Vizier, even while agreeing that his role in the campaign had been inestimable. As Maëlveronde's body passed high above the parapets of the inner ward wall, Burzok had his Captains rally the troops lest they grow distracted and disheartened. With the release of the King's troops from the west wing, the defense of the inner ward had grown sure and the Goblins had lost ground in the east wing. Burzok was confident these losses were only momentary, for both Dwarves and Men were weakened by the siege and their numbers were dwindling. He sensed many had already wearied and given in to despair, and it was only a matter of time before they surrendered to the Goblins or to death.

Zhindarren stared down from a window in the east wing, distraught at the sight of his old friend and mentor slain. He could scarcely believe it. The shock of it left him paralyzed with grief and profound sadness, as though he had suddenly been left alone in the world. Years of friendship stretching over more than five decades had ended abruptly, without even a farewell. Zhindarren struggled to regain his calm. If Maëlveronde was dead, the Dwarves must have recaptured the swords, he thought. But he had to be sure. In any event, he would not remain in the Castle much longer.

Strable stood nearby and saw Zhindarren's disappointment. He wanted to speak but was afraid to disturb Zhindarren. At last the old wizard turned to him. "Gather our men and have them ready to leave," he said.

"And the swords?" Strable asked. "We still haven't found Orven..."

"We shall see. But have them get ready for now," Zhindarren replied.

"Where will we go?" said Strable.

Zhindarren turned to Strable to put an end to his questions. "East," he said.

Strable nodded and left the room. Zhindarren turned back to the window and looked across the outer ward, past Goblin lines to Maëlveronde's tent along the outer wall. A short time later he had slipped out of the east wing and was heading for the tent, letting neither dwarf nor goblin stand in his way.

Battle atop the wall around the outer ward was fierce and bitter. Torches and firebrands swung wildly, clashing steel rang out, and screams and curses rose into the black night air. Under Arlen Frosthelm's command, the Dwarves had retaken the western run of the outer wall, and now held the western gate and gatehouse. They fought on toward the central gatehouse but Goblin forces were too concentrated there for any progress to be made. Holding the western wall was itself a struggle, as goblins and augglins climbed up on both sides. The Dwarves fought them back, trying to keep them from reaching the parapet. Some fell and others hung on, and dwarves were pulled off the wall and killed. A cold moon nearing its last quarter shone down on the war, casting its pallid light and deepening shadows wherever torchlight could not reach.

Zammond and Hobley fought amid the cohort on the western wall, glad they were not in the vanguard with Arlen Frosthelm where the fighting was the worst. To their left battles raged throughout the outer ward, where Prince Varlen's forces clashed against General Burzok's. The Goblins gained ground, lost it to the Dwarves, then gained it back again. Buildings burned and many had been cleared away or lay in heaps of broken timber and ash. Others had been torn apart so the Goblins could build large assault weaponry and other instruments of war. Zammond and Hobley had also seen the dark shape of a body being paraded on spears across the wall of the inner ward, a crowd of bobbing torches below it. It moved along the wall of the inner ward, shouts and cries accompanying it. Even at a distance, they noticed it had a dampening effect on Goblin morale. After the body was seen by all, the torchbearers raised their torches and set it aflame, burning it until it fell from the spears and was dumped, still on fire, onto the Goblin horde who had gathered below it in horror. But the moment soon passed and the Goblins rallied again.

Zammond kept an eye on the battle below. Goblin attacks on the western wall depended on the success or failure of Varlen's troops inside the outer ward. But attacks also came from outside the Castle wall. The Goblin encampment had spread all across the Castle terraces, and the last of the great shaggy Urumak remaining were tethered along its lower edges. A band of highly-trained augglins were brought to immense wooden ladders at the wall so they could reach the parapets and attack the Dwarves. Beyond the wall, the Castle terraces were obscured by smoking campfires and great, steaming cauldrons. The stench rising from them choked the dwarves fighting along the wall; a rotting, foul stink and black, oozing smoke that would not rise but hung in the air and crept and slithered over stone and grass. Smells of oily blood and roasted flesh wafted from an Urumak laid on its side, large slabs and sections cut from its body to be eaten. As smoke shifted in the wind, Zammond caught sight of crude wooden frames and bodies hung by their feet, strange wooden devices, and other evidence of cunning atrocities of which even brief glimpses were enough to chill him.

Zammond and Hobley fought side by side yet had spoken little in the last hour. The noise and chaotic roar of the battle from all sides was relentless and nauseating, and Zammond was shocked at how little organization or strategy there appeared to be on either side. Constant threat and terror had reduced many to raw fear and reaction, their wide eyes wild with anger and desperation. Both Hobley and Zammond were worn and tired as they staggered drowsily, numbed by the cold, their ears deaf to the shrieks and clamor and the booming roar and rumble constantly pounding at them. They were saturated by smoke and ash, and fiery, bloody images of dwarves writhing and clinging and falling. Despair bit at the edges of their minds as they longed for warmth and quiet, even a place where they might die peacefully; then suddenly they would catch themselves, shake such thoughts from their minds, and fight harder as the night dragged on, deep and endless.

Zammond's attention was brought into sudden sharp focus as an Augglin rose up in front of him, swinging a huge clawed hand that snagged his mail, grazing him and drawing blood. "*Hob!*" he shouted, and Hobley was there, swinging his axe at the augglin. Zammond stabbed at the augglin but was badly shaken. The augglin leaned in and pummeled him on the ribs, knocking him down. Zammond held up his sword as the augglin came down on him and pulled back just in time. Massive claws tore across Zammond's mail. Hobley's axe slashed at the augglin while other hands reached in waving torches. Arrows shot at the augglin's beady, hooded eyes. At last they pushed the augglin back and it fell, grasping the parapet with large gnarled hands, until its fingers were hewn off by Dwarven swords.

"Zammond, you're bleeding," said Hobley.

"Am I?" Zammond did not think his wound was bad until he looked at it. He pulled himself up and got to his feet, bending forward and grunting in pain.

"Zammond?" Hobley's voice ached with concern. He wielded his axe as another attack on the wall began, but he was distracted by Zammond's condition.

"It's not... too bad... —Is it?" said Zammond.

"I don't know," said Hobley. "You sure you're all right?"

"I'll have to be," said Zammond. He glanced at Hobley, feeling deep appreciation for his friend, glad they were together and looking out for each other. "They need us here."

"They need us alive," said Hobley, still unsure if he should take Zammond back into the Castle. He, too, had found new respect for Zammond, and noted how the disciplined life in the besieged Castle had already curbed some of his friend's impulsiveness. "If you're cut deep—"

All at once roars and shouts erupted further down the wall near the Castle. While the ground below was his, General Burzok had sent goblins and augglins to attack the end of the western wall. With a concentrated intensity they climbed up one after another, swords slashing and hammers pounding, beating the Dwarves back and pushing them over the parapet.

Hobley stared wide-eyed at the attack. "They've taken the end of the wall," he said, "They've cut us off from the Castle. We won't be able to get you back there." Concern etched his voice and he fought hard, trying to keep Zammond away from danger.

"I'll be all right," said Zammond, "For now, anyway."

An augglin from outside the wall jumped up in front of them, recalling their attention. Zammond swung and stabbed at it, even as bolts of fiery pain shot through his chest and side. He blocked it out as much as he could, fighting the augglin, until they had finally sent it tumbling to the ground. Zammond breathed hard as the pain gripped him tightly again.

Hobley wanted badly to help Zammond, but there was nothing more he could do. When he had a chance, he glanced back toward where the wall joined the Castle and saw the Goblins held it now.

"They want us to pull back and move toward the Castle," said Hobley, "But we've got to hold at least the gatehouse if the Kronivar forces are to get through. We can't let the Goblins hold the entire outer wall against them."

"If troops are coming from Kronivar," said Zammond, "And even if they are, we won't be able to hold it for long."

"No," Hobley said, "Not much longer."

In a sickroom toward the back of the Castle's west wing, Iaven and Orven lay resting. Gusts of wind beat on the windowpanes, and the low, muted sounds of war continued. It was well after midnight and most of the other wounded in the room were asleep. The room was quiet and dark, lit by a candle on a small table set between Iaven's and Orven's beds. Wendolin sat on a chair nearby talking with the twins. He had been eager to hear what had happened to Iaven and to see Orven. Though badly wounded and very tired, Orven was pleased to meet Wendolin and interested in hearing more about the gems and swords, as well as about Maëlveronde and Wendolin himself.

"His death will have an effect on the Goblins," Wendolin said, "Of that we can be sure; for Maëlveronde cultivated his reputation and relished the fearful reverence they gave him. Now it will work against him, as a drain on their confidence. But his death is by no means an end to the war, and there are many Goblins who hated him as well. We can only wait and hope. Be glad you have played your part well."

Wendolin looked upon the torn and stained clothing of the young dwarves, now wrapped with blood-soaked bandages. Iaven had a large gash over the left side of his chest and a slice across his shoulder, while Orven had cuts on his hand and arms and deep lacerations just above his waist where Maëlveronde had stabbed him. "Were I not so weakened, I would have fought Maëlveronde myself, and saved the spilling of your young blood!" Wendolin lamented. "But many of my years have been hard ones. I am an old man now. And so was Maëlveronde, but few goblins knew it; that was another of his deceits. Hale he was for his age, and five years my senior at that! His powers were great, but he was an old man as am I. As his reputation grew, he was able to obtain whatever he desired, without a fight; only the swords and gems were out of his reach. Living as he did for so long, I think he came to believe what others said about him and thought himself invincible."

"I was beginning to think so, too," said Orven, his voice muted by constant pain.

"Fortunate were you, in wounding him as you did," said Wendolin, "He was only toying with you before that. He must have thought you harmless, a mere amusement to enjoy before he took the sword away."

"Well, he found out otherwise!" Orven said proudly in a weak voice.

"Yes, he did," said Wendolin, "His own lies became his undoing. Power without truth only ends in deceiving and destroying itself. Yet such power must often be reckoned with before it does so." Wendolin reached his cane at the footboard of the bed, and with an effort rose to his feet. "And now I must go and rest or I shall be of no use to anyone."

Iaven looked grimly at Wendolin, sad to see his recovery was going so slow. Orven was amazed at how frail Wendolin seemed.

"Were you ever as powerful as Maëlveronde?" Orven asked Wendolin.

Wendolin took the candle from the table and stopped now, considering Orven's question. "Was I? It is not easy to compare; it has been a long time since I have seen him, and much has happened to me since then. And power takes on different forms; one cannot always measure them against each other. The power of wisdom is not that of strength and might, nor can cunning be compared to a strong will. And the nature of power can be quite fickle." Wendolin raised the candle and the small flame lit his face. "One candle's fire can spread until it burns a whole city," he said, "But it can be blown out just as easily." With a quick breath Wendolin put out the candle. "And now good night to both of you!"

After Wendolin left them, Iaven and Orven lay awake. Tired as they were, neither could sleep. Their eyes adjusted to the pale moonlight illuminating the room and they kept talking in hushed tones.

"How I wish I could have met Wendolin sooner," said Orven. "And Maëlveronde not at all."

"I wonder if the Goblins would still have gone to war, if not for him," said Iaven.

"Oh, sure they would have," said Orven, "They're like that. They did before, didn't they? But, you know, I'm still amazed that we defeated him; Maëlveronde, I mean."

"There were the swords and gems," said Iaven, "It wasn't just us. I doubt we could have done it with any other swords."

"Well, it wasn't just the swords, either," said Orven. He turned to look at his brother. "We did it, Iaven. You and I," said Orven. "You know, when Cedric gave us the swords, I was hoping we would use them together..."

"Us, work together?" Iaven laughed, with a bitter undercurrent.

"I suppose it was brave, what you did," said Orven. "Even if you had no idea at the time what you were getting into. And to think you were only just a decoy!"

"Well, I wouldn't have had to go in there at all if you hadn't walked into Maëlveronde's trap," snapped Iaven, "And you knew even less what you were getting into."

"True," said Orven. Iaven expected Orven to say more but he was quiet awhile. "I was glad to see you there, you know," Orven admitted.

"I wonder if you would have done the same for me," said Iaven.

Orven thought a moment. "I would have," he said. He glanced at Iaven again. "Look, Iaven, I know you're still angry about our fight in the tree... I— Well, I got carried away; I mean, I didn't think you'd put up such a fight—"

"And why not?" Iaven retorted, "When have we ever *not* fought, since father died?"

"Well, not quite like *that*," said Orven. "No, no... I was impressed, Iaven, I was; I really respected you for it."

"You left me hanging there," Iaven reminded him.

"Well, you got back up all right, didn't you?" Orven stared at the ceiling, remembering, and a tone of guilt crept into what he said. "I admit I overdid it, telling you Zammond and the others were dead, just to scare you... and during the fight, too." He paused, thinking. "I was amazed at how well you did, especially at a disadvantage. But I always knew you could, Iaven. Do you remember when you were hanging on the roots afterward, and I came to the edge of the cliff, and stood looking down at you? I knew then that you'd be all right, that you'd get back up on the cliff again. I wouldn't have let you fall or left you there to die."

"It didn't seem like that at the time," said Iaven.

"Well, maybe not," Orven smiled a little in the dark. "You really wanted that last gem, didn't you? You wanted it as badly as I did."

Orven was quiet awhile. The twins listened to the wind outside and the faint sounds of war. "It wasn't a fair fight. I'll admit it. And it bothered me; I didn't tell anyone, but it really did bother me afterward. I'm sorry, Iaven..."

Iaven knew he should say something in response, but he let out a breath and lay there, hoping to find the words.

Orven waited and turned a little to see if Iaven was listening. "I mean it; I really am sorry. And I didn't mean for you to lose Halix, either." He looked back up at the ceiling, wondering if that was completely true; he could have found a way to give Halix back, but he hadn't even tried. "I wonder what they're doing with the swords now," he said, "I suppose they'll make some difference now, in the war?"

"I hope so," Iaven said absently.

"If it isn't too late," said Orven. He moved slightly, grimacing as pain flared in his wounds, and then lay still again. "I was foolish, Iaven. If what Wendolin told us about Greywood is true, I could have easily let the swords slip into the hands of the Goblins and Maëlveronde... Well, one *did*, of course, and if not for you they both would have." He turned to look at Iaven again. "Only when Maëlveronde was after me did I see what folly all my plans were. And how mean I was to you. Can you ever forgive me, Iaven?"

Iaven thought about it awhile. "Maybe," he said half-heartedly, "I suppose I will, eventually..." Iaven did love his brother, and the words were easy to say, but he knew it would be some time before he truly felt them in his heart.

As Halix and Gorflange made their way to King Jordgen and Prince Varlen, word spread among the troops that the Lost Swords of the Alliance had been found and would be used against the Goblins. Some caught glimpses of the swords as they passed and even at a distance marveled at their beauty and the power they seemed to exude. Prince Varlen's forces held the inner ward and he led them now in the retaking of the outer ward. He held Gorflange aloft and rallied the crowd. King Jordgen himself took Halix in hand and led the charge to rejoin the troops stranded on the wall, afterwards pushing onward in an attempt to recapture the central gatehouse. Even those who knew little or nothing about the swords were cheered and found their spirits lifted. Although many knew that King Jordgen and Prince Varlen were excellent swordsmen, few had actually seen them fight and were amazed now to see their skills in use. The swords enhanced their abilities even further, and morale rose as the dwarves looked upon their sovereigns leading the defense.

Zammond and Hobley were surprised to hear of the swords' return and wondered where Orven and Ripley were. Like everyone else, they were pleased the swords had been found in time. They knew retaking the wall would be difficult, but had confidence King Jordgen would not fail. The fighting on the wall continued, fierce as ever, and many wondered how long the Goblins would retain the upper hand.

Shouts rose from the outer ward. In a sudden charge, Prince Varlen's forces rushed forward into the goblins holding the center of the ward, pushing them against the wall. The Goblins fought back and all who dared challenge Prince Varlen were slain. General Burzok's horse was killed in the onslaught, but Burzok himself dismounted and led the counterattack. The fighting wore on, in torchlight and shadow, and bonfires burned throughout the ward illuminating the battle. Varlen led the Dwarves and fought his way toward the gates, and at last Burzok met him in battle. Gorflange flew, arcing and swinging, and flashed in the firelight, bright, shining, and terrible to withstand. Varlen skillfully beat Burzok back, but the Goblin General was larger in stature and more powerfully built. The two remained locked in combat as Dwarves and Goblins fought around them. Varlen was faster, and it seemed only a matter of time before Burzok was defeated. Some goblins began to fear for their general, but none dared to step in and aid him, suggesting that he could not hold his own.

As the battle dragged on through the night, many advances the Dwarves had made withered away. The Goblins kept them contained and looked as though they would gain ground if the Dwarves let up their defense for even a moment. The Dwarves fought on, longing for daybreak to end the interminable night and hoping troops from Kronivar were on their way and would not arrive too late.

Aranstone watched the battle from atop the eastern wall by the Castle, which his men were attempting to hold. After a prolonged effort and with help from the inner ward, the east wing was finally theirs again. And with the Goblins turned out and the doors barred, fewer men were needed to hold the east wing; they could now concentrate on retaking the eastern run of the outer wall. Little progress had been made, and it was very slow going. Seeing the fight between Varlen and Burzok, Aranstone was glad Varlen was wielding Gorflange instead of himself. He was fully behind the Castle defense now and sorry for the part he had played in the siege.

The fighting below held Aranstone's attention and he lingered at the parapet longer than he had intended. Varlen was winning, though Burzok fought well, and the outcome was still uncertain. Throughout the ward dwarves and goblins fought bitterly, steel clashing and firelight gleaming on sword, shield, helm, and the faces of all engaged in combat. As Aranstone scanned the scene, his eye caught the shape of a solitary figure making his way through the crowd, apparently unarmed; it was Greywood. He had emerged from one of the tents in the Goblin camp, carrying a small sack on his back, and was returning to the east wing. Aranstone watched with growing indignation as Greywood passed through the outer ward. As Greywood reached the east wing entrances, Aranstone left the parapet and hurried along the wall to the Castle.

Aranstone found a crossbow and bid several of his men to come with him, and together they searched the east wing for Greywood. At last in the northeastern end of the Castle they came to a room overlooking the valleys around Mount Frosthelm. A length of rope hung out an open window and was tied to heavy wooden furniture braced beneath the windowsill. Aranstone rushed to the window and his men readied bows and crossbows at the room's other windows. Outside, near the bottom of the rope, someone was climbing down. In the valley below, a small group gathered by torchlight. Greywood was there, a dozen men or so with him. By the light of their torches Aranstone recognized Rafnel and Strable among the cohort.

Aranstone cut the rope and sent the climber tumbling into the valley with a shout. Those on the ground looked up to the Castle windows, where they found Aranstone's crossbow aimed at them, along with those of his archers who were awaiting his signal.

"*Greywood!*" Aranstone shouted, "So you are a deserter as well as traitor?"

Greywood looked up and stepped forward from the group. Despite the dark and the distance, Aranstone could feel the old man's disdain even before he spoke. "*Traitor?*" Zhindarren mocked, amused that Aranstone had caught up to them. "You accuse me of being a traitor after marching on your own King? And now that you have failed, you would stay aboard a sinking ship and accuse us of deserting!"

"King Jordgen showed me your note to Grawson betraying us all." Aranstone noticed some of the men below glancing at Greywood as he made his accusation and hoped they would hear him out. "You were in league with the Goblins all the while, and have no loyalty to Kronivar," Aranstone shouted. Amazingly, the men stood exchanging glances, but none stepped forward to challenge Greywood. Had they known all along? Seeing Rafnel and Strable among Greywood's cohort suggested that Greywood had indeed been after the swords.

Zhindarren laughed. "Your accusations grow more outlandish," he shouted back. "Do you suppose any of *them* will believe it?" he asked, smiling and indicating the men behind him who stood there amused and did nothing.

Aranstone was about to appeal to the men again, but it seemed they knew about Greywood and had long been a part of his schemes. There was even laughter now among them that infuriated Aranstone.

"At my signal," Aranstone said quietly so that only his archers would hear him. Zhindarren waited below to see if Aranstone would respond, and then turned to lead his men away.

"Now!" shouted Aranstone, and arrows and bolts flew into the valley. Arrows brought down two of the men and they fell to the ground. Zhindarren whirled around, holding up his hand, and all arrows and bolts heading in his direction veered off course and fell away to the side. The remaining men fled into the darkness, and Zhindarren took one last look at Aranstone and followed them. The archers fired where torches bobbed in the blackness, but soon they disappeared behind a rise and all was dark.

Seeing how Greywood had diverted the arrows and bolts, Aranstone was finally convinced of what the King had said regarding Zhindarren. He burned with shame and anger not only for having listened to Zhindarren's advice, but because others under his command had betrayed him as well. Only with a great effort was he able to hold his anger in check. For now, he was needed to lead his men; but after the war he would pursue Zhindarren and hunt him down.

Iaven and Orven lay talking in the darkened sickroom. Bled of his arrogance and swagger, Orven was humble now and his tone softer. "It's a shame we always fought so much," he said, "As brothers we could have been a lot closer than we were. I think that's why I was so upset when you wanted to stay behind on the farm after mother remarried and Cedric gave us the swords."

"I *was* kind of stubborn about letting go of the farm," Iaven admitted, "Even Cedric thought so."

"You were pretty stubborn about giving up the gems, too," Orven joked. "But in a strange way, I was glad to see you put up a fight for them."

"We did fight an awful lot after Dad died, didn't we?" Iaven said, looking up and the ceiling and missing his father.

"Yes, we did," said Orven. His voice was tired as his mind drifted in the past. "But I'm ashamed of it now, of things I did... All those times we fought, I knew there'd be a point where you would hold back, and I could always win. There was a line you wouldn't cross, no matter what I did. I tried to make you cross it, and it infuriated me when you wouldn't. I wanted you to give in; we would have been even then. But you didn't. I think that's why Dad loved you more, maybe; because he knew you were more like him, he wasn't disappointed with you the way he was with me." Orven paused a moment, pained. "You wouldn't cross that line. And I hated you for it; it was a strength I did not have. I used to think it was weakness on your part, but later I saw it was strength. I was the one who was weak. I did things and tried to justify them to myself or shrug them off as nothing; it was too easy for me to do it, and still is."

Iaven was moved and saddened by what Orven said. He turned to his brother. "Orven... don't you think Dad loved us both the same? Why do you say that?"

Orven's voice was quiet and near tears. "I know he did, Iaven. You didn't hear what I heard." He paused again, deciding whether or not to continue. "It was on the night before Dad left to go on the *Yoner*. I couldn't sleep. I just laid there with my eyes closed, pretending to be asleep so they wouldn't worry about me, but I was awake. I heard them, Iaven; I heard them talking out in the kitchen. She didn't want him to go, and he tried comforting her as he could. I can still hear them as they spoke... '*I'll miss you*,' she said, and then Dad said, '*You'll be fine. So will the twins. Iaven will be fine.*' You were always his favorite, Iaven. '*Iaven will be fine.*' He didn't mention me; he didn't care as much about me. From then on I knew it." Orven's voice broke and he sniffed sharply. He looked up at the darkened ceiling as though he could not bear to look at Iaven. "I almost cried right then. But I told myself I'd work harder and try to be the kind of son he wanted. I would prove to him that I was just as good. But he went away and never came back, and I never got the chance to show him."

Orven turned to Iaven briefly and looked back up again. "I hated you for it. It wasn't fair of me, but I did. No matter what I did, that's how it would always be. I couldn't live up to what Dad wanted of me, and I wanted to think you couldn't either. But you did live up to it. I didn't, and it was my own fault." His voice choked off and sounded as though he could say no more.

They were quiet awhile as Iaven considered what to say.

"Orven..." Iaven felt terrible for his brother, "Orven, that wasn't what he meant at all! I'm sure of it; he loved us both the same. We'll ask Mom when we go back to Hillbrook. She knows how he felt."

"When we go back?" Orven sighed, "Oh, Iaven, you're still the dreamer, aren't you? I'm not going to make it, look how wounded I am, I've bled so much..."

"Orven! Don't talk like that, of course you will!"

Orven smiled weakly at Iaven. "I'm paying for my folly now, all my ridiculous plans and self-important ideas. At least I've learned something from them in the end."

"Stop that," Iaven demanded, "You're not going to die. You can be just as stubborn as me, can't you? And anyway, I've long since given up on the farm, so I'll also have to find something to do when we get back home. Maybe we could find something together."

"We'd never agree on what to do and you know it," said Orven.

"Oh, I don't know," said Iaven, "In the last few months I've changed quite a bit, you know."

"Really?" Orven snapped back, smiling, "You've gotten worse then, have you?" He laughed. But Iaven could tell he was still in pain. "Well, you should have seen me, Iaven, after we found that treasure I told you about," Orven sounded more thoughtful now. "All the plans I had for it; outrageous ones. Selfish ones— I only thought about what *I* would do with it. It's yours, now, you know. Max knows where it is in Kronivar. Give some to Mom and Rory."

"Give it to them yourself!" said Iaven, "And quit this talk of dying. You always did like to exaggerate and make everything out to be more than it was, like those hunting stories you and Max would tell."

"You're the one who was always imagining things," said Orven, "Remember when we were kids, that night when Zammond and I gave you that good scare out in the forest? You wouldn't go out after dark for at least three days!"

"That was mean," said Iaven. "You have to admit it was."

"But it was funny," said Orven, enjoying the memory. "I'll bet Zammond still thinks so, too. You were so scared!"

"Not as much as you thought I was," said Iaven.

"Oh yes, you were," said Orven, "And then there was that tree you didn't like and wouldn't go near—"

"We were only five at the time," Iaven reminded Orven, "That didn't last very long, either."

"And you'd always find bones and imagine what they were from," said Orven, "Or find odd-shaped rocks and think they were things made by the Gnomes or Elves or something..."

"I *did* find an Elven arrowhead in the furrows that time," said Iaven, surprised he could still be upset about it.

"It was not and you know it," said Orven. The twins fell to bickering again, finding it comforting to return to their old ways. Gradually, though, their energy ebbed away and they lapsed into silence.

"I'm sorry, Iaven," Orven said again after a while, "I wasn't such a good brother sometimes. Forgive me."

"Well, I wasn't always the best, either," Iaven admitted. "I could be just as stubborn or bull-headed."

"You played your share of pranks on me, too" said Orven.

Iaven smiled. "Yes, I did... I suppose I was mean sometimes, too. But that's how kids are, right? I did sometimes wish things could be different. Even now I do. Especially after Dad died; it just seemed to get worse and worse between us. Cedric noticed it, and I think he kept us from each other's throats more than anyone during those years."

"It's too bad about Cedric," said Orven, "I was hoping to see him again. But we were lucky to have him with us as long as we did."

"He wanted us to be closer," said Iaven, "He thought we should be, as brothers, and as twins. We both disagreed, but now I think he was right."

Orven turned to look at Iaven. "And our fight on the cliffside? You can forgive me for that? And the well in Kronivar, and everything else?"

Iaven was quiet a moment. He realized he was still very upset with Orven. "I'll try to," he said. "I was really very angry. More than I've ever been at you. Or at anybody. It'll take a while to pass. But I think I do want to be closer now."

"I do too, Iaven," said Orven, "I'd like that."

"It must have been difficult for Mom, all those years…" Iaven lay wondering, staring at the ceiling. The faintest hint of daylight was starting to glow in the east now. "With us always fighting, I mean. She needed us the most then, and we were too busy bickering and getting in each other's way. I don't know what we would have done without Cedric." He stopped and lay thinking awhile. "A lot of things could have been better. And you were right about the farm, of course. We wouldn't have lasted more than a season at it. I wanted things to stay as they were and thought I would be content. But it wasn't meant to be." Iaven sighed. "And I have changed. Putting up with me before must have frustrating at times. I hope you can forgive me, too."

Iaven waited for Orven's response but there was silence. Thinking Orven had fallen asleep, Iaven turned to face his bed. Daylight was breaking now and he could see his brother lying there. Orven's lips were parted slightly and his eyes were open, staring unblinkingly at the ceiling. His hands and side were still. "Orven?" Iaven's voice was desperate and edged with tears. *"Orven?"*

Iaven sat up in bed, ignoring the pains in his chest and shoulder. Orven lay motionless, and Iaven felt too heavy with grief to get out of bed. Cold and sorrow weakened him and he lay back on his bed again. Memories of Orven crowded his mind. He let them wash over him, pleasant times that left him longing and sad times that filled him with regret. But underlying it all now was the sense of feeling terribly, utterly alone. "Orven…" he whispered. He closed his eyes and lay mourning his brother in silence.

A short time later Iaven's thoughts were interrupted by noises and bustling outside in the hall. A Dwarven soldier burst into the sickroom, frantic and excited. "The Kronivar troops have arrived!" he exclaimed, "They're marching onto the Castle plateau. The tide has turned in our favor. Prince Varlen has killed General Burzok, the Goblin army is in disarray, and some are fleeing. It won't be long now!"

Shouts of joy came from outside the hall, and some of the wounded who had been awakened sat up cheering and shouting approval. "Long live King Jordgen!" they cried, "Long live Itharia! Long live the King!"

Chapter 44.
Down the Long Road

"Within a day or two, we flushed the rest out and finished them off," said Lexter, "Dozens escaped into the valleys around Mount Frosthelm, and they'll be hunted down over the next few weeks. But most of the Goblins are gone by now."

Lexter was holding forth in the sickroom to an attentive and appreciative audience. Max and Zammond had beds near Iaven's, and Hobley, Wilbur, Aaron, and Roy had pulled up chairs and sat nearby. "When we first came, we didn't know what to expect," said Lexter, "The outer walls could have been held against us. The western gatehouse was still held by the Dwarves, so we made for it, but it wasn't easy going. And the obstacles we had along the way; how I wish I hadn't seen what the Goblins were doing. They held dwarves and men as prisoners of war, even goblins they thought were traitors and deserters; we let them die and buried them. We dumped out those cauldrons they had, and I'll be surprised if grass ever grows there again. Anyway, the Goblins split their forces to meet us, but they didn't have enough. They were hoping to all be inside, holding the entire wall by the time we came. So we fought them on the Castle plateau, and they held out as long as they could. And that was that."

Lexter sat back and took a deep breath. He had been talking almost an hour, and wondered if he had gone on for too long. He smiled at his audience. Iaven, Zammond, and Max were propped up on pillows in their beds, and all three seemed to be recovering well. Max, Roy, and Aaron had even apologized to Lexter for leaving him beaten up on the roadside. Lexter had been eager to forgive them and told them to forget it, and he felt especially sorry for Max, who had been wounded on both arms during his defense of the east wing. Iaven, Zammond, Wilbur, and Hobley had given Lexter a slightly warmer welcome, and were relieved to see he had survived the attack on Halloway. Now that he had finally finished his story, he could see they had a new appreciation for him, even if they did suspect he was exaggerating his own heroics.

"So what will you do now?" asked Hobley.

"Well, I'm eager to see Tolgard again," said Lexter, "and my brothers and parents there." He started to get up. "Once everything's taken care of around here I'll return to Kronivar and stay with Robb Pitford until I leave for Tolgard aboard the *Ahinar*. I'm really looking forward to going home." Lexter smiled. Now that he was so close to returning to Tolgard, he was quite excited and thought of all he had left behind there. For the first time he even wondered if he would miss Itharia.

The dwarves all said goodbye to Lexter, and he wished them well. After he left, they continued talking the rest of the afternoon, sharing whatever news was circulating as reports came in from around the kingdom. Three days had passed now since the end of the war, and during that time they had found out what each had done during and before the war. They worked out whatever differences and grudges remained between them, and all were friends again, as they had been at home in the Foothills before their adventures began.

Throughout the kingdom there was rejoicing that the war was ended. But for every one who celebrated there were two or three who mourned. Families waited for fathers and sons who never returned. Some feared the worst, only to be surprised by the wounded's delayed return. Others received sad visits from friends who related last moments and dying wishes. Still others heard nothing and would never learn what became of their loved ones.

Few were the bodies returned home. Most lay anonymously in freshly-dug mass graves. Yet alongside the sorrow was relief that the war was over, and new appreciation for those things held dear that had not been lost. Many wept tears of joy and sadness as Itharia began its journey down the long road to recovery.

In the swamp where Teska had once stood the waters were gray with ash and floating debris. Beams and poles jutted out of the still waters like broken bones. Cracked and splintering platforms tilted half-submerged, dusted with snow and early-morning frost. Charred logs lurked below the water's surface.

Boats from the remaining ten villages of the *naquihlaaw-ithwatiila* gathered amidst the wreckage. Teskans who had escaped gazed upon the ruins of their village. The other villages had taken them in and there was still no count as to how many had been lost. Many in the other villages had been against collaborative efforts with the Dwarves and this seemed to confirm their suspicions. Ashore, the refuse and litter of the Goblin camp spread across the land where the Dwarves' camp had been, and in the distance, the ruins of Farrenhale, its buildings burned and its few streets empty. Near the crumbling wall the great gates lay askew on the ground, the gate towers now heaps of rubble. Only the Mountain Gate and the wall running up to it remained unharmed.

Across the border in Navrogenaya, all was silent in the Arinzei Valley. Two messenger-birds, sent out in the final hours of the war, had arrived at Ordskell bearing tidings of the Goblins' defeat. King Golhazzar unsuccessfully sought to suppress the news and began planning his exile, though he would fall to assassins before a week had passed. Tolgard felt relief at its borders with Navrogenaya, though some still maintained that their neutrality had been a form of cowardice.

In the northern provinces of Itharia, the towns and villages along the North Road emerged from their sleepy seclusion to help each other. Some had been pillaged and burned by the Goblins while others had gone untouched. Yet every village had lost someone in the war and they consoled each other in their grief. Carts and wagons moved from town to town as neighboring villages opened their doors and rebuilding began.

Towns along the South Road and down in the Foothills waited for fathers, husbands, and sons to come home, mourning their dead as they became known. As word of events spread, many recognized they had suffered less than those in the north, and a few wagon-loads of food and supplies were gathered and sent to the Northern Provinces. Not since the last war nearly a hundred years earlier had talk of events outside the Foothills so dominated conversations there, leaving local gossip struggling to catch up.

Kronivar had braced for attack, and it had not come. In the days following the war, life gradually grew calmer. The defense of the city was dismantled as squadrons and watches disbanded and soldiers became citizens again. Weapons were stowed and other duties were resumed. Grawson had been careful to maintain the balance of power during the war, and the Counts waited to see what would happen once things returned to normal. By now, most in the city had heard of the evidence connecting Orming with the separatists and guessed that a trial was inevitable. It seemed likely that Orming would be deposed, and few could resist speculating how Kronivar would be affected, and how they might profit from it.

Word of the Goblin attack burdened the hearts of the Elves in Miastolas and Northern Feäthiadreya. Horsemen gathered and an Elven company set out. Four days later in the late afternoon they arrived among the ruins of Greensward, where they received word that the Kronivar troops had retaken the Gundithe Plateau the day before and had left for the Castle. The Elven company rode into the mountains, arriving at the Castle just as the war was ending. The Elves remained to help tend the wounded and bury the dead, as well as to celebrate the end of the war and renew old ties with Itharia. Although the Dwarves often had their differences with the Elves, they welcomed them and thanked them for their assistance, even as they were proud to have won the war on their own.

The sun had already set even though it was only suppertime, and a fire burned in the hearth. Iaven and Zammond waited for Wendolin's daily visit and wondered what was keeping him. They envied Max, who had been allowed to leave that morning. His bed was made and his pack lay on it, and many of the other beds in the sickroom were empty now as well. Some had healed while others had been laid out on the Castle terraces with the rest of the dead. Iaven and Zammond were improving, but required more rest. Both were anxious to leave to help the recovery efforts in and around the Castle, where Max, Hobley, and the others now worked. Zammond was so restless that staying in bed seemed more difficult for him than bearing his wounds.

Rhiane came to check on Iaven as she did every day, stopping by in the evening. She and Iaven did not speak very much, nor very intimately, in front of Zammond, but he knew about their audience with the King.

"You think she'd come to Hillbrook with us?" Zammond said once Rhiane was gone.

"I thought of that," Iaven said, "She did say that she wanted to see it, so she might."

"But not to stay," said Zammond.

"No," Iaven admitted. He sighed and rolled over to stare at the ceiling. "I never expected her to, either. She would have mentioned it by now if she was thinking about it."

"It isn't entirely her decision, is it?" said Zammond. "I mean, the Frosthelms aren't like us common folk, are they? They're bound by duties and things are expected of them. So at least you can suppose that if things were different, maybe she would have come to Hillbrook."

"I don't know," said Iaven, "I get the feeling she could, if she really wanted to; they wouldn't keep her here if she wasn't happy. She'd put up a fight. No, I don't think she wants to leave here. And I can see why, too." Iaven turned to Zammond. "But that doesn't mean I'm not going to ask her anyway."

Their conversation was interrupted as the door opened, the candles flickered, and Wendolin entered. Iaven and Zammond looked to him eagerly for news of the goings-on in the Castle. Wendolin still walked with a cane, though he had improved since the end of the war. Wendolin pulled up a chair and set it between their beds.

"And how are my young friends this evening?" said Wendolin. "Still bed-bound against your will? Well, not much longer, they tell me." He sat down and leaned his cane against the footboard. "I would have come by this morning, but King Jordgen required my counsel again. He has been deciding what to do with Aranstone when he returns."

"Returns? From where?" asked Iaven.

"You have not heard?" said Wendolin. "No, I suppose not... Right after the war, King Jordgen, Prince Varlen, and I met with Aranstone. At last he believed all that we had told him about Zhindarren."

Wendolin related what Aranstone had said of Zhindarren's escape during the war. "After his audience with the King, Aranstone and a small band of his handpicked men and dwarves set off down the Ruined East Road to hunt down Zhindarren and his cohort."

"Why down the East Road?" said Iaven.

"From what we can tell, it appears they went east. Had they gone west down the Mountain Road, they would have run into the Elves, though of course they could not have known that at the time. So it seems to me that Zhindarren is making his way toward Arthel Hall. Should Aranstone fail to catch up to him, I have sent word there of Zhindarren's crimes so that they might arrest him and hold him for trial when he arrives."

"What chance does Aranstone have against Zhindarren?" asked Zammond.

"Very little, if Zhindarren knew he was coming," said Wendolin, "That was why they wanted my counsel; so that Aranstone might know what to expect, and how to deal with Zhindarren. He will indeed have to be careful. Aranstone will have the advantage of surprise, though perhaps only one chance to act before his pursuit is known. The lay of the mountains might aid him as well. The ruined road is so narrow in places that Zhindarren's men will have to go single file." Wendolin leaned back, glancing out the window at the mountains in the dark outside. "I do not expect him to succeed; but we shall see. If nothing else, Aranstone will keep Zhindarren from backtracking, and flush him out of the mountains and into the desert. And Zhindarren will not be expecting the arrest awaiting him at Arthel Hall. Fortunately, he never found out that I am here; otherwise he might expect my intervention."

"And what about the rest of the separatists in Kronivar?" Iaven asked.

"They will all be blamed for the siege, even though it was Zhindarren's idea and Aranstone's mistake," said Wendolin. "Orming is sure to be deposed, now that Grawson's connected him with them. That will be the end of separatist activity for a while, though I am sure the sentiment, even if it dies down, will still remain. And King Jordgen will be more likely to take it into consideration in his dealings with Kronivar, after his talks with Aranstone."

"How long are the Kronivar troops staying?" said Iaven.

"Until the dead are entombed," Wendolin replied, "They are carving niches and excavating new tunnels up in the Mountain of the Dead, just beyond the Castle valley. Buildings in the outer ward are being rebuilt, and stores restocked for the winter. And today they were helping dispose of the Urumak carcass the Goblins left behind."

"I heard there were Urumak still alive," said Zammond.

"Four of them remain," said Wendolin. "However, only two *Widiwa* drivers survived. They will have to shepherd all four back up to the Northern Wastes. Elven troops have agreed to escort the Urumak through the mountains and down to Greensward before they ride south. They leave tomorrow." Wendolin looked mildly amused. "The Elves who are still here are quite taken with the Urumak. They had heard tales of them, but none had ever seen one."

"I wouldn't mind seeing one up close, on friendly terms," said Zammond. "I wish they weren't leaving so soon."

"How long are the Elves staying?" asked Iaven.

"Not much longer," said Wendolin. "They are not as fond of winter as you Dwarves are. Most of their countrymen are already settled in their summer homes in Southern Feäthiadreya. A few will stay to help with the entombments, but most will be on their way with the Urumak early tomorrow morning."

Wendolin looked at Iaven and Zammond. "You both seem a little less pale than yesterday. It appears your healing is going well. It would do you good to have some Wilderberry tea, if any leaves of it were to be had. But I fear it is too late in the season to find any."

"Wilderberry leaves?" said Zammond, remembering. "Cedric gave us some before we left Hillbrook."

"They were lost along with Wilbur's pack," said Iaven, "In the storm, in the mountains, remember?"

"Oh, that's right…" Zammond's enthusiasm was punctured. He saw the pack on Max's bed. "Didn't he give Orven some too? It's worth looking, isn't it?"

Hiding a grimace of pain, Zammond slid out of bed and went over and sat on Max's bed, digging through the pack. At last he found a small cloth wrapping, and opened it to find a little wad of small, aromatic, dark green leaves. "Here it is," he said. He handed it to Wendolin and got back in bed. "I'll bet they forgot they had them. It's a shame Orven never got to use them himself."

Wendolin stood slowly, grasping his cane. "I'll have them make some tea out of it, and bring it to you," he said as he turned to go.

"You're joining us and having some yourself, aren't you?" asked Iaven.

Wendolin turned back to them. "I wouldn't miss it," he said.

After tea and conversation with Wendolin, Iaven and Zammond slept more soundly than they had since arriving at the Castle. The Wilderberry tea was more tart and bitter than they expected, but they drank it and found it did have a very soothing effect. Iaven awoke and lay peacefully, staring up at the wash of morning light on the ceiling. Suddenly he remembered something and sat up in bed. "Zammond," he said. "Zammond, wake up!"

Zammond rolled over and opened a bleary eye. "What?" he grumbled.

"It's already morning," said Iaven, getting dressed.

"Too bad," said Zammond and rolled over again.

"They're going to be leaving soon," said Iaven, putting on his coat. "The Urumak. It's our last chance to see them."

Soon they stood looking out from the western gatehouse of the outer ward, along with the guards there and two other young dwarven soldiers, whose resemblance suggested they were brothers. "Look at the size of them!" one said.

"It's a good thing they're such peaceful creatures, isn't it?" said Zammond.

Below them, on the Castle terraces, the four Urumak stood tall, their broad backs hung with shaggy fur damp with frost. They snorted and grunted softly, their breath rising as curls of steam in the wintry air. Elves on horses rode around them, moving them into a line and urging them gently into position. Dwarves on their way down into the Castle valley stared in wonder at the great beasts as they passed.

On the neck of the Urumak nearest the Mountain Road sat one of the small *Widiwa* drivers, while the other was perched on the last one in line. The large, slow-moving beasts moved grudgingly and began to follow one another, as the driver turned and called to them with strange high-pitched whistling sounds. Elves rode alongside the huge striding beasts, controlling their wary and frightened horses. The whole entourage made its way onto the ridge where the Mountain Road ran to the west, into the vast ranges spreading majestically across the land and towering into the sky.

"Do you think we'll ever see them again?" asked Iaven. He suddenly had a great desire to see the Northern Wastes where the *Widiwa* people lived and the Urumak roamed with *irlpiri*-style houses on their backs. He realized he also wanted to see Tolgard, Phamiar, Elluria, and other lands across the sea, and it seemed strange to him now that he did not always possess such a desire.

"The Urumak? Probably not." He looked at Iaven. "Or are you suggesting we go someday to see them?"

"Maybe," said Iaven.

"This is the farthest we've ever been from home," said one of the brothers. "I know what you mean, about wanting to travel. But I'm anxious to return home now, too."

"We're lucky to have both survived the war" said the other brother, "Our parents and sister will be so glad to see us. She was due to have a baby; she must've had it by now. We'll both be uncles!"

"Well, congratulations!" said Iaven. "Yes, I'm looking forward to going home, too. I'm sure my mother is wondering about me." He offered his hand as he and Zammond were leaving. "Nice to meet you both. I'm Iaven, Iaven Ambersheath."

"And I'm Zammond Brockleberry." Zammond offered them his hand.

"Mern" said the elder brother, shaking Zammond's hand. "Mern Thelred, and this is my brother Thom. Sons of Arl and Essie Thelred."

Snow was falling on the crowds gathered on the Castle terraces. A week had passed, and Iaven and Zammond had recovered and stood amongst the throng. The Kronivar troops were there, the few Elves who had remained, and the Castle guard in their brushed woolen coats. Everyone assembled in groups outside the gates, standing in the cold and waiting. All the dead from the war lay across the terraces in rows, stiff and frozen, their arms at their sides. Dwarves lifted the rigid bodies onto wooden stretchers, carrying them in single file through the entire assembly, and all present looked on them and paid their respects in silence. The funeral procession passed across the terraces and down into the Castle valley. From there, in the snowy distance, the line of bearers could be seen ascending the Mountain of the Dead. High up on the slope they entered long passageways of freshly-hewn tombs. There the dead were laid to rest in niches carved into the tunnel walls. Stone slabs engraved with their names sealed the niches and were mortared into place.

King Jordgen stood with Prince Varlen, Erland Clovenstone, and Arlen Frosthelm, all in full regalia as befit their stations. Grim and somber, they watched as the dead were paraded past. Near them, Rhiane stood with Oellia and Tomald. Hamet and Horlen held their mother's hands, wary but curious, their eyes fixed in wonder on the procession of the dead.

Lexter, Pitford, and Gallorne stood with the Kronivar troops, gazing at the faces of the passing dead. Lexter was amazed at how many were familiar; some he had only seen or spoken with, while others he had called friends. He was surprised at how many had died, and felt ashamed to still be alive. So many of the dead had been better soldiers than he, more valiant and courageous, and now they lay slain while he survived.

Cold winds swirled around the solemn onlookers, snowflakes beating faintly on their long faces. Further down in the crowd stood Max, along with Roy and Aaron. As the dead were carried by, they noted those who had defended the Castle with them, and watched anxiously to see Ripley and Orven one last time. At last a cold finger stirred their hearts as they saw Ripley's dark, straight hair in his hood as he lay on the plank the bearers carried past. His eyes were closed and his face pale and strange, his body eerily still and unmoving.

Orven's body followed soon after, and again they were struck with anguish. Orven's face was cold and bloodless, and his beard, hair, and eyelashes fringed with white frost. Tears welled in Max's eyes as he felt the loss of his friend keenly. Roy and Aaron stared sullenly, still finding it hard to believe Orven was gone. They kept their eyes on Orven for as long as they could, the bearers taking him farther and farther away, until they could see him no more and he was just one of the many bodies in the long procession through the falling snow.

Iaven stood with Zammond, Hobley, and Wilbur, and they all were saddened as they recognized Ripley among the dead. They thought again of Tillmore, lying cold and alone, interred in some nameless mountain in the north. As the bearers brought Orven near, their hearts were bowed with sorrow, and they felt sorry for Iaven, who wept softly as Orven passed. Iaven looked upon his twin brother, missing him and feeling strangely alone in the world without him. Orven's cold, pallid face, whitened with frost, gave him a wan, ghostly appearance, unreal and chilling. Iaven felt cold and numb, drowned in a flood of memories and regrets, of troubles and happy times long gone. Even after Orven had passed from sight, Iaven continued standing and gazing at the long procession of body after body, as snow settled and collected on the uncovered heads of the silent crowd. Cold and grief left Iaven drained as weariness overcame him. He stood motionless as snow swirled and touched his face, listening to the soft, regular footfalls of the bearers as the endless procession endured and the afternoon deepened into dusk.

The following morning the troops departed for Kronivar, and Lexter came around one more time and exchanged farewells with Iaven and his friends before he left. They all watched from atop the outer wall as the Kronivar troops marched and rode across the terraces and onto the Mountain Road. Already it seemed much quieter around the Castle, the pace slower as life returned to normal, yet strange because so many who had lived and worked there were no more. The wind blew cold and hollow along the wall and a light blanket of snow covered the terraces and valleys around the Castle. Dwarves went to and fro, leaving fresh tracks across the terrace snow. Two young dwarves came in from the eastern road and hurried toward the Castle gates. Hammers echoed in the outer ward as buildings were rebuilt. The departing Kronivar troops spread out along the Mountain Road, passing around the mountain and turning out of sight.

"Well, Iaven, in not too long a time we'll be heading that way ourselves," said Zammond as he watched the troops disappearing in the distance. "Have you talked with Rhiane yet?"

"I'm going to today," said Iaven, his voice heavy with dread, "It'll be hard to say goodbye." They started walking along the wall back to the Castle.

"You're sure she wouldn't consider coming with us?" Zammond said, "You'll still ask her, won't you?"

"Of course I will," said Iaven. "I have a good idea what she'll say, though. I hinted about coming with us, and she looked at me and didn't say much. I'm not giving up, but I'm not getting my hopes up either. And if she doesn't, well, I understand. Whatever happens, I'm looking forward to seeing Hillbrook again, and I wouldn't mind seeing more of Miastolas someday. Maybe even southern Feäthiadreya. I've heard interesting things about the southern shores and the archipelagoes..."

"We could even journey out to Tolgard and Phamiar," said Zammond, "I'd like to see it all myself, after all I've heard others say about them. And don't forget, we're stopping to see the Carven Halls of Gomirré on the way back!"

"I haven't forgotten," said Iaven. "I'm looking forward to seeing them, too."

"Good," said Zammond. They opened the heavy wooden door to the west wing and stepped inside out of the cold. "Let me know how it goes. You sure you don't want me there to help?" He smiled at Iaven and went off down the hall.

Iaven walked through the Castle halls, looking for Rhiane or someone who might have seen her. He climbed a flight of stairs, and met Oellia coming down them. "Have you seen Rhiane around?" he inquired.

"She was on her way to the King's chamber," Oellia said, "you might catch her if you hurry!"

Iaven went up the steps and down the hall, looking for Rhiane, and finally saw her ahead of him. She was about to turn the corner down the short passage to the King's study when she saw Iaven and stopped.

Iaven caught up to her and realized how nervous he was. "Rhiane, could I talk to you, before you see the King—" Erland Clovenstone came out of the study, greeting them as he passed in the hall, and was gone.

"I'm supposed to meet with him right now," said Rhiane, "why don't you come along?"

"All right," Iaven answered, still recalling their last audience with him.

King Jordgen was seated at his desk, looking at some plans for buildings that Clovenstone had given him. "Enter!" he called as Rhiane knocked her special knock. "Allelia," he said looking up at her, "—and Iaven Ambersheath," he added when he saw Iaven. Iaven noticed a change in the King's tone and attitude as he spoke Iaven's name.

"Good morning, your majesty," Iaven managed. He made a slight bow and wondered afterwards if it had been enough.

The King looked at Iaven and then to Rhiane, as if to ask why he had come. "Allé, have you gone through all the bolts of cloth in the—"

Suddenly a hasty knock sounded and the door opened. Gwaine Clovenstone leaned in and bowed. "Begging your pardon, sire, important news has just come that I thought you would want to hear immediately," he said. The King grunted as though Gwaine had done something like this before. Two young dwarves shuffled nervously into the room, one dark-haired and solidly built, the other sandy-haired and thinner. "This is Osman and Arric, from Aranstone's party, returned from the Ruined East Road," Gwaine told them. He nodded and left, closing the door behind him.

King Jordgen rose and scrutinized the dwarves standing before him. "Where is Aranstone?" he asked them.

"Please sire," answered the sandy-haired dwarf who was Arric. "Zhindarren is dead; Aranstone has succeeded, but—"

"Aranstone tracked down Zhindarren and his men," Osman continued, "When we found them, we held back, so as to take them by surprise. We followed them, waiting for the right place to act. It was along a ruined stretch of road. At one point the trail became a ledge, narrow and treacherous. Zhindarren had set camp near there, and was to cross over it the next day. We waited. In the morning we returned early, and it looked like most of his men had already gone across. But Zhindarren and two others had yet to cross the ledge. They were passing over it when Aranstone sprang, with Khale and Pyrwoed, and killed the two men. Zhindarren reacted and sent Pyrwoed, and later Khale, over the edge, killing them. Aranstone pulled back, out of Zhindarren's reach. They stood there, Aranstone calling Zhindarren a traitor, and Zhindarren laughing and calling him a stooge and fool. Behind him, Aranstone's men came forward, but it was a trap. Zhindarren's men had not gone across, but were waiting to ambush us. Zhindarren laughed, for the ground was unsafe; Aranstone could go no further without endangering himself. But Zhindarren did not count on Aranstone's fury and rashness. Aranstone lunged at Zhindarren, losing his footing as he did so. He grappled with Zhindarren, and both fell over the edge, into the valley. Arric and I were acting as lookouts, on the pass of rock above, and saw it all happen. And we alone escaped Zhindarren's men."

"Aranstone, and the others, are all dead?" said the King.

"All but Osman and myself," said Arric, "We looked for them, and then went down to where Aranstone lay."

"A river ran through the valley below, and Aranstone and Zhindarren landed on the rocks there," Osman explained, "We thought they were dead, but we had to be certain. We climbed down into the valley, and it took us the rest of the day to find a way down there. Zhindarren had broken his neck in the fall and lay dead on the rocks. Aranstone narrowly missed the rocks, but he broke both his legs and his ribs, and was almost dead when we found him. He had been coughing up blood and knew the end was near. Before he died, he sent us to you, to tell you what happened. He said he hoped it had paid the debt he owed."

King Jordgen sat in silence considering the dwarves' tale. "You say that in the morning, it seemed as though the men had crossed over," said the King, "Why was it not known for certain whether they had or not? You were the lookouts at the time, were you not?"

Osman and Arric froze at the question and exchanged guilty glances. Fearfully they turned back to the King, expecting punishment. "We had fallen asleep," said Arric, "We were alternating watches, and..." he faltered, trembling.

"We were all very tired," Osman offered, "We marched for days at a great pace, with little rest, to catch up to Zhindarren. We stayed awake most of the night, but by morning—"

"Please sire, forgive us, we beg you!" Arric's voice was rough and he bowed his head in shame.

"It couldn't have been for very long," said Osman, "we were tired..." He lowered his eyes, awaiting his sentence.

King Jordgen paused in wonderment, amazed at the events that had just been related. Inwardly he was ashamed to admit a certain relief, for he was still uncertain how to deal with Aranstone; whether to punish or show clemency, and to what degree. Now Aranstone had proven his desire to make amends, and that made his loss seem all the greater.

King Jordgen sat contemplating the two penitent dwarves. He was quiet awhile, letting Osman and Arric consider what a grave error their lapse of duty had been. "Such things happen," he said, stern but kinder than they expected, "Though that does not excuse your negligence. Discipline will be needed, but you will not be punished to the full. You will be dealt with later. Go now; and consider well what you have done."

"Yes, sire, we will, thank you, your majesty!" Arric bowed and they thanked the King as though great favor had been bestowed on them. They bowed again and left the King's chambers.

The King pondered what they had said and his mood and attitude had changed. "So Zhindarren is dead, and Aranstone along with him," he said at last. "Hmmph!" he grunted, still considering it.

He turned to Rhiane and Iaven. "My condolences to you, Iaven, regarding your brother," said the King. His tone toward Iaven had changed since Osman and Arric's visit, but it was still not one of warmth.

"Thank you, sire," Iaven said, and averted his eyes.

"I have heard what you and your brother did, and of your stand against Maëlveronde," the King continued, "And of your wounding." He looked at Iaven. "You seem to have recovered well. What will you do now that the war is over?"

Iaven wondered if the King was merely making conversation, or if he was trying to assure himself, and Rhiane as well, that Iaven had no intentions of pursuing Rhiane any longer. He was not sure what to say, and bitterly wished he had talked to Rhiane before coming to see the King. "I'll go back to Hillbrook, I suppose, and find work there." He glanced at Rhiane, then back to the King. "But before I go, I would like to ask whether—"

"You would break your oath, then?" The King sounded surprised and angry.

"My oath?!" Iaven was bewildered and afraid. "What oath do you mean?"

"How quickly you forget!" The King gave Iaven a disdainful look. "Right before the war, did you not stand here, promising *'to offer my service, whatever is needed of me, for as long as you may need it'*? Well, Iaven Ambersheath, you have not yet been released from your oath, nor have you been discharged from service. You have found favor with my grand-niece Allelia, here, and she has requested that you remain with us at the Castle. We should all like to hear in more detail about the vanquishing of Maëlveronde, and see what other uses you may have."

"Sire!" Iaven was shocked, "Then you do not disapprove of Rhiane and I—"

The King stood. "We shall see about that," he said, "I am not yet convinced, but we will give it time and give you a chance, at the very least..."

"Thank you, your majesty!" Iaven bowed his head and did not know what more to say. Rhiane smiled broadly at the King and it was all she could do to keep from jumping forward and hugging her great-uncle Jordgen in front of Iaven. The King saw her delight and nodded kindly toward her, appreciating the restraint she was showing.

"So you'll live at the Castle!" Zammond was thrilled to hear Iaven's news. "Not a bad idea, really. Roy and I were just talking about it. He's made some friends already, and he's even convinced Aaron to stay awhile. There's rebuilding to be done, and, work to be found. I wasn't quite sure what I wanted to do, but now I think I'm going to stay." A mocking smile crept across his face. "Thought you were getting rid of me, did you?"

"Never had my hopes up," said Iaven. "Glad to hear you and Roy are staying, too," he said to Aaron.

"The rebuilding will need all the hands they can get," said Aaron, "And beyond that? I don't know." Fiery images of destruction, of dwarves in agony and dying were still burned into his mind, and he hoped helping rebuild would dispel them or set them to rest. "I may want to travel awhile before I go back," he added, "I'd like to talk with Wendolin more, too; they say the King has invited him to reside at the Castle." They later learned that Wendolin had accepted the invitation. "Time for me to settle down, at last," the old wizard joked with them.

But whereas Zammond, Roy, and Aaron had decided to stay, Hobley, Max, and Wilbur planned to return to the Foothills. "I'd miss the woods and towns and everything down there" said Max, "I promised them I'd come back, too. The hunting's good this time of year, and I miss my dogs." Hobley agreed with Max's sentiment, and the two were looking forward to hunting together again. "But not right away," said Hobley, "Wilbur and I might do some traveling first, out to Tolgard or Elluria, maybe even other lands beyond them."

"We might even go by ship," Wilbur added smiling. "And we'll be back to visit to the Castle, you can be sure of that." Soon everyone wished them farewell and the three were on their way. Iaven wondered what they would be like the next time he saw them.

In the weeks that followed, Iaven, Zammond, Roy, and Aaron aided in the rebuilding of the outer ward and adjusted to life at the Castle. Many dwarves stayed after the war and brought their families from the Foothills, Kronivar, and the Southern and Northern Provinces. Building began in the valleys around Mount Frosthelm, and even on the terraces outside the outer wall. Dwarves who had never been to the Castle before the war found they had fallen in love with the mountains, feeling a connection to their ancestors there. Some even began to wonder why their parents' and grandparents' families had ever moved away to lower ground.

Months passed, winter gave way to a thaw, and spring was imminent. Word spread that a renewing of Itharia's alliance with Feäthiadreya was to be held. Invitations went out and guests arrived at the Castle. Nobles and dignitaries appeared from all over the Kingdom, and Elves came on horseback. Guest rooms were swept and lit.

There would be many meetings, conferences, and discussions during that week, but the event Iaven looked forward to most came the day after everyone arrived. From late morning onward, the Great Hall began filling with people. Everyone was there; Elves from Miastolas, Men and Dwarves from Kronivar and elsewhere in Itharia, the Clovenstones, Vierlings, Ethcairns, and other Castle families, Arlen and his wife Yarra, Oellia and Tomald and their boys, and of course Rhiane, who now preferred "Allelia" again as she readjusted to the formality of the Castle (although family and friends still used her nickname when the occasion called for it). Iaven stood with her, and Zammond joined them. They were amazed at how fast the months had passed, and how much they already felt part of life at the Castle.

A proud, stately blast of horns erupted from the wide double doors of the hall, reducing the roar of conversation to a murmur as the guests quieted and turned toward the entrance. Pages marched in, their young faces disciplined and serious. Following them strode Elven representatives on one side, and on the other, the four Counts of Kronivar with their aides, with Grawson and his wife Luinde behind them. After a short gap King Jordgen appeared, walking with General Ferre Riaswië, the tall, elegant Elven general appointed by Queen Perla herself to represent her in her absence. Enthusiastic greetings and sounds of approval rose from the crowd as the two leaders appeared. Following the King and General Riaswië was another gap, and then came Wendolin, still walking with a cane but tall and unbowed, and next to him Prince Varlen carrying two crimson velvet-wrapped bundles tied with golden cord.

The procession made its way over to the Great Fireplace centered on the south wall, where a fire roared merrily. An enormous wooden ladder leaned against the wall high above the fireplace's huge mantle, where iron mounts had been installed. Ghard Angkelwen IV, the Castle's Master-Forger and great-grandson of the Angkelwen who had made the Swords of the Alliance, waited proudly at the foot of the ladder.

The Elves stood to one side of the fireplace, while Grawson and the Counts gathered on the other side, and the crowd assembled around them all eagerly. Wendolin waited near the Master-Forger and exchanged a nod of greeting with him. In front of the fireplace King Jordgen and General Riaswië received the velvet-wrapped bundles from Prince Varlen. They untied the cord and pulled off the cloth, and an awed hush rose from the audience as two gleaming, ornate swords emerged, brilliant and shining.

"Behold," said the King, "the Swords of the Alliance!"

Iaven smiled to see the swords again, which had been cleaned and polished to a luminous luster. The gems sparkled in the hilts of the swords, catching light from the windows and the fire. King Jordgen and General Riaswië held the swords high for all to see, and shouts of joy and gladness echoed in the hall.

"May an era of peace begin and our swords remain at rest, as these shall be put to rest here today," King Jordgen declared, "And may these Swords of the Alliance, Halix and Gorflange, now serve the purpose for which they were forged; to be a symbol of our friendship with Feäthiadreya, and the Alliance between our peoples, a partnership of equals. May they remind us of our duties as neighbors and allies, as we strive to care for and protect the mountains, lands, and seas over which we have been given dominion and stewardship."

The King was answered with shouts of agreement, and the swords were handed over to Ghard Angkelwen IV, who took them and mounted them on the wall high above the mantle of the Great Fireplace. Blows of his hammer tightened the iron mounts, locking the swords in place. Cheers and shouts rose up again, and many other speeches and pledges were made that day. Elves and Dwarves celebrated together into the evening as Itharia enjoyed its renewed friendship with Feäthiadreya.

And from that day forward for years to come, whenever bright afternoon sunlight fell through the high windows of the Great Hall and swept slowly across the wall, Angkelwen's twin swords gleamed and shone, Aorinthel's six gemstones sparkling within them.

In May of that year Iaven and Rhiane announced their engagement. King Jordgen was as pleased as anyone to hear the news. He had grown fond of Iaven and found that Arlen also approved of him. At the King's orders, wedding preparations began immediately. Guest lists were drawn up and invitations sent out. Zammond and Oellia were overjoyed and took over the planning of the wedding, occasionally letting Iaven and Rhiane in on important decisions. Rhiane also made good on her promise to visit the Foothills with Iaven, and many a party was thrown there in her honor. Sara was happy for Iaven, and took to Rhiane right away, glad to have a daughter-in-law even if she was still a little intimidated by 'Castle folk'.

The marriage of Allelia Frosthelm and Iaven Ambersheath took place later that October. Hobley, Wilbur, and Max returned to the Castle for the occasion, and brought Sara and Rory along with them. Iaven's mother had always dreamed of seeing the Castle and was delighted to be there. Iaven was uncomfortable being the center of attention, but he was grateful for the love and concern of all his friends and family.

The wedding itself was among the grandest the Castle had seen in some time. The train of Rhiane's dress was more than three times her height, and the banquet in the Great Hall surpassed everyone's expectations. At the exchange of vows Iaven thought Rhiane had never looked more beautiful. His heart leapt with great joy as he looked upon his beloved.

During the following spring Rhiane was with child, and late in the year a son was born to her and Iaven. Family and friends gathered around them as Rhiane held the baby in her arms. Iaven beamed proudly at his boy and laughed with delight whenever the child gripped his finger or stared intently at his father with his big, brown eyes.

The adoring onlookers debated whom he resembled more. "He's got his mother's eyes and dark hair," some said, and others, "He looks like his father, you can see it already." But all agreed the child was a handsome little lad who would make his parents proud. A few even suggested he was destined for great things, though they were known to say this whenever babies were born at the Castle. Others commented that a good family life was best thing one could hope for, and with the parents he had, that seemed to be assured.

"And what is his name?" someone in the crowd asked Iaven.

Rhiane laughed, since they had long discussed what to call him. Iaven smiled at his wife and looked lovingly at his little son. "Orven," he said, "His name is Orven."

About the Author

Mark J. P. Wolf is a Professor in the Communication Department at Concordia University Wisconsin. His books include *Abstracting Reality* (2000), *The Medium of the Video Game* (2001), *Virtual Morality* (2003), *The Video Game Theory Reader 1* and *2* (2003, 2008), *The Video Game Explosion* (2007), *Myst & Riven: The World of the D'ni* (2011), *Before the Crash: An Anthology of Early Video Game History* (2012), *Encyclopedia of Video Games* (First Edition, 2012; Second Edition, 2021), *Building Imaginary Worlds* (2012), *The Routledge Companion to Video Game Studies* (First Edition, 2014; Second Edition, 2023), *LEGO Studies* (2014), *Video Games Around the World* (2015), *Video Games and Gaming Culture* (2016), *Revisiting Imaginary Worlds* (2017), *Video Games FAQ* (2017), *The World of Mister Rogers' Neighborhood* (2017), *The Routledge Companion to Imaginary Worlds* (2017), *The Routledge Companion to Media Technology and Obsolescence* (2018) which won the SCMS 2020 Award for Best Edited Collection, *101 Enigmatic Puzzles* (2020), *World-Builders on World-Building* (2020), *Exploring Imaginary Worlds* (2020), *Fifty Key Video Games* (2022), and *Calculated Imagery: A History of Computer Graphics and Hollywood Cinema* (forthcoming). He has published articles in a wide variety of periodicals, and is the founder of the Video Game Studies Scholarly Interest Group (VGSSIG) and the Transmedia Studies Scholarly Interest Group (TSSIG) of the Society for Cinema and Media Studies (SCMS). He lives in Wisconsin with his wife Diane and his sons Michael, Christian, and Francis. This is his first novel. [mark.wolf@cuw.edu]

Glenn R. Engelbart is a software developer who resides in Franklin, Wisconsin, with his wife Dawn, son Finn, and daughter Audrey. In his spare time, he is also a music producer and contributes mods to the open-source voxel video game engine, Minetest.